The Plain City

BRIDESMAIDS

The PLAIN CITY

BRIDESMAIDS

THREE OHIO MENNONITE ROMANCES

DIANNE CHRISTNER

BARBOUR

PUBLISHING

Print ISBN 978-1-62836-166-7

eBook Editions:
Adobe Digital Edition (.epub) 978-1-63058-035-3
Kindle and MobiPocket Edition (.prc) 978-1-63058-036-0

All scripture quotations are taken from the King James Version of the Bible.

For more information about Dianne Christner, please access the author's website at the following Internet address: www.diannechristner.net

Published by Barbour Publishing, Inc., P.O. Box 719, Uhrichsville, OH 44683, www.barbourbooks.com

Our mission is to publish and distribute inspirational products offering exceptional value and biblical encouragement to the masses.

 Member of the
Evangelical Christian
Publishers Association

Printed in the United States of America.

SOMETHING
OLD

DEDICATION

To my mom, who has a good word to say about everybody. Even during a season of intense physical pain, she spread the word about my books. To my mother-in-law, who also experienced a rough year. Yet Anna repeatedly asked, "Is your book out yet?" Finally, I can place it in her lap.

Thanks to my agent, Greg Johnson, who believed in my writing and persevered, opening doors of opportunity that led to the Plain City Bridesmaids series. Thanks to Becky and the superb Barbour Publishing team for enhancing my manuscript throughout editing, marketing, and production.

Dad, thanks for your prayers and my Mennonite upbringing. Jim, I appreciate your daily love and devotion. Rachel, you are my encourager. Leo, you are hers. Mike and Heather, you are patient, especially before deadlines. Kathy and Chris, I cherish your supportive e-mails. Timmy, thanks for your website assistance. Gkids, want to see your name in print? Hi Makaila, Elijah, Vanson, Ethan, and Chloe!

Reader, I'm humbled you picked up *Something Old* and ventured into Plain City to spend time with Katy Yoder and her friends. I hope our paths cross and invite you to meet with me on my website: www.diannechristner.net.

Most thanks go to God, my helper and highest inspiration.

PROLOGUE

Ouch! Stop it!" Ten-year-old Katy Yoder howled, her head pinned to the back of the car seat until she could uncoil Jake Byler's fingers from her ponytail. She glared at the unrepentant boy—though she secretly relished the attention—and flipped her hair to the front of her buttoned blouse. In return, he flashed her a lopsided grin.

With Plain City, Ohio, one hundred miles behind them, the van continued to eat up the asphalt and soon veered off the interstate onto a dusty road that could churn soda pop into butter. The boys whooped, but Katy's stomach did a little somersault. Under normal circumstances, curvy roads turned her green, but she was also fretting over the unknowns of her first camp experience.

The driver shut off the ignition in front of a rectangular, log building. With ambivalence, Katy scrutinized the green-lettered sign identifying Camp Victoria. The side door slid open, startling her as the boys scrambled over her, all elbows and knees, to exit the van. She squealed a protest and piled out after them. Then the children jostled into the parking lot and remained in a cluster like a group of balloons, where they drew attention, not for their festive splash but for their plainness.

Jake, who had pulled Katy's ponytail twice on the road trip, curled his lip and elbowed Chad Penner. Katy turned to see what tickled them. Her cheeks flamed to watch the boys act like first graders over some girls in shorts and brightly colored Ts.

She tossed her black ponytail and nudged Megan Weaver. "Stupid boys. Act like they never saw shorts before."

"Probably not on church girls," Megan replied. "Those girls are looking this way. Should we go talk to them?"

Lillian Mae Landis, the third friend in their tight trio, frowned at her navy culottes. "I wish my mom would let me wear shorts."

For Katy, her homemade culottes afforded more freedom than her normal below-the-calf skirts, and she would die before she showed her legs. She smoothed the cotton folds that clung to her legs and studied the other girls. "I hope they're nice." She gently bit her lip, wondering if they knew how to play Red Rover. Or would they take greater pleasure in calling her ugly names like "Plain Jane"?

One of the shorts-clad girls waved.

"Let's go," Lil urged.

To Katy's relief, it turned out that a girl in green shorts had a cousin who lived in Plain City. The common acquaintance gapped the bridge between the Mennonite girls in shorts and the more conservative ones wearing culottes, which was fortunate since their sleeping bags and duffels all landed in the same cabin.

After participating in a long morning of organized activities, the Plain City girls took advantage of a few minutes of relaxation. Katy squinted up through glistening leaves, trying to locate an angry, chattering squirrel.

Lil propped an elbow on a bare, chubby knee. "Let's name ourselves after something that comes in threes." Their counselor had just divided their cabin in teams of three and given them fifteen minutes to name their group.

Katy gave up on the squirrel and tried to ignore the tight-fitting shorts Lil had already borrowed from a cabin mate. *Things that come in threes.* She twirled her long, black ponytail and thought about the picture books she'd read to entertain her younger siblings while her mother shelled peas. "There's the three bears, three Billy goats, three little pigs—"

"Nah." Lil tilted her leg this way and that. "Everybody'll think of those."

"How about the Trinity?"

"Yeah, I like it," Megan's face glowed. Katy wasn't sure if Megan was excited about her suggestion, or if she sported a sunburn. She was the only person Katy knew whose skin was as pale as white chinaware with hair as light as yellow thread. Lil was light-complected, too, but her freckles camouflaged it.

With a scowl, Lil said, "No way. Too holy."

"She's right." Megan reconsidered, nibbling at the tip of one of her blond braids.

Lil's blue eyes lit with cunning, and Katy inwardly cringed. "Three Bean Salad! Nobody else will pick that name."

"Huh?" The other two scowled. *Leave it to Lil to think of food*, Katy thought.

"Don't you see? It's perfect. Megan is the green bean since her parents are always talking about stewardship and recycling. I'm the garbanzo." Lil shimmied her shoulders and singsonged, "Gar–ban–zo." She pointed at Katy. "And you can be the kidney bean."

"What? I hate it. Do you even know what a kidney does?"

"You're just a kid with a knee. Get it?"

Katy watched Lil pat her bare knee again. "That's stupid. My knees never show." She hoped Lil got the point that at least *she* was a modest person.

"Sometimes they do in your culottes," Megan remarked.

Katy's ears turned pink. "What?"

"I only saw them once in the morning relay." Megan sighed. "Never mind. Would you rather be the green bean?"

"Red's *her* favorite color," Katy tossed her head toward Lil and pulled her culottes down below the middle of her shins. "If Lil's so set on it, let her be the kidney bean."

Megan turned up her palms. "Will you two stop arguing? We'll be three peas in a pod; then we can all be the same."

Lil rolled her gaze heavenward. "It's two peas in a pod, and we're not the same at all."

11

"Got that right," Katy grumbled, thinking about the giant dishpan full of green pellets her mother had shelled. She didn't want to be a pea, either. She'd rather be a bear or a musketeer or even a stooge. What were her friends thinking?

All ten years of their lives, the girls had done things together. They sat in pews at the same Conservative Mennonite church, learned their multiplication tables at the same blackboard, and played tag with the same ornery boys. But their personalities were as far apart as the tips of a triangle. They went to all the same potlucks, but their plates never looked identical. And although Lil and Katy hardly ever agreed on anything, they loved each other something fierce. When they didn't remember that, Megan reminded them.

"Why not three strands to a rope? That's cool." Megan fingered her braid. "Like this."

Lil crossed her arms and wouldn't budge. "Three Bean Salad."

Katy glared. She could blackmail her, threaten to tell Mrs. Landis about Lil's shorts, but Megan would never permit it. So because their leader chose that moment to blow her pink whistle, Three Bean Salad it remained for the rest of the week.

The campfire events *rocked*. A new word Katy had learned. As the highlight of each day, it opened Katy's eyes to a world that existed beyond her sheltered home life. She didn't miss how Megan leaned forward with starry eyes during the mission stories. When they lay in their bunks at night, while Lil and their leader, Mary, did sit-ups on the cabin floor, Megan chatted about Djibouti and Tanzania.

For Katy, the singing rocked most, even though she knew she sang off-key. The words expressed her heart, and she felt like she might burst with love for Jesus. She wished the world could share her happiness. It saddened her to watch Lil mimic the other girls from their cabin.

She glanced sideways now. Lil's freckles practically glowed in the firelight. She was happy, but Katy wished she could hug her friend to her senses. Lil pulled her blue sweater tight around her shoulders, her gaze wistfully trailing the kids now breaking the circle, some heading toward the cabins. "I never want this week to end," she murmured.

"Me either," Katy whispered.

Lil glanced into the shadows where their leader stood talking to another camp counselor. "She's so beautiful."

Megan and Katy leaned forward and looked to their right at Lil. "Who?"

"Mary."

"Oh." They leaned back. All three girls had fallen under Mary's spell. She was kind, patient, and told great Bible stories. To Lil's fascination, she was also beautiful and planning a wedding.

Lil clenched her fists. "I know how we can make this last. Let's make a vow tonight that when we're Mary's age we'll all move in together. It'll be like camp. Only forever."

Katy furrowed her brow. "We'll probably get married."

"Just until we marry. And we'll be each other's bridesmaids, too! Oh, swear it!"

Feeling sad that Lil caught so little of what camp was really about, Katy frowned. "You know Mennonites don't swear or take oaths."

Lil placed her head in her hands and stared at her borrowed jeans.

Megan, who was seated on the log between them, reached out and clasped each of their hands. "The Bible says where two or three are gathered and agree on something, that God honors it."

Twisting her ponytail with her free hand, Katy frowned. "What?"

"Sometimes my parents remind God about it when they pray."

"Really?" Katy asked, amazed.

Megan nodded, and her voice grew grave. "We can agree, but we must never break a promise."

Katy swallowed. Her heart beat fast. Lil's gaze begged. "I promise." Katy squeezed Megan's hand. "And I already know who I'm going to marry."

The other two whipped their gazes to the left. "You do?"

"Jake Byler. He always lets me cut in front of him in line."

Over the next decade, Katy wondered if Lil had made a second oath that night. She must have vowed to never let them break their promise to each other.

CHAPTER 1

Ten years later

Katy Yoder skimmed a white-gloved finger across the edge of the fireplace mantel. The holiday decorations, such extravagance forbidden at her own home, slowed her task. It wasn't just the matter of working around them; it was the assessing of them. Feeling a bit like Cinderella at the ball, she swiped her feather duster, easing it around the angel figurines and Christmas garland. A red plastic berry bounced to the floor, and she stooped to retrieve it, poking it back into place with care.

Her mother, like most members of her Mennonite congregation, shunned such frivolity. Gabriel of the Bible, the angel who visited the Virgin Mary, probably looked nothing like these gilded collectibles. Nevertheless, the manger scene caused warm puddles to pool deep inside her heart, a secret place of confusing desires that she kept properly disguised, covered with her crisp white blouse and ever-busy hands.

The pine-scented tree occupying the corner of the room moved her with wonder. Not the ornaments, but the twinkling white lights, little dots of hope. The cheery music jingling in the background was not forbidden. She mouthed the words to "Silent Night." In December they often sang the hymn at her meetinghouse. But her singing was interrupted mid-stanza as her employer's gravelly voice brought her out

14

of her reverie. Instinctively, she lowered her arm and whirled.

Mr. Beverly's lips thinned and his white mustache twitched. "Katy. We need to talk." Bands of deep wrinkles creased his forehead. "I have bad news," he said. His petite wife stood at his side, twisting her diamond ring.

Apprehension marched up Katy's neck. Could it be a terminal illness? In their late seventies, the couple kept active for their age, always off on golfing vacations. Katy had grown fond of them. Smiles softened their conversation, and their hands were quick to hand her trusted keys and gifts. They even bought her a sweater for her birthday, made from some heavenly soft fabric. Katy gripped the duster's handle with both hands. "Oh?"

"We're going to have to let you go."

Her jaw gaped. Never had she expected such news. "But. . .but I thought you were pleased." Her mind scrambled for some slipup, some blunder.

Mrs. Beverly rushed forward and touched Katy's white sleeve. "No. No. It's nothing like that. Our son wants us to move to Florida." She glanced at her husband. "At our age, it's overdue."

Katy propped the duster against an armchair and smoothed the apron that covered her dark, A-line skirt. "But is this what you want? Is there a problem with your health?"

Mrs. Beverly glanced at the beige shag carpet and back to Katy's face. "Just the usual, but we're not getting any younger." Mr. Beverly squeezed his wife's shoulder. "We'll give you a good reference."

Katy didn't need a reference. She needed a job. This particular job. Her best-paying, two-day-a-week job. To Katy, the tidy, easy-to-clean house classified as a dream job fast becoming a nightmare, if she was to lose it just when the doddy house came up for rent. Forcing a smile, Katy nodded. "I appreciate that. When will you leave?"

"Right away. We're turning the house over to a Realtor. Our son is coming to help us sell some things. There's really no need for you to come again. I'm sorry we couldn't give you more notice. But we are giving you a Christmas bonus."

Katy patted Mrs. Beverly's manicured hand. "Thank you. You have enough to worry about; don't concern yourself with me." She bit her lip, thinking, *I do that well enough for the both of us.*

"We'll leave you to your work, then," Mr. Beverly cut in. He nudged his wife's elbow, but she looked regretfully over her shoulder at Katy. "Come along, dear," he urged. Then to Katy, he called, "Your money's on the counter as usual. Please leave us your house key."

"Yes sir," Katy replied, watching them depart through an arched entryway. Mr. Beverly paused under the mistletoe to peck his wife's delicate cheek before they headed out for the mall. The tender gesture gripped Katy. It never ceased to amaze her when folks who never went to church loved like that. At least she assumed they didn't go to church, for she dusted their wine collection, R-rated DVDs, and sexy novel flaps without noticing any evidence of Christianity in their home except for one solitary Bible. It always stayed put, tucked between *Pride and Prejudice* and *Birds of Ohio Field Guide.* That's why the Beverlys' consistent kindness and loving behavior was so disturbing.

As usual, anything romantic always reminded Katy of Jake Byler. Growing up, she was sure they'd marry, and because of his daring, often reckless behavior, she had dreamed of sharing an adventuresome life with him. In their teen years, he stared at her with an ardor that melted her toes through her black stockings. He'd give her a dimpled grin or a wink, never embarrassed. Every autumn at the youth hayride, he'd claimed her hand. And after he got his own truck, he took her home from fellowship functions and stole kisses at her back door. She'd always loved him.

Just before he'd graduated from high school, their relationship had started to wilt. Katy grabbed a watering pitcher and marched to Mrs. Beverly's poinsettia. Her employer was as clueless about plants as Katy was about relationships. Had she caused him to become restless and distant?

Without addressing the status of their relationship or so much as an apology, Jake had enrolled at Ohio State University and moved near the campus in Columbus. After that, he often skipped church and always avoided her. Then one fateful evening—the night of the incident—he finally stopped coming to church altogether.

Even though rumors circulated that he drank and dated a wild girl with spiked short hair and a miniskirt, Lil continued to defend her cousin. But Katy deemed Jake Byler spoiled goods. Lumping him in the forbidden pile along with dancing, television, and neckties didn't remove the sting and sorrow, but it did help her deal with the situation.

She heard the Beverlys' car purr out of the drive and glanced out the window at a gray sky that threatened snow. It distressed her that the Beverlys could love like that and not know love's source. Love like the many times since Jake had dumped her when the Lord had noticed her wet pillow and sent her comforting lyrics to a hymn so she could sleep.

"While life's dark maze I tread and griefs around me spread, be Thou my guide. . . ."

The Beverlys had the nativity set; she'd give them that. Her hand slid into her white apron pocket and retrieved a small Christmas card she'd purchased. It had a picture of the nativity scene on the front and a Bible verse inside—John 3:16, her Christmas favorite. But was that enough? She could write something more on the card. Smiling, she drew a pen from a rose-patterned cup.

Katy used her best handwriting. *Your love reminds me of God's love.* She complimented them on their beautiful nativity set. *It reminds me that Jesus died for our sin so that we can spend eternity with God in heaven.* If that piqued their curiosity, they might open that dusty Bible. Surely they pondered eternity at their age, especially as they flew south toward their retirement nest.

She set the card in plain sight beside her house key. Then she put the feather duster in a utility closet and returned to the kitchen with paper towels and a spray bottle.

She spritzed the counter with her special homemade solution and polished, musing over her sudden job predicament. What would Lil say if she backed out of their doddy house plans because she could no longer afford it? She buffed a small area until it mirrored her clenched lips. She relaxed her grip. It wouldn't do to rub a hole in Mrs. Beverly's granite countertop right before a Realtor plunked a sign in her yard. Surely the poor old woman had enough to worry about.

Katy loosened the pressure of her seat belt with her left thumb and flicked on her headlights to stare through the Chevrolet's windshield at the silent twirling flakes. Since the news of her job loss earlier in the day, her stomach had worked itself into to a full boil. She veered off the country road onto a crackling driveway, where golden light streamed through the lacy windows of a white two-story.

Megan lived with her parents on the weekends and during school breaks. Otherwise, she lived on campus at the nearby Rosedale Bible College. As an only child and a tad spoiled, she had her own room where the Three Bean Salad could always meet in perfect privacy.

Katy swept up two identically wrapped gifts, stepped into the bright gray night, and slammed her car door. With her face bowed against the wet onslaught, she watched her shoes cut into freshly laid powder. She climbed the porch steps, giving her black oxfords a tap against each riser. Before she could knock, however, the front door opened.

Megan stood in the doorway, her straight blond hair shimmering down the back of her black sweater, and her blue eyes brilliant and round as the balls on the Beverlys' Christmas tree. Katy stepped into her friend's hug. "Hi, green bean. Merry Christmas."

"Merry Christmas, Katy."

After being stirred in the same pot for so many years, Katy and her two friends resembled Bean Salad more than any particular bean. Yet of the three girls, Megan's nickname stuck, because it suited her style, tall and beautiful and prone to type term papers on world peace or ecology.

"Look. Lil's here, too."

Sure enough, Katy recognized the cough of Lil's old clunker, a thorn in her friend's pride and due for a trade-in as soon as she could afford it.

Katy followed the aroma of gingerbread and ham through the house to the country-style kitchen. She hugged Megan's mom, Anita, and removed her wool coat. "So where's the blues man?" It was Bill Weaver's nickname because he restored Chevy Novas for a little extra income. But the unusual thing was that he painted them all his favorite color, midnight blue. Some Conservatives drove plain cars, and although they weren't supposed to idolize their vehicles, his lucrative hobby fell within what the church permitted. Anita Weaver started calling him the blues man, and Katy had picked up on it. Since Bill Weaver was a good sport and loved jokes, she never felt she was being disrespectful.

"Bill's at an elders' meeting at church," Anita explained.

"Oh yeah. I think my dad mentioned that."

"Since Bills' gone and you girls are spending the evening together, I thought I'd get a jump on Christmas dinner. We're having all the relatives over." She swiped at a wisp of hair that had escaped her crisp white covering. Anita Weaver spoiled Katy and Lil like they were her own daughters. Fun at heart, she was the most lenient of all their parents, and she didn't sport dark circles under her eyes like Lil's mom.

"Smells good. We're hosting all our relatives Christmas Day, too." It was a marvel that Lil, Megan, and Katy were in no way related, as many from their congregation were in the small farming community. Their family trees might intersect in the old country since they shared the same European Anabaptist roots, but they'd never dug into the matter.

Megan swept into the kitchen with Lil, whose snowy-lashed eyes sparkled when she spotted the plate of gingerbread men. Katy bit back a smile, watching her friend pull up her mental calorie calculator and consider her options.

"Hi, Lil." Katy squeezed her friend. "You can diet tomorrow."

"Nope." She flipped the hood of her coat back, revealing shiny, nut-colored hair pulled back at the temples and fastened with a silver barrette beneath her covering. "Not a day until January."

Megan picked up the plate of temptations and motioned for them to follow her up to her room. "Not the whole tray," Lil moaned, shrugging out of her coat, but Katy knew she didn't mean a word of it.

"I'll bring up hot chocolate," Anita Weaver called up the stairwell after them.

When they'd sprawled across the Dahlia coverlet Megan's grand-mother had quilted, Katy felt the butterflies in her stomach again. A night purposed for celebration, set aside for exchanging simple gifts and planning their future in Miller's doddy house, now pressed her secret heavily against her heart.

"Let's open our gifts," Megan suggested. They shifted and jostled until they each sat cross-legged with two gifts in front of them. Lil tore into hers first.

Shedding the dignity due her age—she was the oldest of the three by a few months, Katy followed suit. Gifts always stirred up a vestige of childlike excitement that stemmed back to her first store-bought doll. "It's gorgeous." She worked the hinge of the walnut recipe box.

"A cousin made them for me," Lil quipped.

Jake? Katy's protective instincts reared. She cast Lil an apprehensive glance, but she was tossing crumpled wrapping paper across the room, aiming for the trash can. Surely not, Katy dismissed. Inside was a handwritten recipe for Three Bean Salad, a twist from the norm with Lil's special ingredient. She always tweaked ingredients, especially intrigued by spices and herbs. Recently graduated from culinary school, Lil had been working for a month at her first real job at a small Italian restaurant. This set the course for the girls to consider renting the Miller's doddy house. Emotion balled up in Katy's throat.

"I'll keep adding to the recipes," Lil promised.

"Perfect," Megan clapped. "Now open mine."

She had embroidered pillowcases for them with roses and a Bible verse. Ephesians 4:26 read, "Let not the sun go down upon your wrath." Katy smiled. "A good reminder." *If any of us ever got married.* She watched them open the gifts she'd made. "They're lame," she apologized.

"No they're not." Megan jumped off the bed and tied the apron's strings, sashaying across the pine floor and sliding her hand in between each row of decorative stitching. "Wow. Six pockets."

Katy wished she'd done something meaningful or clever. Always the practical one. This was the third year they'd exchanged gifts for their hope chests, another reminder of the vow to be each other's bridesmaids. At the moment, the first part of the vow—the moving in together part—worried her most. She hated to ruin their doddy house dreams. It couldn't be helped. Katy swallowed. "I need to tell you both something."

Lil and Megan turned expectant gazes toward her.

"Did you girls pray for a white Christmas?" Anita Weaver interrupted, carrying a tray of hot chocolate into the room. Lil dove into the treat, and the conversation turned to the snowfall and how special it would make Christmas, drawing everyone to the window.

Anxious thoughts disquieted Katy's mind, but she pushed them aside. Her personal problem was small stuff compared to the miracle of Christmas. She followed the others to the window and made a spur-of-the-moment decision that she wouldn't ruin the spell of Christmas. The news could wait.

Outside, the flakes swirled like little, white feather dusters, turning everything sparkling white. Lil pressed her forehead against the cold windowpane and knocked her prayer covering askew. "Remember when we used to make snow angels?"

Involuntarily touching her own covering, Katy grinned. "I remember."

CHAPTER 2

At four o'clock, Katy was late. The Three Bean Salad had agreed to look over the doddy house as soon as possible after Christmas. Squinting from the glare of sun and snow, Katy hurried around the east side of the Millers' farmhouse and headed toward the little doddy house.

Doddy houses were built for the older Amish folks after their younger family members took over the main house, what the outsiders called guesthouses. She doubted the Beverlys' son had such a sweet arrangement waiting for them. Katy sighed, and a visible puff of breath dispersed into the cold air. This one, a miniature version of the larger house, was picturesque with a snowy porch railing and a glazed blue roof. In shades of white and gray, the doddy house and its surroundings created a peaceful aura similar to a black-and-white photograph of an older era. It probably wouldn't remain that way long, once renovations began. If renovations began, Katy corrected herself.

A window with dark green window shades, partly rolled up, revealed activity inside. She stepped onto a little porch and up to a door cracked ajar. Taking another visible breath, this time for fortification, she pushed the door open.

"Hey, Katy." Lil waved with a joyful bounce.

"Hi, Lil." Trying to act enthused, Katy nodded at Megan and the newly married couple from their church. This was a mistake. She didn't want to get the Millers' hopes up and waste their time.

Aged hardwood planks creaked as Katy joined in the tour of the quaint little house. Ivan Miller explained, "It's been boarded up for years. We've been busy updating the main house and didn't get to this one yet. We figured if somebody was game to fix it up, we'd let them live here rent free for a while."

The girls exchanged hopeful glances.

"When you say fix it up, you mean electricity?" Lil clarified.

A sudden thrill tingled Katy's spine at the idea of painting the walls a cheery color and choosing modern appliances and furniture. But could they swing it? Her pulse quickened. Could she still convince her parents to approve the idea now that her income had fizzled? Her dad took his role as leader of the household seriously. She'd have to convince him she could handle the responsibility.

Ivan nodded. "Whatever you want. Paint, indoor plumbing—"

"We'd like to keep the wood floors, though," Elizabeth said. "We think it adds to its charm."

"I agree." Megan dusted the floor with the toe of her shoe. "Just needs a little sanding and polyurethane."

The kitchen contained a green sink hutch with a hand pump. The refrigerator and stove required propane gas. Elizabeth explained, "You can share the wash room with the main house. It's updated with a dryer, and there's room to hang some clothes inside, too." Katy had noticed a sidewalk connected both houses to the small building.

The bathroom was equipped with a toilet and a hand pump. A large tin tub hung on the far wall. Elizabeth shrugged, apologetically.

Katy made light of the inconvenience. "There's plenty of room to add a shower or tub in here." They moved into the hall, and Lil scribbled furiously on a small pad.

The wind groaned through a broken windowpane, and Ivan fiddled with some loose plywood. Elizabeth rested an arm across the small mound of her pregnant belly. "There's only one bedroom, but it's spacious."

They all stepped into the center of the bare, windswept room. Katy made a slow circle, assessing damages and imagining three twin beds and dressers in the room. "We could build a walk-in closet."

Pointing her pen, Lil added, "Three twins would fit along that wall."

"Or bunk beds," Megan added. "Twins would be tight."

Katy objected, but Lil and Megan volunteered to share a bunk bed and give her a twin.

"We'll leave you girls to talk," Ivan suggested. "Just stop by the house when you're finished here."

Still acting like a newlywed, Elizabeth clasped her husband's hand and, with a parting smile, told the girls she'd put on a pot of fresh coffee.

"Thanks." Katy watched them depart.

"What do you think?" Lil asked at once, her bright gaze indicating her own approval.

"I love it," Megan replied. "I only wish I could move in with you guys. It's hard to wait until graduation."

"But you can stay over on weekends. . . ." Lil started dreaming aloud then broke off when her gaze met Katy's face. "You're scaring me. What are you thinking?"

"It's perfect. Only—" She shrugged and suddenly had to fight a rush of tears.

"What?"

Her mouth contorted uncontrollably, and she fanned her hand in front of her face.

Lil and Megan rushed to her side. "What's wrong?"

She raised her hand to stay them. Her voice broke. "I'm not sure I can afford it."

"Oh." Lil's gaze darted around the weather-damaged room. "Ivan said we wouldn't have to pay any rent right away. We'll need to make a list of what we want to fix and get bids for the work. But we can do it in stages."

"You don't understand. I didn't want to spoil your Christmas, but I lost one of my jobs."

"What!"

Megan pulled her into a hug, patting her back. "I'm so sorry."

Hovering, Lil asked, "What happened?"

Megan dropped her arm, and Katy shrugged. "The Beverlys are moving to Florida."

Lil's eyes widened. "Aren't they the ones who pay you so well?"

With a nod, Katy sniffled. "Yes, and the job will be hard to replace."

"Wow," Lil muttered.

"But you're a good worker," Megan reminded her. "You just need to get the word around that you're looking for more work."

Lil stomped her feet and blew out a puff of cold steam. "We already planned to dip into your savings. And we knew this place needed renovation. Until I repay you the cost of the renovations, I'll be paying the larger portion of the rent anyway. And like Megan said, you'll get more work."

Was Katy overreacting? She rubbed her coat sleeves and shivered. She'd gotten used to a cushioned bank account. And besides the expense of the renovations, there would be food to buy and other necessities.

Megan pulled a tissue from her purse and shoved it in front of Katy's face. "Here. Use this before your tears freeze."

"A heater would make this place more livable," Lil observed. "We should probably get a quote for wiring the whole house. Don't you think?"

Katy nodded, stuffing the tissue in her coat pocket. "I guess it won't hurt to find out if we can afford it. But keep in mind, we'll need new appliances and plumbing and furniture and who knows what else."

"You'll need beds and bedding, too. But my mom would donate some furniture," Megan offered. "It'll work out. You'll see."

"Sure. I want this to work." Katy met their hopeful gazes. "But I planned all along to use my income to sell Dad on the idea. And now. . ." She shrugged.

Lil crossed her arms. "You're of legal age. You can do whatever you want."

Katy shot her a stern look. "I won't go against their wishes."

Raising a palm, Megan stepped between them. "Let's not get ahead of ourselves. We'll talk to the Millers first. My folks won't agree to anything until I graduate and find a job. But out of all our parents, they are the easiest to persuade. If your parents agree, I'm sure they will, too."

"I guess we'll see if it's the Lord's will. I just can't go through with it if my folks are against it," Katy reiterated.

Lil snatched Katy's hand. "I want this so much. Come on. Let's go get warm."

~ৎ~

Later when Katy left the Millers, it was with the assurance that Lil would get the construction bids. Katy needed to obtain her parents' permission and find another job. Not easy feats. Generally speaking, girls from her congregation didn't leave home until they married, unless they attended Bible college. Over the years, her parents had often snickered at her dream, but they had never forbidden it. She had the impression they thought she would outgrow it.

When she reached home, Katy hung up her coat. In the kitchen, her mom poked a long-handled fork into an oblong roasting pan of pork tenderloin done to perfection. Katy's mouth watered. Stepping up to the sink, she washed her hands. "Hi, Mom. I'm home."

"Just in time to help."

Katy took a stack of plates and set one at each place setting: for her parents, herself, and the three siblings who still lived at home. "Just the family tonight?" Often her married brothers joined them.

"Just us. Guess everybody's staying put since Christmas is over."

Katy maneuvered around the pine table her grandfather had crafted in the woodworking shop he'd passed down to her dad. If they didn't have company tonight, it would be a good time to approach her parents about the doddy house. She silently prayed for God to direct her future.

Placing the forks on the left and the knives and spoons on the right of her mom's pink Depression-glass plates, she thought about the renovations and how they would eat up her savings account. When they had first discovered the little house was up for rent, it had seemed like a divine gift. Now she wasn't sure. Maybe it was too soon. They could wait another five months until after Megan graduated. It wasn't like they planned to get married right away.

If they missed the doddy house opportunity, though, they might need to take a city apartment. Already working for outsiders, she fought off a constant onslaught of worldly ideas and temptations. Sometimes at night in the bed she shared with her fourteen-year-old sister, Karen, the darkness would pull up disturbing images from Mrs. Beverly's paperback novel covers. Katy's pulse raced with shame. She tried not to glance at them when she dusted, but inevitably her gaze would photograph the detestable images. Her cheeks burned, and she moved to the other side of the table.

And hadn't the outsiders' Christmas decorations enthralled her? She pressed her lips together and straightened a fork. She hadn't even felt ashamed. Then she relaxed. Her mind was just occupied with this doddy house problem. But she didn't want to live among the outsiders, too. She liked the idea of a safe little place tucked in among her own people. She wished she could find a job with another Mennonite family.

"Katy!" Her mother's sharp tone invaded her rambling thoughts.

"What?"

"I asked you before. Do you want to mash the potatoes or go round up your siblings?"

"Oh." She glanced about confused.

"Karen helped me get supper started and took some clean laundry upstairs. She was going to work on a school report. Your brothers are out in the shop with your dad." The woodworking shop, which now specialized only in cabinets, was located at the end of a long, piney lane. They owned one of the five-acre lots on a Plain City rural road where a farm had been subdivided. Mom wiped her hands on her apron and placed them on her hips. "Are you fretting over that job you lost?"

Katy nodded.

Glancing at the wall clock, Mom said, "The potatoes can wait another five minutes. Let's sit a spell and talk."

Katy sank into the closest chair with a sigh of relief. "It's more than just the job."

"Go on."

"You know how I've been saving to move in with Lil and Megan?"

"Oh that crazy idea." She gave a brush of her hand. "Go on."

"Did you know Ivan Miller's renting out their doddy house?"

"That old thing? There's not even any electricity. Are you so eager to leave us that you'd live like your Amish cousins?"

"You know my friends and I have been planning this since we were little girls."

Her mom poked at the pins securing her prayer covering. "I wish you were more concerned about finding someone to marry. If I know my daughters, and I do, then marriage will make you happy. That Miller boy keeps asking you out. He's such a nice young man. What's his name?"

With a sigh, Katy replied, "David. I can date even if I move into the doddy house, but you're missing the point."

"Okay. What's the point?"

"Lil's been working now for a month at a good job. I've got money saved, too. If we're going to do this like we always dreamed, now's the time. Before one of us does get a boyfriend and gets married." She nibbled on her lip. "Only what if I don't get another good-paying job? That's what worries me. I need Dad's permission, and I want this so much."

Marie Yoder's naturally bright eyes softened. "I see you're serious about this."

"I'm afraid if we don't get this doddy house, Lil will push me to rent a city apartment."

Her mom's brown eyes widened, for she not only knew her daughters, but she knew a lot about their friends, too. "Well, if you are stubbornly set on it, I wish you'd take the doddy house. That is, if your dad agrees."

"Me, too."

With a shrug, her mom said, "I'll mash the potatoes. We won't want them lumpy if you're going to ask your dad about this after supper."

Katy flew out of her chair and threw her arms around her mom's neck. "Thanks." Then she rushed to find her siblings.

Supper lagged forever with Katy forcing down smooth potatoes. A shame she couldn't enjoy the flaky pork, but her stomach was no longer interested in food. She let the rest of her dark-haired siblings chatter while she mentally rehearsed her speech. After dinner, her mom surprised her by shooing the younger children off to do the dishes.

Katy settled on the sofa beside her mom. Her dad took his favorite chair beside the little side table that displayed a worn checkerboard game.

"What's on your mind, dumplin'?" It's what her dad called both his daughters.

"Ivan Miller's doddy house." Katy's words spilled out in a rush. "Since Lil and I both have jobs, and I've been saving for over a year now, and with no marriage prospects, we'd like to rent it. Move in together."

His brows shot together. "Like a bunch of old maids?"

"No—o," Katy drew out the word. "Like girls who are particular about whom they date." Katy tried to tell if he was serious or joking. Sarcasm was part of Vernon Yoder's way of speech.

"And how will I be a good dad to you if you're not living under my roof? Have you thought about that? How can I protect you from the world?"

Moving to the edge of the sofa cushion, Katy straightened her posture and replied, "Of course, I will honor your final decision, but I'm nineteen. I think it would be good for me to learn responsibility. I think the Millers' doddy house would be a safe place to do this." In talking to her mom, she'd happened upon her most persuasive point.

And to Katy's relief, her mother added, "Better than some apartment in the city."

Dad rested his gaze on Mom, who dipped her head. He folded his hands on his lap and turned a stoic face toward Katy. "What are your plans for the doddy house?"

"To renovate it with part of my savings—"

"Hah!" he interrupted, with a wave of hand. "More like all your savings."

Her face heating, Katy ran her palms down the front of her dark skirt. "Lil made a list of our ideas, and she plans to get construction bids on the work. Ivan Miller said we could deduct the renovation costs from rent unless they exceed one year's rent; then he will start to charge rent anyways."

"And what about the job you lost?"

Beads of perspiration collected on Katy's forehead. "I will look for work. I want to work."

He rubbed his slightly shadowed chin, his gaze indiscernible. Finally he nodded, and Kate held her breath. "I will agree on three conditions."

"Yes?" Katy was too pleased to move lest she hinder what could only be a blessing from the Lord.

He thrust one finger in the air. "First, I will look over the bids and the financial arrangements and see if I think they are feasible and fair."

"Yes." She took several quick breaths. "I welcome your advice."

"Second, I will go and speak to Ivan Miller to see if he is willing to keep an eye out for you girls."

Embarrassed because their ages weren't that far apart, Katy frowned. But she gave her head a reluctant nod.

"And third, you must go on three dates with David Miller before you move into this doddy house."

"What!" Katy almost toppled off the couch, and her mouth wouldn't close.

"It would please your mother." He patted her mom's hand. "Her feelings matter in this, too."

Katy stared at her mom, whose eyes widened and then twinkled.

Silence prevailed while Katy tried to tell if he was joking. Her dad cracked his knuckles. Katy swallowed, still mystified over her father's unusual request. Finally, unable to prevent a hint of disrespect from tainting her voice, she asked, "And do I have to report to you after these dates?"

"You can report to your mom."

Still struggling with disbelief, Katy watched her siblings burst into the room. They skidded to a stop when they saw all the serious expressions. Her sister Karen tilted her head. "We're finished, Mom."

"You may go work on your report."

"Dad promised to play checkers," Katy's youngest brother reminded them.

Dad picked up a checker and rolled it between his thumb and one finger. "We're not finished with our talk. I'll call you." The trio shuffled back out, and the checker pinged back onto the game board, bounced, and rolled onto the floor.

Katy quickly retrieved it and placed it back on the board, returning to her seat.

"Where were we?" he asked.

Katy's cheeks heated again. "About David Miller. If after these three dates, I don't like him. Then what?"

"Then you are free to quit him."

"But you must agree to give him a chance," her mother interjected.

Dad patted Mom's hand, as if reminding her who was in charge.

But Katy thought her dad was losing his mind. "Isn't there something you're forgetting?" He bunched his mouth considering but didn't come up with anything.

"I've turned David down twice already. He probably won't ask me again."

Her father's face broke into a satisfied grin. "I have it on good authority that he will. Perhaps as soon as the New Year's skating party."

CHAPTER 3

That night Marie Yoder folded back her star quilt. She'd been restless all evening, anxious to get her husband alone. "Vernon. I can't believe I had to wait all night to find out what you're up to. Spill it."

He chuckled and stepped up behind her to touch her loosened hair, dark like his and streaked in gray. "Ingenious, wasn't it?" he asked.

She turned to face him. "I never would have taken you for a matchmaker. Especially for your own daughter."

His voice turned gruff. "I'm not."

"Then why?"

"You liked the idea, admit it."

She fiddled with the tie to her white nightgown. "Yes, but what are you cooking up?"

With a sigh, he moved to his side of the bed and sat. "Jake Byler is coming back to the church."

Marie's heart pounded with fear. "What? Where did you hear this?"

"At the elders' meeting. He came to talk to us. He's turning over a new leaf. Of course I'm happy for his soul, but I don't trust him. And I don't want him turning Katy's head again."

Marie skirted around the bed and touched his shoulder. "Oh, I don't either. I'm afraid he'll hurt her again. He was so wild. Our Katy

32

needs a gentle man who is strong in the faith like her."

They remained silent a moment. Marie stared at the plain oak headboard Vernon had fashioned with his own hands before they got married. Then she remembered the rest of her questions. "How did you hear that the Miller boy was going to ask Katy out again?"

Vernon removed his shoes. "Through his brother Ivan."

"What? He told you about the doddy house? You already knew of Katy's plans?"

"Of course." His voice held a hint of pride, and he found her hand. "Settle down, Marie. Ivan talked frankly, concerned that the girls would renovate and then get married. He didn't want to cheat them out of their money. He told me of his brother's interest in Katy."

"And what if Katy does spend her savings and then decide to move out and marry David? What then?"

"Then she's learned a valuable lesson. But that's something I need to work out with Ivan. Just in case. He's a kid himself, but he wouldn't have come to me if he planned to cheat them."

Marie nodded and went to her side of the bed. "Seems like you've thought of everything," she said, before flicking off the lamp.

～⌐

Inching along in line at the church's monthly potluck spread, Katy and Lil each grabbed plastic silverware rolled in napkins and a paper plate.

"So what did you bring?" Katy asked, trying to tamp down her excitement until the perfect moment.

"Stew and broccoli corn bread."

"Hope there's some left." Everybody in church knew Lil and her mom were the potluck queens, a matriarchal honor passed down for generations in their family. Katy plunked baked beans on her plate, the serving spoon suddenly fumbling and splattering beans onto the tablecloth. They both reached for it at the same time. "Wish Megan could've come."

"Yeah. Too bad she's got the flu."

"At least she's still on break and has her mom to take care of her. Is that it?" Katy pointed at an empty pot, wondering if it was the stew.

"Yeah. But it looks like it's all gone."

"Your dishes always are. Aha!" Her enthusiasm on eyeing the nine-by-thirteen dish beside the empty pot was overplayed even for one of Lil's recipes. Using a spatula, Katy scooped up a small piece of Lil's corn bread. It missed the empty spot on her plate and plopped on top of her beans. She shrugged. "Clumsy today."

They carried their filled plates down a center aisle, glancing at the rows of long tables at either side of them. "How's that?" Lil asked, nodding her head toward a few empty folding chairs.

They settled in, and Lil glanced over at Katy. "You're acting weird. Jittery. You talked to your folks, didn't you?" Katy opened her mouth, but before she could reply, Lil gave a little squeal. "And they said yes?"

Raising her palms to calm her friend, Katy wavered, "Yes. . .no."

Lil poked her arm with her plastic fork. "Quit."

"Okay. I talked to them. But here's the deal. Dad agreed." She had to pause when Lil bounced and nearly collapsed the gray metal chair. "But he put conditions on it."

"Of course. Parents always do that." Lil shoveled down several bites of tossed salad. "So we just meet those conditions."

Katy shook her head. A part of her wanted to grab Lil by the arms, squeal, and dance with her in a circle as if they were a couple of kids, or at the least do the garbanzo shimmy. But if she didn't tamp down her friend's enthusiasm, Lil would never understand the gravity of the stipulations. And if Katy had to bear this trial, she wasn't going to bear it alone. She pointed a carrot stick at Lil. "Three conditions, to be exact."

Holding her fork at eye level, Lil stared at a chunk of gooey brownie. "Give 'em to me. One at a time."

"First, he wants to see the bids and the financial stuff."

"Easy enough. What else?"

"He wants to persuade Ivan Miller to keep an eye on us."

"Yuck. Oh fine. We can deal with it, I guess."

"You think that one's bad, listen to this." She leaned and whispered, "I have to go on three dates with David Miller before Dad will agree to it."

Lil's lips spewed brownie crumbs, and she slapped her palm over her mouth until she could spit into her napkin to keep from choking. After blotting her face, she stared at Katy. "No way!"

"You heard me."

"*Your* dad came up with that? Your dad, who's on the elder board?" Lil never missed an opportunity to rub it in that Megan and Katy's dads both served on the elder board. Lil's dad was too busy farming.

"With the help of my mom. They're real smug about it, too."

"But are they serious?"

"Dead serious. That's why you've got to come up with those bids fast." Katy lowered her voice to a whisper again, "Because if this whole doddy house thing isn't going to fly, then I for sure don't want to go through with all three dates." She worried her lip. Mostly, she didn't want to hurt David's feelings.

"But. . .then you're going to do it?"

"Well yeah. He's actually a sweet guy. Good-looking, too."

Lil stared at her with stricken eyes. Her face paled. "You like him?"

Feeling uneasy at her friend's unwarranted fear, Katy replied, "No. Of course not. But he's been asking me out for a while."

Lil crumpled her napkin into a ball and tossed it onto her plate. "Well, he's not your type."

"What's that supposed to mean? Wait a minute." Katy narrowed her eyes. "Do you like him?"

"No–o. You just need somebody with more spunk. Since you're so. . .inflexible."

Katy instantly bristled. She wasn't a goody-goody like Lil always insinuated. And she was tired of hearing that she was stubborn, too. Lil pushed sometimes just to see how far she could push. Like the time she actually wore a toe ring to foot washing. Katy still cringed over that. She'd covered it with her palm and slipped it into her pocket while Lil snickered. Giggling at foot washing was a sin in itself. Katy often overcompensated to keep Lil in line. But this wasn't the time to make a case of it, so she turned the heat back at Lil. "Did you ask your folks?"

Lil pushed her plate back and took a sip of her soda. "I did. Round one down. About two more to go, and then we're good. Honestly, Dad seems preoccupied for some reason. And Mom's lost her fight lately.

Now I can tell them what your dad said"—she lowered her voice— "without the David part. So don't worry about them. You know that even if they don't agree, I'm going to do this. "

Dread rippled through Katy's stomach. She hoped Lil didn't end up in a fight with her parents, although that had happened often enough in the past. Their relationship seemed to survive somehow. It was good Lil wasn't the oldest in her family. Her folks at least had practice before she came along. She glanced sideways.

Lil was rubbing her temples, staring down at the table. "I guess this can work."

Thinking of David's feelings again, Katy's meal turned sour. She whispered, "It doesn't feel fair to David. Think I need to tell him what my folks are up to? Warn him up front and see if he'll just play along? That way I don't hurt his feelings. He is a really nice guy."

"What if he won't? Then you won't meet your dad's criteria. Or what if that's even more humiliating for him? You better wait and tell him on the last date that you're not interested and hope that he doesn't ever find out." She gripped Katy's arm. "Wait. Did he even ask you out?"

Twisting away, Katy replied. "No. Dad said he was going to ask me to the skating party this afternoon."

"How would he know that?"

Katy shrugged. "I have no idea. The grapevine, I guess."

"The elders' grapevine," Lil added another dig. "But he didn't ask you yet?"

Katy shook her head. "You think I need to go flirt with him or something?"

Lil suddenly grinned. "I'd like to see *that* happen."

Lil's taunting attitude raised Katy's hackles again. She wasn't afraid to flirt with a guy. Katy just hadn't been interested in anyone since Jake. And she loved to prove Lil wrong. Slanting a brow, Katy scooted her chair back.

Lil clapped her hand over her spreading smile.

During their conversation, Katy had kept tabs on David, scoping the situation. He'd been watching her, too. In fact, he'd smiled once when their gazes had met. Now he loitered by the trash can, the sole of one shoe propped against the wall's baseboard. Her pulse raced with indecision.

David swiped a hand through brown hair that fell neatly back in place—shiny hair a lot of girls would envy—then took a swig of soda pop. *Trying to act cool*, she thought. Normally, the idea that he intentionally waited for her to dump her trash so he could pounce on her would be pathetic enough to make her leave the table empty-handed. But under the circumstances, she decided to put him out of his misery.

She set her shoulders and maneuvered through the crowded room, lifting her plate once to avoid a rowdy child. She reached the gray plastic can and plopped her trash in its black liner. Casually, she stepped aside and allowed her gaze to rest on David. "Oh hi," she said.

"Hi, Katy. Good food, huh?" Even though his trim physique was hidden beneath his plain brown suit jacket, overeating didn't seem to be a problem for him.

"Yes. But you're used to that. Your mom's a good cook."

His hazel gaze darted to the table of casseroles and empty platters. "What about you? Do you like to cook?"

"I can cook, but being friends with Lil, I'd rather not compete in that area. I guess that's why I like to do housekeeping. A girl wants to shine someplace." *That was a stupid pun*, she thought.

He grinned. "I like that about you. You're considerate."

Feeling the light-headed zap that follows an untruth, Katy studied the ground.

"Modest, too," he said.

"No I'm not." She raised her chin. "I'm not as good as everyone thinks."

She didn't know why it bothered her so much today. She wanted to be good. Still, it hurt when Lil called her inflexible or old-fashioned. The paradox confused her. One thing was certain: David didn't suspect her ulterior motives and didn't deserve them, either. She felt herself shrinking back from her dad's plan.

He quirked an eyebrow. She allowed herself to study his pleasantly angular face. He gave her a confident grin, but not presumptuous. "I better not go there. You going to the skating party this afternoon?"

She swallowed. She absolutely wouldn't go through with this.

"If you are, can I take you?"

His eyes pleaded and twinkled at the same time. He widened his smile, and his cheek creased on the left side of his mouth. She'd never noticed he had dimples. And he really was a nice guy. And a great skater. But she had no intentions of stringing him along, doddy house or not. So much rested on her decision. Finally she determined, she'd go with him, but at the first opportunity, she would tell him about her dad's deal.

"Sure."

His shoulders relaxed a tad. "Great. How about three o'clock?"

"Perfect. But you'd better wear knee pads and a helmet. I'm not that good."

"There you go again. I've been watching you, Katy. I know if you can skate or not. You make a pretty picture on the ice."

A spurt of pleasure surprised her. "Thanks, David."

She glanced around and saw that the crowd was starting to disperse. "Guess folks are leaving. I need to put something on the bulletin board before they lock up. See you later." She spun, feeling his gaze on her back, and fought to deny the strange pleasure it brought her.

After she pinned a paper to the church bulletin board that would let others know she was looking for more work, she made her way toward the exit. The moment she stepped into the parking lot, Lil grabbed her arm.

"You did it, didn't you?"

She shrugged away. "Shh! He might be following. Walk me to the car."

"Well?"

"He's taking me to the party." Katy reached for her Chevy's door handle. "Get those bids fast, Lil. Okay?"

"Of course. I can't believe this is finally happening. I'll see you at the party."

Katy started to get in the car, but thought better of it. She jumped back out and leaned against the roof. "Lil!"

Her friend turned, and Katy motioned her back. "Be careful how you act at the party. Don't give me away. And don't tell anybody about this except Megan."

"Duh. I'm not stupid."

"Fine. See you later."

Katy slammed her car door and looked in the mirror to straighten her covering. Her scheming reflection caught her off guard. Was she becoming a stranger to herself? What was happening? She reached up and gave the mirror an angry twist so that it only showed the rectangle of the back windshield. And there was David Miller walking behind her car.

She fastened her seat belt and started the ignition. When she backed out, David was already sitting inside his shiny black sedan. She edged her car onto the street when an angry thought shot through her mind. *It's all your fault, Jake Byler. You've ruined me for everybody else.* She allowed a ball of resentment to expand in her throat. Yes, it was all his fault.

In Plain City, she braked for a red light. Jake was a rat, but it really wasn't all his fault she hadn't moved on with her life. Maybe this date was a good thing, and her dad was doing her a favor. It was time to test the waters and see if she could date somebody besides Jake.

If she gave David a chance, he might even grow on her. Maybe they'd marry and tell their children the funny story of how their mom tricked their daddy into a date. They'd laugh and say the joke was on their mom, because their daddy wanted the date all along. Wouldn't that make a happy story?

Honk! The blare of a car's horn brought her back to her surroundings, and she placed her foot on the accelerator. She needed to get home and get ready for her foolish date.

CHAPTER 4

Dashing toward the door before the bell disturbed her dad's nap, Katy snatched up her skates. She didn't need her dad telling David to take care of his dumplin'. As she passed, her mom looked up from her quilting frame and mumbled, "Have fun with that nice boy."

"Sure." Katy's black, quilted snow boots pattered across the wood flooring. It was bad enough that earlier in the week she'd caught her mom staring at a double wedding ring pattern. Gratefully her siblings, who liked to tease, were sledding out back. Her pulse accelerated. She gripped the handle and swung open the door to be instantly thrown off balance by David's hazel gaze—part warm and part mischievous, as if it held some secret.

David tilted his head, his wind-ruffled hair accentuating his boyish appeal. "Hi Katy." When his mouth quirked at the corner, she realized he was waiting on her, probably expecting to get invited inside.

"Just a moment." She ducked back inside and dove into her wool coat, throwing a scarf around her neck. David held the door for her as she stepped onto the porch. The crisp air nipped her cheeks, and she crunched down the walk with David toward a rumbling, black sedan puffing steam from its exhaust.

"Wow." The word slipped from her mouth unbidden. *Impressive,* she kept to herself. She could have sworn the car was even shinier than it had been at church.

He grinned and opened its passenger door for her, and she slipped into its warm interior. While he went around the outside, she stroked the plush seat with her thumb, inhaling David's intimate ride of leather and aftershave.

He hopped in and paused before placing a gloved hand on the gearshift. "You're stunning in that white scarf."

When she had opened the hand-knitted Christmas gift, her mom had mentioned it would make a nice contrast with her black hair. Usually her mom didn't compliment her children's outward appearance unless it was to affirm neatness or modesty.

Katy had been taught that a woman should be more concerned about her inner beauty and not prideful about the outer, which was fleeting anyway. But Katy couldn't help but be appreciative when she looked in a mirror because her face didn't need the forbidden cosmetics. She had been blessed with good features, and the plain Conservative hairstyles she wore only emphasized them.

Thin like her figure, her face was a perfect oval, and she had dark prominent brows and black-lashed brown eyes that were more exotic than plain. Her mom told her that a missionary ancestor married into Spanish blood. Her nose even protested her Conservative lifestyle for it appeared aristocratic, thin and long. Her lips must have come from the Spanish ancestor, too, because they were full and expressive. She knew that her striking eyes and mouth caused people to imagine more intensity in her emotions than she usually felt or meant to display.

Self-consciously flicking her ponytail out from under the scarf, she said, "Thanks." She dropped her skates on the floor mat, careful to keep her eyes from flirting. With a fluid movement, he put the car in reverse, and they backed onto the country road. "How do you keep your car so clean?" She motioned toward the snowy countryside. "In this?" His cheek muscle twitched as if she'd touched upon a sensitive subject. When he didn't have an immediate comeback, she asked, "What? Am I embarrassing you?"

He shot her a warm glance. "I'm just wondering how you are with secrets."

"Really?" Involuntarily, she leaned toward him. "I'm great with secrets."

His raised brow challenged, "Never knew a woman who could keep secrets."

"Try me."

"I haul buckets of hot water to the barn and wash it, towel dry it."

"How often?"

"Once or twice a week."

Katy rested her head back on the headrest. "Wow. Does your dad know?"

"Yeah. He thinks it's prideful."

"I think it's great."

He cast her an uncertain glance. She leaned forward again and jutted her chin. "I feel flattered to ride in a clean car. I think every guy should take note and learn from you. And I don't think it's prideful to take good care of your stuff. You know Megan?"

"Megan?" He seemed confused at the sudden turn of the conversation. "Yeah."

"Her parents are always harping on stewardship. And it's rubbed off on me, too. It makes good sense to take care of your stuff." He beamed, and she relaxed her shoulders. "All I mean, is I understand. I like things sparkly, too. I clean houses, remember? I just never carried it over to my car in the winter." She troubled her lip. "Maybe I should."

"Maybe I should do it for you."

She glanced over. It was a generous, flirtatious offer. "Ah. I don't think so." She snuck another sideways glance. But was this guy her clone or what?

He shrugged and concentrated on the narrow gravel road lined by low snowbanks and ditches. But the simple offer hung in the air. David Miller had ingratiated himself in only five minutes. She liked him.

He pushed a button and classical music flowed through the car's speakers.

"Can I use your mirror?" she asked.

"Sure."

She lowered the visor and pulled a soft beanie out of her pocket. Staring into a gleaming mirror, she placed it over her covering and pulled it snug over her ears. When she finished, she flipped up the visor and glanced sideways.

He grinned. "And a matching hat. Even more stunning."

"I figured I'd ease you into it, you know, so I didn't knock you off your feet or something."

"You practically ran us into the ditch. Took my brute strength just to keep us on the road."

Lowering an embarrassed gaze to the floorboards, Katy noticed her skates. "You're pretty good on the ice, aren't you?"

"Yep."

Katy sank back against the seat, listening to the music, enjoying the thrill of masculine attention that purred along her spine.

Ten minutes later, David turned into the lane next to the Stuckys' mailbox and drove to the back of the property. Several cars were already parked there. He helped her out, and they trudged over the frozen clods of a dormant cornfield toward a patch of box elders that banked the Big Darby Creek. Lil wasn't among the dozen other young adults already milling down by the ice, and Katy remembered Megan was home sick.

He pointed out a fallen log where the surrounding ground was littered with boots and shoes. "Shall we put on our skates?"

"Sure." Katy dropped to the log, trying to hide the excitement that washed over her. She bent over her gray wool culottes and removed her quilted boots, quickly slipping her black stocking-clad feet into white skates. As she laced, she glanced at David, who was already finished. His elbows propped on his knees, he was watching the skaters. The rink was a wide patch of ice about 150 feet in length, most likely cleared by the Stuckys' red snow thrower that now sat parked against the far bank.

"Ready?" she asked.

In response, his masculine grip warmed her hand through their gloves. At the bank, he glided backward and dug his toe pick into the ice, then skated forward. With surprise, Katy allowed him to clasp her by the waist and lift her down onto the ice.

"Easy. There you go."

At first they stroked forward, hand in hand, and after one circle of the rink, he pulled her into a Kilian position. The back of her left shoulder pressed against the front of his navy jacket, and his hand rested at her waist. She didn't feel uneasy at the intimacy of his touch because skating was one of the permitted group dating activities that allowed such familiarities. Several other couples skated in the group of teens and young adults.

Their skates cut the ice sending sprays of white shavings. The bumpy, air-pocketed river ice didn't hinder their skating; it was all Katy knew. But relying on David's superior skill, she quickly relaxed, their skates crossing in sync and bodies leaning and drawing across the ice as one, even when they dodged in and around other skaters.

When they'd tired of that, he drew her to the middle where a few skaters practiced spins. He twirled her, steadying her when she lost balance. Once she sailed into him, practically knocking his breath away. They laughed, visible puffs of air separating their faces. When she looked up, she saw Lil ahead on the bank, frowning at them. "Oh look, David. It's Lil." Katy waved. "Can we go talk to her?"

Whispering against her soft hat, he replied, "You can call me Dave."

The suggestive tone of his voice sent a startled warning. No, she wouldn't be doing that or anything else to lead him on unnecessarily. He drew her close again, and she felt a bit self-conscious as they glided toward the bank where some of their friends conversed around a big bonfire.

With ease, David jumped to the low bank and pulled her up with him. Then they tiptoed to the fire. "Hi, Lil." Katy beamed. Lil's hands were stuffed in her coat pockets.

"I'll get us some hot chocolate. Want some, Lil?" David offered.

"Sure."

"What's wrong?" Katy demanded. "You're looking at me like I have broccoli stuck in my teeth or something."

"You usually do." Lil chuckled. "Looks like you're having a ball."

"Why not? He's a good skater. Want him to take you a couple spins?"

"Don't you dare pawn off your date on me," Lil snapped.

Katy felt her face heat when David stepped up behind them with steaming drinks in Styrofoam cups. Had he overheard Lil's remark?

Lil thanked him and took one of the cups. "Good thing Megan's not here to see these."

David shrugged a brow. "Because?"

Katy explained. "These are not easily recyclable."

"Oh. Usually we use the thick paper cups, don't we?"

Katy frowned at Lil before she sipped the warm chocolate. "Anyway. This is good."

As they finished drinking and mingled with the rest of the group, Katy felt self-conscious over the curious glances she and David provoked. At least he hadn't hovered or marked his territory. Instead, he'd been considerate and chummed with some of his friends, giving her a chance to visit with Lil. When he asked if she was ready to skate again, Lil waved her away.

When they returned to the ice, he asked, "What's up with Lil?"

"I'm not sure." Katy glanced back at her friend and saw her tapping away at the buttons of her cell phone. Must be preoccupied over her new toy—the elder board had been divided over the issue of allowing its use. With disgust, Katy asked, "You have a cell phone?"

"Yep. Why?"

She shrugged and was saved from getting into a debate when her blade hit a root protrusion. She tripped and David caught her. But the minor incident left them skating face-to-face, with David skating backward.

"Here, put your palms flat against mine," he urged. Then she forgot all about Lil. He even taught her to skate backward, and Katy felt more happy and carefree than she had in months. Within another half an hour, however, her ankles grew tired and her toes frigid. She glanced toward the bonfire, and David was instantly perceptive of her need. "Ready to go in?"

"I am." She scanned the bank for Lil and found her talking to some tall, well-built guy who sent an odd flutter through her stomach. A warning flashed through her mind, and she looked closer. Her stomach clenched. Jake Byler? How on earth—at that instant, her world spun. Her skates tangled, too. David tripped and skidded on the knees of his jeans, pulling her down on top of him. With a grunt, her breath was forced from her lungs, and her elbow slammed the ice. When finally they quit sliding, she rolled over on her side with a groan.

She felt David scrambling out from beneath her, then leaning over her, his hand on her shoulder. "Are you okay?"

"I think so." She tugged at her culottes, but only wanted to curl in a ball and escape the humiliation, escape Jake.

She stared into David's concerned hazel eyes. He apologized, "I don't know what happened."

She did. She also knew she needed to get up before they drew even more attention than they already had. She saw his mouth quirk. "This isn't funny," she warned. "You get up first." Surely his knees were bruised, if not cracked.

With a grimace and some clumsy movements, he was soon standing on his blades. Then he grabbed her under the arms and pulled her to her feet. All his concern was directed at her, and he even brushed awkwardly at her snowy coat.

"I'm fine," she snapped, rubbing an aching elbow.

"Guess we should have quit sooner." He draped a supportive arm around her waist, and they skated toward the bank.

Feeling guilty for snapping at him, she admitted, "It was my fault. I tripped you." She drew in a quick breath. "Is he still over there talking to Lil?" As David glanced over his shoulder, she felt his body tense.

"So *he's* what happened."

"Sorry."

"So you want to talk to them? Or shall we slink off to the car in our humiliation?"

"Definitely slink."

"Sit down then, and let me help you with your skates." She lowered herself to the log. With another grimace, David went down on his knees.

She placed her hand on his shoulder. "You're in pain. I'm so sorry."

"I'm fine. Now smile. Pretend to have fun." He winked. "That'll get him."

She removed her hand. "I was having fun. Now I know why Lil was acting all weird on us. But until he ruined everything, I was having a blast."

David grinned and squeezed her hand. "Me, too, Katy."

⸻

A few minutes before the spill, Lil had explained to Jake Byler, "She doesn't really like him, but David's crazy about her."

Burning with jealousy, Jake Byler glanced down at his cousin, then back out at the ice where David maneuvered Katy around like some ballerina. Her slim form and fine-boned features gave her a fragile appearance, but Jake knew from experience a man couldn't force her to do anything, unless she allowed it. And it hurt to see the way she moved in sync with David. "Since when?"

"I didn't notice until he asked her out. Now it's obvious."

The Miller guy was younger than Jake, and they'd never been close. They'd played some basketball and hockey together. David's brothers were older than Jake so he'd never hung out with them, either. He didn't know what made the guy tick. Except for Katy, that is. And why wouldn't she?

She'd captured his own attention long before he'd acquired any skills to fend off female charms. Katy was younger than Jake, too, but at recess he let her cut in line just because he was intrigued with her bouncy ponytail. After he'd touched it, she'd reeled him in with her black flashing eyes.

Jake had always loved to watch her hands dance when she talked, admiring her tiny wrists and long feminine fingers. But her greatest asset was her face. There was an intensity in her dark eyes that could move mountains. They were deep, dark, and expressive. Her nose was thin and long, merely a gentle slope that drew the eye down to her best feature, those full, sulky lips. The combination of lethal eyes and pursed lips stopped a guy in his tracks. A man instantly sensed the stubborn spirit behind the face. Lesser men shrank back. She wielded her feminine weapons without chagrin, swathing her path through life, unawares that most people did not have such natural charms at their command. She had a hauteur about her that warned others she wasn't used to losing. She probably didn't realize that she could get her way without uttering a word.

As if reading his mind, she turned her brown gaze toward him. Her eyes were naturally so dark that they almost smoldered, causing a man to want to read something sexual in them, when really they were unfathomable. But it caused Jake to feel jealous now that it was David's arms around her.

His stomach clenched when recognition hit her expression and that smoldering gaze riveted upon him. His gaze pleaded with hers. But she denied him. Her eyes glittered, and her expression darkened with repulsion. Her entire body reacted. She actually stopped skating.

David toppled forward, and Jake watched helpless as the couple wiped out on the ice, Katy tumbling on top of David.

Jake lunged forward, but Lil caught him by his coat sleeve.

She grimaced. "Ouch. That had to hurt. You see how both his knees smacked the ice? At least he cushioned Katy's fall."

His jealousy reared again as David untangled himself from Katy and hovered over her. "You sure this is their first date? They seem mighty cozy."

Lil waved a glove through the air. "It's the skating. He's had his hands all over her. That's why I called you. So what are you going to do?"

He knew now this group setting had been a mistake for his first encounter with Katy. He should have waited and gone with their original plan. Lil's plan. She'd hired him to modernize the doddy house. He'd be there when Katy came over. He would apologize in privacy. Beg, if he had to, for her forgiveness.

"Well?"

"I can't go rescue her. I didn't bring any skates. But it looks like they're coming in off the ice." He glared at David. "I've got my work cut out for me."

She put an elbow in his gut. "You deserve it, chump."

"Hmph." He glanced away from the irritating scene where David was now unlacing her skates. Lil had one glove on her hip, looking miffed. She never should have told him all those years ago that Katy meant to marry him. Maybe it wouldn't have made him so confident she'd always be there. Maybe it wouldn't have scared him away. But Lil had meant well. They'd always been close as if she were his sister. In fact, when the family got together, she hung out with him instead of his younger sister Erin. That's probably how he noticed Katy. She and Lil and Megan had always been together.

"They're leaving. I can't believe she's not even going to say good-bye," Lil huffed.

A hand clamped Jake's shoulder, and he turned. "Hey, how's it going?"

"Good to see you, man." Chad Penner held out his hand. Though they had once been best of friends, their relationship had become estranged when Jake had left the church.

Grasping it, Jake replied, "Better get used to it. I'm back to stay."

Chad swung an arm over Jake's shoulder. "I knew you'd be back."

With relief, Jake allowed himself to be drawn into the group of skaters warming up at the bonfire. Everyone seemed happy to see him, forgiving of his sudden absence and eager to accept him back into the group. Meanwhile, he glimpsed Katy and David disappearing into a stand of box elders. But as the group enveloped him, some of his heaviness fled. He roasted a hot dog and caught up with Chad.

Jake wished he'd never left, but all he could do now was prove how he'd changed. He was earnest in his desire to fit back in with his old friends.

When the group began to disperse, Jake walked Lil to her car then squeezed her shoulder. "Maybe this was for the best. It'll give Katy time to digest the idea that I'm back. We'll have to trust God with this, okay?"

"I've been praying for you for a long time, chump."

"I know. Thanks."

Head bent in thought, he strode to his truck and climbed in. Although he'd jumped his first hurdle, facing the group again, he knew the worst was still ahead of him. He'd never forget the incident, the night when he'd been drunk. Furious, Katy had hissed that she wanted him to go away and stay away. But this afternoon, when their gazes latched, he'd felt hopeful for an instant. Then when she'd left without even saying good-bye to Lil, he'd gotten the impression she loathed him.

He drove out onto the gravel road. Nobody had ever loathed him. Wait, hadn't he once heard that love and hate were closely related? For his sake, he hoped so. His mind traveled back to the time before he'd grown restless. He flicked on his headlights and started toward home, involuntarily scanning the snowy ditches and fields for deer and other wild animals that sometimes leapt in front of vehicles.

The farm made him restless. Jake's dad had died years earlier. His mom still lived in his childhood home, but his uncle and brother Cal managed the farm. Jake had never been interested in that, though he'd helped his uncle a lot over the years. He had been interested in construction, seeing buildings erected, swinging a hammer. He didn't regret his vocation decision, but he regretted losing Katy.

Suddenly his vision caught something that made his pulse race. Was God answering his prayer so quickly? There alongside the road was David Miller's disgustingly shiny car. A grin spread over Jake's face; then a chuckle erupted in his throat. A flat tire. Just what the woman-stealer deserved. Trying to tamp down his delight, he pulled in behind the stranded vehicle. Maybe he was going to be able to rescue her after all.

He opened the door and jumped down, leaving his headlights on for Miller. "Hey, got a problem?" David looked up. Even in the dim light, Jake could see the guy's embarrassment. "Need a hand with that?"

"Nope." David jerked the wrench, twisting the lug nuts of the left rear wheel. "Got it under control."

Jake stuffed his hands in his pockets and gazed at the car, where he could see Katy's dark silhouette.

"Don't need your help," David repeated sharply.

"Think I'll just say hi to Katy." Jake strode past his angry opponent and around the back of the car right up to Katy's door. Her face was looking straight ahead. He knocked on her window and startled her. She hit the window's inoperative button. He took that as an invitation and opened her door. It hurt to see her inside another man's car, but he gave her what he hoped looked like a contrite smile. "Hi Katy."

Her chin jutted upward. "What do *you* want?"

Her face was so lovely, flushed and pink, her hair messy under the white knitted beanie. But her gaze smoldered. He'd learned that her gaze could be dark or cool, but one thing it never did was shrink back. Still, he yearned to scoop her into his arms until she no longer despised him. "Need a ride?"

"Not hardly."

"You look kinda lonely and cold."

Just then David jerked the driver's door open and slid in. "Not lonely." He started the engine.

"And warm as toast," Katy added with a shiver.

Jake gave her a salute and eased the door closed, backing away from the car just before it spit gravel in his face.

CHAPTER 5

On Monday morning, Katy took her normal route to work, using routine maneuvers to blend in with the freeway traffic that skirted the west side of Columbus. As she drove, she puzzled over the mystery of Jake's unexpected appearance at Sunday's skating party. It didn't surprise her that he'd come home for the holidays, since like Megan he was probably on break. But why had he come to the river when he hadn't mingled with church friends for over a year now—ever since the incident between them in the church parking lot?

She probed at the matter, furious at herself for gawking at Jake like a lovesick fool. In that one weak moment, his features, wind-ruffled hair, and masculine physique had been burned into her memory all anew, more vivid and arresting than ever. She felt as if months of working to get over him had been destroyed in an instant. He'd stood on the icy riverbank and beckoned her with dark, hooded eyes so scorching and brooding and out of place in that winter playground. It had been all she could do to pull her gaze away. No wonder she'd faltered.

She reached out and flipped the car's heater off. With a glance at the green, overhead sign, she changed into the exit lane. And when David's tire had gone flat, the rat had the gall to butt in where he wasn't wanted. While David had worked on the tire, her nemesis had stepped out of her imagination and appeared in flesh and blood outside her window, wearing a crooked smile and a smug expression.

David had handled the evening's humiliation with more grace than she would have imagined possible, coming to her rescue. Twice.

Leave it to Katy to trip up the best skater at the party. But David had been a great sport—given that Jake had knocked her off her feet, David had played the hero by whisking her away to safety. Only, poor guy, his efforts had backfired.

With the pride he took in the care of his car, she knew that its flat tire probably embarrassed him the most. The tension that sizzled when David slid into his driver's side and glared at Jake would have been intense enough to ignite a forest fire in the dead of winter. Thankfully, Jake had backed away.

After all the drama Jake had caused, she hadn't wanted to humiliate David further by bringing up her dad's stipulations. Her mom had been right. He was a great guy, and she'd had a lot of fun with him, too. Although with the aggravation he'd suffered on their date, including a set of bruised knees, he probably wouldn't ask her out again.

Just when she had started to entertain thoughts of David as a real boyfriend, Jake had returned, sending her heart, mind, and body into a crazy spin. He still wielded tremendous power over her. And she resented him for it. Even if he slipped back into oblivion, his brief appearance had caused her irreparable damage.

Lil could probably explain why Jake had shown up at the party, but Katy hadn't been able to ask her yet with the way their schedules clashed.

As she pulled into the driveway of the Brooks' residence, Katy cringed. She hoped Lil hadn't told Jake about the three-date stipulation. She certainly didn't want him to think she had to buy her dates. Sometimes when it came to Jake, Katy wasn't sure whose side Lil was on. Flipping down her visor, she checked to see that her covering was straight. When she saw her grim lips, she wet them and forced herself to relax.

Moments later, she used her key to enter the house, taking a quick scope of its usual disarray. By the time she hit the kitchen, she'd already scooped up two sets of newspapers and several pink glittery items of clothing.

In the kitchen, her steps faltered. "Oh. Hi, Tammy. I didn't realize you were here, or I would have knocked."

Tammy Brooks snapped her briefcase closed and slipped into its shoulder strap. "No problem." She grabbed a designer purse off a bar stool. "I'm glad I can at least count on you."

Katy took the newspapers to the recycle bin and set Addison's clothing on a bar stool. Her slim, high-heeled employer made a turn toward the door, and Katy knew that she couldn't waste such an opportunity. "Do you have a moment?"

"Sure. I'm already late so what's a few more minutes?" Katy felt her face heat, but before she could reply, Tammy asked, "You aren't going to quit on me, are you?"

"Of course not." She hurried into her explanation so that she didn't take up Tammy's precious time. "I just wondered if you knew of anyone who was looking for a housekeeper? One of my employers moved to Florida, and I could use more work."

Tammy smiled and plunked her purse back on the counter. Her briefcase, stuffed with real estate fliers, slid to the ground. "Why don't I fix us a pot of coffee? We never get to chat. You drink coffee?"

Feeling apprehensive, Katy folded a size 7 sweater. "I'd love a cup."

Tammy flung a wet coffee filter into the garbage, and some of the grounds splattered onto her suit skirt. "Ugh!" she moaned, tearing off a paper towel and blotting at the spot.

"Can I help?"

"Nope." Tammy brushed the air with her hand. "I've got it. Good as new. See?" Then she bent over, and Katy cringed to see a cross nestled in her employer's cleavage, accentuated by her immodest neckline. "What hours do you usually work?"

Slipping onto a bar stool, Katy explained, "I work for you on Mondays and Wednesdays. I clean for an elderly woman who lives in a retirement community every other Friday. The couple that moved to Florida I worked for on Tuesdays and Thursdays. That's the job I need to replace."

The aroma of a popular Starbucks blend filled the kitchen as coffee dripped into a carafe. Tammy moved into a bar stool and swiveled to face her. "I think we can help each other. I need a nanny."

Instantly recoiling, Katy shook her head. "I don't think so. I've never babysat before."

Tammy swept off the stool and got the liquid creamer from the refrigerator. No wonder Tammy was treating her like a guest instead of a servant. The other woman returned with two steaming cups, placing one in front of Katy. "It's not really babysitting. My kids are old enough to take care of themselves. But they need somebody to haul them around and help them with their homework, field problems. Mostly keep an eye on them."

Katy took a sip of coffee, then asked, "What happened to their nanny?"

With a deep sigh, Tammy said. "She quit. Claims her classes are too full next semester. Look, she really left me in the lurch. That's why I was late this morning, arranging for a ride for the kids this afternoon. Tanya didn't even tell me to my face. She just called me last night. I was furious. I can tell you she won't be getting any references from me. In fact, I've a mind to call one of her professors or something." Tammy crossed her long slim legs and forced a smile. "Think about the benefits. A few hours every afternoon until their dad or I get home from work. You'll end up with more hours that way and still have a couple of days off to sleep in, run errands, or read a book. I wish I had that luxury."

Katy felt her face burn. Tammy assumed her life was luxurious? She seldom lounged around reading books. There was plenty of work to be done at home, helping her mom. Her mind raced, looking for a way to politely turn down the offer. When nothing came to mind, she stalled. "How old are they? It's Addison and Tyler?"

"Yes. Addy is seven, and Tyler's an eleven-year-old adult."

Katy smiled. The children seemed well behaved the few times she'd met them. It was Mr. Brooks she didn't care for. Most often, she'd encountered him on his way to the liquor cabinet or sprawled out watching television, both forbidden indulgences in Katy's mind. His drinking reminded her too much of Jake, making her distrust the older man. Maybe he was the reason the nanny quit. She found herself tapping her fingers on the counter.

"Please say you'll do it until I can find another nanny? I like you and know you'll be great for the kids. You'll help me out this once, won't you? I've got several clients this week, and I can't leave them hanging. And you admitted yourself, you need the money."

"You'll look for another nanny?"

"Yes. Oh thanks, so much." Tammy flew out of her seat. "You're such a sweet thing. And I'll ask around and see if anyone needs a housekeeper. Thanks again, honey."

"So when do you want me to start?"

"Tomorrow afternoon. Here." Tammy scribbled the addresses of her children's schools on a yellow sticky note. "Addison gets out of school at 2:30 p.m., and Tyler gets out at 3:00 p.m. Works out great." She picked up her briefcase and left like a whirlwind, leaving Katy to ponder what had just transpired and to stew over the way Tammy had so effortlessly manipulated her.

⟞⟋

The Brooks' home was located in the west side Columbus suburb of Old Arlington. The affluent neighborhood sprawled between two rivers, the Olentangy and the Scioto, giving it a parklike feel. Many of the houses were Tudor style. With Tammy's yellow sticky note stuck to her steering wheel, Katy followed the street signs through meandering, tree-lined streets to a brick elementary charter school and eased into a slow-moving lineup. She noticed teachers lined along the walkway, helping the students into their cars. On Katy's rearview mirror hung a yellow card with a number that would identify her as Addison's ride.

Addison stood in line on the sidewalk with her classmates. The blond second-grader wore a purple coat and pink boots and had a princess backpack slung over one shoulder. Katy pulled up to the curb, and a teacher opened the car's back door. Addison started talking before she'd even buckled her seat belt.

"I'm surprised to see you, Miss Yoder. Why are you picking me up?"

"Didn't your mommy tell you I'd be watching you for a while?"

"Yes, but I forgot. I've got dance class today."

"You do?" Katy asked, easing the car back into the line of traffic. "Well, I'm not sure you'll be going today. Your mom said she'd leave me instructions at the house." Katy felt tense. Dance lessons? She turned west onto another suburban street. "We're going to pick up Tyler now."

"Okay, but where's my snack?"

"What snack?"

"Tanya always brings me a snack so I don't get bored. Sometimes she brings gummy bears or granola bars. But sometimes she brings me pop. I don't like apples. I'm really tired of apples. So don't bring me any apples. Without my snack, it's so boring waiting for Tyler. Today's going to be a boring day, isn't it?"

"I hope not," Katy replied, glancing at the sticky note again and watching for the street signs. "Do you know how to get to your brother's school?"

"Sure, I know where it is. He thinks he's big stuff just because he's in sixth grade, but they don't do anything fun. I don't know why he brags about it."

"Well, tell me if you see where we're supposed to turn."

"Okay. So why don't you just take me to my dance lessons now? I can hang out with my friends, and then I won't be bored."

"Don't worry. We'll figure that out."

"That was the street back there. You just missed it."

"Ugh!" Katy wheeled into a driveway and waited for the opportunity to turn back. Soon she was in another lineup but feeling less apprehensive about the pickup procedure. When Tyler got in the car, he threw his pack on the floorboards and slammed the door. Then he looked at his sister and said, "Hi, brat."

"Stop calling me that. Make him stop calling me that. He thinks he's big stuff. But he's not."

"Be kind, Tyler. I'll soon have you both home."

"Put on the radio," Tyler demanded.

"I don't listen to the radio," Katy explained. "Why don't you look out the window and see how many snowmen you can find?" Such driving games always entertained her little brothers.

"Why don't you listen to the radio?"

Seemed the car games weren't as fun for Tyler as they were for her siblings. She sighed. "Some of the lyrics aren't godly."

"What's that mean?"

"They talk about bad things."

"No they don't. Turn it on. Come on. My mom lets me."

"Sorry, Tyler."

She heard his seat belt unbuckle and then heard him rustling through his backpack. Katy glanced in the mirror nervously. "What are you doing, Tyler?"

"Duh. He's getting his iPod," Addison said. "He thinks he's big stuff because he has an iPod."

"Oh. Well, you need to keep your seat belt fastened." Not that it mattered as they had already reached the children's street. She'd barely pulled into the drive when both children barreled out of the car. While Katy fumbled in her purse for her house key, Tyler walked to the garage door and punched some buttons. The door opened and both children let themselves into the house. Snapping her purse closed, Katy hurried after them. She closed the garage door behind her and followed them into the kitchen, despondent to see empty microwave popcorn bags and bowls on the counter and a stack of dirty dishes in the sink. How hard was it to load a dishwasher?

Tyler jerked open the refrigerator door and stared into it. Addison pushed him and jerked open a bin.

"Stop it."

Their bodies tugged for position, and Addison came out of the scuffle with string cheese, but her brother latched on to it, too. "Let go," she demanded.

Katy walked over, taking each child by a shoulder. "Move aside, and let me see if there's more."

"This was the last one," Addison said, jerking it out of her brother's grip and quickly peeling back the plastic.

Katy glanced at the counter. "How about some fruit, Tyler?"

He gave his sister a glare but moved toward the fruit bowl and took a banana. When he peeled it back, he stuck it under Addison's nose. She squealed. "Stop. Make him stop."

Katy placed her hand on Tyler's shoulder and said sternly, "You sit in that chair." When he hesitated, she sharpened her voice. "Now." The child sulked into the chair. "Addison you sit in that one." Addison bounced into the chair, giving her brother a victorious look. "Now listen up. When I'm watching you, I expect you to respect each other. I have two brothers and a sister at home. Don't think I don't know how to make little children behave." She narrowed her eyes. "Because I do. Do you understand?"

They both gave nods. Tyler's eyes, however, darkened rebelliously. Katy moved to the counter and looked for her instructions. Sure enough, she was to take Tyler to his friend's house and then take Addison to dance class at an Upper Arlington address. She was supposed to walk her inside, watch practice, and afterward relay the instructor's parental information to Tammy.

"I'm done with my snack. Can I go play?" Addison asked.

"Yes. We have a half hour before I take you to your lessons. Tyler you'll be going to your friends'—"

He punched his fist in the air. "Awesome!"

"You may go to your rooms and change clothes, and I'll call you when it's time," she called after Tyler who was already halfway up the stairs. "Tyler, stop! Come back here and take that banana peel to the trash. It's only polite to clean up after yourself." It was no wonder the house always looked like a tornado had hit it.

He turned and marched back, like a bull eyeing a matador and snatched up the peel with a scowl. "I'll do it, but you're the maid. There." He plunked it in the trash. "Satisfied?"

"I'll be satisfied when you can do that with a smile on your face."

"Fat chance of that." He glanced at her covering. "Pilgrim lady."

Katy's jaw dropped, and she found herself speechless. Meanwhile, Tyler took the steps two at a time and disappeared.

So much for the misconception that the Brooks' children were polite. Though it was probably useless and would probably go unnoticed, Katy went through the house, picking up things that were out of place: Barbie dolls, video games, princess socks, and wineglasses.

She had threatened the children by telling them she knew how to handle her brothers and sister, but the truth was, she'd never had to deal with an adolescent boy's smart mouth. The woodshed prevented that sort of rebellion at her house. She would need to speak to Tammy about the appropriate methods of discipline.

Her more immediate challenge, however, would be taking Addison to dance lessons because dancing was forbidden in the Conservative Mennonite Church she attended. In her imagination, the word *dancing* conjured up smoky dens of drink and lust. She'd never given this type of dancing a thought. If she took Addison, as her employer expected, would she be enabling an innocent child to do something sinful?

On the other hand, Addison would continue her lessons regardless of whether Katy continued to be her nanny or not. And if Katy refused to take the little girl to her dance lessons, Tammy might get angry and fire her. Then her doddy house dreams would be ruined for sure.

Considering the options available to her, she placed the breakfast dishes in the dishwasher. Mom would probably tell her to quit her job and remind her that she could live at home until she got another one. Lil would insist that as long as Katy wasn't dancing, she wasn't doing anything wrong. Megan was adept at handling sticky situations. She would advise Katy to use this as an opportunity to witness to the children. So far that tactic hadn't worked with Tyler when he wanted to listen to the radio. But then she hadn't made Christianity sound very enticing, had she? Nevertheless, Megan's imaginary advice was the best.

She gripped the edge of the sink. She wanted to please her employer, but she didn't want to displease God. She definitely believed that bars and nightclubs were not God-honoring places. Lil had watched enough television and passed along enough steamy details for Katy to make valid conclusions about those devil houses. But that wasn't really the issue.

The Bible talked about King David dancing. Katy had wondered about that when she came across the Old Testament passage. She did little joy dances herself when she was alone. Lil had perfected the garbanzo shimmy. Nothing wrong with those. But to move your body seductively, unless it was with your husband, of course, was definitely wrong.

She had picked up Addison's dance costume off the floor several times. It was skimpy, yet how seductively could a seven-year-old dance? She turned on the faucet and watched the water rinse the sink. She washed her hands, dried them, and carefully folded the hand towel, even though she never found it that way.

She didn't want to overreact. Tyler already thought she was a pilgrim. She wasn't sure where he'd come up with that idea. Was he confusing her with Quakers? Still, it was meant as an insult, and she hadn't enjoyed his wisecrack.

A glance at the clock told her she needed to decide now. With a sigh, she opted to follow Tammy's instructions and evaluate the experience. This wasn't a permanent position, anyway. Maybe Tammy had already found a replacement for her. And God knew her heart, that she didn't want to sin against Him.

Church restrictions were put in place to keep a person from falling into situations of temptation that could lead to sin. She would be very careful not to allow temptation in. She pushed the dishwasher's START button and hurried to the stairway.

"Addison. Tyler. It's time to go. Are you ready?"

CHAPTER 6

Katy followed Addison through a lobby decorated with modern chrome furnishings. A bright ballet poster graced one wall, and a rack of glitzy costumes hung from a corner rack, but no one staffed the desk. Katy followed as Addison skipped down the hall and into a cloakroom. Next Addison went into a practice studio where she greeted her enthusiastic friends. Katy hovered by the door tentatively taking in the assortment of girls and a few jean-clad moms.

The girls ranged from about six to ten in age. They chatted and giggled with each other as they did warm-up exercises, reminding Katy of a physical education class. Only these girls were like little princesses. Most wore tights and leotards. A few had frilly tutus, and some wore skin-fitting slacks and glittery tops.

Soon the instructor walked into the room, speaking kindly and clad in a black second skin. The striking young woman intrigued Katy as she floated in and out among the girls, like a breath of fresh air that touched here, repositioned there, causing smiles and looks of adoration on her little students. When she had everyone's attention, she demonstrated a few movements that they all tried to imitate.

Katy bit her lip, amused. Although the little girls looked the part, they were hopelessly out of sync. But the instructor's youthful body and graceful air fascinated Katy. She could almost imagine Megan using her svelte body in such a way. Megan was the most graceful person Katy knew. As she watched Addison, she wondered what it would be like to be a participant and be encouraged to mimic the instructor's movements. As a little girl, it must be great fun.

She remembered learning to skip rope and the satisfaction that came with mastering the little ditties that went along with it. She found herself rooting for Addison to get the movements, and Katy felt a surge of pride when the little girl did them correctly.

As Katy glanced around the studio for a place to sit and quietly observe the class, she had to wonder if her own slim body was flexible enough to bend and stretch like the instructor's. Her gaze rested on a group of moms, and with embarrassment, she realized she'd caught them staring at her. Instantly, she jerked her gaze away. She felt like the guilty party for invading their world.

Even if she never grew accustomed to stares, the odd looks she often drew from outsiders served to ground her in her faith, reminding her of her true identity. She was a citizen of a higher kingdom. She walked in the truth. Outsiders had no idea that the heavenly kingdom was more glorious than the earthly one. It put Katy in an awkward position to be both out of place and right about life. And being right never kept one from being scorned.

She reminded herself that hers was an everlasting kingdom where thieves didn't steal, weather didn't erode, and age didn't wrinkle. At times like this, she wished she could tell the outsiders about her glorious kingdom, but would they listen to someone they considered plain and odd like a pilgrim? What could she say to make them desire her world over theirs?

"Pardon me, miss." a petite blond in jeans and a tight-fitting striped T-shirt jarred her from her thoughts. "Are you Addison's new nanny?"

"Yes, temporarily."

"Oh. Well, we were wondering. Are you European?"

"No ma'am. I'm Mennonite."

"Oh." Another woman with long hair twisted in a messy topknot burst into the conversation. "That's right. You drive buggies and stuff?"

Smiling at their naive curiosity, Katy gently corrected, "I brought Addison in my car. You're thinking of the Amish."

The second woman's face fell, and the blond snickered at her friend's gaffe. "Well, we were going to go watch the older girls. They're practicing for a Valentine's Day performance. Want to join us?"

"Sure." Katy appreciated the kindness of their unexpected inclusion, and with a backward glance at Addison, she followed the two glamorous ladies down the hall. They stopped in front of a glass window to peer into another studio.

Even before Katy looked through the glass, the sudden terrible blare of a worldly song invaded her body, hitting with thunderous force and clapping the forbidden beat through her veins. Her heart leapt wildly from the unexpected assault, and she scudded breathless to a halt. Just as unexpectedly, the music quit, but it left her quite shaken.

With caution, Katy peered through the window. Her eyes widened at the bosomy, witchy-looking creature with wild, coal-black hair, who sashayed about the room. This instructor had dark-lined eyes with fake lashes. The lids were dark lavender even from a distance. Her lips were bloodred and drawn with exaggeration outside the lines. Her skintight top was dangerously low. She wasn't slim and graceful like the other instructor, but embarrassingly curvy and provocative. And old. Katy pitied the woman who must have thought her painting and primping made her appear younger and attractive. It was a wonder her students didn't have nightmares. It was a wonder they ever returned.

The petite blond touched Katy's arm, and she started.

"This dance is so cute. They're going to perform at the mall on Valentine's weekend. Isn't that fun?"

With a slight nod, Katy looked over the girls in the class, junior high age and maybe older. She noticed dancers came in all sizes and shapes, her heart going out to the chubbier ones, the clumsier ones who at this age stuck out in a disparaging way. She heard the instructor—a Mrs. Tenny they called her—tell the girls, "Let's go through the whole thing from the top. Remember to stay in sync with the lead girls."

Mrs. Tenny started the loud, offensive music again, and it assaulted Katy's body just like it had the first time, only it wasn't quite as startling the second time around. The girls started prancing forward then backward, and Katy saw that, as a whole, they moved in sync better than the younger girls. But all of a sudden the dance changed. The girls locked their hands behind their heads and shook their torsos, gyrating their hips seductively.

Katy sucked in a shocked breath.

As if transported into a lower universe, the music changed its cadence to accentuate the girls' sensual movements. Katy felt appalled and violated. With a gasp, she reached out to support herself against the glass, unable to resist the bass that pulsated throughout her entire body, invading where it was not welcomed.

"Are you all right?" the blond asked.

"No. I don't feel so good."

"You'd better go sit in the waiting room."

The blond cast a disappointed look toward the glass as if she'd really wanted to watch every wiggle of her older daughter's performance, but took Katy's arm as if to guide her to the waiting room.

"I'll be all right."

"Well, if you're sure. Just down the hall to the right. You can't miss it. There's a drinking fountain, too."

Katy nodded. "Thanks." She fled for the hall. She would be sure to stay away from the mall on Valentine's weekend—a glaring reminder of why she shopped at the mart discount store. In the hallway, the music finally waned, but her temples still throbbed to the beat. When she reached the sanctuary of the waiting room, she dropped into a purple vinyl chair with cold metal armrests, feeling spiritually raped.

As her breathing slowly returned to normal, she kneaded her temple. Long after her heart quieted from its onslaught, her hands still trembled. She closed her eyes. "Lord, forgive me. I didn't mean to end up here, to witness that. I didn't mean to impress upon those other women that I even go along with dancing. I don't belong in this place. Forgive me for my greed for ill-gotten money. Help me get out of this awful mess."

Katy determined to confront Tammy Brooks about her duties. Knowing Tammy's temper, she'd probably lose her job. Good riddance.

God would provide another job. Unless, of course, He didn't approve of her to moving into the doddy house.

Still rubbing her sore temples, she bargained with God. But as she prayed and then tried to regain her peace, she also struggled with what Lil and Megan would think if she backed out of the doddy house arrangement. And truthfully, she hoped God didn't take it away from her because it wasn't just their dream. It was hers, too. And if she was a Christian, wouldn't a lifelong desire be from God? It had initiated at church camp, after all.

She picked up a magazine and leafed through it. With disgust over a lewd advertisement, she slapped it back down on the side table.

⟋⟍

Back at the Brooks' home, Katy dropped pasta into boiling water, rehearsing her resignation speech to Tammy, all the while listening for her car to rumble into the garage just off the kitchen. Five minutes later, her employer entered the room.

Tammy slung her jacket over a bar stool and dropped her briefcase and purse on the counter. "Smells good. How'd your first day go? Any news from school or dance?"

"I'm not sure."

Tammy lifted the lid off the spaghetti. "Something wrong?"

"Yes." Folding her arms, Katy lifted her chin. "I didn't know I'd be taking Addison to her dance lessons. Dancing is against my religion, you know."

Tammy's jaw dropped. "I didn't even think. . . . Did you take her?"

Nodding, Katy kept up her resolve. "I went inside because you wanted me to hear what her instructor said afterward, but the music and the dancing. . ." She closed her eyes to resist the painful image and shook her head. "I can't do that anymore."

Tammy scooted onto a stool in her short tight skirt. "Wow. They're just little girls. It teaches them grace and poise. It's not like they're strippers or anything."

Katy felt her face heat. "That's what makes it so sad for me. That they're just little girls being exposed to that kind of music."

An angry flush colored Tammy's cheeks.

Katy couldn't believe she'd spoken up to an outsider like that. She remained silent, waiting for Tammy's explosion.

But Tammy removed her designer glasses and pinched the bridge of her nose, then replaced them.

Katy shot up a prayer. *Help me, Jesus. I'm doing this for You.* She lifted her chin, while mentally making plans to apply at an agency.

"What if you just dropped her off and picked her up afterward?"

The oven timer went off. "Bread's ready." Katy shot to the oven, avoiding Tammy's gaze and especially her question. She grabbed a padded mitt and removed the garlic bread. When she turned back again, Tammy was amazingly calm, her eyes pleading.

"I need you, Katy. It's only temporary."

She wanted to help. And if Tammy was willing to accommodate her wishes and respect her beliefs, then maybe she could hang in there for a few more days, just until Tammy found another nanny. "All right. Just until you find another nanny." She moved toward the coat closet. "You could apply at an agency."

Tammy flinched but didn't object.

Katy quickly waved. "I'll see you tomorrow night."

"Okay. I'll leave you a note again, and by the way, Sean will get home tomorrow night before I do."

Dread bubbled up in Katy's throat as she slipped her arms into her coat sleeves. "It's not that I don't like your children, but cleaning is what I do best."

"I understand. I'm sorry about today."

Katy left the house, and although she'd won the battle, she knew she had been outmaneuvered again.

⁓

In her room that night, Katy prayed her evening prayer with an extra dose of humility and several more entreaties for forgiveness. When she unpinned her covering, one of the pins dropped and rolled under the chest of drawers. Katy bent from her waist to retrieve it and found herself almost in one of the positions she'd seen at the studio. The instructor had told the girls it was a cambre. She liked the sound of it. Gripping the edge of her dresser as if it were a ballet barre, she touched her heels together bent at the waist and swept one arm through the air. She heard her sister giggle and went rigid.

Ashamed, she quickly bent, felt under the chest of drawers, and retrieved the pin. She placed it through the organdy and stared at the head bonnet. She wasn't the woman who had been in the dance studio and moved with wondrous grace. She was the woman who kept herself separate from the world. Her sister Karen had already climbed into her side of the bed and was reading *Little Women*.

Katy removed the rubber band from her ponytail and shook her head. Her thick hair fell down the center of her back. Gently, she massaged her scalp. What a day. Premonition told her that the Brooks job was headed toward disaster. She hated when things got out of control. She had been too ashamed to tell her mom about the dance studio. When she asked how the nanny job went, Katy had replied it was unpleasant and she didn't wish to talk about it. But the whole experience left her feeling like she had a sinful secret. She'd asked God for forgiveness now at least six times, so why wouldn't the sad feeling go away? Maybe it lingered because she'd lost a piece of her innocence. That's what the simple life was all about, keeping separate from the world, from temptation, keeping themselves pure.

She should have just quit. But Tammy needed help, and she could put up with it for a few days. Wanting to do what was best, she weighed aiding and abetting the sin by dropping Addison off at dance class against abandoning her employer in her time of need. The church forbade dancing, and the Bible talked about giving every job your best, doing it as unto the Lord. She didn't like gray areas where she couldn't decide what was wrong or right. She liked living above the fray in a place above reproach. She gained much pleasure in following rules.

She tried to block the image of what the next day might bring. Sean Brooks coming into the kitchen and popping the top of one of those beers he kept in the refrigerator. She worked her fingers through her hair and then picked up her brush. What would she do if he got drunk? Like Jake?

She'd only had one experience around a drunkard. The incident had happened during a dark time in her life when she hadn't seen Jake for several months. Megan had let it slip about the rumors that he'd gone wild at college. About the worldly girl he was dating. Then Katy had pressed Lil about it. Lil had yelled at Megan for letting the cat out of the bag, and it had been a big fiasco. But in the end, Katy had found out that the rumors were true.

Jake. . .dating an outsider. Katy jerked the hairbrush through her tangles. Her name was Jessie, and she had short, spiked, black hair. She wore miniskirts and tall boots. Thinking about Jake and that woman brought back the sick feeling in the pit of her stomach that she'd felt at the dance studio. She'd learned Jake had started drinking, too. She'd experienced that firsthand. And who knew what else he'd done? At that point, she always forcefully disengaged her imagination.

She'd been so angry when she'd found out about Jake's behavior, that the next day she'd thrown the dusting can and cracked her bedroom window. She'd been ashamed afterward, but her parents had understood her hurt and never confronted her about her angry fit. In fact, they encouraged her to forget about Jake Byler.

For many weeks after that, she hadn't been able to sleep. That's when she had started keeping a journal of cleaning tips, even going to the library and studying about home remedies. She'd put her energies into her work, but she'd never gotten over Jake.

His shame was her shame. Then one day she wrote his name on a sheet of paper. Beneath it she wrote Leviticus 4:27—"If any one of the common people sin through ignorance, while he doeth somewhat against any of the commandments of the LORD concerning things which ought not to be done, and be guilty." Then she wrote in large script across his name: *guilty and forbidden.*

She drew a line. Beneath it, she listed the qualities of the man she hoped to one day marry. She kept this paper in her Bible so that she could refer to it on those days when she thought she would die from the ache in her heart. It stirred up her convictions to forget Jake and hope for someone who was worthy of her love.

After that, Jake had stayed away from church for several months.

Until the fateful incident. It happened one weekend when he'd come home for his mom's birthday. Katy had come out of church on a Sunday night. She had been standing beside her car when she saw his truck enter the parking lot. He pulled up alongside her car and jumped out to talk to her. He'd told her he'd come to pick up his mom. His breath stank from beer, and she'd tried to get in her car to avoid him, but he'd grabbed her arm and pinned her hard against the car. She asked him to stop. But instead, he'd pressed his body against hers. She'd screamed at him to go away, but he'd forced his rank mouth against hers, pinned her head to the car's window, and kissed her.

Afterward, she'd slapped him. He'd stepped back, stunned. She'd yelled at him to stay away. And crying, she'd left him standing in the parking lot, staring after her. Honoring her demand, he had never returned to church.

She'd felt ashamed and violated. Yet now that time had passed, she also felt guilty. She worried that if he never returned to the church, it was her fault. Mennonites were supposed to be nonresistant and forgiving. But she didn't know how to do that when her heart felt so broken. When the man she loved had treated her with such disrespect.

And now he was back? She felt like the unknown would choke her. She slapped her brush down hard on the dresser.

Karen lowered her book. "What's the matter with you tonight?"

"It's just been a hard day."

"What are those kids like?"

Drawing back the quilt, Katy climbed in bed. "They squabble a lot."

"That's normal." Karen clicked off the lamp.

The image of the older girls dancing flashed in Katy's mind, chased by a Bible verse in 2 Kings: "They followed vanity, and became vain, and went after the heathen that were round about them, concerning whom the LORD had charged them, that they should not do like them."

CHAPTER 7

Somehow, Katy survived the rest of her week without any major setbacks. She had cleaned under Tyler's cluttered bed again so that he could find his BB gun, and she had glued the plastic palm trees to the artificial turf for his science project without getting called a pilgrim. Tammy had kept her word so that Katy hadn't had to enter Addison's dance studio. Katy also survived Sean Brooks. He'd been polite and had even surprised her by seeking out the children instead of the beverage shelf of his refrigerator. To her further astonishment, he'd acted much like her own father might with her siblings, tossing Addison in the air and tussling with Tyler.

On Friday morning, she'd gone to work her half day for Mrs. Cline at the Plain City retirement home, where her most challenging job had been changing the ceiling fan's lightbulbs without falling off the rickety ladder.

"I'm sure it was as old as its employer," Katy now joked to her family over the noonday meal, but nobody laughed because their attention was riveted upon Lil's unexpected appearance. Katy noticed that Lil had a glint in her eyes that warned of trouble.

"Hi, second fam." Lil scooted into a vacant chair.

"Hi Lil. What's cookin'?" Katy's dad asked, as he had every time he'd seen her since she'd started culinary school.

"Fix yourself a plate," Katy's mom invited.

"Thanks but I already ate. Baked a cake to celebrate." She removed the plastic cover to reveal a double-layer chocolate cake, one of Vernon Yoder's favorites. "Just thought I'd drop by the bids for the doddy house."

At her offhanded announcement, Katy's heart flip-flopped. In spirit, she shook Lil for not showing her the bid first. Sometimes Lil didn't have an iota of common sense.

Lil must have read her mind, for she winked at her. Her impetuous friend, as always, seemed in full control of the situation. Lil knew the sum of Katy's savings account as well as she did, so the bid must be reasonable. Still, as owner of that savings account, shouldn't Katy have had the first say in the matter? Then again, Lil had been smart enough to catch her father resting with a full belly.

Katy jumped up and looked over her dad's shoulder. She was unable to mask her widening smile as he shuffled through the paperwork. It was a surprisingly low bid. "We can handle that, Dad." Katy moved back beside Lil to watch his expression as he silently read through the contract again, more meticulously the second time.

Lil's hand clutched hers, and Katy squeezed, perhaps loving her friend more fiercely than ever before.

Her dad tapped the papers on the table, straightening their edges, and handed them back to Lil. "I hate to see the way the world is changing. Now more than ever, you need to learn responsibility. But I have to wonder if this venture will take away from your purpose in life."

"What purpose?" Katy asked, before Lil could blurt out that her purpose was to become a famous chef.

"Marrying and raising a family."

Of course. That purpose. Katy wet her lips. "We hope to someday marry, but we don't even have prospects." She saw her dad's brows arch and had to backpedal, "Oh. There's David. But you know what I mean."

"He's a nice young man," her mom interjected. Suddenly Katy wondered how her mom knew that.

Then her dad went on. "It pleases me that you both have jobs that are preparing you for marriage. You cook and clean and babysit. Suitable occupations for single Mennonite girls." Then he pointed his carpenter-rough finger at them. "You are both good catches. And Megan, she's a good girl, too."

Katy felt Lil tense and hoped she wouldn't blurt out an objection. Lil hated any hint of female suppression or submission; in fact they often joked about the *S* word even if it was a major part of their beliefs. Women were supposed to respect their husbands and allow them to be heads of the household. Many times, that wasn't practiced, but the principle had been ingrained into Katy growing up in the Mennonite culture. Now she increased her pressure on Lil's hand, hoping her friend would exert some of that self-control that allowed her to fast for a day at the onset of every new diet and to adhere to a regimented exercise program.

"I needed to get some saw blades sharpened today anyways, so I'll stop by and have that chat with Ivan Miller on my way home. See if we can seal this deal. Now let's cut that cake. You know it's one of my favorites."

— ❧ —

Early the next week, Katy slid into the ripped seat of Lil's Chevy Blazer, unconsciously poking the stuffing back into place so that it didn't stick to her dark, freshly pressed skirt. "I can't believe this is really happening."

"I know. What do you think I should save up for first? A new car or one of those commercial stoves like they had at school?"

"I wish we could've bought one of those, but—"

Lil reached over and patted her hand. "Oh stop. I'm just dreaming out loud. But someday I will have both of those. You wait and see."

Katy wondered if Lil would ever realize her dreams, for they weren't normal dreams for girls who were born and raised in the Conservative Church. Must have been some other blood in her family line somewhere, too, she mused, thinking of her own Spanish ancestor. Beside her, Lil rambled on while Katy painted her own fantasy of whipping the house into order, clean and inviting, making it a place where she would be proud to—

Her thoughts jarred to a stop. Pride was the sin of the devil. But Mennonites did take pride in the work of their hands. The irony of the plain people had never occurred to her before. Everyone knew the Mennonites were hard workers and honest. They bragged about it among themselves. She tickled the inside of her mouth with her tongue, looking for a different word that would describe her feelings, one that would be acceptable. Responsible? A good steward? That worked.

When they pulled into the Millers' farm, Lil drove to the back of the property and parked in front of the doddy house. For the first time, Katy realized there wasn't any garage or barn to park the car inside. That would be cold in the mornings. Why, she'd have to scrape frost off her windshield. She supposed there were worse things. Next she noticed a truck that resembled Jake's. Lil started to open her door, but Katy reached over. "Wait."

"What?" Lil seemed impatient to go inside.

But the truck reminded Katy that Lil had been avoiding the subject of Jake's sudden appearance. "That looks like Jake's truck."

Lil rolled her gaze heavenward. "You want to sit here and talk about Jake? Or do you want to go inside and see our dream coming true?"

"It's just. . .you've never answered my question about Jake. I saw you talking to him at the skating party. I just want to know why he was there. Did you invite him?"

Lil closed her door again and fiddled with her gearshift. "Okay, here's what I know. He's moved back home. He's coming back to the church. But the important thing is he's changed. He doesn't drink anymore or chase girls. He's over all that wild stuff." She shrugged. "He's changed, and actually he's an improved model from the old one. You'll see."

Kate absorbed Lil's flippant explanation with shock. She released a moan. "No way. He's not back to stay?"

"Yep."

"But I can't face him week after week."

"He told me he's really sorry for hurting you."

"That's so humiliating. I hope you never told him how I moped over him."

"If it's humiliating, he's the one who's ashamed. He regrets his wild fling. He's the one who feels foolish. Just keep your chin up. Take it one step at a time. Now, let's go inside. I've got my list. We need to double-check everything and then go shopping." Lil let out a squeal and bumped her shoulder against Katy's. "Shopping for our own place. Can you believe it?"

Giving in to Lil's coaxing, Katy couldn't help but grin back. "Alright. Let's do it."

She slid out and slammed the door, her boots squishing through the slush caused by several days of higher temperatures. She cast another sideways glance at the truck. If Mennonites swore, she'd swear that was Jake's truck. According to Lil, she was mistaken. Still, the truck brought out a melancholy longing in her, one that gnawed at the pit of her stomach so that her excitement over shopping receded again.

When they entered the house, she heard loud ripping and pounding noises. She stepped onto the plastic flooring protection and started toward the kitchen. "Let's go see what's going on."

Lil stopped and bent to reposition some tape and a portion of the plastic. "I think he's tearing out the plaster and replacing it with drywall. Go on, I'll be there in a minute."

With a shrug, Katy stepped into the country-style kitchen onto more plastic flooring, and saw the backside of a man whose physique made her heart trip before her mind understood the reason. The air between them crackled. The worker must have felt it, too, for he froze, then turned.

His mouth curled into a lopsided grin. "Hey, Katy. You've got a great little place here."

Confused, horrified, and standing in disbelief, she opened her mouth and closed it again. But she could not deny the truth for more than a few seconds. With it came a sudden fury, and she marched forward to throw him out on his ear, or at least demand to know why he was invading her privacy.

"What—" She stopped. *He* was the contractor Lil had hired. She fought for control, not wanting to humiliate herself any further. She wouldn't show him she still cared about him. "I think so." She took a deep breath and coughed, and in the process, accidentally sucked plaster and drywall dust into her throat. She fought the tickle, then got saliva down the wrong track and choked uncontrollably.

Jake moved quickly. He cradled his arm around her and led her to the water pump. Her coughing caused her eyes to water so that she could hardly see, but she soon caught on that the water was frozen. Blindly, she fanned her face and struggled to breathe, coughing and gasping. He left her but quickly returned with a cup of water from his personal water jug. She took a sip, and he lightly rapped her back. When at last she could breathe again, she wheezed, "Stop, please."

"I should have warned you about the dust. Lethal stuff."

"Yeah, lethal," she croaked. Then grudgingly added, "Thanks."

He nodded, and her vision returned enough for her to catch a rare moment when Jake looked uncertain, even vulnerable. But that wouldn't stop her from demanding that Lil fire him. His lips moved as if to speak. Fearing what he might say, certain it would be something personal, she blurted out, "I wish you hadn't come back."

He quickly recovered from her insult. "I wish I'd never left."

Katy rolled her gaze heavenward.

"I couldn't forget you," he added.

She felt uncomfortable in his presence and wanted nothing more than to run. But before she did, she needed to fix something that had plagued her ever since the incident. This time she didn't want to have those nagging regrets. She took another deep breath, careful not to inhale drywall dust. "You remember the night I told you to stay away?"

His eyes softened regrettably. "Yes, I remember. Even though I was drunk. And I want to apologize for that night."

The memories of the incident flooded over Katy, hardening her heart. But she forced herself to continue. "I've felt guilty, thinking my words kept you away from the church."

"I understood it was personal." He grinned, sheepishly. "I didn't think you had the authority of the elders behind you."

She felt her face heat, glad the elders hadn't witnessed that incident, even though she wasn't the one at fault. "As long as you understand that I don't want you to go to hell, I just. . .don't want you."

His brows lowered, creating a dark hood over his eyes as though to shield himself from her cruel remark. A heavy silence loomed between them. Then his mouth quirked to the side, and he grinned. Before, his smile had always charmed her whenever he needed forgiveness. But then his misdeeds were only playful. Still, she had to fight to resist it. Her own lip trembled, and she pulled her gaze back to his eyes. They pierced, searched her blushing face.

"Hi, guys," Lil entered the room, acting as though nothing was irregular, as if this reunion were an everyday occurrence. She wasn't apologetic over Jake's presence. Her behavior disregarded the significance of the awful trick. "Wow, look what you've got done." Lil gazed at the wall, which had jagged plaster and exposed wood.

Katy took her eyes off Jake and stared at the demolition. Yes, he was good at tearing down. And Lil's nonchalance—her play-acting—infuriated her. Sucking in her lower lip, Katy grabbed Lil's arm and pinched hard, pulling her toward the hallway. "Let's go over that list now."

Once they were out of the kitchen, Lil shrugged her off. "Ouch."

"You deserve that and more. Traitor," Katy hissed.

Rubbing her arm, Lil said, "Lower your voice. Jake's going to hear us."

But Katy didn't comply. "You're ruining this for me, you know." She threw up her arms. "Some dream! This is a nightmare! Do you even get it? You're going to fire him. Today. Now. I don't want him here. I don't want him." She crossed her arms. "Go on. Do it. Tell your cousin to pack up his tools."

Lil's arms waved emphatically. "Get a grip. Obviously, you're not thinking straight. He's the reason we're able to remodel cheaply. Nobody else would give us a bid that fit our budget. Don't you see? His guilty conscience is paying off."

Katy narrowed her eyes. "That's despicable."

"Let's go in the bedroom."

Katy stomped after Lil then slammed the door behind them. "This is the most underhanded thing you've ever done to me. You knew that was his truck outside, but you claimed it wasn't."

"I didn't lie."

"You didn't warn me."

"Because you wouldn't have stepped inside."

"You got that right!"

"Look, I know Jake's hurt you, but he's really changed. He wants to make amends at church and with you. You don't have to date him or marry him. Just let him make his peace. Accept him as another human being living in the same universe. That's all."

The wind whipped through a cracked windowpane, blowing pieces of sandpaper and bits of wood splinters across Katy's shoes. She stared at the floor. It hurt so bad to see Jake face-to-face again. And she felt betrayed that Lil had allowed it to happen. That her best friend had arranged it, opened the door, and invited her enemy in. She raised her face. "This place was our dream. I looked forward to fixing it up. Now I won't even want to come over here."

Lil pulled her coat tighter. "I'll tell him to leave you alone. How's that? But we need him to get the work done at the price we can afford. Think of the prize at the end of the race, okay? It is our dream."

With a groan, Katy used her foot to grind debris into the floor. "Does he even know what he's doing?"

"Yep." Lil looked like a proud mama. "He graduated with a bachelor's degree in construction systems management. Most of his classes were on campus at the Agricultural Engineering Building. Anyway, he needs some jobs for his résumé so that he can get his license and start up his own construction company. So this will help everyone in the long run, even though it's a bit awkward now. And you can deal with him here in private, not at the meetinghouse with everyone watching you guys."

The image of her wiping out on the ice with David flashed in Katy's mind. She probably would have made a fool of herself at the meetinghouse if she hadn't been forewarned of his appearance. And she hated pity. "I guess I'll deal with it. Get over it." She'd never get over it—him. She could still feel his arms sheltering her, as they had in the kitchen. If she didn't hate him so much, she'd be running right back into his embrace.

"Guess what? Jake said he'd throw in the beds for free."

"What?"

"He can make furniture."

Katy shoved her finger in Lil's face. "He is *not* making my bed!"

Ducking away, Lil backed down. "Fine."

"You don't get it, Lil." Katy lowered her voice then. "Just having him here is going to cause me pain. Just remembering him standing in the kitchen or looking at a piece of furniture he's made. I'm going to have to work through forgetting him all over again. Especially if he's here at the doddy house. At church." Her voice trailed off. "Everywhere I go." *I see his face.*

"That's just it. He's back to stay. So why not deal with him on your terms? You can heal faster that way. I'm doing this for your own good."

Face-to-face. Those dark mournful eyes, that crooked grin. A mouth she'd once kissed, cherished, owned for her own. No, she wasn't falling for it. "It feels like you're treating me like a child. Giving the contract to my dad before you let me see it, and now this. Why the big surprises? Why couldn't you just be straightforward?"

"Because you wouldn't have been able to see clearly in this situation, to see what's best for you." Lil pulled out her list and made a poor attempt at diversion. "We can talk about this later. We're wasting shopping time. Let's go over this and hit the stores. It's going to be fun."

"I'll tell you what. You go over the list. I'll wait for you in the car, having the time of my life." She heard Lil sigh as she stomped down the hall without even looking in the direction of the kitchen.

⟋⟍

Jake swung the sledgehammer, and a chunk of plaster caved in, some of it crashing to the floor and filling the air with white powder. After Katy's rebuff the night of the skating party, he hadn't expected her to give him an open-armed welcome as her surprise contractor, but her rejection still hurt. He'd overheard much of her ranting and raving, wanting Lil to fire him. Mennonites might be antiwar and noncombatant when it came to flesh wounds, but his fellow brethren could wield weapons that slashed through flesh to the soul. What was the term he'd learned in college? Passive-aggressive. Yeah, that described his Katy. He'd rather she'd just come at him swinging. That he could handle. But when she employed her smoldering eyes and pouty lip, he'd rather scoop her up and kiss her to her senses. Only he'd tried that. It hadn't been successful at all.

Still, her reaction to him today, treating him like he was some lowlife, was a twisted blade to his heart, reiterating the very words she spat at him the night of the incident: *Stay away*. Those words had hardened him then, but now that he'd let God back in, they just plain hurt. And she'd added even more meaning to them today. *I don't want you to go to hell. I just don't want you.*

He knew a few things about Katy. She took life seriously, categorizing everything in labeled cubbies. Six out of ten of these cubbies she labeled off-limits: lying, missing curfew, stealing crackers from the church cupboard marked COMMUNION, watching movies through his neighbor's window when he was mowing, driving over the speed limit, and kissing in the church parking lot.

But being stuffed into a cubby didn't suit his style, and he had no intentions of staying there. The thing was, he knew the real Katy, the little girl he'd teased who loved a good adventure and thrilled at life. She'd always pretended she didn't, but he knew the truth about her. And he intended to bring that inner woman to the surface—the wonderful, vivacious one—then claim her as his own. He wanted to nurture that part of her, not stifle it.

His cell phone jangled in his pocket, and he propped the sledge-hammer and yanked down his dust mask. "Hello."

"Hey, it's Lil."

"So she still mad at me?"

"Yep. But we knew she'd be ticked. That only goes to show how much she still cares about you."

"That love-hate thing?"

"Right."

He sat on the rung of a ladder and stared down at the feminine footprints remaining in the drywall and plaster dust. Tracks that led away from him. "Look, you know how important she is to me. I don't want to drive her away. And I don't think she appreciated the setup. She's not stupid. About our next plan, she's not going to trust us."

"She already doesn't trust you. Just don't go chicken on me. We've got a great plan. You have to show her a little at a time that you've changed. You can't do that if you don't see each other, and she's going to avoid you, so we have to set up some planned meetings like this. And once we move into the doddy house, I'll be able to put in lots of good words for you. She'll come around. I'm sure of it. She loves you, Cuz. Even if you are a chump."

"She tell you that?"

"Yep."

"Lately?"

"No but—"

"You just saw it in her wild eyes? Or maybe you caught that from her sweet talk?"

Lil chuckled. "She's intense, all right."

After their call ended, Jake stuffed his phone in his pocket, stood up, and pulled up his mask. Lil was right. He had to allow Katy the right to voice her anger. He'd just cling to the hope that her anger was evidence that she wasn't dead to him, that their love could be revived. Picking up the sledgehammer, he looked at the demolition he'd accomplished, feeling satisfaction that he was making good time.

He lifted the hammer, and another chunk of plaster met its demise.

CHAPTER 8

Saturday morning, Katy submerged chapped hands in soapy dishwater and looked through a frost-webbed window. Between snowballs and horseplay, her little brothers hand-shoveled the sidewalk, while nearby her dad steered the snowplow through fresh snow.

Was the doddy house blanketed in snow, too? Or had Ivan cleared the drive so that Jake could work? Maybe he didn't work Saturdays. She tried to pull her thoughts away from Jake Byler, but once again they stubbornly fixed upon their unexpected meeting. Every time she went over it, she felt coerced, boxed in, and smothered, clawing to strike out at him and Lil. Katy smiled wryly, remembering how she'd vetoed the patterned dinnerware for plain white plates, just for the sake of defiance. And for once, Lil had backed down. Would they survive as roommates without Megan living with them to keep the peace?

In spite of Jake's return and Lil's manipulations, Katy felt a sense of accomplishment and personal freedom over her anticipated move into the doddy house. She might be trapped in a nanny job she didn't want and forced to accept Jake's return to the community, but she was moving into a new season of life where she could find her own niche in the community. She'd be washing her own dishes from now on, not her folks'. She'd be living out her faith, not theirs.

She dried her hands on her apron and startled. Then pressing her face to the window for a closer look, she watched a familiar automobile turn into the newly cleared lane. The shiny black car that braked next to the snowplow could only belong to one person. At that instant, she was glad she prayed over the little paper she kept in her Bible—the one where *forbidden* marred Jake's name. The husband qualities below it reminded her of David. His smiling face was just what she needed.

Slathering on some lotion, she ran to a hall mirror and checked her hair, straightening her head covering. Then she answered the door. "Hey, you're out and about early."

"Dad sent me out to run errands. I ended up trapped behind a snowplow and thought I'd stop in to stall."

Backing up, she held open the door. "Come in. I'll make coffee."

He glanced down at his snowy boots. "Actually, I can't stay that long. But I wondered if you'd like to go on a sleigh ride tonight?"

Feeling a trickle of mounting excitement, not only because of the time she would spend with David, but also because she'd never gone on a sleigh ride before, Katy nodded. "Sure. That sounds fun."

He brushed back a stray strand of hair and displayed his dimple. He hadn't shaved, and she liked the rugged look. Usually, he looked so perfect, but this natural side of him brought out his masculinity.

"Great. I'll be over about seven. Dress warm. And wear that scarf that makes you so stunning."

Involuntarily, her hand fluttered at her waist searching for her apron pockets, but she'd removed it earlier. "Aren't you sweet?"

A golden glint danced in his eyes. He straightened and rolled his shoulders so that his chest swelled and his coat brushed his chin, drawing her attention back to his intriguing hint of a beard. "We'll see how long I can keep up the charade. Usually after about the third date, most girls dump me."

Katy flinched. Was he flirting or was that a challenge? Had he somehow heard about the three-date deal she'd made with her dad? Her heart raced with confusion.

He touched her cheek with his glove. "See you tonight."

David Miller was an intriguing riddle.

The huge horse, a blond Belgian draft with white feet and mane, was borrowed from David's Amish neighbors. The animal quivered with impatience.

"Is the sleigh the Beachys', too?" Katy asked.

"Yep," David replied. "Ever since I can remember, they've taken me on at least one ride each winter." He helped her up onto the seat of the simple box sleigh. "Now that the Beachys are getting up in years, the horses don't get enough use. The Beachys usually get someone to drive them to town these days. You know they sold Ivan's property to him?"

She nodded. The sleigh heaved under his weight as he climbed up next to her and took the reins.

"Last year, I took their grandkids out a time or two. Now they trust me with their horses. He pulled out a lap blanket and placed it over Katy's skirt. "You might need this till you get used to the cold." He gave the reins a flick. "Giddyup, Jack!"

A full moon gave the snowy evening a pristine glow and provided a soft backdrop for the black goblins that reached from dark trunks toward the passing sleigh. The silent world painted with only black and white seemed unnatural without color, the black so stark against the white. Lil would probably argue it was the other way around. Katy had to wonder if David had felt a bit creepy driving over alone through the lonely countryside. She'd always been a little afraid of the dark herself. Thankfully, the sounds of beast and human made the night less eerie, the soothing clopping of hooves, the creak of leather and wood, and the companionable timbre of her male companion's voice.

The glittering sky, however, gave her an awareness of her insignificance, and the feeling balled up unwelcome in her throat. She wondered if he felt it, too. Glancing sideways, she said, "It's different out here like this. Almost like the night could swallow us up."

"It's pretty." He cast her a glance. "Like you."

"No. It almost feels like we shouldn't be here, like we're trespassing in somebody else's world." She shivered then, not sure if it was from the cold or the idea. It was a familiar one, feeling like a foreigner in an outsider's world. Oftentimes, she felt insignificant. The outsiders' world was confusing. The Conservatives' world was constrictive, yet comforting because it was the most familiar. It was where she fit in best.

His hand slipped over her shoulder. "Come closer."

She inched over so he could still shelter her from the wind, yet their bodies weren't touching, and adjusted the blanket. "Do you ever think about how the Amish live? What it would be like?"

"I've thought about it. The sleigh is nice tonight, great for a date, but I can't imagine life without my car. I don't think I'd like that much. Aren't very many Amish buggies around Plain City anymore, but my dad's good friends with our neighbors, says it's a shame most of the Amish moved out of the community because just having them around added a missing element."

"What's that?"

"The desire for a simple life. Even if we don't choose to follow their way, it's nice to know it's still possible to make a stand like that. It takes courage not to follow the crowd."

She thought about her predicament with her nanny job. "You're right." She warmed her nose with her glove. "I have some Amish cousins."

David burst out laughing. "Doesn't everybody?"

They both laughed.

He drew his sleeve across his eyes and then glanced over to study her, allowing Jack to keep to the road on his own for a bit. "I hear Jake Byler is remodeling the doddy house."

She flinched. Of course he would know because his brother owned the property. "That was all Lil's doing," she clarified. "Jake and I have a history, and she thinks this will help us get past the awkwardness, since he's back to stay. They're close, being cousins, and she thinks we all have to be one big merry family, I guess." Katy gave him a contrite smile. "Plus, he gave us a really cheap bid."

"Is he? The big-brother type?"

"He's the type to avoid. Lil hired him behind my back. I'm still ticked. But he does need the work, too."

"Sounds like you're making excuses for him."

She tilted her head. "I don't mean to. Guess I'm just repeating what Lil said, trying to deal with the situation." She suddenly straightened. "We're headed in that direction, aren't we?"

"Yep. You have a key?"

She grinned. "In my purse."

"Then let's check out his work. Maybe we can get something warm to drink from Elizabeth before we head back."

"I'm not sure that's a good idea." She knew she should avoid dark, secluded places with a date.

"Just a quick look. Elizabeth will see us turn in the drive and be expecting us."

That was almost like having a chaperone, and it was considerate of him. She stole several long, contemplative glances at him. "Okay."

At the doddy house, David worked the key in the lock while she held a lantern they'd found inside the sleigh. She felt a naughty elation, checking out the place alone after Lil and Jake's conniving. Well, not exactly alone.

"Watch out for the plastic on the floor," she warned.

He took the lantern from her. "I see it and a few other obstacles, too. Don't worry, I don't plan to trip you like I did on our last date." He skirted her around a pail filled with a few tools and nails and a roll of electric wire.

Sweet of him to take the blame for that. If it weren't so personal, she'd ask him if his knees still bore bruises. If he'd limped the next day. She bit back a smile. If he'd gotten a new tire.

Jake had torn off most of the kitchen's old plaster and started the wiring. As they walked through the house, she noticed holes in the other walls and some in the ceiling.

"He'll drop the electric down through the walls and put switches and outlets there." David set the lantern on the floor. They stood in the center of the darkly lit room. It grew quiet, the seclusion of their surroundings conducive to a feeling of intimacy. He captured both her hands, and she warmed inside. His voice was low and kind. "Do you know when you'll move in?"

Her breath caught at the intensity of his hazel gaze that bore into hers, drawing her in as though he meant to kiss her. She felt embarrassed when her voice sounded too breathless. "I don't know how long the work will take." She wet her lips, glanced at the walls. "Doesn't look like they started the plumbing." She looked into his eyes again. "Guess I was too angry to ask the important questions."

His thumb caressed her hand through their gloves. "Can I help you move?"

She swallowed, nodding. "Thanks." She drank in his quiet confidence and floated to a higher plane. Not that she was needy. But her toes tingled with anticipation of what he would do next.

He kept caressing her knuckles. It was almost like he was waiting for her to make the next move, but she wasn't sure what he wanted from her.

Finally, he said, "Katy Yoder, will you"—he paused, showed his dimple. His face was now freshly shaved, and he looked younger than he had earlier that morning.

"What?"

"Share a hot chocolate with me?"

He really was a tease. She bit her lip, caught up in the flirtation. "You're practicing for the day you pop the big question to some lucky girl, aren't you?"

"Yep."

"Yes, I will. I'm so thrilled you asked," she played along. "Only, that wasn't as smooth as it could have been. You definitely need more practice. Aren't you supposed to go down on one knee or something?"

"Already did. Both knees. In front of all our friends, too." Grinning, he released one of her hands and scooped up the lantern.

A cup of hot chocolate and a shared blueberry muffin later, they were headed back down the snowy road. "The horses always go faster on their way home, don't they?" she asked.

He squeezed her shoulder. "Wish they'd go slower. Will I get to see you again?"

"You did offer to help us move."

"Before that."

Moved with guilt over her three-date deal—he was making this far too easy—she made a mental note to at least date him four times just for the sake of. . . She looked away from him to the eerie landscape.

"Tough decision?"

"Yes. I'd like to get to know you better." She placed her hand on his arm. "Only I'm not really looking for a relationship. Anything serious."

"I wasn't out looking, either. I just felt attracted to you." Silence pervaded for several moments. "Are you worried my feelings are stronger than yours?"

She dropped her hand and smiled. "So you're a guy who talks about feelings?"

"I'm glad you're good at keeping secrets 'cause that's another one to add to your list."

She laughed. "I won't spread the word that you're a mushy guy."

"Oh man." He shook his head.

She took pity on him. "I enjoy spending time with you. Yes, I'd like to see you again before I move into the doddy house."

His cheek twitched. "How about next Saturday then? We could drive into Columbus and have dinner at a nice restaurant."

"Want to go to Lil's place?"

"Do we need reservations?"

"I don't think so, but if we do, I'll take care of it."

She was pleased because all their dates had been fun, and it appeared the next one would be, too. She'd been wanting to see the restaurant where Lil worked, anyway. They rode in amiable silence except for the soothing horse noises and the creaking of harness and sleigh. When they reached Katy's house, he walked around the front of the sleigh and patted the horse's velvety nose before he helped her down. At the door, she turned to face him, but he was so close, she nearly bumped into him. A nervous giggle escaped her lips, and she saw the dimple dance in his left cheek. She glanced up.

He swallowed.

She winced. He had a prominent Adam's apple. Or was his neck too skinny? Her budding attraction died on the spot, and there wasn't a thing she could do to stop it.

He tipped her chin, lightly brushing her lips with his. "Good night, Katy."

"Good night," she whispered, overcome with the desire to put distance between them.

Inside, she reached the second-floor landing before she realized she'd forgotten to hang her coat in the downstairs hall closet. When his lips had touched hers, not only had it felt strangely cold, but she had envisioned Jake's face, leaving her feeling guilty and ashamed.

As nice as David was and as fun as the sleigh ride had been, she hated herself for using him. She hated how in the end, she would hurt him, because Jake's return had shown her the truth. She wasn't ready to start a relationship with anyone else. No matter how nice of a guy he was or how much her dad desired it.

CHAPTER 9

The churchwomen threw a baby shower in Elizabeth Miller's honor, and since Elizabeth was Katy's new landlord, she felt obligated to attend. The night of the shower, however, Katy had to go alone because her mom needed to stay home with her little brothers, who had caught winter colds.

When Katy arrived at the meetinghouse, the gravel parking lot was already filled with cars. She turned off the ignition, and an unexpected shiver passed through her body, most likely only weariness from a tedious day of cleaning and babysitting and hopefully not the beginning of a cold. When she flicked off her headlights, the dark, moonless night sent prickles along her spine, and she quickened her steps across the parking lot.

Inside the fellowship hall, the buzz of female voices floated to her through the narrow hall, easing her inexplicable jitters. Moving toward the source of the din, she stepped into a large, multipurpose room, and Megan instantly waved her over.

"Hey, green bean. You feeling better?"

Megan looked great, clad in a navy pencil skirt that hit below the knees and a white crewneck sweater. Megan reached up and tucked some hair behind one ear, the rest of her straight blond mane shimmering well below her shoulder blades. "I am. I came home for the shower." Her voice grew animated. "Lil says there's progress at the doddy house."

"Where is she?" Katy involuntarily glanced toward the kitchen.

"Working." She followed Megan's glance and located Lil at one of the two pink-clad tables, stabbing homemade pickles, easing them out of their canning jar, and arranging them on an oval serving platter. "I heard about Jake. Dad told me he came before the elder board to make things right with the church," Megan said.

Katy's head whipped back toward her friend, her mind racing. "You're kidding. My dad didn't tell me about that."

"Probably wanted to spare your feelings."

She remembered her bedroom's broken windowpane. So her dad had withheld important information from her while Lil barged in to control the situation. She clasped her chapped hands together, hating such manipulation.

"They meant well, I'm sure."

Bless Megan's heart, she understood the reason for Katy's rising anger. And as usual, if Katy dug deep enough, she could see that her friend was right. For when it came to Jake, no matter how her friends and family responded, they wouldn't be able to please her. Jake deserved her anger, not everyone else. "You're right. Let's go look at the cake."

When they reached the table, Lil waved a slow-cooker lid. "Hi, guys."

The cake had tiny pink bows for decoration and was scalloped with ribbon. "Cute cake," Katy commented. "Can you do that ribbon thing, Lil?"

"Sure. That looks easy."

As they spoke, a loud crash resonated from the kitchen, followed by an interval of heavy silence. Inez Beachy, an older woman whose head covering still had Amish strings, hurried to the front of the room and used the lull to get everyone's attention. She said a quick prayer over the food, and at the *Amen*, a wave of women started ambling toward Katy and her friends.

Megan elbowed her. "Quick. Let's head up the line."

They grabbed pink plates, and Katy filled hers with a whoopee pie, some nuts, and a meatball.

Katy and Megan found seats near the front, where they could watch Elizabeth open her baby gifts. The party launched and was soon in full swing, with the church sisters losing themselves in the wonder of tiny, hand-knitted booties and doll-sized dresses.

"Make you want to play house?" Megan asked with a smirk. "I heard you're dating David Miller. I miss one Sunday and when I come back, you've already had two dates in one week."

"Hush!"

"You went with him to the skating party. It's not a secret."

"No kidding." Katy pulled an exaggerated frown then with her next breath caught a faint whiff of something abnormal. Perhaps because of her earlier apprehension in the parking lot, she furrowed her brow and inhaled more deeply. She caught it again, only stronger. Touching Megan's wrist, she asked, "What's that funny smell?"

Megan sniffed. "I don't smell anything."

With Megan's allergies, that came as no surprise. Before Katy could disagree, a feminine shriek filled the air, and somebody shouted, "Smoke! Kitchen fire!"

A chaos of activity followed the pronouncement. Women gasped. Chairs scraped and clattered. Aghast, Katy jumped up, too, thrusting her finger. "Look!" Small puffs of smoke wafted through the kitchen's pass-through window. She couldn't hear Megan's response above the mass of feminine hysteria.

Inez flew to the front of the room, her covering strings flying behind her. The older woman clapped her hands until she had most of their attention. Her curt voice shot orders to the nervous crowd. "Everyone. Move out to the parking lot! Move orderly. But hurry!"

Now the women started to act with purpose, crowding toward the entrance, all the while casting worried glances toward the kitchen.

But Katy remained riveted, her mind scrambling for ways to help before exiting.

"What about Lil?" Megan shouted.

Snatching up her purse, Katy unclamped her lips. "There's an exit in the kitchen. She's closer to the door than we are." Starting down the aisle between the rows of vacating chairs, Katy took a final glance behind her and stopped. "Elizabeth!"

Megan swung her gaze around.

The pregnant woman sat stunned, glued to her metal folding chair like a queen ruling over a sea of packages and tissue paper. Quickly running back to her, Katy urged. "Elizabeth! We have to leave the building."

Elizabeth cupped her palms over her swollen stomach and nodded, but still didn't budge.

Katy stepped over gifts and bent over her. "What's wrong?" Surely she wasn't going into labor?

"The baby's gifts. I—"

Understanding, Katy gripped Elizabeth's arm and pulled her to her swollen feet. She glanced toward the jammed exit and made a quick decision. "We'll help you get them."

Katy swept a few gifts off the floor and handed them up to the dazed woman.

"Megan, what are you waiting for?" Anita Weaver suddenly loomed over them with a frightened expression.

Katy shoved a pink gift bag into the older woman's hand. Then Megan and her mom hurried to gather as many gifts as they could.

"Let's go," Anita urged.

The three women juggled gifts and pushed Elizabeth toward the exit, all of their gazes fixed on the thick smoke billowing into the back of the room and the bright flames now visible as well, flickering up through the pass-through window.

"We waited too long," Anita cried. "Hurry, girls."

They tried to run, but the area next to the exit was filled with stifling smoke. Worried for Elizabeth in her pregnant state, Katy yelled, "Hold your breath."

After that, they didn't speak. They reached the rear of the frantic bodies packing and blocking the exit where the smoke-filled multipurpose room narrowed into a hall. A handmade receiving blanket slipped out of Elizabeth's arms and fell to the floor. With a shriek, she halted.

Anita whipped it up off the floor.

The line steadily moved, and as soon as they stumbled outside, they all took welcome draughts of the fresh air. Katy found herself coughing much like she had with the drywall dust, but with each inhalation of uncontaminated air, her breathing became more normal.

Inez urged, "Keep moving so others can come out."

"We were at the end of the line," Katy informed her. The woman nodded with relief and ran toward the other door, which was the kitchen's exit.

Katy instantly remembered Lil and lunged after Inez, but Ivan Miller blocked her path. He moved around Katy and swept Elizabeth into a quick embrace that knocked several gift boxes to the ground.

"Thank God, you're okay." The young husband's voice was husky with worry.

Feeling a touch at her elbow, Katy turned. David gave her a worried nod, his gaze darting nervously to the building and back at Ivan. He moved past her and stopped beside his brother. "We'd better check inside."

Ivan reluctantly released his wife. "Go wait in the car, honey. The smoke isn't good for the baby."

Elizabeth nodded but stooped to pick up the packages her husband had recklessly knocked to the ground. Involuntarily, Katy stooped to help as her worried gaze followed David and Ivan into the smoky building. Torn with which entrance to use to go search for Lil, she watched them until they disappeared.

"No!" Elizabeth lunged, belatedly, after Ivan.

But Anita snatched Elizabeth's arm. "Don't," she reprimanded. "Let the men go."

Megan interrupted her mother. "Do you think Lil and others are trapped in the kitchen?"

Alarm sprinted up Katy's spine at Anita's stricken expression, and she quickly pressed, "Can you take Elizabeth to the car?"

The older woman clamped her lips together for a moment, then replied, "Only if you both stay put, out of danger's way." At Anita's stern look, Megan nodded for the both of them. Katy couldn't promise anything until she knew Lil was safe. Anita draped her arm around Elizabeth, moving the distraught woman toward the parking lot.

Katy's fingers imprinted the soft gift boxes she still clutched. "Oh Lil. Where are you?" She whipped her gaze to Megan. "She must be inside."

Flames now flickered through the kitchen exterior windows. Megan clenched her fists at her side. "We have to go get her."

In the distance they heard a siren. Somewhere along the kitchen's exterior wall, Katy had dropped the gifts. Outside the door, she shrugged someone's hand off her shoulder and grabbed the door handle. But she quickly released the hot metal. Her shoulder jerked back under a firm grip. She glanced back. Inez warned, "Don't do it!"

Frantically, Katy looked around. She needed padding to open the door handle. For the first time, she realized none of them had bothered to fetch their coats or gloves. Hysterically searching her body for something to put over the door's handle, she cried, "But Lil's in there."

Inez clamped her arm on her shoulder again. "I hear the fire truck."

Before she could resist, Megan cried, "Look, Katy! Lil's safe!"

Katy whipped her gaze around, and saw Lil and Mrs. Landis standing by the opposite exit with David and Ivan.

Katy ran to them with relief, her voice laced with fear-induced anger. "Where were you?"

"I don't know. The men found us. We couldn't get the fire out. It blocked the door. When we left the kitchen, it was so hazy we couldn't see."

"Are you all right?"

Lil nodded. "I think so."

A red fire truck screamed into the parking lot. Three men in dark-blue uniforms barreled down and rushed to the building.

Mrs. Landis turned away to speak to Inez. Shivering, Lil rubbed her arms, and the three girls huddled together, watching.

One fireman swung an ax thru the kitchen window. A second stuck a hose through it while the third man ran to them and questioned Ivan.

"What happened in there?" Katy asked.

"Did you hear that crash earlier?" Lil asked.

Katy nodded.

"We dropped a punch bowl. There was a huge mess. Anyway, we all chipped in to clean it up. I think somebody forgot what they were doing. The fire started from the area where there was a slow-cooker and a big coffeepot."

"But how would those start a fire?"

"I don't know."

"I hope it wasn't my fault," Mrs. Landis moaned, stepping into their circle. "Somebody could have been killed."

"It's nobody's fault. It was an accident," Megan assured her, but the older woman looked stricken.

David returned from speaking with some firemen. He looked glum, disheveled, and sooty.

"Everybody out?" Katy asked.

"As far as we know. The firemen are checking now." They both glanced over where one of the professionals was wetting down the meetinghouse.

"You think the meetinghouse will catch on fire?"

"I don't know. The fellowship hall's ruined."

"But you found Lil." Katy's emotions suddenly overwhelmed her. "What if you hadn't been here?"

"I just came to help Ivan pack up the gifts. We came early to sneak some cake. When we got here, we saw women rushing out of the building. Then we saw the fire. While Ivan looked for Elizabeth, I called the fire department." He glanced toward the parking lot. "How is she?"

"I don't know. Anita Weaver took her to the car like Ivan requested."

A crashing noise commanded their attention. They stared at the fire in riveted horror. Part of the roof had caved in, and a new flurry of flames and smoke drove them farther away from the building.

As they stood dazed, more help arrived. A barricade was soon erected. At some point, David removed his coat and placed it across Katy's shoulders. She heard him say, "They want those cars moved. If you give me your keys, I'll move yours."

She dug into her purse and handed him the keys. "Thanks."

"Dumplin'?" Katy nearly broke down at her dad's touch. She turned into his sturdy embrace, clinging to him for a long while.

When she drew away, she asked, "How did you find out?"

"Lil called her dad. Will started the prayer chain." He motioned behind him. "I parked down the street. I had to make sure you were all right. Your mom's real worried."

"I think everybody's okay."

"According to Will, Rose is pretty upset. She's worried she may have been the one who started the fire. She remembers setting a roll of paper towels next to the coffeepot."

"Poor thing. But it was just an accident," Katy replied.

"She feels responsible as head of the hostess committee."

"A punch bowl broke," Katy protested, as though that would explain everything to her dad.

He pointed, "That your car?"

Katy nodded. "David's moving it for me. He and Ivan came to load up Elizabeth's gifts. They were the first men on the scene."

"I'm going to go ask the firemen if there's anything I can do to help. We don't want the sanctuary to burn."

Katy noticed other churchmen who had heard about the fire were starting to mill about the parking lot. "Okay."

"I'd feel better if you'd go home. Your mom's worried."

She realized that even with David's coat, she was shivering. "Okay. But be careful, Dad."

Off to the side, Will Landis was helping his wife to their car. Katy hurried over, asking Lil, "Your mom going to be okay?"

"I think so. It hit her when the firemen checked us over."

"You didn't get burned?"

"No." Lil crossed her trembling arms.

"You in shock?"

"Just cold. My throat's raw, too."

"Want me to take you home?"

Lil's teeth began to clatter. "No. I'm going home with my folks."

Katy watched Lil get in the car. Turning her back to the surreal scene, Katy hugged her arms against the cold and trudged to her own car. Behind her, another crash sounded. When she looked over her shoulder, she saw more of the fellowship hall had caved in. Fire illuminated the winter's night sky. She gripped her car's door handle and instantly flinched at the pain. How would this fire affect their small congregation?

CHAPTER 10

A few nights later, Katy was rebandaging her hand when the telephone rang. From the living room, where she lay on the couch buried to her chin in a quilt and nursing a box of tissues, Mom called, "Git dat?"

Tearing off the medical tape and pressing it in place, Katy hurried to the phone and cradled it in the crook of her neck. David's voice tumbled into her consciousness, low and masculine. "You busy?"

"No, I just finished the dishes."

Her stomach did a little somersault until she remembered the coldness of their kiss. With his bravery at the fire, she had forgotten about that. She brought her attention back to what he was saying. He wasn't saying anything particularly personal, he was just talking about the fire.

"Elizabeth's fine"—David's voice held a hint of hesitance or despondency—"fretting over some handmade blankets that got ruined in the fire, but otherwise good. She told me you got most of the gifts out of there."

Twisting the phone cord, Katy replied, "I just reacted. It was weird."

"You're an angel. Elizabeth thinks so, too. Now she's embarrassed about the way she acted, obsessed over the gifts. She's going to apologize."

"That's not necessary. I'm sure it was just a mixture of shock and probably had something to do with being pregnant."

"That's what Ivan told her. But about the fire, the men are having a cleanup day this coming Saturday. It'll be a long day, and my dad asked me to help with the chores afterward to make up for the time away from the farm. Guess what I'm getting at is, can we postpone our dinner date?"

Disappointment rushed over her. "Of course. We can do that anytime." Unless. . .was he trying to break up? "Or we don't have to go at all," she added.

"Hey, I want to see you. It isn't that."

She didn't reply because everything had become so confusing with David that she didn't know what she wanted anymore.

After some silence, he asked, "Did you do your nanny thing today?"

Leaning against the wall, she worked the kinks out of the phone cord. Maybe he knew about the three-date proposition and wasn't going to give her the third date. Maybe he was going to dangle it. She'd deserve that. "Yeah. Addison broke Tyler's iPod."

"How'd she do that?"

"I have no idea, don't even know how they work, but there was some kind of struggle going on in the backseat on the way home from school. Tyler can be a real imp."

"Boys will be boys. Maybe you need to pack Addison a bigger snack." Katy couldn't help but grin. David's listening abilities amazed her. He really understood and remembered when she'd talked about work. "Did they get in trouble with Tammy?"

"Big-time."

"Oh yeah? She take away his BB gun?"

"She promised him a new iPod. A better one. And Addison is getting her own so they don't have to fight over Tyler's."

"That's a little harsh."

"I know. But I'm sure you've got better things to do than talk about a couple of spoiled kids."

"Nothing's more important than talking to you. Why haven't we talked on the phone before?"

So maybe he wasn't breaking up with her? Unless he was baiting her so he could dangle the third date. She hated to end the call until she knew exactly where they stood. "I made the mistake of asking Tammy what kind of discipline I should administer. She got all white-knuckled and said I should just tell her when they misbehaved, and she'd deal with it."

"By rewarding them?"

"Exactly. Now my hands are really tied. I asked her if she's looking for another nanny. She said the agencies were too expensive. She was thinking of arranging her schedule differently and asked if I could babysit two days a week, on the days I come anyway. She's a pro at getting her way."

"That's not something you want then?"

"Hardly. I told her I'd think about it. If I hadn't stalled, I'd have ended up manipulated into a yes on the spot, and—" She dropped the phone cord, twirled her ponytail, and sighed.

"Guess you need to practice all the ways to say no. There's a lot of country songs on that subject."

She remembered his car radio, although he'd only turned it to classical music on their date. "You like country music?"

"I listen to it sometimes. Anyway, don't practice your no on me, okay?"

"If you're a gentleman, I won't have to."

⟿

Later that night, Vernon Yoder found Marie asleep on the sofa. He leaned over her and lightly shook her shoulder. "Wake up, honey."

"What? I'b just sleeby. How was your meeding?"

"Mennonite Mutual will cover the fire, and we've decided to rebuild, and while we're at it, to add those Sunday school rooms we've been needing."

She sniffled. "Zounds like work."

He grabbed a tissue and handed it to her, easing onto the couch beside her. "We're forming a committee so the elders don't get bogged down."

Dabbing her nose, she asked, "Who's on the gammittee?"

"Maybe your lovely daughter."

Marie jerked to a sitting position. "Why Gaty?"

"First they tried to get someone from the hostess committee. Lil's mom is feeling low right now, so then Lil's name came up. We called her from the meeting. She said she couldn't because she works nights, but she suggested Katy. For some reason, the elders thought she was a good candidate. We tried calling, but the phone was busy."

"Dabe Miller called; then I vell asleeb."

"I didn't want her on the committee."

"Why not?"

"Because Jake Byler will be the project superintendent. They called him, and he's already agreed."

"Oh no."

"Talking to David, huh? I guess that's a good sign."

"Dey sounded habby."

"We'll just have to keep praying about it. You have sick eyes, honey. Let's go to bed."

⟋ᦒ

Later that week, Katy caught lingering whiffs of a smoky odor as she hurried past a yellow ribbon that fenced off the charred disaster. She shouldered the door to the meetinghouse. Low laughter floated to her from the sanctuary, where the building committee was scheduled to meet. She had never served on any committees before and wasn't sure what to expect. She figured she was here as Lil's proxy, but that seemed fair since the elders had asked Lil first.

Curious to see who else would serve on the committee, she stepped through the open double doors that separated the foyer from the sanctuary and made her way down the gray-carpeted center aisle. Dark-stained pews flanked her on either side. She had almost reached the front of the room when her steps faltered.

Her shoulders drooped in utter disbelief. Not Jake again? As if on cue, he turned, meeting her stricken gaze with his own contrite one, the ever-so-charming grin that infuriated her these days. She forced her attention to the elder presiding over the meeting. Her dad had told her he was thankful he wasn't chosen for the position. Instead Megan's dad had received the honor. "Hi Mr. Weaver."

"Hi Katy." He stepped into the aisle and took her hand, but when he saw the large Band-Aid, he treated it with care. "What happened?"

"A few blisters from the fire. But it's healing."

"I'm sorry. We miss seeing you since Megan's away at school."

"I miss you guys, too." Trying hard to ignore Jake's presence, she asked, "Got any midnight blues in the works?"

He held a finger to his lips, pretending nobody else knew that his favorite pastime of restoring cars and painting them midnight blue, but everybody knew.

She took stock of the seating arrangement, and Jake's eyes dared her to sit beside him, but she opted for the painter's pew. Still, Jake's presence beckoned her. He certainly didn't look repentant, coming to church with shaggy hair and wearing a T-shirt. She struggled harder to disregard him, giving her full attention to observing the other committee members.

Besides the blues man, the group included representatives from the finance committee, the grounds committee, and the church council, as well as a layperson who was a painter by trade, Katy as a stand-in for the hostess committee, and obviously Jake as construction advisor. That made seven. To Katy, there were only two people in the room, and that made her want to flee, but she couldn't do that. She'd have to endure the torture of putting in her time at the meeting.

It started with the groundskeeper reporting on the scheduled cleanup and answering questions on easements.

"What if the congregation doesn't want to spend the money for the additional Sunday school rooms?" the painter asked.

"The finance committee will head up the bids, and we'll have all that information before we take it to the congregation for a vote," Mr. Weaver explained.

"What if they think we're trying to push it through by getting on this so quickly?"

Katy hadn't known the painter was such a pessimist.

"There are always a few rumbles, no matter what direction leadership takes. We'll deal with the problems as they arise. We're not trying to trick anybody, just get all our facts together at this point."

As the meeting progressed, Katy's neck stiffened from being held in one position so long to avoid Jake's gaze. Hearing the low rumble of his Dutch accent—his mother's family came from an Amish background— was trying enough, for it brought back yearnings she'd hoped to have stifled by now. Putting a hand to her neck, she twisted to ease the tension. Of course her traitorous eyes sought the most desirable man in the room.

And he knew the moment she looked at him. His brown eyes caressed her, and she found it hard to turn away. Then those sensuous lips of his gave her a private smile, and she remembered how she used to always make him smile. He had once delighted in her, in their relationship. He had that look now, that darkened gaze that clung to her every breath. He probably only wanted her now because she was unobtainable. The thought was enough that she was able to break their visual contact.

She made a show of rubbing her neck and focused once more on the agenda. She gleaned that she needed to speak to the present hostess committee and collect their input on an updated kitchen and get the information to Jake as soon as possible. He needed the details before their next meeting. He was in charge of getting a blueprint drawn, collecting bids for the congregation's approval, and submitting the plans to Plain City's Planning and Zoning Commission.

Now she knew why her dad sometimes returned from elders' meetings looking frayed and worried. Bill Weaver prayed and dismissed them, and finally she could flee. She lurched to her feet and hastened down the aisle, confident that as the only woman present, no one would detain her. She planned to escape before Jake got the opportunity to engage that lethal gaze of his again, the one that made her heart revolt against her will. But she'd not even reached the double doors before a touch sent a shock through her shoulder.

With a frustrated sigh, she stopped. Turned.

"I need to get your ideas before I draw up the kitchen."

So he didn't have anything personal to say to her. Good. That was the way she wanted it, too. "I need to talk to Lil first. I'm sure the hostess committee has ideas."

He raised a brow. Perhaps he hadn't realized Lil was asked first and would be giving her input. "As far as the blueprints go, the plans for the new kitchen are major. Think we could get together sometime soon to discuss it?"

Were those ulterior motives or was he only taking care of business? She troubled her lip. "To be honest, I didn't know I'd be working with you. Otherwise I wouldn't even have accepted this position. I'll have to resign if it includes private meetings with the likes of you."

"That's right. You don't want me. I get that, but if you back out of this committee now, it will just delay the preliminary process. For the congregation's sake, we can surely put our personal feelings aside long enough to get this job done." He gave her a crooked, albeit contrite smile. "Think of all the little Sunday school kids. How would you like to listen to adult sermons without getting any David and Goliath stories afterward to make up for it? And think of all the starving bachelors who count on the church potlucks. And think of—"

"Okay. I get it." She bit her lip to keep from smiling and raised a brow. "What about the doddy house?"

He squinted those intimidating brows. "You're afraid of me, aren't you?" He lifted his arms to show he wore no weapon. "Come on, Katy. I'm just a harmless Dutchman. Totally defenseless."

She ignored his comment and rephrased her question in a voice she might use with Tyler. "Is your work for the church going to slow down your progress at the doddy house? This is a major project."

She saw his eyes darken; anger and lust with him looked so similar, she couldn't tell what was going through his thick, tousle-haired skull. "I'll work overtime, if that's what it takes. I'm not a slacker. I need both jobs to get references for the construction business I plan to start." The painter walked by, giving them a once-over.

"They want to lock up," Katy observed.

"Let me walk you to your car," Jake whispered in reply.

She started to put her coat on and resented the way Jake helped her shrug into it. She moved toward the door. "Regarding the new kitchen, what kind of information do you need?"

He gave her the quick version, one that fit into the distance between the church and her car, and she realized he could be precise and intelligent when he chose to be. He wasn't a boy any longer. He was a stubborn, irrepressible man. When they reached her car, she had a vivid flashback of the incident. It shook her. She only wanted to get rid of him. "I'll make some calls. Talk to Lil and the rest of the committee. Maybe I can stop by sometime at the doddy house and go over it with you." She reached for her car door handle.

"Wait. Do you have paper and a pencil? I should give you my cell phone number so you can call before you come." She frowned and slid into her seat. As if she'd ever call him. But he continued to explain. "I'm usually there, but sometimes I have to run after materials. Sometimes I have to sit with Grandma, too."

Her emotions flickered with instant sympathy, remembering his grandma who now had Alzheimer's. Minnie had been her favorite Sunday school teacher, a vibrant part of their congregation, but now the elderly woman fell asleep the moment her skirt hit the pew, her snores embarrassing everyone within hearing. He must have misread her expression, because he quickly added, "I can always stay late, if I have to do that. But it's one of the reasons I moved back home. To give Mom some support. Sis is staying at a dorm at OSU." He rammed his hands in his jeans.

Trying to tamp down the sympathy she felt for him, she started rifling through her purse. Her bandage caught, and she jerked it free. "I'm sorry about your grandma."

"Thanks."

She handed him paper and pen. "I don't mean to sound like a slave driver. I'm sure you'll do a great job. I just have a problem with you."

He shed off her insult and scribbled seven digits on the paper. Then he started rambling about something totally off the subject, and Katy struggled to follow.

He was saying something about God dividing time into days? "Every morning is a new start. He gave us a new birth, too. There's not much without the hope of new beginnings, Katy."

Getting his drift, she snatched the paper away. "There's always endings."

He stepped back and stuffed his hands in his jean pockets again.

She shut her window.

He turned his back to her and walked toward his truck, and rats if she didn't feel sorry for him.

CHAPTER 11

Parked outside Addison's dance studio, Katy sat in her car and sulked. Tammy Brooks was one stubborn woman who wouldn't get her red-painted claws out of Katy's usually well-ordered life. Surely she wasn't becoming a pushover? Why was everyone interfering with her plans? She had her own ideas of how things should go and didn't like the obstacles she'd been encountering at every turn. She'd had it at home with her dad's matchmaking, in her personal life with Lil hiring Jake, and now at work. She banged her head back against the padded headrest. She was definitely becoming a pushover.

Bored and restless, she opened the glove compartment and withdrew a small testament she kept there, opening the Bible and leafing through it at random. Just as her luck would have it, every verse her gaze fell upon had something to do with newness, reminding her of Jake's oratory in the parking lot. She frowned at God's sense of humor. In the book of Lamentations, she read God's compassions are new every morning. She read passages about new spirits, new hearts, a new commandment—the commandment to love one another—new creatures, and in Revelation how God makes all things new.

Newness? Why couldn't things remain the same? What was wrong with old and boring?

She felt confirmation in her heart that Jake had received God's newness, but that didn't mean she had to let him worm his way back into her affections. More restless than ever, she snapped the testament shut and returned it to the glove box. She glanced in the rearview mirror, involuntarily straightening her covering while she scanned the parking lot. Addison should be out any minute. Not wanting to argue with God about Jake, her fury transferred to Tammy again, who had insisted that Katy try babysitting just two days a week and wouldn't take no for an answer.

Tapping on the steering wheel, she prayed, "Lord, I feel like nothing gets resolved. Like I'm losing control of my life. I need Your help." *I need to be more assertive. Okay, and loving.* She accepted the thoughts that came into her mind as inspiration.

Tap, tap. She jerked her gaze to the passenger's window and saw Addison's bubbly smile. Her small palms were pressed against the window. Her blond hair was piled on top of her head, and sweaty tendrils stuck to her cheeks in spite of the cold temperature outside. Her purple coat was open, revealing a pink tutu beneath it. Feeling a flash of fondness for the little girl, Katy quickly unlocked the doors and allowed her young charge to climb into the backseat.

"We're going to the ballet!" Addison chirped, hopping into the car.

"That's nice," Katy said. "Fasten your seat belt, sweetie." She heard the click and then the shuffling sounds of Addison's dance bag, probably because the girl was retrieving her new, pink iPod.

They swung by Tyler's friend's house to pick him up and then drove to the children's home. Katy had a garage door opener of her own now, and she pulled into an empty stall. The children sprang out and ran inside for their snack. By the time Katy got inside, they were fighting over the last can of soda pop. Tyler snapped it open, and fizz spilled over his hand and onto the freshly mopped floor.

Addison planted her tiny hands on her tutu hips and did a little dance move, posing and gloating over Tyler's sticky mishap.

He burped, grinned, and headed for the stairway.

"Pick up your backpack," Katy called after him.

"I know. I know."

Katy smiled inwardly that he didn't seem quite so resentful, hadn't called her a pilgrim. She gave Addison a faint smile. "How about some orange juice?"

"Okay." The little girl ditched her pose and climbed onto the bar stool, propping pink-clad elbows on the bar, adult-style. "I'm excited about the ballet. It's *Cinderella*."

A brief wave of nostalgia hit Katy, for she'd loved that fairy tale when she was a little girl. But that's all it was. A fairy tale. Pouring the juice, Katy said, "That's nice." Then she wet a paper towel to clean up after Tyler. She was glad it was Thursday. She wouldn't have to come back to the Brooks' until next Tuesday. The coldhearted thought zipped harsh in her own mind, especially after agreeing with God in the car that she needed to be more loving. She slid into the stool beside Addison. "I have some time if you want to play that tea-party board game you have."

"Okay!" Instantly, she abandoned her drink, bounding off the stool and running up to her room.

"Better change first," Katy called after her, wondering if she should follow her up and check on Tyler. When she'd decided to do just that, she'd gotten partway up the stairway when she heard footsteps. She whirled. Sean Brooks was home.

"Oh hi. You're early," she said, retracing her steps so that she could speak to him.

"Tammy told me you needed a break."

"She did?" Katy glanced up the stairway and back with hesitance. "Tyler's in his room. I was about to check on him. And Addison's changing out of her dance costume. We were just going to play a board game. I'm afraid she's going to be disappointed."

"I'll do that with her." Sean started toward the kitchen.

Katy waited with hesitance. To her relief, he didn't grab a beer but returned with an envelope in his hand. She had cleaned around it earlier that day. "Tammy wanted me to give this to you."

It hit Katy that Tammy must have sensed her frustration. She'd misjudged her employer after all. The envelope probably contained a token of apology. She felt a tinge of guilt over her ugly thoughts earlier in the car. The envelope felt like it might hold a gift card. They still needed many things for the doddy house. "Thanks." She took her coat off the bar stool and shrugged into it. "Tell Tammy I really appreciate it."

"No problem. Our treat. Just enjoy."

Nodding, Katy replied, "Tell the children 'bye for me. I'll see them on Tuesday. Thanks again." In the garage, she got into her car and started the engine. But her curiosity couldn't be ignored, and she ripped open the envelope. Inside were two tickets. Not what she'd expected. Furling her brow, she pulled them out far enough to read the print. Tickets to the *Cinderella* ballet! She lay her head against the headrest, pinched her eyes closed, and rapped her forearms against the steering wheel. The horn honked.

~⌒~

By smooth maneuvering on Katy's part, Lil was joining her at the doddy house to talk with Jake about the new church kitchen. Katy refused to meet him alone.

Still, as she approached the front porch, her nerves bristled. Inside the tiny house, Jake turned and gave her one of his crooked grins. She drew in a deep breath at his dark good looks and willed herself to stir up some of those Christian attitudes God had impressed upon her in her recent car devotional. . . . She needed to act lovingly. No, that was just too strong for this circumstance. Arguing inwardly, she substituted the word *sisterly*.

"Hi." For a Christian attitude, it left her feeling a bit breathless. "See you've got a whole crew here today. Where's Lil?"

"In the bathroom, talking to the plumber. The electrician is installing lights. But the rest of the house is ready to start painting."

"Awesome." Now she was talking like Tyler.

Jake caught her slip of tongue. "Somebody's in a good mood."

Maybe being nice wasn't such a good idea. Looking at him wasn't, either. He definitely wore his jeans too tight for a Conservative boy. It made her wonder how much he'd changed or if she even knew him anymore. She sucked in a breath when he looked down at the buckle on his low-slung tool belt, worked the clasp, and dropped it on the ground beside him. *Breathe*, she told herself, *pull up your gaze.* The view wasn't much safer there. His logo-free T worked to his advantage, the black material emphasizing the black, wavy hair that fringed his baseball cap.

"I don't suppose that means you've decided to tolerate me?"

Of all the nerve, after she'd specifically told him she didn't want him and that he bothered her. Truth was, he probably sensed how well she tolerated him—desired him. But trying to act nonchalant, she replied, "Actually, I have." Unconsciously, she fiddled with the shoulder strap of her purse. "I thought about what you said about new beginnings. I'm sure God wants that for you. I want that for you."

His deep-hooded brows relaxed and his brown eyes lit with more enthusiasm than they should have as he bounded toward her, his voice thicker than ever with his Dutch accent. "I won't let you down, Katy. I—"

Throwing both palms in the air, she quickly interjected, "Don't"— and he stopped—"misunderstand. This has nothing to do with us."

His expression wilted, making him seem boyishly vulnerable. He hooked his thumbs in his slim jeans and studied her with tilted head. "You saying you want to be friends?"

She rolled the question distastefully around in her mouth. "More like what you said at first. I'm just trying to tolerate you. It's the decent thing to do. Sisterly."

He made a face. "Sisterly?"

"Christian. Sisterly."

"Oh." His stupid grin returned. He moved forward again. She froze, not sure what he was up to, but thankfully she must have presented a formidable presence, for once again he hesitated. Still, he stood too close. He looked down at her with his dark gaze, and she hoped he said something, did something soon, before she passed out from lack of oxygen. Then he did. Reaching out, he wrapped his forefinger in her ponytail, like he had so many times over the years. He gently untangled it from her purse strap. She lowered her gaze, making it eye level with his neck. He had a handsome Adam's apple. He swallowed as if the gesture affected him the same as it did her. But neither of them would admit it.

"Thanks," he murmured.

"Hey, Jake"—the electrician broke off his sentence when he saw he'd intruded on an intimate moment.

Jake, never one to act embarrassed, slowly turned without dropping his hand.

But she jerked away.

"Yeah?" Jake asked, if anything showing only irritation at the interruption.

"When you get a minute, I'd like to show you something."

Jake turned back to Katy with furled brows, and she knew their business wasn't finalized, but it had gotten more personal than she'd hoped. She was grateful for the interruption.

"Go on." She motioned with a wave. "I'll go find Lil and check out the new shower."

"Okay." His gaze roved over her in a leisurely manner. "Meet me back here in five minutes, and we'll go over the church project." He gave a mocking tip of his ball cap and strode away.

She stood still for a moment longer, both mourning and exulting over the leap their relationship had just taken with its flirtatious undercurrent. It had all happened so quickly that she feared where it might lead in the future if she kept melting a little each time she was in his presence.

She found Lil in the bathroom, flirting with the plumber. Ignoring that, Katy snapped, "You abandoned me." She lowered her voice. "You knew the plan. You were supposed to back me up, so I wouldn't have to talk to him alone."

Lil gave an offhanded frown with a small toss of her hand. "I didn't even know you were here. But now that you are, check out the shower." She opened and closed a glass door. Stepped in and out. "Don't you love it?"

She did. The shower compartment wasn't fancy like the travertine walk-in shower Lil had cut out of a magazine. It was an unpretentious white, but it was new and would serve the purpose. Well, after they scraped the stickers and handprints off, Katy thought, grinning. "I call the first shower." The back of the plumber's neck reddened, and she clamped her hand over her mouth, backing out of the room. In the hall, they both burst out laughing.

"He's kinda cute, don't you think?" Lil asked.

"Married?"

"I don't know. Either that or just shy. I'll have to ask Jake."

They met Jake back in the living room and settled down on the plastic-covered floor for their meeting. Over the next ten minutes, they discussed all the pertinent details of the future fellowship hall's kitchen. Jake asked plenty of questions and scribbled notes on a legal pad, even sketched. While they were at it, he gave them the dimensions they would need to shop for appliances for the doddy house, which was where they were headed next.

"You driving?" Lil asked, popping to her feet.

"Sure," Katy replied.

"Good. I've gotta go find my purse." She winked, and Katy thought it was an excuse to flirt with the plumber again. "Then I'm ready to go."

Jake pinned Katy with his dark gaze, and as soon as Lil left, he jumped right in where they'd left off before his cousin joined them. "You could probably tolerate me better if you'd let me tell you my story. I need to tell you exactly what happened to me the last couple of years. How it's changed me."

She shook her head. "Nah. I don't want to get involved in your personal life."

"Come on, Katy. You already are."

She started to stand, but her foot slipped on the plastic, and he lunged forward and caught her arm, steadying her. Their faces were close, mere inches away, and he whispered. "I hate the word *never*."

When he drew back, she asked, "What?"

"You'll never forgive me, and I'll never forget you. And never's a miserably long time."

Lil popped back into the room. "Found it." She hooked her arm under Katy's coat sleeve. "Let's hit the shops. See ya later, chump."

Katy forced a smile for Lil. At the doorway, she hesitated, but Lil went on outside. Katy glanced back at Jake.

He winked.

Hoping to wipe the smirk from his face, she said, "One thing before we go. I was wondering, is your plumber married?"

His brows furled. "Very."

Katy shrugged and started through the doorway.

But behind her, the amusement in his voice couldn't be denied. "Tell Lil the electrician's single."

Straightening her shoulders, she didn't reply.

CHAPTER 12

Barely able to contain her excitement, Katy grinned over at Lil, whose car was filled with painting supplies. In response, Lil did a little shoulder shimmy. They were both anxious to get started. In a few short weeks, the doddy house renovations had nearly been completed. New purchases were stored in Mr. Landis's barn. Now came Katy's favorite part: cleaning up the place and making it livable.

Lil turned the car into the Millers' drive and honked just as Jake strode out of the doddy house. With a wave, he headed directly to the back of the Blazer. It amazed Katy how those two read each other's minds. They were more like twins than cousins.

Ever since Katy and Lil's spat over hiring Jake to renovate the doddy house, Katy had kept her feelings and frustrations over him private, aware that information somehow magically passed between the other two.

Sometimes Katy's escalating problems seemed overwhelming. She hadn't told anybody about the ballet tickets either. That problem continued to fester, frustrating her peace. Once she would have shared all her job-related problems with her mom, but now that she was operating in a gray zone, she didn't think her mom would understand. With time nearing her move into the doddy house, she didn't want her mom to worry that she was getting pulled into worldly ways.

Katy watched Jake easily tote a five-gallon paint can in each hand—shabby chic yellow for the kitchen and tropical turquoise for the bedroom—jaunting to the doddy house without speaking to her. The sly rat knew how to turn her head, showing off his muscles and ignoring her just the way she wanted him to, all very unfair. Was this something he'd learned at college? How to Win an Old Girlfriend 101?

"Want me to get the white can?" she asked Lil.

"Nah. Too heavy. Let Jake get it. But together we can manage the ladder." Lil struggled to extract it from the back of her car. Katy caught the end just before it dropped to the ground. They did an awkward, baby-step shuffle all the way inside the house with it. "Bedroom or kitchen?" Lil tossed breathlessly over her shoulder.

"Bedroom." *Jake can work in the kitchen*, she hoped, *far away from my work area.*

Lil nodded as they maneuvered the ladder through the hall. Next they struggled to set it upright in the center of the bedroom, next to the paint cans.

"Whew!" Katy said. She removed her coat, taking in the metallic, new-heater smell. Filled with pride and amazement, she thought, *Our heat from* our *new heating system.* Suddenly she had something to show for her hours of housecleaning. Stoking her feeling of satisfaction, she headed for the new closet. "Wow. Have you seen this, Lil?"

Her friend followed at her heels, then did a slow circle inside the large walk-in. "Um-hm. Shoe racks, shelves, clothes bars. It's perfect."

"Which half do you want?" Katy asked, imagining her dark skirts spaced apart in perfect half-inch increments, her long-sleeved blouses classified by colors, sweaters by color, too, in perfectly folded piles on the shelves. With her meager wardrobe, there would be room to spare. She could keep other personal items here, too: some cleaning supplies that she purchased by the gallon, her sweeper bags, her childhood dolls, scrapbooks filled with school papers, and her collection of the *Young Indiana Jones Chronicles.* No, she'd leave those for her little brothers. But she had a stack of unread Christian novels she'd purchased at the Shekinah Festival in September.

Lil pointed at the far wall, the one more visible from the bedroom. "You'd better take that side since you're neater. And we can put a dresser on this wall. I'll take the bottom two drawers."

"That's kind. Thanks." But Lil's reminder that she wouldn't be the neatest roommate sent a tremor of foreboding into her future fantasy vision. When they stepped back into the room, Jake had already started masking off the baseboard.

He looked up. His shaggy black curls flipped out under his hat. The brim had been knocked off-kilter, and he didn't seem aware of how attractive he looked at that moment. Both masculine and boyish. "This wall's ready to go," he offered.

"Now it's your turn to pick. Cut or roll?" Lil asked.

Katy tore her gaze from Jake and stared at Lil, until she could concentrate on the question. It certainly wasn't a difficult one. In the closet, Lil had chosen first. She had given Katy the best, the higher drawers. So Katy chose the chore she thought Lil would least want. "Cut in."

Katy pried off the paint lid and stirred the white swirls with a wooden paddle until she had a solid color that resembled a pale tropical sea. Grabbing a tray and brush, she went to the can, and Jake jumped to her assistance.

"Let me lift that for you." He poured, then placed the can back on the plastic flooring. "Nice color."

She imagined there would be nights when sleep would fail her for remembering his tight jeans-clad form in the center of their bedroom. He was a nuisance in them. Without thanking him, she took the tray to the wall and knelt, straightening her skirt beneath her and then teasing the color along the top of the stained baseboard. She glanced over, "Yes, I love it." His eyes darkened, and then he turned away, filling Lil's tray.

"Me, too," Lil said. "Reminds me of summer." After a few minutes, she called, "Whoala. Look at this."

She'd painted two stripes on the wall with the old green color showing between.

Looking up from her painstakingly straight handiwork, Katy pointed out, "If you don't do it right, it's going to look streaked."

"You think? Okay, if you're sure stripes wouldn't be cool?"

"Crooked stripes are not cool. Neither is that green color. We both agreed on that."

"Your call. Here goes, plain turquoise wall. Love it." She glanced over at Jake. "We'll do the kitchen next, if you want to prep it."

"I can do that, but the closet needs a primer. If I do that first, it might be dry enough for you to paint before you close up the can."

Lil glanced over at Katy. "How does that sound?"

She might as well give in to the fact that with Megan having to finish a school project, Jake's help was allowing them to get more work done, even if it kept him in alarmingly close proximity. "Fine."

Jake tossed her a rakish grin, then disappeared to get the primer.

"He's behaving, don't you think?" Lil asked, her gaze hopefully skittering to Katy.

"Probably up to something."

"Just wants you to believe he's really sorry. . .for everything."

"He has done a good job with the place. Fast, too."

"And cheap."

"Cheap isn't always good," Katy quipped, thinking of the little outsider he'd dated and giving a different meaning to the word.

"In our case it is. Shush. Here he comes."

Jake trudged back through the room, sporting a gigantic grin and barely missing the upturned paint lid. Then he disappeared in the closet.

Out of sight was good, Katy thought, pulling the ladder next to the wall and balancing herself on the top rung to edge along the ceiling. "How's work?"

Lil replied, "Anybody can boil pasta and stir sauce. But it'll pay the rent. The way I figure it, I need to get a good reference and move up to a better restaurant at my first opportunity. Mark my words: I will someday be a top chef."

Katy climbed down and moved the ladder. "David wants to take me out to dinner the next time we go out. I suggested your restaurant."

"Tonight?"

"Nope. He's helping at the church today and has to help his dad do chores afterward."

"One more date, right?"

"Shh!" Katy hissed, nodding her head toward the closet. Jake appeared as if on cue, and Katy fought back a grin at the globs of paint on his hat and in his hair. His cell phone tight to his ear, he walked through the room.

"How's babysitting going?" Lil asked.

Katy's hand paused, unable to shoulder her problem alone any longer. "You're never going to believe it. Tammy tricked me into accepting tickets to the ballet."

"How'd she do that?"

Happy to vent for the next five minutes, Katy explained the details.

"I can't believe she did that, knowing how you feel about dancing," Lil muttered, wearing a mama-lion-protecting-her-cub expression—endearing to Katy that somebody was at last siding for her, and cute, too, given the turquoise freckles. Like her cousin, Lil was wearing the paint. Lil was much prettier than she realized. "It's a test." Lil pushed her hair back with her forearm and some wisps escaped from her ponytail. "She's trying to break you."

Then Katy noticed a clip had been holding her hair in place and not the ponytail rubber band. "You cut bangs!"

Lil grinned, pushed more paint into her hair. "Cute, huh?"

"Has your mom seen them?"

Laying down the roller, Lil clamped her hands on her hips, getting paint on her clothes, too. She faced Katy, directing that mother bear attitude to thwart her now. "When are you going to get it? We've the same as left home. We're adults on our own. We can do whatever we please."

Climbing down off the ladder, Katy felt a rush of fear that one more piece of life was crumbling away. "And what pleases you?" Was Lil going to go crazy wild on her?

"Cutting bangs."

"What else?"

Jake strode back into the room and, noticing the tension, drew back a step.

Katy shook her head and turned away. "I'm done here. Is the closet ready?"

"Nope, wanna help me prep the kitchen?" Honestly, she didn't know which cousin was more frustrating. She followed him into the other room, fretting that Lil was going to pull her further into the gray area or even the black.

Jake stepped close, a tape contraption in his hands. "This is a little tricky. Works like this." As he demonstrated, and they bent over the dispenser, she wanted to reach up and pluck the globs of paint from his black curls. But at least her anger at Lil was easing away. His nearness commanded all of her attention. "Wanna try it?"

"Sure." She took the contraption then mumbled sulkily, "I think you ruined your hat."

"What's a hat compared to a day spent with two lovely ladies?" Then he grinned and, referring to the dispenser, told her, "That's backward."

Katy tried to remove the tape that she now had stuck between her fingers. "Uh-oh."

"No problem." He took her hand, taking his time removing the twisted ruined tape. Their gazes locked.

"I see your hand has healed."

She jerked it away. "It's fine."

"Here, try again."

She nodded and leaned across the counter, running the contraption along the wall seam, amazed at how sweet the tape went in place when she did it correctly. Then she got a prickly sensation that he was still watching her and paused. Sure enough, his hand touched her shoulder and then rested at her waist.

"You got it."

She opened her mouth to reprimand him, but he'd already moved away. Then she heard the sound of tearing tape from across the room.

After that, it went smoothly, the dispenser gliding along seams. They worked at opposite sides of the room, and just when she'd relaxed, his voice whispered, "I miss hanging out with you, like this."

Her hand flinched. She could smell him, faint sawdust and stronger soap. She redid a crooked strip, not daring to glance at him. "Did you know I'm dating David Miller?"

There was silence, and then he replied, "I heard. Is it serious?"

"Now that would be personal, wouldn't it?"

"Hey, you brought it up."

"Only because I want you to back off. Give me some space here. I'm trying to tolerate you, remember?"

"Oh. Right."

—⁂—

Later that evening, Jake opened the back door and stepped into his mom's kitchen. His grandma Minnie sat at the table, and the sight squeezed his heart with tenderness. He strode over and placed a gentle hand on her shoulder. "Hey, Grams."

"Sit down and see what I made," she replied.

Jake dropped into a chair and pointed at the picture in a magazine the older woman was viewing. "You made that quilt?"

"Yeah. I made it for my little girl." As usual since she had developed Alzheimer's, Grams was living in her past memories, believing that Jake's mom was still her little girl.

"That's pretty. I'll bet she loves it."

"Oh, she does. But she's playing now." Then the elderly woman started to her feet. "I need to make supper before the children come in."

He glanced at his mom by the stove. "Mom wants you to enjoy your quilt. She's going to make supper for you tonight."

"She is? How thoughtful. Are you sure, dear?"

"Yes, Minnie," Jake's mom called. "Fried mush, your favorite."

"No, you were always Dad's favorite," she rebuffed. For some time, she'd been thinking that her grown daughter was her sister Martha. Usually Jake and his mom just played along. The only time her confusion really bothered him was when she mistook him for her departed husband, and Jake's grandpa, but the resemblance couldn't be denied.

He kissed her on her cheek. "I need to go change before supper."

"Hurry back. I want to show you what I made for my little girl."

"Okay, Grams. I'll be right back." He looked over at his mom, and she gave him a nod so he hustled up the steps to his room. After his shower, he speed-dialed Lil while he finished dressing.

"So did she say anything about me?" he asked.

"She's not talking to me about you. Except about your work. She's pleased with that."

The compliment gave him a great deal of satisfaction.

"But I can tell by the way she looks at you that she still cares. It's like she's afraid to be around you."

Jake leaned against the wall and crossed his arms. "She told me she's dating David. That she's only tolerating me. She's warming up, but too slowly. I'm almost done at the doddy house."

"There's still the building committee."

He straightened. "She's smart. And you're right about her keeping her distance. I'm scared this isn't going to work. I can't stand the thought of that Miller guy and her together."

"I have an idea. What do people do when somebody's in the hospital or there's a death in the family?"

Jake shrugged and moved to his window. "I don't know."

"Think, chump."

Jake looked down over the flat fields, clumps of snow still evident. "They send cards and take casseroles."

"Exactly. Well, you're going to take her a casserole."

"I know you think a lot about food, but that's pretty stupid."

"A good-deed casserole."

"Go on."

"She's under pressure at work. Her boss gave her tickets to take Addison to the ballet. To her this is a stressful thing. You're going to hold her hand."

"I'm taking her to the ballet?"

"Sort of. Here's the plan."

Jake listened and realized that Lil was a genius at more than cooking.

CHAPTER 13

February brought Katy a reprieve—clear skies and melting snow–with no storms on the personal front, either. Although she still had the ballet tickets tucked inside her cleaning journal, work had been uneventful. The doddy house was progressing nicely in spite of Jake's presence, and the weekly building committee meeting had been postponed.

Also David had asked her out again—date number three, which fulfilled her father's stipulation. But she wasn't a fool. A person couldn't count on a winter's reprieve to hold out much longer than a week.

Katy and David eyed each other over a plastic red rose. The cozy Italian place with its white vinyl tablecloths was the type where waiters could be heard calling out their orders and the clinking of dishes filled any break in the music, a place where David didn't look out of place in his jeans and button-down shirt.

He snapped open his menu and asked, "Know much about Italian food?"

"I know spaghetti and lasagna. Love them both." Katy relaxed in the soft black booth and cast him a smile.

"Lasagna. . .number three on the menu." He set the menu aside. "Since this is our third date, that sounds like a good fit, don't you think?"

The pulse-pounding question caught her off guard, and she peeked at him above her own menu. Was he goading her? His eyes shone with something she couldn't quite read. Straightening, she set down her menu and took a sip of her water. Only she choked. Clutching up a red napkin, she struggled not to send water spewing across the table at David. Quickly she unrolled the napkin and dumped the silverware, pressing the cloth to her face. When she finally could breathe again, she peeped at him through watering eyes. Was he goading? Or just naive?

He looked concerned. "You okay?"

"Fine."

The waiter came, and David gave him their orders. When they were alone again, he asked, "So you love lasagna? What else do you love?"

"Clean black cars," she said.

"Is that why you go out with me? Because you like my car?"

"No. I'm here because I wanted to see where Lil works." When she saw her teasing had hit its mark, she grinned. "And because you're a really nice guy."

His gaze told her he didn't believe that for a moment.

"So what do you love?" she asked him, but instantly knew what he would reply.

"Shiny black cars," they said in unison and then both laughed.

"What about farming?" she asked.

"I like driving the big machinery, but it's pretty dull in the winter. Ivan and I get along good, though. If it wasn't for him, I'd probably be doing something else by now." He studied her a moment, then ventured, "It's not the farming I like, it's the driving. You know, anything with a motor. *Brrrm-brrrm.*"

She smiled.

He leaned close, and his aftershave wafted over her, warm and inviting as his secretive hazel eyes. "I like engines. Speed. You ever go to the races?"

When he leaned back again, the scent was gone but there remained a more vivid impression of the workings of the man across the table, one that might explain the mischievous glint that often appeared in his eyes. Was it a desire for something more than the ordinary, and might that be fast cars? In her imagination, she saw David yanking his gearshift down and racing his shiny black beast down some country road. "No. You drag race?"

"Now that would be breaking the law," he grinned. The smell of garlic, and the appearance of their salad and a basket of buttery breadsticks instantly commanded their appetite and attention.

He passed her the basket then said offhandedly, "How's the doddy house coming?"

The warm bread melted in Katy's mouth. Savoring it, then swallowing, she said, "We're moving in next weekend."

"We missed your friend Jake last Saturday at the cleanup. Was he working at your place?"

She couldn't miss the jealous tone of David's voice and felt instantly defensive. "He did help us paint last Saturday." She tried to make her tone cheerful. "And we finished that today."

A glance across the table caught David's jaw tensing. He'd always been so kind and attentive that she found his resentful behavior unsettling. In fact, he was ruining her appetite. She dangled a fork. "You still want to help us move in?" She pushed her salad, hoping he would redeem himself.

"Yeah, maybe we can make a contest of it."

She pushed her plate aside, no longer able to disregard his barbed comments. He was obviously ticked at her. "What do you mean?"

"See who can carry the most boxes. Me or Jake."

Her face burned. "That would be fun." She slid out of the booth. "You'll excuse me a minute?"

"Sure." He ran a hand through his hair.

Katy slapped her napkin on the table and headed for the restroom, but just as she rounded the corner, Lil appeared, slightly breathless and her face slick with moisture. Her hair was plastered into a smooth brown knot with a hair net securing it, and her newly cut bangs were bobby-pinned. She wiped her hands on a long white apron that protected her white blouse and black skirt uniform. "I wanted to come out sooner, but I couldn't get away."

"Great place." Katy shouldered open the door to the restroom.

Lil followed her. "Hey, what's wrong?"

"Oh, David. He's acting weird tonight." Katy didn't miss the little light that danced in Lil's eyes. "I guess you're happy about that."

Lifting both hands in the air, Lil objected, "Whoa. Don't get me involved in your lovers' spat."

"I'm sorry. This really is a great place. We ordered lasagna. Did you make it?"

"Cooked the noodles and stirred the sauce." She put her hand on Katy's shoulder. "Look. Everything's going as planned. Don't lose sleep over David. If he blows it now, at least you had your three dates. And he had his chance."

"I'm so sick of hearing about *three* dates. One more time and my head's going to explode. I think I'm just going to go back out there and tell him the truth."

"Fine, except please taste the lasagna first. Tell me my noodles are perfecto and not sticky."

Grinning, Katy said, "Okay. And I mean it. I really do love this place. We've got to bring Megan sometime on your night off."

"It's kind of a dead-end job. But it's fun. Did you see how cute the waiters are?" Lil went to the sink and washed her hands, then hit the electronic dryer, raising her voice over the blowing air. "I'll call later."

"No, it'll wake up the household."

The blower shut off, and Lil left.

Katy washed her hands and caught the image of her brooding eyes in the mirror. She fiddled with her covering, wishing she'd brought her purse to the restroom so that she could refresh her lipstick, the only makeup she ever wore. Then it hit her. Lil hadn't had her prayer covering on. She bit her lip. That didn't surprise her much.

When she felt like she could face David's interrogation again, she left and returned to her booth, relieved to see that their meals had arrived. As if they weren't in the middle of a spat, she slid into her seat and took up her fork. "Looks good."

David reached across the table and touched her hand. "I'm sorry for making you mad."

She nodded, avoiding the impulse to shy away from his touch. It was warm and assuring, and her anger melted away. "I wasn't back there sulking. I met Lil in the restroom."

He drew his hand away with a nod. Then he tasted the mild, creamy dish, studying her. "Mm, good. She make it?"

Grinning, Katy said, "She boiled the noodles. And she wants our opinion on their consistency."

He grinned back, holding her gaze until she blushed. The rest of the meal, he reined in his jealousy, and afterward, they even lingered over coffee. She was relaxed, enjoying herself, when abruptly, he started in again. "So what happens after date three? You going to go out with me again?"

He hit the nerve dead-on, jarring her out of her complacency. The dreaded question now hung in the air between them. She tensed. If she didn't go with him again, then she was a user. After her second date, she had already known that she was not romantically interested in him. Her hands clasped her cup, its soothing warmth her only bit of comfort. "Why do you keep bringing up date three?"

"I think you know why. I was allotted three dates to prove myself."

Holding back a moan because her nightmare had come true—he was aware of her despicable behavior—she asked softly, shamefully, "How long have you known?"

His clipped response barely contained his anger. "Before date one."

She sighed, placing her hands on her lap. "So you've been playing me." Her anger suddenly flared, too. Just like everybody else in her life, he'd been manipulating her. She looked at him through the blur of pain-filled eyes. "Why?"

"I wanted to follow the course. See where it led. Are you a user, Katy? Using Jake, too? To get the doddy house fixed up cheap?"

Katy folded her napkin and placed it neatly on the table in front of her. "You figure it out. I'm ready to go now."

David didn't make any moves to leave the restaurant. He had more to say. "Ivan told me about the deal he made with your dad. I'd hoped that after the first date, you'd go with me because you liked me, not because you were using me. I hoped you'd tell me the truth."

"What I told you before is still true. I never intended to look for a guy, but I like you, and I was willing to get to know you. I opened myself to the possibility of falling for you."

"A win-win situation for you, wasn't it? So back to my question. What did you decide? Is there going to be a date four, or are you finished with me?"

"Wow, you are so romantic. So persuasive." She reached for her purse. "Probably not, David."

He took care of the check, and drew his lips in a tight line. "Let's go."

The car ride was dreadful and quiet, except for a country song on his radio about some forlorn man who'd just been dumped by his girl. From the sounds of it, Katy figured the guy in the song deserved it. There was a hint of smoke in the air, emanating from the jacket that David had loaned her the night of the fire. She had returned it earlier, and it now was on the backseat of his car, reminding her of his heroics the night of the fire, heaping more coals to her shame.

When they pulled into her drive, he spoke again. "I guess I could have gone along with the game, but my pride wouldn't allow it any longer. One of us needed to address the issue. Make a new start if there's ever to be a date four. Something real to go on, you know?"

She nodded. "It's been wearing on me, too. I'm sorry for using you. Although you did use the situation to your advantage, too."

"Guess I was willing to settle for scraps."

She gave him a weak grin.

He said, "A promise is a promise. I'll help you move in next Saturday."

"No, please. You don't need to."

"You want to get rid of me?"

"No. I—"

"Good. There probably will be a contest between me and construction cowboy. After all, it's almost Valentine's Day."

"Cowboy?"

"His holster. The tool bags."

She guessed she wasn't the only one who'd noticed Jake wore his pants too tight, and his tool bags only added to his attractiveness. But what had David meant about Valentine's Day? Was he still going to pursue her? The idea of date four had been left hanging. She felt confused but remained quiet.

He walked her to the door, drew her close, and kissed her forehead. Then he tilted her chin up and kissed her mouth, slow and sensual, but he broke it off abruptly. She hadn't wanted to kiss him at all, but she hadn't wanted to humiliate him further by rejecting him. The kiss was calculated, the kiss of a bitter man.

With a sigh, she watched him go, sorry she'd hurt him. She stepped inside the dark interior of the house.

"Do you love him?" came a startling voice out of the darkness.

Katy clasped her heart. "Karen! Don't scare me like that. Why are you still up?"

"To answer the phone. It was Lil." Karen offered, pulling back the curtain and looking outside. "I told her you weren't home yet, and she didn't seem happy."

Katy pushed her sister's hand away from the curtain. Hadn't she told Lil not to call? Maybe she hadn't heard her above the din of the hand dryer.

"So do you?" Karen repeated.

"No. Why are you standing in the dark?"

"I—"

"Were you spying on me?"

"I—"

Suddenly Katy thought better of having this conversation so near their parents' bedroom door. "Come upstairs."

"If you don't love him, then why were you kissing him?" Karen whispered before they'd even reached the landing.

CHAPTER 14

On moving day, ominous purple clouds swallowed the sky. Everyone involved in the move met at the Landis farm, where the furniture was stored in the barn. Katy's car was packed to the roof with clothes, and the rest of its interior resembled a bag of puzzle pieces vying for space. Her new upright vacuum cleaner rode shotgun, and stacks of bedding filled the seats. She crawled out, careful that everything remained wedged in place, and eyed Megan. "I can't believe that leather couch your mom found at a garage sale. What can we do to thank her?"

"Just let her come see the place sometime."

Lil strode away from the place where David and Jake were loading furniture and joined Katy and Megan.

"Maybe we should have a parents' night and make dessert or something," Katy suggested.

"Nah!" They all protested, giggling and then shivering when a fierce gust whipped through the yard. It forced the girls into a huddle then rolled on across the farm's barren fields.

Katy straightened her covering, watching the swirling snow and debris. "Wow, glad my car door wasn't open."

"Careful," Jake yelled.

Looking over to see if the warning was for them, Katy saw Jake nod at David to move slightly to the right as they maneuvered a table onto the bed of his truck. Jake must have felt her gaze, because he glanced over. "We've almost got it, if you girls want to go on over and meet us at the doddy house in a few minutes?"

The scene drew her curiosity, Jake and David working together. Jake winked and brushed his gloves before heading back to the barn. David trailed behind. When he saw that Katy was watching them, he made sport of Jake by mimicking his walk for a few strides, probably to get even for Jake's ordering him around like a hired lackey.

As if David didn't know how to keep things nice, she thought, having always admired that part of his personality. But so far, the two were at least remaining civil enough with each other to have packed their first load of furniture. Katy dismissed their antics and looked back at Lil, thinking about the day's work. "It was great of Jake to take the appliances over earlier this week."

"I love that stainless steel GE stove." Lil did the garbanzo shimmy.

Katy didn't know the difference between a GE or a Viking, but as long as they had sparkling drip pans and working ovens to cook Lil's mouthwatering dishes, they suited her. Grinning at Lil's enthusiasm, she started toward her car. "See you over there."

When everybody reached the doddy house, the unending trips to the cars began. Katy started with the boxes in her trunk—kitchen and household odds and ends her mom had donated—and was sweating by the time she had to struggle with the piles of clothing still on their hangers. Nearly colliding with Megan on the path of freshly laid plastic floor covering—her genius idea—she cried out, "Look out, green bean, or I'll squish ya."

Megan's arms had just been emptied, and she pointed. "Here come the beds."

Every time the guys appeared, Lil became the moving director, which was fine with Katy because Lil had an eye for furniture placement. In this case, Lil's job was easy because the girls had already imagined and reimagined it together many times.

"Last load," David informed her, setting some long pieces of bed support at his feet so that he could take a break. "Feeling pretty excited, huh?"

Jake tried to pass them while balancing similar bed braces on his shoulder. With an irritated huff, he said, "Blocking the way, guys, for us working fellows."

Ignoring him, David smiled at her. "I'll put the beds together next."

"Great."

Just then Jake reappeared. "I'll help you unload your car if you want."

Glancing uneasily at David, she told Jake, "Sure, my sweeper's out there yet and one box in the trunk that was too heavy for me."

"Done."

"Show me which bed's yours," David said, vying for her attention. "Want to help hold the rails in place while I fasten them together?"

"Sure."

After following him into the bedroom and hanging up their coats in the closet, she pointed at a white headboard. "Start with that one. My dad made it. And my little brothers painted it." She'd always admired the white iron set Mrs. Beverly had in her guest room. She tried to get a similar look using wood. Excitement bubbled up inside her that her dream was coming true. But she covered it by saying, "Guess they were eager to get me out of the house."

"I doubt that." She did, too. In fact, the parting with her family after breakfast had been emotional and had left Katy, her mom, and Karen all teary-eyed. David set the frame in place. "Okay, hold that piece."

She knelt next to her hope chest on the warm, restored-wood flooring and involuntarily smoothed her gray skirt around her. To dispel the intimacy of the situation, she blurted out, "You know how to use that tool?"

Working the screwdriver, David grunted, "I've worked on a lot of farm equipment."

"You like fixing stuff? Working on equipment?"

"Nope, like driving—"

"Fast cars," she finished for him just as Jake strode into the room and witnessed the flash of familiarity and ensuing laughter that passed between her and David. She glanced up at Jake's face, and his disapproving sneer pierced her with shame. But a flash of anger quickly followed her guilt, because it was Lil who'd asked Jake to help them move, or maybe he'd volunteered. Either way, if Jake and David hadn't helped, their dads could easily have done the work. She didn't need to *use* them. The remembrance of David's accusation from the night at the restaurant made her eager to finish with the bed assembly.

With her free hand, Katy tugged Jake's sleeve. "Hey, can you hold this for David?" As soon as she touched him, an awareness of his masculinity surfaced old memories and emotions. "I'm going to go help the girls organize the kitchen," she mumbled, backing into her hope chest.

"Don't you think Lil will want to do that?" Jake protested, as he reluctantly replaced her hold on the sideboard.

No ready reply came to her mind so she just fled the room. Let them glare at each other. She bit her lower lip, knowing Jake wouldn't appreciate serving as David's helper. Thankfully, the moment she stepped into the kitchen where Lil and Megan were unloading boxes, the atmosphere lightened.

"We have food, too?" Katy couldn't believe how much their parents had chipped in to make their empty doddy house a real home.

"We'll need some groceries, but we won't starve, either." Lil lifted a small carton. "There's cocoa mix and popcorn, here. The guys have been working hard all day. Should we bust some out?"

"Let's unpack that last box first," Katy replied. "Maybe then the boys will be done with the beds. Gotta make sure we got a place to sleep tonight." *Using them again? They volunteered*, she snapped back at her conscience.

"We can always sleep on mattresses." Lil turned to Megan. "And you have to stay over our first night."

"You sure? I didn't bring any bedding."

Lil gave Megan a playful shoulder bump. "We'll squeeze you in."

"Awesome."

Katy glanced fondly at Megan. Guess Tyler wasn't the only one who used that word. It must be common at the college.

Megan flipped through the microwave's instruction manual, and by the time the last box was unpacked, she had it figured out and was explaining the workings to Katy, who gave Lil the joy of operating the cookstove first.

"I smell popcorn." Jake's thick Dutch accent preceded him and David into the kitchen.

"Sit and enjoy our first meal," Katy motioned toward the drop-leaf table by the window. The boys and Megan settled in, allowing Lil and Katy to serve them. Katy passed out small wooden bowls, old ones that had been made on her father's lathe, then took a chair between Jake and Megan.

When Lil was finished serving, and there weren't enough chairs for everyone to sit around the table, David jumped up and offered, "Sit here."

"Katy can sit on my lap," Jake urged, reaching over and tugging her sleeve.

"Stop it," she hissed, jerking her arm away and glancing up at David, who was acting the gentleman. His expression, however, had darkened.

Lil solved the problem by plopping uninvited on Jake's left knee. "Thanks, chump."

He grinned, supporting her with a hand at her waist, and David slid back into his seat by the window. He glanced out under the dark green, Amish-style window shade. "It's snowing. A storm's been brewing all day. But I'm in no hurry to go. I can always stay over at Ivan's. 'Fraid you girls are going to have to get used to looking at my ugly face. I'm at Ivan's a lot."

Sensing the silent tension coming from Lil and Jake's chair, Katy dipped her smaller bowl into the larger, then offered, "More popcorn, anyone?"

Lil jumped up, "I'll put on more water."

Jake tipped back his chair and stretched his arms lazily. "Let it storm. I'm too tired to move. You gals are slave drivers. I'm ready to hibernate for at least a month. The living room floor will do fine. I'll just roll up in that rug over there and be snug as a bear."

Noticing with worry that the snow really was blanketing the ground, Katy said, "Oh no, you don't. We won't be getting any of that started here."

"Well, you're letting him hang out," Jake lowered his arms, and his chair snapped back to the floor. "And I'm family."

"Your truck too wimpy to plow through a few snowdrifts?" David baited.

"Yeah, pretty wimpy. Maybe in the morning when you go out to do your daily car washing, you can start my puny engine for me. You know, warm it up."

He sneered at Jake. "Puny like its owner?"

"I worked circles around you today, and—"

Katy stood. "Stop it. Both of you."

Megan snatched the empty popcorn bowl from the table and placed her hand on Jake's shoulder. "I'm sure you guys both know that we won't be having either of you stay over. But we can't thank you enough for all your help today." She speared Katy with a warning look.

"Megan's right. We do appreciate your hard work today, but you guys need to quit the bickering. As far as I'm concerned, it's juvenile."

Lil flicked a dish towel at Jake's chest. "Hey, juvie, I'll wash. You dry."

Katy rolled her gaze heavenward. So much for herding the guys out. She could tell Lil was giving Jake an excuse to be the last male to leave. Doing her part to get them both out the door, Katy started toward the bedroom for David's coat. With frustration, she heard him clomping down the hall behind her. He followed her all the way into the walk-in closet.

"I'm not leaving before he does."

She flicked on the light and wheeled to face him.

"I don't trust him." David abruptly pulled her close.

She wiggled free and placed a hand on his chest to separate them. "Stop it."

The golden star in his eyes flickered. "Why?"

She shrugged completely out of his embrace and looked at the floor, rubbing her palms over her arms. "Because we're not—"

"I'm sorry," he interrupted. "It's just that jerk out there acting like he owns you."

"Forget about him."

David's shoulders relaxed, and he nodded.

She saw that as a good sign but wanted to make sure he wasn't getting the wrong idea. "I don't want you to get your hopes up." She hurried on before he could interrupt again. "I'm not looking for a relationship with either of you. Otherwise, I wouldn't have moved in here."

David rubbed his chin, studying her.

"Katy?" Lil strode into the bedroom and stuck her head in the closet. "Oh whoa." She quickly exited.

Katy whipped David's coat off its hanger and flung it at him, scurrying after Lil. "Just getting David's coat."

In the few moments she'd spent in the closet, the house had grown darker. She snapped on a light in the living room. "Thanks again for helping," she told him.

David shuffled to the entry. "See you girls at church tomorrow?"

Katy opened the door and peered out. "As long as we're not snowed in."

"And if we can find an alarm clock," Megan added.

Jake pulled on his coat. "Use your phone." He glanced down the hall where Katy and David had just emerged, then looked at Katy. "We have an extra coatrack I think my mom will donate. I'll bring it over."

She blushed at his insinuating observation.

"Thanks again, guys." Megan waved as they departed.

Just before she closed the door, Katy thought she overheard David challenging Jake to a race. Surely not on these slippery roads? Nah, impossible. Even for those juveniles. She leaned against the door, only rousing from her thoughts when Megan asked, "Wanna make up the beds?"

That night they used Lil's extra set of pale blue flannel sheets for Megan's top bunk, and Katy loaned her a hand-sewn comforter. She snuggled under white crisp sheets and turned on her side to face the bunk bed, a night-light softly illuminating the room.

"Can't believe you sleep with a night-light," Lil teased.

"Don't want Megan falling out of bed," Katy shot back.

Lil looked overhead. "This reminds me of summer camp that first year. Remember?"

Feeling a lump in her throat, Katy murmured, "How could we forget?"

"And this is just the beginning," Lil purred.

But caution ruffled Katy's already exhausted nerves. For so long, they had pushed for this day, for the big prize. It seemed strange to think of it as a mountaintop where they would step off into the unknown. Lil's normal walk—on the Conservative Mennonite edge—filled Katy's spirit with uncertainty. She was tired. Tired of fighting Lil's outlandish whims. They were adults. Living on their own. Would it backfire if she gave in and just allowed Lil to be Lil?

"You think David's gonna keep hanging around?" Lil asked.

"Probably some. Like he said, he's over at Ivan's a lot. I hope Jake doesn't think this is a place for *him* to hang out."

Megan asked, "You going out with him again?"

"Jake? No way."

"No, David."

"Not him, either. I pretty much told him so tonight." Then Katy thought about how her sister had caught them kissing. Though Karen's curiosity had been mostly about boy stuff, it had been a sticky situation. The kind of circumstance a Conservative girl shouldn't be caught in. She needed to set things right. Maybe living in the doddy house could be her new beginning, to be a better person. One who didn't get pulled into the outsiders' world. Lil could be Lil, and she would be the Katy she had always wanted to be. Better than before.

"That what you were doing in the closet?" Lil mocked.

"Pretty much. That and fending him off."

"You should send your scraps my way," Megan complained between allergy sniffles. "Better yet, how about I set you up with a guy in my Bible class?"

"No thanks. I'm going to go solo for a while. Enjoy my freedom."

"That'a girl." Lil handed a tissue up to Megan. "Me, too. Unless that cute waiter with blond hair asks me out."

Giggling, Katy warned, "Better get your beauty sleep then." Nobody but Lil would entertain thoughts of dating an outsider.

CHAPTER 15

The next morning, to Katy's delight, the wind had pushed the storm out of Madison County, and Ivan was able to dig out the drive in time for the girls to attend church. Afterward, Lil made them spaghetti, complaining about using store-bought tomato sauce. It was a given that Lil would cook and Katy clean, although she hadn't envisioned herself hand-carrying all of Lil's empty diet soda cans to the recycling receptacle that Megan had supplied them. And she hadn't decided what to do yet about Lil's unmade bed.

In the afternoon, Megan headed back to her Rosedale dorm, leaving Katy and Lil to experience their first taste of what normalcy at the doddy house might resemble. When the day wound down, they tossed bed pillows in the middle of their tan leather couch, lying head to head with their legs slung over opposite armrests, and allowed the wonder of the moment to settle over them.

"We need throw pillows," Katy remarked, leery of placing her pillowcase on a secondhand couch.

"We need more furniture."

"Maybe we need to invite Anita Weaver over so that she can take pity on us and find us a couple of armchairs, too." Worrying her lip,

Katy mumbled, "I'm such a user."

"Why? Just because you have chapped hands?"

"What?" With a giggle, Katy waved her gloved hands above their faces and corrected, "Not loser. U–ser." She had smeared a home remedy on them, something she did a couple times a week, sometimes sleeping in the goo. It had become an ongoing experiment, trying to find the perfect combinations of ingredients to rectify her occupational damage. She stared at the white gloves, one of several pairs.

"There's so many things I want." Lil sighed. "A new car, a computer."

"Computer!"

"Well, yeah. Someday."

Katy pinched the bridge of her nose. "What else?"

Lil suddenly sat up. "I think I'll make a list in the back of my journal. Anyway, I learned that marjoram adds more flavor to pasta than oregano. And I need to jot down a penne recipe before I forget it."

"Under computer, you can write. . .new roommate."

"Ha, ha, very funny. You want me to bring you anything?"

Katy kept a journal of cleaning tips, but she wasn't in the mood to think about work or which hand-cream concoction worked best. "Grab one of those inspirational novels for me. I have a stack on a shelf in the closet."

"The same closet where you were kissing the moving guy?"

"Stop."

"So when's your next building meeting?" Lil taunted, skipping off before Katy could throttle her.

❧

The meeting was held in the sanctuary again, and Katy passed by the lobby's bulletin board to stare at her unfruitful advertisement. As much good as it had done, she might as well take it down. Yet there was always that distant chance. . .

"Still no job?"

Startled, Katy looked over her shoulder to find Jake standing behind her. "Lil told you I was looking for work?"

He stuffed his hands in his pockets. "Yeah, I'm looking, too. I'll need something after the fellowship hall is done."

Katy moved to find a seat for the meeting. Jake slid into the pew beside her.

"Must you sit so close?" she asked, shrugging her shoulder away from him.

"Mm-hm."

She glanced at the meetinghouse's plain spackled ceiling and back.

The painter settled in on Jake's other side pinning him in place, and Jake grinned.

"You're impossible."

"That often goes hand in hand with juvenile behavior."

She remembered calling him juvenile the day of the move. Was that his subtle way of reminding her that she owed him? "Yes, it does."

Leaning against her—so that she nearly fell off the end of the pew trying to avoid his touch, not to mention his soap and sawdust scent—he dug something out of his tight jeans pocket and flipped it onto her lap.

"Maybe this will make up for it."

She pushed away something that resembled a pair of tickets. "Whatever you're up to, no thanks."

"Come on. They're ballet tickets."

"What!" She snatched them back and stared, her gaze so smoldering it could have turned the offering to ashes. Two tickets to *Cinderella*? Slapping them back at him, she narrowed her eyes into stormy slits. "How did you get these?"

He shrugged. "At a ticket office." When she continued to gawk in disbelief, he added, "At the mall."

The painter leaned forward and stared, too, and to her further aggravation, she noticed they were attracting a small audience. Why did Mr. Weaver have to be late this night, of all times?

"How did you know?" she hissed.

"I'm not uncultured. I thought you might actually enjoy it."

"A kid's ballet?"

"It is?"

She glared at him, not fooled by his feigned act of innocence. "No thanks."

He gave her a lopsided smile and winked. "Let me know if you change your mind."

Bill Weaver, breathless from running into the meetinghouse, strode down the aisle and took his place in the front of the sanctuary. He quickly called the meeting to order. But other than recognizing the welcome distraction of his opening words, Katy became oblivious to the proceedings of the meeting.

The tickets to the same performance couldn't be a coincidence, and the only way he could know she was going to that ballet was through Lil. But why a pair of tickets when she obviously already had hers? Just to keep up the pretense? Why would he think she'd want him along at an already-dreaded event? As the evening wore on, she mulled over the details and poked it from every angle.

Slowly, Lil's part in the incident became glaringly clear. She recalled that Lil hadn't wanted her to date David from the beginning. Because she wanted her to date Jake instead. Lil must have warned Jake about David, and that's why he came to the skating party. Katy's mind rushed on, working out the scenario. That night at the skating party, Lil had been acting cranky. She'd called someone on her cell phone, too. Then she had hired Jake to remodel the doddy house. Katy widened her eyes in further revelation. And Lil had talked Katy into serving on this committee. And just the other night on the couch, Lil had teased her by asking when her next committee meeting was. What a conniving little matchmaker.

"Katy?" Bill Weaver asked.

She felt Jake's elbow in her ribs. "Huh?"

"You look like something troubles you. You don't agree with the size of the storage room?" All gazes turned toward her, eyebrows raised in expectancy.

"No. I mean, yes, I agree," she fumbled, feeling her cheeks heat. Lil was going to pay.

That night after the meeting, Katy waited up for Lil to come home from work. She rehearsed her angry speech as she emptied the trash, the night air nipping her flushed cheeks. She scrubbed toilets and scoured sinks and wrote furiously in her journal about removing unwanted scents from clothing. And when Lil's clunker coughed into the yard, Katy was ready for her, standing five feet from the entry, legs planted and fists on her hips.

The door opened and Lil halted. "Whoa."

"I can't believe you," Katy ground out.

"What? You didn't have to wait up. I'm exhausted. I had to stay and close."

"You told Jake about the ballet," Katy accused.

Flinging her purse on the table, Lil shrugged. "You didn't tell me it was a secret. I only wanted to help."

Katy followed her to the table. "You think I want the whole church to know that I'm participating in a dancing event?"

Shrugging out of her coat and dropping it over the back of a chair, Lil said dryly, "Where's Megan when we need her?"

"This isn't funny. I figured out your matchmaking schemes."

Lil leaned wearily against a chair. "So that makes me a terrible person?"

"Just the other day when you cut your bangs, you told me that we were adults. So why are you trying to run my life for me? Did you ever stop to think that I might like to be treated like an adult, too?"

Lil shot both hands in the air. "Look. Can we discuss this tomorrow after you've cooled down? Like I said, I'm really tired. I just want to go to bed."

"I'm tired, too. Tired of you interfering with my life. You're always trying to change me. I'm sick of it, and I don't think this"—she flung her arms in the air, gesturing at the room—"is going to work out. Us living together."

Lil froze. Her freckles paled. Then she became angry, too. "You don't get it. Jake is like a brother to me. He loves you. If you weren't so stubborn, you'd admit that you love him, too. Because of your pigheadedness, I have to help you guys along."

"You can't decide what's right or wrong for me. Even God gives people free wills."

Lil's eyebrow arched. "Don't go bringing God into this. As if He's on your side. As if I'm not a Christian. You're always doing that for me with your goody-goody attitude. But look at you yelling. What happened to your Mennonite upbringing now? Ever hear of nonresistance?"

"And do Conservative girls go around without wearing their coverings?"

Lil's hand went to her head, then slid back to her side. She raised her chin. "At least I don't pretend I'm something I'm not."

"No you don't," Katy whispered.

"But you do." Lil snatched her coat and purse and flung open the door.

"I do not."

Lil shook her head, then strode out and slammed the door behind her. Shocked, Katy stared at the rattling door. She heard the engine of Lil's car cough to life and then sputter off the property. Katy flicked the dead bolt with such force it popped back open. She slid it the second time, more deliberately, into the locked position. Good riddance.

She marched to the couch, plopped down, and stared at the floor, virtually panting with outrage. What did Lil mean about pretending? She was serious about living a holy life. Sure she fell short, but she didn't pretend.

With crossed arms, she went over their argument, even embellishing it with what she should have said but hadn't. But as much as she tried to justify herself and her anger, Lil's barbs kept darting back. Especially the idea that Katy wasn't honest or real.

Slowly, she came to realize that Lil hadn't been referring to her actions, but her feelings. And specifically her feelings toward Jake. As much as she tried to cover her pining for him, Lil had easily read her. As Katy sat with clenched hands, she allowed the enormity of what had just transpired to flood over her.

Had she really shouted that living together wasn't going to work? Where had that come from? Some hidden fear? She hadn't planned to say any such thing. She thought about all the hateful things that had spewed from her mouth like an uncontrollable and unrecognizable force. She couldn't erase the image of Lil's shocked, pale face.

She sat for a very long time in her desperation. The timbers of the old house began to creak. She felt alone. And just as that angry force had come unbidden earlier, so did another intruder. Fear. She'd known this enemy all her life, the fear of darkness.

Katy heard another bump, and jerked her glance over her shoulder. Though it was the wee hours of the morning, she would never be able to sleep if she went to bed. Miserable, she rose and put a kettle of water on the stove. Lil's stove. She waited for the whistle, blinking back her tears. When the tea was ready, she flicked off the kitchen lights and hurried through the dark hall to the bedroom. The thought shot through her mind that something invisible followed her, but she didn't look back. Heart racing, she shut her bedroom door. The house became a silent, lurking monster that she tried to ignore.

She flicked on her bedside lamp and set her tea on the nightstand. She pulled the drapes and tamped back her panic. Sitting on the edge of her bed, she removed the pins from her covering and placed them on her nightstand. Lil's messy bedcovers flagged her attention, and she couldn't look away.

Calmly she padded across the floor and made Lil's bed. When the last wrinkle was smoothed away, she sat on her own bed again and sipped her tea. What would happen to the doddy-house dream now? She hadn't considered Megan's feelings at all.

Eerie shadows danced in the closet. Strange house noises emphasized her loneliness. Would she have to slink home and admit to her dad she wasn't ready to live on her own?

CHAPTER 16

The next morning upon awakening, Katy groaned and pulled the twisted bedcovers over her tangled locks and bleary eyes, trying to dispel her fragmented dreams and the reality of the mess she'd created. During the night, she'd not only dreamed but woken to fits of unreasonable panic over every creak and moan of the doddy's ancient timbers. Though daylight brought relief in that respect, the promise of future terrifying nights stole from the welcome respite.

Lonely and somewhat isolated, the doddy house was located down a long lane on a rural road, yet received a fair amount of morning work traffic with men gunning their trucks to punch in their time card at Ranco Incorporated or yellow school buses screeching their brakes and picking up students. Most of this noise passed unnoticed by Katy, but one clunker didn't, causing her to throw off her covers at its faintest din before it even rumbled into the Millers' drive.

Thank You, God! She hit the bare floorboards running and fumbled with the dead bolt. She swiped a matted clump of hair from her face, the entire black bramble bush tumbling over her shoulders and tickling her waist. She peered through the frosty window, quickly rubbing a visible circle with her palm. Sure enough, there was Lil stepping out of her Blazer. She had her head bowed and her coat pulled tight. Lil walked toward the doddy house!

Every nerve at alert, Katy turned to face the entryway, waiting for Lil just as she had the previous evening, only her emotions came from a different place now. The door cracked open, and Lil stepped inside with the widening eyes of a burglar caught in the act of breaking and entering. Eerie quiet filled the room with only the memory of bitter words crackling between them.

"Lil," Katy finally managed, unable to form redemptive words with healing power but stupidly muttering the obvious. If she couldn't think how to patch matters up, then she feared to say anything. Had Lil returned to pack her bags or to win another of a long string of arguments that had transpired over the course of their friendship? Katy hoped her friend stood there because the doddy house was their home.

"You're back?" Katy finally asked.

Nodding, Lil blurted out, "I was wrong. I'm sorry."

Overcome with relief, Katy cried, "I didn't mean to push you away. I've been miserable. I had a terrible night."

They flew into each other's embrace and awkwardly swiped at burning eyes. When they drew apart, Lil sniffed the air. "What? No coffee?"

Katy sucked in her bottom lip; her attire, a cotton nightgown that hung to her ankles, vouched for her when she protested, "I just got up. I was in bed with the covers over my head."

Lil gave her a gloating smile. "I forgot you did that."

"I didn't think I did anymore."

"I just got up, too." Lil flung off her coat, still dressed in yesterday's clothes, and started toward the coffeepot.

"We need hooks or something for our coats," Katy mumbled, taking cups from the cupboard. Then she remembered Jake was bringing them a coatrack.

"I got up early 'cause I didn't want to have to explain to my mom why I spent the night. She doesn't need something else to worry about. Anyway, I felt childish afterward."

Katy waited until they stared repentantly at each other over steaming mugs before she ventured upon the delicate subject. "I'm sorry I yelled at you last night. I've been stuffing my feelings." Remembering Lil's accusations, she owned up to her actions with as much honesty as possible. "I just couldn't handle another disappointment. I felt betrayed. But I don't know where all that came from. The terrible things I said."

"I'm sorry you didn't feel like you could confide in me. I called Jake last night."

Conflicting emotions gnawed Katy's insides, fearing to talk about him because a part of her still didn't trust the cousins' intimacy, yet knowing that the problem wouldn't get settled until everything was exposed. At work, she'd never dream of sweeping dirt under a rug, yet lately she'd done that with her emotions. It had resulted in an angry explosion. She didn't want that to happen again.

"I told him I was wrong to get involved. That I didn't want it to ruin my friendship with you. That I loved you both, but I wouldn't be doing any more matchmaking. That he's on his own." Lil held Katy's gaze. "I mean it. I won't interfere again. I want you to know I only did it because I love you both. But I see now I was wrong to stick my nose in where it didn't belong. Like you said, you're an adult."

With a warm smile, Katy acknowledged what this must have cost her take-charge friend. "Thanks."

Lil nodded and quietly drank coffee.

With her anger completely dissolved, Katy thought about Lil's use of the word *matchmaking* and couldn't help but wonder who had initiated that idea, Lil or Jake? Katy's rebellious heart hoped it had been him, but she couldn't be sure because the cousins had similar personalities. It shouldn't matter because the point she was trying to make was that she wasn't going to take him back, regardless. That she was mad about the matchmaking. Yet the question niggled her curiosity.

"What?" Lil asked, peering over her cup and then setting it down.

"Oh, it doesn't matter. But whose idea was it to begin with?"

A sudden glint lit Lil's eyes. "The ballet tickets?"

Katy thumbed small circles on her mug. "I know that came from you. But you know"—her neck heated—"the matchmaking part?"

"Jake came to me. He asked how to win you back. I knew how

much you'd grieved over your broken relationship. I just wanted you both to have a happily-ever-after."

Fighting back unwelcome tears, Katy softly asked, "What if I can't be happy with damaged goods?"

Lil didn't blink at the embarrassing question that had haunted Katy ever since she had heard about Jake's fling with an outsider. "You don't know *that* happened."

Katy raised her chin. "Do you know if it did?"

"No." Lil spit the word out as if it tasted bitter in her mouth. "Guys don't talk about that kind of stuff to girls."

"Exactly." Feeling a mounting resolve that she had every right to brood over the question, she asked, "Don't you think I'd always wonder about him and that other girl?"

"Jessie."

Katy's jaw dropped.

Lil shrugged. "Her name is Jessie, and she's probably not as awful as you picture her."

"If they'd only dated, it would be one thing, but Jake and Jessie went to drunken parties, and I'm thinking"—Katy's lip began to quiver, but she couldn't quit until she'd exposed her imaginations—"she probably went to bed with him." Afterward, she stared at her cup, unable to look Lil in the eyes.

But Lil's voice was soft and sympathetic. "Maybe that's something you should ask Jake. It might change things if you learned the truth."

Swiping a hand across her eyes, Katy protested. "I can't."

"Do you want me to ask him?"

"No!"

"Even if your future depends upon it?"

Katy stared at her, wondering if it would be better to know. If he had kept himself pure, it would make a difference. She opened her mouth to ask Lil if she would do that for her when Lil suddenly waved her hand through the air, as if to erase the offer.

"Sorry. I'm overstepping my bounds again. I promised not to interfere. Let's forget about Jake for a moment. I did a lot of thinking last night. What you said about him being damaged goods, sometimes it feels like you lump me in the same dough as Jake, thinking I'm wild and don't have any scruples. Like I'm not a Christian." Her voice broke. "Like. . .I'm no good."

Hot shame rushed over Katy's face. Lil had never allowed such vulnerability to surface before. "Oh Lil. That's not true," she denied. "I love you."

Lil raised her hand again. "Let me finish. I pride myself on being an open book. What you see is what you get. But here's the thing. I hate being different from everybody else."

Leaning forward, Katy softly probed, "You mean the outsiders?"

"Yeah, everybody." Lil's gaze pleaded for understanding. "I don't like being plain or weird, having people whisper about me when I walk into a room. I don't like being told how to act or how to look by sour-faced men, either." Katy had to swallow her gasp when Lil alluded to the elders, including her own dad, with such disdain. "For once, I'd like to be noticed in a good way. The church discourages dressing in the latest fashions and frowns on focusing on outward beauty. That's why I've just got to be a good chef. I can make food beautiful. There's no sin in that, is there? Jesus made wine out of water. I just want people to respect me. Can you understand that?"

She met Lil's earnest gaze and felt her pain. "Yes. I don't like being different, either. Mostly, I just want to be invisible. Like when I took Addison to her dance class and stepped into a room of glamorous women in jeans with glittery belts. I wanted to disappear through the floorboards. Not to stand out like some oddball. But I swallowed my pride and told myself that following Christ is not an easy thing."

"But we're not supposed to be invisible. We're supposed to let our lights shine."

"Well, the light of God," Katy corrected. At Lil's crestfallen expression, Katy wished she'd refrained.

They both grew contemplative, and the ticking of the wall clock that Lil's mom donated to the doddy house reminded Katy that soon she would need to get ready for work. "I think we both try to express our true selves through our work. I'm thankful we have that."

"Yeah, I obsess about food, and you go around picking up after everybody. What's that say about us?"

Katy shrugged. "That we're weird?"

Lil giggled. "Too bad Megan's not here to get in on this deep stuff. It's right down her alley."

"She's probably smarter than us. But we've got to learn to get along together without her."

"Exactly. More coffee?" Lil got up and brought the pot over.

Katy glanced at the clock again but decided one more cup wouldn't make her late. "Another thing I want to bring up. You're right about us being adults. I'm going to quit preaching at you and just let the real Lil shine."

Lil glowed as if she'd been handed the world. "And I'm not going to try to change you, either. Except it wouldn't hurt if you combed your hair. It looks pretty bad." She lifted her coffee cup. "This calls for a toast."

Rolling her gaze heavenward, Katy relented, "Fine." She mimicked Lil and raised her cup, biting off the urge to ask Lil where in the world she'd learned to toast.

"To adulthood, womanhood, and sisterhood."

Katy felt awed. "And friend-hood."

"Clink your cup against mine, silly."

Clink and *clink* sealed the deal between them.

"Now what are we going to do with our coats?" Katy asked. "We can't just keep hanging them over the chairs. And if we hang them in our bedroom closet, they smell up our clothes."

"I'll ask Jake about that coatrack again. Otherwise, he could make one or put up some hooks for us behind the door. I'll set it up for some day while you're at work."

CHAPTER 17

On Sunday morning, Katy and Lil chatted as they passed a row of cars and headed toward the rectangular shaped—soon to be L-shaped—meetinghouse. A young couple directly in front of them reined in their tiny children, who had spotted the playground and had tried to veer off toward it.

"No. Maybe after church for a few minutes," their mother corrected. "But it might be too cold."

"And no talking in church today," their father added. "Children are to be seen and not heard at times like this."

Katy's eyes, however, lingered nostalgically on the side lawn, now snowy and covered with worn playground equipment. There she and her girlfriends had often sung their ditties. She and Lil had always vied for control on the teeter-totter. Lil, who had weighed more at the time, had often kept Katy airborne at her protest. It had been an act, however, for Katy had always preferred the loftier position.

Now, at last, she hoped the contention was gone between them. She hoped the manipulative games were finished. She didn't wish to be a fraud. She wondered if Megan could sense the change in their relationship or if they would revert back to their old behavior in her presence.

Wrestling with that disturbing thought, she tentatively glanced at Lil, who had moved on from the head chef's ridiculous requests to describe a certain waiter's distracting eyes.

"Speaking of distractions," Katy cut in, "I hope when Megan comes over today, we don't revert to our old style of bickering."

At first Lil's expression blanked, lost in the sudden twist of the conversation; then she smiled. "We won't let that happen." They entered the lobby, and Lil's family called out to her. "Save me a seat, okay? I want talk to my mom."

"Sure." Inside the sanctuary, Katy veered to the left, where the women sat, to locate her favorite pew. Her sister, Karen, spied her and hurried over.

"Hi, sis. I miss you. The bed stays cold all night. And it's no fun being outnumbered. I never realized how much you stuck up for me around the boys. And Mom hasn't gotten me a new night-light yet. Anyway, she says I can sit with you, if you don't care."

"Yes, sit with us." Katy clamped an arm around her sister's shoulders and squeezed. "I miss you, too. After all, you are my only sister."

"Exactly. Please come for dinner today. Mom said to ask you. Please. Please."

"Oh I'm sorry. Lil already has lunch planned. Megan's coming over." At Karen's crestfallen expression, she quickly added. "Tell Mom I'll come next Sunday for sure."

"Promise? It'll be fun."

"I promise."

Lil and a few stragglers shuffled in. Brother Troyer and the song leader strode to the front, causing a hush to fall over the congregation. There was no raised platform. Void of stained glass or unnecessary grandeur, the architecture and interior were plain, reflecting the humble mind-set of the worshippers. But after the singing, the sermon was anything but ordinary.

"Sometimes an unrest blows across a congregation. Like the wind before a storm. Every generation or so, this happens. It has happened again. I believe it's time to address some hard issues like submission and the prayer covering."

If possible, the congregation became even quieter. "In the coming month, I will preach on husband-and-wife relationships, discussing how marriage symbolizes the relationship between God and the church. We will also review the scriptures on the prayer bonnet, which sets us apart from the world."

Katy felt a jubilant little thrill and forced herself not to glance at Lil, whose face must have turned scarlet.

"Rumblings of discontent can destroy a congregation. We've already amended the custom from our Amish friends by allowing our women to take the strings off our bonnets. It's time we take a fresh look at the symbol and explore its relevance to this generation. While it sets us apart from the outsiders, it's starting to divide us as insiders. I don't know if you've ever noticed, but right below the scripture regarding the prayer bonnet, the Lord commands the church not to allow division over unimportant issues."

Katy joined the collective gasp that roused and then hushed the congregation. Was he insinuating that the bonnet was an unimportant issue? Right before that, he had stated the matter was not to be taken lightly. She stirred uncomfortably.

"Some would argue that the covering's not necessary because it was merely a custom in the apostle Paul's time. Others may think it is appropriate for church and prayer but not everyday life. We'll get into all that. And after the series is over, we'll hold a meeting and listen to the congregation's input. We'll encourage the women to participate freely at this meeting. Afterward, a vote will be taken on how we will adhere to the custom. Then I pray that our congregation will abide by the decision, and we can move on at peace with one another. For if we are not at peace with one another"—he raised his arm toward heaven and lowered his voice to a near whisper—"how can we exemplify our Lord?"

Countless questions churned in Katy's mind. Who had complained about the head covering? Was it possible the church would outvote something so vital? Her pulse sped, and her body threw off enough heat to warm the sanctuary.

She knew there were sects of Mennonites who had already abandoned the head covering, but she'd never dreamed the Conservatives would even consider it. Or wouldn't they be Conservatives any longer? Would they move into a higher conference? Was that the ulterior motive of some, bringing televisions and regular clothing into the church, too?

She stared at the elderly preacher. Surely not while Brother Troyer was shepherding the flock. Tension crawled up the back of her neck. As the service wore on, she fought the urge to go out for fresh air. She rubbed her aching temples and glanced across the aisle at the clock near the exit sign.

Fifteen more minutes. She ran the scenarios through her mind again. And only when Karen nudged her, did she discover that she'd been leaning forward and staring at the men's side far too long. But just before she straightened, she met Jake's amused gaze. And he had the audacity to wink at her.

She straightened her spine and looked back at the preacher, then at the plain wooden cross that graced the wall behind the pulpit. Its larger counterpart marked the exterior of the meetinghouse as a house of God, but Katy wondered how pleased God was over the bonnet controversy.

~ ∽ ~

The ride home from church was subdued, neither Katy nor Lil having the courage to bring up the bonnet issue and risk a potential argument. They talked about how good it was to see their families and agreed to spend the following Sunday with them. Lil was worried about her mom, who had been declining ever since the church fire. "I think she's blaming herself, ashamed over all the trouble and expense the fire's caused," Lil explained. "Although even before the fire, Mom was acting depressed."

"But nobody accused her?" Katy asked.

"No, but the fire marshal went to the house and questioned her."

"Because she's chairman of the hostess committee?"

Lil nodded. "Dad told me she felt like a criminal. He's real worried about her. Dad seems more stressed than usual, too."

"Maybe the sermons Brother Troyer has planned will help her."

"No," Lil shook her head. "I don't think it has anything to do with their marriage."

Katy fell quiet, not knowing how else to help. But she determined in her heart to pray for Mrs. Landis.

When they reached the doddy house, David was just getting out of his car, too. As soon as Lil parked, he strode toward them. Before she opened her door, she turned to Katy apologetically. "Do you care if I go on in and start lunch?"

Katy cast a reluctant look in David's direction but relented. "That's fine. I'll be right in." She swept her purse off the floor and stepped out of the car.

David waved. "Lunch ready? I'm starved."

"Well. . ."

He chuckled. "Just kidding. I'm eating at Ivan and Elizabeth's." Before Katy could respond, he added cheerfully, "But I'm available for dessert."

Katy placed her hand on her hip. "I'll just bet you are."

"So is that an invitation?"

Katy thought about the devil's food cake that Lil had baked and hesitated, thankful when she recognized Megan's car pulling into the drive. David's gaze followed the blue Ford, then returned to Katy to wait for her answer.

She finally offered, "You can stop in this afternoon if you're not afraid of the odds."

"What odds?"

"Three to one."

He watched Megan get out of the car. "You've got to be kidding. Those are great odds. Even if they weren't, you should know better than to dare a guy."

She countered, "It's not exactly a dare."

He flashed his dimple. "What is it?"

Katy shrugged, giving in to his good-natured teasing. "We're just hanging out. Drop by if you want. Lil usually makes popcorn mid-afternoon."

He chuckled. "You sure it wasn't a dare?"

Katy smiled, not sure why he was laughing but finding his amusement contagious. "Yes, I'm sure."

"Thanks. Maybe another time."

She waited until David had turned his back and rolled her gaze heavenward. She watched him stride toward Ivan's, seeming more mysterious than ever.

Inside the doddy house, the smell of flank steak and honeyed carrots roused Katy's appetite.

"Wow, look at this place. You guys are all settled in." Megan made a slow circle of the combo dining and living area, then went through the doorway to the kitchen. "This is nothing like my dorm. You guys seem domesticated."

Katy tied her apron. "We are." Then she teased, "Hey, Lil, I'll peel the potatoes if you pitch your own soda cans today."

"Deal."

Megan pulled potatoes from a bag and washed them in the antique kitchen sink. All the while, Katy could feel her quietly observing them. She peeled and plopped the potatoes in a black kettle.

After several minutes passed, Megan spoke her mind. "You guys have jobs and are making this happen. But what about me? What am I going to do after college?" It was a question they couldn't answer since none of Megan's job-hunting pursuits had ever been successful.

Once Megan had applied at the Plain City Laundromat, but when she had been offered a position, she had asked for time off to teach Bible school. They had hired someone else instead. She had checked out the recycle plant in Columbus, but thought the application process was too complicated just for a summer job. Her longest job had been delivery girl at a flower shop. But that fizzled when her allergies worsened.

Katy had hoped Megan would find her niche before she graduated, but Megan's dreams flitted about butterfly-style, matching her personality. While she made the world around her a beautiful place, she flew from one pretty flower to another, never finding a place to employ her special talents. Katy wondered if butterflies ever remained still unless they were pinned to a collector's board. She'd never want to destroy Megan's spirit.

At present it was engaged in praising Rosedale's mission opportunities. "In Nicaragua, people line up to get in the eye clinic," Megan explained. "I was talking to a guy who went last year. He said they had cobblestone roads with palm trees and lizards in the hotels and papayas at every meal and dogfights that woke them at night."

An image of Tyler's science project popped into Katy's mind.

"I can picture you there," Lil said. "Let's fill our plates at the counter so Katy doesn't have such a mess to clean up."

"Hey, thanks," Katy said, giving her friend a little hip-to-hip bump, then forking a serving of tender meat onto her plate. "We can't wait for you to join us here, green bean, but you need to go for your dreams. Maybe God's destined you to be a missionary."

"You think?"

The wistfulness in Megan's voice touched Katy.

"I think you should try a mission trip. See how it goes."

"Even if it keeps me from job hunting? From moving into the doddy house right after graduation?"

"We're doing fine here," Lil replied, shooting a meaningful glance Katy's way. "Committing to a job is a tough thing. Especially a dead-end job. Maybe you're not ready for that yet."

It amazed Katy that Lil would release Megan from their vow so easily, and she wondered if Lil would have been able to do that if they hadn't just had their big argument. They were changing, all of them. It blessed her. And she hoped it would continue for their betterment.

But she could only take a little change at a time. And the one happening at church was too dramatic. As they settled in at the kitchen table, where she and Lil had bared their souls with each other earlier in the week, Katy glanced at Megan. Striving to keep her voice sounding nonchalant, Katy ventured, "What's the deal about the head covering? You guys know anything about that?"

"Not me," Lil quickly replied.

"My dad says we're losing some members to higher churches"—the girls all understood the Mennonite lingo for more liberal churches— "and that although it's up to a husband to be a spiritual leader, the women usually have the most influence behind the scenes. Giving them a chance to express themselves on this matter might appease more of our members in the long run."

"So it's just an offensive tactic? There's not really a group of dissenters?"

"I think there is, but Dad didn't name any names."

"Wow," Lil muttered.

Katy said, "I'm glad Brother Troyer's going to teach on the subject. Like he said, maybe it will help everyone see its relevance."

"Or irrelevance," Lil countered gently.

"Well it's relevant to me," Katy said in a softer tone than she normally would have used.

Megan eyed them carefully. "My dad says it could save the church, but it could also split the church. But if it does, then it probably would have happened some time, anyway. So it's worth a try."

Katy set down her fork. "This is awful."

"Some churches require bonnets at services but allow the people to decide whether they're worn at other times," Megan offered.

Feeling the color drain from her face, Katy strained to keep her poise. "Is that what you think should happen, green bean? Is that what your dad thinks?"

Megan nodded. "Yes. It would be good if everyone agreed to disagree."

Naturally. That had always been Megan's goal. She and her family lived and breathed peace, the fiber that kept the Mennonite church grounded in its nonresistant stand. But Katy didn't get it. "How can it be both ways when it clearly states in the Bible that women should cover their heads?"

"In church and in prayer," Lil clarified.

"Maybe we need to hear all the teaching before we discuss this," Megan suggested. Then she asked, "Is there dessert?"

"Devil's food cake," Lil said, seeming happy to change the subject, too.

But Katy thought keeping the peace came at too great a price. She didn't want the elders to mess with her bonnet. Why, it was almost as sacred to her as her Bible.

CHAPTER 18

In her closet, Katy sighed and scraped hangers across clothes rods, searching through her wardrobe for something appropriate to wear to the ballet. When Addison had shown her the pink confection Tammy had bought her daughter for the performance, Katy's heart had sunk to a deeper level in the downward ballet spiral of doom. Would they even allow her inside the magnificent theater, or would they turn her away at the door? Or worse, would they hand her a broom and point her to the janitor's supplies?

Lil stepped into the closet. "What are you doing in here so long?"

"Barring a miracle, I'm still taking Addison to the ballet, and I don't know what to wear. Do you have any ideas?"

"Yes! I do." Lil dove into her side of the closet and came out holding a black outfit. "Here it is. You can wear this." She held it against her own form, doing the garbanzo dance.

Katy touched the slinky black skirt and its matching top. "It's gorgeous. Where did you get it?"

Lil colored slightly and shrugged. "I had to attend a formal affair at school. Try it on."

"Oh I couldn't. It's way too glamorous. You know I've never worn anything like it. No," Katy protested.

"Is that what you're going to say on your wedding day? There are certain occasions when you need to raise the. . .ah, notch a bit. You don't want them turning you away at the door, saying, 'Sorry, ma'am, the performance hasn't started yet. Cleanup starts at 11:30. Come back then and don't forget your bucket.' "

Katy burst into laughter. "I was thinking the exact same thing." She held the skirt in one hand and the hanger with the top in the other. It is modest, except for. . ." She hung the skirt up and examined the top closer. "I've never worn this type of neckline before."

"It's not a low neckline. Try it on."

Katy faltered, wondering what it would feel like to wear the slinky expensive fabric against her skin. She was thankful the color was basic black. With her dark hair, she'd probably just fade into a shadowy corner somewhere. Yes, every eye would be on Addison, and this might help her maintain a respectability, the invisible air she sought when operating in the outsider's realm. "All right."

Lil helped her slip into the dress. "We need a full-length mirror in here." Impulsively, she said, "I'm splurging on one this week. Then you'll have it in time for the ballet. I'll get Jake to install it. I've got an idea." She left and then toted a kitchen chair to the bathroom. "Climb up on this so you can see yourself in the mirror."

Katy's pulse slammed in her throat when she saw herself. Her figure had transformed into a pleasing hourglass. But the formal attire also maintained a sophisticated modesty. Lil urged, "Hold your hair up." With a nervous giggle, Katy piled her hair atop her head. It flopped to the side, smashing her covering, but she'd fix that later. "Some red lipstick and my black nylons and nobody will ever notice you," her friend teased, reading her mind. "It really makes your eyes smolder."

Ignoring the eye comment, for folks had always raved about her eyes, Katy whispered with awe, "It'll be perfect."

"Not quite." Lil grabbed a fistful of material at the waist. "It needs just a little tailoring. And we definitely need to go shoe shopping."

"Oh I don't know. That looks too tight, doesn't it? I don't want to ruin it for you."

"We can baste it, and we'll remove it afterward."

"Surely I have some shoes that will go?" But Katy's voice trailed off for she knew she didn't have anything worthy of the occasion.

"We'll find you some shoes you can wear to church, too. And afterward, we'll drive downtown and locate the theater and check out the parking situation. Forewarned, and all that."

Feeling a catch in her throat, Katy climbed down and hugged Lil. "Thanks. You're the best. This has just been eating at me, terrifying me. Maybe now I'll be able to endure the whole experience."

"And you won't have to join the cleanup committee," Lil added with a glint in her eyes.

─ ᗡ

Katy held Addison's hand and stared at the scrolled billboard. *Cinderella.* "This is it," she announced to Addison, feeling as if she'd swallowed a glass slipper. A street policeman standing on the corner raised his hand to stay the traffic, and Addison plunged them into a jostling, crowded crosswalk that whisked them directly in front of the Ohio Theatre. They took their place in line, and the touch of Addison's enthusiastic hand was somewhat comforting. Everyone wore smiles and eager expressions, and she forced herself to feign a similar countenance for Addison's sake.

But she didn't have to pretend long. She was awestruck from the moment she stepped inside the marble entry and viewed the high, arched ceilings, gilded and frescoed, from which hung a huge stained-glass chandelier. Spanish Baroque architecture gave the theater a medieval flair, palatial in rich red and gold.

Its splendor was so breathtaking that Katy struggled for comportment, yet Addison took her surroundings in stride and suddenly jerked her hand away. "There's Samantha," she cried and dashed off toward another girl from her dance class.

With a gasp, Katy lunged, but only caught a satin sash that untied and slipped through her fingers, dragging on the ground behind Addison like a pink tail. Involuntarily, Katy clamped her teeth on her bottom lip and helplessly watched the two little girls separate to skirt an elderly couple and join together again laughing. Linking arms, they next burst through a group of teenage girls and vanished. In the blink of an eye, Addison had disappeared. Panic tamped up Katy's spine. She vied to get another glimpse of Addison's pink frothy outfit.

"Hey, Katy."

Startled, she whipped her gaze around to the tall male figure clad in a plain black suit. In all the excitement, she'd forgotten about Jake.

His sister Erin smiled. "Hi Katy. This is my first time here. Great, isn't it?"

Erin's presence momentarily dazed Katy. But the dark-haired girl's enthusiasm and winning smile reminded Katy of her manners. There was no excuse to be rude to Erin Byler just because of her brother, so she took just a moment to engage in some necessary small talk. Then Katy bit the corner of her mouth with frustration. "I lost Addison."

"You want me to help you look?" Jake asked, lines of concern framing his eyes.

Considering that the lobby was filled with children and Jake didn't know what Addison looked like, she wasn't sure he'd be much help. "She's wearing a pink frilly dress."

Jake frowned. Half of the girls were clad in pink or princess outfits.

"What's her name?" Erin asked.

Before Katy could answer the question, the youngster under discussion had returned and grabbed her by the waist. Without missing a beat, Addison urged, "Let's go in."

"Addison!" Katy clutched the girl's hand. "Sweetie, wait. You need to calm down and stay with me. I met some friends." She reeled her charge in and introduced her to Jake and Erin.

Erin bent down and began to tie Addison's bow. "Are you a performer? Are you the dancer who is Cinderella?"

"No, but I take dance lessons."

"Are you sure? You look like a princess."

"That's just because. . ."

"That was unnerving," Katy whispered to Jake.

"I guess she didn't lose you; that's the important thing. Shall we go find our seats?"

"Ours?" Katy raised a brow.

He gave her his notorious lopsided grin. "We're in the row behind you."

Naturally. "So you admit to a conspiracy."

"Yeah, that's old news." He touched her elbow. "Ready?"

With a nod, Katy tugged Addison's hand. "Let's go, sweetie."

"I like Erin. She thinks I'm a princess."

"You are, aren't you?" Katy teased, and the little girl shrugged. Katy held tight so that she didn't skip away again at the first glimpse of someone else from their dance troupe. All the while, her gaze took in the auditorium. More gilt and arches, even more elaborate than the lobby, a perfect fairy-tale setting. They found their seats, and Addison entertained herself by talking to her friend Samantha, who was seated next to her. Katy relaxed and stared overhead at the lighted, coffered ceiling and enormous, tiered chandelier.

Jake leaned forward and whispered, "It's something else."

"I think God must live here," Katy replied.

Soon the lights dimmed, the curtains opened to an elaborate set. Amidst the magic lights and changing colors, a ragged-clad Cinderella appeared on stage, dancing with a broom. Instantly enthralled and swept into the performance, Katy laughed along with the children, enraptured with the ballet movements of the story. When the wicked stepsisters danced onto the stage in bright costumes, Addison whispered, "Look at their funny hats."

In a mere twinkle, it seemed to Katy, it was intermission. "Can we get something?" Addison instantly begged, swinging Samantha's hand.

Katy put off the question momentarily, standing to let others in their row pass. Meanwhile, Addison was skipping impatiently from toe to toe. Katy turned and glanced toward the lobby.

Erin offered, "I'll take the girls. I need a drink myself."

"All right, but stay with Erin," she warned the children, and Addison nodded.

"You want something, too?" Jake asked.

"No thank you. I just want to sit and drink in the splendor." Katy slid back into her seat and Jake climbed over the one next to her and plopped himself down in it. They shared an armrest and spoke about the performance and the costumes. She glanced down at the orchestra pit. "I was nervous about tonight."

"That's understandable. So how does this story end, anyway?"

She spent the next several minutes insisting that he had read far too few books in his childhood and spent too many hours getting into trouble.

At the end of the intermission, Addison squeezed into the row, stepping on Jake's feet, and he reached out a hand to stay the little one. "Can I sit with Erin?" Addison asked. Katy drew in a ragged breath. Addison begged, "Please."

"Me, too." Samantha echoed.

With a shrug, Katy changed places with Erin and trailed Jake back to his row, sliding in beside him. And that's when the afternoon really became enchanted. When the glittery carriage rolled onto the stage, pulled by white-wigged men wearing tights and doublets, she felt like she was living inside the fairy tale. Her shoulder pressed against her prince's, she allowed her guard to melt away for one afternoon and indulged in what it might be like to be Cinderella, or at the very least, an outsider.

When the performance ended, Jake whispered, "We'll walk you to your car." Behind them, Erin kept up a charming dialogue with Addison. Katy was having too much fun to replace her guard. There was always tomorrow. She had until midnight before the spell ended. While Jake opened her door, Erin moved around the back of the car with Addison.

Jake whispered, "I wish this didn't have to end."

Her pulse quickened. She felt the same way, reluctant to ruin a magical afternoon.

He kept his voice low. "I know I don't have any right to ask, but I'd like to take you to dinner tonight. To tell you my story. You did say I need to have more interest in stories with happy endings."

"You're twisting my words."

"Please say yes."

She started to protest. "No. I—"

But he wouldn't have it. "It's not a date. Just two old friends. We're all dressed up." He winked.

She didn't want to remove Lil's dress just yet. *Until midnight, and then I'll get back to reality.* "All right. I need to take Addison home first."

"I'll drop Erin off at her dorm and pick you up at your castle, say around seven?"

She smiled. "Okay."

⁓

Jake stood statue-like, watching Katy back her car out of its parking spot and steer it toward the garage exit.

"Good job!" Erin exclaimed.

He let out a sigh. "I can't believe she said yes. Did you see her, Erin? She's so"—he shook his head unable to express his feelings—"and she's giving me another chance." He stuffed his hands in his pockets. "I can't believe it."

"You've got it bad."

He grinned. "I know."

They walked past a row of cars and stepped into an elevator. "You think she considers this a date?" he asked.

Erin's brows knit together. "What did you say to her?"

"I asked her to go to dinner"—he inwardly groaned as he recalled his exact words—"as two friends."

"That was lame."

He flashed Erin a frown. "It just popped out. While I was begging her."

Erin's mouth gaped. "You begged, too?"

They stepped out of the elevator and went toward his truck. "I guess it's not a date. But it's a chance. She's giving me a second chance, right?"

"When did you get so insecure?"

He reached out and ruffled her hair. "I'm not. Get in." Erin wasn't nearly as helpful as Lil, but his cousin had made it clear that she couldn't help him with Katy anymore because Katy had forbidden it. He was on his own now.

They climbed into his truck, and he put the gears in reverse. Erin's phone rang, and he tuned her conversation out, losing himself in his own thoughts. The ballet had been a new experience for him, and although he had mostly endured it, Katy had been the one enraptured.

When he'd first seen her in the foyer, his heart had nearly stopped. Her eyes were so alive and her lips slightly open; she'd been awestruck with her surroundings. And he'd been awestruck with her, so plain yet elegant in her black gown. He had never seen her so lovely and yet vulnerable. He'd stood and stared, unable to move until Addison momentarily slipped away. When Katy's expression became troubled, he'd come to his senses, snatching at the opportunity to approach her.

He shot Erin a tender gaze across the cab. She had been a natural with Addison, providing him an open door to talk to Katy. When she was off the phone, he thanked her for her help. "I couldn't have done it without you."

"Don't let her get away this time," Erin replied. "By the way, Jessie says hi."

Her remark was just what he needed to bring him back to task. He'd promised Katy to share his story tonight, the one that included Jessie, and he didn't even know where to start. He only knew he needed to express his genuine sorrow over his falling away. Katy wasn't the only one he'd hurt. Now Erin was following his path of folly. "Tell her 'hi' for me." Near Erin's dorm, he pulled his truck to the side of the road. "And be careful. Stay out of trouble, won't you?"

She leaned over and kissed his cheek before she hopped out of the truck. He watched her stroll toward her dorm as if she didn't have a care in the world. He had plenty. He had an hour to figure out what he was going to tell Katy over dinner.

CHAPTER 19

The Worthington Inn, a historical Victorian restaurant, provided a charming atmosphere to prolong the Cinderella spell. Katy placed a cloth napkin on her lap, smoothing the surreal fabric of her skirt, and inhaled contentment. The waiter handed them their menus and disappeared.

"Look." Katy pointed at a descriptive item on the menu. "They use Amish, free range eggs."

"We can dine in elegance and still feel right at home. But Beef Worthington for me. Never hurts to try the house dish, right?"

With a giggle, Katy marveled, "You and Lil could be twins."

He leaned forward. "We are, but our parents gave me away."

"As you well deserved," Katy teased, then folded her menu. "The garden vegetable plate for me." The waiter returned for their orders, and they relaxed over coffee.

"One time when we were kids, I asked Lil why she didn't play with Erin instead of you. She said you were more fun. That Erin could hardly keep up with you two."

"Erin always tried to keep up with me," he admitted with a hint of sadness in his voice. Then he gazed into Katy's eyes and changed the subject. "The Cinderella fairy tale suits you. Especially the pretty part.

You look lovely tonight, your hair swept up like that. Your eyes are amazing. They draw people in, Katy. Did you know that?"

His scrutiny made her uncomfortable. "And the cleaning part. I'm pretty good at sweeping cinders. But I thought we came to talk about you."

"We did. But I want you to know that you've always intrigued me. That has never changed. My problem was a spiritual one, wondering where I fit in. Our family's divided when it comes to beliefs with the whole Amish-Mennonite thing. My mom broke away from the Amish, but my dad was always Conservative. Then my brother moved to a higher Mennonite church. So I never felt like there was only one church or one way to get to heaven or to please God."

He paused when their dinners arrived, and once the waiter left, he asked, "Shall we pray?"

She nodded, pleasantly surprised. Even David hadn't prayed over their meal at Lil's restaurant.

Jake bowed his head. "Lord, we thank You for this food, but mostly I thank You for the opportunity to share my story with Katy. Amen."

The sincerity of the simple prayer touched her with tenderness. "Amen," she breathed. When she opened her eyes, Jake was watching her.

"Anyway, when Dad died, it did something to me. Made me think about how short life is and how trapped I felt. I guess my brother Cal saw my struggle, and he invited me to his Bible study. For the first time I heard about grace."

Katy clenched her fork. "What do you mean? Brother Troyer teaches grace."

"But I never heard it. Never understood."

"Oh."

"Now there was another decision to make on top of wanting to break away from farming. Cal suggested construction, and it appealed to me. So I signed up for some courses. I wanted to get through school as quickly as possible and get on with life, so I took a full load. But I was still torn about the grace thing. At the time, I thought that if I chose grace, I'd have to leave our church and join Cal's. To be honest, I enjoyed his Bible study. But I missed some of the studies and delayed making a choice. I knew that if I moved up to another church, I'd lose you."

You lost me anyway, she thought. But she asked, "Why didn't you talk to me about this? Instead you just withdrew." Remembering how painful it had been, Katy whispered, "You just left."

"I knew where you stood. You've always been rigid in your beliefs."

Rigid. She despised that word. His perception of her matched Lil's. "Was I? Then why was I drawn to the orneriest boy at church?"

"I'm just saying that's how I felt at the time. Then my surroundings desensitized me and pulled me into the world. I didn't intentionally go off to college to sow my wild oats. It just happened one step at a time. There was a new world to explore."

She felt her ears heat. "And new girls."

"I guess. Jessie was in my business class, and she liked to poke fun at me, but at the same time she helped me out, explained things."

I'll bet she did, Katy thought, jealousy rising in her spirit and stealing her appetite.

"She was fun loving and comfortable to hang out with. She convinced me to go to some parties, and the next thing I knew I was drinking. I knew that lots of Mennonite guys drink before they settle down, and I just figured it would help me figure out what I wanted to do with my life. If I even wanted to settle down. But after the initial excitement wore off, I realized that Jessie wasn't for me. I knew I'd lost my most precious gift, you. I tried to win you back that night in the parking lot, but I went about it all wrong. When you smelled the alcohol on my breath, you despised me for it. I want you to know that if I hadn't been drunk I never would have manhandled you that way. I'm so sorry about that. I hope you can forgive me."

She shrugged, not able to answer that question. "I don't know."

The waiter came and refilled their drinks, giving Katy a moment to consider everything Jake had just told her. She realized that he was right that she wouldn't have understood then what it was like to feel the pull of the outsiders. But since she'd started working in their world, she'd experienced some of that excitement, and the lure, too. Wasn't that what tonight was all about? She didn't want to condemn him—maybe a guy was drawn with even more force—but his actions had stolen his innocence. At least sexually, she assumed. And that bothered her a lot.

"When you told me off, I decided to leave the church where I wasn't wanted. The world took me in."

"Jessie did, too." Katy murmured.

"Yes. But I was miserable. Soon after that, I broke up with her. Then one night I ended up drunk on Cal's doorstep. He sobered me up, and we talked a long while. I knew I needed God so I confessed my sins and attended Cal's Bible study and even his church. Once the Lord entered my life, I viewed everything differently. I'd changed and would change even more in the months after that."

He continued. "By then, Erin had come to school and hooked up with Jessie and started following my dead-end path. I tried to talk some sense in her, but she wouldn't listen. Gram got worse, and I decided Mom needed some support at home."

"Why did you come back to the Conservative Church instead of Cal's?"

"Because I love it here. And you're right about grace. It was here all the time, but I was too wrapped up in the dos and don'ts to understand it. Now I realize that church restrictions are put in place to shield us from temptation. They don't get us to heaven. I could attend a higher church without going against my conscience."

Katy wondered how he could be content in either church. Couldn't he see the differences between them? "So you came back because of your friends, and you intend to live Conservative the rest of your life?"

He nodded. "I knew that I had to come back for you. I knew that you'd probably refuse me, but I had to try to recover my most precious loss. Aside from God. Except I don't think I was ever a Christian to begin with."

That startled Katy.

"But I am now," he quickly clarified.

She believed he had repented for his falling away, but she didn't know if she could take him back. She longed to know how intimate he'd been with the other woman, and yet she didn't know if she could handle the truth. The question tickled her lips. "I always thought we would get married. To me, it was like you committed adultery."

"But I didn't. We weren't even engaged. If anything, my experience deepened my love for you."

The admission of his love caught her off guard. She didn't know how to respond, wanting him, yet not sure she could forgive him. She wanted to trust him.

He looked so handsome in his Sunday suit, but it reminded her that this date was still part of the fairy-tale experience. He seemed caught up in it, too. As much as she desired him, she knew she wasn't ready to take him back. But how could she let him go? She felt torn.

The waiter returned to their table. "Are you finished with these?"

Katy nodded.

"May I bring you a dessert menu? We have freshly churned ice cream."

"That sounds good. I'll have chocolate." Jake said.

"Me, too."

When the waiter left, she fiddled with her knife. Jake reached across the table and covered her hand with his. She stilled.

"Thanks for listening. Please. Try and forgive me."

He must have read her mind. She could tell that his asking for forgiveness was difficult. He was such a masculine guy, and he'd pretty much bared his soul. His feelings. He loved her. She looked into his tender gaze and wanted to swim there forever, but how could she settle for less than perfect? Finally, she repeated what she'd earlier told him. "I don't know if I can."

At his crestfallen expression, she quickly added, "I'm sorry. I forgive you as a sister in the church, but as a girlfriend, I don't know if I can. I still resent Jessie. I'm angry you chose her over me. I don't know if I can forgive you for those months of. . .being with someone else." Her lips trembled, and she said, "I'm even angry over the way you and Lil manipulated me."

"You haven't forgiven her?"

"Actually, I did. We're closer now than ever."

He licked his lips and frowned. "I understand your frustration, because I'm just as jealous over your dates with David."

The ice cream arrived, and he released her hand. When the waiter left, he said, "I'm sorry I hurt you. I'll never hurt you again. Just think about it."

How could he promise such a thing? She nodded, unable to speak.

"It isn't midnight yet, and I don't want to spoil our dessert. Let's talk about something else. Addison sure is a cute little thing."

"Much sweeter than her brother, Tyler."

"Girls always are sweeter," he teased, and soon he had her feeling at ease again. When she relaxed, she could almost imagine she was sixteen and nothing had ever changed between them.

When he dropped her off at the doddy house, he walked her to the porch. "Thanks for a wonderful evening, Cinderella." His finger grazed her chin, and drawn like a moth to light, she turned her face upward. He lingered. "See you at the next builders' meeting."

She replied softly, "That's one way to bring a girl back down to earth. Look, don't expect much from me. But I'm thankful for tonight, for a good memory." One that would go far in erasing the uglier, more painful ones.

She thought he might try to kiss her, but then his hand fell away, and he left her alone to the sound of his truck rumbling down the country road and to the blackness that could only be midnight.

Jake shifted gears. Although he'd grown up on a farm, the country road stretched out dark and lonely as his heart. He ached inside for his mistakes, for the beautiful, dark-eyed beauty he'd just taken to dinner. He ached because he was afraid to hope that she might give him a second chance.

Over dinner he'd watched her expressive eyes. He'd seen the desire in them when he admitted he still wanted her. But when she spoke, her eyes had glittered with anger, and when he'd asked her to forgive him, they had saddened with regret. Her lips also held clues. When he spoke about Jessie, they quivered. When he talked about the changes he had made, coming back to the church, she had tucked them between her teeth, showing her suspicions. And when he had wanted to kiss her on the porch, they had seemed willing. But he had made that mistake before. So he left, almost abruptly, to keep from giving in and pulling her into his arms. He knew she was not ready. With a sigh, he turned on the radio.

CHAPTER 20

Katy spent Sunday with her family. They enjoyed a meal of ham and coleslaw, and her married brothers and their wives all played the card game Rook, while Katy's oldest niece entertained the toddlers. The fireplace crackled, and Katy's heart swelled with love for her family that only weeks earlier she'd taken for granted. She considered the new confidence in Karen's behavior.

"Can I bring anyone anything?" Karen had asked between rounds.

Katy realized that Karen had become her mom's new chief helper. It sent a twinge of regret through her to be replaced, yet she knew that just like her married siblings, she would always remain a vital member of the family.

But later that evening it was good to get back to her cozy little doddy house, where Lil fed her popcorn and asked her about the ballet, assuring her that this time, whatever she said would remain confidential. Lil deserved details since she'd donated her beautiful dress to the cause.

Both girls relaxing on the couch, Katy re-spun the spell.

Lil purred, "What a fairy-tale evening."

"Probably my one and only. The church forbids dancing. Do you think the ballet is sinful? That it's wicked to watch men dance in their tight costumes? Now I know why they are called tights, too."

Lil giggled. "I have no idea. Did Jake seem embarrassed by it?"

Katy considered the question. "No. But he never gets embarrassed. I used to think any form of dancing was wrong, but it was so beautiful. Then again, at Addison's dance studio some of the girls were taught seductive moves. " She sighed. "It's confusing."

"The outsiders call it art. I suppose it depends on disciplining your thoughts."

"I was captivated by the entire spectacle. The theater, not the guys." Katy reiterated, nestling comfortably against the leather armrest. "But maybe that was wrong, too. Just basking in such wealth and splendor. Nothing humble about the Ohio Theatre." She shrugged. "I'm struggling with the whole evening."

Lil gazed at her with understanding.

Katy bit her lip then went on, "Especially since I let my guard down with Jake. I don't think I'll ever get over him. What if I turn him away, and he marries someone else? I'll be miserable. After he shared his story with me, I feel partly to blame because when he was restless, I wasn't able to help him. He didn't feel comfortable talking to me about it. He told me that he didn't even think he was a Christian at the time."

"You can't change the past. And if he wants to be with you now, then that's more important. Present definitely trumps past." Katy figured Lil must have played Rook with her family, too. But this was no game. This was her future.

~☙~

On Monday, Katy couldn't help but try out the broom for a dance partner, humming off-key to the songs she'd heard at the ballet. Feeling a stab of conscience, she changed the song to a hymn. But hadn't David danced with joy after one of his war victories? And he was a man of God's heart.

Although dancing was forbidden in her religion, nobody but Lil had ever talked to her about it. She'd never been tempted until she'd stepped into Addison's dance studio. Was it wrong to dance from joy or to express graceful movement of the body that God had created? It was hard to contain joy, and she was joyful over the news that Jake still loved her. But was love enough? That question was more troubling than the first.

Jake's testimony hung in her mind until she picked up Tammy's children from school. Tammy's note reminded her that Sean Brooks was still out of town. That was the reason Katy had taken Addison to the ballet. Now she would have to babysit late. In the note, Tammy asked her to help Tyler with his homework, especially assisting him on a school project.

"So tell me about your school project, Tyler."

"It's kinda dumb. We're supposed to watch certain TV shows and observe people's mannerisms. We have to write down what they say and what they do. Describe how they act. What their faces look like. What gestures they make. Stuff like that."

Her spirit sank to hear that television was involved in the school assignment. "Can I see your notes?"

"Sure." Tyler brought her a thin, bound notebook. Katy flipped through and saw dates on several page and the titles of television shows.

"Did you choose the shows?"

"Nope. I copied them from the blackboard. We have to write a whole page each night."

"Wow."

"But I'm not very good at it, and Mom's been helping me. I can't watch people's faces and write at the same time. That's what you need to do. Write down their lines."

Katy sat on the edge of the couch and rubbed her brow. This was going to be worse than she'd imagined if it included viewing television shows. She eyed Tyler. "You sure you can't do this alone?"

"Nope. And I'll get a bad grade if I skip a night."

"When does the show come on?"

"Seven o'clock."

It was already six forty-five. Reluctantly, Katy rose. "I'll go check on Addison. You get everything ready."

Tyler grabbed the remote and flicked on the television while Katy ran upstairs. She found Addison playing with her Barbie dolls. After explaining she was going to help Tyler with his homework project, Katy started back down, pausing on the stairway at the television's blare.

Once again duty collided with conscience. The way her babysitting responsibilities were pulling her into the life of her charges, she might as well move in and become a part of this outsider's family.

She'd only watched television in the stores a few times as she'd passed through their electronics sections and had caught glimpses of it at various times when she'd been working for her employers. Tyler often had it on in his room, and Addison sometimes watched princess DVDs. In fact, after the ballet it was all Katy could do to refuse Addison when she'd begged her to watch the *Cinderella* movie with her. But somehow, she had prevailed against that temptation.

Katy had never sat down and watched an entire television show. But this wasn't about pleasure; this was a school assignment. And she'd gotten involved in plenty of those lately. Now she considered this one. Surely Tyler's teacher would not have assigned something inappropriate, given his impressionable age?

She'd heard television debated in her congregation, and some claimed all television shows weren't bad, but that it was playing with fire to have a set in your home because it invited temptation by desensitizing you to sex, violence, and greed for beauty and material wealth. In short, it brought the outsiders' world into your own home where you could sit and dream that you were living their life.

She watched Tyler settling in on the sofa and breathed a prayer, "Lord, if this goes sour, then I'm quitting this nanny job, even if I lose my cleaning job with the Brooks. I'll take it as Your will." Then she steeled herself.

She sat next to Tyler, and he handed her his notebook. "You write down something they say, then I'll hit PAUSE. Then we'll play it back, and I'll tell you what to write down about their mannerisms."

"Okay, I'm ready." She thought, *I don't have to watch the show. But I do have to listen to the lines.*

"We have to wait until the commercial's over."

"Commercial?"

Tyler stared at her. "Are you for real?"

177

Katy started scribbling.

"Not yet!" he cried. "It's a commercial." He shook his head as if she was from the dinosaur era. "Just wait, and I'll tell you when the show comes on." Then he displayed an uncharacteristic gentleness. "You'll get the hang of it. I'm gonna get a soda. Be right back."

She started to protest, that he should turn off the television while he left, but her gaze went to the screen as if magnetized. She watched a seductive woman caress a car, and felt the heat rise up her neck. Then some men climbed through a refrigerator and stepped into a bar, and Katy instantly regretted the glimpse into such a dark sinful place. However, she couldn't look away. Next two guys in a truck cracked jokes about fast food, and she laughed at their silly conversation. Just when her interest was growing, Tyler interrupted, "Okay, now. It's starting."

She gripped her pencil. The show was about an Indiana family with three kids. The teenage boy sauntered into the living room in his underwear, and Katy gasped.

Tyler laughed at the actor. "He's hilarious. Did you get that?"

She shook her head, still embarrassed over the teen's bare chest and legs and low-slung boxers. "I don't know. I missed it."

Tyler sighed, then pressed the remote and to Katy's amazement it all reversed back to the beginning of the episode. "Just write what he says, okay?"

"All right," Katy stared at her pad, determined not to watch the screen again and to get it down and get this assignment over with as quickly as possible. After about three more tries, she had his line and Tyler's mannerism description, but listening was almost as bad as watching. Katy was appalled that the teenage actor would talk to his mom with such disrespect. It was eye-opening, how Tyler's behavior mimicked the teenage star's attitude.

The process took forever, and Tyler fast-forwarded through a batch of commercials. The next round of note-taking included a scene with a scantily dressed neighbor. Her eyes had strayed to the screen again, because it made it so much easier to get the lines down. "Are you sure you should be watching this?" Katy asked with concern.

"Are you kidding? My mom loves this show. Remind me not to delete it. She'll want to watch it later. She says it's true to life."

"Maybe your life," Katy mumbled.

"Yeah, well, Miss Pilgrim, what do you do at night? Clean the toilets?" He snickered and flicked the show on PAUSE. "Huh, where do you live anyway? On the Mayflower?"

"I live in a doddy house with my friend Lil."

Tyler laughed. "What's that?"

"It's like a guesthouse."

"Whatcha do there?"

"We cook, read, play games."

"What kind of games?"

"We play Rook."

"A video game?"

"No." At Tyler's confused look, she explained, "It's a card game."

"But you don't watch television and don't know anything about it?"

"Nope."

"That sounds boring to the max. I'll bet you don't even have a computer, do you?"

"No. But it's not boring. I don't like to watch things that aren't God-honoring."

"Whatever. You ready to go again?"

"Yes. . .wait a minute." Suddenly things clicked for Katy. "You can stop and start the show?"

"Duh, that's what we've been doing."

"And you just said you're going to save it for your mom. So why do I have to be doing this with you?"

"Because my mom told you to on the note."

Katy felt her anger flare. "Tyler. We're done now. Your mom can help you when she gets home, or you can finish this tomorrow."

"But my teacher checks my notes every day. I lose points, and you're gonna be in trouble. You may have to do something really crummy for your punishment like"—he looked about the house—"clean under my bed."

She already had done that, many times, and he was right about it being a really crummy job. "Or maybe she'll buy me a new iPod," Katy argued.

He glared at her, not quite getting it, but realizing it was some kind of an insult.

Katy sighed. "We'll wait until eight o'clock, and if she hasn't come home yet, then we'll finish it. Why don't you go up to your room and play now."

"Okay. It's your head, lady pilgrim." He got up and charged up the stairs.

His smart mouth didn't irritate her as much as it had when she'd first started sitting for him, and although she shouldn't have, she let his sarcastic remark pass without admonishing him. She tried to imagine him raised in her own home and thought of her brothers, how they played hard outside and enjoyed working with her dad. Tyler didn't know the disadvantage life had given him.

Then her thoughts went to his mother. Tammy was deliberately asking her to do things that went against her beliefs for no good reason other than Tammy's own inconvenience. Oh, she'd claimed she'd had a workshop to attend on the Saturday of the ballet. But she was just being lazy not to help Tyler with this assignment tonight, especially given her knowledge of Katy's Mennonite beliefs. As she brooded, she picked up the room, placing Tyler's backpack on the stairway, a juice can in the recycle bin, and Addison's princess boots in the hall closet.

"What a day. I'm beat."

The unexpected comment floated within Katy's hearing, and she flinched, thinking the television must have drowned out the sound of Tammy's car. She turned and raised her chin, determining this was the night that she would be more assertive. "Yeah, me, too. Housecleaning's no breeze."

"Uh-oh. Somebody's in a rare mood. The kids acting up or what?"

Once she'd made her mental stand, her frustrations poured out. "I feel manipulated, Tammy. You asked me to help Tyler with his school project when you know I don't watch television. And you can even replay the show."

Tammy's mouth gaped; then she composed her features. "I didn't know you don't watch TV. Anyway, I thought I'd get home too late. I knew I'd be beat."

It was as if Katy had stepped out of her body and the words came from some other source. "Well, I'm tired, too. I've cleaned this entire house. And I'm constantly picking up after the children."

"But this is your job. I pay you. And a high wage."

She saw that some of Tyler's attitude came straight from his mother. "I've made more at other places." Katy shocked herself with that remark and worked quickly to remove the angry glint from Tammy's eyes. Responding in anger wasn't God-honoring, even if it felt right. "I'm sorry. That remark was inappropriate. I don't mean to sound ungrateful for the work. But the nanny part is not working out. I told you from the start, it isn't what I enjoy doing. You've got to find someone else. I won't be picking the children up from school on Wednesday, either." Katy crossed her arms and waited for Tammy's explosion.

"Excuse me?" Tammy ground out with sarcasm. But Katy didn't budge. Then Tammy softened her voice. "You can't back out now. You agreed. I'm working long days so I can be home the other three afternoons."

Dropping her arms, Katy reasoned, "You've always known that I'm a housekeeper, not a nanny. Your kids are great, but the job doesn't suit me." She took a step toward the coat closet. "I'm sorry. I quit."

"Wait! You're not quitting cleaning, too, are you?"

Katy froze. Bit her bottom lip thoughtfully, "Not if you still want me."

"Of course I want you."

If Katy wasn't losing that part of the job, she'd been a fool not to stand up to the woman earlier. "Great. I'll be here on Wednesday. To clean," she clarified, lest Tammy think she was giving in again.

Tammy ran her hands through her hair. She glanced at the stairway and back. "Well, okay. I'll figure something out."

Katy felt a twinge of compassion for her employer, imagining the Realtor trying to show a house with two quarrelsome kids in tow. Or maybe she could handle it. Maybe they'd sit in some corner listening to their new iPods. She caught herself. It wasn't her problem. These were Tammy's children. She was a housekeeper, not a nanny. She needed to be strong, not cave in to her employer's sympathy ploys. She straightened. "Great. We only got halfway through Tyler's homework assignment. 'Night."

Walking to the car, Katy felt like King David must have after his war victories. How she could whip that broom around now! Why her feet were barely hitting the pavement. No more babysitting, and she hadn't even lost her cleaning job! She didn't know how the money would come in until she found another job to replace her loss, but she'd gone nose to nose with an outsider and just shed one hundred pounds of chains. Thank You, Lord!

CHAPTER 21

The next day, Katy and Lil headed to the kitchen door, snatched their coats off the coatrack Jake had dropped by earlier in the week, and started outside toward the washroom. Katy was relating to Lil how she'd stood up to Tammy and gotten rid of her nanny job. Lil set her basket down to close the door behind them and froze.

"What's this? There's a red envelope taped to our door."

Katy's heart thumped. "A valentine?"

Lil tore it free from the door. "Yep. And your name's on it."

Katy dropped her clothes basket, too, and tore open the envelope. Her heart sank. "It's from David."

Lil raised her brow. "Guess he didn't get the message."

Katy opened the envelope of the store-bought card. It was blank inside, but he had handwritten: *Thinking of you and that popcorn! Or maybe dessert?* She bit her lip. When was the last time she had thought about him? She tucked the card inside her wash and picked up her basket. "I hate hurting him."

"Hey, at least one of us got a valentine. That's something, huh?"

"I guess."

They started out for the washroom again, using the sidewalk that connected the doddy house to the workroom that they shared with the main house.

"About our earlier conversation, I'm glad you finally got rid of that nanny job. Don't worry. Something will turn up." Lil plunked her clothes basket on the cement floor, then rifled through it once, then a second time, more thoroughly. "I'm glad you stood up to Tammy. She'll probably treat you with more respect now."

Katy sorted her clothes, making neat piles. "We may be okay with it now, but it will catch up to us eventually. I've got to get a real job soon. Especially if Megan goes on a summer mission trip and doesn't move in with us."

Lil upended her basket until all its contents rained onto the floor, then garment by garment replaced each article with growing frustration as Katy watched with amusement. When that didn't meet Lil's satisfaction, she exhaled angrily and stared at the door as if her missing garment had sprouted legs.

Biting back a smile, Katy poured detergent in the washing machine and added her darks. Then she dangled Lil's work skirt in the air. "This what you're missing?"

Lil snatched it, casting her a dirty look that dared her to make some remark about it. They both knew that if Lil didn't throw her stuff all over the closet, she wouldn't lose things, or at least they wouldn't end up in Katy's dirty clothes basket instead of her own.

"Oops, wait a minute." Lil dug into her skirt pocket and tucked her cell phone into the hollow of her neck. "Hello?" As she talked, she tossed her darks in with Katy's and set the dial.

"Here," Lil shoved the phone in front of Katy's face as they made their way back to the house. "Jake wants to talk to you."

Frowning, Katy held the phone to her ear. "Can you meet me at the new fellowship hall? I've got a quick question about the kitchen cabinets."

"I can be there in an hour."

⎯⎯⎰⎯⎯

The fellowship hall carried the tangy smell of new lumber and in its skeletal state was as much a war zone as a construction site. Voices from the other side of a two-by-six frame wall stuffed with shiny insulation rectangles warned Katy of the presence of workers.

"Okay, boss. See you tomorrow."

"Don't let that baby keep you up all night so that you come crawling in late again."

"No sir. I'll send the wife over instead."

"Can she swing a hammer?"

"The question is, can I change a diaper?" the worker replied. "And the answer is no, I can't."

Jake's good-natured laugh echoed through the nearly vacant building, the crew heading home for the day. As Katy waited for him, she gazed around the kitchen. The island location was chalked off on the floor. Wires protruded at regular intervals through the walls. A piece of sharp sheet metal lay at her feet.

When Jake stepped into the room, like always, his dark good looks caught her unawares. When would she get used to the way the short sleeves of his T accentuated his muscles? The way his tool belt slung low, emphasizing his trim waist. "Hi. Thanks for coming over."

She jerked her gaze off him, stared at the kitchen wall, pretending the building drew her interest more than his presence. "It's like this place went up overnight. Everyone will be amazed on Sunday."

"The framing makes a big difference, but it'll still be a while till it's complete. Over here's the problem. He stepped around a stack of drywall. "We had planned on a countertop microwave, but actually we could fit one in the cabinetry right here beside the refrigerator. What do you think?"

She thought she shouldn't be here, alone with him like this, if she wanted to continue to resist him. And surely she must. Shouldn't she?

He tilted his head. Waited.

Oh! She studied the space he'd indicated and considered the options between less counter space or less cabinet space. "I think we should take it up off the counter if that works." *And yes, I want to resist him.* This could easily have been handled over the phone. Knowing that he had invented a reason to see her, a shiver of delight traipsed up her spine.

185

He stood so close that she could smell soap mixed with the leather from his tool bags. *Or maybe I don't want to resist.*

"Listen, me and some of the guys have been shooting hoops over at Chad Penner's barn."

Chad was Jake's lifelong friend, although Katy knew they hadn't hung around much when he'd fallen away from the church. Chad had gone straight to work for his dad on their farm while Jake was at school. She frowned. Or maybe they had stayed in touch. What did it matter? Was she losing her mind? She tried to concentrate.

"Tomorrow night, they're inviting their girlfriends to come watch. Afterward we're going to roast hot dogs. Would you like to go with me?"

Yes and no. Both. But he wanted her to decide now. On the upside, she wouldn't be babysitting. She did want to explore the possibility of a relationship since he'd explained everything. On the downside, she didn't want to do it in front of an audience. "Who will be there?" she stalled.

Jake's eyes darkened. "Not David, if you're worried about him."

"I'm not. I'm worried about you," she snapped. She knew how to keep an argument going, these days. She didn't know anything, though, about starting or ending relationships.

But her challenge was disregarded as he fixed his gaze on something beyond her. His hand went to his hammer, and he slowly eased it out of his holster. She sucked in her breath, her common sense telling her to be still. He slowly drew his arm back over his head. She closed her eyes. Then a second later, its clang caused her to shriek and open her eyes.

"Got it!"

Wheeling around, the tiny dead mouse caused another involuntary scream to slip out of her mouth, before she shivered and turned back to him. "Ew!"

He grinned and took her into his arms with a whisper. "Sorry about that. Don't think the hostess committee would want him around, nibbling on the communion bread."

"Ew!" she repeated. But she didn't shrink back from his embrace. *I can't resist him. I don't want to resist him.*

The room was darkening. His voice was husky against her ear. "Give me another chance?"

She stepped away. Finally she replied, "Well, you were pretty tolerable on Saturday."

But his touch wasn't, it was deadly. *Irresistible*. As if he could read her mind, he took her hands and pulled her close again. But she bumped his tool bags and the sharp edge of a square dug into her hip bone. "Ouch."

"Sorry." He fiddled with the belt and dropped into onto the floor. He reached for her again, and his touch thrilled and completed her. The question was no longer applicable.

They entered an embrace that removed the last shred of debate. It was just the two of them, and a place of contentment she'd thought was gone forever. Longing for more, temporary as the fix might be, she looked into his face and saw his desire. It wasn't a sexual one, but a soul's longing, and she knew what he felt because she experienced it, too.

He dipped his head and his lips touched hers briefly, igniting a fire that flowed through her veins. When she didn't resist, he kissed her again, more fully. It sizzled with a promise that she longed to give in to. How she wanted to trust this man. Her hands had moved up to his forearms, and she lightly pushed away, breathless.

"Will you?" he asked.

She ran her tongue over her lips then whispered. "It's wrong to claim the prize before we've taken the journey, you know?"

He nodded, rubbing his thumbs against her palms. "You can trust me for the journey."

"How?"

He studied her intently. "Are you talking about our kiss?" She nodded. "Then I won't kiss you again."

Biting her lower lip, she nodded. "Then I'll go with you."

"And I'll do everything in my power to win you."

She grinned. "But no kissing?" When they kissed, she couldn't think rationally.

"Not until you ask. But you were supposed to say, 'And I'll do everything in my power to let you win me.' "

She arched a brow. "Well, that's just not true."

He sighed. "No, I suppose not. That's all right. You'll see. It will all be all right. "

Maybe. She changed the subject. "I quit my nanny job."

"Ah," he groaned. "Addison will miss you. Believe me, I know."

She went on to confide her frustrations with Tammy, the television incident, and even voiced some of her confusion about her emotions over the whole ballet experience. He didn't interrupt her with objections or give his opinions on dancing or television, but just replied, "It's a lot to work through. The Christian walk hinges on our choices. I'll pray for you."

He'd changed. Wasn't the teenager she once loved, but had become a man who prayed and who talked about his mistakes. A man willing to wait and woo. He was the same guy with new intrigue. When she started to leave, she felt his gaze on her back; she turned with a sly smile. "By the way, you're real good with that hammer. That mouse didn't stand a chance." *And neither do I.*

─◌

Afterward, Katy's heart thrilled over the exciting encounter so that when she pulled into the Millers' driveway, she could hardly recall the drive home. But the sight of David's shiny black car brought her out of her daydreams and sent a jolt of anxiety up her nerves. She needed to make it plain to David that she was going to entertain Jake's pursuit. That they were dating again.

The sedan's driver door opened, and David jumped out, tall and perfect as ever. He saw her at once and started toward her car. Tucking the inside of her cheek gently into her bite, she turned off the ignition and stepped outside to face him. "Thanks for the valentine."

He nodded as if it embarrassed him and that he was sorry he'd left it. "Just home from work?"

"No. Church. Going over some stuff with Jake." She carefully watched his reaction, wanting to let him down easy, knowing that was impossible. Once she attended the basketball game, news of her date with Jake would be all over church. Better to tell David in person. "We're dating."

There was an awkward silence. David tilted his head. "Guess his valentine was bigger than mine?"

She gave him a contrite smile. "Older."

His eyes narrowed, and his mouth contorted into an uncharacteristic scowl. "So you're going to give the jerk another chance?"

"I think he's changed."

He crossed his arms and glanced at the doddy house, his expression softening. "And you're not going to invite me in for popcorn?"

"Maybe sometime when Lil's home." She hoped they could remain friends, especially since he was often visiting at Ivan's, but that depended upon him.

Resignation dimmed his eyes. Then they took on a hateful glint. "Think I'll pass on that offer. Popcorn's irritating, the way it gets stuck in your teeth, you know? Don't know what I ever saw in popcorn in the first place. Not when desserts are so plentiful. Think what I want is something real sweet, creamy, and rich. Something that melts in my mouth." He turned abruptly and strode toward his brother's house, leaving her face to turn hot as a stove's burner.

CHAPTER 22

Jake's feet left the ground, his body made a smooth arc as he soared upward, and then his arms suddenly smashed down, slamming the orange ball through the hoop. Some pigeons fluttered in the barn rafters, and Katy shot to her feet with a squeal, clapping just as she had for his previous four baskets.

As the players ran to the opposite end of the court, she settled back onto the bale of hay she shared with a slim blond girl named Mandy, who was Chad Penner's girlfriend.

"He's good," Mandy commented, following Jake with her gaze. A twinge of pride warmed Katy. She glanced sideways. Mandy's eyes followed Jake up and down the court. Or was she watching Chad, who was guarding him?

Jake and Chad had been best of friends yet always challenging each other. Naturally, Jake was a showstopper with his love to perform. Most likely, the show was part of his scheme to woo Katy, but he was also attracting the attention of all the other females inside the barn.

She hated the jealousy that erupted inside her, that desire to possess and control him, even quell him. She'd first felt it when he'd started falling away. She hadn't been able to keep him then, so the familiar grinding in the pit of her stomach also carried a foreboding.

She should flee before he hurt her again. Only she had no place to go since Jake claimed he was here to stay, winning back the community. That made her a part of the spectacle, with everyone waiting to see if she would take him back, too. When Jake winked a roguish blackened eye at her, Katy wished she hadn't allowed their fragile beginnings of a relationship to go public.

Mandy caught the flirtatious gesture. "Glad to see you two back together."

"Excuse me?"

"You belong together."

Thoughts shot through Katy's mind: *If he dumps me it will be even more humiliating this time. If I lose him, the pain will be even worse than it was before. What am I doing here?* With the realization that she was a long way from trusting Jake again, she shrugged, "We'll see."

Everyone inside the barn was paired off, and some were even engaged to be married. Most of the girls were older than Katy and had never been as close to her as Lil and Megan, yet they were more than casual acquaintances. There were few strangers and even fewer secrets within the farming community of Plain City, Ohio, especially for those worshipping together in Katy's small Conservative congregation.

Her hands involuntarily worked tiny bits of prickly chaff from the bale of straw as she watched the guys pound the floor and dart from one end of the barn court to the other. The basketball bounced and flung at various levels of skill. A calico cat suddenly sprang onto her bale and looked at her as if the act surprised the creature, too. Katy rubbed its head, and it tentatively climbed onto her lap.

She wasn't fond of cat hair, and this one had a thick, partly matted coat, but the creature's need drew her and provided a pleasant distraction from the true object of her heart. She quietly stroked the cat's head, and when she eased off, he nudged her hand. Maybe she needed a cat at the doddy house. Lil adored animals, had always taken in strays at the farm. Vernon Yoder hadn't allowed cats at their place because their hair was a nuisance in the woodworking shop, hard to remove from a wet, stained surface.

"What happened to Jake's eye?"

Katy had arrived at the game after it had started and hadn't talked to Jake alone yet. She shrugged, "Probably a construction accident."

Jake commanded her attention with a flamboyant dunk. When he landed, the women heard a loud ripping sound. Katy's hand flew to her mouth in amusement, sure he was in trouble. He made the timeout sign with his hands and backed over to the far side of the barn. When he entered the court again, he had a shirt tied around his waist.

With a giggle, Mandy said, "Serves him right."

"I know." So Mandy had noticed that he wore his pants too tight. Unexpectedly, her jealousy swung to its opposite extreme, where she no longer wanted to flee but wanted to stake her claim before somebody else did. As David had implied, there were plenty of available girls willing to be sweet. But Katy wasn't playing a game, at least that had never been her intention.

The cat leapt down and rubbed its matted fur along the bales. She watched it go and brushed hair off her skirt, realizing the little creature had used her for warmth and affection and moved on.

Later at the bonfire, Katy watched Jake poke a roasting stick into the crackling flames. Their shoulders touching, she asked, "What happened to your eye?"

"Pillow fight."

She grinned. A fleeting picture of the church construction site, however, brought several real possibilities to her mind. Softly, she said, "Now that I've decided to tolerate you, I want you to take care of yourself."

His eyes caressed her. "I like that."

She dropped her gaze, then noticed the fire lapping at the hot dogs and pushed his arm. "Look out."

He jerked the stick from the fire and stared at the charred meat. "Guess these are ready. Let's go fix them." She followed him back inside the barn to a long, metal folding table laid out with buns, hot dog relishes, and paper products. As they fixed their plates, he said, "Hey, about that nanny job you lost? I found another job for you. If you're interested. It's one that might help us both."

Turning back toward the barn door, she replied, "No. I'm not cleaning your room."

He followed her with a chuckle. "I wouldn't want you to. And I'm not joking. It's a real job."

"Oh yeah? What is it?"

They sat on a bale to eat their dinner. "With my gram's Alzheimer's, she can't be left alone anymore. My mom just needs a break. Would you be interesting in sitting with her sometimes? For pay, of course."

"I'd be happy to help for free. I can organize some others to help, too. I'm sorry the church hasn't recognized the need before now."

"That would be too confusing for Gram. Mom mentioned hiring someone. I don't think she'd feel free to go out, otherwise. I'm sure she can find someone else, if you don't want to do it."

It would be good to work for someone within the church; that was what she'd been hoping for. This wasn't a housekeeping offer, but maybe it was God's provision until she found another job. She didn't miss the irony of moving from babysitting kids to babysitting grandmas. "Why don't I give it a try and see how it goes?"

"Great. I know Mom won't have any qualms about leaving Gram with you."

"I've always liked your grandmother. She was one of my favorite Sunday school teachers. Such a great storyteller, and she had so much energy, keeping the boys in line." Katy watched the cat return and rub against Jake's jeans. "Will she know me?"

"Probably not. But sometimes she remembers more than other times. We can't figure out why. The good thing is, she's usually happy."

"I'm sorry she has the disease."

He shrugged, obviously unable to express his grief. He dropped the mewing creature bits of his hot dog, and it ate greedily. "Are you getting a phone soon?"

The question startled her, and she worked it out in her mind as she spoke. "Lil doesn't need one with her cell phone, so I'd probably have to pay for it. As you know, we didn't put in a phone line."

"I meant a cell phone."

Instantly, Katy's spirit rose up in resistance against the unnecessary technology. "I don't think so."

"It might come in handy with work. Or for emergencies."

She nibbled at her lip, her mind conjuring up possible emergencies. "We'll see." Then she thought of the perfect solution. "You can always call the Millers if you can't get a hold of me through Lil."

His expression was clearly frustrated, yet he didn't argue.

—⌒—

Katy's hands grew sweaty. It was the third week into the relationship and marriage sermons, and Brother Troyer had finally broached the topic of the prayer covering. He now directed them to open their Bibles to 1 Corinthians 11:3–16. Only the sound of ruffling pages broke the awesome silence pervading the sanctuary. The pages of Katy's Bible wanted to stick, but she finally found the passage where the apostle Paul clearly stated that a man should worship with his head uncovered and a woman with her head covered.

As Katy followed along, she realized the passage was not as clear as she had remembered it. The verses contained riddle-like prose, and to her great dissatisfaction, the preacher zeroed in on its most troubling portions. Was a woman's hair her covering? Next he touched on what the bonnet symbolized. Even at that point, he had more than one opinion. By the time she rose for the benediction, she felt angry that he hadn't given the congregation clear direction. Instead he had debated the meaning of the passage, playing both advocate and challenger, and had left the matter open-ended. His parting remark admonished them to consider and pray over God's intention. She thought a preacher was supposed to shepherd his flock. Surely the sheep didn't know where to go on their own.

With frustration, she moved into the foyer where another kind of confusion took precedence. Folks were fumbling with babies and umbrellas. Some women waited while their men hunkered down and made a run through the downpour to bring their cars around. Katy's focus on the sermon had been so intense she hadn't even realized it had started raining. She gazed out and sighed. Her umbrella was useless from its location on the rear floorboards of her car.

Just as she was mustering up the courage to make a dash for her car and comforting herself with visions of Lil's bean soup simmering back at the doddy house, the back of a young man's perfectly combed brown hair caught her attention. A tincture of mixed emotions drew her to a halt. She froze.

She had hoped to put off her first meeting with David since his humiliating set down, but the tiny room was too crowded for her to shrink back. She watched him determinedly weave through the foyer toward the door. When a family blocked his path, he glanced up and around. When his unfortunate gaze met Katy's, he flinched. Quite abruptly, he turned and shot through the first opening that led him out into the storm.

Katy gave a gasp. His brief shunning didn't trouble her as much as what she had just glimpsed. David's face was no longer perfect. Battered, with swollen lips, his face bore an ugly bruise on his cheek where his dimple normally played. With a sinking heart, she knew it was no coincidence that both her pursuers sported facial contusions. Why hadn't Jake told her the truth about his black eye? Mennonites didn't fight or brawl.

Already emotional over the sermon, this new revelation fed her churning stomach. Jake hadn't been at church so she couldn't question him. She had seen Ann Byler, so most likely his grandmother was having an off day and he'd stayed home with her.

Sucking in her lower lip, she nodded thanks to a considerate door tender and sprinted for her car. The rain streamed down her face in blinding torrents. The storm pelted her covering. The wind tore it loose. Her hand flew up to catch it. Rain drenched her hair, but she hardly cared. Emotionally, she was drowning. From her first job with the outsiders, she'd started sinking. In every direction, waves swelled. Wind clawed. Decisions loomed. Everyone tossed life preservers at her, but she didn't know which one to grab. If she chose wrong, she was going to drown.

CHAPTER 23

Some smart person started the saying that time heals. Or was that in the Bible some place? Katy didn't know, but she supposed it was true because even an hour had done wonders for her emotional state. So had the heat that flowed through the doddy house, carrying with it the welcoming aroma of Lil's hearty bean soup. Dry clothing and a securely pinned covering also contributed to a better perspective.

After church, Megan had flitted in with her cheery countenance, joining Katy and Lil for Sunday lunch. Their blond friend had chatted about her summer missions options, then flown off to spend the afternoon with her folks before heading back to Rosedale College.

Now Katy lined up her dominoes. Across the table, Lil did the same. As they played, they could look out the kitchen window and watch the steady rain turn the ground into tiny rivulets.

"I didn't see Jake at church, did you?" Lil asked.

"No, but I saw his mom. He probably stayed home with his grandma." Just remembering something he'd mentioned at the basketball game, she added, "He has to bid some blueprints this afternoon." They exchanged a disapproving look, for even Lil knew they shouldn't work on Sundays. "Last night he asked me if I'd like to work for his mom, watching Minnie."

Lil's gaze softened with fondness at the mention of her grandmother. "Mom and I have watched her before. She's a handful, but I love her."

"I'd like to try it and see how it goes. It will be a challenge, but I've always loved her."

"You going to clean their place, too?"

"I don't know. I'll do whatever Ann wants. If it works out, the extra income should help us scrape by. Think Megan will ever settle down with a job?"

Lil matched a yellow domino to another yellow domino. "Hard to tell. Jobs can be disappointing. I need to find something better. Nobody ever sees me back in the kitchen, and the restaurant's not big enough to move to a higher position. No prestige. No extra money. Dead-end job." She glanced out at the rain. "I should drive into Plain City and buy a newspaper."

Trailing her friend's gaze to the dreary weather and back, Katy offered, "I'll go with you, if you'd like."

"Okay. Let's finish this game first. Maybe the rain will ease up by then." They both glanced out the window again, sharing skepticism. Several plays passed without conversing as Katy thought about Lil not liking her job. Her friend had high expectations and the grit to fulfill them. Maybe that was part of her own despair. She didn't have any goals. Just then a shiny black car turned into the Millers' driveway.

"Oh great," Katy said sarcastically. The image of David's bruised face flashed across her mind. Who needed goals when it was hard just to survive each day's handouts? "David won't be coming here."

They both leaned toward the window and watched, but the car disappeared in front of Ivan and Elizabeth's house.

Lil looked over with amusement. "Did you see him today?"

Katy rapped her dominos on the table in disgust. "Yes! How could they? What does fighting solve? Do they think I'm going to throw myself into the winner's arms?"

"I wonder who started it? Jake's been real jealous, but I never heard of him fighting before."

"Probably David. He was quietly furious the other night when we talked. It shocked me." She told Lil about his cutting remark.

"Whoa! Maybe we need to sic Megan on them. Remind them of their Anabaptist upbringing."

"They both know better. It's humiliating. And Jake is going to get an earful the next time I see him, too. When I asked him what happened, he said he'd been in a pillow fight."

Lil giggled. Then she asked, "Is it really humiliating? Or is it a little gratifying?" She slid another ivory rectangle into place. "I'd like that kind of embarrassment—having two guys fight over me." Involuntarily, she waved a domino. "Maybe the blond waiter and that one guy from culinary school that who wouldn't give me the time of day. Yeah, that'd be something. I'd want the waiter to win. The other guy was smug."

"Two things to keep in mind. First, you may be saying good-bye to your blond waiter if you find another job. And second, they aren't really available if they aren't Mennonite men, are they?"

Glancing up, Lil said, "Oh, there's the Katy I remember. Thought we weren't going to get preachy. Especially since you have it all with your dark, smoldering beauty." Lil shook her head. "Pass."

"Don't forget my lovely smooth hands and preachy mouth," Katy reminded her. Then she cocked an eyebrow. "You can't move?"

"Nope."

Making a dramatic gesture with her occupationally chafed hands, she made a winning move. Lil let out a moan and paused to write down her points. Then they turned all the colored dots over until the pile was plain ivory and worked to shuffle the pieces. "What number are we on?" Lil asked.

"Three. I've got it." They kept their peace while lining up their dominos, and then Katy gave Lil a wry grin. "You're right. It's really hard for me not to preach. But you set me up with such lovely opportunities all the time. Speaking of, what did you think of Brother Troyer's sermon? Are you going to be submissive when you get married?"

"Ah, the awful *S* word. You did hear him say that men and women are equal? One's not superior over the other?"

Katy nodded. "He was talking out of both sides of his mouth, 'cause in the next breath, he implied that the husband was in charge." She knew that her own mom showed deference to her dad in a lot of ways and that Lil's folks had modeled the same type of marriage, but she couldn't picture Lil settling for that type of arrangement. And to be honest, she had to wonder if she could settle for it, either.

Lil thoughtfully tapped a domino on the table. "I like what he said about it being purely an order issue. Adam was made first to reflect God's glory. Then woman next, to reflect man's glory."

"Glorious man," Katy taunted, and Lil burst into giggles. Then Katy pushed back from the table and stared out the window. "Seriously, I don't get the glory thing."

Lil glanced out the window and back. "You agree that God's creation shows His greatness?"

"Sure. Nature draws me to God."

Lil explained, "Man's the highest of his creation. When a man shows honor to somebody, he removes his hat. So Adam worships with his head uncovered. But mankind sinned. When Adam and Eve sinned, what did they do?"

Katy shrugged. "Hid and covered themselves with fig leaves."

Lil pointed to her own covering. "So when woman wears a head covering, it's a symbol of mankind's fall."

Inadvertently, Katy touched her own covering. "Wow. What a spiritual picture."

"For the angels to witness."

Katy felt drawn to Lil's depiction of equality. "So what about the angels?"

Lil shrugged. "Honestly? I don't know. I'm not *that* smart."

Katy would have laughed if it wasn't such a crucial topic. "So it's not just about the woman submitting to her husband?"

"If it were, only married women would wear it."

Katy demanded, "How do you know all this?"

"Duh? Brother Troyer preached it today. Weren't you even listening? Sometimes I get the impression you think I'm totally lost and going to hell or something."

"Lil! Don't say that. Of course I don't think that." Katy felt contrite.

"But I did think you'd be happy to ditch the covering."

"Not really. At work, but not at church. The important thing is that the church doesn't split apart over it."

Katy hoped for more than peace. She hoped nothing would change. Since their big argument, Lil had seemed softer, more sensitive toward spiritual things than Katy had given her credit for, and yet she couldn't picture Lil taking a submissive role. "So back to the *S* word. You going to submit to your husband?"

"I'm hoping to find a man who'll welcome my opinions, but right now I can't even find a man." She pushed back her chair. "I think we need a hot chocolate perk or we're never going to finish this game. And I need that newspaper." She started the teakettle, then returned to the table. "Since you've got two guys fighting over you, the *S* word seems to be more your problem than mine."

Katy cringed. She didn't like the idea of submission. Thunder cracked, and she glanced out the window at the dark sky, considering God.

When Lil returned to the table with two steaming cups, she placed one in front of Katy. "Just take your time with Jake. I don't want to lose you as a roommate."

After the game was finished, they left to get Lil's newspaper. While they drove, they discussed the benefits of Katy getting a cell phone versus a landline. Lil finally persuaded her that just because cell phones were more modern didn't make then any worldlier than landlines. A phone was a phone, and it was a safety precaution to have while driving.

When Lil brought up driving, it touched a chord with Katy. She did get nervous when she drove alone in the dark.

After they got back to the doddy house, Lil gave her a demonstration of how a cell phone worked, and Katy finally relented to the idea. After that, Lil circled two job ads that she meant to check out the following week.

"You think once you get married things get easier?" Katy asked.

"Nope. Then you get kids. That's when your trouble really starts." Lil moved to the floor to begin her regimented sit-ups, and Katy knew the conversation was over.

She opened the jar that contained her latest concoction and rubbed the greasy cream on her hands. After that, she slipped into her night gloves and jotted notes in her journal. She had an entire section devoted to her hand-cream experiments.

Since her journal had become a handy tool for housekeeping, she decided to add a spiritual section. Nibbling on her pen, she came up with a practical heading: The Prayer Covering. Below it, she copied the scripture Brother Troyer had given them to study.

CHAPTER 24

The telephone store might not have been so intimidating if it hadn't been located inside the indoor mall, which screamed to Katy *lust of the flesh, lust of the eyes, and pride of life*—all phrases from a Bible verse. Lil told her she was lucky it wasn't the weekend for that's when it became a breeding ground for weirdness. Katy didn't even want to know what that meant.

Young moms in tight-belted jeans and high-heeled boots pushed strollers and shushed babies without dropping their gaze from the window displays that carried the latest fashions. Some hurried by as if they were participating in a shopping marathon in which they wouldn't hesitate to run over stragglers. Others stared at her and Lil, their gazes sweeping over them from their oxfords to their coverings, but Katy kept her shoulders ramrod straight. She had as much right as anyone to spend her money. To own a cell phone without being frivolous or self-centered. Or so Lil maintained.

A sudden face darted in front of her. "Ma'am, try this ring cleaner?" Katy halted and stared at the teenager, who blushed when he discovered that she wasn't wearing any jewelry.

"No thank you." Katy sidestepped, bumping into Lil.

"Over there." Lil pointed.

Katy glanced at the store's sign. When they stepped inside the phone store, Katy felt more out of place than a guy at a quilting.

"I already looked the phones over and can point you to a couple of good deals," Lil advised. She pointed out various features of the display phones that rested on tiny glass shelves throughout the store. Next a sales representative explained the terms and told Katy about rebates. After Katy chose a phone, she followed him—careful not to stare at his low-slung pants—to the cash register and got out her checkbook. She wrote the check out for the amount he had indicated and pushed it toward him.

"Um, if you write a check, I need to see a debit card."

Katy glanced at Lil, then back at the young man behind the counter. "I don't have any cards." A card had come with her checking account, but she had filed it away, refusing to use it.

"Sorry." He glanced up at her covering. "I can't take this then."

She returned the wasted check to her checkbook and dropped it inside her purse, pulling out her billfold instead. "I'll pay cash then."

The young man seemed surprised and patient as Katy worked to get him the correct amount. He programmed the phone and handed it back to her. Her pulse quickened unexpectedly as she stared at the shiny rectangle in her palm. Beside her, Lil snatched Katy's shopping bag off the counter and nudged her toward the door.

"Thanks," Katy tossed over her shoulder. The clerk smiled.

"Let's celebrate. I'll buy lunch," Lil urged.

After everything happened so quickly, Katy did need to catch her breath, so she agreed to dine at a Mexican restaurant. Over the chips and salsa, Lil entered some of her phone numbers into Katy's phone and demonstrated its unique features.

"Thanks for going with me. It was pretty intimidating. How did you ever have the nerve to go by yourself?"

"I didn't. Jake went with me. Here, let me show you about texting."

"No thanks. I only bought this for practical purposes."

"That's why you need to learn how to text. Watch, I'll text Jake and tell him your new number."

"No. Wait. I'm not ready for that yet."

"What good's a phone if you don't use it?"

"Oh fine," Katy relented.

Moments later she got a reply from Jake. Can u come to dinnr Fri nite to c how Gram does?

Lil showed her how to reply: Yes.

I'll call w d tails.

Amazed, Katy wondered how she could have feared something so convenient and practical.

$$\sim$$

Jake's familial home was a typical Plain City farm. It consisted of a two-story house, barn, silo, and more than forty acres of flat, tilled cornfields. Large ash and buckeyes shaded the house, and Katy recalled her first kiss happened under the huge weeping willow by the circle drive. She had been sixteen years old. Trying not to think about it, she stepped up onto the front porch that cooled the Bylers' guests in the summer and sheltered them in winter.

As soon as she touched the bell, Jake opened the door. His hair was still damp from the shower, and his face clean-shaven. For a moment he just grinned at her, looking rakish with his one black eye.

She flashed him a timid smile. "This feels strange."

"Not to me. You belong here." He took her hand and drew her inside. "With me."

She wet her lips, choosing to ignore his remark. "Where is everybody?"

"In the kitchen. Come on."

Ann Byler's kitchen reflected her cheery disposition. She celebrated sunshine, welcoming it through rows of windows dressed in perky yellow valances. The window and ledge above the sink displayed a collection of stained-glass sun catchers. An antique cupboard held a sun chime. Its soft jingle had always intrigued Katy. In the summer, Ann grew sunflowers in her garden, and in the winter, silk ones decorated the table.

Rocking in a corner stream of late-afternoon light, Jake's grandmother bowed her head over a lap-sized hoop. She didn't look up when

Katy moved closer to observe her project, watching the old hands work a needle up and down through taut material. To her pleasant surprise, the stitching was small and even. The old woman's hands were steady, and the tips of her fingers that weren't covered with thimbles were dry and cracked from the continuous push of the needle. Sympathy curled inside Katy's heart. She would bring Minnie some of her healing hand ointment.

"Mom loves to quilt pillow shams," Ann said, then returned to her stove.

"I sell them for her on eBay." Jake winked and moved to give Minnie a side hug. When he saw Katy's confusion, he explained, "An Internet store. On the computer."

Katy touched Minnie's arm. "That's very good stitching."

The older woman looked up then focused on Jake. "Who have you brought home, Jacob?"

"This is Katy Yoder."

"Oh. I taught her in Sunday school, you know. Such a lovely girl."

Katy beamed that Minnie remembered her, but sadly Minnie thought Jake was his grandfather, his namesake. "I loved your stories about David and Goliath. The way you marched around the room with a pretend slingshot."

Minnie giggled then covered her mouth, whispering between her fingers. "I should have been a movie actress."

Shocked, Katy replied, "I'm glad you were a Sunday school teacher instead."

"Dinner's ready," Ann called.

"Are you hungry, Gram?" Jake asked.

"No, I need to finish this while there's still light."

"We're having meat loaf."

"Well that does sound good. Maybe I will." He helped her stand, and then she walked to the kitchen table, confused.

"In the dining room. Since Katy's visiting."

"Who's Katy?"

Katy's heart sank.

Giving Katy a sympathetic look, Jake guided Grandma Minnie by the elbow to her place in the dining room. "What a pretty table." She stopped mid-step and smiled at Ann. "You shouldn't have gone to all this trouble."

Jake whispered to Katy, "Most of the time she thinks Mom is her sister, and I'm Grandpa."

"You always looked like him," Katy whispered.

Once Minnie was seated, Ann smiled at Katy. "I'm so glad you came tonight. I've missed you."

Katy had always appreciated Ann's gentle manner. Rumor was she didn't have any backbone, and that's why she allowed her only daughter to traipse off to OSU and why Jake went wild. With his dad gone, there was simply no discipline. Katy tried to rein her thoughts back to the conversation. Ann was asking polite questions, inquiring about Katy's work and skirting around Grandma Minnie's periodic interruptions with a practiced skill that was both sad and heartwarming. Sipping water from a sunflower-patterned glass, Katy listened to Ann's summer plans for a fruit and vegetable stand, and cast smiling eyes Jake's way, pleased with him for returning home to help his family.

Before she left, Katy and Ann planned for Katy to stay with Grandma Minnie one day a week. If that worked, they might extend it to two days and include some cleaning. Around eight o'clock, Jake offered to walk her to her car.

Taking her gloved hand, he said, "How about you start the heater, and I'll join you for a few minutes. We haven't had any time alone."

Instantly, Katy remembered times they'd sat in his truck after a date and talked. Sometimes they kissed, but he'd always remained a gentleman. Would he keep his word tonight, about not kissing her until she was ready?

Inside her car, he took her hand and leaned close. "Thanks so much for helping with Grams."

"We'll get along fine. She remembered me for an instant."

"She loved you. Back when we were in high school, she encouraged me to date you."

Resisting the nostalgic pull, Katy drew her hand away, taking hold of the steering wheel. Light shone through the living room windows. Everything inside had been faintly familiar yet different. Jake's dad was now gone, Cal was married, and Erin was away at college. Jake seemed changed, too, older and more mature. But should she trust him? It would be so easy to fall under his spell.

Take it slow, Lil had warned, in spite of her earlier matchmaking. Did Lil know something about Jake she wasn't sharing? Or was it just Lil's way to hang on to the doddy house dream?

Katy glanced over. "What really happened to your eye?"

The corner of his mouth quirked. "I just collided with something."

She arched her brows. "Did you know David had a similar accident?"

Finally he replied, his Amish-Dutch accent thicker than usual, "It's a good thing you dumped him. He's a real hothead."

"He started it then?"

"He came to the church one night after the crew left. I tried to reason with him, but in his condition it was useless. I'm surprised he even made it home without ending up in some ditch."

Her pursed lips slackened. "He was drunk?"

Jake nodded.

"But everybody thinks he's such a nice guy," Katy protested.

Jake looked hurt. "Everyone makes mistakes."

She considered his statement. David Miller had gotten drunk and started a fight because of her mistakes. She tightened her grip on the steering wheel. "I know what you're thinking. That I used him to get the doddy house. But I wanted to find out if I was over you, too. I hoped my dates with David would turn into more."

He touched her cheek. "Thanks for your honesty."

She dropped her hands in her lap and stared at him, blinking back threatening tears. Silence hovered between them, and she knew instinctively when he thought about kissing her. She saw his inward struggle, but he refrained.

Should she ask him more about his relationship with Jessie? Would there ever be a more fitting time? Before she could trust him, she needed to know exactly what she was forgiving.

But he spoke again first. "The doddy house has always been your dream. I want you to enjoy it. Although I made mistakes when I was out on my own, it helped me find my way. I want that for you, too. It will help us in our relationship."

It seemed contrived now to bring the conversation back to Jessie. Instead, Katy asked, "What if I become too independent and never marry? I like being my own boss."

"You still have Lil."

She chuckled, glad they'd lightened the tone of the conversation. "I don't get to boss her around, but we do have some great argu— discussions."

His laughter rang in her ears long after the car had grown quiet. Then he said, "You have a pure heart, Katy Yoder. It draws a man."

But it was his heart Katy wanted to explore. She needed to know if they still meshed. "What do you think about the prayer covering?"

He didn't answer directly. "If we ever married, I'd give you lots of freedom to be yourself."

She considered the implications of the *S* word as she studied his moonlit face. He seemed serious.

"You wouldn't boss me around?"

"Would you listen if I did?"

She shrugged.

He stared at her lips. "I'm finding it hard to behave."

Involuntarily, she twirled her ponytail.

He swallowed. "I'd better go." Once he was out, he ducked his head back inside. "I'll call."

As she watched him go, she had to wonder if he offered a relationship with plenty of freedom because he wasn't willing to settle down himself. If she pursued a relationship with him, even marriage, would there be more things to condone? Or worse things to forgive? Freedom was a frightening thing. Was his newfound faith in God enough to make him a faithful husband?

CHAPTER 25

Ann Byler lingered at the door, a worrisome gaze flitting over her sunny nest, and Katy sensed the other woman's reluctance to give her elderly mother over to someone else's care.

"Grandma Minnie will be fine with me. Take as long as you like." Katy knew Ann needed a break, regardless of her own niggling apprehension at spending time in Jake's home, where even in his absence, his presence permeated every corner.

Was she overly sensitive that everything about that man attracted and cautioned her at the same time? That everything about him screamed, *Tread carefully*?

The door closed and she braced herself. She owed Grandma Minnie. In Sunday school, it was Minnie who had instilled in her to color inside the lines. And taught her faces weren't purple, but legs were black. Minnie had guided generations, campaigning against prideful adornment whether it be a necktie or lipstick. Normally, Katy used a lip moistener with just a touch of shine, but in case Minnie was having one of her lucid days, Katy had avoided that luxury.

No need to vex the woman in her old age. Katy couldn't imagine the pain Minnie must have endured over the years as changes invaded their tight-knit community. It was sad, but Katy didn't know another woman in the church who could follow in Minnie's stead to keep the church from conforming to the world around them.

Minnie sat on the couch, staring across the room where her gaze was transfixed on a tree outside the window. Her quilting hoop lay discarded on the cushion next to her.

"Hello, Minnie."

The woman jerked her gaze away and squinted at Katy. "Are you here for firewood? That old tree isn't dead. Only dormant, waiting for spring." She folded her arms. "My swing's in that tree."

The homestead had been Minnie's childhood home. No wonder she was so confused now. "I'm just here to visit."

The deeply folded face belied the childlike spirit. "Then let's go swing." Minnie pushed up from the couch and started toward the kitchen with amazing agility.

Scurrying after her, Katy objected. "It's really cold outside."

Minnie's chin jutted up. "But I want to swing."

Seeing there was no stopping the older woman, Katy went to the coat closet. "Put this on first."

Thankfully, Minnie shrugged into her black, Amish shawl.

"Sit down. I'll help you put your boots on, too."

Minnie sat, a wide smile on her face.

Katy grabbed a pair of winter boots that appeared to be the appropriate size and knelt in front of Minnie. The action reminded her of foot washing service, and it humbled her and sent warm fuzzies up her back to serve the woman who had once served her. She untied the black oxfords and set them to the side, then tipped the boots. Minnie obediently poked her black-clad toes into the opening. She tilted her face to the side, studying Katy.

"Who are you?"

"Katy Yoder. A friend of Jake's. All done. Let's go." Minnie took her hand, and they went outside. For an instant the older woman braced herself, confused and blinking at the sudden glare of sunlight. The sting of cold air nipped Katy's face. "This way."

She led the five-foot-two woman around the side of the house to the old ash tree. She helped Minnie onto the swing's board seat, which was supported by two thick ropes. "Hold tight. I'll push you." Minnie pumped her legs and giggled. Her blue skirt billowed out, exposing thin, black-clad knees. Minnie was always barely over one hundred pounds, and now seemed more waiflike than ever, and as Katy stepped away to watch, a melancholy lump formed in her throat.

How many human generations would the old tree know? It was sad to see Minnie's life end in confusion. It hurt to learn that even when you colored inside the lines, life was still not a safe place to inhabit.

"I can touch heaven," Minnie said, pointing her toes. "God's smiling at me."

Katy swiped her coat sleeve across her eyes.

After they finished playing, Katy fixed Minnie the leftover chili that Ann had set aside for their lunch. Her face still aglow from the crisp cold, Minnie had the spoon to her mouth before Katy was even seated. With a smile, Katy said, "I'll pray."

She closed her eyes and, still feeling melancholy over Minnie's condition, she waited for peace to settle over her before she started speaking. "Lord, I thank You for Minnie's life, for her years of leadership and love to us. I pray that You will fill her heart with joy and peace. May she always feel Your presence. We thank You for this food. Amen."

Katy opened her eyes and looked across the table. Her jaw dropped. Stunned, she stared at Minnie.

The Alzheimer's victim had removed her prayer covering and placed it upside down in her bowl of chili. Her hair was partly unpinned, and she was struggling with its remaining pins.

Katy jumped up and fairly flew around the side of the table. She grabbed Minnie's hand, but the older woman jerked it away and knocked over her water glass. With a yelp, Katy ran to the counter for a roll of paper towels. Minnie had jumped up now, too, and was holding her apron out, staring at a giant wet spot, her lower lip quivering. Her hair was as wild as a bag woman's Katy had once observed on a Columbus street corner.

Dabbing at the puddle of water spreading across the tablecloth and dripping onto the floor, Katy soaked up as much as she could. Then she glanced at Minnie, still not believing the woman had stuck her covering in her chili bowl. But when their gazes met, Minnie must have felt her displeasure because she started to cry.

Katy set down the roll of towels and touched her shoulder. "It's all right. Let's just take off your apron and find a dry one."

The woman whimpered and eyed Katy suspiciously. She tried to keep her voice soothing. "Why don't you sit in this other dry chair?" Minnie eased into it like a frightened child. Katy smiled, pulling the woman's bowl over. But Minnie beat her to the covering and whipped it out of the food, plopping it onto the table. Katy tightened her lips at the ugly orange stain on Ann's white tablecloth. She snatched another paper towel and scooped up the covering, taking it to the kitchen sink along with the wet apron.

She quickly returned to the table and gave Minnie a weak smile, handing her a spoon. The woman clamped her hand around the spoon but didn't eat. Remembering how Jake had gotten her to the table the other night, Katy started talking about how good the soup smelled. Minnie took the bait.

Katy wanted to push the woman's hair back over her shoulder so it didn't hang in her chili, but she didn't want to frighten her again. Instead she returned to the sink and ran water through the covering, reverently patting it dry and trying to plump out its shape, setting it in a sunny spot.

Next she seated herself beside Minnie and forced herself to take a few spoonfuls of the soup, wondering how she was going to get Minnie's hair combed and the covering back on her head. She knew that if Minnie were in her right mind, she'd want to wear her head covering. She'd want someone to make sure she kept it on when she wasn't thinking clearly anymore. Katy determined to make that happen.

Eventually after much maneuvering and gentle urgings, Katy managed to get the contrite woman to her bedroom. She combed out Minnie's hair, plaited it and replaced her covering. While Minnie settled under the bed quilt, Katy read a few scriptures from a Bible on a nearby nightstand. She patted Minnie's back until the old eyes closed. Even afterward, Katy lingered outside of the bedroom door until she heard

Minnie's snoring. Then she leaned against the wall a moment to collect herself, wondering how so much damage could happen in such a small fraction of time.

Next she returned to set Ann's kitchen to rights. Katy set the dirty dishes on the counter and removed the white tablecloth, running water over the tomato spots, then dabbing vinegar on the stain. She draped it over the washing machine and returned to the kitchen to wash the dishes.

When she had the kitchen finished, she went to listen outside Minnie's bedroom door. But she only heard silence through the walls. Sensing that Minnie could get in more trouble than Addison at seven years of age could even dream of, she slowly turned the doorknob and eased it open.

Her heart leapt in her chest. Katy cried, "Stop!"

Minnie's hand paused. Orange-handled scissors interlocked a long shank of thin white hair. Hair that had hardly ever been cut. Minnie blinked. Then Katy saw a rebellious glint enter the old eyes. Was this some sort of showdown? It was becoming obvious where Jake got his rebellion.

Katy was afraid to step into the room. If Minnie jerked, she might snip off her hair. She willed her voice to calm. "Your hair is so lovely. If you give me the scissors, I'll brush it for you again."

"No! That hurts. I'm cutting it so it doesn't hurt." The woman lifted the shank of hair and dropped her gaze to it, pressing the scissors handles closed. With a gasp, Katy watched twelve inches of growth slip to the floor.

Katy flew into the room and wrestled the scissors out of Minnie's hand, all the while being sure to keep it away from her face. When Minnie saw she had lost, she curled into a ball on the bed, making a noise that sounded like an angry cat. And Katy had a moment to take inventory. Minnie's wet covering was squashed on top of the pillow. Not only was a large chunk of Minnie's hair gone, but now Katy noticed that part of the cape on Minnie's gown was shredded.

Katy pressed her eyes together in agony and regret. Had she been too rough when she'd brushed Minnie's hair, giving her charge the idea to cut it off? Then remembering she couldn't give Minnie a scrap of time unwatched, she flashed her eyes open again. But Minnie was still curled on the bed making unearthly sounds. Katy rubbed her sweaty palms on her skirt, wondering how to rectify the situation.

Suddenly Minnie sat up. "My dress is ruined."

A flash of anger shot through Katy, but she quickly reminded herself that it wasn't Minnie's fault that the cape was shredded. It was the disease. And Katy's own neglect. First, she needed to get rid of the scissors. A glance at the door told her Minnie's lock had been removed, but she still didn't trust her alone. Katy backed toward the closet, stood on her tiptoes, and shoved the scissors on a high shelf that the shorter woman wouldn't be able to reach. While she was by the closet, she saw a clean dress and removed it from its hanger. Draping it over her arm, she started toward the bed. "Let's put this on before Ann comes home."

Minnie swung her legs over the side of the bed. "Where is Ann?"

"She went to town."

"How? Did she go with her daddy?"

Katy realized Minnie thought her daughter was a child again. Taking advantage of the older woman's contemplative state, she unfastened her dress and managed to remove it from a compliant body. "May I pin up your hair? Jacob likes it that way." Minnie shrugged, and Katy used her fingers to inspect the damage. The shearing was noticeable, but could be disguised when plaited. After that she shook open the covering. "A woman should always wear her covering," Katy soothed, starting toward her.

"No." Minnie stuck out her foot and kicked Katie in the stomach.

"Ugh!" The unexpected blow took her breath away and brought tears to her eyes. But Katy quickly recovered. She narrowed her eyes. Her voice came out harsh. "Why not?"

"I'm sick of it. I always wanted to be an actress."

The words hit Katy with a force equal to the earlier kick. This was more serious than she'd thought. Katy began to perspire. She tentatively bent toward Minnie, softening her voice as though she spoke to a four-year-old. She pointed, "I'm wearing one, see?"

Then quick as a viper, Minnie's hand struck out and swiped Katy's covering from her head, taking pins and hair with it.

"Ouch!" Katy's arms flew up, but she was too late.

Minnie now waved Katy's covering, from which several long black hairs dangled.

Setting an angry jaw, Katy placed a firm hand on Minnie's shoulder and with the other tried to snatch her covering back. But Minnie waved it overhead like a white organdy flag. This was far from a truce. Katy made several swipes through the air, and the last one toppled them both back on the bed with Katy landing on top of the weaker woman.

But Minnie fought like one twice her weight and hollered like she was being murdered, crumpling the head covering and pulling it close to her body. Katy feared Minnie would scratch herself with the pins. Then in a quick flash, the wily woman stuffed it inside her bodice.

With both hands free now, Minnie started to beat Katy and kick. She landed several blows to Katy's face. "Get off!"

Katy thrust up a protective arm and tried to capture Minnie's battering fists. "Stop. Give me that! This instant!"

"What on earth!" a feminine voice wailed from the doorway.

Katy flinched then sat up, her own hair now nearly as disheveled as Minnie's. Minnie crawled to the far side of the bed and pulled the covers up around her protectively. Katy's cheeks flamed to see Ann burst into the room with Jake at her heels. Katy slid to her feet and withdrew a few steps.

Jake swept past her and fell to his knees, gently embracing his grandmother. "Grams. You all right?"

The gentleness in his voice and his total disregard of Katy enraged her. Ann wore a pained expression. How could they think this was her fault? "Just keep it!" Katy spit out. She faced Ann. "She cut her hair and her dress. The scissors are on the closet shelf. And my covering is in her bra!"

Ann's face paled, and she took a backward step, her hands going to her chest as though she might have a heart attack.

But Katy ignored it and stormed out of the room.

"Wait!" Katy heard Ann call after her.

Utterly humiliated and in spite of the footsteps clamoring after her,

Katy fled from the nightmare. She flung open the closet door, threw her coat and purse over her arm, and ran for the car. But she slipped in the gravel driveway and fell, bruising her knees.

Behind her she heard, "Oh Katy."

She struggled to her feet and didn't look back.

CHAPTER 26

As two of the most important women in Jake's life fled from the room, his mom screaming after Katy, he sat on the bed and draped his arm around his gram. On the floor lay a pile of discarded clothing and a covering with strings. His gram's.

Instantly, he understood what had happened. Gram had been removing her bonnet a lot lately, and Katy probably tried to force her to wear it. They should have warned Katy about that. But struggling with scissors? What had Katy been thinking to allow it to come to that? Headstrong and hotheaded. Maybe it was good he'd seen this side to her. He couldn't believe the image that lingered over what he'd witnessed when he entered the bedroom. Katy on top of his little grandmother, manhandling her. Unbelievable!

Minnie shivered, and Jake realized she was still recovering from the ordeal. He pulled the quilt up over her shoulders. He needed to dress her. He rose and sorted through the mess on the floor, and his hand touched the discarded head covering. Wet? How on earth? With a frustrated sigh, he let it lay and retrieved the fresh dress from its hanger. "Let's get you dressed."

"Is that awful woman gone?"

"Yes. You're safe now."

Minnie nodded obediently. "Wait." She stuck her hand through her torn bodice and withdrew another smaller covering, thrusting it forward like a great prize.

Jake blinked. She did have Katy's covering in her bra! How in the world?

He narrowed his eyes. "Grams, what did you do?"

"She's a wildcat! Do you want it or not?"

He obviously wouldn't get to the bottom of it by talking to his gram. Katy would have to explain the situation. He tightened his jaw. Her version of it. Her sanctimonious version of it. At his grandmother's contrite expression, he relaxed his jaw. "It's all right, Gram." He opened his hand, and she dropped it into his palm.

She tugged at her bosom. "It scratched me."

Surprised, he noticed the pins. He'd never paid much attention to the little caps, although he'd seen plenty in his day. For years, his grandmother had designed and sewn them for others as extra income. He dropped the straight pins in his shirt pocket, but left Katy's hair in the organdy cap and stuffed it into his jeans pocket.

"She's gone," Ann declared, entering the room with a sullen expression. "We scared her off." She swept a painful gaze across the room, like he had earlier. Then she looked at Minnie, and her eyes softened. "You tired, Mother?"

"No. I think I'll swing," Minnie declared.

Ann sighed.

Jake handed the dress to his mother and left them, intending to get to the bottom of the incident. In the kitchen, he saw the bare table, the open closet door, the wet boots. There'd been plenty of action in a few hours' time. He strode to the window and looked outside. Gone were all but the tire tracks of Katy's Chevy. He turned and scaled the stairs, hurrying into the privacy of his room. Moving to the window that gave view of the barren fields, he speed-dialed Katy. But she wasn't answering. Of course, she wasn't, he fumed, jamming his phone in his pocket and striding to his door.

Stomping into her bedroom and jerking open the drawer of her nightstand, Katy took out a fresh covering and marched to the bathroom. She was taken back momentarily when she saw her disheveled state. Her face was bruised on the right cheekbone just below the eye. Well, now she matched Jake and David! She washed her face and quickly put herself to rights, pinning on the fresh covering.

"Ouch!" She stuck her thumb in her mouth. The physical pain subsided, but not the pain over the incident with Minnie, and worse, getting caught in the midst of it.

Her stockings had a hole in one knee. She removed them and washed gravel from the wound, placing salve over it and a bandage. Then she put on her slippers and went to the kitchen.

Not knowing how to rectify the situation, when Ann and Jake so obviously blamed her for everything, she got out a pint of chocolate ice cream. Absurd images flashed through her mind. Her hands shaky, Katy licked the tasteless dessert. Shame flooded over her. How had she lost control of a petite, eighty-five-year-old woman? An innocent babe who didn't know what she was doing? And worst, why hadn't she stayed to explain her actions instead of running away like a guilty criminal?

Because Jake betrayed her. Again.

Still she could have heeded the soft warning, the quiet voice that had warned her to cease struggling. She could pinpoint the exact moment when she'd let her anger take control, overstepped her bounds, and pressed ahead in anger instead of retreating in love. She hadn't done anything wrong. Until the struggle. Then she'd chosen the same childish behavior as Minnie's. But it had all happened so quickly, she rationalized. She would have quit struggling if she'd had only a moment more. She didn't want Minnie to get scratched with the pins. But Ann had returned at the most inappropriate time.

As she thought back to the incident, she remembered Minnie's bloodcurdling screams. No wonder Jake and Ann had burst into the room with looks of horror on their faces. She jammed the spoon into the frozen mound and pushed it away.

Her cell phone rang. Jake again. She groaned and didn't answer it. He'd called at least six times now. She wasn't ready to talk to him, couldn't forget the condemnation in his eyes. She put the carton of ice cream away and got out her journal instead.

Tomato stain—run cool water until clear, then blot with white vinegar.

Next to the tip, she wrote: *Removing the stain does not remove memory of the incident. I remain in search of that particular cleansing agent that can renew thoughts.*

She remembered reading something like that in the scriptures and went to her bedroom to get her Bible. When she passed the window, however, she caught movement outside. Her spirit sank to see Jake's truck pulling into the drive.

Squaring her shoulders for battle, she started toward the door. *He just doesn't know when to give up!*

When Jake stepped inside, his face was grim. He looked around the spic-and-span doddy house with snapping eyes. "Am I interrupting something?"

"No."

"Then why didn't you answer your phone?"

"Because I saw your name on the screen."

His face flinched. He lifted his gaze to the top of her head and dropped it again, his expression burning with accusation. He swept her covering out of his pocket and slapped it on the table. "Guess you don't need this."

Her cheeks heated.

"She's a frail old woman," he admonished.

"How dare you come blaming me without giving me a chance to explain what happened?"

"You're the one who ran. You let her alone with scissors? What were you thinking?"

Katy placed both hands to her temples. "Okay, stop. Just sit down. Listen to my side of it."

He hesitated.

She tilted her head to the side impatiently, "Isn't that why you came?"

He brushed past her and strode into the living room. She wasn't expecting to win him over, but she wasn't about to let him leave without defending herself. She followed him and sat at the opposite end of the leather sofa, keeping an awkward distance between them.

She folded her hands on the lap of her dark skirt and painstakingly conveyed the entire story. Surprisingly, he didn't interrupt. His expression had softened when she told him about swinging with his grandma, but it hardened again as the story continued. "Then you burst into the room, and you know the rest," she finished.

"But how did she get the scissors?"

He was one-tracked. Katy shook her head. "I'm not a fool."

He lifted a brow.

"I don't know. Maybe she slipped into the living room. Maybe she was pretending to sleep. Honestly, it's almost like she was testing me, playing me."

He rolled his gaze toward the ceiling.

Katy insisted, "You know as well as I do that the covering was once important to Minnie. If she were in her right mind, she would want us to keep it on her head."

"You can't control the congregation's vote, so you control someone too weak to defend herself."

"Minnie may be small, but she's not weak. My face has the bruises to attest to that. And you won't find any bruises on her!"

Jake studied her face, perhaps seeing the bruises and scratches for the first time. His voice calmed. "God knows my grandmother's heart. After years of service and faithfulness, do you think He's going to reject her now when her physical mind has grown senile? She's our family. It's our responsibility to keep her safe and happy. And if she doesn't want to wear her covering, then so be it."

Were they going to encourage her to become an actress, too? She pushed the bitter thought aside and faced the truth. She had failed miserably, neither keeping Minnie safe nor happy. And she wasn't part of their family. Jake and Ann had the right to decide what was best for Minnie. Feeling the depths of her failure and desperation over what she'd done that might never be set right again, Katy slumped, resting her head in her hands. A grievous mistake. So many mistakes. Her shoulders convulsed uncontrollably.

Within seconds, she felt Jake's arms drape across them, sheltering her. She closed her eyes, inconsolable, not knowing how to make things right. Unconsciously, she curled into the comfort of his embrace.

"It's okay," he murmured again and again.

When she opened her eyes, his face hovered over hers, lined with empathy.

She squirmed then froze. When had she crawled into his lap? His hands cupped her face, caressed it. "Katy. Katy," he whispered.

"I'm sorry." She tried to sit up, but he stayed her.

"Me, too," he breathed into her ear.

She nuzzled into the crook of his neck, slid her arms around his waist, and rested there, not knowing what else to do until a creaky door and a surprised *Whoa!* brought Katy to her senses. At Lil's voice, Katy tried to leap off Jake's lap, but his arms tightened and firmly held her in place.

"Don't mind me," Lil chirped, walking past them and disappearing into the bedroom.

Katy groaned in the crook of his neck. "What else?"

"Be still," he whispered. "I'm not letting you up until we understand each other. I lost you once, and I won't do it again."

She looked into his eyes. "You're not angry?"

"No."

She gently bit the inside of her cheek. "I handled it all wrong. Do you think Ann will forgive me?"

"Yes." His voice was low and soothing.

"Minnie?"

He smiled and shrugged. "Don't know what's going through her mind."

Just then Katy remembered something. She wiggled her arm free and reached into her pocket for a small container of her homemade hand cream. "I meant to give her this. For her cracked fingers. Will you take it to her?"

With reverence he stared at the small Tupperware container in the palm of his hand. His voice grew gravelly. "Oh Katy."

CHAPTER 27

Katy watched Mr. Weaver walk to the front of the sanctuary, and her gaze went to the plain wooden cross on the wall behind him, a humble symbol of the Lord's ultimate sacrifice. She hoped today's special meeting addressing the head-covering ordinance would be God honoring.

Lil sat to Katy's right, whispering to Mandy. On Katy's left, Megan fiddled with her purse strap, no doubt nervous for her father and well informed of the many facets of the issue.

Mr. Weaver cleared his throat, and the congregation quieted. He held up his left arm and pointed to his watch. "The board of elders has elected to allow one hour for discussion, and then we will conclude the meeting with a vote. Women are invited to give their opinions on the matter. Keep your comments short. Everyone will be allowed to speak no more than twice per household to avoid any heated personal debates. Who will begin?"

A young mother stood up with a toddler straddled on her hip. He squirmed and swatted at her face, poking her eye. Blinking, she handed him down to her husband, who was seated beside her.

"Yes, Sister Irene."

"I think we should wear the covering because it's like baptism. A symbol that reflects an attitude of heart and spirit, one of love and submission and obedience to God."

The congregation remained quiet, and another woman shot to her feet.

"Sister Terri."

"*Symbol* is the key word here. But home's a private sanctuary. I don't need to wear a symbol at home. I don't have to prove anything there." She glanced fondly at the tall, thin man beside her. "Simon knows my heart. God, too. That's all that matters."

Irene stood, holding the baby again, this time patting his back. "It's not about proving anything. It's about honoring God's order. The design of the body attests to it. Men are designed to lead. Women nurture." She cradled her little boy into her arms to demonstrate her point. He reached up and batted her face. She rubbed her face into his playful arms and sat back down.

Next Mandy stood. "I'm not opposed to wearing a covering, but if we're going to be biblical, why not wear something that actually covers, like a larger veil?

Mr. Weaver recognized someone at the far side of the room, who had been trying to get acknowledged earlier. Katy strained to see who had stood. Lori was a single woman, self-educated, and rumors were that her learning included how to use the Internet for other than business purposes. Her sisters had all married into a higher church. She was also the church librarian. "I say it's all a principle. The actual cultural practice is old-fashioned and not applicable to today when women hardly even wear hats any longer. I love the people in this congregation. You are my family. I'd hate to have to move to a higher church because of this little piece of organdy."

Katy stifled a gasp, and Megan touched her hand, whispering out of the side of her mouth. "She'll leave if this doesn't go her way."

It would be sad to have to replace her in the library, and she was an excellent quilter, too. An elderly woman stood, leaning heavily on the pew before her. "I've never talked in church before. But I've prayed over the years for most everyone here tonight. Or at least one of your loved ones." She took several deep breaths. She had severe asthma, and speaking was difficult. "You probably think I'm old-fashioned, but I've seen a lot of changes in my day. And change is not necessarily good." After several wheezy inhales, she said, "The church ordinances were put there for a reason. We—"

Beside her Lil rolled her gaze heavenward.

The woman spoke longer than was necessary, as if she took to being in the limelight, making the entire congregation uneasy with her struggle to breathe and her incessant rambling. Mr. Weaver grew antsy, moved to the head of the center aisle. Eventually she got around to her point. "We know that we are not to conform to the world. Once the prayer covering goes, it's only a matter of time until we will blend in with mainstream society."

"Mainstream?" Lil whispered. "Where'd *she* learn that word?"

"Probably reads the newspaper," Katy replied.

Next a man spoke. "Just as every action we perform throughout the day is a choice that reflects our relationship with the Lord, I consider wearing the covering a personal choice, not something to be forced. Just like salvation." He sat down. For this meeting, couples had been encouraged to sit together instead of taking separate sides of the room as was customary during regular church services. Now his wife nudged him. He popped back up. "And the style of the covering should be personal choice, too." He started to sit and popped up again and grinned. "Long as it's not a baseball cap."

Titters filled the auditorium. Everyone realized that last tidbit was the only original part of his spiel.

"Anything more to add?" Mr. Weaver asked, with a teasing glint in his eyes.

The speaker shook his head and crossed his arms. His wife leaned into him with a proud smile.

Then one of Megan's professors stood. He spoke clearly, enunciating every word as he might in a classroom when he wanted to make a point. "Free choice? As in women wearing male attire like blue jeans? As in abortion? Or feminism? Or perhaps women ordination?"

A second collective gasp resounded in the sanctuary. All those issues seemed far-fetched, even to Katy, but she respected him for reminding them of the pressures of society.

Her own experiences lately had shown her how easy it was to get pulled into worldly ways. She wanted to remain in God's will. The shelter of His wings was the only place where one could find stability and safety. Minnie came to mind. God hadn't prevented her from getting Alzheimer's, but when swinging, she'd been aware of His presence, even joyful.

Katy considered her most recent encounter with Jake. When he'd held her and comforted her, she'd felt safe, yet tried to jump off his lap. But he'd clamped his arms tightly and lovingly until she'd submitted. They had resolved their problem. Was that the meaning of submission? Did it bring a woman to a better place? And wasn't the covering submission to God?

The elder in charge of the meeting looked at his watch. "There is time for a few more comments."

Katy had butterflies, yet her opinion welled up inside her and threatened to spew forth. But she didn't know if she could express what she understood in her spirit. Like many of the others who had not made the best impression, she'd never spoken up in church. She might even hurt the cause. Many of the husbands sat red-faced, grim-mouthed. But she didn't have a husband. Jake was present. Ann, too. If she spoke, would they be reminded of the recent covering incident?

The next speaker was another man. He read the long passage of scripture in Corinthians. Katy felt like he was stealing from the congregation's discussion time, for they had already covered the scripture several times in the course of Brother Troyer's sermons. She tried to calm herself, to listen. She tried to remain open-minded. To silently pray. But after the man sat down, she found herself on her feet.

"Yes, Sister Katy," Mr. Weaver said gently.

"I—" She closed her eyes a moment and swallowed, trying to put her thoughts into a short summary. The image of God's sheltering wings shot into her mind again, along with the scripture she'd just heard. "But we are to wear the covering on behalf of the angels. According to the scripture just read, they are present in this room." She paused. "Right now." Nothing else came to her mind so she sat.

Silence prevailed for a long moment. She dipped her head and stared at her skirt, thinking she had not expressed her opinion logically. Megan took her arm in support. The silence prolonged. And amazingly, nobody else stood. Her heart drummed inside her, for she wondered what everyone was thinking. Still nobody spoke. She slowly raised her head. Across the sanctuary, several heads were bowed. A rush of shivers passed over her.

Then a sweet note filled the silence, and she turned toward its source. One of the women had started to sing from her pew. Her words rang pure and sweet wafting over the otherwise silent room: *"Angels from the realms of glory, wing your flight o'er all the earth."* Katy joined her voice to the rest of the congregation's. *"Ye who sang creation's story, now proclaim Messiah's birth; come and worship, come and worship, worship Christ the newborn King."*

At the end of the song, Mr. Weaver spoke in a reverent tone. "I believe the angels are observing our meeting. In the awe of this holy moment, let us pray." His prayer held reverence and worship. A few *Amen*s sounded afterward.

He looked over the congregation and explained, "If the vote to keep the present headdress ordinance does not pass, then the elders will appoint a committee to write a new ordinance. That one will be brought to the congregation for a vote of approval. Let us take our vote now regarding the original ordinance. Remember, only church members are allowed to participate. All those who wish to keep the head covering ordinance as it is, please stand."

Katy stood. Megan and Lil both remained seated. But Katy joyfully noticed a large number of men and women stood with her. After they were counted, Mr. Weaver asked them to please be seated. Then he said, "All opposed to the present ordinance on the headdress, please stand." Lil and Megan stood, and a lump of despair and unbelief filled Katy's throat when she saw that the opposing side was equally represented. Her heart drummed inside her as she waited for the count to be concluded.

"Be seated." Mr. Weaver coughed into his hand. "The opposed have it. The ordinance will be amended. This meeting is now adjourned."

Stunned to silence, the congregation slowly rose and, Quaker-like, filed out of the meetinghouse. The winning side did not gloat, and the losers did not protest. Generations of practicing nonresistance came to the fore and governed the congregation's actions. Everyone seemed to understand that it was best to just disband until everyone had time to pray over the elders' decision since it was such a controversial matter. Katy followed the suit of the others, but inside, she felt turmoil. Soon the turmoil turned to anger.

When they'd reached the parking lot, Megan said, "I want you to know that I stood because I believe the only way we can keep the congregation from splitting is to allow everyone to make their own decision. I'm sorry. I know it hurt you. I hate to go, but I've still got homework."

A black veil shuttered Katy's vision at the glib explanation. "Bye," she mouthed, woodenly.

As she and Lil walked toward the car, she was pleased Lil made no small talk, and even more pleased to note that nobody unpinned their covering in the parking lot. She had a mental picture of what Megan said happened with caps at graduation ceremonies.

"Katy, wait up."

She halted, squared her shoulders. She wasn't feeling up to small talk, even with Jake, who knew where she stood on this matter.

"I'll wait in the car," Lil said softly.

She nodded and turned, unable to fake a smile.

"I'm sorry." He took her hand.

Chapped and ungloved, she felt his touch on her bare skin. She'd been too shocked to remove her gloves from her purse. He rubbed his thumb across the top of her fingers, and she almost warmed to the physical contact. Yet she resisted, unable to give in to defeat.

"It should make Minnie happy," she said sharply.

His hand fell away at the cruel remark. The shock in his expression sent a pang of regret through her. "Katy," he said sadly.

"I'm sorry. I don't know why I said that. I just can't deal with this."

He cast a quick glance over his shoulder and stuffed his hands in his jeans pockets. "Can we drive into New Rome, get some coffee?"

"I don't think so. I'm not good company right now." She longingly glanced toward the car. "Lil's waiting." She knew she should invite him over to the doddy house, but she really wasn't in the mood. With that, she turned away from his hurt expression and walked across the crackling parking lot. Only headlights broke the darkness, each vehicle heading off to their solitary places.

CHAPTER 28

On Monday morning, Katy tossed her cell phone on the nightstand, then quickly grabbed for a Kleenex. She sneezed twice, her eyes welling up in tears. "Ugh."

Lil perched on the edge of Katy's bed. "How did Tammy take it?"

"She wasn't pleased I called in sick. She asked if I could come in tomorrow instead, if I was feeling better. I do need the money."

Lil nodded sympathetically. "Here's coffee. Maybe it will help. I'm going to make a big pot of chicken noodle soup. It'll be ready in a couple of hours, and you can sip on it all day. And I'll even clean up the kitchen."

Katy took the coffee with little strength to protest. "Thanks."

"Hey, you know how we've been hoping for a chair for the living room?"

After taking a cautious first sip of her coffee, Katy nodded.

"My mom's willing to give us her green-striped armchair. And if you agree, I can get Jake to haul it over."

"Why is she willing to let it go?"

"Well, you know how she's been moping around ever since the fire?"

Katy nodded.

"Her birthday's coming up, so Dad told her to pick out some new furniture. He wants her to get a recliner-rocker that's just her size. He's worried about her."

"I was sorry to hear that she resigned from the hostess committee."

Lil's shoulders sagged. "We're all worried about her. We've never seen her so depressed."

"I know the fire's bothering her, but do you think empty-nest syndrome has anything to do with her despondency?"

Lil's eyes widened. "You think? I guess I was her baby. Maybe I need to visit her more often."

Katy crooked her mouth in mock deliberation. "Nah. I can't imagine why she'd miss you. Can't say as I would."

Lil's mouth flew open, and she countered, "If you weren't sick, I'd make you eat those words. I know how ticklish you are."

"But I am so sick right now." She popped a throat lozenge in her mouth and glanced at the tropical turquoise wall and longed for summer. It had been a long, hard winter in her soul. And she was growing weary of it. She sighed and took another sip of coffee. "Yuck, those two don't mix."

Lil chuckled. "Dummy. So it's okay to take the chair?"

"Of course. It will add some color, too. Though without two chairs, I suppose we'll fight over it."

"You bet we will. Just like everything else." Lil studied her a moment, and then ventured, "I haven't told you, but I'm sorry for you, about the outcome of the head-covering vote. But at least you'll be able to still wear yours. That won't change."

"It is a symbol. I feel like Megan's professor. That without it, we'll just become part of the world."

"I don't want to argue, but if it's a symbol and someone's heart isn't really in it, then it makes them feel like a hypocrite. That's how I felt. That's not good, either. You know how Jesus hated hypocrites."

She knew, because sometimes she felt like one, too. She'd felt like that after the ballet. "I know. I'm surprised you're still wearing yours."

"I figured it would break your heart if I didn't."

Katy saw the caring in Lil's eyes. It brought back a memory flash.

That first summer at camp. In one of the group games, Lil had taken a different trail from Megan and Katy. They'd needed to pair off, and Lil had gone with one of the Mennonite girls who wore shorts. It was a scavenger hunt and race to a designated clearing. Katy didn't remember who won, but what she remembered was the reunion and excitement at the clearing, and how they'd each shared their adventures.

She saw that's how it was with them. How it always would be. They were always going to go at the goal from a different path. Her throat thickened, whether from the cough drop or her emotions, she wasn't sure.

She whispered, "Bend down."

"Huh?"

"Just do it."

Lil bent, and Katy reached up and unpinned Lil's covering. Lil straightened, her eyes round. In a sudden rush of emotion, she hugged Katy.

"You're going to catch my cold."

"I don't care. I love you."

"I know. But I expect to see that covering on at the church meetings."

"Duh."

"Okay, go start that soup. I need something to get me out of this bed."

Lil started toward the door, then looked back. "Thanks for understanding."

Once she was gone, Katy spit the cough drop into a small trash can and turned onto her stomach. Her own covering sat on her nightstand beside her cell phone. She punched her pillow and released her sobs.

⌒⌒

That afternoon, Katy lay on the couch, reading an inspirational romance novel, but she was jolted out of the story when the heroine used the phrase *sensational solo woman*. The heroine was bragging that she didn't need a man to find happiness. Since it was a romance novel, she assumed the heroine would change her mind somewhere in the plot. Still, she paused to toy with the idea. Could she remain single and be happy?

It was the Mennonite way for a woman to prepare herself for marriage and children. It was presumed that every woman sought fulfillment in wifely duties and motherhood. She'd always gravitated toward that end herself, dreaming of one day marrying Jake or after they'd broken up, some other godly man.

Much like the heroine in Katy's story, Lil scoffed at the idea of a man fulfilling a woman. Lil liked guys, all right, but she was super-independent for a Conservative girl. During the church's recent series on relationships, Brother Troyer had made it clear that fulfillment came from the Lord, not marriage. Perhaps that's where this story was headed. Her interest piquing, she turned the page and started reading. But seconds later, she was interrupted again, this time by a knock at the front door.

"Come in," she croaked, then clutched her neck. Realizing that nobody could hear her raspy voice and that Lil had locked the door, she stuffed her feet into slippers and shuffled off to see who was calling.

"Jake," she said, staring through the cracked door with surprise.

Dressed in his work clothes, a dusty T, and sweat-stained baseball cap, he said, "Yikes, you okay?"

Katy mumbled, "Fine thing to say to a woman," and turned to shuffle back to the living room. They'd only talked once since she'd been rude to him in the church parking lot. The phone conversation had been another attempt to patch their tempestuous relationship. She sank back on the couch, and looked up at him. "This is a house of germs, you know."

He gave a wave. "I never get sick. Too ugly."

She couldn't resist the grin that belied that preposterous remark. "Real ugly," she added.

"I've got the chair from Lil's mom."

She sat forward, "Great!" Then, involuntarily, her hand clutched her neck again.

"Can I leave the door open for a minute?"

"Sure. You need my help?"

"Nope."

She soon heard a *plunk* in the kitchen. Then the door closed. Then a shuffling, and he manhandled the green-striped armchair into the room, lowering it in a vacant place off to her right. "Where you want it?"

"Move it about three feet to your left. Though we both know Lil will change it later."

He chuckled, moved the chair, then flung himself down. "Nice," he said, leaning back and making himself at home. Then suddenly he jumped up. "Oh sorry. Forgot how dirty I am. I came straight from work."

"You're fine," she said uncharacteristically, too weak to bother with protecting the chair. "I could use some company."

He glanced at her novel and sat more tentatively on the edge of the chair. "Wish you weren't under the weather. I'm playing basketball later. Could use a fan."

She thought about his flamboyant dunks. "Yes, I suppose you could."

"Next time." He took off his hat, set it on his lap. His wavy black hair stuck up in disarray, and she figured with her bed head, they made a pair of bookends about now. He fiddled with its brim. "We're good. You and me. Right?"

She gave him a wry smile. "I'm tolerating you pretty good, yeah."

He grinned. "Here it is, then. Mom wanted me to ask you if you'd like to clean for her."

Katy grew serious. "Yes, but. . ." Her voice softened. "As you know, watching Minnie is a full-time—"

"She'd take Minnie with her. She knows Gram is a handful and thought that arrangement might work better. Mom could use the help."

"Of course, I'll do it. I'm just relieved that Ann would still want me."

"She does." He grinned. "So do I."

CHAPTER 29

The elders of the Big Darby Conservative Mennonite Church came up with their revised head-covering ruling and took it to the congregation for a vote. The new decree stated that a woman should wear a head covering of an unpretentious style to public meetings of worship and prayer. It was approved. Outside of that, the wearing of the head covering was a personal matter for a woman. Or if married, between a couple.

The new ordinance held no surprises, and neither did Katy's interpretation of it. Since she'd became a Christian at church camp all those years earlier, prayer had become a natural habit for her whether it was congregational prayer, devotional prayers, or one-word prayers of praise or agony shot heavenward at various unplanned moments throughout the day. And she wasn't going to be caught uncovered and unable to commune with God whenever she pleased or needed. The only time she removed her covering was when she showered or slept. She figured the water would be her covering in the shower, and her bedding would serve at night. She'd taken to heart her own mother's advice on those two exceptions. As far as Katy was concerned, she was covered. The Lord knew her heart, and she was set on doing her part to please Him.

After the official vote, she determined to put the painful issue out of her mind. She didn't want to stir up coals of anger against her church family who had disappointed her by voting down her precious tradition. There was nothing left for her to do but tamp down her feelings. It was the nonresistant way, the Mennonite way.

Even though Katy had initiated that moment when Lil quit wearing the covering around home, sometimes Lil's uncovered head still shocked her and caused a niggling of anger to resurface. When that happened, Katy rehashed their conversation and forced herself to consider Lil's point of view. She didn't want her friend to wear it hypocritically. But as the days passed, Katy found it easier just to stuff her feelings.

Even so, the first time she went to clean the Byler residence, she primed herself to be ready for the unexpected. If the female members of Jake's family were bareheaded, she would simply disregard it. Jake had already explained how they felt about Minnie, and as for Ann, it wasn't Katy's place to fret about her decision. She needed to let it go so that it didn't interfere with her fragile relationship with Jake. She determined to allow nothing to go wrong like it had the last time she'd watched Minnie. This day would be all about mending bridges and restoring relationships.

It was a pleasant surprise then, when upon Katy's arrival at the Bylers, both Ann and Minnie wore their head coverings.

Ann acted first, hesitantly drawing Katy into a quick hug. "Thank you for coming. I'm happy we didn't scare you away."

"I'm sorry it ended so badly, the other day. I guess I wasn't prepared for"—she glanced over at Minnie, whose head was tilted, intently trying to follow their exchange.

"Let's just put it behind us." Ann suggested. Then she brightly added, "Today Mom and I are going shopping at the discount mart and then meeting Erin for lunch at Der Dutchman."

Minnie spoke up, "I'm having raisin pie."

Katy smiled at the older woman's enthusiasm.

As they slipped into their coats, Ann cast Katy a final glance. "I feel guilty going off to have fun and leaving you to do my work."

"Don't. You need to do something fun. I'm sure Minnie does, too."

Ann gave her a few quick instructions, and once they'd gone, Katy brought her own cleaning supplies in from the car. In most instances, she preferred her homemade mixtures to anything store-bought. She took a quick walk through the house before she decided where to start. The kitchen was all Ann, but as soon as she left that room, the house carried Jake's presence. A pair of his jeans lay folded beside an armchair, waiting to be mended. She forced her mind away from his tight jeans and the man who wore them.

She noticed a handmade magazine rack. In it was a *Fine Homebuilding* magazine. Her heart warmed to think of Jake's love for building things. He was like her father in that regard. When Jake had brought their new chair to the doddy house, he'd ended up staying much longer than either of them had planned. In fact, he'd almost forgotten about playing basketball. They'd eaten chicken noodle soup, and he had even joined her in a game of Concentration, Jake denying he'd get sick. She wondered now if he had.

He'd talked about his dreams of starting his own business and getting his general contractor license. He told her he was going to be a hands-on boss, doing some of the work himself. At least while he was young and able. He thought it would allow him to keep better tabs on the construction process and cut down on mistakes and wasted materials. This, in turn, would allow the job to be more economical for him and the customer. It was his desire to put out a quality project. He thought that by hiring other Conservative men, who weren't money greedy, they could build at a fair price. A quality house at a fair price. And when he got older, he wanted to design new homes. He'd explained about the software that helped with home design, and her distrust of computers had lessened one notch. She smiled, dusting the magazine and replacing it.

After cleaning the bathroom and kitchen and then dusting and sweeping the downstairs, she moved into more dangerous territory, the upstairs bedrooms. Jake's room wasn't on the list, and she remembered him once teasing her that he wouldn't want her cleaning his room, yet she felt drawn to it as powerfully as she was to the man himself.

In all the times she'd been at his home, she'd never been inside his room. She ventured up now. She noticed a bathroom and another room with a closed door. Feeling the prickles of wrongdoing, she glanced over her shoulder then turned the knob. When would she ever get another opportunity to learn more about him? She pushed.

Stepping into the room, she smiled and closed her eyes, letting the scent of sawdust and soap waft over her. After a moment of basking in his scent, she opened them and surveyed his domain. His bed was made, yet the blue-and-white quilt lay uneven and lumpy. Definitely could be a twin to Lil, she smirked.

He had a desk beside the window. She moved to the blue-draped panes and peered down at the fields below. A crow flew down and landed on a furrow, poking at something with his beak. He looked in her direction and cawed.

They were fields that Jake hadn't wanted to farm, glad his brother Cal and his uncle had taken over that responsibility, yet this was the view that Jake had gazed upon ever since he'd been a little boy. She took it in now, the barren fields, the barn, the road. She imagined his truck leaving the drive, heading to—she broke off her thoughts because she didn't want to remember his falling away. Not while they were mending their relationship.

No, she didn't want that. But what did she want? She wanted to trust him. To love him. To marry him and raise a family that never veered from God's truth. That was what she wanted. She'd always wanted that since she could remember. But she'd been denying it for the past couple of years. She'd been denying her innermost longings. No wonder she'd been miserable.

There were deeper facets to his personality now. She hoped with the new Jake her dreams could come true, after all. She wondered how many times he'd stared out this window, thinking about his dreams. Hadn't Jake talked about new beginnings? And with God, all things were possible.

The crow flew off, and she turned away from the window. Some rubber-banded blueprints were propped up beside his desk. She skimmed her palms over them. A laptop computer was open on his desk. His screensaver flashed galactic patterns, galaxies, and stars. It was beautiful. Another surprise. She hadn't known he was interested in astronomy. Her curiosity suddenly piqued. What else didn't she know about him?

She glanced at the door, feeling a bit guilty for snooping, but crossed the room to his nightstand. Her breath caught. He had a Bible, one she recognized, and sitting on top of it was a framed picture of two girls. She froze. Then slowly, she picked up the photograph and looked closer at the two young women. Across the bottom of the picture was cursive writing:

Love always. I'll never forget those steamy, starry nights. Just Jessie

Feeling hateful thoughts toward the girl with her arm around Jake's sister, Erin, Katy stared long and hard at the woman who had caused her such grief. She resembled pictures she'd seen of fairies, petite, slender. Her hair was black with white-streaked bangs. It was short and spiked. Her eyes were bright blue and lined with black pencil. So different from Katy's own dark ones. She wore bright lipstick. While Katy was plain and natural, this woman was worldly. Katy drew the photo closer, and her jaw fell open. She wore a nose ring. Katy's eyes narrowed, taking in the tight jeans and slim, yet appealing silhouette. A black lacy tank top revealed a tattoo on her upper arm. The other arm was wrapped possessively around Erin. A wide belt emphasized her figure. Both girls were exhibiting a seductive pose.

Katy felt stricken, as if she couldn't breathe, would never breathe again. She felt as if Jake had taken a spike and driven it through her heart and all her will to live had poured out the open wound.

She read the inscription again. Every word held intimate implications of what had passed between them. Romantic nights under the stars. Steamy even. She tried not to envision what those nights might have entailed. She couldn't stand the thought of this stranger touching Jake, kissing him, embracing him. And *Just Jessie*. What did that mean? It insinuated a lot of time spent together, a relationship so cemented that it didn't need further explanation.

She turned the despicable photograph around. Nothing was written on the back. But he kept her picture on his nightstand, on top of his Bible of all places. He probably read his Bible every night, and first he picked up the photo and looked at her. The last image he saw before he closed his eyes at night.

Jake's betrayal fell over her afresh. Darker than anything she'd ever experienced because this time there was no window left for renewed trust. No chance of making things right. No hope. He cared about this awful woman. He'd lied. He would never change. There was no future with him. And she would never be able to love anyone else. All these truths swept over her like a storm with no warning and no escape. She thought she would die. Or worse, she might live.

CHAPTER 30

Katy drove blindly, the tears streaming down her face, her car headed for the Rosedale Bible College. She had to find Megan. She couldn't face Lil yet. She had to do something to make the pain go away.

At the college, Katy hurried straight to Megan's room. The door was unlocked, but the room was empty. Katy let herself in. Impatiently, she studied the posters on the wall. The one over Megan's twin bed had bare hands stretched up, most likely toward God. It read: *He is able.* Swiping her cheeks, she wished it were that simple. She climbed into Megan's bed and curled up in a ball. Nothing was simple any longer.

"Katy? Katy!"

Katy felt something shaking her shoulder. Slowly she came out of her stupor, feeling as if she'd slept for one hundred years, but when she took in her surroundings, her memory returned along with her sense of Jake's betrayal. She met Megan's gaze. "It's over."

Megan plunked on the edge of the bed. "What? Did something happen at the doddy house?"

"No." Her voice trembled. "It's Jake."

"What happened?"

"He loves Jessie."

Megan's usually serene face furrowed around her blond brow. "Who's that?" Then before Katy could reply, Megan's eyes narrowed. "That girl from OSU?"

"Yes."

Megan looked aghast. "He told you that?"

"No. But he has her photo on his nightstand. On top of his Bible."

"I don't believe it. Wait a minute. Why were you in his room?"

Katy knew that Megan was only questioning her so that she would know how to help. "I was cleaning their house. And it's true. Jessie has her arm around Erin, like she's wiggled her way right into the family. Don't you see? He keeps her picture on his nightstand. He has feelings for her. Yet he had the nerve to tell me he loves me. He's such a rat, chasing me and acting like it's me he wants."

Megan sat in quiet thoughtfulness. Then she asked, "You love him, don't you?"

Katy nodded and looked at the floor.

Megan stood. She began to pace. "Then you're going to talk to him about this. And you're going to ask him why he has Jessie's picture on his nightstand. Maybe there's some simple explanation. The last time you guys broke up, you never talked it out. It tore you up afterward. You have to confront him and listen to his explanation."

"So he can squirm out of it?" Katy demanded angrily.

"Something's not right about this. I feel like you're missing some of the pertinent facts."

"Believe me, I discovered more than I wanted. Now her picture is etched in my memory. Tramp." Katy clenched her jaw and gripped the bed covering, allowing her jealousy to consume her.

Megan pulled up a chair and sat facing Katy. "Just because she's an outsider doesn't make her promiscuous."

Katy's mouth flew open. She'd thought of all people, Megan would understand. "You didn't see her."

Megan leaned forward, imploring, "But you can't just accuse him and ruin your relationship without knowing for sure that he loves her. Sometimes things just aren't the way they look."

"Yeah? Well, it's too late for that." Katy felt her face heat. "I left him a note."

Megan moaned. "You didn't."

Katy stared at the green comforter. "I was so angry that he betrayed me again. He told me he didn't like her that way."

Megan patted Katy's knee. "But there has to be an explanation. You said Erin was in the photo. You want me to tell you what I honestly think?"

Looking up into Megan's gaze, Katy replied, "Of course. That's why I'm here."

Megan's pink cheeks indicated that she knew Katy came because she needed a caring shoulder more than someone who would lecture her, yet she was going to do it anyway. "I think you've never forgiven him. That you'll never be able to move forward in your relationship until you quit judging him for what he's done in the past. You live in fear because you can't control the situation, and you don't want to get hurt."

"Of course I don't want to get hurt!" Katy cried in her own defense.

"It's not your job to control everything. It's God's."

Katy trembled with resentment. "That's a terrible thing to say. Especially when I'm hurting."

"But it's the truth. You don't trust God in this."

Katy stood and moved away. "Maybe."

Megan followed her. "There's something else."

Katy crossed her arms. "What?"

"You and Lil are like night and day. I've been mediating between you two for years. But did you ever stop to think that it isn't Lil who starts the arguments or works herself into a huff?"

Katy hung her head. "That really hurts."

Megan's hand pressed Katy's shoulder. "I'm sorry. I'm tired of watching you pull the world down crashing around you. It's just that you get so fired up, when a soft word could ward off so much of the distress you bring upon yourself."

Katy shook her head. "I'm not wrong about this one. Jake loves Jessie."

"Maybe so. But you need to give Jake a chance to explain the photo before throwing him into the discard pile."

That illustration gave Katy pause. Not only discarded, but *forbidden* in big bold letters across his name on a paper in her Bible. She narrowed her eyes. Maybe Megan was right. She needed time to think about it.

"Do you want me to call him?" Megan asked.

⁓

Freshly showered and wearing boxers and a T-shirt, Jake padded down the hall in his bare feet. The cold medication he'd taken the moment he'd gotten home had made him drowsy. His sinuses ached, and all he desired was a tissue box and bed. Finding Kleenex in a linen closet, he plodded into his room and crawled under the covers with great relief. *Too ugly to get sick.* Yeah, right.

Earlier he had tossed his cell phone on his nightstand, and he remembered he still needed to plug it into its charger before he fell asleep. With his eyes closed, he reached over and patted the top of the nightstand. But his fingers touched something out of the ordinary, something out of place.

He propped up on his elbow and frowned at a piece of paper stuck between his Bible and the photo of Erin and Jessie. The only items on his nightstand should be his Bible, the photo, and his cell phone. He kept his watch, billfold, and change on his desk, so it couldn't be a sales receipt. He didn't remember placing any paper on his nightstand.

He brought it up to his face. *We are through. I hate you. Just Katy.* He frowned, turned it over, and saw his mom's cleaning list on the other side. A shudder of dread struck him. His mom hadn't told him that Katy was coming. His pulse quickening, he read it again. He closed his eyes in agony, knowing it was about the photo that Jessie had signed similarly.

A long time ago, when he'd asked Jessie her name, she'd told him it was Jessica, but she was just Jessie. So he often teasingly called her Just Jessie. Now he picked up the photo, and although he had the inscription memorized, he read it again, flinching at her pun, using the word *steamy*, and easily imagining how that had sounded to Katy. *Love always, Don't forget about those steamy, starry nights. Just Jessie.* He wasn't a fool. He understood exactly the images and insinuations that would have gone through Katy's mind. And she thought he kept the photo there because he still cared about Jessie. He moaned, shoved everything back on the nightstand, and turned his back to it. He heard a crash. *Women. Way too much trouble.*

Jake awoke to music from his cell phone. With a groan he rolled over and swiped the nightstand for it, knocking it onto the floor. As he came to his senses, he remembered that Katy was mad. Was that her calling? Muttering at himself, he stumbled out of bed, bringing half the bedcovers with him, and scooped the phone off the floor. He glanced at the phone's rectangular face, noting that the caller wasn't Katy or anybody else he had in his address book.

"Hello," he growled.

"Hi. This is Megan."

"Yeah?" There was silence on the other end. He tried to sound more civil. "Megan?"

"I thought you should know that Katy came to see me this afternoon. She was really upset. With you."

"I figured."

"You sound weird. Is this bad timing?"

"No. I've got a cold."

He could hear a feminine sigh. "I'm sorry. Anyway, I told her she needed to hear your explanation of why you keep Jessie's photo on your nightstand. I'm hoping you have a reasonable explanation?"

"You bet I do. It's not what she thinks. Thanks for sticking up for me. So. . ." He looked at the ceiling and sent up a quick prayer. *Please, God.* "Is she willing to listen to reason?"

"Maybe. You're not going to hurt her again?"

He sighed. "No. Is Katy there? Can you put her on?"

"Just a minute."

Listening to feminine protests, he grabbed up an armful of blankets and tossed the soft ball back onto the bed. Fortunately, Megan was trying to patch things up for him.

Finally, a familiar voice snapped angrily, "This is Katy."

She acted like he'd called her instead of them calling him, waking him up, too. He really wanted to snap back at her for snooping in his room—for getting him sick—but he knew that when he felt better, he'd regret it. He gentled his voice. "I got your note. But I think you jumped to the wrong conclusions."

"I thought she didn't mean anything to you." Now she sounded pouty. He could visualize her sulky lips, her smoky eyes. "I trusted you." Now she sounded heartbroken, definitely vulnerable. That clenched his heart because he knew how much it cost her to reveal her jealousy.

For weeks he'd worked at earning her trust. Now if he wasn't careful, he would lose her over a stupid misunderstanding. "Remember when I told you that Erin and Jessie became friends? That Erin was going down the same path I went? That I'd give anything to prevent that?"

"Anything, huh?"

He lay back on his pillow, disregarded her heated barb, and continued to speak softly. "I love my sister. And I worry about Jessie, too. I keep the photo on top of my Bible so that I remember to pray for them every night. It's simple as that. There's no attraction there. It's you I love. Not Jessie. That's the truth." There was a silence, and he waited.

"You love me?" He'd told her that the night at the restaurant, too.

He quirked his mouth. "Yes I do."

"But the inscription on the photo was so intimate. I was jealous."

"You love me, too?"

She paused too long.

"Sorry. Dumb question."

"I want to."

He swallowed his disappointment. He'd just lost major points on trustworthiness. Her anger and jealousy revealed that she cared deeply for him. She said she wanted to love him. That probably meant she did love him but couldn't trust him. If she wasn't ready to do that, he shouldn't push her. He might scare her away. Instead he needed to convince her of his sincerity. He needed to win her over, but not now when he felt so sick. "I wasn't too ugly after all."

"You're sick?"

"Yep."

"I warned you."

"It was worth it." Losing his battle against the drowsy side effects of his cold medicine and starting to shake with a fever, he pulled the rumpled covers up around his sore throat—that was getting more painful with talking—and off his bare feet. Shivering, he curled them up under the covers.

"I didn't know you liked stars."

He closed his eyes and managed, "Took a class in school."

Her next sentence was long, distorted, and dreamlike, and then his mouth and hand went slack.

CHAPTER 31

Katy stood in the open doorway and glared at Jake. Then she slammed the door in his face and strode through the doddy house into the living room. Behind her, the door creaked open. She heard heavy, intruding footsteps.

"That was rude." Jake's voice was laced with irritation.

"Yes, I'm rude and obviously boring," she replied. Then dropping to the sofa, she pulled a pillow onto her lap and hugged it to herself.

She felt the couch sink, and his shoulder brushed hers. "It was the cold medicine. I can't even remember what I said to you yesterday. When Megan called, I was sleeping."

She jerked her shoulder away from him. "We were discussing our relationship. Our crumbling relationship. I was baring my heart, and you started snoring. Or was that just an excuse not to have to talk about steamy, starry nights?"

He didn't speak, and finally she glanced over at him. His face was pale, stricken. He still looked sick. "You told me you loved me?"

"No, I did not!"

"Well that's a relief. I wouldn't want to miss that." He rubbed his jeans with his palms. "I vaguely remember telling you—"

"What?" She arched a brow.

He shook his head. "Never mind about that. Just tell me again why you're mad. So I can make it right."

She gaped at him. Then she spat out. "It hurt to see Jessie's photo on your nightstand. And you didn't care. You fell asleep on me."

"What is the big deal about Jessie? I told you she's just a friend."

Hugging her pillow, Katy corrected, "*Girl*friend. With whom you shared steamy, starry nights!"

"Like David was your *boy*friend. Come on, Katy. This is childish."

She felt heat rising up her neck and into her cheeks. "You know there wasn't much between David and me."

"Did you kiss him?" he demanded. Katy pressed her lips together. "And did you skate in his arms?" he asked. Her eyes narrowed painfully. Jake's voice softened. "I know how you felt when you saw the picture because I felt that way when I saw you with David."

"But I wasn't emotionally involved with him."

He eyed her skeptically. "So you want to hear about Jessie?"

She nodded.

"Fine. I'll admit to some flirting, some dancing, a few kisses, toying with the idea of a relationship, and then dismissing it. Because I knew I was in love with you. It was the whole idea of exploring the world that she was part of, but it was only a fleeting attraction."

It hurt to hear him admit what was between him and Jessie, fleeting or not, yet she also understood because it had been similar with her and David. There had been moments when David caused her pulse to race, and she had entertained a deeper relationship. Though she had wanted the relationship to deepen, it was always Jake who she loved. But had there been more between Jake and Jessie?

She needed to know. She felt her blush returning. She searched deep in his eyes, wanting to watch his facial reaction to the question. Then her heart fluttering like a caged bird seeking freedom, she asked, "Kissing? Was that all that happened between you two?"

His eyes didn't dart away in fear, but softened and pleaded for her to trust him. "Yes. That was all. I'm saving everything else for you. If that's been bothering you, I wish you'd asked me sooner."

With relief she admitted, "Me, too."

"And for the record, the steamy, starry thing was just a pun about a dud of a field trip. It was nothing romantic, just a joke because a group of us got stuck in a flash rainstorm."

She gave him a skeptical look. "Everybody knows you don't go stargazing on a cloudy night."

"Now everybody knows."

She couldn't help but smile.

"Just a class project. That's all it was, Katy. Nothing at all for you to worry about."

He pulled her close, embraced her, and whispered, "I'm yours. Whenever you're ready."

She nodded against his shoulder. "Thanks." Then she pushed away. She gave him an embarrassed smile. "So tell me about your astronomy class. And don't fall asleep this time."

꩜

Katy stood beside Jake's truck, staring at the bejeweled sky. "So that's the Milky Way?"

"The galaxy where our solar system is located," he explained. His arm was draped across her shoulders. "You're shivering. Want to go inside?"

She glanced up at him and troubled her lip, uncertain. His invitation included the use of his computer to post an Internet housekeeping advertisement.

By unanimous consent, Katy and Jake had decided it would be better if Ann got somebody else besides Katy to help with the cleaning and with Minnie. They just didn't think their relationship could stand any additional drama. But this left Katy missing a chunk of income again. And the church bulletin board had been unfruitful.

Earlier in the evening, she'd watched Jake play basketball at the Penners. On the drive home, they had discussed a popular website where people could post free ads. Since the Byler farm was on the way to the doddy house, they had pulled in and parked in the circle drive to continue their conversation.

"It's not forbidden." He repeated the same argument he'd been using all evening. "The church permits computers for business purposes." Jake's Dutch accent grew thicker when he was adamant about something, as he was now.

She had already relented that the computer was necessary for his future as a businessman. He was right that the church allowed its members to use the computer for business purposes but strongly discouraged its use as a social outlet. They frowned upon browsing the Internet just for the sake of entertainment for the same reasons they discouraged owning televisions.

"Let me show you the site; then you can decide."

The light shining through the kitchen window assured her they would not be alone in the house. "I guess."

Inside the house, there was an awkward moment when Ann acted surprised to see Katy. It grew even more awkward when Jake explained, "Katy needs to use my computer."

Ann glanced at the clock. "I guess it's not too late."

Katy felt the other woman's disapproval. "We can do it another time," she protested.

But Jake grabbed her hand and started leading her toward the stairway. "It won't take long."

"You want to come with us?" Katy threw over her shoulder.

"Sure. Let me just get Minnie situated. I'll be right up."

"Chicken," Jake whispered.

At the top of the steps, they turned right, and he opened his bedroom door and motioned her inside. She forced her gaze to his desk rather than across the room to his nightstand.

Behind them, Ann called up the stairwell, "I'll bring cookies."

"Is she nervous about us being up here alone? Or is she mad at me?"

"Just playing the chaperone."

Katy nodded, hoping that was true while Jake slipped into the chair and booted up his computer. While he was fiddling with his mouse, she couldn't resist the urge any longer and glanced over at his nightstand. To her glee, the photograph was gone.

"What did you do with it?" she asked.

He knew what she meant and quickly replied, "I took it out of the frame and stuck it in my high school yearbook."

"What about praying for them?"

"Funny. After our spat, I realized it had become such a habit to pray for Erin that I didn't need the photo to remind me."

"Of course you can pray for Jessie, too." She couldn't be that controlling. Could she?

He gave her a lopsided grin. "Thanks. Here's the site I was telling you about." He pushed back from the desk. "You sit down."

Feeling a tad nervous, for she hadn't used a computer since high school, which made it a couple of years now, she took his chair and stared at the unfamiliar screen.

"You just type your ad"—he hovered behind her and pointed at a blank space—"there."

"I see. But I'm still considering if I really want to do this." She brought up a new argument. "By using the computer, it's pretty certain anyone who replies to the ad will be an outsider."

"The church bulletin board hasn't helped you," he reminded.

"I know. I just hate using the Internet."

"If you get work with an outsider, you can always quit if you get a better position."

She worried her lip. "Oh fine." She started typing, surprised when her keyboard ability returned easily:

Need housecleaning jov,

"Oops." She backspaced and typed again:

job, one or two days a week. Experienced with references.

She paused and glanced over her shoulder. "Now what?"

He rested his hands on her shoulders. "You need to type in my e-mail address."

"You have e-mail?" she snapped, instantly regretting her judgmental tone when she felt his hands tense in frustration. "Never mind. Give it to me." She typed it into the appropriate space. "Guess you're now my agent."

He gently kneaded her shoulders and whispered, "That and anything else you allow me to be."

His patience struck her. He was waiting for her to express her trust, her love. He was also waiting for her to initiate their next kiss. He could have stolen one earlier when they were stargazing, but he hadn't. For years, Jake had carried the knowledge that Katy wanted to marry him—she had blurted it out to Lil at age ten—but now he had become the uncertain one.

She grinned. "I like that." Katy filled in a few more spaces and took in a deep breath, hovering the mouse over the SEND button. "You're sure I should do this?"

He squeezed her shoulders. "Yes."

"Here goes." She hit SEND. "I did it!" She threw up her arms.

"And now the job offers will come rolling in," he teased. "So will the money."

"Ready for cookies?" Ann asked, stepping into the room.

Katy turned and rose from the chair. "Yes, they smell delicious. But do you mind if we eat them downstairs? We're finished here."

"Those look delicious," Jake said, then leaned over his computer and placed it in sleep mode.

"Yes, let's go downstairs." Ann gave a relieved smile.

As they followed her down the stairs, Katy basked in the approval she'd seen in Ann's eyes. It wasn't that Jake's family was hard to please, but just that she'd already made so many mistakes. She prayed that placing that ad on the Internet would not be another one.

~⟶⟶

Katy was cleaning at the retirement center for Mrs. Kline when she felt her apron pocket vibrate. Setting aside her dusting mop, she punched a button and placed her phone to her ear. "Oh hi, Jake."

"You want to be a working woman?"

She chuckled. "I am one. I'm working right now."

"I mean every day."

Excitement coursed through her veins and quickened her pulse. "Someone answered my ad?"

"You have three replies. Want me to read them to you?"

She gave a happy sigh, as she imagined him sitting at his computer, his broad shoulders bent over his desk while working on her behalf—a rakish agent with his tousled hair and lopsided grin. "Yes."

" 'Elderly woman needs a housekeeper for two days a week. Small house. Can pay $12 an hour. Barbara White.' And she leaves her phone number."

Katy found a pen and pad on Mrs. Kline's desk and scribbled the information. "Interesting that she needs two days with a small house. Okay next."

" 'Can hire for one day a week at $10. Widower with three children. Harry Chalmers.' "

"Not as appealing." But she jotted down his information anyway. "Go on."

" 'Looking for housekeeper. Can pay good.' No phone number. You'll have to e-mail that one back to get more information."

"Great, thanks," Katy said. "So what are you doing home in the middle of the day?"

"Figuring a blueprint. Pricing a job. A referral from Mr. Weaver."

"That's good. Guess we better both get back to work. Thanks for the information."

"You bet."

As Katy slipped her phone back inside her apron pocket, she read over her notes. She would start with Barbara. In her mind's eye, she envisioned someone sweet and kind like Mrs. Beverly, who had moved to Florida.

CHAPTER 32

Katy stared at Barbara White's tiny home in a downtown section of Columbus. The weeds thrived, but the grass was scarce. Nothing like Mrs. Beverly's picture-perfect, country club home, but Katy tried not to judge Mrs. White by her home's exterior. Maybe she was too old to do any gardening.

Through burning eyes, Katy observed that, indeed, Mrs. White was stooped, and her overall impression of the job didn't improve when she was bombarded with a strong odor of cat urine.

"Come and sit. We'll have tea." A large-boned, top-heavy woman led her across the living room's dirty carpet. The coffee table was laden with stacks of glued jigsaw puzzles. Boxes of unsolved puzzles filled every corner. A calico cat sat in a sunbeam, using its claws on a threadbare sofa.

Wide-eyed and venturing with trepidation into the kitchen, Katy was motioned toward a chair. The table had puzzle pieces spread over its surface. The sink held unwashed dishes.

Katy's stomach clenched at the idea of taking tea in the midst of such filth and rank odor. Trying to keep her nose from wrinkling, she asked, "Have you had a housekeeper before?"

Barbara straightened a few inches from her bent position and let out an uproarious bout of laughter. Then she brushed at the air in front of her face. "Does it look like it? I wouldn't be looking for one now except my kids threatened to put me in a retirement center if I don't"—she twisted her lips in a snarl—"meet their high and mighty expectations." Then she smiled, again. "Chamomile or Licorice?"

"Chamomile."

Barbara eyed Katy's covering. "Figured you for that sort."

The older woman lifted a grimy teapot from a white cookstove cluttered with pots and crusty spatulas, allowing time for Katy to assess the room. Besides the dirty dishes, filthy hairballs covered the floor, and her chair felt sticky. Something touched her leg, and she jumped. Then she heard a purr and looked down at a Siamese cat that wove in and out between her chair and her legs. She gasped when a large white Persian jumped from the floor onto the counter.

"Stay away, Goblin. Stove's hot." Barbara scooped up the cat in her arms, patting its fluffy head, shuffled a few steps, and dropped the cat. White hair floated down over the stove and teapot. "She's white like a ghost, but I liked the sound of Goblin better. Catchy, don't you think?"

"Scary." Katy nibbled her lip. She nudged the Siamese away from her ankle and, making a spur-of-the-moment decision, stood. "How many cats do you have?"

Barbara's gaze skittered nervously from the Siamese to Katy. "Only three. And Sergeant spends most of his time outside. They're sweet little kitties. You'll see."

"This isn't going to work out for me."

"I expect it's the smell scaring you off, but if you keep up the litter box more regular than I do, that should fix that problem. I can't smell it, but my daughter says it's bad."

"I'm sorry." Katy shook her head and started toward the door. She wasn't going to get herself in a fix like she had with Tammy. She would nip this disastrous job opportunity in the bud.

Barbara clambered after her, huffing by the time they reached the entryway. "You didn't even give me a chance to ask you any questions. I thought the one doing the hiring was supposed to ask the questions.

I ain't so sure I want some Amish person working for me anyway. You didn't mention that in the ad."

"I'm Mennonite. Don't forget about your teapot, Barbara."

With that Katy turned and opened the door. With a gasp, she reached down and caught the white cat just before it escaped and pushed it back inside. Behind her, she heard Barbara say, "What a shame. I liked her, Goblin. The kids ain't gonna be happy about this, either."

Katy regretted not being able to help Barbara, but there was no trying to fool herself. She was too fussy to fit in with the woman and her cats. And this had seemed like the best opportunity of the three replies.

───⌒───

Katy glanced across the truck's cab at Jake and gave a tremulous smile. After a few e-mails, they had discovered the third response to Katy's ad was a dud that ended up flooding his computer with spam. This added to her apprehensions about the entire Internet process and also about her interviewing with complete strangers.

Playing it safe with the widower, they had scheduled the last interview for a Saturday so that Jake could accompany Katy. Now his truck braked in front of a multilevel house in a nice neighborhood with huge lots.

"Wow." She leaned forward to look past Jake. She'd never cleaned such a large, beautiful home. Surely Harry Chalmers could afford more than ten dollars an hour. She determined right then she'd ask for more. Then she remembered how Jake wanted to build better homes at more affordable prices and felt ashamed over her greed. But she quickly rationalized that, after all, she needed to be able to afford her expenses.

They opened an entry gate and walked up a long brick sidewalk flanked by camellia bushes with white blooms. Jake rang the doorbell.

They heard rattling on the other side of the door. Then little footsteps and a youngster yelling, "Daddy! Daddy!"

When the door opened, a tall, good-looking man in jeans and a polo shirt greeted them. One of his hands rested on the red head of a preschool-age boy. Harry Chalmers glanced at Jake and then at Katy's covering. His eyes crinkled. "You're Katy?"

She made the introductions, explaining that she'd brought Jake along as her escort.

"With the way the world is today, I totally understand. Come in."

The entryway was impressive, two stories high with an iron-and-glass chandelier hanging from a domed ceiling. There were two armchairs, a table, and a large mirror. She looked up at the chandelier and wondered how she'd ever clean it. They went into a large great room and sat in dark leather furniture that was grouped around a fireplace and entertainment area. Katy had never seen such a huge television. The room was dusty, but not as cluttered as Tammy's home usually was.

Her gaze rested on the little red-haired boy who was still plastered against his dad. The child's stare had never left Katy.

She placed her references on the coffee table that separated them and folded her hands on her dark skirt. Harry Chalmers briefly scanned the page and nodded. "I just need the normal stuff. I don't even know what that is. I haven't done any cleaning since—" He broke off. "I'm a bit of a perfectionist, so I hate the house like this."

It seemed his loss was recent. Katy gladdened to hear that he was the type who would keep things orderly. "I could clean your house in one day, but it would be a long day, and I'd need to rotate some of the cleaning. But $10 is low for this size of house."

He studied her, his gaze slowly raking over her entire body as if trying to decide if she was worth the money. She tensed, instinctively knowing that he was using the wrong gauge. The uncomfortable moment was broken when an older girl, about Addison's age, called down from the stairway, "Is Mommy here yet?"

Harry's face colored. "Not yet, sweetie."

The little red-haired girl started down, one small hand gliding along the wood hand railing, the other dragging a wheeled, pink-handled backpack behind her, allowing it to bump awkwardly on each step.

Katy considered the implications of the little girl's question. Had her interviewer been married twice? She searched his face and then quickly scanned the room for photos, trying to piece the puzzle together.

Next, the doorbell chimed.

"Excuse me." Harry Chalmers rose. His son took a fearful look at Jake and churned his little legs, running after his dad.

Once the family had left the room, Katy looked at Jake and shrugged. He seemed as uneasy as she. From the entryway, angry voices carried into the great room. Jake patted her hand. The voices escalated.

"But I want to go with Mommy, too," the little boy begged.

"No, it's not your turn today."

Then an older boy, whom they hadn't seen yet, entered the room from the direction of the entryway. He was almost as tall as his father and wore jeans and a black T-shirt. He was using an iPod and halted when he saw them sitting on the couch. Then he hitched up his backpack and strode past them with a curious look. Once he reached the stairway, he bounded up to the second level and disappeared, but Katy heard him slam a door.

The situation grew increasingly uncomfortable with Harry and the children's mother still arguing in the entryway. The little boy increased his cries whenever his parents allowed a silent moment. It seemed Harry wanted her to take all the children at the same time, and she wanted to spend quality time with each one. Harry claimed she just wanted to make it hard for him to have any time to go out with his friends. He accused her of being jealous of his secretary and trying to control his life. He didn't sound like a grieving widower. Their youngest son's cries suddenly drowned out their conversation.

Jake squeezed her hand. "Sorry," he whispered.

"I'm so glad you're here," she whispered back. "We can't leave; they're blocking the entrance."

"Let's wait." His Dutch accent thickened. "Maybe Chalmers will enlighten us about his personal situation. Otherwise, this is not the job for you."

Before Katy could decide if Jake was overstepping his bounds by saying the job was not for her, Harry rejoined them, carrying his son. The little boy struggled in his father's arms, his face tear-streaked. When the boy calmed a bit, Harry gave Katy a sheepish grin. "Sorry about all that." Then his voice hardened. "She's such a—" But his voice broke off, as if he suddenly realized he didn't want to speak harshly of the woman in front of his son. Or perhaps in front of strangers, for the couple had been arguing in front of the children. Shoulders slumped, he tenderly patted the little boy's back.

When she felt Harry intended to let the matter drop, Katy withdrew her hand from Jake's and squared her shoulders. "Normally, I don't pry into personal affairs, but under the circumstances. . .well your ad stated you were a widower."

Harry placed his son on the floor and ruffled his hair. "Your brother's home. Why don't you scoot up and say hi?"

The boy nodded and tramped partway upstairs. Then he turned back and jutted his lower lip out. "I wanted to go with Mommy." He swiped his forearm across his eyes and sullenly went up the stairs.

With a sigh, Harry sank back onto the sofa. "Okay, look. I'm not a widower. I'm divorced. I haven't been having any luck getting a housekeeper. I just thought if I implied I was a widower, it might help. I can't afford an agency. The divorce really cost me. I'm a good guy. You'd be safe working here. We need help. But I can only pay ten dollars."

Katy met Harry's gaze, unswayed by his sentimental act. "Implied? You gave me false information."

"I just thought that once you met me, you'd see I was a good guy."

She narrowed her eyes, wondering if that was what his secretary thought. Then she snatched her references off the coffee table and stood. Jake quickly jumped to his feet, and reassuringly, touched her elbow.

"I can't accept the position," Katy said. "It's not about the money anymore. But if you lied to me once, I don't feel I can trust you."

"But you can trust me."

Did all men think trust could be earned so flippantly? She wanted to add that she didn't like the way he'd looked her over, either. Instead, she said, "I'm sorry, Mr. Chalmers."

He rose, following them to the door. "You're sure? I wouldn't even be here. The kids, either. You'd have the place entirely to yourself."

She hesitated. That did sound inviting. Her gaze swept over the grand entry, taking in the elegant furnishings and marble floor, but her heart sank when she felt uneasiness in her stomach and recognized the little warning voice. This time she listened to it. "I'm sorry."

Chalmers opened the door, and they stepped into the sunny March afternoon. Jake matched her hurried strides.

"Good choice. I didn't like him," he said. "I didn't like the way he looked at you. Especially after what his ex said about his secretary." So she hadn't imagined that. But while Jake intended to show his support, he made her feel worse, reminding her of how deceptive a man could be. This new peek into the outsiders' ways disturbed her peace of mind.

Jake opened the truck door for her, and she climbed up into the cab. As soon as he jumped up and seated himself behind the wheel, he went on, "We'll put another ad online. I know there's the perfect job out there for you."

"No. This isn't working out."

⸺☙⸺

Jake turned the key, and his truck rumbled to life, but he let it idle while he studied Katy. There was an edge to the tone of her voice that insinuated more than disappointment. She had shot the remark at him as if she were speaking of their relationship and not the computer ad service. As soon as she'd gotten inside the cab, she stiffened her shoulders and clenched her jaw, not looking his way but straight ahead out the windshield. No doubt, she blamed him for owning the computer that set up the failed interview.

How illogical. He'd only wanted to help her see that she needed to come out of the Dark Ages. He pulled onto the suburban street and glanced over again. Her shoulders had relaxed a bit so he tried to put it as logically as he could manage. "The point of job interviews is weeding out the undesirables. The right one will come along. There was no way of knowing that man was a liar."

She turned glittering, brown eyes in his direction. "I should have known. He's an outsider."

Again, her frustration seemed personally directed at him. "That's rather harsh."

"Is it? Or are you so close to. . .them. . .that you can't see the difference anymore?"

How did Katy always manage to turn everything inside out and hurl it back at him? "But you like your job at the Brooks. There are a lot of good outsiders, Katy. Good jobs waiting for you."

Her jaw dropped open momentarily. Then she flew into a passionate protest. "Surely you know how many struggles I've had with the Brooks' job? It's tested me in every aspect of my faith."

He quirked his mouth, trying to lighten her mood. "And that's a bad thing?"

"Of course it is," she snapped.

Her narrow-mindedness was increasingly irritating. "I disagree. It's how I found my faith."

"At the expense of others. Your little fling caused damage, Jake. How can you be so flippant?"

Her retort cut deeply. He braked for a light, hurt that she felt the need to continually punish him. He lived with the pain of his sister's rebellion and of the damaged relationship with Katy. He had already bared his past like an open book, hoping she would understand that he hadn't intentionally set out to hurt her. But Katy wouldn't forgive him or believe that he'd changed. She kept ripping open the old wounds. She would never let them heal. It was unfair.

He slapped the steering wheel with both palms, and then gripped it firmly. "You think you are so perfect, living your self-righteous life. But I'm not your puppet, and I don't want a mean-spirited woman."

Her eyes widened and her sulky lower lip dropped. Then suddenly her nostrils flared. "Right. I remember your type."

"At least Jessie was an honest person. She didn't pretend. She was kind and fun to be around. You may look good on the outside, but you have an unforgiving heart."

"Don't try to put the blame on me. You *are* just like Tammy, trying to get your own way and not caring how it affects people around you."

Jake laughed out loud in disbelief. Katy crossed her arms and jerked her gaze to stare out the passenger window. He shook his head. No use in talking to someone so stubborn and deceived. They drove in charged silence until they reached the doddy house.

He hurt bad inside because he knew this time there would be no reconciliation. They'd spoken words they could never retract. He needed to say something before she jumped out of the truck. He reached over tentatively and touched her arm.

She looked up at him, the stubborn set of her face slackened lightly, and he glimpsed something vulnerable. Somewhere in there was the woman he had once known. That was the woman he loved. He wanted nothing more than to lean over and kiss her. But she'd forbidden that, hadn't she? She'd kissed David, but she refused him. His pride swelled, and his resolve hardened. This woman was impervious, and he just didn't have the heart for it anymore, so he told her what she'd been trying to tell him all along. "You're right. It's not going to work between us. We've both changed. I'm sorry."

She yanked her arm away. "I'm sure it won't take you long to find a woman on *the Internet.* Somebody who understands you. Or maybe Jessie will take you back." Tears streaming down her cheeks, Katy jerked the door handle and jumped out. In her wake, the door slammed and shook the cab.

He refused to watch her walk away and kept his gaze straight ahead. It was all he could do not to spin his tires in the gravel. In his mind's eye, he could see her marching to the doddy house. Stubborn, foolish woman who made him furious. If he had a hammer in his hand, he would surely demolish something.

Jake drove, hardly noticing the traffic signs, his mind churning with anger and guilt. Finally he pulled over, his wheels partly on the road and partly on a sloped embankment. He no longer felt like swinging a hammer; he felt like crumbling. He couldn't talk to Chad or Cal. Guys didn't take much to weakness, weren't good at helping a guy deal with a broken heart. He'd never had one before, but he felt like he'd explode if somebody didn't help him. He tried calling Lil, but she didn't answer. For several minutes, he sat with his phone against his forehead. He tried again. Still no answer. Then he tried his sister. When she answered, he blurted out, "Katy and I broke up. Can I come over?"

"Sure. I'll meet you outside the dorm."

"Twenty-five minutes?"

"Okay."

When Jake reached the southern edge of the manicured lawns and red-bricked university buildings, he calmed a bit. It helped just to get away from the country and everything that reminded him of Katy. He pulled to the side of the road in a no-parking zone and glanced at Canfield Hall, wondering if he should text Erin.

But then he saw her standing on the sidewalk near the residence halls. When she started running toward him, he jerked his gearshift in PARK and jumped down out of the cab. Erin pulled him into a firm embrace.

"I'm so sorry," she said.

He didn't say anything. Erin knew how much he loved Katy. She'd conspired with him the afternoon of the ballet, jumping in to entertain Addison so that he could spend time with Katy. He clung tight to his little sister, leaning his head on top of hers. Just feeling the beat of her heart brought him a sense of assurance. Finally, Erin drew back, touched his cheek. "You can't park here. Can we go someplace? Wanta go get coffee?"

"No." He shook his head. "Someplace private."

"Let's go down to the lake."

He agreed, and at Mirror Lake, they found a vacant bench, but the location probably wasn't ideal. Many lovers strolled through the park, reminding him of his great loss.

He slunk forward. "It's over."

"You want to tell me what happened?"

"She'll never forgive me. She thinks I'm contaminated. Says my falling away has done irreparable damage to others." He looked at Erin, and her face had paled. Yet he needed to get it all out. "She's right. Because of me, she's changed. I've ruined her."

Erin sucked in a deep breath. "No. She's responsible for who she is. She can't blame you for that." Erin brushed his hair with her hand. "I don't understand why she can't see how you've changed."

He shrugged. "You're the one taking psychology. The thing is, I want the old Katy. It's hopeless. All we do is fight when we're together."

Erin rubbed her forehead with a ringed hand. She lifted her gaze out across the water. "This is awful," she said. "I thought Katy would take you back."

He stared at his sister, who had changed so much in the past six months. She dressed in jeans and wore jewelry and makeup. Although her hair was still long, in many ways she resembled Jessie. He grabbed her by her upper arms. "The Bible's right about one thing."

"What?" she asked, widening her eyes.

"We reap what we sow. Erin, don't let the same thing happen to you. Promise me, you won't let your falling away ruin your life."

"You're scaring me. Your life's not ruined." She cupped his face with her hands. "It's all reversible, right?"

He gently pushed her hand away. "Once I thought it was. Now I don't."

"Sure it is. Before you know it you'll be reaping the good stuff. The blessings."

"Maybe. But it's too late with Katy. And that's something I'm going to regret the rest of my life."

―⟨⟩―

Katy flung herself on her bed. Jake had dumped her. He'd begged her to forgive him, and then he'd dumped her. The cruel words he'd tossed at her burned through her mind: *Self-righteous, mean-spirited, unforgiving.* If she was any of those things, it was because he'd caused it. Still, it hurt so bad to know he felt that way about her. She hated him for putting the blame back on her. She hated herself for giving him reason to do it.

She had known from the start that she was wrong to blame him for the bad interview, but still she had gone down that destructive path. And to what end? She'd left him with no way out because she wanted to punish him. She'd brought this on herself because she couldn't forgive him. She thought she had, but she must not have, because she wanted to punish him again and again for his rejection, his betrayal. Now she disgusted him. She disgusted herself.

He wouldn't care that he'd lost her, but she would. And she would never get over him.

She bunched up her pillow and released pent-up pain and anger. She punched it and moaned. She hated him. She hated herself.

CHAPTER 33

Katy, wake up."

"Go away." Katy pushed at Lil's hand. She didn't want to wake up. "I'm staying home."

Lil laced her voice with concern. "But you never miss church."

Katy tried to focus her eyes through swollen slits. "Then today will be a first because I'm not facing Jake."

"But you can't stay in bed all day."

Katy turned her head toward the wall, wondering why not.

"I know you're miserable. Look, you gave it a shot. Now you can both move on. . .without regrets. No more what-ifs."

"That's easy for you to say. Nobody's ever dumped you. Twice."

Lil's hand retreated.

Instantly, Katy regretted her harshness. Her failed relationship wasn't Lil's fault. "I'm sorry. But he said horrible things to me."

Lil sighed and lowered onto the edge of Katy's bed. "He was only angry. We both know he's a hopeless chump."

"When people are angry, they say what they mean. And chump doesn't cover the half of it."

"Sometimes they try to lash out to cover their own hurts, too."

That's exactly what Katy had done. Lashed out at him for no reason yesterday, even when he'd only been kind. She had lashed out because of her own fears.

"You can still be friends. You were great at that."

Katy tried to imagine a brotherly relationship with Jake, one built on kindness and an intimacy gained from knowing each other so well. It would never work because one of them would flirt, and then they'd end right back where they were today. But he was Lil's cousin so he couldn't be avoided, either.

"Megan's coming over for lunch. She's made her mission-trip choice. Wants to show us her Bangladesh brochure."

Katy moaned. She wasn't interested in Bangladesh. She had her own *Bungled-mess*. But weekends were the only time she saw Megan. And Katy didn't want her to think she was mad over the discussion that had taken place in Megan's dorm. "Okay, but when she wants to patch me up with Jake again, stand with me on this. You agree we're hopeless together, right?"

Lil hesitated. "I haven't heard Jake's side yet. But it does seem that way."

Katy bunched and cradled her pillow. "I can't do this if you won't help me."

"All right." Lil nodded. "I'll back you up. But Megan won't push you."

"She might. Seems to have some honest streak going."

"You think so, too?" Lil tapped her freckled cheek. "The other day she lectured me about self-respect. Had the nerve to say that if I didn't chase guys so hard, they'd be chasing me. Like that would ever happen. She said some other stuff, too. Brought up my mom's depression. Gave me a bunch of advice." She dropped her hand. "Usually, she's not so pushy. I thought she was acting weird, too. Maybe it *is* an honesty thing."

Katy rose up on an elbow. "I'll bet she's taking some psychology class and testing it out on us."

Lil's voice grew animated. "Yes. I'll bet that's it."

Nudging Lil with her hand, Katy snapped, "Move off my bed. I've gotta hurry if we don't want to be late."

Lil jumped up and smiled brightly. "Great, I'll be in the kitchen."

—⌒○

The sermon was on spiritual seasons. The preacher brought up Dutchman's breeches—little, white, spring flowers that resembled a row of upside-down breeches on a clothesline. They represented summer's promise. He compared spring and summer to God's love and blessings. Winter symbolized the hard times. He stressed the beauty of faith in winter. Katy recalled the beauty of the barren wintry countryside when she took that dark sleigh ride with David. How long ago that seemed.

Applying the concept to her situation, she figured she was experiencing the bleakest winter of her life. Her latest fight with Jake must be dead winter. According to Brother Troyer, spring was around the corner. He claimed the key was trusting God. She thought about God and wondered if it really was that easy. Did God take a personal interest in her? Was He planning a spring and summer for her? Or was it all wishful thinking? Was He a judge, watching to see how she handled adversity?

Normally, Katy didn't like change, but living in bitter cold forced her to welcome it. She jotted down a few notes on her bulletin, thinking she should start a spring-cleaning section of her journal and incorporate the spiritual season theme.

Brother Troyer ended the sermon by challenging his congregation to trust a loving God with their winters. The idea invaded the core of Katy's heart like a live coal. As it burned deeper, she prayed, *I want to believe, Lord. Please help me.*

Before she knew it, Megan and Lil were singing on either side of her. She felt glad Lil had urged her to come to church. The sermon had given her hope, and she couldn't wait to find some time alone to pray and ask God to give her direction and shower her with an emotional-spiritual spring. She had to believe that the burning sensation she'd felt at the conclusion of the sermon was God's drawing her, wooing her.

Time after time, she had ignored God's voice. Yet He still wooed her. That was amazing.

But after the closing prayer, Katy remembered Jake. She returned her hymnal to the rack in the back of the pew in front of her and slowly turned. Her eyes scanned the sanctuary. Thankfully, he wasn't anywhere in sight. Relief flooded through her. Either he hadn't come and was at home lying in a bed of misery like she had been, or he had shot out the back at once, dreading their meeting as much as she did.

"I'm going to go find Mom," Lil said.

Katy watched her friend depart, feeling a bit forsaken. But she understood that Lil was still worried about her mom's depression. Feigning a smile, she turned to Megan. "I'll bet you're excited about your trip."

Megan's blond head bobbed. "So excited. I don't know how I'll ever wait until June."

They moved down the center aisle, maneuvered around clusters of farmers eager to get in the fields and discussing disking and planting.

Megan added, "The sermon was awesome. I kept applying it to my life. Graduating and my trip. I can't wait for summer to come so I can get to the good stuff, you know?"

Awestruck that God could use a sermon to speak to an entire congregation in a personal way, Katy nodded. "I feel the same way."

Megan gave her a curious look. "Something's happened, hasn't it?"

"Yes, but I don't want to tell you about it here."

"All right. But I hope it's a good thing. You deserve something good."

The comment struck Katy as odd. Did she? Hadn't Jake said she was self-righteous and ugly on the inside? Sometimes she felt like she was two persons, the proper one on the outside, and the enemy on the inside. How did anyone ever get that inside woman to jive with the outside one? If only Megan knew the real her, she'd realize she didn't deserve much. No. What happened wasn't good. At least not now, while she still hurt.

They shook hands with Brother Troyer and stepped into the foyer, and then Katy's heart plummeted straight to the carpet. There stood Jake next to the exit. She had a view of his profile, and he had a happy expression. She ground her teeth. Happy to be rid of her. Happy because he was talking to two girls. Her eyes narrowed, and she tightened her grip on her purse. Then she noticed with relief that one was his sister, Erin.

She felt conflicting emotions. Katy should be happy that Erin was back in church. It was an answer to Jake's prayers. But a selfish meanness arose in her that resented any kind of happiness for him today while she was hurting. At the same time, she felt ashamed.

Erin started laughing. She was dressed in her normal conservative clothing. Had Jake made all that up about her falling away? But Erin's guest was a definite outsider. Jake was staring—or more like flirting—with a blond girl. A definite outsider, so maybe Erin hadn't changed. Jake, either.

Jealousy flooded through her. How could he be able to flirt and forget her so easily? Then the blond girl moved, and Katy saw her face. The girl wore a nose ring. Katy gasped. Her jealousy reared like a wild stallion, an uncontrollable beast. Jessie! With bleached hair. Her entire hair, not just one strand.

For an instant, she stood spellbound and incredulous. The waiflike woman wore the highest spiked shoes Katy had ever seen. Her slender legs showed way too much skin, even though her skirt swirled around her calves in some clingy, flowery material. She couldn't believe the elders had even allowed her inside the doors. Her pale hair had dark roots, not natural and beautiful like Megan's. The change of hair color was why she hadn't instantly recognized her. But her clothes had given her away even though her tattoo was covered. No, she had another one low on one leg. Katy blushed at viewing such a shocking, worldly display. Her face burned to think that Jake had been attracted to this type of woman. It seemed he still was, the way he was responding to her bright smiling lips and seductive eyes. Katy longed to turn away from the display, and at the same time felt riveted to watch it play out.

She should be happy she was rid of Jake, yet she felt like ripping Jessie's hair out at its fake roots. Her eyes narrowed as she envisioned doing just that.

Then she felt Megan's touch at her elbow. "It's Erin!"

"And Jessie," Katy ground out.

Megan's face paled as she took in the significance of the scene. "Oh. And they're blocking the door."

In case her friend didn't get the whole of it, Katy said between gritted teeth. "Get me out of here." *Before I make a scene.*

But before that happened, Jake turned his gaze in her direction. He was in the middle of a sentence and stopped speaking. He closed his mouth and tightened his jaw. When he did so, Erin and Jessie turned, too, following his gaze. All three stared at Katy, and Katy stared back, feeling nothing but hatred for the three of them.

Megan's arm shot around Katy's shoulder, and she was propelled around, probably heading back through the sanctuary and out a side door, but she wasn't sure because her surroundings blurred into a swirling green that swallowed her vision. Green movements, green people, a green cross, and green shrubbery. She felt her feet moving, but all she saw was Jake and that despicable girl.

Like a drowning person, her mind struggled. Had he run straight from her back into Jessie's arms? Slowly, Katy realized that was exactly what she'd told him to do. In fact, it was her parting jab. *Maybe Jessie will take you back.*

Incoherent thoughts shot through her mind. *Spring? Darkness. Did God cause this? Or was this His warning against testing Him? Jake loved Jessie all along. Just Jessie. Steamy, starry nights with Jessie. Maybe they'd marry, and he'd leave. Please let him leave. God's not listening. Help me, God.*

Then she saw they were standing on the passenger side of Megan's car. She looked up at her with confusion.

"You're not driving like this. Get in. I'm taking you home."

CHAPTER 34

By the time they'd reached the doddy house, Katy had tearfully told Megan all about the breakup and had recovered somewhat from the initial shock of seeing Jake with Jessie. Her thoughts still skittered chaotically, but she was able to divert some of her frustrated energy into setting the table. Aware of Megan's sympathetic glances, Katy set the plates on the vinyl tablecloth. "So much for spring," she said sarcastically.

"It will come."

Pressing a firm crease into a paper napkin, Katy remembered Megan's earlier excitement over her upcoming mission trip. "I'm sorry I've ruined your news. You were so happy before—" She fumbled with the napkin.

"Don't even—"

The door burst open, and they both turned to watch Lil enter. She plunked her purse and Bible on the counter. Then she placed both palms flat on the counter, looked at them, and burst into tears.

Katy's mouth gaped, and the napkin she had been holding floated to the floor.

Megan rushed forward. "What on earth?"

"It's Mom," Lil gasped.

Katy went rigid, thinking the worst.

Lil waved a hand in front of her face. "I'm sorry. I didn't know I was going to do that. It's just. . .she won't get out of bed. My dad doesn't know what to do with her. I've never seen him so worried. So stressed."

Relief flooded over Katy that Mrs. Landis wasn't injured or worse. She'd never had to deal with anyone plagued with depression. "Has she been to the doctor?"

"No. She won't go." Lil swiped a hand across her eyes and met Katy's gaze. "I know this is such bad timing, but she needs me. I told Dad I'd come home for a while to help out and try to get Mom out of her slump."

Katy bit her lip, and her stomach knotted. What was she saying? Was Lil moving out? She searched her friend's face, looking for some other explanation, but when she saw the grief etched on Lil's countenance, she knew she hadn't misunderstood. She remembered talking to Lil about her mother's empty-nest syndrome and realized that this was probably the right thing for Lil to do. Wrong for Katy, but right for Lil and her family.

Earlier in church, Katy had thought that she'd already faced dead winter. How wrong she'd been. Within a short twenty-four hours, Katy had lost so much. First Jake. Now her roommate. Megan would soon be going off to her mission trip. It was hard to accept that Lil was actually moving out. She gripped the back of a chair, her mind searching for something to hold on to, something. . .anything stable. For in actuality, Lil was the motivating force of the trio of friends. Without her, Katy might shrivel up and. . . No, she wouldn't. She could be just as strong as Lil. Even if she was afraid of the dark and afraid to be alone in the doddy house at night. She bit her lip. She would show Jake that she was a survivor, that she didn't care if he flew back into Jessie's arms.

Matters with Lil's mom had to be serious for Lil to abandon her dream. Katy didn't blame her. But if she moved out permanently, Katy wouldn't be able to afford the doddy house. As it was, she could only afford a few more months on her present income.

Then a disturbing question shot through her mind. Was God punishing her for pursuing such a selfish dream to begin with? For testing Him? Would she end up moving back home, having failed at everything?

"I'm sorry, Katy. I saw what happened to you at church," Lil said. "The pastor's sermon was so good, and then all this happened. Where is spring in this?"

"I don't know," Katy replied.

Megan stirred uneasily. "He didn't promise us spring today. His sermon was supposed to give us hope. Remember, he said faith is the beauty of winter."

Katy and Lil exchanged glances, reading each other's minds and wanting to tell Megan they weren't in the mood for wishful thinking. Their friend couldn't relate because she didn't have any worries. Her parents allowed her to do whatever she wanted and paid for it, too. They meant well, but Megan hadn't experienced much in the line of hard work or disappointment. Megan could always say the right thing, but was it heart knowledge or head knowledge?

Yet watching her now, just her sunshiny appearance lightened the room. She was always the exquisite butterfly, the epitome of spring manifest, and who could squash her optimism? If they did, then who would be there to brighten their lives? Someday life would challenge Megan. In the meantime, Katy couldn't bring herself to put a tear in Megan's wings.

Evidently, Lil's thinking followed the same path, because she said, "Thanks." Then she looked at Katy. "I hate to leave you like this. I haven't talked to Jake, but I want to wring his neck. What was he thinking?"

Feeling her eyes narrow with a sudden surge of her own hatred, Katy tried to think of a nasty retort to describe Jake, but she got stuck in the dark recesses of her mind until Megan spoke again.

"I'll stay with Katy tonight. It's spring break! I have a meeting tomorrow about the mission trip. And I have some stuff planned with my folks, but I can stay tonight, for sure. We'll pick up your car later or tomorrow. Then maybe I can stay another night, too."

"See. I'll be fine. You need to go," Katy urged Lil with a wave of her hand. "Take lunch over for your dad, too."

Lil turned and lifted the lid off a pot of stew. "I will take some.

There's plenty for all of us. You sure you'll be alright?"

"Yes. Go."

Lil started toward their bedroom. "I need to pack a few things. I'll call you soon as I can."

Katy turned and smiled at Megan, wishing her friend hadn't volunteered to stay over, even though she needed a way to get her car. Always the optimist, Megan would make it her job to help Katy out of her grief, but all she really wanted was to crawl into bed and revisit those dark recesses of her mind. Even if she was afraid of the dark.

⁓

That night, Katy sprawled across the bed from Megan while they looked at color brochures of the Bangladesh mission project.

"Tell me about it. Everything." Anything to get her mind off herself.

"I'll be going through SEND Ministries. An acronym for Service, Evangelism, Nurture, and Discipleship. The trip is June 25 through July 11."

"That's not so long. I thought you were going to be gone all summer?"

Megan raised a blond eyebrow. "Then you haven't been listening."

Katy frowned. Had she tuned Megan out? "I'm sorry. I'm listening now."

"Forgiven. So far there's four of us going. They take up to eight. We'll be involved in English Bible camps doing manuscript studies, worshiping, learning activities, and maybe some prayer walks."

"Wow. So you're not building huts?"

"No." Megan tilted her head, studying her like she was a foreign specimen, and Katy felt ashamed that somehow she'd distanced herself from her friend, hadn't been listening to her dreams.

"If this is an English camp, what language do they speak?"

Megan smiled. "Bangla."

"Of course." Katy smiled back then tried out the word. "Bangla. Where is it?"

"In Asia, between Burma and India."

"You're kidding! I thought you were going to Africa."

Megan ruffled Katy's hair. "You're a mess." They giggled, and then Megan said dreamily, "I wish you could go with me. You could. They still have four more openings. Will you think about it?"

Katy tried to imagine herself in Asia, teaching English Bible. There was no use even considering it; it wasn't anything she felt interested in. "No. It's not for me. Strange as it might sound to you, I've never had the desire to be any kind of missionary."

Megan scrutinized her, and Katy inwardly squirmed. Some people had to carry on with life, working to pay the way for others to go do the mission work or live together in doddy houses. That's what Katy was. A worker, she rationalized. She enjoyed working. She enjoyed seeing the completion of what she'd done with her own hands. "If I ever went on a mission trip, it would have to be some kind of cleanup. Like after a hurricane or tornado or something."

Megan waved a slender finger at her. "I'll remember you said that. With Mennonite Disaster Service, there's lots of opportunities for cleanup. I'd like to do that myself sometime."

They lay back on their pillows, silently studying the ceiling, each thinking their own thoughts. Then Katy said, "I wonder how Lil's doing. I thought maybe she'd call by now."

"Let's call her." Megan closed her brochure and placed it on the nightstand. She pulled out her phone and punched in a speed-dial number. The conversation was short with Megan mostly listening. Katy heard her end with a promise to pray.

"So?" Katy prompted.

"Her mom spent the day in bed, but Lil got her to eat. Lil said tomorrow she's making a doctor's appointment for her." Megan's expression turned contrite. "She was on the other line with Jake when I called."

Katy felt as if she'd taken a blow to the stomach. "And?"

Megan shook her head. "She didn't say anything about him. But she said her old room seems strange, and she misses it here."

"I miss her, too." Katy pushed Jake out of her mind and smiled. "Honestly, at first I thought one of us would murder the other one."

Megan didn't seem surprised. She teased, "But then your nonresistant teaching brought you to your senses."

"Maybe. Mostly, I started to understand her. She has a lot of insecurities."

"I know. If only she could realize how great she is," Megan replied. Then she sighed. "We all have our insecurities."

"You?" Katy gently probed.

Megan twisted a long shank of shiny hair and shot Katy a reproachful glance with her blue eyes. "You're kidding, right?"

Stretching her arm beneath the coolness of her pillow, Katy yawned, but not from boredom. This conversation intrigued her because Megan was the one who always had it together. "But you're so gorgeous and smart."

Megan rolled on her back and stared at the lamp-lit ceiling. "This trip we've been talking about? After that, my folks expect me to find a job. You and Lil expect it, too. I'm part of that pact we made, living together and everything."

"Don't you want to?"

"Move in? Sure." Then Megan yawned. "Wow, why are those so catchy? Anyway, not the job part. I'm not lazy. I'm just scared. August. That's when I'll have to go job hunting. Yuck. I have no clue what kind of job to get."

Katy winced inwardly. If she didn't get more work soon, there wouldn't be any doddy house for Megan to worry about. "Something will turn up. Something that suits you."

"You really think so?"

"Yes."

❧

Late the following afternoon, Katy stepped into the quiet doddy house and plopped an armful of mail onto the kitchen table. After breakfast, Megan had taken her for her car, and Katy had gone straight to work. In addition to her normal cleaning, she had tackled some dreaded tasks she'd been putting off, like defrosting Mrs. Kline's ancient freezer and going through her storage boxes to locate her spring wreath.

Weary and discouraged, she glanced at the stove. Even though Lil hadn't always been home when Katy was, it felt lonely to know that her friend wouldn't be preparing their dinner. She glanced down the hall, her bed beckoning and tempting. She wanted to answer its call, curl under her covers, and sleep for at least a year. But that wasn't reality. Her growling stomach was demanding nutrition. Anyway, if she went to bed too early, she might not be able to sleep later, when the house was creepier.

She trudged to the refrigerator and found some cold roast beef. She added Swiss cheese from the local Amish cheese house, store-bought tomato, and pickles, then headed to the kitchen table.

She rolled up the dark green shade and peered outside. The trees were budding, but she lived in perpetual winter. She noticed David's shiny black sedan, and her interest perked. His car hadn't been there earlier. He certainly was a contradiction, not the nice boy her mom always raved about, but hot-tempered and still holding a grudge toward her.

She took a bite of her sandwich, wishing things weren't strained between them. She'd enjoyed his company, shared his obsession for cleanliness. That day at Megan's dorm, her friend had pointed out that Katy had a temper. She had that in common with David, too. Feeling melancholy over all that had happened between them, she wondered if she might have grown to love him if Jake hadn't returned.

She shook her head at the turn of her foolish thoughts and noticed her unopened mail. Using her table knife, she sliced through the envelope. Her car's license needed to be renewed. Great. She flipped through a spring clothing catalog, frowning at the worldly styles and wondering how she'd gotten on that store's mailing list. She turned it over to see if it had Lil's name on the address label, and an envelope fell out of its back cover.

She had almost missed it. After setting down her sandwich and wiping mayonnaise from the corner of her mouth with her napkin, she took a closer look. The letter was addressed to her. It was from Florida. She only knew one family from Florida. Sure enough, the return address revealed that the letter was from her old employer, Mrs. Beverly. Her heart sped up with anticipation, wondering if she was returning. Her hands anxious, she opened the envelope and unfolded a rose-patterned stationery that displayed artful, beautiful handwriting:

Dear Katy,

How I've missed your dear face. I don't know if you're still looking for any jobs, but a neighbor from the old neighborhood is looking for a housekeeper. She's looking for someone two days a week, and she'll probably even pay more than I did. She's a sweetheart and will be easy to work with.

The first line of the letter filled Katy with warm nostalgia, envisioning the sweet old woman sitting at her white, rolltop desk, her aged hand taking a pen from a rose-patterned cup. It brought a lump to her throat to realize that Mrs. Beverly was still concerned over her welfare. But when she read about the job opportunity, her heart leapt with excitement. Quickly she read on:

I never thanked you for your handwritten note inside the Christmas card you left us. I was so flustered that day. But I just wanted you to know that I am a Christian. Jesus was my anchor when I lost a daughter to leukemia, giving me peace and hope to continue on.

Katy hadn't even known she'd lost a daughter. Poor Mrs. Beverly. She quickly read on:

I remember how I'd wake in the middle of the night with a song on my lips, the words just what I needed to see me through the next day. The Lord has helped me to make the transition into a retirement facility. I always thought retirement centers were the end of the road, but knowing that I have heaven to look forward to, gives me joy.

With shock, Katy received Mrs. Beverly's testimony into her heart. It rang of truth. As she took it in, she felt a heat in her bosom, like

279

she had the previous Sunday at church. It was a confirmation that her past employer truly knew Jesus. The same Jesus Katy knew, for Mrs. Beverly had the same experience with Him, the reassuring songs that came in a time of despair. Surely, it was God's way of showing her that Mrs. Beverly was a Christian. She stared at the letter with a new understanding of her past employer.

> *We aren't ready to give up yet, however. We're still golfing and enjoying life and good health. If you're ever in Florida, stop in and see us.*
>
> *Love,*
Sonja Beverly

> *P.S. My friend, Betty Rucker, is a godly woman, too. But watch out for her husband, Herb. He's a hopeless tease. Here's Betty's address and phone number, 777 Springtime. . .*

Springtime? Katy's jaw gaped. God couldn't have made His reassurance any plainer had He penned it across the sky. Either God was exhibiting a sense of humor, or else He thought she needed things spelled out in a clear manner. This was her spring. This job was from Him. Another dream job, according to Mrs. Beverly, and working for a godly couple. An even better job, moneywise, than her other jobs. God had heard her prayers. Gripping the letter with both hands, Katy's vision blurred, and her shoulders shook. She didn't deserve this. She hadn't even been trusting God. If anything, she'd been blaming Him. And here was God smiling down on her.

She felt ashamed for all the times she'd cleaned for Mrs. Beverly and felt sorry for her, assuming she wasn't a Christian just because she was an outsider and did things Katy would never have the conscience to do. She remembered the embarrassing pictures on the paperback novels, and the R-rated movies. The dusty Bible. Perhaps Mrs. Beverly had kept a different Bible in her nightstand drawer? How could she have been so quick to judge? She didn't understand it all, but she couldn't doubt Mrs. Beverly's sincerity. As she looked back, she remembered how the older woman always acted with love and kindness. How could Katy have been so blind?

Bitter remorse sickened her for all the times she'd judged outsiders. How many times had she dismissed people as if they were unredeemable? Suddenly her words came to her, the ones she'd spat out at Jake and their ensuing conversation: *All outsiders are the same.* She remembered his shock. *That's rather harsh. Isn't it?* And then she had lashed out at him. *Or are you so close to them that you can't see the difference?* His description of her was accurate. *Self-righteous. . .mean-spirited. . .good on the outside. . . unforgiving.*

Katy brought her fist to her quivering mouth. *Oh God. Forgive me.* She'd been so wrong. So foolish. Crossing her arms on the table, she hid her face in their cradle and sobbed over her sins.

She saw her own ugliness, and as she prayed and asked for forgiveness and renewal, she felt God's flames of love burning through her, cleansing her. She prayed and pleaded and thanked the One who was in control. She realized that only God deserved to be in control. She'd been wrong to usurp that privilege, trying to move other people like checkers on a game board. Grievous as she felt, when she lifted her head, she felt spring bubbling up inside her.

Never could she have drummed up that much hope for the future on her own. But it now fell over her like a fresh rain. God cared. The Lord was with her. And finally, she wanted to trust Him with her life.

She wasn't sure how to do that, but God would teach her. Rising from the table with a smile, a song bubbled up inside her. She took a fresh tissue and blotted her eyes, then broke into song, not caring if she was hopelessly off-key.

She remembered how Brother Troyer's sermon had seared her heart. Then her hand stilled, and she had another epiphany. This was how Jake felt after his falling away. This was what he'd been trying to explain to her all along about the feeling of a new beginning. With that, she also realized that she didn't hate him any longer. God had removed that burden. It was like she could see him in her mind's eye like God might see him. With compassion. Not all-knowing, but with a patient love.

As she moved around the room, cleaning the table, she spoke out loud to God as if He was a friend present with her in the room. *I give Jake to You, whatever Your will is for us. I might actually be able to be his friend now. With Your help. And forgive me for my poor attitude toward Erin and even Jessie. I know You love them, too.* Then she paused when she caught movement from her side vision. Outside, David was walking to his car. She saw him glance at the doddy house, and she felt a surge of God's love toward him and a powerful urge to make things right between them. Quickly dabbing her eyes again, she ran to the door, acting before she lost her courage.

Swinging it open, she called out. "Hey, David."

He froze. Stared at her.

"Can you come over a minute?"

CHAPTER 35

Katy waited in the open doorway, her heart racing at her impetuousness yet unable to deny the prompting she had felt in her spirit.

David reached the front stoop and halted.

Katy smiled, her eyes pleading for his forgiveness.

His narrowed. His jaw hardened.

She ran her tongue over her dry lips. "I have chocolate mint ice cream. I thought maybe you'd like some."

He glanced back at his car, his expression telling her that he remembered their last conversation as clearly as she did. She knew she was opening herself to another curt rebuff.

He rolled back his shoulders. "Not really."

Lord, help me here. "Please?"

He shifted his stance. "Why?"

She shrugged. "I miss our friendship." When he still seemed skittish, she flashed him another tentative smile that came out a bit more tremulous than she'd intended.

"I heard about Lil. I guess you're real hard up for company."

"That's true," she grinned. "I have some mocha ice cream, too."

"Oh, in that case." He strode past her into the doddy house.

Wondering if she should apologize again, she got the ice cream out of the freezer and placed the containers and some bowls on the table. "Here we are."

In silence, he dipped a scooper into the round container of mocha. His hand paused. "So you miss our friendship. And?"

"Yes." Their gazes met as she tried to convey that reconciliation—not dating—was her intention.

He handed her the ice-cream scoop. "I heard you broke up with Jake."

So that was it. He thought she was on the rebound. She felt her face heat as she scooped ice cream into her bowl. "Yes, we did. I couldn't forgive him. . .until now. . .after it was too late."

"Slow down. You forgave him. After you broke up?"

She took the ice-cream containers back to the freezer and joined him at the table with a sarcastic chuckle. "Right. I need to work on my personal problems. I'm a mess. But with God's help, I plan to change. Anyway, I hate the way it was left between us. You and me."

He displayed his dimple. "Such a pretty mess."

Her face heated again. "So is there any way that you and I could, um"—she took a spoonful of ice cream, feeling self-conscious, and once it had melted in her mouth, she finished—"be friends again?"

He twirled his spoon, making her squirm. "Let me make sure I'm getting this right. You only want to be friends? Or do you want to start up where we left off?"

She couldn't help but smile at his frankness. "No. I just want to be. . .buddies. Play games, chat. I want you to flash your dimple at me like you are now, instead of your nasty scowl. I didn't like that much."

He shrugged. "I overreacted. It's no big deal anymore." Then as if it was settled, he took a spoonful of ice cream.

She settled back, relieved. After a comfortable pause, she asked, "How's Elizabeth doing?"

"Good. Better than this ice cream. How long's it been in the freezer anyway?"

She laughed and made a face. "It's awful, isn't it?" She pushed her bowl away. "We don't have to finish it."

"Too late. I sacrificed myself for friendship." He leaned back in his chair and studied her intently.

She squirmed. "Do I have chocolate on my chin or what?"

"I don't get it. You wanted me to forgive *you*. But you can't forgive Jake."

"I forgave him after it was too late," Katy corrected. She didn't explain that she'd just forgiven him an hour earlier, that she'd just had a renewal experience right before she'd invited him inside. But now that they'd made their peace, she questioned the wisdom of entertaining him inside while she was living alone in the house. She worried her lip. If he lingered, she would call Megan and ask her to join them. They could play Rook.

"So why don't you tell Jake now? That you forgive him?"

She stared at him, having lost track of their conversation. "What?"

He repeated the question.

She reasoned aloud. "Because he hates me. Anyway, he was with Jessie on Sunday."

"Who's that?"

She felt a twinge of pain. "A girl from school. I think they may be getting back together."

"That girl with Erin? Standing in the foyer?"

Katy nodded.

"I didn't get a good look at her. I was too busy looking at Erin. But Jake would never go back to her."

Looking at Erin? She raised an eyebrow. "How do you know that?"

"Because he came back to the church, and unless she changes a lot, that's not going to work out."

"Maybe he'll leave again."

"Not if he's changed."

"Maybe she'll change."

"I doubt it."

She wanted to ask him if he thought Jessie was pretty, but he'd claimed he hadn't looked at her very much. Instead she argued, "But she's friends with Erin."

"That is strange." He wore an unreadable look, one that made her wonder if he had a crush on Erin. Then he shook his head. "Forget about Jessie. You should tell Jake you're sorry."

Katy planted her elbow on the table and cradled her head in her hand. "It's over."

He shrugged. "Maybe you haven't really had a change of heart."

"Don't say that. I have so."

"Prove it."

She narrowed her eyes with suspicion. "Why are you so anxious to see us get back together? You don't even like him." She didn't want to bring up the fistfight.

"I have my reasons."

She stared at him, saw a vulnerability in his expression. Maybe he didn't want Katy to be available because he didn't want to get hurt again. Or maybe David wanted to square things with Jake so he could date Erin. Whatever the reason, he had the right to his opinion. She swallowed.

"Call him," he urged.

_____ ɔ

Loud, uplifting refrains filled the cab, and Jake tapped his palms on his steering wheel keeping time to the beat. He willed the inspirational message into his wounded spirit as he mouthed the words. Meanwhile his truck sped across miles, putting distance between him and the object of his heartbreak.

When he stopped for gas, he checked his phone, surprised to see he had messages. His heart wrenched. Three calls from Katy in the past two hours. He could only hope he wouldn't have answered her calls anyway. Two missed calls and one voice mail.

He hesitated, wondering if he should listen to the voice mail. It would be like her to leave some message saying she was sorry. If he listened, he might be tempted to take her back. He wouldn't do that again. He wouldn't weaken. He needed to move on with his life. Clenching his jaw, he erased the message. Grimly, he set the phone to vibrate and jammed it in his pocket.

Climbing back in the cab, he worked the interior lights and checked his road map. After breaking up with Katy, he'd jumped at the opportunity to get away. He needed time to heal, time to forget about her, and mostly time to resolve that he wouldn't go back to her again.

He pulled back onto the highway, sparse with traffic now, intending to go at least a hundred miles before he stopped for the night.

After another thirty miles, his radio started to break up so he turned it off. It was peaceful at that time of night with nothing but twinkling stars overhead and the occasional headlight. Up there somewhere was God. He drove on. Peace stole over him because he knew God answered prayer.

The afternoon he and Katy broke up, he'd driven straight to OSU. Erin had listened to the entire story, helping him work through it. But the most amazing thing was that God had used Jake's pain for His glory. For when Erin saw how his falling away had destroyed his relationship with Katy, the only girl he'd ever loved, and when she saw how this had devastated him, she determined that she wouldn't allow the same thing to happen to her.

They'd talked until late that night, and he had witnessed the miracle of seeing his sister repent of her rebellion. That's why she'd come to church on Sunday. And after the services, the impossible had happened. Jessie had actually stepped inside the meetinghouse, too. She hadn't come for the services, but she had come, nevertheless.

He grinned inwardly. Erin and Jessie made an odd couple, about as odd as he and Jessie had once made. But they'd met through him, and Jessie had helped convert Erin to the world. He wondered if Erin would now be God's instrument to draw Jessie. Would that be the ultimate good that came out of his repentance?

Nah. Jessie would never become Mennonite. He remembered their talks, and Jessie's arguments against the Conservative way. But she might become a Christian. He wouldn't give up praying until it happened.

Erin's repentance had given him a joy that softened the pain of his broken relationship with Katy. For the first time in his life, he didn't center his future around her, and the joy of answered prayer was quietly upholding him. He knew that God was behind the Texas job opportunity he had received. Everything had fallen into place so quickly and perfectly, with Erin moving back home to help his mother. He'd felt compelled to jump in his truck and follow his dream.

CHAPTER 36

Katy paused on the Bylers' front porch. A robin's chirp drew her attention to the large ash tree on the side of the house. The empty swing reminded her of her escapade with Jake's grandma. The robin swooped down to the ground, then flew into the weeping willow, the same tree where she'd gotten her first kiss from Jake.

She felt like an intruder, embarrassed to be chasing a man who'd undeclared himself. She couldn't bring herself to step up to the door. "He's not home. His truck is gone."

"Maybe it's in the barn," David replied, undeterred.

Katy glanced in the direction of the barn. "If he won't answer his phone or return my calls, then he doesn't want to see me," she argued. "He made it clear to me that we were through."

"We've already discussed that. I'm a guy. Trust me. He needs to know you've forgiven him."

"I didn't know guys could be such nags." She scowled at David and stepped up to the doorbell.

When the door opened, Katy's mind reeled from shock, her hand involuntarily covering her pitching stomach as she stared across the threshold at the woman responsible for much of her grief. Jessie was the last person she had expected to see in Ann's kitchen.

On the other hand, Jessie seemed nonplussed with her. She merely tilted her blond head, quietly studying them, until her smoky rimmed eyes widened. "You're Katy." When she sensed Katy's confusion, she added, "I saw you in church."

Jessie didn't seem resentful or jealous. Rather she acted like she was genuinely glad to meet Katy. Her personality came across much softer than Katy had imagined it. There was something beneath all the makeup that was refreshing. But that didn't keep Katy from feeling like she'd walked into a daytime nightmare. Praying for Jessie and actually speaking to her were two entirely different things. She bit her lip and looked up at David.

He quickly introduced himself and asked, "Is Jake here?"

"No. But come in. I'll go get Erin."

Katy's feet seemed nailed to the porch flooring, but Jessie motioned them in as if she were hostess, and when David pushed her elbow, Katy found herself begrudgingly inside Ann's kitchen.

As soon as Jessie left the room, Katy hissed at David. "Let's get out of here. This is a mistake."

"Not so fast. Let's find out what's going on first."

"No. It's obvious. I'm out. She's in. I need to leave before Jake comes back and finds me here."

"You know they're going to tell him anyway. She must be visiting Erin. Otherwise she'd be with Jake."

"Not necessarily. I think—"

Erin burst into the room, ending the argument, her expression bearing delight. Oddly, so did Jessie's. Katy was curious. Maybe David was right. Still. . .

"Have a seat." Erin motioned at the table. "Can I get you guys a soda?"

"No!" Katy quickly replied, her pride pushing aside her curiosity.

"Yes, please." David gave Katy an obstinate look.

She tightened her lips and placed her hands on her lap to keep from yanking his perfect hair from his stubborn head.

"Great." Erin talked while she moved with ease about her mother's kitchen. Her gaze flitted from David to Katy. "What are you guys up to?"

David elbowed Katy. "We were looking for Jake."

"Oh?" A flicker of wariness crossed Erin's expression.

Katy felt both girls studying her with inquisitive gazes but couldn't think of anything to say that would satisfy their curiosity without giving herself away.

"He's not returning her calls, and she needs to tell him something important," David clarified.

Katy's jaw dropped open with disbelief, and her face heated from humiliation. Now she wanted to pull his hair out by its perfect roots.

Erin joined the others at the table, her eyes so like Jake's now filled with concern. "Then I'm very sorry you missed him. He's hurting bad."

It seemed the only one with the brains to skirt the issue was Katy. Her face still burning, she glanced at Jessie, but even she wore a sympathetic expression. David squeezed her arm. The encouragement was her undoing. Her pretense fell away. "Me, too," she admitted, easing gently from his touch.

"I know it wouldn't be the same, but I could relay a message for you," Erin offered hopefully. "It isn't any of my business, but if it would help you guys get back together?" Her gaze held a definite yearning, then it dropped to the table, and she continued more softly, "But if I'm reading this wrong, then I don't want to—"

She looked up again. "I love you, Katy, but I just don't want him to get hurt again."

"I don't blame you." Katy wanted to tell her that she'd changed and how she'd forgiven Jake, but it felt awkward with Jessie present. She studied the petite woman who had her chin propped by a silver-cuffed hand. Katy sucked her lip in then released it. "Are you and Jake back together?"

Jessie pointed at herself and the bracelet jangled. She tossed her short blond mop and laughed. "No. Absolutely not. We're just good friends." Her smoky gaze shifted to Jake's sister. "I'm just hanging with Erin over spring break. Taking a country vacation."

"Lame, I know." Erin shrugged.

Katy could tell that they spoke the truth. Otherwise, Jessie wouldn't have been acting so nice. It appeared that Jessie wasn't as stuck on Jake as Katy had expected her to be. There was no evidence that Jessie was experiencing any kind of pain. This new piece of knowledge lightened Katy's heart and planted new hope.

Nodding, Katy explained, "I've been a fool. God showed me some things about myself, some ugly things. After that, I was finally able to forgive Jake for. . .the past. I know it's too late. But David keeps nagging me, telling me I owe it to Jake to let him know I forgive him."

Erin's eyes filled with respect for David, and she cast him a smile. "He's right. Even if you don't get back together, it'll make Jake happy to know you've found peace. When you guys broke up, he came to see me. He blamed himself for causing you to change. I'm sure that was hard for you to admit. Thanks for sharing it."

Katy sighed. "But he won't answer my calls. He hates me."

"He's hurting," Erin repeated. "He's protecting himself. Now that I know the importance of what you want to tell him, I believe it would be much better hearing it from you. I'll tell him you dropped by and ask him to call you."

"He won't," Katy replied. "I don't blame him."

"I know," David said. "Just give Katy a call when he returns, and she can come back. I think he'll listen if they're face-to-face."

"There's the glitch," Jessie piped up, tapping a red fingernail against a porcelain cheek.

Katy and David both snapped their heads in her direction.

Jessie's hand fell gracefully to the table. "He's run away."

"What?" Katy exclaimed, glancing fretfully at David.

"He got a job offer," Erin explained. "In Texas."

Katy reeled from yet another hard blow then sat in stunned silence. She covered her mouth with her hand, taking in all the implications. How many different ways could she lose him? "I guess we're not to be," she said, glumly.

Jessie leaned forward. "I know you're more important to him than a job. Let me call him. Maybe he'll listen to me."

"No!" Katy blurted, unable to accept Jessie's interference.

For the first time, Jessie's eyes snapped with indignation. "Look. I'm not an idiot."

"I—" Katy started.

But Jessie interrupted, her gaze softening again. "I know I'm partly to blame for all this. I want to help. Make it right somehow."

Katy met her gaze and held it. "That's not necessary."

The foursome sat in quiet contemplation. "There must be something we can do," Erin blurted out as she rose. Katy thought she was getting up to pace, but then she saw she was getting a bowl of chips and dip. She plopped it on the table as if food would provide a solution to their problem.

David dove in, crunching happily.

"I know!" Jessie exclaimed. "You can e-mail him. Pour out your heart. It's perfect because you can say everything you want to say without him interrupting."

A flutter of hope tickled Katy's spine. Jessie was right. He might read an e-mail. Her heart began to race, and she shot Jessie an appreciative look. "You're a genius. It is a perfect idea because our last argument started with a disagreement over using the Internet. It would shock him and at the same time validate my change of heart."

Jessie glanced up at Katy's covering, then back down to her face. Katy blushed, realizing how silly such an argument must sound to an outsider, much like all her many run-ins with Tammy.

But Erin caught her enthusiasm. "This could work."

"Got any more of that dip?" David asked.

All three girls rolled their gazes heavenward. Ignoring him, Katy went on, "Only. . .he might not read it when he realizes it's from me."

"But that's the beauty of it. He'll think it's from me!"

Katy gave Jessie a sideways frown, trying not to let her irritation show.

Jessie went on undeterred, "And once he gets into it, he'll be too hooked to stop reading. Come on. Let's go do it before you chicken out."

Katy worried her lip and glanced at David, wondering how everyone pegged her inner wavering so easily. He motioned as if she were a five-year-old. "Go."

Erin blushed. Katy understood why when she offered, "I'll stay and get David some more dip."

Starting to feel like a third wheel, Katy scooted her chair back and followed the enthusiastic Jessie, who seemed to be as self-willed as David. In the short time she'd known Jessie, she saw that Jake's assessment of the girl was accurate. She was helpful and straightforward. Didn't make a big deal out of social differences. And she looked like she would probably be fun, too. To her own amazement, she could see how Jake had gravitated to her when she extended a helpful hand through the maze of campus life. And she imagined Jessie hadn't intentionally led him astray. Well, possibly she had an ulterior motive at the time, too. Jake was good-looking, even in his conservative clothing. To someone like Jessie, it had probably only made him intriguing.

Still, she couldn't believe that she was taking advice from Jake's old girlfriend. A worldly girl's advice. When they passed through the living room, Jessie drew her finger to her lips. Katy saw that Minnie was resting in an armchair. Her head hung to the side, and her mouth emitted soft snoring noises. They tiptoed past.

"Is Ann gone?" Katy whispered.

"Yes. Grocery shopping. Should be home soon."

And to think they weren't having a bit of trouble with the ornery older woman. The longer she stayed in this home, the more her pride was brought down from its lofty throne. The only thing that would clinch it would be for Ann to come home and find her chasing after her son. Katy hoped she was gone before then. Ann might not want Katy at the house again after all her blunders. Yet if things went as she hoped with Jake, she would have to face Ann sometime.

When Katy realized where Jessie was leading her, she instinctively hesitated.

Jessie placed a hand on her black belted hip. "I'm staying in Jake's room while he's gone. I brought my laptop along."

A pang of hurt shot through Katy. But she quickly closed her mind to it, and when she did, the thought came to her that it was just her pride rearing up again. Pride was a hard foe to quell. Much of the hurt and jealousy she had battled against was caused by the injury to her pride. No wonder God had allowed her to get to this place. Feeling more humbled than ever, she followed Jessie into Jake's room.

Jake's room was different, chaotic from all of Jessie's belongings. Even her perfume overpowered his masculine scents. His computer was missing on his desk, replaced with her backpack and her laptop. Katy couldn't tell if the objectionable photograph was still gone because the nightstand was draped with feminine clothing. So was the bed. Clothing also spilled from an open suitcase. Katy's gaze lingered on the high-heeled shoes cluttering the floor in the middle of the room, the ones Jessie had worn on Sunday. Katy couldn't imagine how anyone could wear them without breaking their neck.

She felt a touch on her arm and looked up.

"I know this is hard for you. It's kind of weird for me, too. First Jake getting all religious, and now Erin. Then Jake running away. You showing up while I'm staying in Jake's room—"

Katy interrupted, "Erin's religious? Was that why she was at church on Sunday? Do you know? Is she returning to the church?"

"Yep." Jessie's face contorted. "Claims she's had some epiphany." She stooped, picked up the heels, and dropped them into the suitcase. "That's why I followed her here for spring break. I'm trying to figure out how this family operates."

Katy gave Jessie her first genuine smile. "It doesn't have to be weird with us. I never thought I'd say it, but I kinda like you. In fact, you're a little like my roommate." Her lip quirked into a smile. "Wouldn't you love to see the look on Jake's face when he realizes I e-mailed him from *your* computer?" It wasn't necessary to add, *Because you were the reason I couldn't forgive him.*

Jessie's dark-rimmed eyes lit with amusement. "He's going to flip!" As they booted up Jessie's computer, they giggled.

Jessie pulled up Jake's e-mail address and a page from which Katy could send her message. "You want me to leave?"

"Do you mind?"

"Not at all."

"Thanks, Jessie."

Jessie waved her appreciation away as if it were a natural thing for the two of them to conspire together. She started to leave then paused. "I'm going to go see what's going on between Erin and David. I didn't see that one coming. Did you?"

"Actually, he hinted to me earlier that he had a thing for her."

"They're cute together. Does he always look so. . .perfect?"

"Yes, he does. But he doesn't always act that way."

"Interesting."

Katy couldn't blame David for his ulterior motives. Once Katy was alone, she glanced at the empty e-mail form. This was it. Her last chance, albeit a slim one. After that, it was up to God.

Breathing in Jessie's perfume in the quiet of Jake's room, Katy paused to collect her thoughts. "It's up to You, God. Whatever Your will, I accept it." She began to type.

CHAPTER 37

Jake stood on the newly laid street, looking over the construction site. In a sense, the streets were laid with gold because the barren dirt lots would someday hold fifty new brick two-story houses. The project could line his pockets and secure his future if this interview went right. But he hadn't driven across the country for the lure of money. He'd never been money hungry. He'd come for peace of mind. Working with his hands and building something for other folks to enjoy brought him satisfaction. And he needed that now to forget about Katy. He needed to make new dreams and to numb the raw pain that kept him on his knees.

Inside the mobile office earlier, he'd noticed that the project's landscape mock-up included grass and trees and winding roads, even a few ponds and playgrounds. The houses would be for middle-class people, but definitely upscale, a worthwhile project.

Yet he held some reservations. Texas wasn't what he'd expected. He wiped the sweat from his forehead with the back of his sleeve. He hadn't known the place could be so hot in April, but the newspaper he'd read in his hotel room the night before had predicted eighty degrees for the afternoon. In April! Would he be able to get used to the heat?

He'd checked Houston out on the Internet, and the temperature could rise past one hundred degrees in the sultry thick of summer. He tried to imagine what that might feel like. And then there was the threat of hurricanes.

With this project, the grid of lots would soon face change, and if he accepted the position so would his own life. He hoped he presented himself as confident, but he felt out of place, an Ohio farm boy gone to the big city. Why, he'd even seen his first palm tree.

"Wasn't easy diverting the bayou," the contractor drawled in his southern manner of speech. "Even had to transport a stubborn alligator."

Jake crossed his arms, mirroring the other man's stance. "Never dealt with alligators, but I had a mad bull chase me around the pasture one summer."

Ben Rawlins, of Rawlins Construction, chuckled. "I think that would be worse." He tilted his face, studying Jake. "I like you. And Tom gave you a high recommendation."

Tom was Jake's college professor. He was a brother-in law to Ben Rawlins and had recommended Jake to the contractor. The job opportunity was a superintendent position for Rawlins Construction's current land-development project.

Rawlins excused himself to take a call, stepping away and turning his back to Jake. They had spent the better part of the day together, going over the project, the job requirements, and just getting to know one another. Jake had been invited to the Texan's home for barbecue. When the contractor got off the phone, he told Jake he had to go take care of a problem. Rawlins dismissed him with directions to his place, hollering over his shoulder, "I'll e-mail you those blueprints, and you can look them over before you come out to the house later."

Back at his hotel, Jake popped open a cola from the little refrigerator in the kitchenette and cranked on the air conditioner. Then he sank in a comfortable chair and pulled out a phone book. He propped his feet on the desk and leafed through, checking to see if there were any Mennonite churches in the area. He found one, but it didn't mention anything about being Conservative Mennonite. Another change he'd have to make. He'd told Katy that he could fit in at a more liberal church, but he had no idea how liberal this one would be. Maybe he just didn't know the names of all the suburbs. Hopefully, there was a Conservative church in the area.

With a sigh, he checked the time on his phone and saw he had a few minutes before he needed to shower. That was just enough time to check the computer for those blueprints the contractor had promised to e-mail.

While he waited for the computer to boot, he considered the pros and cons of the project. He liked the contractor, although he didn't really know him. Yet if Jake's professor was recommending him, in a backward sort of way, he was recommending the contractor, too. The job had dropped in his lap as if it was God's doing. And the offer was better than he'd expected, but since he'd arrived in Texas, he'd had a niggling unease that something wasn't right about it.

Rubbing the back of his neck, he tried to figure it out. Was it the job or the move that bothered him? He wasn't one to run away from his problems, and he'd discovered how long the road was between Texas and Ohio—from his family.

He worked the mouse, considering Erin. She and Jessie were staying at the house over spring break. Then they would return and finish their semester. After that, Erin would move home for good. The timing was right, for Erin would be available to help their mom. Still, he'd learned not to proceed when he didn't feel peace about a situation.

He had e-mail. Only it wasn't from the Texan. His brow rose. From Jessie? That surprised him, although they did e-mail on occasion. Inquisitive, he clicked open the message.

~⌐

Katy dipped a long-handled squeegee into a bucket. Starting at the top and stroking downward, she removed winter's grime from the exterior of her kitchen windowpane. Although she was tired from already working at the Brooks', she wanted to get the window cleaned before dark. As she worked, she prayed for Lil and Mrs. Landis. They were seeing a doctor today. She also prayed about the e-mail she'd sent Jake.

Normally under such circumstances, the waiting would have been unbearable, but amazingly, God had provided her with peace. Oh, she had moments when she wondered if she'd been crazy to send that e-mail, but then she remembered that God was in control, come what may.

She heard the crackle of gravel and turned, expecting to see Megan. Surprised to see Ann Byler's car instead, Katy dropped her squeegee in the bucket. Her heart tripped when she saw Jessie crawl out from behind the steering wheel.

"Hey!" the short blond hailed with enthusiasm.

Katy waved back, but her nerves were acutely aware that she probably bore news about Jake.

"Wow. Show me how that works," Jessie said, eyeing the partly cleaned window and the squeegee.

With a chuckle, Katy gave her a demonstration. "Want to give it a try?"

"Sure."

The girl wore a supple leather jacket, jeans, and high-heeled boots— so different from Katy's own calf-length skirt. Jessie gave a little shriek when water dripped over part of what Katy had already cleaned, and then she surrendered the tool.

"Don't worry. I'm going over it again."

"Guess I'd better live in apartments until I can afford a maid." Then Jessie clutched Katy's arm. "I'm sorry. I didn't think."

Katy's face went hot. "I like my job."

"I just wish I *had* a job. My dad always makes me get a summer job. I'd like to keep one all year, but it never works out that way."

Katy bit her lower lip, considering. Earlier that day, she'd discovered that Tammy was still having trouble finding a replacement nanny. "You like kids?"

"I love them. Kids are so fun."

"One of my employers is looking for a nanny for a seven-year-old girl and an eleven-year-old boy. They live in Old Arlington. Think you'd be interested?"

"Are you kidding? That's close to campus!"

"Tammy, the wife, had a bad experience with another college student. But I think she'd like you."

Jessie clutched Katy's shoulders, and she suddenly felt herself pulled into the smaller woman's embrace. At first she flinched, but then she awkwardly patted Jessie's back. When they drew apart, Jessie exclaimed, "Thanks so much!"

"You're welcome. I can finish this later. Want to come inside?"

"I'd love to. Jake told me he did the remodel."

So they'd been in touch since he'd come back to Plain City. Pushing that out of her mind, Katy led the way into the doddy house.

"This is so cute," Jessie exclaimed. After their tour, she admitted, "You must have thought I was a slob when you saw Jake's room."

Katy remembered with a grin. Then she pointed a finger at Jessie. "If you get the Brooks' job, don't let the kids tear up the house."

"Oh man." Jessie sighed. "But I need the job. You've got a deal."

"I'm going on an interview myself. Tomorrow. My dream job." They sat in the living room, and Katy explained about Mrs. Beverly and the loss Katy had experienced when the older couple moved to Florida. She found herself talking about the letter and its effect over her. She watched the vulnerability cross Jessie's face.

Afterward, Jessie sighed. "I could never become like you. I'd have too much to change, too much to give up. I don't want to lose Erin as a friend. But it seems we're doomed. She's not going to be going to parties with me anymore. I'll have to move on."

"Perhaps our lifestyle isn't what God has for you." Katy thought of Mrs. Beverly and said what she'd never thought she'd say, "But you could still be a Christian in another denomination."

"That's what Erin says. We'll see. I really came over to say that I hadn't gotten any e-mails from Jake. Wondered if he'd called."

"No."

"I'm sorry. Maybe he just needs more time. You sure you don't want me to call him, give him a little push?"

"Please don't. It's just the way it should be."

⁓

As hard as it was for him, Jake didn't call Katy. Instead after the barbecue, he told the Texas contractor that he was going home to think over the offer. Ben Rawlins had seemed surprised that Jake hadn't jumped at the opportunity. Even slightly offended, although his southern hospitality kept him from saying so.

Jake had explained that first he had some business to take care of that would determine if he accepted the superintendent position. He explained that although it was a great opportunity, he wanted to be able to give it his all once he accepted. The cross-country move would be life altering, and Jake needed to make sure it was the right move.

That appeased the other man somewhat, and he agreed to wait one week. After that, he'd call his brother-in-law for another name. Jake agreed, and they parted on good terms.

Later along the interstate, Jake mulled over the offer. By the size of the insects that plastered the truck's windshield and splattered the front grill, the saying that everything was big in Texas seemed true. This job offer was a giant-sized decision, too. It was the type of decision that could affect his entire future. As he weighed his choices, a major portion of the return trip was spent praying.

He also listened to Christian radio stations. At times he broke out into audible laughter, trying to imagine Katy and Jessie conspiring together. That was what made Katy's e-mail smack of honesty. She couldn't have faced Jessie without forgiveness. It seemed she had really changed.

Still, he wanted to see her expression when they talked about it. In order to believe her, he needed to see that her guarded expression was gone. It had been shadowing her eyes ever since he'd come back to the Plain City church. He hoped his childhood companion had returned. Because anything less was not enough any longer. He was done chasing a past love. His future companion needed to be a soul mate who would accept him in every way.

He couldn't take Katy back if she was going to slip back into her judgmental attitude or go through life with the emergency brake on. Yet hope kept him buzzing along Interstate 40. If God could change his own heart, filling it with a love that saw beyond the outer facade, then God could have done a miracle in Katy's life, too. Maybe even Jessie's. He breathed another prayer of thankfulness. He wouldn't be headed home if he didn't believe God had already performed such a miracle.

Katy relaxed on her sofa, her legs flung over the armrest and her phone cradled against her ear. "It's going to be a dream job, just like Mrs. Beverly said. She accepted me on the spot. Mrs. Beverly told her Mennonites are hard workers."

She heard Lil laughing on the other end. "Guess I need to remind my boss about that. I think he senses my lack of interest at the restaurant. I need a better job, too." She sighed. Katy knew Lil had quit searching the newspaper ads. "But not until Mom gets better. Anyway, congrats. We'll celebrate soon. I can't wait to move back to the doddy house. I miss it. Miss you. You're being such a great sport about this."

"So what did the doctor say?"

"He suggested counseling, and we have a follow-up appointment. He'll have the results of the blood work by then. And if that doesn't help, then there's always medication."

"What does your mom think about that?"

"She claims she won't take any drugs. But I think she might agree to see a Christian counselor. I'm going to set up an appointment."

"So is she still in bed all day?"

"She gets up late and takes long naps. But she's up some. I came up with a great idea, but she turned me down flat."

"What was it?"

"I wanted her to take a cake-decorating class with me. Get her back into the kitchen."

"That would have been perfect. Maybe soon she'll—Someone's at the door, Lil. Can I call you back later?"

Katy stuck her phone in her pocket and squinted through the peephole that Jake had installed in the front door when they'd remodeled the doddy house. She nearly fainted to see her handsome remodeler in the flesh, holding a bouquet of daffodils, no less. Her heart racing, she flung open the door.

"Jake?" It was all she could do to keep from flinging her arms around his neck.

When he grinned, she realized how much she'd missed him. "Can I come in?"

"Yes!"

Inside, he tentatively held out the bouquet. "For keeping you waiting. I wanted to talk to you in person."

She clutched the flowers. "I can't believe you came. I mean, I hoped you would. That you'd give me a chance to explain some things. But I didn't think you would."

He leaned one shoulder against the wall. "Your e-mail definitely piqued my interest."

Although his stance was nonchalant, she knew that this was her one moment in the universe when she was being given the chance to restore their relationship. *Just say it*, the quiet voice insisted. "I was wrong."

"Wrong?" He crossed his arms, tilted his face.

"Not to forgive you. Not to believe in you. I was too proud." She gave him a tremulous smile. "But I've changed."

He straightened. Then slowly he reached up to touch her cheek. "Can you tell me what happened?"

She nodded, never allowing her gaze to leave his. "I got a letter from my old employer." Katy poured forth the entire story. She ended it by telling him about her visit to his house and Jessie's idea of sending him an e-mail. When she finished speaking, she was still standing in the same place, clutching his bouquet.

The corners of his eyes crinkled with sympathy. "That must have taken a lot of courage."

"I had my eyes set on the goal."

"What goal?"

"I hoped you could forgive me, too."

He tilted her chin up, looked deeper in her eyes. "Is that all you hoped, Katy?"

Another sliver of her pride slipped away, and she thought surely there must not be a shred remaining. "I hoped you'd give me another chance."

He released his hand, studied her with a serious expression, and she thought it was too late. Her hopes sagged.

And then he quirked the left side of his mouth. "Maybe I could learn to tolerate you a little bit."

She grinned. "If you could, then would you please. . ."

"Yes?"

"Prove it," she whispered.

He lifted a brow. "What do you want, Katy?"

She stared at his lips.

He pulled her close, crushing the flowers. Although his arms held her close, his lips remained gentle and tentative. She threw both arms around his neck and drew him closer, eager to express her love and joy and drawing him into a deeper kiss. When she finally drew back first, she gazed again into the face of the one she thought she'd lost. His return was as glorious as the kiss. He stood there before her, accepting her and giving her another chance. But his gaze didn't hold the awe she felt. It held something else. . .satisfaction, amusement even.

He touched his lip. "That was tolerable, but I think we ruined your flowers."

"That doesn't matter," she said, turning and tossing them on the counter. She turned back and leaned her head against his chest, her arms slipping around his trim waist. "Spring has arrived anyway."

CHAPTER 38

Where are you taking me?" Katy asked.

The black-fringed scarf that Jake had tied over her eyes kept her from seeing where he was driving. Even without the blindfold, she would have known he was up to something because their date was scheduled later than usual. He'd mumbled something over the phone about picking her up after dark to take advantage of a full moon.

His voice broke into her thoughts. "We're almost there, and I don't want to spoil the surprise."

Katy gripped the passenger-seat armrest, deliriously happy ever since Jake had accepted her apology. In the past two weeks, they'd been making up for wasted years. Emotionally, Katy had opened up to him without reservation. The vulnerability of placing her heart in a man's hands left her a tad breathless. Not frightened, exactly. More like exhilarated, climbing a mountain, anxious to see the view from the top, and unsure what was on the other side.

They had both grown so much since their high school dates. They hadn't talked much yet about what was on the other side of the mountain, except that he had turned down the Texas job and planned to stay in Plain City.

Getting to know him was surprising in many ways. She had discovered that he preferred dawn over sunset, because it symbolized new beginnings. He wore his pants tight because otherwise his leather tool belt pulled them too low, making it uncomfortable when he worked. She was glad to know that wouldn't change.

Although he couldn't always express himself eloquently, he was a good listener, a tease who knew how to bring a smile to everyone's lips, whether it was Minnie in one of her moods or his hired help after a day of hard manual labor. It took a lot to anger Jake, but she'd discovered that when he was frustrated, he always stuck his hands in his pockets and his eyes saddened around the outer fringes. Best of all, he'd admitted that he prayed for her every night before he fell asleep. How had she ever doubted him?

Through an open window, a gentle breeze brushed her cheeks. With the distinct scent of wet fields and the absence of traffic sounds, she knew that they were still driving on rural roads. The truck slowed and gently bounced onto a rougher surface that crackled like gravel. He killed the engine.

"Are we there?"

"Yes. I'll come around to your side and help you down."

She waited, eager to find out what he had planned. Had he gotten a job and taken her to a construction site? Would it be a prelude to talking about building or buying a house of their own one day? No, a construction site would be too dangerous after dark.

As she waited for him to open her door, her thoughts continued along that vein, sharing a house with Jake. Of late she dreamed more about marrying him than fulfilling the vow of living in the doddy house with all three of her friends.

The door opened, interrupting her musings and quickening her pulse. He reached in and caught her by the waist, then swung her down and set her on her feet. Tottering a bit, she gripped his firm arm until she had her balance. Then he led her across gravel onto softer ground. Something tickled her face, and she swatted it away.

He stopped. "Ready?"

"Yes," she replied.

Gently he untied the scarf. She blinked, looked around. "Our tree?" The weeping willow made a romantic canopy around them beneath the moon's soft glow. In wonder, she added, "Where we first kissed."

"I remember."

He grinned and drew her close. His lips claimed hers. It wasn't a tentative kiss like that first one so long ago, or even like the one a few weeks ago when they had finally gotten back together. It was a confident kiss but urgent. When she opened her eyes, the silvery moonlight shone across his face. His expression held a need that delighted her.

He buried his hand in her long tresses and said in a low rumbling voice, "I love your hair. When I was a kid, it was such a temptation."

"I remember."

"I like it down like this, too."

"You're getting romantic on me, aren't you?"

"Maybe I am."

His work-roughened hand captured hers again. His calluses made her proud of him, of his hardworking attitude. They helped her accept her own work-worn hands. His husky voice turned her thoughts toward him again, "Come with me," he urged.

Her heart swelled with affection. She wondered why he was taking her away from the house until she saw a circle of stones and a pile of firewood topped with tinder. "What's this?"

He answered with a self-satisfied smile. "Do you remember the summer we went to camp?"

"Of course." How could she forget about the vows she and her friends had made around the campfire? It was there that Katy had blurted out, *I know who I'll marry. Jake Byler.* Later she'd found out that Lil had told Jake about it before they'd even left the campgrounds. And even though they'd been mutually attracted to each other for years, Katy had always surmised that his crooked grin had something to do with being privy to that information.

Her gaze next took in two lawn chairs, and she suddenly understood. The kissing tree. The campfire declaration. He was going to propose. She tried to pretend that bubbles of joy were not dancing inside her as she feigned ignorance. "The surprise is a campfire?"

He nodded, then released her hand and motioned. "Sit down. I'll light it."

She eased into the lawn chair and watched him stoop before the fire pit. As he struck the match, his muscles bunched his shirtsleeve. She felt flushed even before the flames leapt from the neatly arranged firewood. While he worked over the fire, a shrill bird cry broke the silence. Some crickets chirped from the direction of the weeping willow. When the sound of crackling wood joined the other night sounds, Jake stood and brushed his hands.

He strode back to her and settled into his chair with a wink that curled around her heart. His hand caressed hers possessively, but he looked into the fire when he spoke. "You had some dreams that year. When I heard about them, they ignited a fire inside me. I didn't know it at the time, but it's been burning there ever since I heard you wanted to marry me."

She stared at the growing blaze, aware of the burning desire he alluded to but wanting to hear more from him than a smug reminder of her own feelings. "That was a long time ago. I was just a little girl."

He turned his gaze on her. The firelight cast golden glints of determination in his eyes. "I want you, Katy. I've always wanted you." He leaned close and kissed her. "Marry me?"

Breathless, she touched his cheek. She wanted him, too. And he knew it. And she didn't care if he was smug. His self-assurance was part of what she loved about him.

"Yes, I'll marry you."

"I love you," he breathed. He slipped his arm around her shoulders, leaned his head against hers, and whispered, "I don't have much to offer you."

Heads bent together, peace and contentment settled over her as they whispered their most intimate thoughts. After assuring him that he was more than enough to meet all her dreams, she asked, "Are you sorry you turned down the job in Texas?"

"Not at all. This is exactly where I want to be."

CHAPTER 39

In Katy's mind, one couldn't have spring without doing some spring-cleaning, and she'd enlisted Lil and Megan to help her prepare the doddy house for her upcoming marriage. The wedding would be just before Megan left on her mission trip in June. Katy and Jake would live in the doddy house. The three friends had set up a tentative plan that by September, Lil and Megan would take over the doddy house. They hoped that was enough time for Katy and Jake to find a place of their own, for Megan to find a job, and for Lil's mom to recuperate.

Now Katy stood on a small ladder she'd borrowed from Jake and handed dishes down out of the cupboards while Lil and Megan stacked them on the counters, the green sink hutch, and the kitchen table.

As Lil restacked plates, she announced, "I have news."

"What?" Katy asked.

"I complained to my mom that I didn't know how I was going to manage your wedding cake, that it was more than I should have agreed to do, and that I was worried about it."

Katy's jaw dropped. "But I didn't know you felt that way. I would never—"

"Ah!" Lil lifted her hand to interrupt Katy. "I don't really feel that

309

way. I just had this hunch, and it worked. Mom's mothering instincts took over, and she told me she'd help me. We'd get through it together. That maybe we should sign up for those cake-decorating classes I had mentioned, after all."

Katy paused from wiping down the cupboard. She turned and perched on the top rung of the ladder. "So you want to do my cake?"

"Yes, silly. And Mom's agreed to help me with it. This is going to be so good for her."

"And she even suggested it? That's great." Katy shook her head, thinking how great Lil was at helping others to move in positive directions. "You're amazing."

"And our first class is next Tuesday."

Megan put a bucket in the sink and ran some water. Once she'd turned the faucet off, she said, "Things are coming together, aren't they? Hey, Katy, you're not still scared at night, are you?"

"Not scared. Just lonely." Katy pointed at the cupboard under the sink. "Can you add a little vinegar to that?"

Megan opened the green cupboard door and found the vinegar.

"I do still use my night-light. But something amazing happened. When I trusted God for Jake and my job, my terror of the dark fled." She tilted her head, thoughtfully. "I don't think I'd ever choose to live alone. Nights aren't exactly pleasant. But I can make it a few more weeks."

Megan lifted the bucket up to Katy and filled a second one to wash the baseboard and windowsills.

"This place really isn't that dirty," Lil stated. "It hasn't been that long since we moved in."

Considering that remark came from someone who didn't make her bed or pick up after herself, Katy couldn't help but protest, "I think some of that construction dust settled after we moved in."

Lil shrugged and started on the baseboards. "Jake told me you guys had decided on your honeymoon, but he wouldn't tell me where you're going."

Megan turned from where she was working at the sill to listen.

"Sarasota, Florida. I want to thank Mrs. Beverly in person."

"That's awesome," Megan replied. "You'll love it."

Katy knew that Megan's family often drove down over the Christmas break during her school years. They had extended family in Sarasota, and there was a Mennonite community there.

"Jake's going to do some research on the Internet to find us a place to stay."

"The Internet?" Lil asked, drawing out and exaggerating the word *Internet*.

Needing to move her ladder, Katy came down. She got herself a cold drink and couldn't resist placing the cold glass against the back of Lil's neck.

"Ah! Stop!"

"Actually, Jake was willing to get rid of the computer, knowing my reservations. But I suggested we keep it for business only, and that any other use should be discussed between the two of us first. That way, it won't be so easy to use it for frivolity and get pulled into the world."

Lil had turned away from the baseboard and now sat cross-legged on the floor. Her expression turned dreamy. "That sounds like a great plan."

Megan poured two more glasses of water, handed Lil one, and joined them. "While we're on the subject of computers. . ." Her voice became tentative. "There's something I wanted to give you for a wedding gift if you don't think it's too worldly."

Katy tilted her head. "It sounds like you're up to something. Let me guess. A computer cam so that we can talk to you in Bangladesh?"

Megan scowled, looking beautiful as ever. "How did you know about those?"

"Jessie explained them to me."

"Oh. I knew you wouldn't agree to that. Anyway, you'll be on your honeymoon. But one of my friends at school is great at photography. He does his photos on the computer. I'd like to arrange for him to shoot your wedding."

Katy smiled with pleasure. "I'd love it. As long as we keep it simple."

"Great. You won't even know what he's up to, I promise. I think my parents will chip in. We'll definitely keep it simple."

"I'm so blessed," Katy whispered. "I wish your photographer was here today. This is a day I always want to remember. . .with the three of us together."

"Don't worry," Lil said. "We won't let you forget anything." She reached out to give Katy a hug and knocked her covering askew.

With her heart swelling with fondness for her friends, Katy reached up to straighten it, suddenly realizing that neither of her friends wore theirs, and it didn't hurt her any longer. She said with choking emotion, "Once Jake and I find another place and you guys live here, if Jake ever has to take an out-of-town job, I'm joining you for a sleepover."

Lil scowled. "Duh? That's just a given."

EPILOGUE

Katy and Jake faced each other for the first time as husband and wife. She drank in the masculine planes of his clean-shaven face, his fresh haircut, the softening of his dark eyes, and three things struck her at once: the intensity of his love for her, its sincerity, and that it was hers for the taking. She stood on tiptoe. His head lowered to give her the traditional wedding kiss. When she heard clapping, she drew away blushing.

"I love you," he whispered.

"Love you, too," she replied.

A white rose petal drifted down and landed on the grass at their feet.

Their kissing tree had become their wedding tree. Katy's idea of placing satin bows of purest white and sprinkling white primroses throughout the weeping willow branches made it a lovely altar for their vows. Since they'd had their first kiss beneath it, and since Jake had proposed there, the Byler farm had been deemed the perfect place for their June wedding.

They turned and looked out over their guests. Jake had made benches for the ceremony, and together they had painted them white. The picturesque white sparkled clean against the lush summer lawn and the more distant green cornfields. Their friends and family brightened the benches with color and laughter.

Holding hands, they moved down the center aisle, greeting guests as they moved along. Her gown swished over the freshly mowed grass, but for once, Katy wasn't worried about stains.

Her gown was everything she'd ever dreamed it could be. Her mother had sewn the satin dress in a simple, yet elegant style with a high neck and quarter-length sleeves. She had embroidered the neck and the hem. Now it glistened in the late afternoon sunlight.

The mothers of the bride and groom had conspired to find a stringed head covering that Minnie had once made—when she designed and sewed bonnets for extra income. Mrs. Yoder had removed the strings and added longer, wider satin ribbons that now streamed down Katy's back, serving as her wedding veil.

Katy's hair was twisted and pinned up beneath the covering. Before the wedding, when she'd fixed her hair, she daydreamed of her new groom removing the pins. For once, she wouldn't slap his hands away, like she had so many times before when he was just a mischievous little boy who took pleasure in yanking her ponytail.

Now as they edged forward, Katy's left arm held her bouquet so that the white roses nestled in the hollow of her skirt, adding the perfect adornment to her plain gown. From her tiny cinched waist, the fabric draped elegantly over the slim curve of her hips to the ground. Having taken a good look at herself in the full-length mirror Lil had purchased for the doddy house closet, she'd felt more of a Cinderella than she had the night of the ballet.

She blushed now to remember the silk white negligee that was packed in her suitcase. It had not been cut with such modesty. Thankfully, it was not being captured on film. It had been a gift from Lil. And Katy had wondered if Jake had put his cousin up to it.

Beside her, Jake looked handsome in his new black suit. He wore a white shirt and a vest made from the same material as Katy's wedding dress. But it was the possessive look in his eyes that made Katy's heart turn somersaults. She hoped the photographer would catch that look as well as the lopsided grin sometime before the day was over.

Their attendants trailed behind them. Lil was paired with Cal, and

Megan with Chad Penner. Karen walked with their oldest brother, and Erin with David. The bridesmaids wore simple lavender dresses, hand-sewn from a Butterick pattern Katy had found at the discount fabric store.

When they reached the last row, Jessie stood beside the Brooks, holding Addison's hand. When Jessie gave Jake a hug. Katy didn't resent it one bit. In fact she took pleasure in seeing the rare occasion of Jake's blush.

"I didn't initiate that," he whispered, his voice thick with his Dutch accent, as they moved toward the table that had been set up for the wedding party.

"We'll discuss it later," Katy replied, feigning displeasure.

He glanced at her to see how much trouble he was in, and she affectionately squeezed his hand.

When it came time to cut the wedding cake, Katy and Jake took their places to do the traditional first bites. Their arms interlocked, Katy stared at the piece of cake that hovered in front of her face. He pushed it closer, and she closed her lips, teasing him. He had already licked his bite greedily clean. His mouth quirked in a grin, then his lips grew serious, and he gave her a most sincere gaze, one she'd come to love of late.

"I'll never force you to do anything, Katy. I'm not that kind of guy." Forgetting about their enraptured audience for a few seconds, she touched his cheek, inadvertently getting frosting in his black hair. She opened her mouth and accepted the creamy confection. Maybe the S word woouldn't be so bad after all. "You're getting more tolerable all the time."

"And you haven't seen anything yet."

When they stepped away from the table, Katy pointed toward his sparkling truck. "Did you see what David did?" When she had enlisted David to wash it, she forgot how easy that would make it for him to tie a string of cans from its hitch.

Jake gave her a sideways frown. "I saw. He's after Erin, you know. I mean to have a frank talk with him when we get back from our honeymoon."

"But he's such a nice guy," Katy couldn't resist saying, thinking of her mother. Just before the wedding, her mom had predicted again, *I know marriage will make you happy.* And although she hadn't added that Jake was *such a nice boy,* Katy knew that Jake had won her mother over the day he took her little brothers fishing so that Mrs. Yoder could run some wedding errands.

With fondness, she also remembered how her dad had called her *dumpling* when he walked her down the aisle. Although he'd given his blessing on the marriage weeks earlier, he'd also given Jake a private talk, a rather stern one if evidenced by the pale expression Jake had worn afterward.

She blinked out of her reverie. "I need to talk to Mrs. Landis before the cake table is inaccessible."

"All right. I'm going to go see what damage David did to my truck."

Katy praised Mrs. Landis for her work on the triple-layer cake. "I'm so glad you took care of finding servers for me."

"Oh, it's nothing. I enjoy doing this," Mrs. Landis replied. The woman seemed happier than Katy had seen her in months.

A few minutes later, Jake returned and drew her off to the side.

"Everything all right?" she asked.

"Elizabeth went into labor. David went with their family to the hospital."

"How exciting!"

Jake glanced around the milling crowd. "How much longer do we need to stay here?"

Everyone was having fun, but now that the cake had been served, the party would soon wind down, and they wished to make their exit before that happened. "Why—" She cut her comment short when Minnie marched up to them.

The older woman stopped, toe to toe with Katy, her eyes squinting at Katy's covering, staring far longer than normal or polite. Katy began to feel uneasy. She'd seen that look in Minnie's eyes before. And when Minnie stretched forth her arm, Katy squeezed Jake's hand, hoping he saw what was happening, too. Minnie was going to make a move for her covering again!

But the old woman was too quick for Katy or Jake, and her hand flashed out and up, nabbing one of the satin ribbons. She wound it around her age-worn fingers, cracked from hours of quilting. Katy froze, waiting for her to yank it off her head. This time, she determined, she wasn't going to make a fuss. Yet she had envisioned allowing Jake to remove it. It was her wedding veil, and it symbolized so much for her. She sucked in her breath, afraid to move.

"Now Gram," Jake began, "that's Katy's wedding veil."

"I made this, didn't I?" Minnie asked, ignoring her grandson and narrowing her eyes with unmistakable mischief.

"Yes, Minnie," Katy softly gasped. "And I'll always cherish it."

Emotion flashed in Minnie's eyes, and she dropped the ribbon. Her mouth moved almost fishlike. Then she suddenly shook her head in protest, emphatically thrusting her finger against Jake's suit jacket. "This! This!" she insisted loudly.

Aghast, Katy looked at her groom. Then slowly, understanding dawned. "You want me to cherish your grandson instead? Oh Minnie, I do cherish him."

Minnie didn't reply, but she dropped her hand and got a big grin on her face as she dismissed them by marching off toward the cake table.

Katy let out a sigh of relief then grinned up at Jake. "That was a close one. She's right, you know."

Jake demonstrated *his* agreement by sweeping Katy into his arms right next to the willow tree, for all the world to see. He kissed her until there was no doubt left in her mind that he cherished her, too, and that it was time to make a dash for that shiny, black pickup truck.

Katy's Journal

Cleaning Tips

Cold or hot coffee cleans drainpipes.

Vinegar in front-loader washers kills mildew on seals.

Keep home cleaner by sweeping driveways and entryways.

Use paintbrushes to dust cracks and hard-to-reach places in telephones, stereos, etc.

Shine a stainless steel sink with vinegar or a touch of oil on a cloth to make the sink sparkle

Cleaning my feather duster: Keep dipping and swirling in soapy water and rinsing in clear water until the water stays clear. Then dry with feathers up.

Miscellaneous Tips

Ice cubes sharpen garbage disposal blades.

Chopping onions takes rust off knives.

Outsiders: peel like an onion to see what's really inside before discarding. Stop judging their actions without understanding their motives. "Every way of a man is right in his own eyes: but the LORD pondereth the hearts" (Proverbs 21:2).

Do not underestimate the elderly. Though their feet move slower, their hands remain lightning fast and their thoughts are as mysterious as the universe.

Kissing trees make wonderful wedding altars.

Stains

Burned food in dishes: fill with water and 2 tablespoons baking soda. Soak. Scrub.

Ring around the collar: shampoo cleans the body oils away.

Gum: first cool and harden, then scrape most off with hard edge, then rub remainder with egg whites.

Tomato stains: run cool water until clear, then blot with white vinegar. Note: Removes the stain but does not remove memory of the incident. I remain in search of that particular cleansing agent, that can renew my mind.

Later entry: It is forgiveness.

Removing Jake's scent: sprinkled a pinch of baking soda on my white blouse where our shoulders touched. Do not give in to temptation to sleep with untreated blouse under my pillow.

Hand Cream Home Remedies

Recipe One
2 ounces beeswax
1 cup sweet almond oil
1 cup water
Heat, heating water separately, then blend. Cool and store in jar or tin.
Use as hand lotion.

Recipe Two
½ cup olive oil
A few drops of scented lavender drops from dollar store
Wear gloves until it soaks into skin

Recipe Three
1 banana
1 teaspoon honey
Juice of one lime
1 tablespoon butter
Mash banana and add to honey, lime juice, and butter. Blend and put in container. Leave on at least two hours with gloves.

Spring-Cleaning Tips

Use a natural sponge. Wash down kitchen backsplashes with
vinegar water.

Use dishwasher to clean odds and ends.

Check expiration dates of medicine-cabinet and refrigerator items
and make a shopping list for employer.

Check smoke alarms before they go off in the middle of the night
and frighten little Addison.

Window blinds: use a white glove and dip in vinegar water (equal
parts vinegar and water).

Toss shower curtains in washer.

Personal note 1: to survive winter until spring arrives, stir up my
faith, wrap myself in God's hope, and watch for Dutchman's
breeches. God is able.

Personal note 2: new beginnings are not only possible but
wonderful!

Cleaning Recipes

Wood-Paneling Recipe:

1 pint warm water

4 tablespoons white or apple vinegar

2 tablespoons olive oil

Apply with a clean cloth. Let soak a few minutes, and wipe off
with a dry cloth.

Windows Recipe:

2 cups water

3 tablespoons vinegar

½ teaspoon liquid dishwashing detergent

Squeegee

Tip: Clean one side horizontally and the other vertically so you
can determine which side has streaks

Cleaning the Microwave:

1 cup coffee

1 slice lemon

Microwave a few minutes, let it set, and it softens the spills. Wipe
down with warm, soapy water.

The Head Covering

"But I would have you know that the head of every man is Christ,
and the head of the woman is the man; and the head of Christ is
God. Every man praying or prophesying, having his head covered,
dishonoureth his head. But every woman that prayeth or prophesieth
with her head uncovered dishonoureth her head: for that is even all
one as if she were shaven. For if the woman be not covered, let her
also be shorn: but if it be a shame for a woman to be shorn or shaven,
let her be covered. For a man indeed ought not to cover his head
forasmuch as he is the image and glory of God: but the woman is the
glory of the man. For the man is not of the woman: but the woman of
the man. Neither was the man created for the woman; but the woman
for the man. For this cause ought the woman to have power on her
head because of the angels. Nevertheless, neither is the man without
the woman, neither the woman without the man, in the Lord. For as
the woman is of the man, even so is the man also by the woman; but
all things of God.

"Judge in yourselves, is it comely that a woman pray unto God
uncovered? Doth not even nature itself teach you, that, if a man have
long hair, it is a shame unto him? But if a woman have long hair, it is
a glory to her: for her hair is given her for a covering. But if any man
seem to be contentious, we have no such custom, neither the churches
of God."

1 CORINTHIANS 11:3–16

Journal disclaimer: Cleaning tips and recipes try at your own risk.
Same with applying Katy's personal tips.

SOMETHING NEW

DEDICATION

To Jim, my own Plain City sweetheart.
I hope this story honors your fond memories
of growing up on a farm.

PROLOGUE

Ten-year-old Lillian Mae Landis inched her toes to the edge of the tiny square platform fifty feet above the ground. She ran clammy hands down her glittery red costume and poised them. Her heart rose to her throat as she watched the trapeze swing through the air toward her. She counted one, two, three and then leaped forward.

Lil's stomach somersaulted, and she exulted when her hands clasped the swinging bar with perfect timing. The crowd gasped. Her body jerked, but she held fast and tightened her tummy and leg muscles as she brought her body into perfect form. The air rushed across her face. The music came to a crescendo. Every eye was riveted on her performance.

A second trapeze carrying the teenager Rollo—a handsome boy with flowing blond hair—made its descent. Rollo's knees gripped his trapeze bar. Keeping silent count, Lil let loose of her bar at just the correct moment, and Rollo's sure, strong hands caught her arms. The crowd roared in delight. She basked in their admiration.

"Ouch! Stop it!"

Lil blinked, torn from her fantasy. She pulled her face from the open van's window and looked sideways to where her cousin Jake Byler was pulling Katy Yoder's black ponytail. Lil tucked one foot under her homemade culottes and twisted so she could look him square in the eyes.

"What was your favorite part of the circus?" she asked. Their families had attended the Ringling Brothers and Barnum and Bailey Circus together when it had come to Columbus, Ohio, earlier that month.

"The tigers." Jake growled in her friend Katy's ear then sank back in his seat and started tussling with his buddy Chad Penner.

Lil rolled her gaze heavenward. Forgetting about Jake, she told Katy, "I liked the trapeze artists." She had already described the circus to her two best friends—Katy Yoder and Megan Weaver—repeatedly, but she didn't think they really understood how magical that experience had been for a girl whose normal day consisted of gathering brown eggs and snapping green beans. Lil lived on a farm.

Katy bit the inside of her cheek thoughtfully, and Lil let the conversation drop.

The van veered off the smooth interstate onto a rural road and rattled over a cattle guard. Lil could hardly contain her excitement. At last she was getting a break from her farm chores, a chance to have some real fun. "I heard Camp Victoria has a huge swing that goes right out over the river."

Katy's eyes widened. "Where'd you hear that? You think they'll make us do it?"

"It's true." Megan turned around, fingering a long, blond braid. "But I don't think they'll make us do it."

"I'll do it!" Lil replied.

"I hope you don't try any of those circus tricks," Katy replied, her dark eyes fretful.

"Look. There's the camp." Megan pointed ahead. Through the window, they saw a green-lettered sign on a rectangular log building.

Sure enough, the van turned into a gravel parking lot. As soon as the door slid open, the children piled out of the vehicle. Stretching, Lil quickly scanned the campsite. She didn't see any swings. She heard her cousin Jake's snickers, however, and glanced over because he was usually in the middle of any fun activity. But he and Chad Penner were only staring at some girls about her age. Instantly, she understood why.

Those girls wore shorts and brightly colored T-shirts. Their hair was cut, too. The other girls were observing their group's arrival. Lil felt a pang of envy, as she so often did, wishing she hadn't been born on a hog farm, of all things. Her family attended the Big Darby Conservative Mennonite Church in Plain City, Ohio. Now she wished she'd been born in a different Mennonite church like those girls so she didn't have to wear ugly, homemade culottes. She muttered to her friends, "I wish my mom let me wear shorts."

"I hope they're nice," Katy replied, ignoring Lil's comment and eyeing the girls in shorts.

As if a mind reader, one of the girls waved.

Lil grabbed Megan's arm. "Let's go." Heart skipping, she released Megan's arm and waved back.

A girl with brown bobbed hair and blue eyes said, "Hi, I'm Lisa."

Lil stared at the other girl in amazement. "I never met another Lil before."

Lisa smiled. "I think you misunderstood. It's Lisa."

"Oh, sorry."

"Hey, you're in our cabin. I saw your name. Come on. We'll show you where it is."

The girls got acquainted as they strolled down a freshly graded dirt road edged with white daisies. It led to a row of brown cabins with blue roofs. All the while, Lil kept sneaking peeks at Lisa's green shorts and suntanned legs, wondering how such a freedom would feel.

"This is it," Lisa announced, skipping up the steps to the cabin. Lil almost stumbled when she noticed Lisa's painted toenails glimmering through her sandals. The girl didn't know how lucky she was to have been born in a more lenient Mennonite family. Lil studied the names posted on the door of Cabin Colorado, relieved to see that she and Katy and Megan would all be bunking together. Inside the cabin, a friendly blond woman greeted them.

"I'm Mary, your counselor. Our group is complete now. Go ahead and choose a bed. Soon the tractor will come around with your bags. We're going to do an icebreaker in about a half hour, so stick close by."

Katy rushed to claim a vacant bed, and Megan took its top bunk. Lil asked Lisa where her bed was. She took the top bunk over Lisa's bed.

"I wish the tractor would lose my bag," Lil admitted to her new friend.

"Why?" Lisa asked with surprise.

"'Cause my clothes are ugly. I love your shorts."

"You can wear them if you want. I've got more, and my bag's right here." Clearly Lisa understood Lil's situation.

Pleasure shot through Lil, and her hand covered her heart. "Are you serious? You'd let me?"

"Sure. It's no big deal." Lisa unzipped her bag and riffled through, sizing up her new friend. "Actually, these might fit you better. Want to try them? Here's a tee that matches."

Lil didn't even get offended that Lisa had noticed she was a bit chubbier. She was out of her culottes in a flash, squeezing herself into the borrowed shorts. Red! Even better. And the T-shirt had ruffled feminine edging. She wasn't allowed to wear T-shirts at home because Conservative girls could not dress like men. She flung her culottes up onto her bunk, and they hung down over the edge like an ugly navy flag that waved "here's plain old Lil's bunk." She wished she could toss them on the campfire. Looking away, she embraced Lisa. "Thanks so much!" Then she rushed over to Katy and Megan's bunks.

Katy's naturally sulky lips parted. "Lillian Mae!" she scolded.

But Lil ignored her rebuke just like she always did and gracefully raised her arms—circus performer style—twirling to give them the 360-degree view.

Lil didn't miss that Megan placed a calming hand on Katy's shoulder and whispered something in her ear. Whatever it was, Katy continued to narrow her eyes in disapproval.

"Well I like them. Wish there was a mirror in here," Lil replied, flouncing away.

⁓ৎ

Lil propped an elbow on her bare knee, making sure she sat in a sunny patch so that she could tan her legs like Lisa's. She could tell that Katy was still mad at her, but she wasn't going to allow her friend to ruin her week of fun and freedom. She'd worry later about any consequences there might be when she got home. Megan was always good at getting her out of scrapes and patching up any spats between her and Katy. With that in mind she insisted, "I say, Three Bean Salad."

Their counselor had divided them into groups of three, and they were supposed to come up with a name for their group. She and Katy had been arguing about whether or not to call themselves "Three Bean Salad" which had been Lil's choice. The argument was really a battle of wills, and all three girls knew it. When Mary blew her pink whistle, Lil knew she'd won. She ran over to Katy, who was lounging under a tree, staring at a squirrel on a high branch with glistening leaves. She touched her friend's shoulder. "I'll let you choose the next time. I promise."

Megan intervened softly, "You can be the green bean, if you want, Katy."

"That's okay," Katy replied. "I'll be the dumb kidney bean."

Lil did a little shimmy with her shoulders and sing-songed, "Gar-ban-zo, Gar-ban-zo," for the bean she had picked for herself. Soon she had Katy grinning. Camp was great, way better than shucking corn.

—⌒〰⌒—

On the last night of camp, the three friends sat mesmerized by the campfire. Lil brushed her hands down her borrowed jeans. She was lucky to have such good friends. She knew they would never tattle on her, even if they didn't approve of her wearing shorts and jeans all week. Although Katy and Megan would always be her best friends, she had enjoyed her time with Lisa, too.

Not only that, but their counselor, Mary, had shown Lil some exercises she could continue to do when she got home. She envied Mary's flat tummy, but it was hard to stay slim when Lil's mom was such a great cook. They came from a family of wonderful cooks, and Lil enjoyed cooking, too. She already knew how to make piecrusts, and she also made a tasty meatloaf.

The young man who played guitar and led the singing each evening put away his instrument and dismissed the group to return to their cabins. Seated on a log next to Megan and Katy, Lil looped her arm through Megan's and watched the rest of the group disassemble. "Mary's still standing over there, talking. Let's stay here until she's finished."

"I can't believe tomorrow's our last day," Megan bemoaned.

Lil wasn't ready to go home, don her dark skirts, and get back to chores. She glanced desperately at the sparking campfire. "I never want this to end. It was the best week of my life. And that swing over the lake was the scariest thing I ever did."

"Better than the circus?" Katy asked.

"Just as good." Lil clenched her fists. "Let's make a vow tonight that when we're Mary's age, we'll all move in together. It'll be like camp. Only forever."

Katy furrowed her brow. "We'll probably get married."

"Just until we marry. And we'll be each other's bridesmaids, too! Oh, swear it!"

Katy frowned. "You know Mennonites don't swear or take oaths."

Lil dropped her head in her hands and stared at her jeans, feeling desperate enough to cry.

Megan, who was seated on the log between them, reached out and clasped each of their hands. "The Bible says where two or three agree on something, God honors it. We can agree, but we must never break a promise."

Lil felt rising hope. She leaned forward and sent Katy her most earnest gaze.

Katy bit her lip, then nodded. "Oh all right. I promise. And I already know who I'm going to marry. Jake Byler."

"Ew! Yuck!" Lil made a face because it was gross to think that Katy would want to marry her cousin. But from that day forth, Lil did everything in her power to make sure that their campfire dreams came true. Someday she would break free from her stifling, navy-blue chains. Someday she would own her own pink fingernail polish. She would move in with her two best friends. They would be each other's bridesmaids, and when she married, she would shine in a beautiful lacy gown.

CHAPTER 1

"Don't tell your mother."

Lil clutched her father's dirty breakfast plate and glanced down the hall to make sure Rose Landis was, indeed, still asleep. But then, why wouldn't she be? Her depression kept her abed most mornings.

"Oh Dad. Things will get better. They always do." She'd been hanging on to that hope for weeks now, ever since her own desires had been temporarily deferred.

Although Mom had been suffering from depression for months, she had temporarily rallied for Katy and Jake's wedding because Lil had asked her to help with Katy's wedding cake. Lil had even gotten Mom to take that cake decorating class with her, but the day after the wedding, Mom fell to her bed in exhaustion, and afterward, she reverted to her earlier depressed state, even more tired than before.

"This didn't happen overnight, girl." Dad broke into her thoughts. "And it's not getting any better. Only getting worse." He placed his elbows on the newly cleared table and clasped his unshaven face between his work-worn hands. "It wouldn't be so bad if it was just me, but the farm is the life of this family. All your brothers depend upon it for the livelihood of their families, too."

Lil had inherited her dad's grit, which was why it was unusual for him to cave in to despair. He'd always been the hundred-year-old girder truss that held the Landis family together. But he should have given his sons more leadership. They were grown men, and one old truss didn't have to hold an entire barn together by itself when other trusses were ready to share the load.

"You shouldn't shoulder this alone. You need to share your burden with the boys. Maybe one of them even has an idea."

The Landis men had farmed for generations. Willis Landis owned 140 acres, inherited from his father. The farm had two hog barns, and most of the acreage was used for corn and soybeans because the government made those crops more profitable and they fed the hogs.

Lil had detested those hogs since she was old enough to know that raising them carried a stigma, sometimes even among other farmers. Oh she didn't hate the animals themselves, just the chore of raising them. As a child, she'd even had a pet or two. Hogs were smart animals, and the piglets were cute in their fat-bellied, flat-snouted way, each with their individual personalities, but she would rather have been raised anywhere other than on a hog farm. Katy's dad had a respectable woodworking shop. Jake—Katy's husband and Lil's favorite cousin— was in construction. Megan's dad worked at an automotive shop and even restored Chevy Novas for extra income. But of all the possible scenarios, Lil had been born to a family who raised smelly, squealing hogs.

Picking up the aqua-colored canning jar that served as the centerpiece for the kitchen table, she unscrewed its silver lid and removed the candle. From habit, she swirled a green-checkered dish towel around the inside of the jar. Holding the candle in the palm of one hand, she stared at her dad; her heart broke over his humble and disappointing lot in life. Such a hard worker and doing the only job he'd ever known. She'd never seen him so worn as he had been this past year. The continual struggle against the raw elements of nature had sapped his strength. The recent stress of finances and Mom's depression had shaken his morale.

Lil replaced the candle and put the jar back in its distinctive place, her hands dusting the tea towel over a set of green Depression glass salt and pepper shakers. Just when Lil had been so close to fulfilling her own dreams, everything had been snatched away from her.

Last winter, she'd finally moved into the Millers' doddy house with Katy Yoder. The freedom to chase after her own dreams had long been coveted, along with the fun adventure of rooming with her closest friends. So when the house originally designed for a family's grandparents became available, the three friends had jumped at the chance to rent it. Megan Weaver had been set to join them in the fall after her mission trip. Once Megan helped pay the rent, Lil would have been able to start buying the other things she dreamed about, too, like a new car to replace the brown tin can she drove and referred to as Jezebel.

Mechanically, Lil twisted the tea towel and untwisted it again, considering how the three friends had taken such delight in renovating the doddy house with modern conveniences. Once Lil had graduated from culinary school and gotten her first restaurant job, everything had fallen into place. That is, until Mom had become depressed, and Dad had asked Lil to move back home and help take care of her.

Not knowing anything about depression, Lil thought the illness would only last for a couple of days or weeks at the most. But once she came home, she'd gotten stuck in a sinking routine, trying to keep up with all the chores her mom had once performed. There was cooking and cleaning and laundry and some farm chores, too. But one thing she refused to do was the garden.

Under those circumstances, once Katy and Jake had married, they took over the doddy house. The only fragment of Lil's dream that remained intact was her restaurant job. Low paying and rather dead-end, it didn't provide the career opportunity of moving up to head chef position, but it was still a respite from the farm and her family's troubles. Not only did the farm finances affect her dad and brothers, but this grave problem could be the final blow to her mother's emotional state and affect Lil's future, too.

Replacing the dish towel on a homemade wooden towel bar inside the pine cabinet beneath the sink, Lil quickly turned back to face Dad.

"Maybe you need to modernize."

He stared at her and tugged one of his large ears—which pitched up his hat's straw brim like soil to toadstools. "That's what Matt always says."

Lil's middle brother was the one most likely to challenge Dad. Matt had Lil's personality and was open to modern ways, changes that might keep them out of bankruptcy. Like her, he had often tested the church elders, too. "I know it's hard for you, but couldn't you ask Matt about some of his ideas? If all the other farms are utilizing new methods, well. . ." She shrugged.

Dad abruptly rose. "Got chores to do. Thanks for breakfast." He started toward the door and snatched his truck keys off the yellow peg shelf that had served the family for as long as Lil could recall. "So you won't tell your mom?"

With a heavy sigh, Lil glanced regrettably down the hall again. "No. I won't tell." She looked back toward the yellow shelf visible through the doorway that separated the kitchen from the mudroom. It had been there ever since she could remember. Five feet in width, it was firmly secured to the wall studs to bear the family's offerings. Its row of sturdy six-inch pegs provided a stopping off place for the family's odds and ends, mostly hats and coats and items of clothing the boys used to bring home for their mom to mend.

A basket containing gloves and garden tools perched in readiness for her mom's frequent trips to the garden. Of late, the basket had been neglected. Beside it was a folded set of clean overalls. The shelf harbored items both entering and departing the house. Beneath it was a matching bench where family members sat when tugging on their boots. Things on the farm didn't change much, and Lil had always hungered for change. She only hoped it wouldn't be change for the worse.

⸺૭⸻

Lil replaced the gas nozzle into its receptacle and jerked open her car door, then lifted it so that it would latch. She was going to have to get those door hinges checked before the whole door fell off. She locked it for good measure and reprimanded herself for forgetting that Jezebel needed gas. Now she was going to be late to work again. She grabbed for the seat belt before she'd even slid onto the vinyl seat cover that protected her skirt from bare springs and stuffing, and was soon pulling back into traffic.

Nearing the four-o'clock rush hour, the traffic moved slower than she would have liked, especially when she needed to make up the ten minutes she'd lost at the gas station. But she came alive to the hustle and bustle of the Columbus streets that were so different than the rural Plain City roads.

Being a few minutes late wouldn't have been such a big deal if she weren't already on the manager's bad list. He'd had to rearrange the restaurant's work schedule several times lately to accommodate Lil's personal needs, which revolved around her mom's care. Doctor appointments and Mom's neglected household chores all bubbled together like a boiling pot that Lil barely managed to keep from overflowing. A smart cook either removed such a pot from the fire or turned down the heat, but she could do neither.

Yes, she was overworked, but she didn't want to let her job at Riccardo's slide; it was her door of escape. Sure, she wasn't using all her culinary skills, but at least she was working in her area of expertise and building a résumé. She shuddered to think how her dad would react to her use of *résumé*—such a worldly word. He would rebuke her for striving to become a famous chef. He thought her ambitions were foolish and unladylike. He thought she should be pursuing a life that included marriage, children, and homemaking. It wasn't that she didn't want those things, but she wasn't ready to settle down without pursuing her dream first.

At last Lil saw the Riccardo's sign and whipped Jezebel into the parking lot. She pulled next to head chef Beppe's expensive SUV then realized she was far too close. If he came out to the parking lot and saw her car, he would yell at her again because he claimed somebody was repeatedly dinging his car door. Quickly putting Jezebel in REVERSE, Lil backed up to adjust her car's alignment.

But with that action, her car unexpectedly jerked. Simultaneously, a loud crashing sound filled her ears. With it came the awful realization that she'd backed into another vehicle. She yanked her gearshift into PARK, finagled her car door open, and jumped out, not bothering to turn off the ignition of her sputtering engine.

"Move your car forward. I can't open my door," a curt male voice demanded.

One look at the shiny silver Lexus caused her heart to sink. Quickly, she hopped back inside Jezebel and pulled back into the parking spot, still remaining too close to the chef's car. She got out again, so flustered that her car door banged hard into Beppe's SUV.

"Do you always go around destroying cars?" Feeling the rise of indignation, she jostled her door shut and turned. Her lips tensed with an angry retort. The derogatory question had been asked by a strikingly handsome man who now stood glaring at her, waiting for an explanation.

"Of course not!" Unless she had been the one putting dings in Beppe's car. Her mind had been preoccupied lately with personal problems. Was she the one? She'd been so frustrated lately with her rickety door. For the first time, she entertained the possibility that she might be the culprit dinging Beppe's car door. Her voice carried her growing dismay. "At least not until my car door broke."

The blond stranger eyed her clunker, and pity softened his glittering brown eyes. Lil despised pity. Her pride always raised its hackles at any pity or scorn directed her way.

"Do you have insurance?"

"Yes. Just a minute." She opened her sagging car door again to get her insurance card out of the glove box, and his hand shot out and caught the edge of the door so it didn't bang against the chef's SUV again.

Drowning in embarrassment, she scooted across the vinyl seat cover and retrieved the card. When she moved back, he still hovered outside, holding the top edge of her car door. Eyeing his shirt, she thought, *He certainly is a tall one.* The way he towered over her and the manner in which he protected Beppe's car while assuming the worst of her, provoked her to fulfill his expectations with a shove of her door. It gouged into his body, and she heard his surprised grunt.

"Excuse me," she said, holding back a smile and easing out.

His gaze narrowed onto the card she waved. "I'll go get a pen," he said warily, starting toward his car.

She fumbled inside her purse. "No wait. I have one." She saw him stare at his creased car door with droopy shoulders. *At least his door has two working hinges.* She sighed. If she had a nice car like his, she'd be feeling pretty discouraged about now, too. Her fingers still groping every cranny of her purse, searching for that pen, she muttered beneath her breath, "Too bad he's such a cute guy."

"Too bad she's such a beauty."

She jerked her gaze over at him, wondering if she'd spoken her thoughts aloud. Was he referring to her or his car?

Whichever, his expression had softened, making him even more appealing. "You didn't get hurt, did you?"

"No. You?"

She watched him shake his head then glance back at his creased car door. With disappointment, she figured he must have been referring to his car.

She shoved the pen and paper at him. "You can use the roof of my car to write if you want."

Protective as he was about cars, he must have agreed that another scratch on her clunker wouldn't matter because he took her up on her offer.

"Another year or so, and I'll be driving a beauty like yours," she remarked.

He ran his gaze over her. "You work here?"

"Yes. You eat here?"

Handing back her insurance information, he gave her his first genuine smile. "This was going to be my first time."

She stared at the tiny dimples on either side of his mouth. "You'd better be nice to me if you're going to order pasta."

Surprise lit his brown eyes. "I ordered takeout. It's probably in there getting cold. You're a cook?"

"Line cook, soon to be head chef."

He chuckled. "I like that."

"Look, mister." Not having his name, she continued. "The least I

339

can do is get you a free meal."

"Fletch Stauffer." He held out his hand to shake.

Something familiar tickled Lil's brain, but when she placed her hand in his palm, the pleasant firmness pushed the murky thought away.

He released her hand. "Here's my boss's insurance card. Better write down his information, too."

She pulled a face, about to ask him if he thought Jezebel really needed fixing, when she caught the *boss* part. She stared at the card, suddenly understanding his dismay.

"It's my boss's car," he explained unnecessarily.

With a penitent nod, she realized she wasn't getting Fletch Stauffer's personal information at all. She'd never have the nerve to call him anyway. And Jezebel certainly didn't need a new bumper. Today's scratch was just another wrinkle. Trying to cover up Jezebel's age with some shiny new chrome would be about as foolish as the bright red lipstick some elderly outsiders wore into the restaurant. In Lil's opinion, it would only make the car appear more ridiculous.

As if their minds were running along similar tracks, he said, "Let me add my phone number." He shrugged. "Just in case something comes up."

When she read his information, it finally hit her. "The name Stauffer sounds familiar. You're not a Mennonite, are you?"

His shoulders relaxed. "I am. I was wondering. Are you, too?"

She felt a moment of embarrassment that he must have noticed her plain clothing. "Yeah, I attend the Big Darby Conservative Church." She lowered her gaze and was surprised to see that he wore red tennis shoes. Nope. Nothing conservative about him.

"No kidding. Small worl—parking lot."

She laughed. "Exactly. Too small. If they just made these spaces a little wider, none of this would have happened." But she couldn't deny the pleasure she was feeling at his expense. She hoped his boss wasn't as ill-tempered as Beppe. "Where do you go to church?"

"Crossroads Mennonite."

Just as she had earlier surmised, he was an Ohio Conference Mennonite. Envy and disappointment rushed over her. It seemed the good

things were always just out of her reach. She longed to attend a church
with fewer restrictions on things like television and more modern
clothing, but she didn't want to leave her family and friends or feel
condemned by them.

Another car honked, and Fletcher looked over his shoulder. "Guess
I better move my boss's car before somebody else hits it."

"Sure," she said, slapping at a pesky mosquito.

When she looked up, Fletch had already turned away. Maybe she'd
get a chance to talk to him inside. *Inside,* where she should have been a
half an hour earlier, or more. Beppe was going to be mad. Quickly she
started toward Riccardo's, breaking into a run.

CHAPTER 2

Y ou're late," Beppe, Lil's Italian boss, snapped, just as she'd known he would. Once again she'd managed to light his short fuse, and she wasn't sure how far his patience with her would last before he showed her the exit sign.

"I'm so sorry. I had an accident. . .with Jezebel. . .in the parking lot."

Beppe's eyes flared, and his voice barked, "You didn't hit my car did you?"

"No. Of course not." Well she hadn't had the accident with his car. She really needed to start avoiding his car altogether. But his choice spot was close to the restaurant, and none of the other employees had the nerve to park next to him so that spot was usually vacant. Since she was usually running late, it drew her like a moth to flame.

"That car of yours is an annoyance. Maybe you'll get a new one now?" His expression was hopeful.

"Didn't hurt Jezebel. But the car I hit, it was a Lexus."

Beppe cringed as if his own car had taken the blow.

Lil explained, "And it was the driver's first time at Riccardo's. Do you think we could give him a free meal?"

Beppe suddenly turned all business. "You paying?"

"If I could afford that, I wouldn't be driving Jezebel, now would I?" she quipped.

"How many are in his party?"

"I don't know. He has a take-out order."

"Yes. You hand deliver the bill, tell him it's covered, and be sure to smooth things over. And for the love of good food, be more careful."

Lil glanced anxiously toward the take-out counter but couldn't see Fletch. She needed to catch him before he paid. "Okay. Thanks. Sorry I was late."

"Again."

She cringed. Beppe was chalking up another offense for her on his mental blackboard.

"You're wearing my patience, Lil. You really are. Now go to your station."

"Yes, sir. Just as soon as I hand deliver that bill." Hurrying away from him before he changed his mind, past the stations to the hall, she rushed to the take-out counter, where Fletch was already thumbing through his billfold. She exchanged a few words with the clerk, scratched paid on his check, and slid it across the counter to him.

"I took care of your check."

He accepted the receipt and stuffed it in his billfold, which he jammed into his jeans pocket. His smile flashed more than appreciation; it possessed all the elements that could make Lil's toes curl inside her black oxfords.

"Thanks, Lily."

"I thought you should have my number, too, so I put it on the back of the bill."

"That's considerate."

Lil felt her face heat. "No problem. Well let me know if. . .you know. . .you need anything. For your boss's car, I mean."

"I will." Concern briefly clouded the sparkle in his toe-curling gaze, and she figured he was thinking about his boss's reaction, but honestly, she couldn't afford to offer to pay his deductible. She was saving up her meager paychecks to move back into the doddy house as soon as her mom got better.

"It was the least I could do. Well, better get back to my station. Sorry about everything."

Fletch motioned as if he was tipping the bill of an invisible hat, and Lil turned away while her feet could still carry her.

"It wasn't all bad."

She halted at the soft statement. Turned. When their gazes met, she recognized the look of male appreciation. "Thanks." She paused momentarily, but when he didn't say anything more, she smiled and clambered to the kitchen. Her heart peddled faster than her little nephew Scott on his new John Deere tractor trike. Would Fletch give her a call? How long had it been since a guy had shown interest in her?

The idea lingered. Even after a half hour bent over a steaming black pot, Lil was still dreaming about Fletch Stauffer. She brushed her sweaty forehead with the inside of her forearm, aggravated that the bangs she had impulsively cut had slipped out of their bobby-pin moorings to mercilessly tickle her face. They needed trimming, but she couldn't do that while she was living at home again, at least without getting a lecture.

The restaurant had been what Beppe called in-the-weeds busy with the pregame crowd at the nearby SportsOhio complex. Her stomach rumbled from working around the aromas of the Italian sauces she loved so much. Usually, she skipped dinner on the nights she came in early. It helped to keep her rebellious waistline trim, although it was never small enough to suit her. That was probably one of the reasons guys weren't interested in her. Why should they be?

She was a plain woman in every aspect. Born on a farm. Born into a Conservative Mennonite church where the women were forbidden to adorn themselves in the latest fashions or paint their flesh with cosmetics. And having come from a family of wonderful cooks, she'd had to battle her waistline all her life. Oh she had it under control now, but only because of a regimented exercise program and bouts of deprivation.

Clumping her black oxfords to the back room for another crate of tomatoes, she hoisted them with a grunt into her arms and placed them on a prep counter, all the while persuading herself that he wouldn't call.

She had plain brown hair and freckles to boot. No, a tall, blond, good-looking guy like Fletch Stauffer wouldn't be calling the likes of her. He was just being kind. She remembered how he'd looked down his nose at Jezebel and gazed with pity at her. Fletch certainly wouldn't be calling her. She leaned over the sink and washed her hands.

Glancing around the kitchen, she squared her shoulders and started washing tomatoes. She still carried high hopes of becoming head chef, and then her life would change. She would make her dreams happen. She blew a puff of air at her bangs, but one stubborn strand still obscured her vision. Oh, she knew she wouldn't be replacing Beppe at Riccardo's. For now she was biding her time, scrubbing vegetables and cooking plain pasta. Plain, plain, plain. But someday—

—☙—

For a Conservative girl, Lillian Landis was anything but plain, Fletch thought as he strode out of Riccardo's and headed toward his boss's car. Her shiny brown hair was pulled up in a knot, but many cooks wore their hair secured. He'd noticed the restaurant's customary uniform was either black slacks or black miniskirts, but Lillian wore a modest-length skirt that teased her curves. Instead of a tight-fitting T-shirt beneath her apron, she wore a crisp white blouse. But the tell-tale sign that Lillian was Mennonite was in her voice, which carried the thick slur that came from the Pennsylvania Dutch accent of many of the Mennonite's older members. She must have family still from the old order.

He shook his mind from her cute image and relived the accident. He'd been so mad when her old brown clunker had backed into Vic's expensive car. Until he got a look at Lillian Landis.

She was average height, lots shorter than him—but then five foot four seemed short when a guy was six foot one—and such a curvy little thing with a waist tiny enough to encircle with his hands. Her modest clothing added to her feminine allure, following her movements and tightening in the right places for the briefest of moments and skimming over her curves as if draping an exquisite piece of art that was not on exhibit for public viewing.

Her eyes were multiple shades of blue that in their brief encounter had ranged from a soft sky blue to a sparkling glacier green. What a contradiction they were to her cute freckles and upturned nose. How refreshing to meet an honest, candid woman, startling him by admitting she was a car destroyer. In the next breath, her Dutch accent slayed him with the news that she found him attractive.

He reached Vic's car door and crouched to examine the damage, disbelief and regret rushing through him anew as he ran his hand along the whitish-green horizontal crease. Fletch had never owned a car this nice and hoped Vic's car insurance premium wouldn't skyrocket.

He slid into the driver's seat and started the engine. As the Lexus glided out of its doomed parking space, Lillian's face flashed in his mind again. What an intriguing woman. Mennonite woman, of all things. Was that some kind of God sign?

Fletch made it a habit to observe everything that happened around him, watching for God's direction. Could it only be coincidence that in the big city of Columbus, Ohio, he'd run into a Mennonite girl? Well, strictly speaking, she had run into him.

In church, he hadn't met any single women half as attractive as Lillian. He was tempted to call her just to listen to her cute Dutch accent again. Unconsciously, he raked a hand through his fine blond hair. Although he could make a pastime out of thinking about women, he shouldn't be doing so as busy as he was with his studies and trying to please Vic.

He had been placed at Vic's veterinarian clinic as part of an offsite selective experience, a senior requisite of the veterinary school at Ohio State University. As intense as these final requirements were, the last thing he needed to knock him off course was a romantic fling, especially with a Conservative girl. He didn't even know how their faith differed.

Fletch eased into Dublin's traffic and headed toward Plain City, where Vic's practice was located close to the farms that sprawled across acres of plowed fields and pasture lands. Fletch's cheap apartment was near the practice. Vic's brother owned the small apartment complex, and he allowed Fletch to live there rent-free as long as he worked for Vic. The veterinarian paid his utilities and gave him a small stipend for his other living expenses. Fletch was grateful for that, because all the veterinary students weren't so fortunate. Vic had his generous moments, which was why he had offered Fletch his car for the food run. He could only hope that Vic's attitude wouldn't change when he saw what had happened.

A siren's shriek tore Fletch's glance from the surrounding landscape to his rearview mirror. At the flashing lights bearing down upon him, he groaned with the realization he was speeding. Brooding over his unbelievably rotten luck, he pulled to the side of the road and lowered his window. He had removed Vic's registration from the glove box by the time the police officer stepped up to his door.

"May I see your registration and insurance information?"

Fletch handed the officer Vic's registration and insurance card, relieved for the second time that day that his boss kept his documents in his glove box.

"This is my boss's car." He pointed at the food bag. "I was getting his lunch."

The officer hardened his gaze. "I'll need to see your license."

Fletch removed his billfold from his pocket and nervously fumbled through his cards, which spilled onto the floorboards. He leaned forward.

"Stop right there. Step out of the car." The officer's voice was curt, nonnegotiable.

Fletch froze. The officer seemed suspicious that he might be going for a gun under the seat. "Sure." Fletch opened his dented car door. "I was just going after the cards that I dropped on the floorboards." Was the officer about to pat him down and throw him up against the car like he'd seen in the movies?

Instead, the officer quietly studied him, securing the information Fletch had given him to his clipboard. "Did you know you were going 55 in a 45 mile-per-hour speed zone?"

"No. I was a bit preoccupied. I was just involved in a minor accident." He pointed toward his car door. "I guess I was still thinking about how my boss will react. The accident wasn't my fault. A woman backed into me in the restaurant's parking lot." Too late, Fletch realized that admitting he'd just been in an accident probably hadn't been the brightest thing to do.

Eyeing the crease in the car door then looking back at Fletch, the officer's expression softened. "You a resident?"

"I'm attending OSU's veterinary school. I graduate in the spring."

"Have you signed a rental lease?"

"No."

"Own a car?"

"Yes, sir."

"Gainfully employed?"

"No, sir." He didn't think there was anything gainful about the housing stipend Vic provided.

"I'm giving you a warning." He finished scribbling, tore off a sheet of paper, and handed it to Fletch.

"Thanks, sir. I appreciate that."

The officer eyed him again, then smiled. "Figured you needed a break."

Fletch uttered another thanks. Of all the scenarios zipping through his mind—owing a hefty speeding ticket, having to register his car, applying for an Ohio license—he'd gotten off easy.

"Drive safely," the officer said, then strode back to his patrol car.

With a sigh, Fletch got back in the car. Dare he get back on the road? he wondered, leaning and sweeping his hand along the floorboards to retrieve the fallen cards. The restaurant receipt slipped out of his grasp and floated farther beneath the seat. He abandoned it for the sake of getting back to the practice before Vic's hunger added to his distress.

CHAPTER 3

Rose Landis had lost interest in life. Lil's mom kept her bedroom's heavy brocade drapes drawn and her antique German lamps snuffed. It took daily bouts of coaxing just to get her to rise and dress. And this morning, Lil had to get her inside the car, too.

"But Mom, we have an appointment with that nice counselor today."

"Don't be fooled. It's his job to be nice. That's all. He'll just have to fill in my appointment slot with some other lunatic. I'm not up to it today. And I didn't ask you to make that appointment, anyway."

Lil gazed at her mom. Until spewing out her objection, she had looked like a small lifeless lump in a big bed. Her long hair was plaited in one white-streaked brown braid. Her lips were pulled tight and thin. Lil softly reasoned, "You're not crazy, Mom. Everyone has times when life becomes unmanageable. That's why God made friends and family."

"To force their moms to go to counseling," Mom huffed back.

Lil knew that counseling was a bit out of the ordinary in their Conservative circles. In their church it carried a stigma of personal and spiritual failure because everybody knew that God was sufficient, and if a person couldn't cope—and it wasn't God's fault—putting two and two together added up to a faulty faith. Even for Lil, who had no clue where Mom's problem had begun, it was hard not to judge her in some way. But now she gave her a patient smile. "Just like you forced me to brush my teeth and learn my ABC's. It's not that you don't know what you should be doing. You just need a little nudging." Mom turned her unconvinced expression toward the wall.

"I'm going to turn the shower on now. Nice and hot like you like it. I wish I had a new massage showerhead like the one Dad installed for you. He sure does love you, catering to you like he does."

Rolling toward the edge of the bed, Mom muttered, "Hmmph. Cater, my eye. And making me feel guilty doesn't make it any better." Then she murmured so low that Lil almost didn't catch it, "It's too late for that man."

Lil wondered about the meaning of that snide remark. Were her mom and dad having marriage problems? She remembered telling Katy a while back that she was positive her mom's depression had nothing to do with their marriage. But love was a mighty force, and just by watching Katy and Jake's tumultuous relationship and how it had affected her friends, she could attest to its strange powers. Did she dare question her mom on the topic? Mom and Dad never talked about their relationship. It had always been a private thing without much public demonstration. Or should Lil encourage Mom to bring the topic up to the counselor?

Meanwhile Mom had placed her bare feet on the oval, braided rug beside the bed. Her shoulders slumped. "I don't know why I don't have any energy. I hate getting old. Don't know what your dad even sees in me. And I never asked for a new showerhead, even if the old one dripped for two-and-a-half years."

"Dad sees the same things we all do," Lil went on, without acknowledging her mom's complaint about the house's old and faulty plumbing. "You're a wonderful person. Of course your cooking has nothing to do with it," she teased, hoping to stir up some of her mom's old confidence. Mom's laughter used to fill the home, and her sense of humor had kept everyone on their toes. She had passed that gene along to Lil's brother Matt.

"I do miss baking. If only I had the gumption, I'd make us some cinnamon rolls with brown-sugar icing. Maybe tomorrow."

"I'll help if you like," Lil replied, staring at the starched head covering on her mom's nightstand, though she knew from experience that when tomorrow rolled around Mom wouldn't feel like baking. Something terrible was wrong, but nobody could pinpoint the problem. This was only their third session with the counselor, and Lil hoped he would get to the bottom of it soon. Mom had lost weight, too—judging by the way her waistband hung, probably at least twenty-five or thirty pounds.

Later that morning after the appointment concluded with the kind, but noncommittal counselor, Lil brought her mom home and settled her in the new rocker Dad had purchased for Mom's fiftieth birthday. Dad's tenderness toward Mom, of late, baffled Lil, too, because as her mom had earlier insinuated, Will Landis had never been the thoughtful, caring type. He'd always just been sturdy, hardworking, and dependable—the practical type.

Leaving her mom by the living room window so she could watch it rain, Lil hoped to get to town and back before the actual downpour hit. She used her purse for a makeshift umbrella and made a dash for Jezebel. On the road, her windshield wipers did little to clear her vision as she drove to the Plain City pharmacy to get the pills the therapist had prescribed for her mom. She wasn't sure if she could get her to take any, but maybe if Mom knew they were already purchased, she would comply with the psychiatrist's wishes.

The canopy in front of the pharmacy beckoned with its dry patch of sidewalk but traitorously startled Lil with a gush of water down the back of her neck. Inside, she agreed with the pharmacist that the farmers would be glad for the rain and paid the bill with her own money, not wanting to burden her dad after learning the farm was about to go bankrupt. Assuming pharmacists took oaths of privacy, she was glad that she didn't see anybody else she knew while she purchased a prescription of bottled happiness.

Outside, the awning baptized her again, and clutching her small white bag of hope, she made a run for Jezebel. Drenched, she finagled the warped door and tossed her purse and bag on the plastic slipcover.

A shiver tingled up and down her spine as she stuck her key in the ignition. Jezebel wouldn't start.

—⸱◡⸱—

On the same side of the cow as Vic, Fletch leaned his shoulder against the heifer and tightened his grip on the animal's green-and-black-striped lead rope. Water dripped off his red ball cap, and with one hand he flipped the hood of his slicker back up over it. Impatient, for it seemed to be taking the vet examining the cow far too long, he called, "Can you see anything?"

"The leg wound is infected. We're lucky she's still on her feet. But we're going to have to get her back to the barn before I can treat it, or the bandage will just get soaked."

Thinking of the truck's cab with desire, Fletch remarked, "Would have been nice if Johnson would have already had her confined."

"He probably wasn't expecting the rain. It's all part of the job. You might as well get used to bad weather and contrary animals. Believe me, if it's not the animals, it's their owners."

"I suppose so."

"Or are you going to take one of those cushy jobs taking care of pets?"

Fletch figured every job had its drawbacks. "In school, they warned us that house cats are as deadly as a mountain lion."

Vic scoffed. "Pure exaggeration. Well you've got the lead rope and I've got the truck keys. So I guess I'll see you and this heifer back at the barn in about an hour."

"More penance?" Fletch teased.

"Just exposing you to a wider range of experience," the thin, red-haired vet replied.

"Exposure, all right," Fletch muttered, stepping in front of the cow and gently pulling her forward. Ever since he'd returned to the veterinary practice with Vic's dented car—correction, Vic's wife's dented car, for Fletch had discovered that the couple had exchanged vehicles that day—the veterinarian had mustered up every conceivable dirty job for him to perform. Fletch didn't mind getting his hands dirty. After all, he was raised on the mission field and used to all kinds of adverse and unexpected conditions. But Vic was getting far too much pleasure out of watching him slosh around in manure and probe stool samples for parasites.

He guessed the honeymoon had worn off between them. For all Fletch knew, maybe Vic's ire stemmed from the fact that he was sleeping on the couch at home. Fletch hadn't been around Britt enough to determine her personality type. He didn't know if she was supportive or resentful of Vic's practice. Part of their schooling had prepared them for the hazards of choosing a career that demanded long, irregular hours.

Most of the students spent their summers involved in some sort of on-the-job experience, and Fletch had been fortunate to get on with the same veterinarian he was going to help once the fall term began. At least he had previously thought he was fortunate. Though they were barely getting started, he had to wonder what the next year would hold.

Fletch hunched his shoulders against the rain and urged the heifer toward the dirt tire tracks that crisscrossed green pasture, where he and Vic had earlier driven to reach the field where the animal had been last seen. Fletch's muckers sank deep in the muddy track, making his progress slower, and the animal must have felt the change of terrain, too, because it suddenly balked, practically jerking Fletch's arm from its shoulder socket. With several tugs, he got the animal moving again, but Fletch still couldn't see the barn. He spoke as softly as he could over the wind and rain to urge the animal forward, but a bolt of thunder changed the animal's will.

The cow reared back, and Fletch frantically strove to secure his grasp on the slippery lead. But the strong animal turned and dragged Fletch backward until the lead slid through his gloves. Moments after that, he found himself sprawled facedown in the muddy lane. He lay there, momentarily stunned, until a current of rain made its way onto his bare skin between the hem of his hiked-up slicker and his belt. Rising to his elbows, he sputtered between mud-caked teeth, "Stupid cow!"

Staggering to his feet, he glared through the rain at the animal that had stopped only a short distance away. The heifer stared him down with a frightened curiosity. The animal's injury had to be severe if she hadn't bolted away, Fletch thought, yanking his slicker back in place and starting toward the frightened animal. Regardless if Vic was dry and sipping coffee with Johnson or not, he needed to get the animal back to the barn as quickly as possible.

—∽—

Later that week, Lil slid five pieces of pie onto her mom's Autumn Leaf dessert plates and placed four of them in front of the men seated around the kitchen table. She glanced nervously down the hall, assured that her mom was in her room. Mostly, she was nervous for her brother Matt's sake. Dad had called a family meeting to tell the brothers about the farm trouble. She just hoped he gave Matt a chance to express his ideas. Matt had recently started attending a more liberal-minded Mennonite church, and she knew there was still underlying friction between him and their dad.

Hank, the darkest and oldest of the Landis siblings, looked up at her from his seat at the table. "Thanks, Lily Mae. This looks good."

"You deserve it for coming to my rescue the other day. I don't know what I would have done without you."

"Anybody can replace spark plugs."

"Yes, but you got drenched doing it while I stayed dry in the car."

"That's what brothers are for, but I worry about you driving that piece of junk."

"It's my piece of junk, and usually it gets me around." Lil's face heated. "I'm sorry. That was rude."

"Mom still not cooking?" her youngest brother, Stephen, interrupted.

Stephen's waist size reflected his main interest in life was food—with a partiality toward his mom's cooking. All the sisters-in-law had an inferiority complex when it came to their cooking. They were good cooks, just not as good as the Landis women.

"No." Lil lowered her voice. "But she went to the counselor again and even took some medication this week."

"You think that's a good idea?" Hank frowned. Unless he shaved twice a day, her brother sported a dark shadow of a beard, which added to his formidable countenance. As the eldest, he was always looking out for everyone, appearing grumpy and overbearing at times.

Dad came to her defense. "It's more serious than you know. Lil's doing her best with your mom."

Hank nodded. Dark, serious, and traditional, he was clad in his usual short-sleeved, button-down shirt and a pair of jeans, his only fashion vice his penchant for the John Deere label. He could always be found in the classic green J. D. hat. He splurged on the more expensive J. D. farm boots, too, and loved to buy his sons J. D. pedal tractors and push toys.

Hank's wife, Sara, claimed he spoiled their children, Scott and Sammy. His feisty wife came from Kansas, and Hank's nickname for her was Sara Cyclone, taken from *The Wizard of Oz* book.

Lil took a small wedge of the peach pie for herself. "You care if I join you?"

Dad narrowed his eyes as if wanting to get the meeting going and dreading it at the same time.

"Go ahead and start your meeting. I won't interrupt," Lil urged. She figured after picking all the peaches—which was an itchy job— freezing them, and baking the pies, she had a right to sit and eat at the table with them. Anyway, she really wanted to hear what was going on with the farm's finances. She had to wonder if her mom knew about it and if it had anything to do with her depression.

Dad tugged gently on the lobe of his large ear, considering her request. "I guess we can talk in front of Lil." Then he thrust a warning finger at her. "But you have enough to worry about helping with your mom. Remember to leave the farm problems to us men."

Although his voice remained gentle and he meant his warning for her own good, she resented his male finger pointing and shutting her out just because she was a female. She had hoped he was changing his attitude when he'd confided in her the other morning. Now she realized he'd been sharing with her only because he didn't have his wife to vent to any longer. Will Landis didn't usually ask anyone for advice. He was the girder. He didn't expect her to help him find a solution to his financial woes. Probably didn't think she was capable of such things. She gave a small nod and dropped her gaze to her pie.

She intended to linger and listen even if she had to set a record on how slow a body could eat one piece of pie—the same piece for which she would have to add extra sit-ups to her nightly regimen. After eating her dessert, she could refill coffee cups, if need be.

"I missed my loan payment this month," Dad announced.

The brothers' gazes swam in confusion. Lil remembered how painful it had been to receive the bad news. Her brothers understood that Dad referred to the farm loan, which had accumulated with various farm needs from equipment to seeds. On a row of good years, it was temporary, enough to get by until harvest. On a row of bad years, it provided the payroll and carried the farm. But the confusion came because the boys hadn't known the farm was in trouble.

"Do you need some money to tide you over?" Hank asked. "The cyclone and I can spare a few thousand temporarily."

Dad gripped his coffee cup. "It's too late for tiding over."

Stephen pushed another heaping fork of pie into his mouth and chewed, his brows forming a frustrated *V* as if they might take wing and fly off his face.

Hank's forehead furrowed. "Let's sell off some hogs."

"We can do that, but it will only delay the inevitable. The last couple of years should have been good ones; instead we're steadily sinking."

"Can I have a look at the books?" Hank asked, as eldest son.

Dad rose without comment and left the room.

In his absence, Hank muttered, "I should have taken over the books years ago." Lil knew he had taken accounting courses in college. Hank had gone to Hesston Mennonite College and returned one year later with his wife, Sara, but had never finished his bachelor's degree. Instead, at Dad's urging, he'd gone straight back to farming. But he had been a natural with numbers and spreadsheets.

"Shh! Here he comes!" Matt warned.

Dad pushed a ledger across the table. "Look all you want. It won't change a thing. But at least I won't have as much to explain."

Matt exchanged glances with Lil, and she knew exactly what he was thinking. Dad should have computerized his books by now. Matt had finished his degree at Hesston and was the most liberal of the brothers. Not that it would have magically corrected all their financial woes, Lil imagined. But surely every problem had a solution. Even multiple solutions. Hank had just turned thirty. It was high time that Dad let her brothers help shoulder the farm burdens besides doing the manual labor and receiving a paycheck.

The men bent their heads over the books while she refilled their coffee cups. Then they spent an hour probing at the situation from different angles. Finally, Matt spoke up. "Dad's right. Without a major change, we'll be bankrupt before harvest. Our only hope is to modernize."

All gazes fastened on Matt to see if he was joking, because their middle brother had a corny sense of humor. He liked to pull practical jokes on the others, and since he'd begun attending a different church, he'd started wearing T-shirts that bore messages like "Tractorologist" or "Farm fed and rural raised." But this time, Matt appeared to be dead serious.

Stephen motioned at Lil for more pie, clearly wishing to escape.

Hank set down his John Deere mug. "He's right."

Dad took a long swig of coffee, then set down his cup so hard it clattered and spilled brown liquid onto the plastic, lilac-flowered tablecloth. Lil jumped up and returned with a green-checkered tea towel. She pushed it toward her dad, but he ignored her efforts. "Guess it won't hurt to listen to your newfangled notions."

With relief, Lil sank back on her chair, the cloth dropping to her lap. Her eyes stung, knowing how much that statement had cost her dad. She barely breathed, hoping Matt really did have an idea. He didn't disappoint. He started talking about factory farming where more animals could be raised in tighter, modern pens. His ideas brought out some scoffs and raised some questions, yet most of it was taken to heart by the other men. Lil sat engrossed as they batted around possible scenarios and discussed what the church would allow and what might be forbidden. Suddenly, the room became quiet as a morgue.

Lil looked up. There stood Mom in her bathrobe, her disheveled head tilted to the side. "You having a party without me?"

Dad paled, quickly scooting back his chair and then easing Mom into it. With one meaningful look in Hank's direction, the books were snatched and hidden beneath the table.

"Peach pie, Mom," Lil said. "Would you like a piece?" She quickly wiped up the spill to protect her mom's ribbed, terry-cloth sleeve.

"I think so," Mom replied, oblivious to Lil's ministrations. "For some reason, I can't sleep tonight. Just restless, I guess."

Lil exchanged a look with her dad. Were the pills already causing a change and bringing her out of her stupor? Mom had not gotten out of bed on her own for weeks.

The business discussion was dropped on the spot, and all the attention was riveted on Mom. Even with the dark circles under her eyes, she was a pretty woman. Lil's sister, Michelle, looked like their mom, but Lil took after their dad. Mom's long braid was draped over the front of her mint-green robe, and she'd taken the effort to put on her covering. "What are you boys talking about? Sure sounded lively out here."

"Just farming," Hank explained.

Mom's expression fell in disappointment. "Oh?" She looked at the untouched wedge of pie before her. "I'm more worn out than I realized. Help me back to bed, Lil?"

Lil rushed forward. "Sure."

"Give those grandbabies kisses," Mom said flatly as she shuffled along the wood floor that, like her, had lost its luster, for Lil didn't buff it like her mom had always done. Mom's terry slippers had a piece of elastic hand sewn across the ankles. She used to do small things like that, paying attention to all the little details that make a family a home. Her appearance at the table now was not much in comparison, but it had been an unexpected effort.

It took Lil a while to get her mom settled.

"It was good to hear the boys talking about the farm," Mom said. "Will's finally allowing them a say?" she asked, hopefully.

"Yes, I believe he is."

She sighed deeply. "There was a time when he used to talk to me about the farm. Now he just clams up." Her voice took on a childlike hope. "Maybe if the boys do more, your dad won't be so busy."

Not if they lost the farm, Lil supposed, though she kept that opinion to herself.

"Get me one of those sleeping pills, will you?" Mom asked.

Lil touched her mom's forehead and unpinned her covering. "They aren't sleeping pills." Sometimes she gave her mom an over-the-counter painkiller. "And you already took your new pill."

Mom suddenly clutched Lil's arm. "What if I can't sleep anymore? I can't bear it if the days get any longer." She tightened her grip. "I just can't."

CHAPTER 4

At the rooster's untimely crowing and intrusion upon her wonderful dream, Lil awoke with an overwhelming desire for one particular chicken cooked with tender dumplings. Of course she shouldn't have been dreaming about Fletch anyways, because it only made each passing day that he didn't phone her more difficult to endure. Even though she knew he wouldn't call, she charged her phone's battery every night while she slept. Hopefully time would remove the sting of his rejection.

Wistfully, she dismissed him from her mind, dressed, and prepared breakfast for her dad. When she had placed the last hand-washed breakfast plate in the drying rack—for the farm kitchen didn't have the latest appliances—she went to see how Mom had slept and if she couldn't coax her out of bed and into making those cinnamon rolls she'd mentioned.

Lil padded into the dark room and frowned at the lump of empty bedcovers, for it was unusual for Mom to rise on her own. Once again, her thoughts turned hopeful that the new pills might be helping.

Light filtered beneath the bathroom door's threshold. With a rap, Lil softly called, "Mom. You in there?"

There was no answer so she knocked again, calling a little louder,

"Mom!" Still no reply. Lil twisted the knob and inched the door ajar, but it hit an obstacle that kept it from fully opening. Looking down, Lil gasped to see her mom's bare leg. Diving through the narrow opening, she quickly took in the scene and dropped to her knees beside Mom's rigid body.

"Mom!" She didn't respond. Her eyes were rolled back, and her body was contracting in some sort of seizure. "Oh, no. Oh, no." Trembling with fear, Lil scooped her mom's head under one arm and used her free hand to grab her cell phone from her apron pocket. "Matt! Get Dad. Quick! Something's wrong with Mom! We're in their bathroom."

Lil's gaze fell on the empty painkiller bottle. Helpless to know what to do, she held her mom's shuddering body. "Oh Mom, what did you do?"

By the time Dad arrived, Mom's body had gone limp, and she'd either fallen asleep or fainted. Dad quickly scooped Mom up into his arms and ran for his truck. On her way out, Lil snatched the generic painkiller bottle, Mom's covering from the nightstand, and her own purse from the mudroom.

Since they lived too far from the nearest emergency vehicle, they planned to drive Rose to the hospital themselves. Lil jumped in the cab of her dad's truck, clutching her mom's limp form and praying all the way to the Dublin Methodist Hospital. Matt had called ahead, and when they arrived, a gurney was waiting outside the emergency entrance. Hospital attendants promptly strapped Mom to the gurney and rushed her through a set of glass doors.

Dad went with Mom, and Lil was left with the admitting paperwork. Her hands trembled too violently to use the kiosk, even if she knew how, so she stepped up to a clerk. He motioned her into a chair where she clenched her hands on her lap to keep them from shaking. Still wearing her apron, she answered the questions as best she could, but the hospital clerk eyed her inquisitively. "Plain City?"

"Yes." She gave her address.

"You Amish farmers?"

The farmer part should have been obvious, the way her dad had whisked through the room in his overalls without even removing his straw hat. The clerk's probing glance and nosy questions made her feel like an oddity and served to ruffle her farm-girl feathers. Jutting her chin, she asked, "Is that a question on your admissions form?"

"No, just curious."

"We're Mennonites. We drive cars," she snapped, knowing from past experiences that would probably be his next question.

The young man quirked a brow, and after that he stuck to the questions needed to fill out the admittance forms. "Wait over there. I'll take this form back and have your dad sign it."

"Thanks."

She found an empty chair in the waiting room just as her brothers filed through the entrance. Several strangers in the room lifted their gazes to the newcomers. Lil motioned her siblings over and told them everything that had happened. After that, they all settled in to wait for word from Dad or the doctor.

Lil's heart throbbed with fear for her mom and family. Although she didn't want to think about such things, this hospital visit would add additional financial strain to an already serious situation. She brushed away the negative thought and prayed for her mother to pull through and come out of her coma.

About an hour passed before Dad finally stepped into the waiting room, looking quite lost. At once, Lil jumped to her feet and waved. "Over here."

When his gaze lit on her, he seemed relieved. With hat in hand and heavy steps, he crossed the room to his children.

"Is she okay?" Hank asked.

"Yes. She's sleeping." He explained how Mom had been treated using uncustomary words such as *activated charcoal* and *gastrointestinal tract*. "They started an IV."

"Does she need to be admitted?"

"Yes. They want to keep her at the hospital and give sodium bicarbonate until her urine reaches a specified pH level."

"But she will be all right?"

He gave a weary nod, and Lil heaved a huge sigh of relief, as did her brothers. To hear her dad use medical terms reminded her that he was an intelligent man, even though he usually didn't use big words. Actually, she corrected herself, he usually didn't talk much at all.

His worried brow caused Lil concern. "Can we see her?"

"Not yet." Dad shook his head wearily. "I'm going to stay with her. The rest of you best go home and take care of the farm."

Lil knew that the chores needed to be done, but she didn't want to go. "Me, too?"

He studied her and shook his head. "You've been taking her to the doctor visits. You'd better stay with us."

⸺৽⸺

Fletcher moved his hands over the steering wheel of his blue Ford Focus. The car was a gift from a donor who supported his parents' mission work and had been third-handed off to him. All his life, Fletch had survived on hand-me-downs. His missionary parents lived mainly on donations and a few odds-and-ends jobs—from working at the local discount stores to mixing pesticides for migrant workers—along with piecework his dad picked up when they took leave in the States. Frank Stauffer once hauled Amish people to Florida, returning with a load of citrus fruit to sell. The family had always been thankful to God for each job or donation.

Although Fletch's family never owned many valuable possessions—unless you counted various trinkets given to them from the natives—their real wealth was in their experiences. Fletch had received a good education, both from personal experience and the classes he took at Ohio State University. His college tuition was being covered by one of his parents' longest and most dedicated supporters, Marshall Lewis. Marshall was also Fletch's mentor and second father figure. This kind, generous man had guided Fletch in his career choice when it seemed that his own father was too busy to be bothered with such details.

Fletch pulled up to his apartment complex's mailboxes, shifted the Focus into PARK, and got out to check his mail. At present, his parents were in the Congo, trying to put their camp and ministry back together for the third time in a war-torn land. They were too occupied with the Bambuti, Congo Pygmies, to write. E-mail was sporadic.

Phone service random.

Fletch flipped through the usual junk mail and a utility bill he would pass along to Vic, who still harbored a grudge over the accident between Britt's car and Lillian's brown rattletrap. Her ugly vehicle was a reminder of some of his experiences with embarrassing clunkers. Recalling bits and pieces of their conversation, he had to admire Lillian's determination to acquire a prominent chef's position and own a nice car like Britt's. Given Lil's Conservative Mennonite background, her goals had been surprising to him.

His own goals were not so surprising. His vocational direction evolved out of his natural love for animals.

Although he was a Christian, he didn't feel driven to evangelize people, like his parents. In fact, he wanted to keep as far from the mission field as he could. His focus was on obtaining his degree, starting a veterinarian practice, and living a normal life. If anything, Fletch's dream was to be ordinary because he'd always been different than most people.

Entering his apartment with a whistle for his pet, he dropped his mail in the trash and tossed the utility bill on a small table. The room was sparse, containing only the barest of necessities, and he easily spied his companion bounding toward him from across the room. Fletch scratched the dog behind one droopy ear. He'd gotten the dog at veterinarian school, where the students were encouraged to adopt abandoned animals from their hospital. Fletch didn't regret his decision to adopt Buddy. The basset hound finished sniffing his leg and went to the front door.

"Wait a minute." Fletch snatched a package of frozen burgers out of the freezer and set it on the counter before he picked up Buddy's leash and an empty grocery bag. The dog wagged his tail, anticipating their customary walk. Once around the block, and Fletch was home again, tossing burgers on the grill that came with the apartment's eight-by-ten-foot walled-in patio. When he opened the slider to return inside the apartment, the basset's nose sniffed the smoky scent that had entered the room.

As Fletch ate his dinner, his thoughts returned to Lillian. All week long, he had squelched the urge to drive back to Riccardo's, but he didn't even know which days she worked. He would look pathetic hanging out at Riccardo's until their paths crossed again. But he was still entertaining the notion. Driving over there seemed the only way to reach her since her phone number was on the back of the take-out check that had floated under Britt's car seat.

His shoulders slumped with regret that he hadn't remembered to look for her phone number. At the time, he hadn't realized his mind would become obsessed over her. Considering the differences in their faith, he should just forget about her. That was his original intention, but his thoughts riveted on the image of Lillian Landis and the idea of pursuing her.

Calling Riccardo's could get her in trouble with her boss. Hadn't she mentioned something about him having a temper? He let out a long sigh. *Lord, could You just prompt Vic to send me to Riccardo's again? Either that, or please help me forget her?*

One thing he'd learned from the Bambuti: if you asked God for direction, He would send you a sign. The native group had signs and superstitions about everything. Only they didn't seek Fletch's God, they turned to nature for their answers, considering the forest their god. Fletch's personal theology had naturally evolved from his own experiences; if God created nature, He could certainly use it to speak to mankind. Fletch believed that God cared about details. If Vic sent him back to Riccardo's, Fletch would take that as a sign to pursue the object of his imagination.

⁓

Rose Landis clapped her hands to the sides of her head. "My ears are ringing. Sounds like a swarm of bees in the lilac bush. Only they are inside my head. I can't stand it."

"Just a hangover," Lil's dad joked, but nobody laughed. Lil didn't understand why her dad would jokingly allude to drinking alcohol when the church forbid it, unless it was his passive-aggressive reminder that the ringing was a direct result of ingesting too many pills.

"It will fade," Lil consoled her mom for the third time. But in actuality, the physician that was assigned to Mom's case hadn't guaranteed that the ringing would ever go away. The causes and cures of tinnitus weren't understood by the medical world. Lil could only hope Mom hadn't ruined her inner ears with the overdose.

Mom clawed at her bedcovers. "I want to go home. When can I go?"

Dad patted her arm. "As soon as they release you."

"Don't treat me like a child, Will. Do you know, or don't you? Why do you always try to keep things from me? You treat me as if I don't have a brain in my head. Of course I may not if these bees keep buzzing around in there."

He kept his voice calm. "Because you can't cope with stress these days."

Mom jerked the sheet up to her chin. "What do you know about anything?"

With a sigh, Lil snatched up her purse and retreated to the hallway. She wished she could call her friends and vent. But Katy was still on her honeymoon. Jake was on it with her. And Megan was on a summer mission trip. All her friends were busy, getting on with their lives. Frustrated, she dialed her sister, Michelle.

Her sister's voice sounded breathless, probably from chasing after her three children, all under the age of six. "How's Mom?"

"I think they'd release her now, but they've called for a psychoanalysis."

"Oh no." Michelle groaned. "What will Brother Troyer think? And the elders? Do you think they'll make her get up in front of the church and ask for forgiveness for trying to commit"—her voice broke—"you know?"

Lil sympathized with her sister's anguish. Suicide was almost nonexistent among the Mennonites because they believed that killing was a sin, and if a person committed sin without asking for forgiveness, he or she might not get to heaven. The few bereft families who did experience such a loss clung to the consolation that nobody could know for sure that the dying person hadn't asked for forgiveness on their way to the other life. Suicide was something that happened in the outsider's world, not in Lil's congregation.

Even though a nurse's station was ten feet to her right and a hospital hallway stretched out to her left, Lil found it hard to accept that Mom had tried to commit suicide. It hurt to think she was that miserable, that her family wasn't important enough for her to fight to survive.

With grief thickening her throat, Lil replied, "No. But Dad said Brother Troyer might make a house call. I think it'll be kept hushed. I'm hoping the staff here will call her psychiatrist and then discharge her."

"What can I do to help?"

Lil's gaze darted around the sterile hall. How could Michelle help with her active little ones who needed constant care? When her gaze rested on a clock, she gasped. "Oh no. I forgot to call Riccardo's. Beppe will be mad."

Michelle replied, "He has to allow for family emergencies. Do I need to bring Mom some clothes or anything?"

With irritation, Lil brushed back a fringe of bangs and repositioned her bobby pins. "I can't think right now. Beppe claims I've already had too many family emergencies. I've got to call the restaurant. I'll call you back later."

"Okay," Michelle's hesitant voice insinuated what they both knew— that nothing was okay. "Call me."

Lil ended their call and quickly punched in her speed dial.

"Riccardo's."

"Hi, Beppe. I'm sorry I'm late." She tucked her hair behind her left ear.

"You know there's a baseball game tonight. It's going to be busy."

"I had an emergency. My mom's in the hospital. She took an overdose of aspirin. I'm not going to be able to come in tonight."

There was a long pause on the other end. "I'm surprised to hear that. Didn't think your people—Look, I'm sorry about your mom. But this restaurant has to operate regardless of personal problems."

Lil glanced back at her mom's room. "Fine. I can be there in an hour. But I don't have my uniform."

Suddenly his tone became overly sympathetic. "Maybe you need a leave of absence. Just wait to come back until things settle, and meanwhile, I'll hire somebody else to fill in."

Panicking, Lil knew that once she was replaced, the door to Riccardo's would be forever closed to her. "No! I'll be there," she cried.

Ending the call and stuffing her phone in her purse, Lil ducked her head into her mom's hospital room and motioned for Dad to come to the hallway.

He stepped into the hall beside her, his brows creased in worry. "What is it? Did the doctor speak with you?"

"No, nothing like that. I have to go to work. I'm already late. Call me if Mom gets discharged. Otherwise, I'll come straight back here."

"But you can't go. You know all about her depression stuff. I don't know what to tell that shrink."

"I have to go, Dad. Otherwise I'm losing my job."

"You don't even have your car."

"I know. I need to borrow your truck."

Dad's eyes narrowed in anger. He glanced into the hospital room and back at Lil. "You can't be in two places at once. You cannot ride the fence any longer. It is time to quit your job and help your family. It is the right thing to do."

"You sent the boys home to work. I have work, too."

"Yes. To help with your mom."

Lil stilled. Her job was her last grasp for freedom. She loved both her parents, but she couldn't give up her job. She shook her head. "I'm sorry. I'll call someone then."

"Don't go. We need you."

"I know. It's just for a few hours." Lil had never truly accepted the path her parents had chosen for her life and had become accustomed to continually scrapping with them. They usually gave in pretty easily, as they weren't nearly as strict with her as they had been with Michelle or Hank. But with the recent turmoil that had entered her parents' lives, she found it painful to add to their burdens. She bit her tongue and turned her back to him.

Her dad remained silent.

Feeling sick to her stomach, she walked away before she changed her mind and somehow ended up forever trying to fill her mom's shoes at home—the very shoes that had led her mom into a bout of depression.

She started running. She punched the elevator button. It would take Michelle too long to come for her. Her brothers were busy, and her friends were out of town. Mustering every bit of courage to keep her job, she decided to ask one of the hospital clerks how to call a cab.

⌒

After her shift, Lil took a cab back to the farm, eating up more than her night's wages. Beppe had been hard to please, and her emotions were frazzled. Bone-tired, she trudged toward Jezebel, intending to go straight to the hospital. Curiously, her dad's truck was parked in the driveway. Turning, she went into the house.

She hurried through the mudroom and kitchen to the hall. Her parents' bedroom door was closed. Not knowing if her mom had been released or if her dad had come home to sleep, Lil would have to wait until morning to unravel it all. She would rise early and make a good breakfast to appease her dad's anger for going against his wishes.

But the next morning, Lil's special waffles and raspberry syrup did not mollify him.

"I suppose hamburger gravy is too plain for you to make?"

Lil was taken aback. Her dad had never once complained about her cooking. Nobody had. He knew he was the luckiest man alive to have married into the matriarchal line of Mennonite potluck queens. Hurt, she swallowed. "I'll remember next time."

He shot her an angry glance and then looked back at his plate. "You'd better go through the medicine cabinet and make sure your mother won't find any more pills." The tips of his ears pinked, and Lil knew he was shamed that his wife would seek such a route of escape. He probably blamed himself for all the troubles at the Landis farm.

"Is she here? Did they discharge her?"

He looked up again. "Now why else would I be sitting here eating your fandangled waffles?"

"Maybe because you like them," she quipped, her eyes mirroring his. "Just maybe they're the best waffles you ever tasted." Lil tried one of her mom's tactics from before her depression. She had been an expert at making Dad laugh when times were tough.

"And maybe you need to get your nose out of the air. I never thought my own daughter would be too proud to wear her covering."

Stunned at his out-of-the blue dig, Lil steadied her hand against the countertop. "I didn't know it bothered you." The church had recently changed the ordinance allowing women to have the freedom of choice when it came to wearing the covering outside of worship services. She had quit wearing it when she lived at the doddy house. She had been living on her own at the time and hadn't thought to ask her parents' permission. They had never spoken of it.

He didn't reply, just finished eating.

Hurt, Lil tried to reason with him again. "I had to go to work. It's the only thing left of my—" She broke off. He would scoff at her dreams. Her dad seemed broken. How long would it be until she was broken, too? "We're a lot alike, you and me. Matt is like us, too."

"That's not much to brag about," he replied. "By the way, you might have to help with the chores come Saturday."

"Why?"

"Because Matt's dragging us to some farm seminar." He stuck a warning finger in the air. "I'm allowing him his chance. But if this doesn't work, well let's just say there might not be any chores for any of the Landis clan in the future."

"I'm glad you're open to new ideas, Dad. But sometimes one chance isn't enough. I imagine it will take plenty of hard work, too. You'll have to give it time. It's only fair."

He shook his head and rose from table, then stepped into the mudroom and plucked his straw hat from the yellow peg shelf. As she watched, he squared his shoulders. "You should know by now that one thing I never shirked was hard work."

His presence filled the small mudroom. She watched the broad shoulders of his plaid shirt slouch again beneath his worn overalls. One sleeve was rolled higher than the other, exposing a tan forearm and sun-freckled hand. It clasped the screen door, and he was gone.

She looked up at the ceiling and, falling into a Dutch accent, demanded, "Do You see what's happening here, God? Do You even care?"

CHAPTER 5

Fletch looked out the passenger window of Vic's white Chevy pickup at the low, sleek facility with neatly trimmed hedges. Strong winds strewed lavender phlox across the rolling green lawns that made the property an appealing place for a farm seminar. A row of newly planted trees bent low to the onslaught. The country feel of the landscape would aid in setting the farmers at ease, allowing them to be more receptive to new ideas and equipment.

The concept of attending a farm seminar to drum up work was something he hadn't considered as part of his future job description. They pulled into the parking garage, and Fletch asked, "How many of these do you attend in a year?"

"Depends on how busy I am." They exchanged glances, and then Vic said almost grudgingly, "Three this year. The kids have to eat." Since the accident, Vic had remained in a sour mood.

"Did you get the car fixed yet?"

"It's in the shop. Britt's driving a rental. Has to take the boys to school and all their activities."

"I'm sorry for the inconvenience." It wasn't as if Fletch had been a careless driver, but Vic had made it plain that he regretted allowing

Fletch to drive his wife's car.

"I shouldn't have bought that car anyway."

Fletch felt it was better to let that comment alone and focus on the seminar.

Inside the entry, they followed signs to a room designated for the meetings. A brunette in a trim, chic suit handed him a packet of material and a name tag that he stuck to his button-down, short-sleeved shirt. Vic had warned him that the farmers didn't show up in suit coats or even long sleeves in summer, and they needed to fit in with the farmers, present themselves as people who could be trusted and even befriended. He pointed out that in a small community like Plain City, businesses treated their clients like family.

Several dividers had been opened to make one room large enough to display various types of farm equipment for differing livestock, such as mechanical devices to facilitate the feeding, reproduction, and nursing of hogs. The usual computerized units for temperature control, including sample misting equipment, also were being exhibited.

When Fletch looked at the equipment, most of which had been set up the day before, he wasn't thinking about profit and convenience; he was thinking about how it would affect animals' health and well-being.

Fletch helped Vic set up their booth, which consisted of one large banner representing the practice, a table, two folding chairs, some flyers, and a notepad to take down names and phone numbers. By the time they were finished, the farmers were trickling in for the workshops that would be starting within the hour. Fletch enjoyed observing the farmers.

"How long have you been practicing?"

Fletch turned left to see a man who looked faintly familiar. He had a sun-freckled face and the rough hands of a farmer. He wore a graphic T-shirt under a pale-blue, button-down shirt, and some bold lettering that Fletch couldn't quite read showed through the fabric. He tilted his head inquisitively.

"Vic's been practicing for almost twenty years. I'm his assistant."

"The vet we always used just retired. We'll be expanding soon and will be looking for somebody new."

"What kind of livestock do you have?"

"Hogs."

"Vic's really good with all animals. Why don't you take one of our flyers?" Remembering Vic's comment that clients were treated like family, he said, "By the way, my name's Fletch Stauffer."

"I think I've seen you at my church. That's another reason why I stopped at your booth. I haven't been going to Crossroads Mennonite that long."

"Me either. I've only been going there since I enrolled at OSU, and it took me a while to find a church."

"Matt L—" The young man's introduction was cut off as another man carrying an insulated John Deere mug stepped up to join them.

"There's a great buffet over there. Too bad Steve's not here. Dad's saving us some seats." The newcomer motioned to the far side of the room.

"This is my brother Hank."

Both men looked familiar, though Hank was darker than his brother, but Fletch didn't recall seeing either of them at his church.

Hank picked up one of Vic's brochures and placed it on top of a flyer he had on pressure washers.

Matt turned his attention back to Fletch. "What kind of classes are you taking?"

"Oh, didn't I say? I'm going to veterinary school." Fletch finally caught the wording barely visible through Matt's shirt: *hog heaven*. He bit back a smile.

Hank had been thumbing through his brochures. "You familiar with the slatted flooring? These pressure washers?"

"Yes. I understand they work best when the waste is flushed out of the building into a lagoon and later spread over the fields." Fletch was pleased to share the information he'd learned in one of his agricultural classes. The way this was going, he might be drumming up some new customers for his employer. "Vic's giving a workshop about antibiotics. It might be worth your while for one of you to attend, especially if you're expanding."

Matt tapped Fletch with his brochure. "Thanks for the tip. We're all taking different workshops. I've already decided I'm taking the one on contract growers and integrators. How about you, Hank?"

"All?" Fletch asked, curious now. "How many brothers do you have?"
"Just two. More than enough." He pointed to a farmer who was headed
their way. "And that's my dad, Will Landis."

Landis? At the name, Fletch stared at the farmer who was now
extending a hand toward him. Landis? His mind scrambled. As in
Lillian Landis? No wonder Matt and Hank looked familiar. This was
Lillian's family! He clasped the older farmer's hand. Gripped it solidly
in hopes of making a good impression.

"Pleased to meet you, Mr. Landis." More than ever, he didn't want
to lose this customer. Special customer. God hadn't prompted Vic
to send Fletch for more Italian food, but to the One who made the
universe, there was more than one way to answer a prayer.

"If you register with us today, Vic Fuller, the owner of the veterinary practice, will give you a discount on his services or even on vaccinations." When he saw interest in the farmer's eyes, he quickly grabbed
the notepad off the table, supplying him with a pen as well.

As Mr. Landis scrawled his name, he said to his sons. "I found us
some seats next to the coffeepot so Hank can stay awake."

Hank shrugged. "Coffee is my best friend most mornings."

"Wait until I tell Sara that," Matt teased.

"She already knows, blabbermouth."

Fletch watched the farmers leave his booth, almost dumbstruck
that God had brought Lillian's family to him. A future encounter with
her might happen naturally, not with him playing the part of a lovesick
fool who stalked her at her place of work.

Even if the Landis men did not seek Vic's veterinary services, Fletch
now had her address. This changed everything. Instead of spending his
time daydreaming about how to contact her, he needed to embrace
the likely possibility and consider the consequences of pursuing a
Conservative girl. Matt Landis had left the Conservative Church.
Would his sister be willing to do the same? Fletch had to have one more
look at Lillian Landis.

⁂

Lil literally blew into the mudroom. She swiped her hair out of her eyes
and spit grit from her parched lips as she removed her barn shoes. It was

the kind of dry wind that downed wheat and damaged fields. This time of year, wind could be real trouble for farmers.

Now midmorning, she'd already put in a full day's work. She'd risen early and rearranged her schedule to help with the chores since her dad and two of her brothers were at the farming seminar. But she was glad to do it if it helped them find a solution to the farm's financial woes.

Lil went to the kitchen to wash her hands and halted with surprise. "Mom? Hi."

"You got up early. What's going on?"

A pang of resentment shot through Lil that her dad remained so secretive with her mom these days. Intuition told her it was only adding to her mom's depression. "Dad had some farm business and asked me to do some extra chores."

Mom dipped her head. "I'm sorry everything falls on you. I wish the doctors could find out what's wrong with me. I'd like to do my share around here." Then she tilted her face and studied Lil curiously. "Why, you have your covering on. I didn't think you were wearing it anymore."

Lil shrugged, unwilling to make any commitments, and pulled out a chair across the table from her mom. She wondered if the medication had given Mom the desire to get out of bed. Aside from the overdose incident, she hadn't been complaining or sleeping as much anymore. Lil searched her mind for something enjoyable to occupy her mother's time. "I do have something you could do for me. Michelle's zucchini are starting."

Mom actually smiled. "And so the battle begins."

They both knew that keeping up with a zucchini crop took plenty of ingenuity. "Anyway, she lost her relish recipe. Maybe you could jot it down for her again, along with any other good zucchini recipes." Lil raced to the drawer that held their recipe cards and plunked a couple down in front of her mom. Stephen's wife, Lisa, had gifted Mom with some special-order cards that read ROSE'S YUMMY RECIPES.

Mom tapped a pencil on the table. "Yes, I believe I know it from memory." She started to write, glancing up at Lil. "And the men love your chocolate zucchini cake." She became totally absorbed in the zucchini project until the sudden chime at the front doorbell announced a potential visitor. She instantly paled. "Quick, Lil! Help me back to my room."

Lil placed a steadying hand on her mom's tense shoulder. "No need for that. You look fine. Let me just go see who it is." When she entered the living room, her heart sank to see Brother Troyer's car through the windowpane. Though it was partly hidden by blowing tree limbs, she knew in her heart it was him. The entire family had been anticipating and dreading his call. She wondered if he'd purposefully chosen a day when the men would be gone. She sped back to the kitchen. "It's Brother Troyer. Look busy so he'll think you're doing well."

"Oh no."

"It will be fine."

When she saw her mom relent, Lil patted the wrinkles out of her apron and hurried to the door. "Hello," she said as the screen door blew wide open and hit the outside wall. "Come in."

Brother Troyer pulled the door closed behind him and entered the front room with his hat in his hand. "Whew, hope that wind passes on through the county without doing any harm to the fields."

Lil nodded. "Yes, the recent rains shot the crops up, and now they are vulnerable."

He looked toward the back of the house and attempted a joke. "Well you know the old saying about what the wind blew in." He shrugged and his black collarless coat bunched around his thin shoulders. "Guess that's just me."

Lil gave an uncomfortable smile, hoping her mom hadn't slipped back to her bedroom. She didn't want to face the preacher's questions alone. "Yes. Here you are. How may I help you?"

He cleared his throat. "I hoped to have a chat with Rose."

"Of course. She's in the kitchen. Please follow me."

The older man followed Lil into the kitchen and smiled kindly at her mother. "Don't get up, Rose. I'll just join you at the table, if I may."

"Yes," Mom said, dipping her head.

Lil felt her mom's shame, felt her own face heat. "Would you like some iced tea or lemonade?"

"Iced tea would be nice. That wind parched my lips." Brother

Troyer settled into a chair and gazed at Mom. "Are you writing one of your splendid secret recipes, there?"

"Oh no. Just jotting down a few old faithfuls for Michelle. Her zucchini's in. Besides that, she's got her hands full with those little ones."

"Yes, she does." He studied her a moment. "Our hostess committee has their hands full, too, without you, Rose. You've been the hub of that committee ever since I can remember. We could use your help."

"I'm really tired these days. Why I even had a little hospital stay."

The glass in Lil's hand clinked as she set the preacher's iced drink before him. Listening to the conversation progress, she slipped into a chair at the table with them.

"I'm sorry to hear that. There's many ways to get weary. I remember a time about ten years after I'd entered the ministry when my soul got so weary. For me, I was trying to do too many things on my own and lost the will to keep up the battle. We can't do it on our own, you know."

"What happened?" Mom asked.

"Why there wasn't any one thing I did to snap out of it, but it was a journey, let me tell you. Learning to lean on God and not on my own strength."

"Oh."

Lil heard the disappointment in Mom's voice. She'd probably been hopeful that there was a simpler solution.

"Looking back now, I'm glad it happened. God walked me through it and taught me little things that altogether brought me out of my slump. The key was realizing I'd come to my end and really depending on God to help me out of it."

"Yeah?"

"Do you have the strength to pray?"

To Lil's surprise, Mom answered honestly with a negative shake of her head.

"I thought so. That's how I felt back then. But people prayed for me. And I'll pray for you. I'll pray that God will give you enough strength to pray for yourself. Promise me you'll just try. You have to ask to receive.

See if God doesn't provide. Remember, when Jesus healed the lame, they had to try to walk to find out if they could."

"I suppose."

Brother Troyer patted Mom's hand.

CHAPTER 6

Lil poured herself a glass of well water from the kitchen sink and peered out under the lilac-print window valance. Clothes gently flapped on the wash line just beyond the flower beds, where monarch and swallowtail butterflies flitted around Mom's scraggly perennials. The only flowers this year were the ones that had survived of their own accord.

The bird feeder remained empty, but she had noticed that occasionally a small flock of goldfinches came in to investigate. Over the years, Dad had grumbled that birdseed was a waste of money, and in a sense it was, because God provided plenty for the birds to eat. But she knew Mom used the feeder to draw the birds in close to the window where she had to while away so many hours washing dishes and preparing food. Conservative women didn't have televisions on their countertops for entertainment, and Lil's mom had few modern conveniences—like the dishwasher Lil and her friends had installed in the doddy house—so chores took plenty of time. She determined that if Mom ever got well enough to do kitchen chores, she would buy birdseed for that feeder whether Dad thought it was a waste of money or not.

Farther out, barn swallows swooped over the corn and soy fields to snatch insects. After the rain, the insects seemed to flourish. Earlier in the week, the wind had brought just enough moisture to raise the humidity and officially bring in the dog days of summer.

Lil's gaze followed the long circle drive that ran all the way to the barn. She leisurely scanned the hog pastures, wondering if Dad would be in late again. She had no way of telling, because she would already be at work. She was not going to be late. Beppe's insolent attitude had not improved.

Lil's thoughts returned to her dad, curious over his recent behavior. Since he and the boys had gone off to that farm seminar, he'd been silent. On the nights when she hadn't worked, she'd noticed that Dad and her brothers were having frequent meetings and lingering longer than usual after their chores.

When Lil didn't stay home for supper because of her work schedule, she always set the table for two, hoping Mom would join Dad for the meal. Usually Lil needed to be at work by four o'clock. Then she would scribble last-minute instructions about the meal for Dad.

With a sigh, she set down her glass and went to fetch the clothes off the line. Since the preacher's visit, Mom seemed more determined than ever not to lift a finger. It was as if her spirit had vacated her body, especially when Dad was in the room. But Lil had noticed something new. Mom often had her Bible open. At least she was taking Brother Troyer's advice.

Lil got the clothespin bag off the mudroom shelf and grabbed the clothes basket off the floor. At the clothesline, she spied Dad coming across the drive from the direction of the barn. When he got within earshot, she called out to him.

He waved and joined her at the clothesline. "Do you have enough food for the boys and their families?"

"What?" Lil sputtered, placing her hands on her skirted hips. "No. Did you invite the entire family?"

He stuck a thumb under his overall's suspender. "Yep."

"But Dad, I can't just whip up an entire meal. Usually it's just you and Mom."

He reached out and tussled her hair. "Sure you can, sweetheart. You can do anything with food. Just whip out those fandangled waffles and that fancy syrup of yours."

Lil straightened her head covering, wanting to scream. *But I don't have time. I can't be late to work again.* But it had been so long since her dad had ruffled her hair. So long since he'd even smiled. Since anybody had smiled. Including Beppe at work.

"I'll finish my chores, then come in and shower and get your mom up myself."

Lil gazed down the row of clothing as if an idea would pop off the clothesline. Amazingly, one did. "All right. I'll throw a big batch of chili together, and Michelle can finish it up when she gets here."

"Why Michelle? Where are you going?"

"Uh, Riccardo's?" The moment she'd said it, she realized her voice had sounded disrespectful.

"Oh." He waved his hand as if to dismiss her job as a mere inconvenience. "Well you're going to miss the big announcement then. When I told Matt to come, he asked if he could bring along the vet." He stopped speaking and eyed Lil speculatively. "Somebody we met at the farm seminar."

"He's bringing company, too?"

"Yep. A good-looking guy. Nice enough. But don't get your hopes up about him. He's a Mennonite, but not Conservative." Her dad twisted his mouth in an unpleasant grimace. "He goes to Matt's church."

While her subconscious probed the bits and pieces her dad had flung at her, trying to make sense of the information, she wondered what a good-looking stranger would think of chili in the middle of the summer. *Not a stranger,* her brain corrected. *Mennonite vet.* She breathed a sigh of relief that she wouldn't be there to witness a good-looking Mennonite vet's reaction to the meal. "Maybe you can just tell me the news, since I have to work."

Ignoring her last remark, Dad kept on talking about the invited guest. "His name's Fletch Stauffer. Did I mention he goes to Matt's church?"

She felt her face heat, momentarily forgetting all about the big

381

announcement. "Did you say—" She choked off the words. No need to bring the minor car accident and object of her daydreams to her dad's attention. She tried to stay calm, to still her speeding heartbeat. "And you say he's a veterinarian?"

"Yep." Dad rocked back on his heels, then slapped his straw hat on his leg and placed it back on his head before he strode back toward the barn.

It had to be the same Fletch Stauffer. *Well!* Lil quickly unpinned the dry clothes, folding and dropping them into the clothes basket, all the while trying to digest what had just transpired. Dad was happy, almost boyish. And Fletch Stauffer, the handsome blond who never called her, was coming to dinner.

Emotions battled inside her, making her want to skip work to see Fletch again. Wanting to hear every little detail about the big news that would be discussed over supper. She especially wondered what had Dad seeing blue skies. Next he'd be singing and filling the bird feeder. Her heart raced with hope. He had promised to get Mom up for dinner, and with his new cheery attitude, Mom might come out of her shell.

But Lil had to go to the restaurant. She hadn't mustered up courage to call a cab when Mom was in the hospital just to lose her job now. With a disappointed sigh, she realized she could get Michelle's version of the big announcement later. And if Fletch was going to do veterinary work at the Landis farm, surely she'd get an opportunity to talk to him another time. Wouldn't' she?

But what if after tonight, Fletch didn't want anything to do with the Landis bunch? What then? She'd miss her one and only chance to connect with him.

With the basket propped on one hip, and her phone at her ear, she started toward the house. "Hi, Beppe," she said, passing through the mudroom. "Can I switch nights and come in at six tonight and four tomorrow night? If not, that's okay. Just checking."

She heard Beppe's irritated grunt. "I don't have to ask who this is."

"Oh sorry. Yeah, it's Lil."

"Hold on." She waited, never so hopeful over missing a few hours of work. Finally he returned. "You can be here by six?"

"Yes. Thanks."

"Don't be late," he warned.

She set the clothes basket on the washing machine and jerked open the freezer door. She grabbed some frozen ground pork and slapped it on a riveted thawing board. After that, she diced tomatoes, fresh from Michelle's garden. She could slice fresh corn off the cob, and she'd add some cilantro and maybe some summer savory. As she worked, temptation came to her. *Don't go to work. Stay home and see Fletcher. If you lose your job, you could work on a recipe book. Dad's been after you to quit, anyway.*

She shook aside the fantasy she sometimes had of writing a fabulous recipe book. If she lost her job, the farm would suck her in and sap the life right out of her. There'd be no time for recipes. *I love my job,* she argued.

It's a dead end, temptation beckoned.

No. If Fletch wants to ask me out, he has my phone number. And now he has my address, too.

Temptation warned, *Matt's bringing him. They go to the same church. He's coming as Matt's friend. Maybe he doesn't even know that Matt is your brother.*

Back and forth her thoughts went. Even as she slipped into her freshly ironed black skirt and white blouse uniform, she debated. Before she left the house for work, however, she gave the dining room a final once-over.

Mom's Autumn Leaf dishes were set on a pristine, white lace tablecloth. The chili concoction simmered in two slow cookers that the family used in the summer so they didn't heat up the kitchen. And strawberry cobbler would do for dessert. It was the best she could do on such short notice. An easy meal that could be served without the cook's presence, she determined.

With the decision made to fulfill her responsibilities at the restaurant, she took her purse off the peg shelf and bolted for the back door, confident that for once, she'd be right on time for work.

"Oophf!" she exclaimed, ramming into something solid. Splaying her hands on a firm, shirt-clad chest, Lil saw the familiar red tennis shoes. Her face burned with embarrassment as she looked up into soft brown eyes. She quickly dropped her hands.

He shook his head. "Never saw a more accident-prone woman."

"You're early." She instantly regretted the slip of tongue that made him aware that she'd been expecting him. Didn't want him to judge her cooking when it had been so hurriedly tossed together. Didn't want him to think she was trying to avoid him. Beans! Just didn't want him to think she was thinking about him, period.

And she wasn't thinking, she was feeling. Tingling from her palms to her black-toed oxfords. She wet her lips, frozen to the spot. Frozen and tingling.

But he hadn't missed her declaration. His brows arched. She'd remembered he was good-looking, but she had forgotten about the interesting brown brows/blond hair combination. It intrigued her because the darker brows made a nice frame for his eyes. But intriguing as he was, she snapped her mouth closed, determined not to stick her foot back in it again.

He gave her a dimpled smile. "You aren't running away, are you?"

She tucked her errant bangs behind her ear, and her response came out in thicker Dutch than she would have liked. "I am on my way out. I'm off to work."

His expression fell. "Riccardo's?"

She nodded.

"I'm sorry. Ever since Matt gave me the invitation, I've been looking forward to seeing you again."

She stared at him, still unable to fathom his presence. Almost as if she was conjuring him up like her imaginary Rollo. But his comment reminded her of the disappointment she'd felt when he hadn't called. "If that's true, maybe you should have called."

"I wanted to. But I lost your number."

Lil frowned. It would be nice to believe him. Even though she didn't date much, she was able to recognize a flimsy excuse when she heard one. No matter how tingly he made her palms and heart and toes, she wouldn't tolerate feeble excuses. She narrowed her eyes. "A likely story."

He raised both hands in objection. "It's the truth. Our accident was just the beginning. After I left Riccardo's, I got stopped by a police officer for speeding. The dinner check with your phone number floated under my seat, and when I tried to get it, the officer thought I was going for a gun and made me step out of the car. Later, my boss had me so flustered, I forgot to look for it." He shrugged. "It turned out the car belonged to my boss's wife."

Lil's lips twitched, and it was hard not to smile and fall under Fletcher's dimpled charm. The story seemed too far-fetched to be fiction. "That's an interesting story."

That was when she noticed Matt, leaning against the wall with crossed arms.

"Hi, Matt."

"What's going on with you two?"

"Oh Fletch can explain. If I don't leave this instant, Beppe's going to give me an earful."

"You're afraid of a Beepie?" Fletch asked, refusing to step aside.

"Beppe," she corrected, with a grin. "Yes, because he's my boss. Maybe, I'll see you. . .sometime." Lil started toward the door, but it was too late. Michelle flounced in with her three little girls in tow—in birth order, Tate, Tammy, and Trish. Tammy reached up and wrapped her arms around Lil's waist. "Hi, Auntie Lily. Swing me?"

The nieces were dolly stepping stones all dressed alike in homemade dresses that were tinier versions of Michelle's own dress. Their little dresses hung well below their knees, but unlike their mommy, the girls wore no stockings. In spite of the heat, they looked pretty with their light brown hair freshly braided.

Lil swung Tammy in a circle like she always did. After that it was Tate's turn. And next, she took Trish from Michelle's arms to give her a row of cuddly kisses. Her nephews barreled in too, and after that, Lil couldn't have gone against the tide of incoming bodies even if her future position as head chef depended on it. But when she was able to get away, she slipped into the living room to call the restaurant manager.

"Guess what, Beppe?"

"Lillian, please don't start."

"Remember that guy with the Lexus, the one I ran into in the parking lot?"

A frustrated sigh came from Beppe. "Yes, what about him?"

"My dad invited him for supper tonight. I haven't had a date in a really long time, Beppe. Surely you don't want me to miss an opportunity like this?"

"Actually, I don't care about your personal life, Lillian, because you don't work here any longer."

"Come on, Beppe. You don't really mean that." But no reply was forthcoming. Only a click and silence. With a moan, Lil returned to the kitchen. Regardless of her best intentions, it seemed her fate had been decided for her.

CHAPTER 7

Stephen lifted the slow cooker lid and sniffed. "Wow, chili in summer? Now that's a crazy idea."

His red-haired, pregnant wife, Lisa, elbowed him.

"Summer chili," Lil corrected.

"Then you should have served it cold." Now why hadn't she thought of that? Because her brain had malfunctioned after learning that Fletcher was coming to supper. That's why. She'd have plenty of time to tweak recipes now. Plenty of unemployed time.

As usual, it was a major production to get the Landis clan all seated and situated. Everyone knew their places, for a natural pecking order had been established over the years. All the chairs around the extended dining room table would be filled, as well as the children's table, and a high chair for Trish beside Michelle and her husband, Tom.

Hank's wife, Sara Cyclone, made several trips to the kids' table before she was satisfied that Scott's ant farm was still intact and Sammy's shoes were securely tied. Seated next to Sara, Lisa rested her arms over a bulging belly, and her errant red curls bounced each time her gaze followed Sara's movements. Most likely, Lisa was observing and gathering future mothering skills in preparation for her own baby's arrival.

Lil's dad presided at one end. Sitting next to him, Mom wore a pasted but somewhat pleasant smile. Being single, Matt claimed a man-sized space which crowded into Lil's. Across from them, a chair had been squeezed in for Fletch, who watched all the commotion with mild amusement.

Although it seemed to be a typical family gathering, it was anything but normal to Lil, whose heart hammered from its proximity to the *good-looking Mennonite vet.* The very idea that she had the next half hour to scrutinize him and, if possible, impress him with her feminine charms was too good to be true. Now if only she could breathe.

"I'll ask the blessing," Dad announced, still uncharacteristically happy, even after what must have been a draining half hour of getting Mom out of bed and dressed for the occasion. The prayer was spoken in that reverent tone the Mennonite heads of house used, barely audible except for a recognizable phrase or two.

Afterward, Lil gestured toward the crocks of chili at each end of the table. "Sorry supper is informal. We'll just have to pass the chili and serve ourselves." If Fletch thought it strange that the youngest daughter was acting hostess, he didn't let on, but Lil still felt her face heat as Stephen lifted the ladle. Why had she kept things so casual? What would Fletch think of them? Better to underplay his presence, she finally concluded.

With Stephen's help, Lisa passed a large citrus-and-lettuce salad that she had contributed, and Lil passed the rolls. Sara had brought cucumber salad, and Michelle had contributed zucchini bread. Thankfully it all went together wonderfully even though nobody had called to ask what to bring.

Michelle opened her cloth napkin and sprang to her feet. "Matt! You scoundrel!"

Lil bit back a smile and craned her neck to see what had happened. You'd think Michelle would be more cautious since Matt loved to single her out for his practical jokes, probably because she screamed the loudest and was the most gullible. She shook out her napkin, and straw floated to the floor. Her daughters giggled.

Michelle reseated herself, jutted her chin, and speared Matt with a fake glare. "You can sweep the floor."

"Sure." He shrugged. "Think we live in a pigsty?"

"But we don't live here. Neither do you, Uncle Matt," four-year-old Tammy pointed out from her place at the children's table.

"No, sweetie. It's just an expression," Matt explained.

"Don't pay any attention to him, girls. Better start eating," Michelle warned with a smile.

When everyone had been served, Lil stole a glance at Fletch. His lean face, planed in masculine angles, sported a wide forehead and those dark expressive brows. She watched him taste the chili. His soft brown eyes lit with pleasure. He raised them and met her gaze with a slightly dimpled smile that made it hard to forget that there were more than a dozen other people in the room.

Stephen mumbled, "Delicious. Really good, Lil." There were several affirmative murmurs around the table.

"Thanks." She glanced at Fletch again. "Tell me about your work. Dad said you're a veterinarian?"

"Not really. I'm still in school at OSU. But I'm doing what the course calls an off-site selective experience, working with Vic at his clinic. It's a senior requirement."

She tried not to blush as she asked, "How long will you be helping there?"

"Until next spring when I graduate."

On learning that Fletch would be around for a significant length of time, she did a mental garbanzo bean dance, her personal way of celebrating ever since childhood camp days.

He leaned forward and said softly, "I'm glad you didn't go to work after all." His expression was seductively smug.

"I—I hadn't seen my nieces and nephews for a while. They're hard to resist. I guess when they came in, I had a change of heart."

"Yes. Very hard to resist."

The room grew stifling hot. What had she been thinking? Chili in summer?

"I met your family at the farm seminar where Vic was giving a workshop. Matt recognized me from church."

Fletch Stauffer in the flesh was a gorgeous contradiction. Flirting one minute and in the next breath forewarning her that he was merely Matt's friend. Was his flirtatious behavior part of a natural charm and not meant to be taken personally? She needed to tread carefully. After all, he attended a Mennonite church that didn't hold to the same restrictions that her church maintained. She glanced warily at him. In the background, her dad cleared his throat. Fletch glanced down the table at him. The gesture reminded Lil that they had all gathered for a specific purpose. Hearing the big announcement.

Dad cleared his throat a second time. "I suppose you all wonder why we gathered you together on a weeknight?" It wouldn't have been unusual a year earlier when Mom was healthy, but of late, they'd mostly gotten together for birthdays and holidays.

Lil glanced around the table, observing her family's reaction. Sara's blush meant that Hank had already filled the Cyclone in on the big secret, but Michelle seemed surprised that Dad had an announcement to make. A general hush fell over the gathering, except for Stephen's nervous slurping. He wasn't much on table manners; even now he had his bare arms resting on the tablecloth. Lil figured he tried to cover up his growing pouch by displaying his muscular arms. Beads of perspiration dotted Lisa's pretty forehead.

Dad continued. "It's time for change." He explained about the farm's decline. "I don't know if I've told you lately, but I'm proud of all you kids." Lil noticed Mom's eyes get teary. "It's time I let you modernize. We're going to expand, put up one of those newfangled metal barns so we can handle more hogs. We're going to contract with one of them big integrator companies. And I just wanted to get everybody together and make it official."

Beside her, she felt Matt's shoulders swell with pride over his modern ideas. His green T-shirt—that no Conservative farmer would wear—said it all: PROUD TO BE A FARMER.

All around the table, conversation buzzed with excitement and questions, mostly from the wives. Lil gave Fletch a curious glance, wondering why Matt had invited him and what he thought of their family's modernizing plans. "How do you fit into this, Fletch?" she asked, softly.

He glanced at Matt with hesitation.

Matt shrugged. "Just thought it would be a good opportunity to get to know us better."

As a friend or professionally? she wondered.

"Actually," Fletch grinned, "I aim to do what I can to keep the Landis hogs happy."

Matt broke into laughter.

Lil felt her face redden for Fletch, but he seemed impervious to his gaffe. *Happy hogs?* She could just envision the sort of practical joke Matt would play on him because of that foolish remark.

When Matt stopped laughing, he started the rolls around again. "I ran into Ivan Penner at the farm implement store. He said that Katy and Jake have returned from their honeymoon."

The good news caused Lil to forget all about Fletch. She broke into a happy squeal and did a garbanzo-dance shoulder shimmy against Matt. "I can't wait to see them. Thanks."

She missed them so much and wanted to tell them all that had happened lately. As she thought about all the changes, she quickly sobered. Too many changes. It had hardly sunk in.

Beppe had fired her.

Across the table, their visitor grew quiet, perhaps overwhelmed by their large, talkative family. The conversation skittered in a million directions. Her brothers eagerly discussed a tentative meeting with the Plain City Bank.

Lil caught Mom's gaze. Her face had become stoic again. "What's for dessert, dear?"

"Strawberry shortcake."

Over at the children's table, Tate clapped her hands. "My favorite."

Everybody laughed, surprised the six-year-old had been following the adult conversation.

"She's been helping me in the strawberry patch." Michelle smiled at Mom. "You should come over and spend a day with us, Mom. The girls would love to show you the garden—wouldn't you, sweethearts?"

The tiny heads bobbed in agreement, and the children broke out in chatter which included a cute string of mispronunciations.

Mom let out a ragged gasp, her shoulders convulsing.

Dad scooted his chair back and draped an arm around her. "Honey?"

He looked over helplessly at Lil. She didn't know if she should help Mom back to her room or let her cry. Nobody else knew either, because they were all looking at her to do something.

—⬨—

"None of us knew what to do," Lil told Katy. "I've never been so thankful for my nieces' spontaneity. When they saw Mom crying, they jumped up and crawled all over her, throwing their little arms around her neck. And it was so weird. Mom went straight from weeping to laughing. And when she started laughing, so did everybody else, including Fletch, even though I don't think he had a clue what was happening. Honestly, he must think we are the strangest family."

"Wait." Katy shook her brunette ponytail, pushing a glass of lemonade toward Lil. "Who's Fletch?"

"Oh, no. He can wait. You tell me about your honeymoon first." Lil examined the glass. "Where'd you get this?"

"Jake's mom. She adores sunflowers." Katy pointed to the window. "See the sunflower chime?"

Lil giggled. "What's it like to have a mother-in-law?"

"First I have to tell you what it's like to have a husband."

Widening her eyes, Lil hoped her friend wasn't going to go into details about her cousin.

"Jake is the greatest." Katy's dark eyes turned dreamy. "Marriage is better than I thought it would be."

Lil was relieved to see Katy so in love with the man who was like a brother to her, and probably even closer to her than Matt. "That chump?" she teased.

"We got sunburned on the beach, took a cruise that was so romantic." Katy quickly highlighted their trip from sunset strolls to a reunion with her old employer—a sweet elderly woman who had played a big part in deepening Katy's faith. Only a year earlier, she had been experiencing a personal winter. Lil couldn't be happier that Katy had found happiness, even if her own future seemed uncertain.

"And Jake's mom and I found some common ground." Katy suddenly tilted her head. "I noticed you're wearing your covering again."

Shrugging, Lil replied, "My dad said something to me about it."

"So it's just temporary?"

"I don't know."

Lil gazed wistfully around the doddy house, wondering if she would be able to move in, come September. So much had changed. The little farm table now sported Jake's computer. Sunflowers splashed bits of new color. Only six months earlier, she and Katy had moved into the tiny Amish guest house, renovating it together. Their other best friend, Megan, had helped them and had planned to move in with them as soon as she graduated from Rosedale Bible College. It had always been the friends' shared dream, but especially Lil's. She came up with the idea all those years ago at camp—to room together and be each other's bridesmaids.

But when Lil had moved home, Katy married Jake. The doddy house became their honeymoon cottage. Megan went on a mission trip as soon as she graduated. The new plan was for Katy and Jake to find another house. Megan and Lil planned to move in together in the autumn. September, to be exact. Lil was counting the days.

But now that she had lost her job, she would not be able to afford her part of the rent. And Mom was still struggling with depression. Moving back into the doddy house seemed impossible. How could she admit to her friends that she had been fired?

"Who's Fletch?" Katy asked, returning to the earlier question.

"You're never going to believe it." Lil started telling the basics of the story: how they met, the farm problems, the farm seminar, and how Matt had invited Fletch to a family supper. But some important adjectives like *good-looking, Mennonite,* and *veterinarian* found their way into the narrative. Then Lil caved altogether and crooned on and on about his dark brows and soft suede eyes.

Katy's mouth gaped. "How could so much happen in three short weeks?"

"Three weeks may seem short to somebody on their honeymoon," Lil teased, "but they've been an eternity for me. I've missed you so much."

"Well, it's good to be home."

"I'm glad you're happy." Lil hugged Katy.

When they drew apart, Katy brought the conversation back to Fletch. "But a cute guy delivered right to your back door. Now that's amazing."

Lil grinned, thinking that Katy made him sound like a brown UPS package. "He wasn't exactly wrapped and delivered to me. He's Matt's friend." And just in case Katy maintained the brown parcel image, she added, "Did I mention *good-looking* and *charming* friend?"

"I did catch that. *Mennonite veterinarian.* Got it. But just because he's Matt's friend doesn't mean he's not interested in you."

"Matt told me later that Fletch was drumming up work at the seminar. Matt plans to use their practice for our veterinary services. Fletch's interest in Matt might be work related."

"Their practice?"

"He works for Vic Fuller. Fletch is doing some sort of internship."

"Interesting. You never fell for a Mennonite guy before. This could be the one."

"But he's not Conservative Mennonite."

Katy bit her lip.

Lil saw her friend's hesitation and understood it. In their friendship pattern, Katy always tried to persuade Lil to be more conservative in her thinking and actions. In her black-and-white thinking, Katy closely adhered to all the church restrictions. But last year, her friend had learned forgiveness. She wasn't as judgmental against the outsiders anymore. But would she approve of Fletch and his red tennis shoes?

CHAPTER 8

Fletch patted Buddy on the head, deliberating over his dinner at the Landis farm. Lil's huge family was so different from his own. He and his sister had been raised on the mission field. Often it felt like his parents had been more involved with their ministry than concerned about their children. He and Erica had been close, but now she was married to a Canadian she had met in Africa. They lived in his country and were involved with Wycliffe Bible Translators. Erica and Fletch hardly talked anymore. Watching the Landis family interact had made him aware of his personal loneliness.

Sure, he was a friendly sort, and people were always around him, but that wasn't the same. Right now, his closest friend was his mentor, Marshall. The man who funded Fletch's tuition came from a wealthy family who had acquired money in Texas oil. He was a southern gentleman and a bit of an eccentric. Like Fletch's own dad, Marshall was passionate about life. Not only did he support his favorite causes, but he got involved in them.

Marshall had first discovered the Stauffers by visiting a Mennonite church to learn about their peace stance. That Sunday, the Stauffers were on furlough and reporting on their Congo mission work. Before

Marshall left the church foyer, he'd pledged his financial support to them.

Marshall was the Stauffer family's most consistent supporter. Over the years, he'd visited the mission field three times to see firsthand where his money was invested. On those visits, he'd noticed Fletch, especially his love for animals. Marshall shared this passion and had been influential in encouraging Fletch to chase his dreams and become a veterinarian. And now he was financing his schooling. Fletch owed Marshall. He missed him.

Acting on impulse and loneliness, Fletch pulled his cell phone from his jeans pocket.

Soon Marshall's southern voice drawled, "Ya can't throw in the hat now."

Fletch grinned. "Don't worry. I'm not calling for a pep talk. I just miss you."

"So this isn't one of them 'I'm out of money' calls?"

"Of course not. I'd call my dad if I needed money."

They both laughed over that irony. "So how's it going, working for Victor?"

"It was going great until I wrecked his wife's car."

"Oh Fletch, ya didn't?"

"Afraid so. But it wasn't my fault. A girl backed into me in a parking lot. But Vic's been acting like he's got a chip on his shoulder ever since."

"Hm. His recommendations were excellent."

"Don't get me wrong. He's a good guy. I like him, and I'm learning a lot."

"Has he taken ya to the farm shelter yet?"

The shelter was a farm that took in abused livestock. "No. I'd almost forgotten about it. That's one of your charities, isn't it?"

"It's more than a charity," Marshall drawled. "Marcus is running that place now."

"Give me the address. I'd like to go see him."

After the conversation ended, Fletch wondered why he hadn't been informed earlier that Marshall's son was in Plain City. The farm shelter was all his mentor had wanted to talk about. In their conversation,

Marshall insinuated that Vic was one of the shelter's volunteer vets, but Vic had never mentioned it to Fletch.

Buddy licked his arm, and Fletch ruffled the basset's head. "Wanna go for a walk?" Buddy responded by dancing in circles.

Fletch went for the dog's leash, remembering Marshall's positive reaction to his description of dinner with the Landis family. Marshall had thought it was hilarious that Lillian was the one who'd backed into Britt's car.

"Ya better ask her out before some pasta maker plucks her off to Italy."

For a rich world traveler, opportunities were endless. Marshall could make anything sound feasible.

But then, Lillian had skipped work after Fletch asked her to stay. She told him that her nieces and nephews had changed her mind, but he hoped it was his invitation. He'd like to believe that he would get one more look at her angelic, freckled face.

─◦

Lil heard the door to the mudroom slam and quickly shoved the newspaper ad into the trash bin, while turning and pretending a calm demeanor. Her guilty conscience ebbed when Dad stormed into the room.

Red-faced with anger, he stated, "Heaven is against us."

Lil's blood went cold. Her dad never said such blasphemous things. Well, at least not in her presence.

"Matt said the Plain City Bank won't even listen to him. They want to talk to me, or I have to give him legal authorization."

"Well that can be worked out," Lil soothed.

Her father slumped into a kitchen chair. "And the hogs are sick."

"Oh, no!" Lil paced to the sink and back. "Well, you can call the vet that Fletch works for, can't you?"

"Hank already called him." He pounded his fist on the table. "He should have been here by now."

Lil quickly went to the refrigerator and poured her dad a glass of lemonade, sliding it in front of him. She touched his arm. "You mustn't lose heart."

He chugged the drink and pushed the empty glass away, turning to Lil with a bitter expression. "Why not? I'm losing my wife, my farm, and now my hogs. What is left?"

"Your faith?" Lil reminded him, although she didn't feel as though she should be the one to talk about God to a person as devoted as her dad, when she was not that. . .well, just was not. She tried to remember the last time she'd prayed. It had been on the way to the hospital when she'd petitioned for Mom's life. God had spared her. She was about to remind her dad about that, but he spoke first.

"Well we might be losing that, too. We might even be kicked out of church."

"Why?" Lil demanded, hoping she hadn't done something to provoke the elders. Had Matt?

"The preacher called again. This time he talked to me. He said that gossip is going around the church about your mom about why she doesn't come to church anymore. He suggested it would be better for the unity of the believers if she comes before the congregation and publicly repents for trying to commit suicide."

Lil clutched the table.

"He says the congregation will gladly forgive her. That it will help her recover. He asked me how I thought she'd respond to the idea."

"What!" Lil cried. "She'll never do that. She's too weak. She'd be humiliated. Why, he never talked like that the day he visited Mom. He—"

"I know that. He claims the elders came up with it. He said they're not demanding it, just recommending it. They want to help her."

"Well! They can recommend it to the moon!" Lil replied. She wondered how Katy and Megan's dads, both elders in the church, could come up with something so hurtful for their friends. Tears burned her eyes. Surely that was what was riling her dad up, too.

The house phone rang, and Lil resented the interruption, but Dad, who didn't own a cell phone, jumped up to answer it. "Yah-low." He nodded. "Be right there."

"What is it?" Lil's hand flew to her heart fearfully, wondering what else might befall them. Perhaps the barn had collapsed, like in the book of Job. Surely her dad was right about heaven being against them.

"Vet's here." He turned and strode away, leaving Lil to bear the burden of her hurt alone.

She rushed to the window and saw a white Chevy pickup. The vet must have already gone inside the barn. Fletch drove a blue car. She wondered if he was out there, too. She watched her father's squared shoulders, the image of a man bracing himself for the worst. *Oh Lord,* she prayed, *I'm sorry I only pray in need. But there goes a man who's been faithful to You. Please, won't You help him? He's my dad.*

—ᘓ—

Fletch felt his heart sink. Six piglets were coughing and two inside the creep, the portion of the pen that the sow couldn't get into, had already expired. Vic examined one of the sick piglets and asked Will Landis, "Is this the first sign of pneumonia?"

"Yep."

"Do you have a regular vaccination program?"

"We did. We were using antibiotic feed, too. But we've been strapped and let up a bit."

The fear in the older man's voice tore at Fletch, for they all knew that once something like Porcine Reproductive and Respiratory Syndrome got into a herd, it was a costly, lengthy process to rid the herd of the virus.

Vic placed the piglet back in the straw and made a nest around the baby animal then picked up another. "Introduced any new breeders into the herd?"

"Yep, last fall. Surely we would have seen signs before now if that was the cause?"

Vic's expression softened. "These are just routine questions. Could be parasites, could just be a sick sow. I'd like to get a blood sample from her and take the two dead corpses back to the lab. Either way, we should get you started back on a vaccine routine and feed precautions."

Will gave a frustrated nod.

Vic placed the piglet down and stood. "Fletch? Can I have a word with you?" They moved to a nearby corner, and the vet placed his hand on Fletch's shoulder. "I've seen this kind of thing sweep through a herd. It's hard to eradicate."

"The Landis farm is already in financial trouble," Fletch replied.

"I can give them a discount, but if you'd want to volunteer your time for the vaccinations and some ongoing blood draws, it would help me and the Landises, too. I know you've become friends with Matt. Would you be willing to do that?"

Fletch was eager to help Matt—and Lillian, too, for that matter. He didn't hesitate. "I'll do it."

Vic warned, "You'll be busy. I've agreed to volunteer at a local farm shelter, and Britt's already on my case about being away from home so much. This could turn into a big project here, and. . .well, I appreciate it."

"I'll do whatever it takes to help."

"Thanks." Vic turned away and strode back to the farrowing pen. "Fletch has agreed to volunteer his time to give vaccines and take blood draws, if that will help."

Matt grabbed Fletch's arm. "You'd do that?"

Fletch nodded. "Sure. I told you I'd do what I could to make the Landis hogs happy."

Will Landis gave a huge sigh, and Fletch wasn't sure if it was from relief or dread of what the future had to hold for all of them. "Guess you know about our struggles here. We thank you. And for the discount, too."

Fletch wished he could do more. As they continued to discuss the Landis hogs, he got an inkling of the emotional turmoil this job would entail. With clients treated like family, their pain was felt as one's own. Just the other night, he'd been feeling sorry for himself, engulfed in his personal loneliness. Getting close to people carried a price. Now he shared their fears.

After further examination of the sow and disinfecting again at the barn's entrance, Fletch and Vic took their leave.

"See you at church," Fletch called, while sneaking a peek toward the house. Lillian's car was there, but he hadn't caught a glimpse of her.

"You bet. Thanks again," Matt replied.

On their way back to the practice, they discussed the Landis hogs some more, and then fell quiet, content to watch the landscape of green cornfields and soybeans. When Fletch saw Vic's eyelids drooping heavily with sleep, he started up another conversation, hoping to keep them out of the ditch.

"What can you tell me about the shelter?"

Vic sent him a startled look. "I thought you knew all about it."

"Not really. Marshall mentioned it the last time we talked on the phone. I meant to ask you about it before."

The truck bounced over a pothole, causing Vic's hands to bounce off the steering wheel. He tightened his grip. "It's in rural Plain City. Just getting started, actually. It takes in abused or abandoned farm animals and lets them stay for the remainder of their lives. The place is operated solely on contributions and volunteers. They work with a multitude of institutions. For instance, their summer volunteers can earn credits towards certain degrees. Right now they have two other vets on call. I'm offering more of a routine rounds type of service. I think they'll take whatever they can get."

"What's their purpose or function besides animal rescue? Surely they can't afford to just keep accumulating animals?"

"I don't know that I can answer all your questions, but I think they get endorsements from certain vegetarian food companies and activist groups that want to introduce certain animal protection laws. Usually, activist groups don't deal with people like me who endorse vaccinations and antibiotics. But Marshall claims they need all the help they can get."

"His son Marcus is heading it up. He's a friend, but I haven't seen him in a long while."

Vic's eyes lit up. "Maybe I can pawn the routine stuff off on you. You can catch up on old times."

Fletch grinned.

———◦———

Thank the Lord, when the callers came, it was one of Mom's good days. Lil had set up the ironing board in the dining room so she could keep an eye on her mom and intervene if necessary. From her vantage point, she could hear the ensuing conversation between Marie Yoder, Anita Weaver, and Mom.

"We've missed you at church," Marie said.

"I haven't been feeling well." Mom used a diversion tactic with which Lil was altogether familiar. "How are the newlyweds?"

Mom was an expert at avoiding important matters by placing emphasis on the little things. Like the time that Lil asked her if she could get her driver's license, and Mom had shoved an envelope in her hand, telling her to run to the mailbox or they would miss the mailman. Or the time Matt wanted to purchase a high school lettermen's jacket, and her mom had marched him off with a spiel about making them proud by finding his pole and catching a stringer of trout for their supper.

Lil set down the hissing iron, wondering what Marie had to say about Katy and Jake.

"Doing well. In love and happy," Marie replied. "The wedding cake was so lovely. You did such a good job."

Aha. Marie was quick, directing the conversation back to her friend.

"Thanks, and Megan? Have you heard from her?" Mom asked.

"No, but she gets home this weekend. I'll be glad when she's back in the country," replied Anita Weaver.

The room grew quiet for a spell. Then Anita said, "Rose, we came with an ulterior motive today."

"Oh?"

"We need your help. The church is having a fund-raiser, and we need someone with experience to head up the food."

"What kind of event?" Mom asked.

Lil picked up a white blouse and smoothed out the yoke, wondering if her mom was considering helping or just being polite. Or maybe she just felt out of touch and was curious about the event.

"It's an auction. There will be food and quilts sold, and a few used items that folks donate. It's to go toward the cost of the new Sunday school rooms."

"I wish I was up to it. I owe it to the church."

"What do you mean?" Anita asked.

"You know that I'm the one who caused the fire. And now they need money to rebuild."

"You are not responsible for that!" Marie scolded. "It was a combination of things."

"But you weren't there. You were home sick with a cold that night. How would you know?" Mom demanded.

"Because Vernon is on the elders' committee."

"That's right," Anita vouched.

Lil set the iron upright and strained to catch every word. Had these women—who were as close to her as second mothers—come to persuade Mom to repent? The idea made Lil burn with resentment.

"It was old wiring. And then the punch bowl accident."

"And the paper towels fell against the coffeepot."

"Those contraptions catch on fire all the time. You are not to blame. Is that what this is all about, your quitting the hostess committee?"

"You don't understand."

"Help us to understand," Anita urged.

"That committee was my life. The one place I shined. And I failed. And now nothing else matters."

"Nonsense," Marie argued.

Although relieved they hadn't brought up the elders' notion of repentance, what had just been revealed to Lil pierced her heart. She now understood the reason behind her mom's depression. And she felt her mom's pain. Because it was the same for Lil.

Lil's life was ordinary except for her hopes of becoming head chef, becoming known for beautiful presentations and perfection of flavor. She dreamed of writing a bestselling recipe book. But she'd never known until now that her mom felt the same way about her job on the hostess committee. Lil wanted to cry. Her mom had failed at the one thing that brought her joy and purpose.

"That's just it," Marie argued. "The hostess committee *needs* you. Your church family misses you. We need you."

"But it doesn't matter anymore. It will never be the same for me. You know why. I'm sure everybody knows by now."

Lil held her breath. As far as she knew, her father had not told her mom about the preacher's second visit. She hoped it did not come up in the ongoing conversation.

"We are not here to judge you. We love you. How do you know until you try it again?"

Lil exhaled with relief.

"I just know," Mom replied.

"I don't suppose you'd want to try your hand at quilting?" Anita asked. "Those bring the most money."

Lil could feel the resignation in Mom's voice. "No. I'm too tired and too old to learn something new. I'm too tired to do the things I used to do."

"Over at Plain City Druggist, they sell some herbs that pep folks up. Why don't you give those a try?" Marie urged.

Lil determined then that, whether her mom was able to pull out of her depression or not, she wouldn't end up like her. Lil would accomplish her dreams. She would find that happiness if she had to claw her way to the top. Because if she didn't, she might end up just like her mom—passing her days doing dead-end chores on a hog farm.

CHAPTER 9

After Mrs. Yoder and Mrs. Weaver left, Lil struggled with anxiety and churning emotions for the remainder of the afternoon. She felt like she had swallowed Scott's entire ant farm. Her parents had problems that she couldn't resolve, but worse, their problems were keeping her from reaching her own happiness. She should be working more hours instead of getting fired. She needed to find another job.

When she couldn't stand the emotional upheaval any longer, she fled the house for her favorite spot of refuge. As a little girl, she'd spent hours in the back pasture's cottonwood, watching its fluffy wisps burst from their capsules and float up into the air. The robins would snatch the cottony substance midair and fly away to line their nests with it. When life was easier, she would stretch out on the grass and watch the triangular leaves sparkle as they fluttered in the slightest of breezes.

Her brothers had put up a swing the summer she turned ten, inspired by the circus and church camp. She used to pretend she was a circus performer. The old swing was still there, but she didn't fit into it nearly as well as she had as a child. She came less frequently now. She clutched the frazzled rope and looked over the grassy field.

It was overgrown. Her dad moved their hogs from pasture to

pasture, and this one had been vacant long enough for wildflowers to mature and bloom, creating a charming patch of nature at its wildest.

It had been months since she'd touched the splintery board seat. As soon as she rested on it, she felt as if she'd come home—to a place where truth resided, where God used to come to meet her and touch her soul. Here many dreams had been birthed and many sins had been confessed and forgiven. She felt a shudder rake over her shoulders, thinking about Mom's predicament. And when had she grown so far from God? Lil covered her face with her hands and allowed her sorrow to manifest itself before she sought divine intervention, before she even knew how to pray.

"Lillian?"

She jerked up her head with a gasp, Fletch's voice sending a tremor down her spine. Quickly swiping an arm across her face, she caused the swing to swivel awkwardly. She used her feet to stop its movement. "Hi." Her thoughts scattered. *Now he thinks I'm crazy. Just like Mom's performance at dinner the other night.* Of course Lil shouldn't have entertained any hopes for this man anyway. He wouldn't want a Conservative girl when he could date some cute girl in jeans and toenail polish.

Fletch removed his red ball cap and slapped it across his jeans. "Sorry to intrude."

"I didn't think anyone was around."

"I came here because Matt mentioned it might make a good place for the lagoon."

"You're kidding," she snapped. She didn't want to lose her paradise hideaway. "This is the prettiest place on the farm. Surely it's not going to be ruined?"

"I don't know. I had to come out to that pasture"—he pointed off to Lil's left—"to check on some hogs. While I was this close, I came to see what it's like. I didn't mean to barge in on a private moment."

Her shoulders slumped. "It's all right. I'm just dealing with a lot of stuff right now."

He sat on the ground and crossed his arms over his bent knees. "Want to talk about it?"

She looked at him. Really looked at him. His blond hair was neatly trimmed, but it was long and fine enough to waft in the breeze. He looked so different from her brown-haired brothers and cousins. More refined, like Megan with her silky hair. Even in his mucking boots, he looked city bred. But he wasn't; he'd been a missionary's kid. Why was she judging him when his eyes shone with kindness?

⁓

Fletch didn't know why he hadn't turned and hightailed it out of there when he saw Lil, especially when she was crying. But the tender scene had gripped his heart, and he found himself drawn to her instead. And now he'd asked her if she wanted to talk about it. Either fate or God was drawing them together, and he hoped it was the latter.

"Today I overheard my mom talking to her friends. I found out why she's depressed."

So that's what Mrs. Landis's odd dinner behavior had been all about—depression. Fletch nodded, not knowing what to say.

"Mom's a plain woman. Like me," Lillian explained.

He definitely had an opinion on that, and he blurted it out, "You're not plain at all."

She pulled an ugly face, as if he'd just said something disgusting. "Never mind. Someone like you in your red shoes and red hat would never understand, anyway."

How could such a captivating creature think that she was plain? Or was her plainness a badge of self-righteousness? He frowned. "That's hardly fair. Anyway, haven't you noticed I have my mucking boots on?"

"Yeah, well you're still a pretty boy. You wouldn't understand about the dreams of plain people."

He frowned, shocked and disgusted to be referred to as a pretty boy. "You have a low opinion of me." Maybe he didn't understand what it was like to be plain, whatever that meant, but he understood about being different. "Look, Lillian. My parents were missionaries. We survived on charity and hand-me-downs. Have you even noticed that the car I drive isn't that much newer than yours?"

Lil's jaw dropped. "I had no idea."

They stared at each other.

She must have changed her opinion of him on the spot because she began to explain, "Cooking is the one place we Landis women shine. For my mom, it was being the head of the hostess committee. I already told you my goal."

"To become head chef."

She nodded. "That and more. Anyway, one night during a baby shower, a fire started in the church fellowship hall. Mom blames herself for burning down the entire fellowship hall. It was humiliating for her. After that, she resigned, and then she fell into a depression. She even took an overdose of pills. She almost died. As you know, Mennonites don't commit suicide."

He wasn't sure that was true. He always figured that depression and suicidal inclinations could hit anybody going through hard times. He wasn't entirely familiar with how the Conservative Mennonites' beliefs differed from his own—and his own beliefs might even be a bit convoluted from the norm just because of his upbringing. But he didn't argue the point. "Wow. That's tough."

Lil went on to explain how she moved out of the doddy house that she and her friends had renovated to help her family, and Fletch was reminded again what had first attracted him to her. She was a woman with grit and conviction. Not only that, but she didn't shirk back from helping others. He liked that a lot. But he didn't like seeing her so dejected.

He jumped to his feet and brushed off his jeans. "I know just what you need."

She eyed him warily. "What?"

"Somebody to push you until your feet touch those branches up there." As he hoped, he caught her off guard. She smiled, and before she could protest, he hurried behind her. "Hang on."

She did. Her black oxfords reached for the sky, and her navy skirt billowed. He felt a fond tug for the petite girl in plain, Conservative clothing. He'd never known a Conservative girl before and would never have imagined one would have big-city dreams and man-sized grit.

"Enough! I feel silly," she cried.

He caught the rope and slowed her down. The swing careened, and the small black oxfords scuffed the grass. He reached for her hand to help her off, but the old weathered rope chose that moment to snap in two, propelling Lillian's seat out from under her. Her bottom hit the ground with a hard thump, and Fletch toppled helplessly on top of her.

"Ouch!" Lil exclaimed.

His heart sped when he realized they lay in each other's arms. He rolled slightly to the side but hadn't the will to leave her. He breathed, "Lillian? Are you all right?"

She whispered back, "My friends call me Lil."

He knew he needed to get up and would, just as soon as they finished their conversation. He stroked her face. "I heard your family calling you that. I think it's cute." At the moment, he was interested in more than friendship. Tentatively, he tilted her chin, closed his eyes, and tasted her sassy lips. The kiss was brief, and like he expected, her lips were naively eager. He pulled back.

Wonder brightened the blue of her eyes.

In that moment, she seemed so naive that it almost frightened him. He needed to slow down before he hurt her. His sister, Erica, had always called him a natural flirt, and he didn't want to mislead Lil. But if she was plain, it was plain irresistible.

"Always dreamed about kissing someone like you," she said breathlessly.

Definitely time to get up. He laughed nervously, rolled away, and got to his feet.

She jumped up and brushed off her clothing. A rosy blush covered her face. "I need to go back to the house and start supper."

He glanced toward the path that wound through a stand of tangled oak and maples and concealed them from the house and barn, suddenly remembering his purpose at the farm. He wasn't here to seduce the farmer's daughter. Of course he was. He had been after her all along. And now she was mad, misunderstanding his sudden withdrawal. She had no idea how hard it had been for him to be a gentleman and pull away. "I'll go with you."

"Suit yourself." She ran her hands down her skirt and started walking away from him.

Quickly moving to her side, he said, "I have an idea about your mom."

She glanced sideways, warily. "What's that?"

"It sounds like she's lost her purpose. While we were talking, an incident popped into my mind about one of my dad's friends who had to leave the mission field and come stateside because of health problems. He fell into depression, and my mom said it was because he lost his purpose. You need to find her a new one."

"Like what? Her friends tried to get her to quilt, but she refused."

"My mom always told me that even if you don't really want to do something helpful, afterward you're glad you did. She lives by the motto that service brings joy." *That and kissing the farmer's daughter.*

"I like that, a guy who listens to his mom." She grinned, warming up to him again. "So helping animals, is that your purpose? Does that give you joy?"

Had she read his mind? He gave a scoffing laugh, thinking of the past couple of weeks working with Vic and all the sleepless nights studying. "So far it's brought me a lot of hard work."

"Service usually does."

"I suppose so. Right now my main focus is getting a diploma." That sounded as ignoble as his earlier advice had probably sounded trite, especially for a guy who wanted to get as far away from his parents as possible. A guy who just wanted to live a normal life. He tried to explain, "There's this person in my life, in my family's life. . . . His name is Marshall. He's given a tremendous amount of financial support to my parents over the years. He became a family friend and saw my interest in animals and is paying for my tuition."

"So you don't want to disappoint him?" she concluded.

"He's my person. The one who is always there for me. I can't let him down."

"Do you think if you hadn't met him, you'd still feel drawn to work with animals? I always knew what I wanted to do. Just kept gravitating toward it."

Fletch couldn't resist asking, "And do you feel this same gravitation toward me?"

Her face reddened, swallowing up her freckles. "Surely you don't expect me to answer that?"

If her blush was any indication, she might be gravitating. They walked a little way in silence, and then the barn came into view. Lil glanced sadly toward it. "Tell me. Is the herd infected?"

"We don't know yet," he answered gravely.

CHAPTER 10

It was a happy occasion for Lil. Megan had just returned from her mission trip, and in celebration, Katy had rallied the friends together at the doddy house. Megan's enthusiastic stories had captivated Lil for well over an hour, before the conversation shifted its focus. Now Lil found herself in the spotlight, being grilled about Fletch.

For Megan's sake, she glowingly described his attributes. After that, she went on to share her reservations. "So he's telling me my mom needs purpose in her life, but then when I asked him about his choice to become a veterinarian, he seemed more concerned about pleasing the man who was paying his tuition." She shrugged. "I thought that was unusual."

"Guys have to be concerned about financial obligations," Jake pointed out.

Lil thought about her dad and knew her cousin made a valid point.

"You're falling for him," Megan observed, twisting a long strand of blond hair.

"He's amazing. But he wears red shoes and a red cap, and I never should have let him kiss me."

"What!" Katy squealed. "We need to meet him. Give him the once-over."

Lil glanced at the braided area rug and back up at Katy. "The point is, if I don't quit drooling over him, it's going to be too late for me to let him go. And I don't know if I can really commit to a guy who might take me away from my church."

Katy grinned.

"What?" Lil asked.

"It's not like you to worry about a guy. You always just drooled, even if he was an outsider. And usually you complain about the church."

"Which means she didn't really like those guys," Jake observed from the sofa with his arm draped over Katy's shoulders. They were a picture of happiness now, but Lil recalled how difficult it had been for them to finally get together. Jake had fallen away from the church and even pursued an outside girl for a brief time before he'd settled down with Katy. But he'd come back. He surely understood her dilemma.

Katy was still perplexed. "Don't you remember how you wore shorts and jeans at church camp? You registered for culinary school *before* you had your dad's permission?"

"Remember the toe ring at foot washing?" Megan interjected.

"So now you're concerned about church?" Katy asked, as if her jog down memory lane validated her point.

"Of course I am! It's one thing to wish and another to actually do something that will force me to step over the line of no return. I don't want to be forced. I want to do it when I'm ready. Katy, you're the conservative one. I'm shocked you're encouraging me to consider Fletch. I depend on you to reel me in when I drift away."

"I'm just trying to understand you."

"Women. I'm in the middle of too many women," Jake protested.

Megan's eyes lit up. "Know how they court in Bangladesh?"

On the back of Jake's taunt, Megan's serious yet out-of-nowhere question set them all into a fit of laughter.

Except for Megan, "No seriously, they have a lot of rituals." She pushed her shimmering blond hair off her shoulder, and it fell into a straight line across the middle of her back.

Sweet, naive Megan, Lil mused. Always lovely, gentle, and graceful. The exact opposite of Katy, with her dark smoldering beauty and feisty personality. At times, Lil envied them both. She worked hard to maintain a trim figure. She had plain brown hair and freckles. But it was always a mild envy. Her sin, not theirs. No matter what, Lil experienced a fierce love and devotion toward them. How she'd missed them.

Megan ended her explanation with a flourish of one slender finger. "So you see, it involves various gods, touching their elders' feet, and bathing in pond water."

This raised Lil's hackles. After her church elders' request for Mom to repent in front of the entire congregation, Lil would not touch their feet. But even in her anger, she was not ready to confide in Megan and Katy about her problem with their elder-dads. She frowned, having missed some of the story. "You mean like the foot-washing service at church?"

"Kinda," Megan's perplexed expression revealed she had never connected the two events.

Lil grew contemplative, too. What kind of rituals had Fletch been exposed to as the son of missionaries? Working through her thoughts, she said, "I don't know if I could touch the elders' feet and swim in pond water for Fletch, but I did lose my job over him."

"What!" Megan exclaimed, scooting to the edge of the sofa.

Lil explained everything, trying to keep her voice upbeat. "Looks like we'll both be looking for a job if we hope to boot Katy and Jake out of their honeymoon shack."

Megan sneezed into a tissue. "Dad suggested I try Salvation Army or Red Cross." She rolled her gaze toward the ceiling. "Mom mentioned Mennonite Disaster Service."

"Your allergies bothering you?" Lil asked.

"Yes, and it was the strangest thing. I wasn't bothered at all in Bangladesh."

"Maybe you're allergic to job hunting," Jake teased.

Katy elbowed him. "Before you boot us out, we need to find another house."

They were a sorry lot. Lil sank back into the armchair her mom had donated to the doddy house. To replace it, Dad had bought Mom a small rocking recliner for her birthday, hoping it would cheer her out of her gloom. That was before they had discovered the truth—nothing would cheer her. "My mom said that, after the church fire, she felt like she'd lost her purpose in life."

"Yeah?" Katy urged, gently biting her lip.

Lil's heart sped. Could she expose the fears that had been plaguing her ever since she overheard her mom's confession? She lowered her voice to a near whisper. "What if I don't find another job? What then? Will I be just like my mom?"

Megan shook her blond mane fiercely. "You're not your mom. If anything, you're like your dad."

Lil objected, "No. I'm like her, too."

"It's a good thing that you can relate to her." Katy pushed up from the sofa. "Because that will help you to find a way to help her. You're always helping people. You're good at that. And Megan's right. You have your dad's determination. That and God will get you through. I know you don't like me to preach, but Lil Landis, enough gloom and doom."

Katy went to a drawer and pulled out some Rook cards. "I don't mean to minimize what you're going through, Lil, but God is faithful." Katy handed the cards to Jake. "You deal, and I'll go cut the strawberry pie."

"I'll help." Megan jumped up as though she wanted to get as far away from the talk of job hunting as she could.

Lil blinked the mist from her eyes as she watched her friends leave the room, pondering Katy's remarks. She had gone through a rough patch. And she probably did understand what Lil was going through in the romance department. She was right about needing to enjoy the evening. She and her friends had been apart too long, and they couldn't possibly solve all of their problems in one evening anyway.

Jake hadn't moved to do his wife's bidding yet. Lil grinned at him. "So does Katy get on you about picking up after yourself?" She remembered how Katy was always the neat one when they'd lived together. It worked out to her advantage, however, because while Lil had cooked, Katy had cleaned. At the farm these days, Lil was doing it all.

He tilted his face, and a shock of wavy black hair fell over his eye. He brushed it back, looking sheepish. "Yeah. Sometimes she's a little bossy, too, but I wouldn't change her much."

Lil could only wish she was at that place in life. "Can I ask you a guy question?"

"Sure. You helped me win Katy."

"No kidding, chump." She wet her lips, thinking how to phrase it, and opted for bluntness. "It's about Fletch's kiss."

"You've come to the right person. I'm an expert in this category."

Ignoring his boast, she explained, "Afterward, he couldn't get away from me fast enough."

"Hm. Either he didn't like it, or he liked it too much."

"What do you mean by too much?"

"He didn't trust himself to be a gentleman without pulling away."

"Oh." She sighed with confusion.

"If he likes you enough, he won't be able to stay away long."

Megan popped her head back into the room. "Pie's ready."

Lil smiled at Jake. "Thanks. I've missed you." At the table, she was impressed with Katy's pie-baking ability. "This is absolutely mountainous. Heaping with strawberries."

"Scrumptious, just how I like it." Jake winked at Katy.

Megan poised her fork in the air. "Hey, Lil. What about that cookbook you always wanted to write? Maybe we could do something creative with that instead of getting a real job."

Once again, everybody burst out laughing.

"What did I say?" Megan raised her palms in frustration.

"You come up with a lucrative way to do that, and I'll supply the recipes." Lil looked at her cards. "Now come on, green bean, we've got to make a good team. These two are hard to beat."

"That's what I mean," Megan countered. "We'd make a great team."

A tug of sympathy dismayed Lil. Megan was terrified to go job hunting. The interviews didn't frighten Lil as much as the commitment she would need to actually keep her next job. "Say, if you decide to apply at those places your parents mentioned, I can help you fill out your applications."

"That's not what's bothering me," Megan argued, slapping down a card. "Actually, I don't know what's bothering me. Just settling back into everyday life, I guess."

Lil nodded, understanding how hard it must be for her friend. She smacked her trump card on top of Jake's suit king and winked. "Got them this round!"

———❧———

Gawking at the countryside, Fletch's tire hit a pothole that shook his car so violently that it resonated throughout his entire body. Belatedly, he hit the brakes and drove at a slower speed. Only five miles lay between the Landis farm, where he'd been doing some more blood draws, and Marshall's Plain City Farm Shelter.

He was supposed to meet Vic at the shelter. He turned the steering wheel and entered the long gravel lane, glancing over the pasture. There was even a pond for waterfowl. An old barn appeared to have been remodeled. When he hit the brakes, a small cloud of dust rose over the hood of his car. When it settled, he saw the welcome sight of his mentor's son striding toward him.

Fletch jumped out of the car and waved at the muscle-clad bodybuilder. "Marcus!"

"Hey, man. I recognized your car." The two men embraced and then stepped apart. "How's it going Fletch?"

"Good. I lost track of you. I had no idea we were living right next to each other. Until I spoke with your dad."

"I was on my way to the barn. Walk with me?" They fell into step as Marcus explained, "All along, Dad intended to head this project up himself. He wanted to surprise ya with it. But he's been having some health issues, and his doctor set him up for some testing. He sent me out instead."

"Marshall didn't mention any of that. I hope it's nothing serious."

"I doubt it. Probably just an old malaria flare-up or something. He's still as forceful as ever."

Fletch knew that Marcus often resented his dad's take-charge attitude, but mostly they got along. He and Marcus often joked about their domineering dads. Amazingly, there had never been any jealousy or animosity between the two of them. Rather, they'd gotten along like brothers, estranged by location rather than choice, always happy to get reacquainted after long periods of separation. Of course, they were as different as night and day. Marcus came from a family of money and opportunity.

Fletch was happy to spend some time with Marcus on this new project. He was sure his benefactor had been delighted to put his two favorite people together. They entered the barn, and Fletch halted at the sight of a tall blond woman kneeling over a shivering lamb.

Marcus didn't seem to notice his hesitation and introduced her as Ashley. The blond stood and dusted off her low-slung jeans.

"Nice to meet ya, Fletch."

Marcus ran a hand over his shiny, shaved head. "Hey, man, Ashley's going to be our other staff person."

Fletch arched an inquisitive brow. "Other?"

"Well you're coming on board, aren't you?"

"Didn't Marshall tell you why I'm in Ohio?"

"Yeah, working for Vic's veterinary clinic."

Fletch felt an unfamiliar bristling that Marshall and Marcus both took his involvement for granted. His schooling and work were both difficult and time consuming. "Actually, I'm meeting Vic here I'm on his timecard these days."

As if Ashley had read his mind, she smiled and went for the throat of the matter. "That's just a technicality. Everybody is overworked. That's life, right?"

A voice from the open barn door interrupted their conversation. "I guess I'm at the right place?" Grateful for Vic's timely appearance, Fletch made the introductions. Vic's attention instantly riveted onto the lamb. "What have we got here?"

Marcus replied. "A couple out for a country drive found the little guy discarded on a pile of dead carcasses. They saw the lamb move."

Ashley handed Vic a clipboard containing documentation of the treatment the lamb had already received.

"When was its last feeding?" Vic asked.

"It's recorded there," Ashley pointed out. "It's time now."

"Good. Fletch, let's increase the formula. You get the pleasure this time."

Fletch mixed up the formula according to Vic's instructions. He twisted the bottle's screw cap and dropped to his knees. Taking the lamb in his lap, he felt himself melt when it started sucking the large rubber nipple.

As Fletch fed the animal, Vic explained, "Lambs need gentle treatment because even trauma can lead to pneumonia. Most likely, though, it was just inadequate colostrum in the ewe's milk. Makes the babies more susceptible to pneumonia. Could also be lungworm. The lamb's on the same medication I would have prescribed." He scribbled some notes on the clipboard. "I see nobody's done a blood draw, but you should keep the lamb isolated, anyways." While Fletch continued to feed the baby, Vic examined its hindquarters for fly-strike, but explained that all looked good on that account.

"Will the lamb pull through?" Ashley asked.

"It's too soon to tell," Vic replied.

When he was finished, Fletch nestled the baby into some straw and went with Vic to complete their rounds. There weren't many animals yet. Only two needed treatment: an old horse that a farmer had brought in to live out the remainder of its life and a cow that had managed to escape on its way to the slaughterhouse.

As they worked, Marcus talked about the farm shelter. "That cow brought us newspaper publicity."

Fletch discovered that Marshall had purchased the sixty-acre farm, donating it to the animal shelter. The farm included a white, two-story house that was getting some updated wiring to satisfy the inspector's code. The house had several bedrooms that had been turned into dorms to house their volunteers. Ashley was in charge of donations, and she'd gotten the farm connected with a university's agricultural program that supplied them with volunteers and grants.

"You've already done an amazing job with this place," Fletch said, holding the steer's lead so that Vic could examine its mouth.

"Yeah, man, the barn has been totally reinforced. Ashley got some contractors to donate new siding, paint, and roofing."

"Do you put the animals up for adoption?"

"Yeah, but not to get butchered. So keep your eyes and ears open." Marcus chuckled. "It's kinda like getting religion. These animals got saved, and now they receive life."

Fletch frowned, thinking it was a blasphemous analogy, but he got the point. "I'll let you know if anything turns up."

"Great. Can I take ya out to dinner when you're done here?"

Fletch glanced over at Vic.

Vic nodded. "Sure, I'm headed home after this. Come straight to the clinic in the morning."

Fletch agreed, glad to catch up with Marcus but hoping his mentor's son didn't exert more pressure on him to help out at the farm shelter.

"Calm down," Lil told her sister over the phone. "Where are you now?"

"At the hospital."

Lil couldn't believe a family member was in the hospital again. "I'll be right there."

"No. That's not necessary. Tom is taking care of everything. The neighbor girl's sitting the kids. It's just that the x-rays show that my ankle's broken, and I don't know how I'm going to manage."

Lil anxiously thought about the six weeks or longer that her sister would be laid up with a cast on her ankle. Michelle's garden was in full swing. It was her sister's pride and joy. As Lil's mind scurried for some scrap of assurance to give Michelle, she saw herself adding her sister's work to her already heavy load. It was impossible. Unless. . .a plan began to formulate.

"Look, sis. I know it seems bleak, and you're probably in a lot of pain right now, but I think we can make this work for the good."

"How is a broken ankle good?" her sister bemoaned.

"It might be the motive Mom needs to get out of bed."

"You're thinking if you help me, she'll get up and do her work? But she wasn't doing anything before you moved home. I don't think that will change."

"But I'm not coming to help you. I'm dropping her off at your place."

"What! You're going to make me deal with her depression, too? You don't understand. I don't know how I'm going to manage as it is." Thinking with resolve about Fletch's advice that her mom needed a purpose, Lil didn't back down from her newly formed plan. "I'll do whatever it takes to get her in the car. Then I'm dropping her off at your place and driving away. And you're not getting out of your bed until she helps."

"But Lil. . . I called for reassurance, not more complications."

"I really think it will work. She can't resist her grandchildren. She won't let them go hungry or run around looking like those ragdolls we used to have. Remember those?"

"Yeah." Michelle still seemed leery. "The girls do miss her. I do, too."

"Meanwhile, you pamper yourself. Haven't you always wished for some time for yourself?"

"That part sounds good. But I don't know if I can turn a blind eye to what's going on in the house. What if Mom just sits on the couch and stares out the window? What then?"

"She chipped in when I needed her to help me with Katy's wedding cake."

Michelle's voice heartened. "Maybe."

"It will work. You sure you don't want me to come to the hospital or go sit with the girls?"

"No. I just needed to vent. We're fine here. I can't believe I fell down the porch steps. What a klutz."

"Everything's going to be fine, sis. I'll go tell Mom about your accident. Give her some time to stew about it. Who knows? She might even offer."

"She won't."

"You're right. But I'll be over tomorrow morning with Mom in tow."

"Ouch! Oh! Careful! Ow! Gotta go."

Lil flinched at the sound of her sister's pain. In the background, she had heard a stranger's voice, no doubt a physician or nurse who had come into the room to examine her injury. She wondered if she'd asked too much of Michelle. It would probably take both Mom and herself to adequately fill in for Michelle, because honestly, if anybody was the family cyclone, it was her sister. But they would make do. They always did. And just maybe, if Fletch was right, her plan would work.

For an instant her thoughts went back to the last time she'd schemed. She had teamed up with her cousin Jake, working as a matchmaker, to help him win Katy's love. When Katy discovered her interference, she'd been furious. Mom would get mad, too. Lil hoped this didn't backfire on her.

CHAPTER 11

Fletch squinted at the blinding glare of the sun rising over the horizon. Beside him, Buddy squirmed on the car seat. As he drove, Fletch processed the conversation he'd had with Marcus the previous evening over dinner.

"Ya do realize that Dad strategically placed you in Plain City? He thought you'd be thrilled to help him." Marcus had given him a look that translated to *after all he's done for you and your family.*

"Fourth-year selective internships are hard, and anything below C minus is failing. The last thing I want is to disappoint your dad with failing grades and the cost of an extra semester. Anyway, everything I do has to go through Vic. He's covering my cost of living, you know. But he'll probably let me provide a lot of the shelter's animal care. Maybe that's what Marshall had in mind all along?"

"Ya can stay at the shelter."

"No." Fletch shook his head. "I have to follow the school's protocol—what's already been set up—and Vic is paying for all my living expenses. But I have a dog that would love to spend some time out there. A basset that's either stuck at my apartment or in the tiny fenced yard at the clinic."

"Sure, bring him over."

"Thanks."

"Tell me about your work. About the farms you visit."

Fletch had talked about the Landis family after that and had even shared about his attraction to Lil. Marcus showed interest in the discussion. Finally, his friend had relented. "I can see ya don't have time to run down donations, but Dad mentioned something specific ya can do for him."

"He did?"

"He wanted ya to take some video footage of sick animals."

Shocked and repulsed, Fletch asked, "Why?"

"We're putting together a documentary-type film to use at fundraisers. It would just be a little filler, ya know, to play on crowd sympathy."

"Why can't you use the animals here at the shelter?"

"Oh we are. But we don't have many animals. It's one of those 'which comes first, the chicken or the egg' things. We need the fundraising events to buy feed for the animals, but first we need animals for the fund-raising film. You're around sick animals all the time, and it won't hurt anything. It will help us."

Fletch understood but wasn't eager to film sick animals. Who would view the film? What would the narrative contain? How might it affect the farmers where the animals were filmed? Thankfully, after Marcus had presented the details and stressed Marshall's wishes, he'd let the issue drop. Fletch had to wonder if next Marshall would call him.

They pulled into the farm shelter, and Fletch ruffled Buddy's fur. "You're going to love this place. Even ducks. I know how you love to chase birds." He leashed Buddy, and after seeing nobody outside, walked him to the farmhouse. The front door was propped open with a paint can, and Fletch let himself in. Paint fumes drifted from the dining room, which was situated off to his left, and he followed his nose, stopping short in the entry.

His gaze involuntarily caught the backside of Ashley, who was kneeling on the floor and stroking some unfinished pine cabinetry with a paint brush. She was clad in rolled-up jeans and a yellow T-shirt splattered with white paint. He couldn't help but notice she was an attractive woman, from her white tennis shoes to her hair that was swept up in a perky ponytail that didn't even reach her neck. He must have released some kind of unintentional sigh, because she suddenly looked over her shoulder. When their gazes met, her eyes lit up.

"Hey, Fletch. You here to help?"

He gazed around at several pieces of unfinished cabinetry. "What is all this?"

"Our new office furniture."

Buddy let out a yip, and Ashley smiled. "Who's that?"

"Didn't Marcus tell you?"

She shook her head, and her ponytail swung from side to side.

"My dog. Ashley meet Buddy." He released his end of the leash, and the dog sidled over to the girl, wagging his whole backside.

Ashley laughed. "You're adorable. I love your saggy eyes. And you're so plump and cute." She placed her paintbrush down and bent to pet the dog.

"Marcus said I can drop him off sometimes."

"Oh good. I need a break anyway."

"At seven a.m.?"

"Coffee break, silly. Don't you drink coffee?"

"Yes, I have a mug in the car. Which reminds me, I've got about twenty minutes to get over to the clinic. Vic wanted me to be there when it opens this morning."

Ashley looked a little disappointed but offered, "I'll show Buddy around and keep an eye out for him."

"Can you keep him inside until I've driven away? So he doesn't chase me?"

"Sure. Wait a minute." She strode to her desk and opened a drawer. When she came back, she thrust a palm-sized video camera at him.

"What's this?" Fletch asked, warily.

"Marcus asked me to give it to you next time I saw you."

"I didn't. . ." Fletch wet his lips, trying to figure out how to turn her down without offending her or Marcus.

She snatched his hand and pressed it into his palm. "Just keep it. You'll know when to use it. That's all. And I'll take care of Buddy."

Fletch stuck the camera in his jeans pocket, thinking he might not be dropping Buddy off that often, after all, if doing so brought ultimatums.

"Thanks." He bent and gave the dog a pat. "Stay." Buddy studied him with soulful eyes, and Fletch almost regretted leaving him.

As he headed toward the car, he heard, *Woof!* Next he heard Ashley's soft feminine voice. He could see why Marshall had hired her to get donations, why he'd asked her to give him the video camera. If anything, the incident opened his eyes to the power of an attractive female. Ashley wasn't his type. He saw how she used her looks to get what she wanted. She wasn't at all like Lil, who was honest and forthright.

He shook his head. Too many distractions. He needed a cool head. He needed to get his diploma and—

His thoughts came to a dead end, startling him. He'd been so set on getting that diploma and making Marshall proud that he hadn't thought much beyond that one event. Oh, he had a vague idea of his options. He would probably take an internship and try to work himself into an existing practice. He'd never have the funds to start up his own place. Probably not the experience, either.

Sometimes it was easier to probe an issue from the opposite direction. He knew what he didn't want to do with his life. He didn't want to follow his parents' footsteps. He didn't want to make his children feel unwanted. When he settled down, he wanted to provide the sort of home where kids had an ordinary life.

With a mother like Lil? With a sinking heart, he realized that dating wasn't even included in his limited budget.

⁓৹

Mom fastened her seat belt. "It's a pity you have to drive such an undependable, ugly car."

Lil glanced at her with a glint in her eyes. "Now, Mom, don't go putting ideas of rebellion in Jezebel's head."

"I'm so tired of all these sessions and appointments. If you really loved me, you wouldn't drag me through all this. Nothing helps anyway."

Her heart picking up a speed to match Jezebel's engine, Lil replied,

"We don't have an appointment."

Mom snapped a panicked gaze in Lil's direction. "Then where are we going? You're not taking me to the church. I told you I didn't want to help with that fund-raiser."

"We're going to Michelle's."

"Oh Lil. I'm not up to that. I know she needs help, but surely you can't expect me to—" Mom cut off midsentence, probably because she realized how selfish her remark was going to sound.

In silence, they passed a few farms where colorful combine harvesters moved through the golden wheat fields, kicking up a swirl of dust and chaff. When they pulled into Michelle's driveway, Lil pulled as close to the house as she could. "Let's just go see how she's doing."

Mom shook her head. "I know it sounds awful, but I can't go in there because I know she needs me, and I don't have anything to offer her. I'm sure you can't understand. I don't even understand it. But I feel paralyzed. Useless. We didn't even bring any food. We should have brought a casserole or something."

"We're here now. Michelle has plenty of food stocked up and ready for use. I'm sure you want to see the grandchildren?"

"You know I love them," Mom snapped.

"Let's go inside. You can tell them."

"No." She turned her face away, toward Michelle's huge vegetable and flower garden.

It was a reminder to Lil that not only was she trying to help her mom, but Michelle really needed them. Lil was ready to roll up her sleeves, but she had to try her plan first. "Mom." Lil hardened her voice. "We are sitting in this car until you go inside. I'm not backing down."

Mom put her hand on the door handle. "Then I'll just walk home."

"Good idea. And when one of the neighbors stops to pick you up and asks how your daughter's ankle is doing, you can explain that you don't know because you're out for a leisurely stroll."

When Mom flinched, Lil felt her pain. And Mom was correct; Lil didn't understand it all completely, how a woman could turn her back on her family. But she saw the pain involved and thought she understood the root of the problem. Lil's thoughts went to Fletch, and in her mind's eye she told him, *You better be right about this.* But Fletch seemed world-wise with his multicultural upbringing. She trusted his judgment, happy to have somebody help her through unchartered waters.

Lil's thoughts snapped back to her mom when she heard the car door open. "Fine, but let's not stay long. Maybe we can take some laundry home or bring the children back to the house for you to watch," Mom suggested.

Lil grinned inwardly. Mom was already focusing on the problem. Sure, she was figuring on Lil doing the actual work, but then she didn't know about Lil's plan.

⟋⌣

Over an hour later, Lil pulled Jezebel into the Landises' large circle drive and slipped into her usual parking place near the house. It would seem strange going into the empty house. As she headed toward the mudroom, she realized she should have told Dad about her idea before she toted Mom off to Michelle's. But it was too late for—her thoughts broke off when she spotted a red dot peeking over the other side of the azalea bush. She scurried over and stopped in amazement.

The tomatoes had reseeded themselves in a place that was out of the way and hidden by the house-hugging shrubbery. That is until they had gotten leggy and scrambled over the azalea bush. Amazingly, the tomatoes were doing great without any human help. She yanked out a weed, tossed it in the yard, and brushed her hands against her brown skirt.

Normally, Mom kept a garden, but she also kept a couple of tomato plants near the house for quick use. These were experiments, too, using different hybrids and species. But this plant had survived without any human help. Lil cupped the ripest orb in the palm of her hand, thinking about her mom and wondering how she was doing. With a sigh, she stepped back and went to get a watering hose. When Mom returned, she'd have tomatoes to tend. Even if there wouldn't be enough to can, it might give her mom a little joy.

Lil unwound the hose and dragged it toward the bush until it caught on something. Retracing her steps to see what hindered the hose, she stopped short. A blue Ford Focus was driving onto their property, moving along the far side of the drive.

It stopped, and Lil's heart did a little flip to see Fletch step out of the car. With her free hand, she waved.

"Hi, Lil." He gave his red cap a nudge so it didn't block his vision or his gorgeous brown eyes. "I come bearing good news."

"About the hogs?"

"Yes. It's not the PRRS virus."

Lil gave a relieved sigh. She knew that the threat of Porcine Reproductive and Respiratory Syndrome was a dreaded threat to any hog farm. "I'm so relieved. You have no idea."

"I think I do."

He stepped nearer, causing her mind and body to act all befuddled. He hadn't put on his mucking boots yet, and there was something intimidating about those red sneakers. Her mind picked up the warning, but his smile charmed her traitorous heart, as if it had never learned anything about men. His eyes sent dual messages. When flirtatious, she was defenseless. When sincere and caring. . . . Wait! She was defenseless then, too. Had the Africans he'd grown up with been as confused about the blond-haired boy? She swallowed uncomfortably.

And he stepped nearer. "The vaccinations are done, but I'll still need to take some random blood draws."

She nodded, grateful to see him again. No. She shouldn't fall for him or his red sneakers. He didn't fit on this farm, wearing his clean white T-shirt and standing more than a head taller than any of the Landis men. He was different. Even if he was a Mennonite. He reminded her of her imaginary Rollo. Why had she made her imaginary circus performer tall and blond?

The closer Fletch came, the more she worried that he might try to kiss her again. That she might let him. Right here in the yard, where her dad or any one of her brothers might observe them. She turned away and yanked on the hose, freeing it from its obstacle. Her voice came out thick with her family's Dutch accent, as it usually did when she was emotional about something. "I was taking your advice, just now."

Keeping her back to the wonderful intruder, she dragged the hose toward the tomato bed, her pulse speeding when she heard the soft sound of red sneakers following.

"I don't remember giving any advice on watering tomatoes, but I can tell you that you need to turn the faucet on."

Biting back a smile, she tossed the end of the hose to the ground at the edge of the tomato plants and started back toward the faucet, tossing over her shoulder, "I just got back from Michelle's." When she turned, she noticed his intriguing dark brows formed a sharp *V*.

"Matt told me about her ankle. That's too bad. How's she doing?"

"She's in pain because she doesn't believe in taking medicine unless it's a last resort."

"I'm sorry to hear about her accident. Who's taking care of your nieces?"

She watched the water gush into the dry soil surrounding the tomato plants and adjusted the flow. "My mom. I hope. I tricked her into getting into the car and then convinced her to go into Michelle's house. Then after visiting a few minutes, I snuck out the side door. I left her there," she admitted. Her eyes widening over the gravity of her deed, she glanced over at Fletch.

His left cheek twitched. He glanced at the barn and back. "Are they in on the scheme?"

"No. I acted on impulse. So if this backfires, it'll be my fault. But I think Dad will go along." She shrugged. "Nothing else is working."

Fletch arched his brow. "Will Landis does not seem very flexible."

Lil glanced toward the barn, wanting to disagree. Actually, her dad was compromising a lot these days. She admired him for it, too. But when she saw the teasing light in Fletch's eyes, she let his comment slide. "If you're scared of him, you'd better not let him see you loafing like this. Anyway, I just wanted to tell you that I'm testing your theory about Mom needing a purpose."

"From what I saw that night at supper, the grandchildren will lift her spirits. There's general need, and then there's family needs. And family trumps everything else."

"You play Rook?"

"Poker."

Lil's mouth dropped open. But before she could reply, he laughed. "You'd be surprised at some of the games I've played. But even across continents, most games are similar."

She nodded, intrigued by the mysteries of his background and understanding what he meant about family. "Michelle will call if my plan backfires."

Fletch touched her arm. "Let me know how it turns out. You're right, though. I need to get to work. To give your dad the good news." After another reluctant gaze toward the barn, he turned away. But he'd only taken a few steps in that direction when he turned back to her.

Embarrassed that he'd caught her watching him, she quickly dropped her gaze to the ground.

"Lil? Would you like to go out with me sometime?"

She raised her gaze. "Yes!" Instantly regretting her eagerness, she qualified, "But I shouldn't."

He tilted his face with confusion. "Why not?"

"Because we don't go to the same church."

"But we both attend a Mennonite church."

She arched an eyebrow at him. "You know what I mean."

"Could we just talk about it? Maybe it's not the big obstacle we think it is. Look, I'm still in school, and I don't have much money. But what if we went on a picnic?"

Lil glanced toward the barn, saw her dad striding toward them, and wondered what he would have to say about the matter. She wanted to settle her internal conflict over Fletch once and for all. Would a date do that? She didn't have much time until her dad would be able to hear their conversation. "All right."

Fletch grinned. "Great! How about Sunday after church?" He explained that Vic gave him time off to attend church, so it shouldn't be too hard get the extra time off for a picnic.

"Yes. That will work." She whispered, "I'll provide the food."

"Great!" he repeated. "I'll see you then." He turned and ran smack into Lil's dad, who let out a surprised grunt. "Oh! Sorry, sir," Fletch quickly apologized. "I was just. . . ."

Dad shoved his straw hat back and frowned. "Was what?"

Lil tried not to smile at Fletch's reddening neck. She really should have warned him.

"Just coming to give you the good news."

They started toward the barn together, and she hurried inside, doing the garbanzo dance all of the way through the mudroom.

CHAPTER 12

Most mornings, the clinic was open for drop-in clients, but Vic didn't set regular appointments because his loyalties were with the local farms, and he wanted to be available for emergencies. Fletch was glad that Vic often trusted him to work unsupervised. He had just finished muzzling and treating a house cat for infected animal bites. When the waiting room had finally emptied, he felt Vic clutch his shoulder. "You've been a great help. I wish I could afford to hire somebody full-time."

Glowing under the praise, Fletch turned. "Well you have me full-time for a while yet."

Vic gave him a halfhearted smile. "About the time I get you trained, your term will be over."

"Maybe you'll get a quicker student next year."

"Huh?"

Fletch saw the momentary confusion in Vic's eyes. "You thinking of quitting the program with the school?"

Vic turned and washed his hands in the basin, talking over his shoulder. "This is the first time I've ever had a student. I wouldn't have even thought about joining the program if Marshall hadn't approached me with his offer."

"What offer?" Fletch probed, grabbing a bottle of bleach and water mixture.

Vic dried his hands and stared at Fletch. "You didn't know that Marshall set us up together?"

"He only told me he knew you, highly recommended you, and that he'd gotten the school's approval. He thought it would be ideal because it was close to OSU."

Vic gave a sardonic laugh. "Probably bribed the school with donations just like he did me."

Fletch didn't understand Vic's insinuations. "It's true that Marshall is a generous man. What is it you have against him?"

"I don't like being coerced."

Fletch spritzed a table and wiped it down with paper towels, trying to tamp down a rising premonition. "So he gave you money to join the off-site program?"

"Don't you get it? It's all about the farm shelter. I didn't get it at first either. I thought I was just taking his gift and returning a favor, but now that I've been out to the shelter, I see there's strings attached."

Fletch swallowed, feeling a bit coerced himself when it came to the farm shelter. He put the bottle back in the cupboard. "Do you mind telling me the entire story?"

"This stays between us?"

Fletch quickly considered. "Yes."

Vic grabbed the broom, his strokes matching his frustration as he explained. "Somehow Marshall found out that I was in financial trouble. It was my own fault. I took too much money personally. But Britt was always nagging me, wanting this and that. Anyway, he bought me some equipment I needed and paid off a debt I had. In return, I was to apply at the college for the off-site experience. He led me to believe that I was supporting the veterinary school. Like that was his main objective. To me, it seemed like a win-win situation. For me, the school, the student—you."

"But now you believe that he handpicked you because you were close to the shelter, and he wanted me to get involved there?"

Vic stopped sweeping and studied Fletch a moment. "He recently called me and requested that I volunteer at the shelter. Britt was already upset because I work so many hours. A lot of the work there is routine, so naturally, I can turn that over to you."

Fletch swallowed, hating to blacken Marshall's character without knowing the full truth, but also feeling like he owed Vic some loyalty. "I think Marshall wanted me to help at the shelter. Marcus wants me to video sick animals for a documentary they're doing."

Vic ran his hands through his hair. "So that's it. You understand they'll use it against the farmers? The shelter is probably connected with organizations that hope to abolish animal abuse by establishing laws that make it harder for the farmers to make a living."

"I don't like abuse. You don't either."

"Of course not. And I'd do something about it if I came across it. But my clients are good people. I don't want to get in the middle of an issue, right or wrong, that could ruin my practice. I'm not going to that shelter any more than I have to until our agreement is over. I'll send you in my stead, like Marshall wants. But I want you to be discreet about this. And don't be taking any videos. Marshall may have me by the throat, but just remember that you need my recommendations to get a passing grade. Until the new term starts, I can still back out of the program."

Fletch wondered. Surely he'd signed a contract, but he didn't know that for sure. "Yes, sir." But he determined to call Marshall that very evening. He didn't like being caught in the middle.

⁓

The next day, Lil punched the speed dial and waited for her sister's voice. "How's it going over there?"

"You checking on me or Mom?" Michelle asked.

"Both. It's hard not knowing what's happening at your house. I feel like I should be there."

"Let's just say that I smell fresh zucchini cake, and I hear giggles coming from the kitchen."

"Whew!" Lil blew out a sigh of relief. She twisted a lock of her hair.

"It's too soon to come and get her. If I bring her home tonight, most likely she'll take to her bed tomorrow to recuperate."

"She thinks you're coming back to get her. Last night she slept in our attic bedroom. Does Dad care if she's here?"

"He's skeptical, but he's all right with it."

"Ouch!"

"What?"

"Oh I just bumped my foot."

"You're not out of bed?" Lil demanded.

"No. Tammy just left some toys on the bed. But I can't stay in bed forever."

"How quickly you change your tune. I thought you were always complaining that you needed rest."

"I know. But now I'm rested."

"Are you in much pain?"

"It's bearable. But I need some magazines or something."

"What about hand sewing?"

By the time Lil finished her conversation, she felt confident she was doing the right thing for her mom and Michelle. And even though Michelle was already growing restless, she could use some pampering.

───✑───

On Friday, Lil joined Megan for lunch at a restaurant near the company where Megan was interviewing for a job. Although Megan claimed she didn't need the moral support, she'd allowed Lil to come along. Right across the street was the Italian restaurant that Beppe had always raved about. It was his model for running Riccardo's. Lil wanted to scope the place out to see if it might be a place where she could apply for a job.

Megan parked her dad's restored dark-blue Chevy Nova at the far edge of the parking lot to avoid paint dings. Even so, a few heads turned at the car's rumble and watched the two Conservative Mennonite girls step out of the classic car. Megan seemed used to it, but Lil always enjoyed the attention. Megan locked the Nova with her key, and they started toward the restaurant.

Lil's excitement mounted over dining at Beppe's favorite restaurant.

"They have valet parking here in the evenings."

At the entrance, a hostess greeted them. They passed stone pillars that imitated ancient Roman architecture. Lil saw that the eating facility was upscale and received a lot of corporate clientele. She understood Beppe's obsession.

They ordered soft drinks, and a menu was placed in front of each of them, but Lil resisted the temptation to open it because once she did she would be absorbed with it. Instead, she leaned forward on her elbows. "So tell me all about your interview."

Megan's eyes lit up. "I think it went well. It sounds like a dream job. Char Air is a charter service that has achieved a superb reputation for the service they give their customers. They are looking for individuals to build relationships with a portfolio of clients who regularly need to charter commercial jets all over the world."

"Wow. I never pictured you in a place like that."

"Sometimes they charter sports teams and private corporations, but they do a lot with humanitarian workers and relief organizations. The name Char stands for charter and charity. Clever, huh?"

"Aha." Lil leaned back as the waiter came to their table and asked if they needed more time to select their food. "Yes, sorry."

"No problem. Take your time." He dipped his head and backed away.

"I want to hear more, but we'd better order." Lil scanned the entrées, her eyes passing over the lasagna and penne, but she took her time reading the descriptions of the items that many Italian restaurants didn't carry.

When the waiter returned, Lil ordered the gnocchi that Beppe always raved about. They had never served gnocchi at Riccardo's. Megan went with an antipasto salad. When the waiter left, Lil confided, "I should order salad, too, but since I'm checking this place out, I wanted to order one of the entrées."

"A nice place like this, you have to try the food. I'm just too excited and nervous over the interview. I don't think I'll be able to enjoy my meal."

"Of course you are. Anyway, if you get the job, you'll have plenty of chances to eat here."

"Or if you get a job here."

They grinned at each other, thrilled over the possibilities. Then Lil came back to earth. "I'm just checking it out; I didn't bring a résumé. I need to make sure Mom's doing okay before I botch up another job."

"So how's it going with her over at Michelle's?"

Plucking a roll from a bread basket and swirling a small chunk in herbed olive oil, Lil smiled. "She's working hard, and Michelle said she seems happy. Like her old self again. I'm bringing her home on Monday. That will be the real test. I'm hoping she'll want to continue going over to help Michelle with her garden. Or at least do more at home, so I can help Michelle."

"How long will Michelle be in a cast?"

"She'll probably get it off in six weeks, but I doubt it will stop her once she's feeling better."

Megan nodded somberly.

Lil thanked the waiter for bringing their meals. "Back to the interview. Would it be strictly office work or would there be travel?"

"Both. I love the airport location. I always had a fascination with planes. As you saw, it's right by one of their hangars. The view from the office is amazing."

Lil took a bite of the creamy, peach-colored sauce. Delicious. Beppe was right. "I didn't know you were interested in planes."

"But I am! Especially since Bangladesh. I saw some charter planes bringing in supplies, landing on makeshift runways. It was thrilling."

"You think this company lands on runways like that?"

"Maybe not. But listen to this. If I got the job, I might get to go on some foreign trips. He said that the last girl who worked there went to Haiti and India, free of charge by the company who chartered the plane."

Lil couldn't deny the spark of excitement in Megan's blues. "What happened to her?"

"She had a baby and decided not to return."

Lil took another bite of pasta, noting its perfection, and glanced up. "He probably liked that you were single?"

Megan nodded. "I think so. But he says he's got a couple of more interviews. He'll call next week. I hope I get it. There's nothing else out there in my field. Well there was a payment coordinator. How dull does that sound? I guess they deal with money for relief projects."

"Maybe that sort of job would have the same travel opportunities."

Megan shrugged. "It sounded like dull paperwork. Anyway, there was a news position with a local Christian television station. Can you imagine how that would go over at church? Television?"

Lil rolled her gaze. "I don't think it would suit you."

"I had no idea, but so many of the jobs I am interested in are military or government organizations, and the church wouldn't be happy about those either."

Lil nodded her understanding. Because of the commandment "Thou shalt not kill," the Conservative Mennonite Church took a stance against war or anything supporting war. That ruled out members' participation in the military and law enforcement and most government positions, too.

It wasn't that the Conservatives weren't appreciative of their freedoms, but they gave their thanks to God, who they believed used outsiders to move in areas that their people would never consider, such as the military. Lil had grown up being taught that Conservative Mennonites were not of the world, only passing through it, and that God was their provider.

The war-and-peace issue had never been that important to Lil because it hadn't touched her life in a personal way, but Megan was very involved in causes related to world peace. She would like nothing better than to work for an organization that would help bring world peace.

"I suppose you've checked out all the Mennonite organizations like Mennonite Mutual Aid or Mennonite Disaster Service? What's that organization that deals with world peace?"

"Mennonite Central Committee. It has a few positions but nothing local. I'd have to move. Many humanitarian jobs are headquartered in another city. There're plenty of volunteer positions in Columbus. Oh"—she reached across the table and touched Lil's hand—"I found a job opportunity for head of missions in Sudan, with no education required."

Lil gripped Megan's hand. "Oh please. Don't consider that. You have to get *this* job. I've never seen you so excited over a job before." She released Megan's hand and relaxed back in the booth again. "I want you here. I want us to move into the doddy house together."

"Of course! That's why I'm job hunting instead of volunteering someplace."

Lil urged, "I'm really hoping that by September, things will fall in place for us." Unlike Megan, who was insecure about finding a job, Lil hoped to find something quickly. If her present scheme, her mom helping at Michelle's, didn't work. . . It would work. It had to.

"I need to work," Megan admitted. "I'm starting to get bored. Antsy."

"I know that feeling. But I know I won't be bored on Sunday."

Megan tilted her head. "Why not on Sunday?"

"Because I have a date with Fletch."

"And you're just now telling me that?" Megan reprimanded. "I can't wait to meet him."

"He's taking me on a picnic. After church."

"How romantic!"

"Yeah, but you know what? I'm scared."

"Those red sneakers, huh?"

"No. It's definitely the guy who wears them."

CHAPTER 13

Fletch was uncharacteristically nervous. He felt more like he was facing an important exam than going on a date. But he was also excited to see Lil again and certainly didn't regret asking her out, at least that's what he told Buddy on the way to the Landis farm. But Buddy didn't seem interested in romance if the basset's droopy eyes and saggy jowls were any indication. He seemed more interested in the passing scenery.

"Yeah, that's how you feel now. But once you see her, you'll change your tune."

And Buddy did. He literally drooled when he gazed into Lil's eyes. And when she knelt down to pet him, he licked her face. When she stood up, he whined. So she got down again, and he licked her face again.

Seeing that somebody was going to have to break the cycle and intervene, Fletch took Lil's arm and helped her back to her feet, whispering, "I think Buddy's in love. I don't blame him. But this is my date." He whisked her toward the car, but she kept glancing back at the pooch, who panted at her heels. Fletch was pleased to see Buddy capturing Lil's heart, too. If he was lucky, he'd at least get the leftover scraps of affection.

Glancing to the backseat, Lil laughed. "I didn't know it was going to be a trio or I would have packed an extra sandwich." Staring at Buddy, she added, "He's irresistible. In fact, if you're not careful, Fletch, I might just give Buddy your portion of my special avocado BLT's."

"Have I mentioned how happy I am to be dating a cook?"

"I'm not sure we're dating. More like having a picnic to talk about dating," she corrected.

"I stand corrected but not dissuaded. Regarding Buddy, I had no intention of having a pet while going through school until I saw this dog."

"Kind of like us," Lil said, straightening in her seat and blushing. "I mean the 'no intentions' part."

"I guess so. But that doesn't sound very romantic."

Lil sighed, "Intriguing though."

Fletch grinned. "My thoughts exactly."

When the river became visible in the passing scenery, Lil remarked, "I've never been to Antrim Park."

"It's close to the university. Buddy loves it. That's why I didn't have the heart to leave him at home."

The Olentangy River park was divided in to two portions. The west side of the park had tennis courts, a basketball court, several baseball diamonds, and soccer fields. It included a parking lot, where they unloaded. Fletch gave Lil Buddy's leash, in exchange for the blanket and picnic basket.

"This is a real picnic basket. I expected a cooler."

"It's old. Handed down in the family. Could probably tell us some tales."

"Like your parents dating?"

"And my grandparents."

"Then I'm glad I asked you on a picnic for our first date." He figured he must be wearing her down, because she didn't protest about it not being a date this time. Of course that could have been because Buddy had discovered where they were and was straining and pulling on the leash.

"If you wrap the leash a couple of times around your hand and pull him in closer, he'll be easier to control."

"I don't want to hurt him."

"You won't."

"Funny, I don't think I've ever walked a dog before."

That struck Fletch as painfully sad. "Ever wanted to?" he asked.

"I do now," she replied. "It's fun."

Her answer satisfied him. Placing his hand at the tiny waist he'd been itching to touch, he asked, "How does this spot look?"

"Perfect!"

While Buddy sniffed the grass, they spread out the mouth-watering picnic of Lil's special sandwiches, fruit, and homemade cookies. Fletch whistled, and the dog came and laid beside the tattered quilt, panting and gazing steadily into Lil's face.

"Obedient," Lil noted.

But Fletch was more interested in the food and the girl than in Buddy's manners. "You told me you always knew that you wanted to be a cook, but it's hard for me to imagine you as a baby, babbling, 'Sauté it, Mommy.'"

Lil giggled. "I'm glad you know a little about cooking."

"I live alone. Have to fend for myself."

"How long have you lived alone?" she asked.

"Nope. We're talking about you first. I don't know that much about Conservative Mennonites, but I have a hunch that most of the women aren't career-minded. Tell me more about your journey to become head cook." He took a bite of his sandwich and muttered, "Wait. First tell me what's on this sandwich. This is awesome."

Lil grinned as if he'd just given her the moon. "That's my special avocado spread, and it's a secret this early in a relationship."

He loved the challenge but played along. "That's cruel."

Her expression became serious, even serene. "I think the cooking thing is a Mennonite gene that my mom's family inherited. My sister has it, too, only she's busy raising a family and really enjoys the gardening part of it. I always had to help Mom, and I loved both cooking and baking."

"But that doesn't explain your dream to take it beyond cooking for your family."

Her blue eyes lit up. "At an early age, I received praise. Heard Mom's friends telling her I was talented. It was probably the attention, and then my imagination just fueled it."

He was utterly intrigued. "What do you mean?"

"I always had a strong imagination. . . . I remember the time we went to the circus. It was one of those rare outings where I got a glimpse of life beyond the farm. We went with my cousin Jake's family. We went to a real sit-down restaurant, which was unusual with all us kids. I was mesmerized by the whole thing. After that, my life came down to the fact that I had two choices: I could join the circus or I could become a famous chef. The latter seemed the better choice."

Fletch burst out laughing. "I'm sorry. It's just I wasn't expecting that."

She blushed.

Fletch eased close and touched her arm. "You're such a delight. So fascinating. Did your parents encourage you to pursue your dreams?"

"Not exactly. They let me go to culinary school because it was a talent I could use once I got married. But Dad thinks my goals are foolish and unwomanly." She squirmed. "You don't really know me. Growing up, I was a bit of a trial to my parents. I've always been a little rebellious."

He thought she would probably still be a handful for a man.

"As you know, the family's under a lot of other strain right now, so I'm really trying to cooperate. But I can't wait to leave the farm." She sighed. "Well, it's my turn to eat. You talk."

"What was it you wanted to know again?"

Her expression softened. "How long have you lived alone?"

"My folks sent us to a school where a lot of the missionary kids went. I wasn't always alone, but I was always lonely for family. I hated being sent away. My sister and I were close, but then she married a man she met in Africa. He's Canadian, and they live in his country now."

"I'm sorry. My friend Megan is an only child. Sometimes I see the sadness of it in her eyes. Then again, sometimes I'm envious of all the attention she gets from her parents."

"Well I didn't get much attention. We moved around a lot, too. I had to make new friends. At the university, I lived in the dorms or shared apartments just to be around people. Usually, I lived off donations. Marshall's helped me because my dad wasn't financially able. Right now I'm living in an apartment furnished by Vic, in a complex owned by his brother." Fletch shrugged. "Maybe I haven't always lived alone. But I mostly fend for myself. I look forward to the day when I can pay my own way, too. Settle in some place for real. Quit moving around. That's one reason I'm dreaming of that diploma. One more milestone."

He quit speaking and glanced at Lil to see how she was receiving the information. She smiled and passed him a cookie. He took a bite and thought he'd gone to heaven. He started talking with his mouth full. "Mm. I can't tell you the last time I had a homemade cookie. And never one as delicious as this."

"Do you compliment all the girls? How many girls have you dated?" she asked.

He almost choked from her blunt question. He swallowed. "My sister says I'm a flirt. But I really mean it when I say this cookie is delicious. As to the other question, I've dated a few women, the usual school functions. Not so much lately. What about you?" Trying to play down his past experience with girls, he nibbled on his cookie. But as he waited for her reply, he felt as if the question was the most important one he'd ever asked anyone. He wanted her all to himself.

She grinned. "My friends tell me I'm a flirt, too."

That hit him painfully, but he remembered thinking that about her the day she backed into Britt's car. "Are you?"

She laughed. "I don't know. I've always liked guys. I think I'm just honest and friendly."

"Go on." *How many guys?*

Lil shrugged. "I've had a few dates, but like you, nothing serious. Never a real boyfriend."

No serious boyfriend. Fletch felt as if the weight of the world had just been lifted off his shoulders, and if he wasn't careful, he was going to float up off the old quilt. Now if he could just get her to turn all that friendliness his way. Only his way.

⎯ৎ⎯

Lil felt cherished, the way Fletch held her hand in his. After taking their picnic supplies to the car, they started along a gravel path that encircled the lake. With Fletch's free hand, he threw a stick for the basset.

"What happens if it goes in the lake?" she asked, wondering if she'd have a wet dog panting down her neck on the ride home. Buddy was a sweetheart, but she needed to know what to expect.

"He doesn't like the water. He'll just shuffle back and expect me to find a new object."

"Smart dog."

She was trying to think of a question that would get them on the topic of their religious beliefs, but Fletch beat her to it.

"When you mentioned you were a little rebellious, what exactly did you mean by that?"

Lil figured the easiest way to explain was to show him. She removed her bobby pins and slipped them into a pocket. When Fletch saw her bangs fall down and sweep across her eyes, his mouth opened in surprise.

"Wow. So you still feel this rebellion? I noticed you're wearing your covering, but you weren't the day we met. Does that mean anything?"

"The church recently voted to change the ruling on the covering. We only have to wear it to worship. I had stopped wearing it other places, but when I moved back home, my dad seemed so disappointed in me that I started wearing it again. Look. I was the girl who borrowed shorts at church camp and wore them until I had to return home. I once wore a toe ring to foot washing."

Fletch burst out laughing. "Now in the church I attend, that wouldn't be a big deal, but I can only guess what happened to you."

"My friend Katy took it off and hid it before anybody saw it. I loved to get her flustered. She always covered for me and always tried to boss me around. It was like having a second mother. I figured Katy would keep me straight. But I think she's quit doing that now."

"I don't understand. Are you saying that you wouldn't have a problem going to a church like mine? It sounds like you might even welcome it."

"Once I thought I might change churches. I always wished I'd been born in a different church."

"You're a Christian, right?"

"Yes, but that's what I'm trying to tell you. Since I moved home, I'm seeing things differently. That's why I'm pinning back my bangs and wearing my covering. I'm not so sure that I can leave the Conservative Church, after all. I saw the way it hurt my parents when Matt left. And all the people I love are in that church. They are wonderful people." With that she blushed. "You know what I mean. And my conscience has been bothering me lately. I've been praying more. Seeking God, and I don't know yet what that's going to mean for me."

"I understand how you don't want to hurt your parents, but faith is a personal thing. I have to be honest; I can't picture myself attending your church. This is all very revealing. I think we are going to need another date to figure out the puzzle."

Lil stopped walking. Removed her hand from Fletch's and faced him. "I thought that was what today was all about."

"This is going to take time. I don't want to give up on us though." He pulled her close and whispered, "Do you?"

She knew that her friends wanted to meet him. If anybody could help her work through her concerns, it was Katy, Jake, and Megan. On one hand, it wasn't fair that her allies were all of the Conservative faith. But an evening with her friends might help them come to a solution. Maybe Fletch would see that living the Conservative lifestyle could be fun, too.

"Yes, but we can't skirt around the issue either. One of us might get hurt." *Probably me.*

"If you won't see me again, then that somebody is me," he insisted.

"Would you like to meet my best friends? Spend an evening playing Rook with them at the doddy house?"

"Yes," he said. "And if we don't get any time alone, we might have to go on a third date to talk about this again."

"Don't count your chickens before they are hatched," she warned, pulling away before he could kiss her. But then she let him hold her hand all the way back to the parking lot.

⎯⎯ ⌒ ⎯⎯

When Lil returned from her date, her dad met her in the kitchen. "So you are dating the vet," he said.

"I thought you knew. That you heard him ask me the other day."

"Lillian, I don't understand you. I have tried to teach you the difference between right and wrong. But you are like your mother. You have your own ideas." He pressed his lips together and stared at her.

Her heart pounded, wondering if he was going to say more about her mother. Things she wasn't ready to hear. "But I thought you liked Fletch."

"I do. That's not the point. If you insist on dating him, then at least bring him to church. Maybe then Matt will come to his senses, too."

"He might not want to come to our church."

"Be real careful, Lil. Don't be like your mother and live with regrets."

Lil was relieved he hadn't forbidden her to see Fletch again. That was something.

"You need to start making good choices. Dating a Conservative man would be a better choice. Choosing to follow the Lord."

"I understand your concern."

He narrowed his eyes and said gruffly, "I think it's time to bring your mother home. It's time that she makes her choice, too."

"What do you mean?"

"We can't make her do anything. She has to choose to live."

Lil nodded. "I'll go get her. Unless you want to?" she asked hopefully.

"It was your idea. You get her," he said. "I have enough to worry about around here."

"The hogs?"

"The Plain City Bank turned down your brother, even after I signed all the paperwork. After all these years. They said the loan was too high. But it's what we need."

"There are other banks," Lil suggested hopefully.

"You sound so much like Matt. I'm going to go read my farm magazine."

All Lil had wanted was some time to reflect on her date with Fletch. That had just been stolen from her, like everything else she wanted. But she wasn't the only one in the household who was disappointed or had problems.

She snatched up her purse and headed for the door.

Later on the drive back home, Lil's mom seemed miffed, too. As soon as she arrived at the house, she announced she was going to her room to rest. From the miracle Lil had witnessed firsthand at Michelle's earlier—the pretty rows of canned tomato sauce, the delicious aroma coming from the slow cooker, and the way she handled her granddaughters with a cheerful ease—Lil was sorely disappointed. She'd hoped that Mom would walk into her own home, see the details that had been neglected, and just carry on. She had envisioned Mom bustling about as though she'd returned from a trip and had never sunk into her earlier depression.

Instead, the moment Mom had gotten into Jezebel, she'd stiffened her shoulders. When they got home, she had started toward the house as if she was heading for her execution. Lil couldn't figure out what had caused the change between Michelle's house and the Landis farm, unless it was coming home to reality.

Surely Mom wouldn't hold a grudge against her?

When Rose had been sleeping or hiding in her room for at least two hours, Lil slipped into an apron. Swiping at the tears that welled up in her eyes, she opened the fridge door. She needed to make supper for her father, who was presently napping off his bad mood.

"What time is it? I slept like a rock."

Lil whirled around, astonished to see her mom's hair combed and her head covering on crisp and straight.

"Oh."

If Mom noticed the condition of Lil's red eyes, she didn't comment. Her gaze went to the rooster clock in the kitchen. "Six already? The clock in the bedroom said eleven. I knew that couldn't be right."

Coming to her senses, Lil said, "It must need batteries. You look rested." Afterward, she feared she'd said the wrong thing again. Usually any positive remark incited a negative response or reaction, with her mom refusing to be drawn out of her gloom.

"I am. I don't know how Michelle does it. Those little girls are so active. But why are you standing with the refrigerator door open?"

"Oh." Lil released the door with a grin. "I was figuring out what to make for supper."

Mom grabbed the refrigerator handle. "Let's take a look and see what you've got in there. I'm starved."

Stunned, Lil found it hard to step aside or move at all. She watched Mom pull out remnants of a ham, which had always been a Landis staple. "Grab that lettuce. Do we have any cheese? We'll make a chef's salad for supper."

"Okay!" Lil said, breaking free from her stupor and jumping to do whatever Mom bid.

Mom donned an apron from the yellow peg shelf, and they began chopping and dicing. She snacked on bits of ham and told a cute story about Trish and a garden frog. Then as the reminiscence ended, her gaze rose to Lil's. "I was furious at you. But you did the right thing. Taking me to Michelle's. I didn't realize how much I'd missed my grandchildren."

"Thanks, Mom. In the car I thought you were holding a grudge against me."

Mom straightened her shoulders. "I was exhausted, is all. You should know by now that Mennonites do not hold grudges."

Her transformation was surreal, and Lil could only hope it was permanent. She hadn't taken on a mother's role for such a long time, it almost seemed foreign for Lil to receive instruction and not be the one giving it.

Suddenly Rose laid down her knife, her eyes panicky. "I'm afraid, Lil. I don't want to slip back into the darkness again."

Lil slipped her arms around her mom's waist and whispered, "I won't let you."

After the embrace, Rose wiped her hands on her apron. "Well! I guess we're done here. I'll put plastic wrap over the bowl and chill it till supper."

"I think Dad fell asleep with his farm magazine, but he'll be hungry as soon as he wakes up. I've got something to show you first. Get your shoes."

Mom glanced at the bowl of freshly cut vegetables with uncertainty. "It'll just take a moment."

She shrugged and went to the mudroom's yellow rocker that she had once painted to match the shelf. Mom loved the colors of yellow and lilac. When she was finished putting on her shoes, she followed Lil outside.

Lil noticed a sad pallor fall across her mom's face when she glanced toward the barns. "This way," she said quickly.

They stepped onto the grass and went around the corner of the house. "What?" her mom squealed. She looked at Lil skeptically. "You planted tomatoes?"

"No. They're yours. They reseeded themselves."

"But they're doing well," she observed, touching the twisted vines that bent to the ground, laden with ripening tomatoes. Rose plucked one and turned it over in her hands. Suddenly she started laughing.

"What?" Lil asked.

"I'm so sick of tomatoes right now, canning all that tomato sauce at Michelle's. And yet this bush excites me."

Lil laughed, too. "Sorry about that. But I thought this would make the perfect addition to our chef's salad."

"It makes the perfect addition to my homecoming," Mom said cheerily as though she'd been gone for months. In a real way, she had.

CHAPTER 14

Fletch came out of one of the Landis barns to notice Lil standing by the back door of the farmhouse. That was odd. She usually bustled around like a hummingbird. Yet there she stood, absolutely motionless.

He watched her staring at some shrubbery, and his curiosity escalated. Then his phone jangled. He pulled it out of his jeans pocket, and it was an unidentified caller. Since he'd been getting weird calls all day, he stuck his phone back in his pocket and kept his gaze riveted on Lil. The caller could leave a message.

As he drew nearer, he called out so that he didn't startle her. "Hi, Lil."

She raised her finger to her lips, warning him to proceed quietly, and motioned him forward. More curious than ever, he quietly joined her, surprised when she gripped his hand.

"It worked," she whispered.

He didn't know what had worked, but surely his heart wasn't working given the way it was flopping insanely inside his chest. Her unexpected touch had sent his entire body reacting as if they were back at the lake, hand in hand. Following her silent gestures of instruction, he leaned forward and peered through the bushes, even more startled to see Lil's normally glum dad kissing Lil's mom. Dismayed, he jerked his gaze away. "Didn't anybody ever tell you it's not nice to spy?"

"As the youngest kid, I spied on all my siblings. Anyway, in this case, I can't help it," she whispered. "My mom is happy again. I can't see enough of that." She tugged his hand. "Come with me."

He allowed her to lead him around the opposite corner of the house, which faced the road and front porch. "I'm glad," he said, knowing his words weren't nearly strong enough to match Lil's elation. He took her free hand, drawing her close to face him. His voice low, he said, "I mean, it's a miracle, isn't it?"

"I probably shouldn't be telling you this, but I was beginning to think there was something wrong between Mom and Dad. But they seemed okay, didn't they?"

"I'm not a great one to judge relationships, but it seemed to me like they were getting along fine."

Lil didn't seem to catch his humor. "And I have you to thank. I don't think I would have had the brains or the courage to dump Mom off at Michelle's if you hadn't told me that she needed to get involved again."

"I'm happy for all of you," he said, wishing he didn't have to tell her or her dad what he'd just told Matt out in the barn. Besides that, Rose's improvement could be just the beginning of a long process of healing. "Is she still going to help out at Michelle's?"

"I'm not sure what she'll do." He felt Lil's grip tighten on his hands, as if she was experiencing a moment of panic.

"I've been praying for her. For you." He didn't add that he'd been praying about their relationship as well.

She looked up at him with misty blue eyes. "Thanks." She released one of his hands and touched his cheek. "That means a lot. I've been praying, too."

Standing so close to her, taking in her sweetness, he felt himself pulling her close. He bent his head and whispered, "It's natural. You're special to me."

Her eyes widened then filled with longing.

She melted into his embrace, and he cupped the back of her head, forgetting all about the fact that they were standing in broad daylight in the Landis front yard. He'd given her a brief kiss after their date, but this one was the most meaningful. It gave him a warm feeling, the "I've come home" feeling for which he'd always longed. Afterward, he could only marvel and wonder over its meaning. Lil was precious, and he had to treat her with care so that he didn't harm her or lose her. He couldn't bear that. "Very special," he repeated, giving her a winsome smile. Lil smiled then, and his world brightened like when the sun came out on a cloudy day. "Sunshine," he said, feeling instantly foolish.

"What?"

"You're like sunshine." Then he clamped his mouth shut before he blurted out, *I can actually feel you on my skin.* Foolish or not to admit, it was exactly how she affected him, making him all warm and tingly.

"That's the nicest thing to say." From around the back of the house, they heard a door close. Lil's gaze lowered to the ground and swept up again. "So I guess I'll see you on Saturday? To meet my friends?"

Her question momentarily caught him off guard. He was still thinking about sunshine. "I'm looking forward to it. I just need to get off work."

"Oh? Do you think that'll be a problem?"

"I'll be persuasive." At her worried expression, he added, "And persistent."

~~~

"Hello," Fletch snapped, interrupting the caller midsentence. "No, my car is not for sale. You have the wrong number." The call was one of a dozen he'd received that week asking if his car was for sale. At first he'd thought that it was merely the matter of an ad gone awry, his number getting posted by mistake. But every time someone called, they described his exact car.

Puzzling over the situation that was getting increasingly inconvenient and aggravating, he strode toward the Landis barn.

"What's that all about?" Vic asked.

Fletch explained the situation to Vic, adding, "I guess I'm just on edge. I hated to hear that there's more sick hogs."

Inside the barn, Matt led them to a batch of sick piglets and a couple of other hogs they had isolated. After a thorough examination, Vic explained, "See the sow's ears—the blue tint? I'm afraid this is the beginning of PRRS, after all. As you know, we found it in one of our most recent blood draws, too."

Just then Will entered the barn. "Saw your truck." He stopped when he saw their glum expressions. His shoulders sagged.

Vic explained, "This is nothing to be overly alarmed about. Although we've found evidence of PRRS in the last batch of blood draws and this sow has the blue ears, I think we've caught it early on. The fact that it was in the blood before we saw sick hogs means it could be a mild strain. There's over twenty strains, and some are mild and don't cause major loss. They can even help to bring immunities into the herd."

"So the other piglets were infected, after all? We need to isolate that sow?"

"No. They were all negative. Just a coincidence. But lucky for you, it brought us in to start vaccinations and be here from the start of your first real outbreak."

"Maybe not luck. Maybe God?" Fletch suggested.

Matt gave him a sadly wistful smile.

"So what now?" Will asked.

"Early weaning of pigs at fourteen days. Clean and disinfect the nursery and allow it to rest for two to three weeks. We can give antibiotics to infected hogs. We can sacrifice one to come up with a custommade vaccination, or you can use a commercial one that works for various strains."

"You know we're strapped for money," Will reminded the vet.

"I think a commercial one will work for you since it's my gut feeling that this is a milder strain.

"Back to treatment," Vic continued, "Practice a sixty-day isolation for new breeding stock. We've already done the vaccinating, but we need to keep vaccinating the weaned pigs. Those need to be tested at sixteen weeks and again at twenty-four weeks, and if they are negative, they can be entered into the herd."

Will lifted his straw hat and ran a hand through his hair. "I don't know where we're going to get the room to isolate all these hogs. We need another barn, but we just got turned down at the bank. You know that whenever we fill out paperwork, they ask about the health of the herd. And now this." He shook his head and replaced his hat.

Vic replied, "Fill out the paperwork as soon as possible. I can give you a letter that gives the small percentage of infected hogs. Really, it's a rare farm that doesn't have some infection."

"Then I guess we've been fortunate until now. We never should have let up on the vaccinations."

"We can only go forward," Fletch said. "But disappointing as this must be, remember that Vic brought up a lot of positive factors."

Fletch followed Vic to his truck.

Vic jumped in his cab and cracked his window. "Meet you back at the clinic after your next appointment."

They exchanged knowing looks, for Fletch's next appointment was the farm shelter, but Vic had been discreet not to mention it in front of Matt. "Right. I'll see you in an hour or two," Fletch replied.

Matt placed his palm on the hood of Fletch's car. "You know, this is a real nice car. You wouldn't be willing to sell it would you?" The tone of Matt's voice clicked in Fletch's mind. Of course. The practical joker had been at work. Fletch shook his head at his own thickness. "You had to have put a really cheap price on it. I must have gotten a dozen or more calls today."

Matt grinned. "I don't know what you're talking about."

Fletch reached into his car to the passenger's seat and withdrew a shopping bag. "Well, here's your payback." He thrust the bag at Matt. "You wear this, and I'll call it even."

With a surprised expression, Matt cautiously accepted the gift. He held the T-shirt up in front of him and started laughing. The T-shirt featured pictures of a wolf and three little pigs and bore the message "Big Bad Wolf."

"Never saw this one. Where'd you get it?"

"I noticed it at the feed store when I was buying my muckers. Then when you showed up every day wearing a funny shirt, I couldn't resist it the next time I had to go in there for Vic." He didn't add that it had been marked down 60 percent, which might be indicative of Matt's poor taste. Fletch patted his car, acting as if he'd known what Matt had been up to all day. "Trying to blow my house down."

Still examining the shirt, Matt admitted, "I like it. But I hope it doesn't scare the girls away."

It probably will, along with all your other T-shirts.

Fletch grew serious. "You know I've been thinking about what your dad said in there about the loan for the new barn and equipment. I remember hearing about a thing called hoop barns, tent-like structures that are cheaper than the metal barns most factory farms use. It might be a way for you to start your expansion."

"Thanks. But all I need is a good contract with an integrator company. I'm going to work on that next."

"You think? Maybe Vic had a point about getting his letter now before more of the herd is infected."

"I guess there's more than one way to go about it. But the integrator companies require the same documentation a bank does. And I want to be better prepared the next time I go face a bank officer. It's demeaning to get turned down cold."

"I'll see if I can scrounge up some information on the hoop barns. At least look at it, won't you?"

At Matt's frown, Fletch realized he'd just stepped on the other guy's testosterone. "I hope I wasn't out of line, just now." He shrugged. "It's just another angle."

Matt still frowned, and Fletch figured he'd better just shut up before he dug himself in deeper.

"You have a thing for Lil?"

The question hit him like a sledgehammer, forceful and unanticipated. Matt could be as blunt as his sister, and the disapproving tone of his voice made Fletch squirm. Had Matt seen them kissing in the front yard? "Well. . ."

Matt tossed the shirt over his shoulder and narrowed his eyes.

Fletch took off his ball cap and tapped it against his jeans. "I guess I do."

"I haven't figured out if Lil's unhappy because she doesn't want you chasing her or if it's because she thinks you're toying with her. It better not be the latter." He took the shirt down and opened it up again. "Big bad wolf, huh? I hope that's not a theme with you."

Fletch felt his face heat. If it had been, that was long before he'd met Lil. "Of course not!" But then he remembered their kisses.

Matt's expression softened a bit.

"The thing that's troubling both of us is that we go to different churches."

"Dad wasn't happy about me leaving the Conservative Church. I can't blame Lil if she wants to do the same thing, only the timing is tricky." Matt tossed his shirt over his shoulder again. "I don't like to see Lily get down in the dumps." He glanced at the house. "This family's got enough of that already. I don't want it to rub off on her."

"I'll back off if she wants me to." Fletch swallowed, wondering if he could or would really do that.

Matt nodded. "Fair enough. Thanks for the shirt." He started to walk away.

What a strange character, Fletch thought. *Most practical jokers aren't hotheads.* "So how long is the ad going to run?" Fletch called.

Matt looked back with a triumphant grin. "I have no idea what you're talking about."

Getting in his car and starting the engine, Fletch grimaced. That hadn't gone well at all. First delivering the bad news of the infected herd then getting called out for dating Lil. And now having to head over to the farm shelter.

─◌

Fletch had never felt so powerless. "I understand, Marshall, but if I do that, it could place Vic in a precarious situation, and I still have an entire term to finish with him. He can make it so that I fail the class."

"Oh I think that's an exaggeration. It's such a simple thing. More simple than the last thing I asked ya. Let me see, help me here, do ya remember the last thing I asked of ya?"

Fletch switched the phone to his other ear. "I don't believe you ever asked me to do anything," he admitted, feeling lower than a worm.

"No kidding? This is the first thing?" Marshall drawled in his southern accent. "Well that surprises me. And we've known each other for years."

Fletch squirmed like a spider under a giant thumb, pacing to the sliding glass door of his apartment. "Will I be able to see the film before it's available for public use?"

"Well sure, Fletch. We can arrange that. Your commitment and integrity is commendable. That's why I. . .well, why I like you so much."

Fletch felt his face burn with humiliation. Marshall had never manipulated him like this that he could remember. But how could he object to one request, even if it wasn't quite on the up-and-up? Buddy sidled up to him and stared out the sliding glass door. Fletch heard himself relenting, "If I can see the film and hear the narration, I guess I could raise any objections later."

"Just trust me, Fletch. I won't do anything to harm ya."

"I wouldn't want to harm Vic's practice. Actually, he warned me not to do any video taping."

"Maybe ya should be more discreet. Just so there won't be any misunderstandings."

"I suppose," Fletch whispered.

As if in tune with his master's feelings, Buddy lifted his nose and gave a mournful howl.

⁓

Exhausted from spending the day at Michelle's, Lil entered the Landis kitchen and stopped short. She didn't know if she'd ever take such a sight for granted again. Mom stood over the sink, paring potatoes. Her apron was tied in a perfect bow that rested just below her newly slim waist. Lil swallowed, hoping her mom's first day alone had gone as well as it appeared.

"I'm home."

Mom dropped her peeler and turned, wiping her hands on her apron. "You look awful."

Lil smiled, thinking how their places had taken such a reversal. "Thanks."

"Seriously, I know how exhausting it is over there."

"Yeah, and it's not going to get any easier for Michelle."

With concern, Mom asked, "What do you mean?"

Lil hung her purse on a peg and wiped her hand across her sweaty brow, knocking her covering askew. "She thinks she's pregnant."

"What!" Mom exclaimed. Then she put her hand to her mouth and started laughing.

Lil couldn't help but catch the joy in the situation, too, for they all loved babies, despite the work they created. "I know. Well, it's not for sure. She's making Tom pick up a pregnancy test at the store on his way home from work."

Mom shook her head. "Such modern conveniences. Won't be necessary. A woman knows such things. If she thinks she is, then it's probably so."

"I suppose. What can I do to help?"

"You can wash the broccoli. I'm making a broccoli salad."

Lil headed to the refrigerator to get the broccoli that her mom had brought back from Michelle's garden. "Are these from the second growth?" Lil asked, staring at the small, tender shoots.

"Yes. So tell me about Fletch."

Lil jerked her gaze up to her mom's, surprised because their date was before her mom had come home from Michelle's. That meant that her dad must have told her about it. She guessed it must not be troubling him too much if he'd discussed it with Mom. He usually tried to keep things like that from her. "You heard about our picnic?"

"So that is why the picnic basket was moved? No, I've seen how you look at each other."

Lil didn't know when her mom had seen them together, but that hardly mattered. "I really like him."

"And he goes to Matt's church?" She had learned that when Matt brought him to supper.

"Yes."

"Are you seeing him again?"

"Yes."

"I don't suppose you'll look to me for advice, the kind of mother I've been to you lately."

"That's not true, Mom. I always welcome your advice." *But I have to make up my own mind.*

Mom placed the potatoes in water and dumped the peelings into the trash. "Hand me the potato pot?"

Lil reached in the cupboard beside her for a medium-sized pot and handed it to her mom.

"All I know is I want you to be happy. But then there is also duty to consider. I only wish happiness were not so elusive."

Lil was grateful that her mom had remained philosophical, because if Mom forbid her from seeing Fletch or even cautioned her not to see him, she would have become defensive, like she had with her dad. "Thanks, Mom," she said. "But I already invited him to go with me to Katy's on Saturday night. Maybe we can talk more about it after that?"

Instead of a worried expression crossing her face, Mom's eyes brightened. Lil figured it had something to do with the promise to confide in her again.

CHAPTER 15

Fletch opened the passenger door for Lil and placed the dessert she had made in the backseat.

"You sure you don't want to take Jezebel?" she teased.

"Maybe next time. That is, as long as you don't mind riding in a car that's up for sale and could get sold right out from under our noses."

He watched his petite date slide into the seat. He walked around the front of the car and wiped his clammy hands on his jeans. In the car, he turned on the air conditioner to combat the hot, sultry evening. The soothing breeze which came from the vents played with the fringes of Lil's hair. He splayed the steering wheel and gave her a smile. The fiery highlights in her hair made it a color that needed an exotic name description other than brown, like he'd described to Marcus. It was shiny and beautiful. His heart swelled with joy to be alone with her again.

Lil smiled back at him. "So what's this about putting your car up for sale?"

"Maybe you ought to ask your brother about that."

"Okay. Which one?"

"How about Matt, the prankster?"

"Uh-oh." Her blue eyes twinkled. "He pulled that on my cousin Jake when he first bought his truck."

Fletch's mind flashed to a red Dodge he'd seen on a vacant corner he'd passed on his way to the farm shelter. Someday he would own a truck like that. First he had to get his diploma and a real job. "What kind? He still have it? 'Cause the offers are wearing me down."

"You can ask him yourself. Tonight."

"Common ground. That always helps. So, are your friends going to give me a hard time?"

Lil tilted up her cute freckled nose. "Maybe if we keep sitting here and show up late."

With a grin, Fletch put the car in gear and brought it around the circle drive. "I wouldn't want to disappoint you and get on everybody's bad side."

She smiled. "Thanks."

He nosed onto the road. "Which way?"

"Turn right. The doddy house isn't far."

"Doddy house?" He remembered she'd told him about it before, but it had only sparked his curiosity.

Over the next several miles of narrow country roads edged with deep weedy ditches, Lil told him all about the doddy house. She talked about her childhood vow and her few months living there with Katy. As she talked, he tried to imagine three Conservative Mennonite, ten-year-old girls huddled around a campfire.

When she finished, she gave him a sideways glance. "You think that's dumb?"

"Are you kidding? I think it's sweet."

He was about to add *like you,* only her arm flew out. "Turn! Turn!" she cried, pointing at the lane directly in front of them on the right.

He whipped the wheel and slammed on the brakes, veering off the drive and clipping the ditch with a bump, before they stopped.

"Sorry about that." Her Dutch was thick and apologetic. "Wasn't paying attention."

"We're okay," he said, feeling like she really must have a penchant for destroying cars.

"Just pull around back. That's it." She pointed proudly.

A small, white-sided house with a blue roof and a cute porch that ran the entire length of the front sat at the end of the lane. "Looks like a dollhouse," he commented. Then his eyes swept over the rest of the farm. It was nice. Something about the country drew him. He spotted Jake's black truck and let out a low whistle. Involuntarily, he turned off the ignition, startled to notice Lil reaching for the car door. He tore his thoughts from the truck and caught her left hand.

"Wait."

"What?"

For some reason, his dad's Pygmies came to mind, and the ceremony they performed for luck before they went hunting. He knew that being in God's plan wasn't about luck at all, and he wasn't sure why the memory had struck him, but since it had, he decided to have some fun with it.

"What?" she repeated.

He nodded toward the house. "These are your best friends, right?"

Lil nodded. "Yes, best in the world."

"Then I think this calls for a good-luck kiss."

Her eyes lit up with surprise. "I never heard of those."

"What? But it's our tradition."

Lil pointed at herself, then Fletch, then back at herself. She shook her head. "We don't have any traditions. This is only our second date."

"Exactly. But it won't be our last, so let's start the tradition."

She tapped her chin, as if trying to decide. "What will this good-luck kiss be like?"

He turned sideways in his seat, resting his left arm on the steering wheel. Considering that he'd just seen a couple of females peek out a window with a green roller shade, he figured it would be pretty chaste. "Oh they're very short. Nothing like the ones we had before." His heart tripped when she blushed. He liked how the rosy glow swallowed up her freckles. He really liked that he was the one who caused it. He stared at her mouth. "Just a mere brush of the lips." He curled his finger, inviting her closer.

Breathless, Lil unfastened her seat belt and inched closer. He leaned forward, closing the distance between them. Good for his word, only moments later, he drew back again. Even though it was a brief encounter, she looked breathless. Her freckles returned.

"Good luck, then," she said, pulling away.

But Fletch grabbed her hand. "Wait. That was for your luck."

She grinned. "And why do I need luck?"

"You need the most because they're your friends."

She laughed. "On one hand you are so right. But on the other hand, that doesn't even make sense."

Rather than argue, he brushed her lips, which stilled against his touch. Then he released her.

"See. It worked."

"How do you know?" she asked.

He beamed. "Because now I don't feel like I need any luck." It was true. A little assurance went a long way. Not that he was shy about meeting people. It was more about winning Lil over—not botching his chance with her.

He jumped out of the car, and the hot, humid air struck him like a wall. He stuck his head back inside. "Don't move." He liked that she allowed him to open the door for her. He didn't want to miss a second of their time alone or an opportunity to touch her soft little hand again.

When he opened the door, he reached for her. "Let's go, before it wears off."

She glanced at their hands. "You sure a hand squeeze couldn't have done the same thing?"

"Probably, but it wouldn't have been as much fun. Don't you think?"

She wrinkled her nose. "You're right. I haven't had that much fun since I accidently put salt on my cinnamon toast."

Sassy-soft. That's what she was. He'd never known anyone like her. She was the most intriguing little thing. But his thoughts shifted when a man about his own age opened the door. He offered Fletch a friendly smile and firm handshake.

Lil gave Jake a hug and made the introductions.

During this interval, Fletch didn't miss the look that passed between Lil and Jake. He remembered that she once referred to Jake as a friend who was as close as a brother. Oddly, it gave him a twinge of jealousy. He wondered if Jake felt it, too, or some brotherly protective emotion. Was the friendly demeanor only on the surface? She seemed to be giving Jake the eye, warning him to behave. As if Fletch needed Lil's protection. He saw the moment that Jake acquiesced.

"My wife, Katy, is in the living room, talking to Megan. Come on. They're anxious to meet you."

Lil rolled her gaze to the ceiling. "Chump and blabbermouth," she muttered.

Fletch glanced at her with amusement, pleased that she'd been talking about him to her friends. Pleased to see Lil squirm with embarrassment. Surely that was a good sign.

As soon as they entered the living room, Megan and Katy quit talking and shot to their feet. Jake's wife was beautiful with a black ponytail and exotic features. Megan was just as pretty, only she was the exact opposite with long blond hair and a sweet face. No three women could be more different in appearance, yet more striking.

As they were introduced, Katy touched his arm. Megan cupped his hand in both of hers. Their warm welcome was family-like, and he could see that their friendliness was genuine.

"While we're up, let's move to the table." Katy played the perfect newlywed hostess and led them to a country-style kitchen. He tried to imagine Lil living here with Katy, as she had related to him on their ride over. He imagined curvy little Lil in an apron, cooking up her fancy dishes in the plain but refurbished Amish kitchen. Quaint. He loved the image.

"This is new," Lil said, fingering the table's centerpiece.

Jake entered the room, carrying an extra chair, and Fletch moved some of the other chairs to the side so it would fit at the table. It didn't match the other four chairs, and he hoped that wasn't some sort of sign that he would never fit in.

"It was a wedding present," Katy said, eyeing the rose-patterned teapot sporting a blooming African violet. "From Mrs. Beverly." Her eyes softened. "It's not really my style. Too fancy and delicate. See the gold edging? Since I moved the plant here, it's thriving. It deserves to live since we dragged it all over on our honeymoon. Anyway, seeing it every day is a good reminder for me."

"Reminder?" Fletch asked, not wanting to be the mismatched chair when everyone else knew exactly what Katy meant.

"There was a time I was pretty judgmental regarding outsiders."

"Outsiders?" Lil teased.

"Well, most people," Katy corrected, touching her covering. He'd seen her do that earlier, as if it served as a security blanket. He remembered Lil telling him how Katy liked to adhere to rules. Recalled the face Lil made when talking about it. From the little he'd seen of Lil, he knew she didn't like them. She was this beautiful creature trying to break free from her chains. Sometimes it almost hurt to see her trapped at the farm. But his thoughts returned to Katy. Would she accept him? By Katy's blush, Fletch wondered if he shouldn't have pried.

Lil warned, "A year ago, you would have been discarded or at least labeled forbidden for your red shoes."

As if on cue, everyone stared at his shoes. Thankfully, he was wearing dressier ones. He shrugged, wondering if Lil even liked his shoes. She mentioned them a lot, but he wasn't sure if she liked them.

He considered Lil's dreams of a new car and a head job at a restaurant with a fancy signature dish, her complaining about being plain. He knew she didn't like the plainness associated with the Conservative Mennonites.

"So you two are pretty opposite then?" he asked.

"Wow, you know Lil pretty well," Megan said, clutching his arm. "All my life, I've been refereeing those two. They're like cats and dogs. Black and white."

"No we're not!" Katy and Lil denied in unison.

Lil wouldn't let the comment go without rectification. "When was the last time you had to do that?"

Megan tilted her face and tapped her chin. Then her eyes widened, and her hand fell away from his arm. "It's been months. Of course I was gone for a while."

"Anyway, Mrs. Beverly was Katy's employer," Lil told Fletch. "But she retired and moved to Florida, where they honeymooned."

"I misjudged her and didn't think she was a Christian, but she sent me a letter explaining things about her faith that opened my eyes. So I think you're safe to wear the red shoes around me."

He wasn't sure he'd followed the entire story, especially with so many pretty mouths sharing in the telling. "Thanks."

Lil turned back to Katy. "The plant must be hardy. Look at all those blooms."

Katy looked at her husband with admiration. "Jake has the green thumb."

Lil made a face. "You guys are too mushy. Even when you aren't being mushy, you're mushy."

"Lil!" Megan flipped her hair to the side. "Be thankful they finally get along."

Lil blushed, and Fletch wondered if she was thinking of their budding relationship and the good-luck kisses they had shared in the car. When she glanced over at him, he quirked an eyebrow, delighted to make her freckles disappear.

"Fletch, I hear you traveled a lot, growing up," Katy said.

Megan instantly came alive, peppering Fletch with questions. He was used to it. Missionary life intrigued most people. He found that his experiences usually made interesting conversation, and he was a skilled storyteller. He fed on Megan's enraptured expression and explained to her how the Bambuti Pygmies climbed more than one hundred feet to the tops of the trees to collect honey, stunning the bees with smoke from burning wood clubs.

Then she told him about her trip to Bangladesh. He could relate to her experience. With Megan it was more than fascination over an unusual topic. She had missionary-fever in her eyes. She reminded him a lot of his mom, what she must have been like in the early years of her marriage. In moments, he could tell that Megan was destined for the missionary lifestyle.

At a nudge against his arm, he remembered his date. He glanced up, surprised to see that her expression had cooled. Her face was paler, and her freckles danced boldly.

"I need your keys. I left my dessert in the car."

He feared he was responsible for the change he saw in Lil and knew that it was not a good change. "I'll go with you."

As they started to the door, Jake taunted, "Talk about mushy, Lil."

"He's just being protective," Lil snapped.

"Am I?" Fletch asked, shooting Jake a grin.

"Just give me your keys."

"Nope," he dangled them and started toward the door.

Lil faltered and he could see she was struggling with something. Finally she relented. "I suppose there could be a rabid squirrel out there."

"Or a vicious fox!" Megan teased.

"An angry deer."

"Or a bear!"

"All right!" Lil exclaimed. "Let's go."

Although there was no real reason to protect Lil in the short traipse to the car, having his date clutch his arm was a good thing. "What was that?" he whispered. "Did you hear that crackle?"

"Yeah. It's good the car is so close." She played along, but her voice had lost its zest.

At the car, he swung her around. "Hey, what's wrong?"

She shook her head too quickly. "Nothing."

"It's something."

She sighed. "I was just thinking that maybe the reason we met. . ." She paused then started again. "Was so you could meet Megan."

"What? I was just trying to be friendly in there. Because she's your friend."

"But you have the same interests. She's really into missions."

He lifted her chin until their gazes met. "But I'm not into missions at all. My folks are. Not me."

She studied him carefully. Her voice was unusually timid. "You seem alike. You're pretty. She's pretty. And if you two want to date, I'm okay with that."

"I'm pretty?" He moved on to his next objection. "How can you ditch me? That really hurts."

"Okay, I'm not exactly okay with it, but—"

"Let me explain something. I was minding my own business, going to school. I was never out there looking for girls until you captured my attention. Lily, you're every bit as beautiful as Megan. But it's more than physical attraction with me. It's everything about you. The attraction is there," he quickly added, when he saw her expression fall. "You just strike a chord with me." He pointed to his chest. "In here. Remember? You're my sunshine." He knew that their relationship would have plenty of obstacles in store, but Megan certainly wasn't one of them.

"Thanks, Fletch."

"You're not going to be one of those jealous girls, are you?"

"I hope not."

He had to smile at her honesty. "Great. Now you keep a lookout for the squirrels while I duck in and get your cake."

"And foxes. Don't forget about the foxes, and careful you don't tip it and let the icing hit the sides," she warned.

He scooped out the cake and did a fake juggle act with it.

"Why do I adore ornery guys?" she asked.

"I thought I was your only boyfriend."

"I was thinking of Jake and my brothers, silly."

When they reached the house again, he paused. "That didn't go so well first time around. I might need a little more luck."

"Forget it, buster," she said, opening the door.

Fletch hurried after her and placed the cake in the kitchen, and then they joined the others waiting at the table for them.

Before the meal, Jake prayed. Afterward, he passed the chicken dumpling casserole and said, "Katy and I have an important announcement."

Fletch watched Lil's eyes widen.

CHAPTER 16

Lil's gaze sought Katy's, wondering what Jake's announcement would be. Was he going to announce a baby was on the way? Whatever it was, Jake's expression was both joyful and proud, and Katy's was that of adoration, like usual. *Total mush,* Lil thought, glancing over at Fletch.

"We made an offer on a house."

Lil's gaze returned to Katy, allowing the information to sink in. Her stomach twisted, yet her heart rejoiced. She wanted to do the garbanzo dance. She wanted to weep. This was all part of the plan—her door to freedom, but she was unprepared to make the move. She had no job. If she missed this opportunity, the doddy house might go to someone else. Her doddy house. Dollhouse, Fletch had called it. Her dream. She took a deep breath. "When will you move?"

"A lot has to happen first, but if everything goes according to plans, we will close the end of August and this place will be yours in September."

"So soon?" Megan asked, exchanging a worried look with Lil.

Katy's expression turned puzzled. "What's wrong? I thought you were so eager to boot us out."

"It's great news," Lil said. "Tell us about your house."

471

"Jake got a contract with a local land developer, and one of the original model homes became available. They're giving it to us at a great price."

"Which development?"

"The Pines. And it's near the Columbus outer belt. I won't have to live in the middle of the city someplace," Katy explained. "It's perfect." Her expression fell. "For us. But what's wrong? Is it your mom?"

"It's just that. . ."

Across the table from her, Katy bit her lip, waiting.

Lil's mind mulled over her circumstances, and she thought out loud. "Mom *is* doing better. By September, Michelle should be back on her feet. I guess the only obstacle is I need to get a job." Her voice turned uncertain. "That shouldn't be too hard."

"I didn't get the job at Char Airlines either," Megan said, nervously twisting a shank of shiny blond hair.

"Oh no," Lil exclaimed. "You wanted it so badly."

Fletch leaned forward. "Wait! Did you say Char Airlines? I might be able to pull some strings for you there."

All eyes turned to him, expectantly. Lil studied him and then saw Megan's awestruck gaze. They were doing it again, connecting.

"What do you mean?" Lil asked. She wanted to move into the doddy house. Megan needed that job. But she didn't need Megan staring at her date that way, ready to melt into a puddle on the doddy house kitchen floor.

"My mentor, Marshall. The man who contributed to my education," he explained. "He has a connection with them, uses them."

"Really? I can't believe it. This is my dream job," Megan gushed.

"Dream job?" Jake taunted. "Since when do you have a dream job?"

Everyone except Fletch knew that Megan had always floundered when it came to jobs, and Katy and Jake had been left out of the loop altogether regarding her most recent interview.

"This one was different. It came with opportunities to travel to various mission sites. It seemed perfect."

"And it's really close to my dream job," Lil added. "I plan to apply at Volo Italiano."

Katy frowned, obviously frustrated over the turn of conversation. "We don't get together often enough anymore." She thrust out her sulky lower lip. "Why am I just hearing about these jobs?"

Ignoring Katy's remark, Lil turned to Fletch. "Do you really think your friend could get her the job?"

His coloring deepened a bit, and Lil was sorry that she had made him self-conscious around Megan. Fletch wasn't normally the blushing type. He was the resourceful type.

"He's pretty influential. It's worth a try."

Megan shot out of her seat and flew to Fletch's side, tossed her arms around him. "Thank you so much."

Lil saw his neck redden deeper. When Megan withdrew, he shrugged. "Sure. No problem." Then he grabbed Lil's hand and squeezed.

She looked into his gaze, appreciating his reassurance. She wanted to believe that their relationship was intact and moving forward. She needed to shake off her ridiculous jealousy. It was a new emotion for her. She never would have thought she was the jealous type. But if she didn't relax, she was going to ruin their date. She would drive Fletch away. Now she understood how awful Katy must have felt when Jake was dating a girl from college.

Lil squeezed his hand back and forced a smile. "Happy endings all around. Just the way we like it."

Just as Megan was the peacemaker for the three friends, Lil realized she was the tone setter. She was the lively and cheerful one, the schemer who kept things interesting and fun. Up to that moment, the tension had expanded into a giant balloon over the dinner table, but her decision to put on a cheerful front was the pin that pricked that balloon and successfully drained the tension from the room. Everyone seemed grateful.

Afterward on the ride home, Lil realized she had overreacted to the connection between Megan and Fletch. Megan had given Fletch her family's phone number, but Megan didn't have a betraying bone in her.

"It's amazing that you have a connection with Megan's dream job," she remarked.

"God's the amazing One."

She studied him thoughtfully. "Do you think He cares about our dreams?"

"I think He plants them in our souls. Possibly in our DNA, too."

Lil gave him the awestruck smile that Katy reserved for Jake. She couldn't help it. When they pulled into her drive, he turned off the ignition. "Don't want to wake up the house," he teased.

"It's kind of weird moving out, then coming home again. September won't come around fast enough for me."

"But I'll miss seeing you here. I'll miss stealing kisses behind the azalea bush."

She remembered their first kiss, when the swing broke and they fell onto the ground together. She felt her cheeks heat.

He touched her hand. "Can we go out again?"

Her dad's advice came to mind. She shrugged it off. She remembered how the first time Fletch had asked her out, she'd hoped a date might clarify her feelings for him. But it hadn't. They had only scratched the surface in getting to really know each other. Before their relationship went much further, though, they needed to discuss their beliefs and talk about church.

"I'd like that."

"It's my turn to think of something to do. Unless you have something in mind?"

She shook her head.

"I should be by this week. Maybe I'll see you. Otherwise, I'll call."

"Great!" She opened the door, jumped out, and gave him a little wave.

He lurched out of the car and called after her, "Wait! Lil?"

She blew him a kiss, almost giggling at his astonished face. He probably had more kisses in mind, but she figured it was time to play a little hard to get.

—⟳

A crowing rooster did its best to awaken the humans on the Landis farm, but it didn't irritate Lil like it did some mornings.

Wrapped in a towel, she stared at the clothing she'd tossed onto the colorful pinwheel quilt. Even the plain garb—calf-length jean skirt; faded, tiny-flowered, yellow blouse; and white tennis shoes—didn't seem so drab today because of her date with Fletch.

Correction. Two dates, and another one lined up. She yawned. A smile replaced her yawn as she donned her clothing and pinned on her head covering. Her smile remained when she hung up her towel in the little bathroom at the end of the hall, and it was still in place when she went downstairs to start breakfast.

But when she stepped into the kitchen, her smile vanished, replaced by astonishment. Syrup, butter, and steaming sausage links graced the table, and her mom was already flipping pancakes on the griddle. "Mom?"

"Hi, honey. Hope you're hungry."

Lil scratched her head. Was she still dreaming? Surely all these wonderful miracles weren't happening to her. First a Mennonite guy appeared in her life, God-planted right under her nose. And now her mom was making breakfast again? This was, indeed, a morning of hope.

If God meant to bless her now, she'd better go job hunting, too.

"Lillian!" Her mom laughed.

Coming out of her reverie, Lil stepped into the room. "Sorry, I was daydreaming."

"I saw. That young man has you befuddled."

She opened her mouth to protest, but the rebellious smile came back. She figured it was best not to deny it. "I'll set the table."

"Use the Autumn Leaf set. We're celebrating."

"Okay. What are we celebrating?"

"Life, Lil. Just life." Mom studied her, then added with a half smile, "And perhaps love?"

"I'm all for life, Mom. You don't know how happy it makes me to see you feeling good." Even with her mom in such a glorious mood, the old fear lingered that one wrong word would send her back into depression. "Let's celebrate life. But if by love you're referring to my date, then I think that's a bit premature."

"Where's the Lily I know? You've always chased after the boys."

Chased them away, Lil thought, wondering why her mom was

promoting Fletch. "Yeah, I tried to keep up with my brothers and Jake, but—"

Mom plunked the platter of steaming pancakes on the table and removed her apron. "Well that must have been good practice, because I think you've finally caught one." She winked. "Okay, I'll humor you. We'll just celebrate life."

Lil hugged her, happy to see her zest for life returning. "This is a good day." Over her mom's shoulder, her gaze went to the window, and she stepped back. "Are we early, or are the men late?"

"They're late. I hope the pancakes don't get cold."

Lil swallowed. Her mom seemed better. This might be the only time that she would be receptive to Lil's plans. "Mom, I need to tell you something. Jake and Katy found a house."

"How nice," she said with uncertainty.

Pushing aside the light tension, Lil went on. "I would like to move back in with Megan the first of September."

Mom sank into the nearest chair. "But today is the fifth of August. That's less than a month away. Anyway, how can you afford it?"

Lil pulled out the chair next to her mom. "That's plenty of time for me to find a job. In fact, I thought I'd go looking today."

Staring at the sausage, Mom shook her head. "You are forgetting that Michelle needs our help." She looked over at Lil with hurt-filled eyes. "Or was that all some farce to get me out of bed?"

"Mom! Of course not. I just figured that by the time I actually started working, you'd be able to handle chores here. That you would want to do the things you love doing. I can put in all my spare time at Michelle's. Her cast will be off by September."

"Love doing?" Mom said mockingly. She sighed. "Look. I'm trying Lil, but I'm not ready for this. It was so lonely here the last time you left."

Fear gripped Lil as she watched her mom's fragile expression flit from emotion to emotion. She remembered that day at the doddy house when Katy had suggested that Mom's depression might have something to do with an empty-nest syndrome. Panic cupped Lil's heart, and she tried to reassure Mom. "This time I'll drop in all the time, and you can come to the doddy house, too. We'll do stuff together. You can help me start an herb garden."

"You know I don't drive," Mom snapped.

Lil scratched her damp, freshly showered hair. "But one of the boys can drop you off. It's not far. It will be different this time. You'll see." *I won't be so selfish.*

Mom tipped her chin upwards. "I see you will have it no other way. I hate when you act like your father."

The hope Lil had felt when she'd caught Mom and Dad kissing dissipated. Her mom had a myriad of problems. But Lil couldn't miss the especially bitter tone she directed at Dad. Was it resentment over her lot in life? Did that come from some distant "outsider's gene" that got handed down to Lil, too?

Only moments earlier, her mom had announced they were celebrating life. Now Lil regretted bringing up the doddy house. She should have gone job hunting without mentioning it. Her mom was too delicate. A setback now would be disastrous for all of them.

She touched her mom's tensed fist. "Let's not fret about this, Mom. This morning we are celebrating life. Remember? Let's—"

Mom stood. "You celebrate life, Lil. You are young. Yes, you go and fetch your dreams." She started across the kitchen.

"Mom!" Lil called out with panic.

But her mother slumped her shoulders and left the room.

Lil followed as far as the hallway, watching her mother turn into her bedroom and slam the door. From behind, she heard her father and brothers entering the mudroom. Needing to escape, too, she ran the other direction, through the living room. She turned the deadbolt and ran outside, shutting the door behind her. Her back against the door, she looked around. She needed to escape! To get away from this madhouse before it pulled her down and sucked away her life.

Her heart beating wildly, she hurried around the side of the house, unconsciously starting toward the cottonwood at the back of the farm. But she came to a halt at the sight of the blue Ford Focus. That meant Fletch had come without Vic. With the men inside eating breakfast, Fletch would be alone in one of the barns. She glanced at the woods, then at the barns, envisioning his strong open arms.

She wanted to feel his tight embrace. To pour out what had just happened and tell him about her mom's downturn. She longed for words of affirmation, telling her it was all right to go job hunting. She needed somebody who would understand.

Lil slowed her steps as she neared the first barn. When she reached it, she tried to calm her rapid heartbeat by going through a rote routine that everybody used before they entered. She squirted disinfectant on her hands. Next, she pulled on a pair of men's muckers over her white sneakers. They were one of her brother's extras, several sizes too big, and made her walk like a duck, but she'd done this a million times, even if never in front of a boyfriend.

She shuffled past pens filled with routing, snorting hogs devouring their breakfast. She needed Fletch. He understood her like nobody else and wasn't concerned with her appearance. He'd told her that on their date.

Once she would have run to Jake. Those days were gone. She missed him. And some of that need had been transposed onto Fletch. He was more resourceful than Jake had ever been. And with Fletch, there was more. There was the physical attraction, the need and desire. She hurried deeper into the barn, her eyes gradually adjusting to the darkness.

Then she saw him. But she froze in puzzlement at his peculiar behavior.

Fletch moved slowly about the stalls, slightly crouched. He peered through a palm-sized camera aimed at the sick piglets, pushing various buttons. Next he leaned over a short wall and aimed the lens at the sow. He slowly backed away and turned.

When the camera caught Lil, he jerked it away from his face.

He stared at Lil as if she were someone horridly intrusive and shoved the video camera into his jeans pocket. The alarm on his face was all she needed to know that she'd caught him doing something wrong. Even though she didn't understand what, her heart sank.

"What are you doing?"

"I'm working," he said defensively.

"Why were you taking pictures of our hogs?"

Fletch turned more pale than when she'd first caught him. "It's not what it looks like."

She tried to think. What did it look like? What did he mean? She strode forward with growing distress, forgetting momentarily her huge waders, and stepped out of her boot. Angrily, she stopped to replace it, then marched forward. She placed her hands on her hips. "Perhaps not, but I'm waiting to hear the reason. Why are you filming our sick hogs?"

She hoped for a reasonable explanation, perhaps some protocol that Vic demanded since Fletch was a student and Vic hadn't accompanied him to the farm. But in her heart she knew that there was no reasonable explanation. Something was terribly wrong.

Fletch acted increasingly uncomfortable. Finally, he sighed and started toward her. "You've heard me talk about Marshall?"

She could tell this wasn't going anywhere pleasant. "Yes."

"He has a farm shelter."

"What's that?"

"It's a place where they take in abused farm animals."

She narrowed her eyes in confusion, feeling pangs of betrayal. "Go on."

"Vic and I volunteer there. Marshall asked me to take some videos of sick animals. That's what I was doing."

"Why?"

"The shelter is doing a documentary that they'll use for fund-raising."

"I can't believe this. You're going to put our farm on a documentary for abused animals?"

"No. The name of your farm won't be mentioned."

"Are you doing this behind Vic's back?" Lil's hands flew to her temples, holding her head, which throbbed with betrayal and disillusion.

"You don't understand. Marshall paid for my tuition. He's never asked me for any favors before this. I had no choice."

"You betrayed us, acting like you were Matt's friend, and my—" *Boyfriend?* She clenched her jaw. When she could speak, she said, "I'm getting the men." Her trust in him crumbled like chaff.

"Wait!"

She paused, turned around. "You are unbelievable! I never want to see you again!" Her eyes burning, she started to run, but her feet came out of her boots. For fear that he would catch up to her if she stopped, she left them behind. She ran through the muck, the squishy sound of her white tennies adding to her hopelessness.

She broke into the morning light and ran down the lane, scattering a group of squawking chickens. In a blind flash, she passed the clothesline, Jezebel, and the azalea bush. She hit the house screaming at the top of her lungs. "Da-a-ad!" She didn't care about tracking up her mom's house, but ran straight through the mudroom into her father's solid arms.

He towered over her, so strong and comforting in his worn overalls. "What? What's wrong?"

Two of her brothers stood behind him, their eyes wide and frightened.

Her chest heaving, she spat out, "He betrayed us!"

"Who?" Dad asked, looking fearfully over her shoulder.

"Fletch. He's filming our sick hogs."

"What?" Matt demanded, his eyes darkening in anger.

Lil wept and gasped, "He's doing a documentary on animal cruelty. He's. . . He's. . ." She couldn't finish.

Dad pulled her into his arms, but her brothers rushed past them. She heard the screen door slam. But she couldn't be consoled. She tore out of her father's arms and pushed him. "Go. See for yourself." She placed her fist to her mouth to keep her sobs at bay and ran down the hall. She hesitated outside Mom's closed bedroom door. Removing her fist from her lips, she opened it and stepped into its dark interior. Kicking off her ruined shoes, she climbed into bed with her mom and let the anguish spill.

Mom's arms clutched her, pulled her close. "What's wrong?"

Lil hiccupped, "I didn't catch one after all, Mom. Fletch is a big disappointment."

"Oh, honey."

Lil broke into inconsolable sobs.

CHAPTER 17

Fletch followed Lil out of the barn and watched her run toward the house, his own heart breaking for her. She thought he had betrayed her and her family, which was so far from the truth. At least his intentions. Part of him wanted to run after her, but he knew that given the state she was in, she wouldn't listen. Her eyes had become green frigid glaciers when she shouted that she never wanted to see him again.

He hoped he would get the chance to explain things again once she calmed down. Maybe he had done the wrong thing, but if he hadn't gotten caught, the video would have pacified Marshall without hurting anybody. Nobody would have known the hogs came from the Landis farm. He would have made sure of that.

When Fletch had asked Marshall about Char Air, the other man had used it for negotiating power. He would get Megan another interview if Fletch got him the requested footage. Fletch had wanted to refuse, but he couldn't dismiss Megan's enthusiastic face.

Fletch knew that once Lil reached the house, the Landis men would come after him. Feeling like the traitor he was, he hid the camera in his car until he could decide what to do with it. His survival instinct told him to drive away and never look back, but of course he couldn't do that. He needed to finish this. It wouldn't end at the Landis farm either. He would need to deal with Vic next. The vet would be furious if he lost the Landis account.

Fletch had only taken a few steps back toward the barn when he saw the men barreling out of the house like a herd of angry boars.

"Stop!" Hank shouted.

Fletch clenched his jaw and set his feet.

Hank screeched to a halt just a few feet from him. But Matt pushed past Hank and grabbed Fletch's arm. "Is it true? Are you filming our farm for a documentary on animal cruelty?"

Fletch jerked his arm away. "Not exactly."

Infuriated, Matt brought his arm back as if to hit him. Fletch's arm automatically went up to block the blow, but it never came. Will had caught up with his sons and snatched Matt's arm in midair.

"Don't lower yourself to his level."

Matt shook off his father's hand.

"I know you don't abuse animals," Fletch explained in his own defense.

"Of course we don't! So why are you filming our hogs?" Matt demanded.

"The man who is footing my college tuition owns a farm shelter and wanted me to film some sick animals to use in his fund-raising documentary. But it was just to stir up some sympathy. The footage would remain anonymous and not indict your name or farm in any way."

"That's pathetic," Matt sneered. "And I thought you were a friend. If you needed pictures, you should have come to us first."

Fletch said wryly, "As if anybody would let me film their sick animals." In truth, he would have asked Matt the last time they were together if Matt hadn't been in such a foul mood.

Will accused, "We are just trying to survive, yet you perch here like a vulture, waiting for us to do something wrong so you could film it? Is this the kind of stuff they teach you at your church?"

Matt cringed. "This has nothing to do with church."

"Doesn't it?" Will demanded. "Is Vic a part of this?"

"No," Fletch replied.

Will thrust a finger toward Fletch. "You tell him we want to see him. He has some explaining to do. And I want *you* to stay off our property."

"And stay away from our sister," Hank added.

"I'm going. But regarding Lil—"

Hank grabbed Fletch by the shirtfront. "You sleazeball. Don't even say her name."

"Let him go. Violence is not our way." The older man looked Fletch in the eyes. "She doesn't want you, anyway. You betrayed her."

"Stay away from Lily," Hank warned in a low, deadly voice.

Fletch's own anger flared at the way the others were attacking him and had so readily turned on him. If Hank didn't let go of his shirt soon, he was going to find himself sitting on his John Deere pockets. Just when Fletch thought he couldn't contain himself any longer, Hank released his shirt. Fletch jerked it down into place, gritting his teeth.

Glaring at the lot of them, he restrained himself. It wouldn't serve any purpose to say another word to this clan of blockheads. They were not receptive to any reasoning, especially regarding Lil. Words were finished.

Fletch turned away. Strode toward his car. Once he reached it, he started the ignition and backed down the lane, understanding why his dad had preached so many times about having to turn the other cheek—the Mennonite's practice of nonresistance. He imagined all of them had been tempted to break that stance today. Lil's brothers had wanted a piece of him as badly as he'd wanted to knock sense into them. The adrenaline continued to course through him. He didn't look back but peeled out of the lane.

⁓⌒

When he arrived at the clinic, Buddy heard Fletch's car and was at the door waiting for him. He knelt down, scratching the basset's head. "It's over. I got what I needed on film, but I lost the girl, and I detest myself." The anger was gone. He should have refused Marshall. What he'd done was unethical.

Even if Marshall had withdrawn his support, he could have applied for a college loan. It might have added an extra year to his education, but it would have been better than this mess he'd gotten himself into. He should have let Megan find her own job. Buddy licked his hand, but it did little to lessen the hard lump in the pit of Fletch's stomach.

"How's it going at the Landis farm?" Vic asked. "Any more sick hogs?"

"No, but there's a problem."

Vic turned from the notes he'd been writing, giving Fletch his full attention. "What kind of problem?"

"They caught me filming their hogs."

Vic closed his eyes and pinched the bridge of his nose. "So you did it anyway? Well congratulations. In this small town, word will get around. By this time tomorrow night, not a farmer in town will trust me with their animals."

Fletch grew even more glum.

"I don't suppose we could get somebody from the shelter to apologize?"

Fletch shook his head. "Not a chance."

"You cover here. I'm going to the Landis farm and see if I can get them to listen to reason. Maybe they'll understand Marshall's hand in this if I explain it."

"You don't have to mention your part in this," Fletch said. "I don't want to be responsible for taking your company down. Just blame it all on me."

"Yes. That was my intention."

Fletch realized that if he couldn't set foot on any of the farms, his time with Vic was finished, and just when the fall term was starting. He probably wouldn't be able to get another vet to work with. He didn't think he could muster a passing grade if Vic let him go.

"If nobody wants me on their farm, how are you going to fulfill your obligation to Marshall?" Fletch asked.

"You're going to get him off my back."

That wouldn't likely happen. "What if the farms won't let me help you?"

Vic sighed. "Let's just take this one step at a time."

Fletch nodded, but the moment the vet was out the door, he sank to his knees in prayer.

⁓

Lil clasped her teacup, glancing up at her friends. "I'm so humiliated. To think that the first guy I fell for was only using us for some farm footage."

"He seemed so down-to-earth, so honest," Katy replied.

"I thought he had a good heart, being a missionary and everything," Megan bemoaned.

"He's not a missionary!" Lil corrected, still a bit miffed that to Megan anybody associated with mission work was more than holy. "His parents are. There's a big difference. He's just a student who will do anything to get his degree."

"Well sure, I knew it was his parents, but I still thought he had a good heart."

"I'm sorry." Lil gazed out the doddy house window. When she looked back, she said, "I guess he fooled us all."

"I know how you must feel," Katy replied. "Jake betrayed my trust, too, when we were dating."

Lil pinched the bridge of her nose and tried to focus on her friend's analogy. "But he repented."

"Maybe Fletch will, too," Megan said hopefully.

"These things take time to work themselves out," Katy advised. "You might have to talk to him again before you can move on."

Lil stared at the African violet in the center of the table.

"Jake and I started reading the Bible together, and I came across a verse that I wanted to give you. I know you don't like me getting preachy, but this really is meant for your mother. It's an encouraging verse. I copied it on a recipe card for you. Would you like it?"

Lil wasn't sure why Katy was changing the subject, for she didn't feel as if she had finished ranting about Fletch. But then would she ever be? "Of course."

Katy got up and moved to a small side table in the living room. "Let me see. Here it is."

"Thanks." Lil gave it a quick glance and put it in her purse. "It has been a rough couple of months. I can use any encouragement." She blinked back her tears. "But I'm not letting you both down because of him. I have a job interview on Thursday."

"You do?" Megan's expression remained sad. "That's wonderful."

Lil touched Megan's hand because her friend didn't sound like it was wonderful to her, probably thinking of how Fletch had betrayed her hopes at Char Air. "Somehow this will still work out for us."

"We must believe," Katy added.

Megan placed a hand to her temple. "I better get out there again. If you can do it, then I can, too."

"That a girl," Lil replied.

She saw Katy glance up at the clock.

"Time for the chump to come home?"

"Yes, but you don't have to rush off. Stay for dinner."

"Thanks. Maybe another time. I'm not up to it."

Lil's despondency continued on the drive home as she rehashed their conversation. She grasped at the only thread of hope she'd received from her chat with Katy and Megan. If her interview went well on Thursday, she could land the job and go forward with her plans for the doddy house.

At home, she stepped into the mudroom and placed her purse on the shelf until she remembered Katy's verse. She pulled out the recipe card, brushed off a piece of purse lint, and read:

> *Then they cried unto the* LORD *in their trouble, and he saved them out of their distresses. He brought them out of darkness and the shadow of death, and brake their bands in sunder. Oh that men would praise the* LORD *for his goodness, and for his wonderful works to the children of men!—Psalm 107:13–15*

Usually Katy's habit of acting like Lil's personal Holy Spirit was intolerable, but this time, the words touched her soul. Lil brought the card up to her mouth to shield the sob that erupted from her throat.

These words weren't just for Mom. They were as personal as if God was speaking directly to her. Lil hurried to her room, shut the door, and fell to her knees, crying to the Lord to save her from her distress.

⁓∾

Fletch crouched in the lamb's stall and wished he could crawl under the straw and hibernate for a couple hundred years. He was alone in the world, like the lamb. No place to really call home, nobody waiting for him at his sparse apartment. Nobody to ask him how his day had gone. Now that his budding relationship with Lil had been prematurely ended, he felt bereft. Bereft and alone. He put his back to the wall and cradled the lamb.

"*I am the Lamb.*"

Fletch flinched. Where had that thought come from? His heart raced to think that the Lord was speaking to him. Comforting him. He replied, *Lord, I guess You know what will happen next, but things seem pretty bleak right now.*

He knew what he'd done was unethical, but nobody cared enough to listen to his reasons for caving to Marshall's request. He supposed that he shouldn't expect more out of Vic than his shifting of blame, because if Vic had been a strong man, he wouldn't have accepted Marshall's monetary help in the first place.

Vic had talked his way out of the trouble with Lil's family. He'd put all the blame on Fletch. He'd let on as if Fletch's actions had been a bewildering shock to him, as well. Now Fletch lived under the cloud of dread, that when he least expected it, some farmer would demand that he not be allowed to treat their animals.

If the whole thing didn't blow over quickly, his chances at starting any kind of practice or finding an internship around Columbus were doomed. And if his college instructor found out what he'd done, he might even be kicked out of the program. Why hadn't he thought of all that before he took the video?

The lamb stirred, gave a small bleat. Fletch felt a stirring in his heart. *Thank You, Lord, for reminding me that I'm never alone.*

"Isn't this a pretty picture? I saw your car," Ashley explained, for she

487

wasn't usually in the barn much.

Fletch jerked his gaze toward Ashley. "You caught me loafing, enjoying the little guy."

"Hey, you're a volunteer. You can loaf a few minutes."

"Except Vic always has work lined up for me."

"Cottonball is enjoying this as much as you. It's good for him."

"You name them?"

"Yes, but their files have case numbers, too." Fletch rose to finish his rounds, but Ashley stopped him. "I have something for you."

"Yeah?"

She handed him a yellow sticky note with a date and time written on it.

"What's this?"

"An interview for your friend."

"For Megan?" he asked, staring at the note and wondering why Marshall had set that up before Fletch had even turned in the video.

"I thought you'd be happier about it than that. What's wrong?"

He let out a sigh. "I got busted taking video at the Landis farm."

Ashley's eyes widened. "Oh no. What happened?"

Fletch briefly sketched the fateful events.

"I'm sorry it was the Landis farm."

He wondered how she knew that farm was special to him. Fingering the sticky note, he said, "Megan probably won't accept this from me now."

"Maybe she will. It might help you win your girl back."

With a start, Fletch asked, "How did you know about her?"

"I'm here twelve hours a day. I have eyes and ears." Then she blushed. "Okay, so Marcus and I are pretty close. He told me."

Fletch fought the lump that came to his throat. "Her name's Lil."

"I know."

"She hates me."

"Understandable. But that can change if she loves you."

Love? The word cut his heart like a knife, because it carried some truth. In their brief acquaintance, he had come to love many things about her. But surely it wasn't *the* love. The kind poems were written about. Was it? He blew a puff of exasperation, staring at the little sticky note. "You think?"

Ashley touched his hand. "Yes. Look if there's anything I can do to help, I'm here for you."

Marcus stepped into the barn just then and stopped short when he saw them together in the stall. Ashley jerked her hand away. "What are ya doing here?" Marcus asked in a harsh tone.

"I work here," she replied.

"You know what I mean."

"I was giving him a note from Marshall. He got busted," Ashley explained.

"Oh, man. I'm sorry. Ya still have the camera?"

Fletch had the camera. It was still on the carpet, where he'd flung it. And his heart was urging him to go to it. To delete the footage he'd taken.

CHAPTER 18

At Volo Italiano, Lil sat across the black tablecloth from Giovanni and handed the head waiter her résumé.

Her interviewer was a light-haired Italian with a thick accent that missed many of the English vowel sounds. "The school is a good one. Everything seems in order, but. . .eh. . .I will have to check with your last employer."

"Beppe didn't like me, but I can explain. First of all, he thought I was putting dings in his car. Then there was a family illness, something unexpected, and I had to help my parents. I had to switch my hours several times, and finally I had to give up my job altogether. But all that is over now. I'm able to give one hundred percent. I don't think Beppe can complain about my cooking."

"You ding cars, no?"

"No. He was a fanatic." *Well maybe just that once after I backed into Fletch's.* Lil jerked her mind from that errant path and shook her head emphatically. "No."

"And how do I know that when another family problem pops up. . .eh. . .you won't have to help out again?"

"Because I have a rent payment. And I've determined to meet my goals."

"Is it too personal to ask about these goals?"

Lil squirmed. *To get your job.* But she knew that admitting she was eventually after a head-cook position like his wouldn't help the interview. She supposed it wasn't even very Christian-like to imagine it, but it was the truth. Instead, she replied, "To pursue my cooking career. I've been miserable these past months. Cooking is what I live for. It's in the genes. I come from a line of potluck queens."

He twisted his mouth with disdain, "Eh. . .potluck?"

"It's a church thing." She saw his gaze go up to her covering and back down to her face, seeming more puzzled than ever, and she knew she was botching her interview big-time. "I'm tired of driving a clunker. I'm putting my needs first this time."

Now he tilted his head. "Above your family's, no?"

"Yes. I will be the best employee you've ever had."

He pinched his Roman nose and frowned. "You sound bitter. My experience is that bitterness spreads and infects." He shook his head. "Eh. . .I do not like to be around bitter people." Then under his breath, she thought she heard, "I have enough of that at home."

"I love my family. But my mom has been experiencing depression. She's much better, but if she slips back into it, now I know that there's nothing I can do. Believe me I tried, but I didn't think you'd be interested in personal details."

"Thank you for sharing this. . .eh. . .which gives the better insight."

"And if I sounded bitter, that was because I just broke up with my boyfriend. But I'm naturally a very upbeat person." She shrugged. "My friends say I light up a room." She couldn't believe she'd just told him such personal details and even boasted about herself. She should have waited a few days until—

He touched her arm. "I understand."

She glanced at him, and he removed his long thin fingers and folded them together, studying her with smoky eyes. Now they brooded, but she had a hunch that this man could be as explosive as Beppe and that Giovanni's eyes could storm with the best of them. Only they bore a hint of sadness and a tremendous depth as if he would be the type of man to experience everything with intensity.

He blinked, and she asked, "You do?"

"Yes, my wife has these bouts with. . .eh. . .the gloom. But hers stems from bitterness because she cannot have babies."

Lil glanced from the Saltillo tile to the live potted plants that sent trailing tendrils around their adjacent pillars. "My mom is bitter, too," Lil admitted.

"Now I see that you are the victim, like me. Maybe we can support each other in this, no?"

His last sentence drifted away, as if he was talking to himself. Feeling awkward, Lil gave a hesitant nod.

"When can you start?"

The abrupt question nearly brought tears of joy to her eyes. "How about right now?"

"Good. I like that. Let's go find a uniform. Eh. . . There's a box of tissues in the stockroom, too." He pointed at her. "But no. Not today. You start tomorrow."

In spite of her general sadness over losing Fletch, it was hard to resist the garbanzo dance. Her new boss understood her situation. She nodded. "Thank you so much. I won't disappoint you."

His brown gaze settled on her, and before he opened the door to the stockroom, he said, "Eh. . . One more thing. In your case, I believe we will give you assigned parking." He pointed, "It will be way out at the end of the parking lot. Eh. . . We will even put your name on it. Just until you have proven you do not ding the head chef's car."

"Thanks a lot," she said sarcastically, wondering if he was teasing or serious. Well she didn't intend to be late to work anymore. This was a new start.

—⌒◡

Fletch stared at the video camera in the corner of the room. It still lay on its landing spot, drawing Buddy to an occasional sniff. He slouched down in his chair. He'd acted unethically by going against client privacy. Lil never wanted to see him again. He would have to face Matt at church on Sunday. Matt might tell other people in the congregation. The Landis family might tell other farmers. Vic might tell his instructor.

Feeling trapped in a corner with no way out, he flung his red ball cap. It sailed across the room and landed near the camera.

If he deleted the film, Marshall might abandon him. He remembered the Lord's nudging back in the barn. He was not alone, he reminded himself. But his situation remained grave. The entire semester might be wasted. Fletch might have to pick himself up and find a new school. He hoped his credits would transfer, that he wouldn't be blackballed from the veterinary program. He was just a student. Weren't student's allowed to make mistakes?

He snatched up his phone and pulled up Marshall's name from his contacts. "Hi Marshall. How's it going?"

"Hi, Fletch. Actually, I'm talking from a hospital bed."

"I heard you were taking some tests." Fletch overheard bits of conversation in the background. "Marshall, you still there?"

"Can we talk later? I have to go."

"Sure. I. . .wish you the best."

"Maybe send up a prayer or two?"

"Of course I will. I'm sure you'll be fine."

Fletch dropped his phone in his lap. Was there something serious going on with Marshall? He'd never asked Fletch to pray before. The longer Fletch dwelled on the matter, the more he wondered about Marshall's faith. Growing up, he'd just assumed that Marshall was a Christian because he contributed so generously to his parents' mission work. It hit Fletch hard that maybe Marshall was trying to earn his way to heaven and had never heard about God's gift of forgiveness.

Fletch had heard fear in Marshall's voice. He racked his brain for a time when he had discussed Jesus with Marshall. Did his mentor know that Jesus had died on the cross for his sins? Had his father ever shared his faith with Marshall? Or had they all assumed?

He dipped his head and prayed for Marshall. While he was at it, he prayed for Marcus, and ended up by praying for his present situation. Time passed, and Fletch heard Buddy's whine. He looked across the room. The dog was sniffing his hat. The video camera was still there to mock him, but he no longer felt hopeless.

"Wanna go for a walk?"

Buddy jumped to his feet, and his rear parts wiggled. "Go fetch it."

The dog snapped up Fletch's hat and brought it to him. Buddy was smart. He was a good companion. Fletch's life might be a disaster, but he definitely wasn't alone.

By the time they had returned from their walk, Fletch had a new perspective on his situation. He felt that he needed to let matters with Marshall and the video rest. He was going to concentrate on mending his relationship with Lil and Matt.

———

On Sunday, Fletch held his head up as his heart and the rest of his body slunk into his usual church pew. He didn't expect Matt to sit next to him, but he was surprised to see that he chose the seat directly across the aisle. Inhaling a breath of courage, Fletch turned and gave Matt a contrite smile. He saw Matt's cheek muscle twitch, but Matt gave him a frosty glare.

Fletch would have welcomed a sermon on forgiveness or even some practical advice about frostbite, but it was the middle of summer, and the usually captivating preacher droned on and on about the Israelites' march through the wilderness. Fletch tried to listen, but the message wasn't getting through to him.

He found himself absently counting the stained-glass sections of the nearest window. He counted it from the top down and from the bottom up until he was completely satisfied it was exactly fifty-five sections. He was about to count them in individual colors, too, but the excruciating sermon came to a conclusion.

Fletch waited while Matt spoke to a pretty girl who had been sharing his pew. She was the reason they always sat on the tenth row up from the back. Matt was interested in her. Fletch felt conspicuous standing and waiting alone. It didn't help when the girl glanced over at Fletch as if they were discussing him. A chill ran up his back, but he wasn't going to turn coward. He took her glance as an invitation and crossed the aisle to face Mr. Frost.

"Hi, guys."

"Hi, Fletch." The girl squirmed and shot a quick glance at Matt.

"I gotta go." She squeezed past Fletch and whispered, "Hope you guys work out your differences."

"Thanks a lot, Stauffer, for chasing her away."

Fletch wanted to reply, *Thanks, Landis, for squealing on me.* "I came to apologize. I need to make things right with you. Can we go to lunch?"

"You pack us a picnic?" Matt asked sarcastically.

Ignoring the remark, he gave a half smile. "No, but I can afford fast food."

Matt looked at the exit and then back at Fletch. "Looking at you makes me lose my appetite, but I won't stop you from walking me to my car." With that Matt started down the nearly vacant aisle.

Fletch fell into stride, one hand slipping into his pocket and rubbing the few bills and change he'd scraped up in case Matt had taken him up on his offer. As they walked, Fletch spilled out his story, giving the bare facts, which in his own mind justified his motives though not his actions. "I thought we were friends, and that you'd help me out." He bit back his tongue from saying, *I was volunteering a lot of hours at your farm so you could afford treatment for your animals.* "I was going to talk to you about the filming the day you jumped me about Lil. I was going to ask your permission."

As they reached Matt's pickup, he replied, "You told me that day that if Lil didn't want you bothering her, you'd back off. Well she doesn't. So are you going to keep your word now?"

"I can give you my word that I'm not giving up until I win back your friendship. And your family's trust. I'm hoping that Lil will at least hear me out, too. I made a mistake. Can you forgive me? Give me another chance?"

"Look, I know it takes guts to ask that. I can forgive you. But what are you going to do about this mistake? Are you going to destroy that video? You said you wanted to make things right."

"Yes. I will. I was going to do that last week. I called Marshall to tell him, to face the music even if it meant losing my tuition and dropping out of school. But when I called, he was in the hospital. He was scared about some tests he's undergoing. He asked me to pray for him. It didn't seem the right time to approach the subject. But I'm going to tell him.

I just need time."

"I guess time will tell then. I hope it all works out for you." Matt turned and hopped up in his cab, obviously still angry even though he'd said he forgave Fletch.

Fletch stepped back and watched Matt drive away.

~☐~

Sunday afternoon, Fletch grew weary of waiting for time to tell. Since Lil wasn't answering any of his phone calls, he decided to try Ashley's advice. He pulled the yellow sticky note off the screen of his laptop and headed for the house that Lil had once pointed out as Megan's.

Walking up the steps to Megan's front porch, he patted his shirt pocket to make sure he still had his admission ticket. He rang the doorbell, hoping his plan would work. Thankfully, Megan came to the door, leaving it ajar behind her.

"Fletch?" Uncertainty clouded her face. "Hi."

"Hi, Megan. I brought you something." He pulled the yellow sticky note from his pocket and handed it to her. "It's another interview with Char Air."

"No kidding? That's wonderful. I don't know how to. . .wow." Her tone of voice descended, losing its excitement. "I don't know. This makes me feel like I'm in cahoots with the enemy."

"I hoped to talk to you about that. Lil's not taking any of my phone calls."

"I'm afraid I can't accept this." She tried to give him back the yellow note.

He quickly stuffed his hands in to his jeans pockets. "Please, keep it." Her face reddened. "I can't. Not after what you did."

"It's true I made a mistake taking that film at the Landis farm." He saw her face softening.

"It was unethical. But it was a personal request from the man who financed my schooling. He also donated lots of money to the mission field, supplied a lot of personal needs over the years for me and my parents. And it was the first thing he'd ever asked me to do for him. Just take some pictures of some sick animals."

Megan's face contorted. "Why?"

"He's starting a shelter for abused farm animals. It was for a movie they would show at fund-raisers. He promised nobody would know whose farm was filmed, that I could see the film when it was finished. Honestly, it had nothing to do with Lil. The Landis farm is the only farm where I could take the pictures, because it's the only one I go to without Vic." He toed the porch flooring with his red sneaker. "If I hadn't got caught, nobody would have gotten hurt."

Megan closed the front door behind her and turned back to him with an arched brow. "Do you read the Bible?"

"Of course."

"Does this sound familiar? 'Your deeds will be brought to light.'"

Fletch cringed under her rebuff but knew she was right. "Yes, but it was a situation where no matter what I did, somebody could get hurt. I did what I thought was best at the time."

She twisted a shank of blond hair and said sympathetically, "We all make mistakes."

"You think Lil will forgive me?"

"I doubt it."

Fletch cringed.

"She's really upset. Feels betrayed. She thinks you used her. And you were the first guy she really liked."

He dipped his head. "Her family hates me now, too." He lifted his gaze to meet Megan's again. "But I'm not giving up on her. I can't. I don't want to give up on Matt either, but he's stubborn."

"This is all very interesting Fletch, but. . ." She shook her head.

Out on the road, a car stirred up dust and a flock of blackbirds from a neighboring field. He nervously jangled the coins in his pocket. "Will you help me if I try to win her back?"

Megan sighed. "I'm not going to betray Lil. Why should we trust you?"

He didn't miss the *we*, which meant she wanted to trust him. "Because that's the only way to fix this mess. And because all I was trying to do was repay a debt."

She leaned her shoulder against a porch post, crossing her arms and studying him. "Do you have a plan?"

"My plan is to talk to Lil."

"And you want me to convince her to meet with you or pick up the phone or what?"

"You could tell her about the interview? Ask her to give me just a few minutes on the phone. Think she'd help you out?"

Megan straightened, her face paling with anger. "No! Lil doesn't need somebody who's scheming and using other people again. You're disgusting me right now, Fletch. I won't be a party to anything like this. I think Lil was right about you."

She reached out, and for an instant, Fletch thought she was going to strike him, but instead she slapped the sticky note on his chest. "I don't want your interview." She wheeled and opened the door.

"Wait! Please!"

She paused, turned, and looked at him as if he was lower than dirt.

"It was a stupid idea." He took the note off his shirt and held it out toward her. "Please keep this. No matter what. I want you to get that job."

Megan crossed her arms. "Under the circumstances, I can't go on that interview."

He licked his lips. He hadn't expected it to go this poorly. Megan was supposed to be the peacemaker. "Look, I have an idea."

She rolled her gaze toward the porch ceiling impatiently, and he knew that any second she was going to leave him standing alone on the stoop.

"Come to the farm shelter. Meet the people and see what it's all about. I need an advocate, Megan. Please?"

Her hands flew up in a gesture of refusal. "Absolutely not. If Lil finds out—"

He touched her arm, and it stilled.

"She told me how she tried to help her friend Katy. If it was you, Lil would try to help. I thought you were a peacemaker."

Gently, Megan pulled her arm away. "And that backfired on her."

His eyes pleaded. "At first. But Katy did end up with Jake."

Megan pinched her eyes closed. Her hand went to her temple. Her voice was barely audible. "I want Lil to be happy. Tell me more about your shelter."

"It's not my shelter. It's not my cause. See that's the whole point. But it's not really a bad cause either."

"Fletch." Her tone warned him she was losing patience.

"Okay. Marshall bought a farm and donated it to be used as a rescue farm. They operate on donations, volunteers, and grants. They need donations to operate. The film is to garner sympathy at fund-raisers."

"You work there?"

"Vic volunteers our veterinary services."

Again there was a moment of silence. "Okay, Fletch. I'll help you, but I'm going to be honest with Lil about everything."

"You won't regret it. I'll call you the next time I'm going over. Probably tomorrow afternoon." Fletch stuck the yellow sticky note on the nearest post and sprang off the porch, afraid if he lingered she'd change her mind. "Thanks!"

CHAPTER 19

Lil turned Jezebel into Michelle's lane and hopped out of the car while it was still sputtering.

She opened her sister's screen door and yelled, "Hello! Michelle?"

"In the kitchen. Come in."

The moment Lil stepped into the sunny room, little Tammy clamped her by the leg. Without missing a beat, Lil knelt down and scooped the girl up, cuddling her as she went. Michelle sat at a rectangular farm table, snapping green beans with her casted leg stretched out. "Next year, I had planned to do a vegetable stand. But now that, you know. . ." She glanced at Tammy, "I guess that will have to wait."

Lil heard the wistful note in her sister's voice and knew that when Michelle had the baby, she would be far too busy for a vegetable stand. "I imagine by next summer, Tate will be a good helper."

"Yes, she will. Tammy, go tell your sisters that auntie is here."

Lil let her niece down. "Are you feeling morning sickness?"

"No, I never have."

"That's good news. I have news, too. I got the job! Got the job!" Lil did a little garbanzo shoulder-shimmy dance around the table.

Laughing at her antics, Michelle reached out and snatched a handful of Lil's skirt.

Lil took Michelle's hand and slipped into the chair next to her.

Michelle squeezed her hand. "I'm so glad for you, sis. Glad everything's turning out good." Then sadness touched her eyes. "I mean with Mom and the new job."

Lil determined not to allow Fletch's betrayal to steal her joy. "Me, too. But I need to get to work here. I'll get my apron while we talk."

On the way to the pantry, she gave Tate a hug and spun her in the air until she squealed. When she set her down, Tammy jumped up and down. "I want to show you what Mommy did with her *gassed* on!"

Both girls scampered out of the room. Lil understood they were talking about Michelle's *cast.*

"Don't wake your sister," Michelle warned. "They want to show you the doll clothes I made."

With a chuckle, Lil returned to the table.

"When do you start?"

Lil began snapping beans. "Tomorrow."

"Does Mom know you had the interview?"

"Yes. At first she was angry." Lil remembered how her mom had comforted her after Fletch's betrayal. "Now I think she understands. But Dad is another story. He thinks it's foolish for me to work outside the home. He said that once the farm got on its feet again, he'd pay me to help around there, like he does the boys. And he's dead set against the doddy house and can't understand why I want to move in with Megan. Claims I should have 'that folly' out of my system. Honestly, he can be so—"

"Pigheaded," they said in unison. It was an ongoing joke Mom had started because he always had hogs on the brain and he was stubborn, too.

"He's not going to budge."

"Will you go against his wishes?"

Lil's nieces bounded into the room, holding out their dolls and new doll clothes. They wore miniature outfits that matched the girls' own look-alike Conservative-style clothing. Lil oohed and aahed, and then the youngsters skipped off to the quilt in the corner of the room, which was designated as a play area.

"So will you go against Dad's wishes?" Michelle repeated.

"Yes," Lil nodded. "I don't want it to be that way. But I don't belong on the farm. I never have. . . . I've been praying about things. I'm asking for God's help. I hope God will work things out between me and Dad. Funny, I used to think of Dad mainly as an authority figure. But lately I see him as a person." Her glimpses of his pain had changed her attitude toward him.

"That's a strange thing to say."

"The only thing is—" Lil stopped, choked up.

"What?"

"I don't want Mom and Dad to get in a fight over it. I don't think they get along that well behind closed doors. It would have been better for me if I'd never moved back home."

Michelle nodded. "This gives me a better understanding of how to pray. I'm so thankful for you. For the way you've helped Mom. For your help here. You can't imagine how hard it is for me to wear this cast."

Lil smiled. "You mean your *gassed?*"

‿͡ᴗ

Megan followed Fletch into the two-story farmhouse, pausing inside the front door. He motioned her to a side room that had been fixed into an office, where he introduced a woman named Ashley. Megan vaguely remembered his mentioning her, and she wondered how this woman played into everything.

Ashley jumped to her feet and offered Megan a handshake. In one sweep, Megan saw that Ashley was beautiful in typical outsider style, dressed in snug jeans and a bright tank top and sporting a stylish bob.

"Have a seat," Ashley offered. She flashed Fletch a dazzling, teeth-brightened smile. "Why don't you leave us alone for a few minutes?" She waved her manicured hand. "I'll bring Megan out to the barn when we're done chatting."

Fletch hesitated.

"It's okay," Megan urged, her curiosity mounting over Ashley. Once Fletch had gone, she looked at the other woman expectantly. "I don't really know what I'm doing here."

"You came because you have a kind heart. I see it in your eyes."

"That's a nice thing to say. What is your job?"

"I get donations from suppliers and companies that help us stay afloat. I guess I'm kind of a receptionist, too. There aren't that many volunteers yet, so I have to juggle quite a few jobs right now. Marcus, Marshall's son, is the person who heads everything up. Fletch comes a couple of times a week to give care to the animals. Most need veterinary care when they arrive. I can answer any questions you have about the shelter, but it's Fletch I wanted to talk to you about. You know, girl to girl."

Megan felt her face heat. "You know I'm not his girlfriend, right?"

"I know about Lil and the interview with Char Air."

Following Ashley's lead, Megan decided to be forthright and set the other woman straight. "I'm not going on that interview. But I'm willing to hear more about Fletch, for Lil's sake. Right now she despises him."

"Most of what I know comes from Marcus. We're dating." She sighed. "When we have time." She waved her hand in a feminine gesture. "Sorry. Off track. Marcus told me that Fletch got tossed around as a kid. He told me about the time that he and his dad flew to Africa to see firsthand what the Landis mission work entailed."

Megan was hooked. "Go on."

"They hired somebody in a Jeep to take them into the field, to Fletch's family. It was a shack with limited resources. Out in the boonies. But the natives would come to them from every direction and at every hour of the day. They brought all sorts of needs. Fletch's mom had medical training, and his dad was resourceful and also taught them about God."

Megan could picture it in her mind. "That's a beautiful story."

"There's more. Fletch's sister followed his mom around, but Marshall noticed that Fletch seemed rather lost. Marcus was allowed to play with him. When Marcus asked him about his friends, Fletch told Marcus the animals were his friends because they looked at him when he spoke, and they were the only ones that ever listened to him."

Megan felt a lump in her throat. "That's so sad." She remembered Fletch's pleading expression when he told her on Sunday that he needed to talk to Lil. To make her listen. "And you think that's why he went to veterinary school?"

"Marcus told me that Marshall felt sorry for Fletch. That Marshall knew Fletch's dad was a powerful man and expected his son to be the same way. But Fletch is different, real tenderhearted. Marshall saw that Frank was too hard on his son, being gentler with the daughter." Ashley leaned close as if to share a confidence. "Now from what I hear, Marshall is a bit overbearing sometimes, too. But Marcus loves him in spite of it." She relaxed again. "Anyway, Marshall loves animals, too. He's a great philanthropist, and it was only natural that he wanted to help Fletch with his career."

"I see." And Megan did. Fletch had been torn between refusing his longtime mentor or taking advantage of his new friends. She still had questions, but she wanted to save them for Fletch.

Ashley fiddled with a pencil. "Fletch is a caring person. Perhaps what we did was unethical, but it was to help his friends and a lot of abused animals. I don't know how some people can be so cruel."

Megan could see how his friends had helped him rationalize his actions. "Thank you for sharing."

"You're welcome. Now let's go to the barn. You'll fall in love with Cottonball. Everybody does."

Megan allowed Ashley to lead her toward the barn, feeling torn about Fletch. She could only imagine how he felt. She didn't know if she should drag Lil back into Fletch's world, where he was obviously still finding his way, or tell her to run as fast as she could in the other direction.

⁓

Monday night, Lil had just finished helping her mom with the supper dishes when the doorbell rang. "I'll get it." Her heart sped hopefully. She'd just been thinking that if Fletch really cared about her, he'd quit calling and present himself on her doorstep. Taking a deep breath, she opened the door.

"Megan?" With fleeting disappointment and growing concern, Lil pulled her friend inside. Untying her apron, she drew Megan to the couch. "Everything all right?"

"Kind of. We need to talk."

Megan's nervous manner worried her. Was she going to back out of the doddy house?

She knew she would have to wait to find out when Mom stepped into the room. "I thought I heard your voice."

"Hi, Mrs. Landis."

"Hi, sweetie." She touched Megan's shoulder. "Talking about the doddy house plans?"

"Sorta."

Mom confided, "I'm trying to wear Lil's dad down."

Megan looked surprised. "That's great. Thanks."

Mom sat down and made a little small talk, but apparently sensing the girls' unease, she stood again. "I need to make sure I turned off the stove."

"Okay, we'll be up in my bedroom."

Megan furrowed her brow. "What's that all about? You have to get permission all over again?"

Lil snatched Megan's hand and led her toward the stairway. "Dad's just worried about Mom. I'm moving out no matter what. Unless. . .are you here to talk about the doddy house?"

"No. It's about Fletch."

Lil almost missed her footing. She was glad that Megan was following her up the stairway so she couldn't see her shock. Had they seen each other? She didn't know what the man was capable of when it came to destroying her heart. Now that she knew Fletch was deceitful, it seemed possible that he could have been attracted to Megan all along. Why wouldn't he be? Megan was way prettier. And ever since Megan had arrived, she'd sported a guilty expression.

Lil closed her bedroom door behind them. "So don't keep me in suspense. What about him?"

Megan sat uneasily on the edge of the bed. "He came to see me."

Lil wanted to scratch the man's eyes out. Instead, she snatched up a white eyelet pillow and hugged it to herself. "Oh?"

"He tried to make me his ally."

She lowered the pillow to her lap. "What do you mean?"

"Fletch asked me to help him win you back."

Lil tossed the pillow aside. "What?" It was exactly what she'd hoped for, but it was still unbelievable. "But—"

Megan moved to the middle of the bed and crossed her legs. "Why is that such a shock? He really likes you. He always has."

Although it was a relief that Fletch hadn't asked Megan out, Lil was wary about his intentions. She propped her back against the headboard. "So he's winning you over? I have to warn you, he's persuasive. You can't be naive around him, Megan."

"There's more." Megan fleetingly touched her arm. "This is hard for me, so please, just listen while I try to explain."

Lil nodded. Even though she'd just warned Megan not to trust Fletch, her rebellious heart grasped for a ray of hope, willing Megan to say something that could mend their broken relationship. "Okay. You talk. I'll listen."

"He and Vic both volunteer at a farm shelter for abused farm animals. It's just getting started, but his mentor has other ones already operating. He's the man who helped Fletch get his education."

"Marshall. I know all about him."

Megan frowned.

Lil's hand went up to muffle her mouth. "Sorry. I'll be quiet. Go on."

"He asked me to go with him to the shelter to meet the people there."

"You didn't!"

Megan nodded. "I met a girl there named Ashley. She told me a story about Fletch. Do you want to hear it? Because it might help you understand him."

"You know you can't bait me like that. Yes, I want to hear the story she told you."

Lil listened, and the story meshed with what Fletch had already told her about himself. Megan helped her see that Fletch had been backed into a hopeless corner.

"But if he liked me, why did he take pictures at our farm? Didn't Matt's friendship account for anything?"

"Because he only has a few farms where Vic leaves him alone. He hasn't had that many opportunities. And he thought since you were his friends you'd understand."

"He should have asked for permission. Why didn't he take pictures of the animals at the shelter?"

"They don't have very many animals yet. You should ask him these questions."

"I don't know." Lil shook her head. "I'm afraid to talk to him. I like him so much, and he's so persuasive."

Megan twisted her hair. "There's more. Now keep in mind that the only reason I listened to Fletch was for your happiness. If there was a way for you two to make amends I. . ." She shrugged.

"I know how you like to see things get resolved. I understand."

"I hope so, because I never asked him to, but he set up that interview with Char Air."

Lil's mouth fell open in disbelief. He'd won over Megan by dangling her dream job. Lil fought back the tears. "He bribed you. Surely, you see that."

"I do. It was a rotten thing for him to do, and I told him so. I also told him I wouldn't go to the interview. And I won't. But he was desperate to win you back. And that's why I went to the farm."

Lil sighed. "If you get the job, would you be working with Fletch?"

"No. Of course not. Marshall uses their company. But it doesn't matter. I'm not going on the interview. This isn't about that. I just came to convince you that I wasn't trying to betray you. My intentions are pure."

"I can't believe you guys talked about me behind my back. That you went to the shelter."

"Fletch told me you'd understand because you had intervened in Katy and Jake's relationship. That's why I went. I thought it was what you would have done for me if our situations were reversed."

Lil narrowed her eyes. She wanted to object, but it was similar to the situation with Katy. She had even tricked Katy into seeing Jake. She guessed it was true that she reaped what she sowed. Now she knew how humiliating and infuriating it felt to be on the recipient's end of a matchmaking scheme. She should apologize to Katy again. Only Katy was in love, living the happily ever after. "I don't know what to say."

Megan nodded. "You have a lot to think about. I don't know if Fletch is right for you, but if you want him, the next time he calls, you should pick up the phone. Now that you've both had time to think about everything, just listen to what he has to say." Megan released her hair and gave her head a little shake so that it fell down her back again. "I need to go, but can you forgive me for interfering?"

"It hurts, but you're right. I did the same thing to Katy. And I feel bad for Fletch that nobody listens to him."

Megan moved off the bed. "Sleep on it. We'll talk tomorrow."

Lil stood. She resented her friend's interference, but Megan's intentions were too sincere to rebuke. She remembered how happy Megan had been to hear about her successful interview. She felt terribly guilty that she had landed her dream job while Megan was sacrificing hers. Whether Fletch was trustworthy or not, she couldn't stand in the way of Megan's second chance. She clutched her friend's arm. "You have to go on that interview."

Megan's eyes lit up, and Lil saw how badly she wanted the job. But her friend shook her head. "I can't. That's not why I met with Fletch. I didn't come here because of that."

"I know. But let's do it for the doddy house."

"I don't know. We better pray about it."

Shrugging, Lil replied, "Okay. But I promise I won't hold it against you. I want you to get that job." She followed Megan downstairs to the door and gave her a forgiving hug before letting her go.

When she returned to her room, Lil considered Megan's petition. If what Megan said was true, Fletch still wanted to date Lil. He wanted her to give him another chance. Like Megan suggested, she prayed, but she still didn't have an answer. Contemplatively, she stretched out on an heirloom rug and started her sit-up routine. "One. Two. Three. Four," she counted, getting warmed up.

Then her mind fell into a chant. "Five. I'll answer the phone." She sucked in her abs. "Six. I won't. Seven. He deserves a chance." She took a deep breath. "Eight. He's a deceiver. Nine. He loves me." She puffed, "Ten. He loves me not."

CHAPTER 20

Y ou have the natural instinct. . .eh. . .take this pan a moment. I'll be right back."

Volo Italiano was not a typical restaurant because Giovanni was not a typical chef. He didn't go by the books. Lil quickly discovered that her boss was temperamental and acted on his whims.

Lil stirred the sautéing ingredients and watched Giovanni push open the door to the cooler. She had flourished under a week of the chef's praise and instruction. To her utter amazement, he'd personally taken her under his wing, allowing her to do jobs that were normally reserved for the cooks with more seniority. She'd gotten to do more than polish the stainless and stir the sauce. Giovanni was a hands-on boss. He ran an orderly kitchen, and nobody complained because he was a likeable man who had earned their respect. Most likely, he'd given them all breaks at one time or another.

Volo Italiano was nothing like Riccardo's, where everybody had been on edge and out to get one another. The politics of her old workplace had not been a new experience for her because she had experienced the same type of rivalry at culinary school. She had thought it was just the way of the outsiders. But Volo Italiano had a friendly, family-like atmosphere, where everyone had welcomed her, not even questioning her about her plain clothing or head covering.

At Riccardo's, she had opted to quit wearing her head covering even before the church elders lifted the restriction. She'd never appreciated the little piece of organdy like her friend Katy, who thought it represented her faith.

With Lil, it was just a necessary contrivance, even an embarrassing one, that made her an object of curiosity to the outsiders. How she envied the Mennonite girls in progressive churches who never wore theirs, even to church.

When their congregation had taken a fresh look at the ordinance last year and then voted to change it, Lil had rejoiced that she only needed to wear it to church meetings.

She thought sadly of her dad's recent disapproval, how she'd donned it again to make life at the farm easier. She considered it a temporary nuisance. Yet she had found herself wearing it to Volo Italiano's. But she would make some changes when she moved into the doddy house. The first thing she would do was get her hair trimmed.

Giovanni returned to her side. "Now! Remove. Now!"

She jerked the pan from the gas burner and looked up in confusion, for even though she'd been daydreaming, she had been watching, and the vegetables were only half cooked.

"Most cooks leave it too long. I remove it before the celery and onions are clear. They will keep cooking after you remove them from. . ." His hands made a circular, churning gesture as if she would fill in the words for him. "Eh. . .the fire."

"Yes, sir." Another little secret to store in her mind's recipe box. She set the pan on a heat-safe surface for him to add in his tomato mixture. She felt the vibration of her cell phone in her apron pocket and turned slightly to peek at its screen. Her heart drummed beneath her white blouse and bib apron. Fletch again. She hadn't quit with ninety-nine sit-ups instead of her usual one hundred for nothing.

Turning her back to her boss, she pressed the send button and without any small talk said in a breathless voice, "I can't talk. I'm at work."

"I'll call back."

Her thumb pressed the red button, and she dropped the little heart-stopping rectangle back into her apron pocket. Her hand shaky, she moved back to the chopping board to resume the dicing she had been doing before Giovanni had taken her aside for special instruction.

"Grab some new gloves," Giovanni said, more snippy than usual as he passed behind her.

Embarrassed that he'd caught her phone conversation, she snapped off her little white gloves, tossed them in the garbage, and wriggled into a fresh set. She quickly apologized. "I'm sorry. I had to get that call."

"Your old boyfriend?"

"Yes."

"I hope that was wise, no?" Then he turned away. "Elaine, take over. . .eh. . .I have my ordering to do."

Lil felt crushed under Giovanni's sudden change of attitude. She peeled an onion and chopped and diced until her eyes watered.

⌒ᴓ

In the clinic's side yard, where Buddy often lounged and chased birds, Fletch pumped his arm in the air. Although Lil's voice had been curt, she had finally answered her phone. That was a good sign. He hoped Megan had convinced Lil to accept his apology. He watched a cone-necked collie sniff around the yard's perimeter.

Vic was treating Fletch better now, as if he wasn't that kid who had been plunked into his life just to make it miserable. And he wasn't. He wanted to take some of the strain off Vic's shoulders, if he could. He was grateful that Vic had allowed him to do the surgery on the collie. The tumor had been successfully removed. The dog moved slowly, not chasing birds like Buddy, but his teeth dazzled whiter than Buddy's. Fletch didn't like putting an animal under unnecessarily, especially his own companion, but Buddy would need his teeth cleaned one of these days.

Vic stuck his head out the door. "Got an emergency call. Take over here?"

"Sure."

The vet's head disappeared just as Fletch's phone rang. When he saw the name on the screen, his heart leaped. Stuffing one hand into his jeans pocket, he answered it with an enthusiastic, "Lil!"

"I just wanted to ask if you'd please stop calling me."

His hand flew out of his pocket, and he switched the phone to his other ear. "I don't think I can do that until I have a chance to explain some things."

"I have a new job, and I don't want to lose it."

Whatever that meant. All she needed to do was set her phone on vibrate. But she was opening the door to him, even if it was only enough to get one toe inside. He tried to remember what he'd planned on saying, only his mind froze. All he could think to say was, "I can't quit calling. I'm falling in love with you."

"What?"

Not the response he had hoped for. "Look. Can I meet you after work?"

"No. You're not listening to me. I don't want you to know where I work."

"Okay. Then let's meet someplace else. Any place. You name it. I have to see you."

"How about my living room?"

He could tell by her tone of voice it was a challenge. "I don't think your family would let me remain there long enough to properly beg your forgiveness. Matt forgave me. On Sunday."

"He told you that? Wait. It doesn't matter. You don't have to beg for my forgiveness. I forgive you, too. Just quit calling, all right?"

Fletch could tell she hadn't forgiven him at all, but her contrivance might be a small start. "I'll meet you at your swing at. . ." He didn't know what time she got off work, so he made it late. "At midnight."

There was a brief silence. "Don't bother coming," she said. "I won't be there. You're wasting your time." Then his phone went dead.

He took off his cap, slapped his knee with it, and put it back on. He didn't believe her. Lily would be there.

⌐⌐

Lil stood in front of her bedroom mirror. She ran a brush through her hair, then replaced her head covering and pinched her cheeks. *I'm falling in love with you.* It had been all she could think about. She heard the downstairs grandfather clock chime on the quarter hour. *I'm falling in love with you.* She wouldn't go until one minute after midnight. That would make her at least ten minutes late and give Fletch time to change his mind. She didn't wish to appear eager. She moved to the edge of her bed and prayed. *Lord, help me to know if I can trust him. Please reveal the truth to me. Help me let him go again, if he's not the one You've chosen.*

Grandfather Landis's clock chimed again, and she counted its bongs. One, two. . .and finally the twelfth bong. One more minute, and then she'd go. *I'm falling in love with you.* She watched the face of her cell phone with anticipation until the time finally changed. Her heart thumping louder than the clock's bongs, she crept down the stairway and made her way stealthily to the mudroom.

She opened a utility drawer and stuck her hand in, groping for a round handle. When she clutched the flashlight, she tucked it into a fold of her skirt and cast a glance over her shoulder and down the hall to her parents' bedroom. Thankfully, nobody stirred.

Lil flicked the deadbolt and slipped through the door, quietly closing it behind her. She stepped into the night. Overhead, a million crystals sparkled. All around her was the hum of nature's nighttime. The moon was full, and although she didn't need it, she turned on the flashlight, making zigzags across the tall grass so she didn't surprise any snakes or other night creatures.

I'm falling in love with you. Me, too, she breathed. Her heart drummed wildly for she felt as though she was Juliet sneaking out to meet her Romeo. She felt guilty because the family didn't like him. He was a traitor, after all. But she couldn't resist the urge to let him have his say. Even if she didn't fully trust him, it would be thrilling to hear words of love from the man who resembled the Rollo of her daydreams.

She hadn't told anybody about that because she didn't want to provoke snickers, but one morning she had awakened after a night of restless dreams, remembering that Fletch was the exact image of Rollo.

He was the boy she had always imagined in her childhood daydreams. Without the long flowing hair, of course. That coincidence, along with everything else that had culminated since she smashed into Fletch's car, made this rendezvous seem all the more fated. Traipsing through the darkness, she had the eerie sensation that Fletch was supposed to be a major part of her destiny. If only she could trust him.

A sudden hoot from an owl brought her hand over her heart. She paused, momentarily, thinking there would soon be one less mouse to keep out of the mudroom, then picked up her pace. By the time she neared the swing, the intensifying night sounds had her running.

"Over here."

Now breathless, she shined the light. She saw Fletch standing with both hands in his pockets. It tugged her heart, for she'd often seen Jake do that when he was troubled. But she tried to remain strong. "I almost didn't come. I shouldn't have. I felt sorry for you out here alone with the foxes."

He smiled. "I'm grateful you came."

She cast a backward glance. "I don't think I've ever been out here this time of night. Alone, anyways."

"You aren't alone." He stepped toward her.

One of her hands flew up to ward him off. If he touched her, she would lose all her good intentions to think rationally and block out his words: *I'm falling in love with you.* She hoped he didn't say that again. She prayed he did.

She warned, "Don't come any closer. You can talk from over there."

Fletch raised his palms in a gesture of truce and began talking as if he understood his time allotment was ticking away.

"When Marshall asked me to take pictures of sick animals for his fund-raiser film, I knew it was wrong. It made me sick to my stomach to betray a farmer's trust and right of privacy. But Marshall is special to me, my best friend ever. It was the only thing he'd ever asked from me."

"I understand that. But why our farm? Didn't we mean anything to you?" She realized one farm wasn't worse than another, but going behind a friend's back seemed worse.

"Because Vic let me come to your farm alone. It was the only place I could take the video. I was going to ask Matt's permission, but that day we got into a little spat. It was about you, and I never got the chance. If I could turn back time, believe me, I would tell Marshall no."

Lil saw the yearning in his expression. She remembered the story Megan told her about the little boy who had to talk to animals because nobody listened to him, and her heart melted.

He went on. "It's true I hid that from you, but I didn't lie about my attraction to you. That's real. You must remember that our meeting was purely accidental."

"Very funny."

He gave a dimpled, playful smile, and in Lil's opinion, an adorable and endearing shrug. Then his moonlit features grew serious. "I couldn't deny the instant attraction."

"To Jezebel, you mean?" *Don't tell me you love me. Please say it,* her conflicted heart begged.

He gave a nervous laugh.

"Attraction isn't the most important thing in a relationship," she pointed out, mimicking what he'd once told her and forcing herself to remember his shortcomings before she threw herself in his arms.

"I'm just saying I didn't go after you intentionally to use you or trick you. I wish there was a way that we could start over."

Lil's eyes brimmed with unshed tears. His explanation was reasonable. What he'd done didn't seem nearly as unforgivable as it had appeared that day in the barn when she caught him filming. "My brothers are stubborn. And now my entire family is set against you. I don't think they trust you anymore."

"I promised Matt I'd destroy the video. I want to talk to your dad and your other brothers, but Vic ordered me to stay away from the farm. I've got myself in a tight spot."

"I can see that. Matt's right. Destroying the video would be a start."

"I need to tell you what I already told Matt."

She listened to his explanation about Marshall being in the hospital. She thought he might not go through with it. The thought leaped into her mind that he might be trying to make amends only to restore his good name with the farmers and with Vic. Confused, she needed time to think and pray. She swiped her arm across her cheeks. "Thanks for the explanation. I have to go now." She turned and started toward the house. But the flashlight slipped out of her hands. She knelt, groping the ground under a patch of tall, brittle weeds.

"Ouch!" She drew back her hand, now filled with fine stickers.

"Here." Fletch moved into her vision and found the flashlight. "At least let me walk you back to the house."

She took it from him and flashed it across her pathway, walking silently.

"I don't want to make you mad, but there's something I have to tell you."

"I'm listening."

"I thought you were the sunshine in my life, but when I said that, I was thinking of the way you made me feel, all tingly. But tonight, in the moonlight. You're. . ."

She looked at his face, so serene, and felt her breath catch. When he hesitated, she pressed. "What?"

"Don't you know?"

He touched her cheek, and she gasped.

"Your light goes deeper than skin. You touch my heart."

"How can you say such things," she blurted out in a Dutchy accent. "We don't even go to the same church!" The house was looming ahead. "I have to go." She sprinted for the house, never looking back.

CHAPTER 21

On the drive home from his midnight rendezvous with Lil, Fletch's mind was determined. The very first thing he was going to do when he reached his apartment was to erase the video. Regardless of the consequences. He was going to act like a man and do the right thing. No matter how much he wanted to please Marshall or pay him back for his years of support, he had to do the right thing before God and the people in this community. Surely, Marshall would understand his decision.

He kept to the deserted country road, automatically watching for deer that might leap across the dark road, and remembered a game he used to play with his sister. It was their version of Pick Up Sticks they'd seen in the States. They would collect straight twigs, dump them in a tight pile, and take turns trying to remove one stick without moving any of the others. But sometimes the entire stack tumbled down.

Fletch knew that his next move would bring the stack down, and he would have to pick up the pieces of his life, but as much as he loved Marshall, he couldn't hurt the Landis family. He needed to make this right. He needed to erase the video he had taken even if it caused his veterinary career to come crashing down. He couldn't disappoint Lil and Matt one more day. One more hour. With his decision came relief.

He turned into a parking space, turned off the ignition, and locked the car. Walking briskly, he started toward his apartment. But a dark shadow moved on his door stoop, causing him to slow warily. The black silhouette moved. A man larger than himself blocked his door. He was sitting, hunched over, and Fletch couldn't see his face. He wondered if it was a homeless man. Unless he planned to spend the night in his car, he would have to find out. Swallowing, Fletch ventured closer. "Hello, there?"

The man looked up.

"Marcus?" Fear clutched him. "What on earth are you doing?"

"I'm sorry, man. I know it's late. I just need to talk."

Dread crept up Fletch's spine. "Let's go inside." Marcus stood and stepped aside, swiping his arm across his face. Fletch couldn't remember ever seeing his friend break down before, even as kids. He worked the key in his lock. "Come in."

Inside, they went to the small table, and Fletch moved his laptop out of the way. "Want some coffee?"

"No. You can make some for yourself."

Fletch thought better of it and took the chair across from Marcus. "Is this about your dad?" he asked.

Marcus nodded and broke down again. Fletch waited while the other man fought for control of his voice. "He's been diagnosed with lung cancer."

Fletch closed his eyes in despair. "Oh no. Are they sure? I mean. . ."

"Yeah, man. He's sure."

Fletch didn't know much about cancer, but it sounded serious.

"It's deadly. Probably those stupid cigars," Marcus bemoaned. "He always thought going to the gym would make up for it."

Fletch felt stricken. "Is he in pain?"

"He has a lot of coughing and chest pain."

"Is there a treatment?"

Marcus stared at his folded hands. "It's his call. Without chemo, the doctors claim he won't last more than four months."

The prognosis hit Fletch like a blow. "And with it?"

"Probably not any longer than five years."

"Well then he needs to do it."

"That's why I need to go home. That's why I need your help."

—◌—

It was the early hours of the morning before Lil could finally sleep. Her Romeo and Juliet rendezvous with Fletch was paramount in her waking mind. The things that man could say, calling her sunshine and moonbeam. No wait, a light that goes deeper than skin and touches his heart. She wished there were no obstacles to overcome, only blissful romance. But that wasn't the truth of the matter. Like the fictional Romeo and Juliet, they had their problems.

She'd already forgiven Fletch. She did that the night Megan told her his story. But everything was befuddled. If Lil jumped into the fray with him and all his unsolved issues, her heart might become the real victim. Yet she was drawn to him, like basil to tomato sauce. Even her job and doddy house plans were trifles compared to her feelings for him. The words he'd confessed were the feelings in her own heart. He was her sunshine. His light touched her heart. She was falling in love with him.

And so the day lagged on, tamping down longings and rehashing his explanations. It lagged through the ironing and her trip to the grocery store, and by three o'clock, she was desperate to break the cycle. "I'm off to work, Mom," she called, snatching her purse in the mudroom and heading outdoors.

In the circle lane, however, she saw Fletch's Focus parked near the barns, where he used to park when he came to care for the animals. Her heart tripped with anxiety as she hurried past Jezebel—all thoughts of work gone—moving purposefully toward the first barn. At the open door, familiar voices made her hesitate.

Lil placed her back to the barn and prepared to eavesdrop.

"I can't do this to him now. He's been diagnosed with terminal cancer."

"I'm sorry. I know what he means to you."

Lil couldn't figure out who had cancer. Marshall? Why hadn't Fletch mentioned it to her?

"Look, this is very sad news. But the video still needs to be destroyed."

"I know. I'll do whatever it takes to make things right with your family and Lil."

"Lil? You agreed to back off."

"I can't."

"It's wrong to pursue my sister when you don't even know if you have a job. You need to get things straightened out. I don't want her hurt any more than she already is."

Their voices stilled, and Lil's heart ached for Fletch. Would he do what Matt asked and pull away from her? She swallowed a thick lump in her throat.

"What about the farm? Have you isolated the hogs?"

"We started to, but we've run out of room."

"Hoop farming, Matt. It's cheaper. Maybe the Plain City Bank, the one that already knows your family, will finance a couple hoop barns."

"How do you know so much about this?"

"We studied it under our agricultural section. On the metal barns, the slatted floors are uncomfortable and dangerous for the animals. It prohibits them from following their natural instincts of rooting and nesting. The animals injure themselves on the metal stalls because when they are confined they bite the walls and attack each other. The slats allow the waste to collect. If for nothing else, your family would someday regret the slatted floor for the smell. But with hoop barns, you could isolate the animals. When you get your contract, you could expand without really changing your present methods."

"Why are you, just now, telling me all this?"

"Matt, I tried. You wouldn't listen before."

Lil's insides twisted. Poor Fletch.

"And you think those integrator companies would go for hoop farming?"

"It's cutting edge, but I think you should at least check into it. I've got to meet Vic just down the road. He's probably already there. . . ."

Not wanting to get caught at her eavesdropping, Lil took off for her car. A thunderclap sounded, and a small flock of frightened chickens ran in front of her. With a shriek, she threw up her hands. The chickens scattered, but the rooster went after her ankle. "Oh no, you don't, you irritating alarm clock." She swung her purse at him, and he flew off after his hens.

Dark clouds churned over the farm. Lil jumped into Jezebel and shimmied her door closed. If it stormed, the freeway would be congested. While she had been eavesdropping, she had lost track of time. She was going to be late to work even without a storm. As quickly as possible, she coaxed her rattletrap out of the lane and set the dust to flying.

—⋐૭

Fletch met Vic at the dairy farm, one of the vet's biggest accounts. He had accompanied him on several of the routine herd checks, and this one wasn't much different. Fletch followed Vic along the row of bovine backsides, while the herdsman walked along the cow's heads. He pointed out the ones who hadn't come into heat and needed pregnancy checks.

As they worked, Vic explained some things about udder health and how to check for food consumption, and then they switched places with the herdsman and checked eyes and ears. There wasn't an opportunity for any personal discussion until they headed back to the vehicles.

"Late night?" Vic asked.

Fletch quickly covered his yawn. "Marcus came to my apartment last night. Marshall has lung cancer."

Various emotions flitted across Vic's face before he ventured a reply. "I only met him once. He took me to dinner. Afterward he smoked a cigar in the parking lot." He sighed. "I wouldn't be a vet if I enjoyed suffering. I'm sorry."

Vic's behavior was a mystery to Fletch. At times, the vet was easily provoked to anger. Other times, he displayed compassion. Fletch was appreciative for Vic's show of sympathy. "Marcus is going home to try to convince Marshall to take chemo. Marcus asked me for a favor. But I don't want to make any more mistakes."

Vic took off his hat and swatted at flies. "What does he want?"

"He asked me to stay at the shelter while he's gone, just in case something comes up. They have a couple of volunteers there and Ashley."

"Thanks for running it by me. I don't blame you for everything that's happened, but this is a sticky situation. It reminds me of the Menno Coblentz farm. It has a shallow pond that's more of a mudhole than anything. In the heat, it lures the livestock in, and the animals get stuck, like they're in quicksand."

"Why don't they fence it off?"

"They do. That's not the point. That shelter is your quicksand."

Fletch saw truth in the statement and nodded.

"Did he say how long?"

"Three or four days."

"As far as I'm concerned, we didn't have this conversation. I'm not responsible for where you sleep nights. But if this all comes crashing down on my reputation and practice, you won't be getting a passing grade. And you won't be practicing in this county."

"I understand." Fletch grinned. "Kind of like the CIA."

Vic rolled his gaze toward the sky. "I wouldn't know about that."

"I'll be discreet as I can. And I'll try not to get my boots muddy either. Thanks."

Vic waved his hat in front of his face. "Pesky flies. Let's head back to the clinic. Then go together to the Miller farm."

Fletch started to nod, but it turned into another yawn.

CHAPTER 22

The storm had passed. Its minty-musty smell seeped through Jezebel's open window. Giovanni had reacted to Lil's lateness with silence and a steely gaze. Someone had whispered that he was having trouble at home, but Lil knew he was watching her, expecting her to fall into her old habits. It hurt that she had disappointed him. But as she started home, the landscape was peaceful and soothing to her weary soul. She breathed it in and tried to shake off her stress.

She watched her headlights illuminate the road's dotted white lines, her mind drifting until it latched on to the conversation she'd overheard in the barn. She sympathized with Fletch and wanted to fan the indomitable flame of romantic hope that should have been snuffed out long before now.

If her family accepted Fletch's apology for the filming, would they be able to accept him as a possible son-in-law? That's where Lil's mind was headed. If she dated Fletch again, it would be with permanent intentions, at least on her part.

If they married, they would have to choose a church to attend. Did she want to raise her children within the restrictions of the Conservative Mennonite Church? If she didn't, she would stir up a heap of trouble at the Landis house. Once such trouble wouldn't have bothered her. Lately she was more cautious.

Or did she want to raise her children in a progressive Mennonite church like the one that Fletch attended? Such a church would allow more freedom for their members to recognize sin by their hearts' own interpretations of the Bible. At least that's how she imagined it would be. Lil thought she could trust her own heart, but could she risk giving such freedom to her children?

If she extinguished the flame of romantic hope, she wouldn't have to make that decision now. But her life would be cold and painful. She was so tired of the pain.

Lord, she prayed, *Fletch told me my dreams come from You. I want to believe that You formed me in my mom's belly like the prophet Jeremiah wrote about in the Bible. That my personality is not a mistake. I see the fields and woods all around me, so diverse and interesting. I find it hard to believe that You would want me to walk a boring restricted path when creation beckons me to come and explore life.*

I'm not an outsider; I don't want to be one either. I agree with the beliefs that set the Mennonites apart from other denominations. I want to walk the life You created for me. Not my mom's or my dad's. Or the elders'. Just mine. Help me make the right choices. I don't want to be disrespectful and disobedient. I believe Your Spirit lives in me and is molding me to be a better person.

She turned onto a road that no longer had the hypnotic white ribbon. Lingering clouds made the night pitch-black. She blinked back tears. *Don't let me fall away from You again. Please don't lose me.*

You can see into my heart. I can't deny it to You. I want Fletch, Lord. I think he wants me, too. You put his face in my mind's eye many years ago. I called him Rollo. Fletch is part of my dream. If You love me, please help us. And, please, don't lose me.

Lil felt God's peace so strongly that she pulled over to the side of the road to bask in His presence. It was a rare moment for her. One in which she would willingly give up all her dreams, if He asked. She wasn't foolish enough to believe that she lived in this serene, almost holy place. But in this moment, her soul cried out for God's truth. She trusted the God of grace as the Father of her spirit.

She sat in the inky silence, longing for God and longing for Fletch. The desire melded together. It seemed so right. The peace and the sweet longing.

Thanks, Lord. Lil groped the black interior of her purse and pulled out her phone. It was late, but if she was right, Fletch wouldn't care.

$\sim$

"Hello," Fletch said drowsily, not having the sensibility to look at his phone before he answered. Over the years he had become used to receiving calls at odd hours because his parents often lived in different time zones and made use of phones whenever it served their purposes.

But the feminine voice that hesitantly pronounced his name wasn't his mom's. Its sweet quiver brought him wide awake.

"Lil? Is everything okay?"

"Sorry it's late. I was driving home from work. Thinking about you. Everything you said."

His heart thudded. "That's great to know."

"I overheard you talking to Matt in the barn. Thanks for doing that."

He rolled over on one elbow. "Aha. Eavesdropping again?"

"Yes. Thanks for trying to help Matt."

"He's my friend." The line grew quiet. Fletch savored the moment as if they were actually together. He drank in her presence. "It's so good to hear your voice."

"Yours, too. I'm sitting beside the road in Jezebel."

"What! Now, I'm torn. I'd like to imagine you sitting there in the moonlight. But that's dangerous, Lil. I don't like it. Why don't you go on home and call me back?"

"This from the guy who asked me to meet him in the pasture at midnight?"

"On your property, with me to protect you," he reminded.

She laughed. "Not tonight. But you can call me sometime."

"Does this mean. . .you'll see me again?"

"I suppose that depends on your persuasion and persistence."

He knew exactly where he wanted to take her. "Would a mystery date entice you?"

She sighed. "You know it would."

"Then hang up. I'll call you right back. Only, don't answer. I'll leave details that you can check when you're safe at home. I can't wait to see you again."

"Sweet dreams, Fletch."

─◦◦

"Where are you going?"

Lil halted her steps before she reached the mudroom and turned. Her mom looked pretty in her long, night-tousled hair and snug slippers with the home-sewn elastic around the heels. "Hi, Mom."

Rose padded across the kitchen's hardwood. "Off to Michelle's so early?"

The day that Lil had rushed into her mom's bedroom, bearing the fresh wound of Fletcher's deception, her mom had become her advocate. It had been the turning point where Mom regained her ability to plant her slippers in the real world again. Otherwise, Lil might have bitten her tongue instead of revealing her plans.

"Fletch invited me to meet him. He claims he's falling in love with me."

The scoop in Mom's hand trembled, scattering coffee grounds across the counter and onto the floor. Grabbing a dishrag, she asked, "When did you and Fletch start talking again?"

Lil got the broom and cleaned up the floor. "Just yesterday. It's something I need to do."

Mom poured water into the coffeemaker then turned to face Lil, taking the broom from her hand. "I understand. You're at that age where a girl has choices to make that will set her life's course. Some decisions cannot be reversed. Tread carefully, daughter."

"I am. That's why I must see him. If he's the one and I let him get away, I may regret it the rest of my life."

Mom turned thoughtful. "On the other hand, I married my true love, but even so, life is not what I imagined it would be."

"There is still time," Lil urged. "Tell me what you imagined, so that

I can help you find your dreams, too."

Laughing softly, almost bitterly, Mom shooed Lil away. "Nonsense. Dreams are for young women. Women my age are meant to get the work done." Her voice faded. "So that when I'm feeble, I will have something to show for all my years. Now go."

"Thanks, Mom."

Lil knew their mystery date location was a rural address. She was familiar with the general location but didn't know the exact property. Perhaps Fletch was going to let her go on a job with him or maybe another picnic. Fishing? The day at the park they'd watched some kids fishing and talked about doing it sometime. Lil's mind was occupied trying to outguess her persuasive and persistent suitor.

When she got close, she matched the number from her paper to a mailbox and steered Jezebel into a farm drive. Fletch's eager face popped out of a barn. He was dressed in jeans and work boots. She jiggled her car door open and jumped out, shimmying it closed again.

"Isn't this the old Stutzman place?"

"I wouldn't know about that." His eyes sparkled with enthusiasm, and his mouth tilted into a winsome smile. "But I heard you a mile away. Why don't you just marry me, and we'll haul Jezebel to the auto graveyard?"

Lil put her hands on her hips. "Is that supposed to be persuasive? Cause it sounds a lot like bribery."

"Just dreaming."

She grinned at him.

"Come and let me show you the nursery first. I can't get anything done; I just keep ending up in there. This place grows on you. The animals seem more like pets than livestock."

Of course! This was the shelter. Clasping his offered hand, she allowed him to lead her into the barn. It was nothing like their smelly hog barn. This one carried the scent of fresh straw and pungent hay.

"Over here."

The sound of their voices provoked a little bleat from behind a stall's enclosure. Fletch pulled the gate open and drew Lil inside. Still adjusting to the dark interior, she let her gaze follow the soft bleating and rustling of straw to the little fellow standing on shaky legs. Instantly, she dropped to the floor. "Oh! You're adorable."

"He's something, isn't he?"

She petted his wrinkled fleece, and he cupped his nose into her hand.

"Name's Cottonball. But there's a baby next door that still needs a name. When Ashley heard you were coming, she suggested you name the other lamb."

Lil took a sharp intake of breath. "Ashley?"

"Yes." Fletch knelt beside her. "I have some things to tell you." She listened to his explanation of all that had occurred since the last time they were together. "Since I'm staying here for a couple of days, I thought I could show you Marshall's farm, that it might help you understand some things about me."

"I'm so sorry about Marshall."

She sympathized with his grief over Marshall's cancer, understood his need to help Marcus. Regarding the video, she believed Fletch intended to eventually destroy it. But until it was done, it remained a threat to their relationship and to her family. So many things hinged on that silver hunk of technology that most people in her church didn't even know how to operate. Their innocence made them all vulnerable to situations like the one that had happened at the Landis farm. The Conservative people would not place lawsuits. Was that why Marshall had sent Fletch into their community? To take advantage of them?

Fletch interrupted her thoughts. "I sent my dad an e-mail this morning, telling him about. . .everything. About you, too. I can't contact him by phone right now, but he checks his e-mail every time he gets into Goma."

"You asked him for advice?"

"I guess."

The real-live man beside her was not an imaginary Rollo, and life was no circus. Fletch had gotten himself into a fix, and she wondered how it would all end. How it would affect her.

The lamb nudged her again. The skinny little creature melted her heart. "How can the lamb we are to name be any tinier than this sweetie?"

"Come see for yourself."

She hated to put the lamb down.

"We'll come back in a minute. I'll let you feed Cottonball his bottle."

"Really?"

The newborn was tinier, but fortunately it had a mother. "Oh my," she murmured. Fletch didn't take her inside the stall because the ewe was still recovering.

"It's a male."

"How about Flannel? And when he grows up, he can be Sir Flannel." Fletch grinned approval. "I love it."

"I just want to take you home," she purred through the slatted gate.

"I'm all yours," Fletch replied.

After Lil returned to Cottonball and gave him his bottle, Fletch finally managed to pull her away for an outside tour of the farm, explaining the renovations that had taken place and about the many donors Ashley had found for supplies. He told her about the volunteers who lived and worked at the shelter.

"Honestly, a month ago, I didn't even know there was such a place as this. I never thought there would be a need."

"Let's head for the house, and I'll introduce you to Ashley."

Lil stumbled to a halt. "Wait a minute. You're staying here with a girl?"

"She's Marcus's girlfriend. There are other volunteers here, too. Mostly guys. A couple of girls. But you're the only girl for me." He gently touched her chin, tilting her face up. "Remember? You're my sunshine."

And don't forget moonbeam. The light in your heart. Her insides went as soft and warm as marmalade pudding, and she might not have been able to resist if he'd tried to kiss her in the barnyard under the sun he raved about. Only Buddy chose that moment to come bounding across the yard. His ears nearly swept the ground, his droopy eyes fastened on Lil.

She crouched down, and he licked her face and then nuzzled into her touch. She felt Fletch's smile. The basset, the lambs, and his work all reflected his love for animals. She loved both the passion and gentleness he demonstrated.

Buddy wagged his tail, and his whole behind did a little jig.

Lil giggled. "He's doing the garbanzo dance. Only with the wrong end."

Grinning, Fletch said, "What's that?"

The basset was as soft as the lamb. How, when she lived on a farm, had she missed the wonder of the animal kingdom? She had tried to make pets of the baby pigs, but her parents had warned her away from such affection and cautioned her that hogs were dangerous animals. Eventually, she'd grown indifferent toward them and most animals. It felt amazing to feel the stirring of awareness now.

She answered his question about the garbanzo dance as they walked to the farmhouse. He stared at her as if he'd just tasted her best-ever entrée.

When they went inside, Ashley was a wonderful surprise. Lil wasn't sure what kind of woman she'd been expecting, but surely nobody as classy yet friendly as the blond woman who greeted them.

"There's a job for a cook here. Doesn't pay much, though," Ashley admitted. "Except room and board. But it's fun working here."

The offer did not appeal to Lil, except the part about being near Fletch. But she understood that was only a temporary arrangement. "Actually, I'm already set at a great restaurant."

"But as head chef?" Ashley probed.

Lil gave Fletch a hurt glance, wondering if he'd shared her personal dream with Ashley. Had he even made sport of her? He quickly threw his hands up. "I never said a word. Ashley's perceptive. That's how we manage to survive around here."

Giving a skeptical nod, Lil told Ashley, "Thanks for the offer, but like I said, I have a great job with opportunity for advancement." Not head chef, but Lil figured if she wanted to cook on a farm, she could continue to live with her parents. That wasn't her idea of a good job.

"Okay, well while you're here, how about you stuff some flyers?"

Lil laughed at the other woman's ingenuity and doggedness. "Can I see them?"

As she eyed Ashley, the blond waved at Fletch. "Scat. Go brush a horse or something."

"I get no respect around here," he joked. But it wasn't a joke to Lil because she saw the setup for what it was: a time to ask Ashley some questions about the man who claimed he was falling in love with her. Only she wasn't about to stuff any of her propaganda. She did look it over, making sure there weren't any Landis hogs inside. Thankfully, there weren't.

CHAPTER 23

Later that day, as Lil set her mom's table for lunch—her dad and brothers were all coming inside for a special treat of mush and eggs—Lil relived the thrill of being with Fletch. Their mystery date had only lasted a couple of hours because he had to go in to work, but it had been long enough to leave her with many unanswered questions.

Fletch was a lot like Jake, responding to life from the inside, rather than judging himself against what the church allowed or didn't. Even the mistakes he had made came from the loyalties he felt toward Marshall, something on the inside. Fletch was funny, gentle, and compassionate. Smart, too, and he was falling in love with her. She was his sunshine. The light in his heart. He. . .

"Here. Be careful—it's hot," her mom warned.

"Mmm. Smells good," Stephen said, washing his hands at the sink.

"You should do that in the sink outside," Mom scolded.

"Too crowded."

Lil figured the smell had lured him in. If anything, Stephen was predictable. Soon the others could be heard removing their shoes in the mudroom.

It blessed Lil to watch Mom scurry about the table, making sure there was ample tomato gravy for those who liked that better than syrup. Once the men were served, Lil and her mom sat down to join them.

About midway through the meal, Matt told his brothers, "I took a new proposal to the Plain City Bank."

"I thought you were going to try some banks in Columbus?"

"Dad and I talked about it, and we think this might work better. We need the new barn quick, to isolate the hogs. Hoop barns are cheaper, and we think the bank might go for it."

Hank's fork clinked against his plate. "Have you been talking to that Stauffer spy?"

Lil didn't even feign an appetite any longer, but folded her hands on the lap of her skirt. "He's not a spy."

Hank frowned at her. "Why have you changed your tune? Are you talking to him?"

Lil wished she'd had the discipline to remain quiet. She raised her chin. "I am a grown woman, and I will make my own decisions about who I talk to. Anyway, this isn't about me."

"You won't be dating him," her dad interjected. He placed his fist heavily on the table. "And that's final."

"I don't believe it is final," Mom disagreed.

Every gaze swiveled to fasten on her.

Stephen's face showed stark horror.

"What do you mean?" Dad asked, with a gravelly voice.

Mom's eyes glittered with anger. "I mean Lil should make up her own mind who she wants to date."

Dad stood up and slapped his napkin down on the table. "She needs to date a Conservative man!" He marched into the mudroom.

Mom's face turned beet red.

Matt told the others, "Fletch just made a mistake. He isn't a bad guy."

Hank's expression hardened. "Don't be leading our sister down the wrong path."

"What does that mean?"

"It's one thing for you to leave the church, but she is a woman.

533

Chasing after Fletch would be leaving the protection of her father and family. This is dangerous ground."

"I did not leave the church. I only moved to a different one," Matt protested.

"I will back your idea about the hoop farm, but don't get too big for your britches, little brother."

Matt pushed back his chair and stood, seething with anger.

Lil stood up, too. "Stop it. Please."

Hank turned to Lil, softening his voice but still clearly angered. "You don't know anything about making a farm prosperous. You just stick to cooking, little sister, and stay away from Stauffer, because one way or another, he's going to hurt you. That's all. It's for your own good." He seemed to have something more to say, but after a glance at their mother, he grew quiet.

Stephen wiped his mouth with his napkin, the last to stand. He asked Hank, "Think we need to pay Stauffer a visit?"

"Don't you dare," Lil objected.

"We're just worried about you, Lil."

"I know. But this time, you're all wrong."

"Thanks for the mush, Mom," Stephen said, following Hank out of the kitchen.

Matt stepped up to Lil. "You didn't make things any easier for me just now."

Her mouth flew open in disbelief. "I—"

"I like Fletch, too. But the others are probably right about you and him."

"I can't believe you're saying this. He's your friend. He's helped you, and you even told him you forgave him."

"I see you've been talking to him. Be careful. Like the others said, I don't want to cause you to stumble."

Hearing the tender catch in his throat, Lil could only nod.

"Sorry, Mom," Matt said, before he left them.

Once the men had all gone, Mom put trembling hands on her hips.

"Well that was about as bad as a fox in a henhouse," Lil observed.

"It was the roosters causing the trouble."

"I guess!" But even with her mom's attempt at humor, Lil could see that the whole incident had shaken her. "Thanks for sticking up for me."

Mom's hands slipped off her hips; her head sadly dipped. "More than one of us is being a bad example for you."

Lil wished they all didn't make such a cackle about protecting her. Couldn't they see she was a grown woman?

"I don't make it a practice of going against your dad's wishes, because I believe a woman is to be submissive to her man, but sometimes I just can't keep quiet." She grabbed Lil's sleeve. "But child, a woman must pick her battles. You do realize I'll have to apologize to him later? But maybe in the meantime, what I said will sink in a little bit."

Lil wanted to roll her gaze heavenward. What kind of twisted theology was that? She started to clear the plates, scraping the leftovers into the trash.

Mom sighed. "A shame to waste that much food. Especially when frying it takes so much time."

"I'm sorry, Mom. It was a lot of work." Reasoning with men was tricky business, especially stubborn Mennonite men. Lil had always fantasized about taking five minutes at Brother Troyer's pulpit. She would politely ask the congregation if they thought taking away worldly goods such as fashionable clothing and flashy cars really made people less prideful? It had never worked for her. And from her observations, it hadn't stifled the male egos coming and going in their household either.

⁓⤳

On Sunday Lil did not take over Brother Troyer's pulpit. The sermon was about sowing and reaping, and she wasn't about to argue with that. Afterward in the foyer and sprinkled throughout the churchyard, she was relieved to see family members mingling as if yesterday's argument had never happened. The only family member missing was Mom. She still hadn't returned to church. But Lil knew her mom was struggling with the issue.

As far as Lil knew, nobody had told her mom about the elders' recommendation. But Sunday morning was the only time she didn't get out of bed, and the guilt of it was becoming too much for Mom to bear. Each Sunday, Lil expected her mom to join them and was sorely disappointed when she didn't muster up the courage. Lil knew that her first time would be hard but that her mom had friends who would surround her with love.

Standing under the shade of a huge elm, Lil took in the clusters of dark-suited men and modestly dressed women in starched white coverings. Inside the plainness were hardworking saints and sinners of varying personalities—some gentle and some spirited. But one thing they all had in common was that they cared about each other. That's what made the thought of leaving her church family so hard for Lil. These godly people loved her in spite of herself. Maybe that assurance, that broader sense of a caring family was the reason she hadn't been afraid to push the boundaries. Even her brothers meant well.

"Lil."

Megan squeezed under the shade beside Lil and the other parishioners who sought to escape the heat. She whispered, "I got the job!"

Lil squealed and did the garbanzo shimmy.

Megan giggled. "People are staring."

"Well my heart's dancing," Lil exclaimed. "So when are we moving into the doddy house?"

Megan snapped opened her purse. "I have a calendar. Just a moment." They both peered into the small datebook. Megan's slender finger slid over the numbers. "This is the second Sunday of August. Katy and Jake are moving out the last Saturday in August. We could take our stuff over on Sunday, if you don't think that's working on Sunday. Do you?"

"I only have clothes to move so I don't have a problem with it."

"I can get my dad to take my stuff over on Saturday. My mom's donating some more furniture. I'm sure Katy won't mind."

"This is going to be the longest two weeks of my life," Lil moaned.

"I suppose learning my new job will make the time fly for me." Megan's enthusiasm over her new job was undeniable.

Smiling dreamily, Lil replied, "And I've got a date with Fletch tonight."

"Oh, Lil." Megan clasped her by both arms. "I couldn't be happier for you."

"Well at least somebody sees it my way."

"Your family doesn't?"

"Dad and my brothers are all warning me away. Dad ordered me to date a Conservative man. Stephen claims he'll pay Fletch a visit. Matt even warned me to be careful."

"Oh no."

"But things are looking up for us. They must be."

⌒☙

"You're going to love this place," Fletch said, juggling two fishing poles in one arm and carrying a small tackle box in the other. "Amos Miller owns this land."

Lil carried her grandma's hand-me-down quilt, the same one they'd taken to their picnic. "I thought his farm was just down the road."

"He told me I could come use his fishing hole any time I wanted. He even let me borrow his poles. And being the cheapskate that I am, I thought it might make a fun thing for us to do together."

"You're not a cheapskate." Lil stepped over a log that lay across the narrow footpath. "After I got my first job, I made a list in my journal of all the things I wanted to buy. Kind of selfish, wasn't it?"

"Only natural. I didn't know you kept a journal."

"A recipe journal. I'd like to publish a recipe book someday."

"So this journal's kind of a wish list?"

"Maybe it is." She glanced over at him.

"I hope you've written my name in it."

"Yes. Right under: Need a man who'll turn my world upside down."

"What a sweet thing to say."

"And that was next to: Need a man who'll misconstrue everything I say."

"The important part is that you need a man. And I'm a man."

Lil gave him a slow, intentional once-over, taking in the way he towered over her and how the river's breeze pleasantly tousled his hair. His eyes danced with mischief and charm. His shoulders were broad and his waist trim. And then there were those long slim legs and, of course, red tennis shoes. "Yes. I noticed that."

In the animal kingdom, the male species was the most striking. In humans, women were lovely. But in their case, she thought Fletch outshined her. *Even if her light did shine in his heart.* She just couldn't figure out why he was attracted to a plain Conservative girl and even more specifically to her. She hoped to find out today.

"Be careful what you say, or I might have to kiss you."

Lil made the gesture of buttoning her lips and turned her gaze back to the path.

Tucking the tackle box under his arm, he reached for her hand. "Let me help you down the embankment."

"Fletch. I think I can manage. I am a farm girl." But she found she really couldn't. The moment the boast was out of her lips, one foot slid ahead of the other. Her arms flew out awkwardly. The quilt fell to the ground. Thankfully, she caught her balance without falling and making a complete spectacle of herself.

Fletch chuckled.

She swept up the quilt, gave it a little shake, and straightened her shoulders, keeping her gaze forward and not giving him the satisfaction of a backward glance.

When she reached the bottom, she looked out over the Little Darby. Behind her, she heard him settling his tackle then felt his hands settle atop her shoulders. They slid down her arms, and he whispered in her right ear, "I noticed you, too. The day you backed into Britt's car. I thought you were the prettiest little thing I'd ever seen."

Before she could respond, he drew away. He took the quilt, making them a pallet to sit upon, and easily prepared both their poles.

"Where'd you learn to do that?" she asked.

"My dad taught me."

Lil had gleaned from their earlier conversations that he had a chip on his shoulder when it came to his dad. "That's nice."

"It was," he admitted.

They cast their lines in the water and enjoyed their natural surroundings. She noticed the way the water swirled around some rocks farther down the river, but the stream's current grew calm where they were fishing. "This is better than any place you could have taken me."

"I'm glad you like it. Glad Amos Miller called us to take care of his sick cow."

She ventured, "Yes, he's a nice man. Today in church I looked around me. The people in the congregation are like family to me. It was hard to think about leaving them."

"Do you really want me to give up my sneakers?" he teased. "Are the restrictions of your church important to you? Or can you be a Christian without them?"

"That's a good question. I've discussed these things with Matt and Jake, too. He left the church for a while. His conscience wouldn't bother him if he went to a more progressive Mennonite church, but it would Katy's, so he chose to stay Conservative. Like me, his friends were in the church. But he says that the restrictions are just there to make it easier for us not to sin. Take television, for example. I believe the television, itself, is not sinful. It's just a chunk of metal."

"Metal?" he questioned.

"Fine. I don't know what televisions are made of, but you know what I mean. It's what you choose to watch that dulls your conscience against sinful behavior. So if you don't have a television, you don't have to deal with those temptations."

"But if the church forbids the television, and you have one, then it's sinful?"

"Going against the ordinances set by the elders is an attitude of rebellion. If you are a member of the church, that kind of rebellion is sinful."

After that, they spent another hour discussing their personal beliefs. Finally Fletch asked, "Could you go to my church if you dressed the same, wore your covering, and I agreed not to bring anything into our home that you found offensive? Could you do that with a clear conscience?"

So he was thinking about marriage, too, and not just joking about it. "Yes. I think as long as my heart was at peace with God and my husband."

"Lil," he whispered, gratefully.

She raised a palm, quickly clarifying, "But I don't know if I want to leave my church. I don't believe it's the only way to heaven. But it's still hard to change."

His voice saddened. "I think I understand."

"Could you be happy to go to my church and abide by all the restrictions? Like Jake does?" she asked, hopefully.

"I've tried to imagine that. But it feels hypocritical because I don't feel the need to follow those particular rules."

"You don't even know what they all are," she argued.

"You're right."

Her shoulders sagged. "My family had a huge argument the day I met you at the shelter. It was about you."

He picked up a pebble and threw it off to his right. It thudded into a thick patch of weeds. "I'm afraid to ask about it."

"Everyone but my mom and Matt warned me away from you. Stephen even threatened to pay you a visit. Dad told me I had to date a Conservative man."

"And what did you do?"

"I told them that I would date whomever I wanted. But it hurt to see my family arguing. And they accused Matt of leading me astray."

"Away from the church?"

"Yes. So I need to think carefully about it. Leaving the Conservative Church will cause more family trouble."

"And your family has had their share of trouble. I understand that. I will just have to wait and see what you and God decide. But I have to warn you, I'm very persuasive—"

"And persistent. Which is why you just caught a fish. Fletch! Reel it in!"

CHAPTER 24

Lil carried an armload of skirts into the doddy house, passing Jake and Fletch, who were carrying a blue sofa in the other direction. Katy had insisted that the girls move in on Saturday, and they'd make it one big "moving-in/moving-out" party. If the boxes hadn't been clearly marked JAKE'S or DODDY HOUSE with large black markers, it might have been chaos. While the others moved boxes and furniture in and out, Katy furiously cleaned every vacant inch of refurbished wood flooring and the empty cabinetry.

"You're working harder than any of us," Lil fretted, placing a hand on Katy's wilted sleeve.

"I'm thinking it may never get cleaned again." Katy gave a teasing grin.

"You're probably right. But you can clean whenever you come to visit."

"Oh no. That's called abusing your friends."

"No, it isn't. You love cleaning."

Katy swiped her arm across her damp brow. "Not the cleaning part, Lil, just the results. But go"—she waved—"I'm fine here."

"Okay, then I'll invite you for supper soon."

"I'm happy that you'll have your own kitchen again. Happy for both of us."

"I know. Me, too."

Lil hung her skirts next to some clothes she had left in the closet when she moved back to the farm. It looked as though Jake had just shoved them aside. Megan would fill Katy's part of the closet.

On her way to the car for another load, she met Fletch. By the silly expression he'd sported most of the day, he was as happy as Lil about the move, especially since he'd lost his welcome at the Landis farm.

"I think your little dollhouse needs a kitten to keep you company. That is, when I'm not here."

"I don't think a barn cat would feel at home in a doddy house," she retorted.

"I think Slinky would think he was in heaven. I know I would."

Given the kitten was named, she thought it must be from the farm shelter. "He sounds sneaky."

"No, he just does this stretching thing then curls up like a slinky toy. You won't be sorry. You'll love the little guy and his antics."

Falling into her Dutchy accent, she protested, "Oh, but I won't love it, because I didn't say yes."

They had reached the car, and Fletch put his arm on the roof, blocking her from her belongings. "It's only temporary until we get married. Then I'll take over Slinky's care. I'd take him now, but he's still so tiny, and I don't trust Buddy around him."

Lil widened her eyes. "Is this your way of warning me. . . ?" She faltered. It seemed silly to keep joking about marriage when they weren't that far along in their relationship. "Warning me that you come along with a whole entourage of animals?"

"Is that so bad? You explicitly warned me that you're a farm girl. Of course that was right before you fell down the river bank like a city girl."

She tapped his chest, emphasizing each word. "I did not fall down." Her hand dropped. "Anyway, I don't really want to be a farm girl. You're not planning to live on a farm, are you?"

"Not really. But I love pets."

"Won't you be tired of taking care of them all day?"

"Do you get tired of cooking? If you do, do you quit eating?"

She frowned, unable to follow the correlation.

"What do you hate about the farm?"

Lil stared, not really seeing Ivan Miller's house but only the country road that stretched off in the distance like her thoughts. What did she hate? "I hate the rooster that wakes me up so early."

"Surely a good cook could think of a way to solve that problem."

Without the rooster, there wouldn't be any cute chicks. But she wasn't telling him that. "I hate the chores."

"Who doesn't?"

Actually, she liked her mom's cheery kitchen and the picturesque window that looked out over the farm. She thought about the past couple of months. As much as she complained to herself and others, she had enjoyed rattling her Grandma Landis's pots and pans and ironing the heirloom tablecloths. She loved rubbing her finger over the golden rim of her mom's Autumn Leaf dishes when she set the table.

"I hate the smell of hogs, but not the scent of lilacs or the grass after rain."

"You hate the hogs?"

"No." Her eyes widened in the realization that she didn't hate the farm as much as she just wanted her own place. "Fine. I don't hate the farm. But I'm ready for something different."

"Me, too."

She smiled seductively. "You have a way of twisting everything I say to suit your intentions, don't you?"

"I confess when it comes to you my brain is only wired one way."

"Mu-shy!" Jake called, shaking his head.

"Busted."

"Now if you will kindly move to the side."

"All right. You don't have to commit to Slinky just yet. I'll bring him along next time for you to meet."

"Oh no you don't. That's not fair."

"Exactly." He opened the car door and pulled out a box of cookbooks. "You don't have to commit to me yet either. But I'm hoping if Slinky and I remain on our best behavior we'll wear down your resistance." He grunted. "What do you have in here? Bricks?"

He headed back toward the house, and Lil paused to watch him. He was definitely wearing down her resistance. She wondered if her mom had ever felt that way about her dad.

Later after everyone was gone except Megan and Lil, they were in the kitchen, unpacking some dishes that Mrs. Weaver had donated.

"I don't mean to dampen your spirits, but I have to ask if your dad ever gave us his blessing," Megan said.

Lil threw a wad of crumpled newspaper into an empty box. "He told me that if Mom slipped back into depression it was all my fault. That he expected me to get this nonsense out of my head quickly and get back home where I belonged. He said I wasn't behaving like a Conservative woman with my worldly ideas of living on my own and wanting to be my own boss."

"Yikes."

Lil rested her hand on the counter. "My family's divided over Fletch, too."

"One day, you'll make the perfect couple. The best things don't always come easily."

Although they didn't talk about it after that, the next time Lil went to her sister's home to help out, Michelle had plenty to say on the matter. Her sister joked that Lil should be glad they were not Amish, because if they were, the family would have shunned her by now. Their father was angry because Lil was supposed to be under his authority until she married. Michelle had heard him call Lil a rebellious child who didn't care about her family. Michelle claimed their mom had responded to his comment by slapping the mashed potatoes on his plate and muttering something about choking. Hank and Stephen were scheming revenge on Fletch, even threatening to pay the shelter a night visit to free the animals. At that, little Flannel and Cottonball popped into Lil's mind, and she felt ill. She wondered if she should warn Fletch.

Thankfully, Michelle had ended their conversation on a positive note. Her cast had been removed, and she no longer required Lil's help. The way Michelle rushed Lil out the door, she had to wonder if she wasn't being shunned, after all.

Work was the one place that Lil forgot her family problems. Giovanni took her under his wing again. He hovered and flitted like a mama bird and left her in charge while he took a personal phone call.

When he had shouted out the order, Lil was embarrassed that he chose her over others with more seniority. That was a mere technicality. Everybody knew what to do. Giovanni wasn't an ordinary manager. His employees did not expect him to stick to procedures. Anyway, Lil didn't actually take charge of anything. If a problem cropped up that she could not handle, she would delegate it to somebody with more expertise. Nobody would criticize her.

Still, Giovanni's gesture set her deepest core into a secret garbanzo dance. For five whole minutes, she took charge of the kitchen that mean old Beppe had always envied.

In the sixth and seventh minute, her happiness fizzled. Giovanni hung up the phone with a face the color of a mozzarella cheese ball.

"Is something wrong?" she whispered.

"Eh, it is my wife." He gripped the countertop then looked up at her with wide eyes. "She's pregnant."

The kitchen became as quiet as if Giovanni was taking a bite from a new recipe. Lil sensed his fear, knew his emotions were at war with the news he had just received. On one hand, he was happy for his wife's joy, and for his own. He loved children. That was evident when he made napkin airplanes for the little ones as he mingled with customers. But on the other hand, he had taken this path before. It had led to disappointment over his wife's miscarriages and her ensuing bouts of depression.

"I will pray," Lil replied. "God is able."

"Is He?" Giovanni asked.

Lil flinched. But Giovanni whispered, "I am the reason this restaurant has been successful, no?"

"Of course you are," she replied, wondering why he was going down that track.

He whispered, "I see myself in you."

Lil nodded with confusion. "Thank you."

545

CHAPTER 25

The following Saturday, Lil stirred pasta sauce, shaking some basil into her palm and brushing it off into the contents of a cast-iron pot. "I hate using dried herbs. I want to start an herb garden in the windowsill." She stared dreamily out the window, "And a bird feeder would be nice, too."

"Those are great ideas." Megan pushed aside the study material for a children's Sunday school class she taught. "I don't know if I can stand the aroma if this simmers all afternoon. I'm going to get fat living with you. How do you keep such a tiny waist?"

Lil stared at her naive friend. She'd always been envious of Megan's thin figure and beauty. "You do realize I skipped dinner last night and did one hundred sit-ups before bed?"

Megan rose and stretched. "Yes, but I've always told you that you shouldn't skip meals like that."

"It doesn't hurt to skip meals as long as you eat healthy."

"Maybe you're right. We sent food boxes to Mexico last week. I'm sure the recipients of those boxes didn't stand around having this discussion. We are so fortunate."

Lil bit back a smile. Living with Megan was almost like living with

Katy. Only the sermons Megan gave took a different spin. While Katy hoped to narrow Lil's perspective, Megan tried to widen her worldview. Megan was all about saving the world.

But her friends' personalities differed so that Lil needed to take care that she didn't prick Megan's tender heart. Katy made a competent sparring partner with her black smoldering eyes and sulky lips, but Megan delighted in dismantling arguments. So Lil didn't dispute with Megan if she could avoid it. Instead, she used her mom's trick of changing the topic. "Your job is perfect for you. Have you met any cute guys?"

"Actually, my boss is probably the handsomest man I've ever met." Megan clamped her hand across her mouth, and her blue eyes widened in horror. "I can't believe I just said that."

Lil slapped her wooden spoon on the counter, forgetting all about her sauce. "What? Why haven't I heard about him before?"

Megan's eyes grew softly regretful. "Because. I think he's divorced. You know that makes him off limits." Her gaze fell to the braided oval rug Lil's grandma had made. She shrugged her shoulders. "I don't even know why I mentioned him."

"Oh no." Lil knew that if Megan made that comment about her boss, she had already fallen for him. The elders in the church would never honor a second marriage.

Megan glanced up again and tried to explain, "When I started working there, he was wearing a wedding ring. Now he isn't. He hasn't told me what happened, but I've heard rumors that his wife left him."

Lil's hands went to her apron's waistband. "So he's not pursuing you?"

"No! Of course not!"

"But you're attracted?"

Megan shook her head. "No."

"But you said. . ."

"Okay, I noticed him. He's a nice man. I feel sorry for him."

Lil's hands left her hips and rose to the air making a helpless gesture. "His wife must have had a reason for leaving him."

"It might not be his fault," Megan defended. Then she said, "If

I'm attracted, I'll get over it. I have to. I don't want to leave Char Air because of some silly crush. How childish would that be? I love this job. I'm really careful around him so that he doesn't see my admiration."

This news unsettled Lil. Megan, the butterfly, had never lit—romantically speaking. She'd never fallen in love. Why did this have to happen just when Megan had found her niche? Why couldn't she have fallen for some clean-cut Rosedale College student? "Be careful, green bean. Love is a sneaky thing."

Megan slowly nodded, then ran long fingers through her fine hair, pushing it behind her shoulder. "You're talking about Fletch?"

"Yes. Yesterday I stopped in to see my mom, and Matt pulled me in the barn to lecture me about causing problems between Mom and Dad." She placed a lid on the slightly simmering pot and stepped away. "He said I was going to ruin the family. Naturally, we ended up in a disagreement about Fletch." Turning her back to Megan, she went to the big, farm-style sink to scrub some utensils. Blinking, she whispered, "I hate what's become of our family. Matt and I used to be close."

"I'm sorry. Here, let me do that." Megan nudged Lil aside just as she was squeezing liquid detergent, and a billow of tiny bubbles rose above them.

"Oops." Megan waved her hand through the airborne bubbles and stared aghast into the bubbly sink. "That's wasting resources."

"It's just one squirt of detergent."

"Lil," Megan said with a soft but reprimanding tone. "My mom says that if everyone wasted a squirt, it would soon become an ocean."

⁓

Fletch watched Vic's scalpel move with expertise as he performed a necropsy. Animal autopsies were invaluable to Fletch's hands-on education, and he found the internal workings of the horse fascinating. But when his phone rang, the caller's identity was equally amazing.

"Vic, can I take this call? It's from my dad in Africa."

"Sure. Go on."

Fletch snapped his phone open and stuck it in the crook of his neck so he could wash his hands in the clinic basin. "Dad. It's good to hear your voice."

"Yours, too. It's been a long time."

"How's Mom?"

"She's great. She's out purchasing some medical supplies. I got your e-mail. I was sorry to hear about Marshall. He's been a friend to us over the years. A generous man."

"Yes." Fletch moved out of doors. "The news is hard."

"I know. So is your predicament. Do you want to talk about it?"

Fletch sat on the ground, and Buddy rubbed against his hand. He touched the dog absentmindedly, telling his dad about Marshall's request and how it had affected the Landis family and his position as Vic's assistant. "So the camera is untouched, but I have to do something."

"Yes, you do. If we aren't moving forward, we are losing ground."

His dad always peppered his conversation with frustrating maxims. Fletch pressed, "What would you do?"

"Without hindsight, I probably would be standing in your shoes about now. Tell me who deserves your loyalty."

"I knew Marshall first."

"If he's the one you serve, you shouldn't be feeling regret."

Fletch caught his dad's meaning. "You know I serve the Lord first."

"Exactly."

"So you're not going to tell me what to do?"

"You prayed about it?"

Fletch yanked a clump of grass from the lawn, and Buddy moved away. "Of course."

"Then trust God and follow your heart. The circumstance won't heal itself or go away on its own."

He let the grass filter through his fingers. "And you won't be upset if Marshall withdraws his support from your ministry, too?"

"I appreciate all Marshall's done for us, but the Lord is our provider. Anyway, we might not be needing his support. I was calling to tell you that we decided it's time to come home."

With surprise, Fletch sputtered, "You mean. . .the States? A furlough?"

"We think it will be for good this time."

Fletch felt his adrenaline spike from the shocking news. He worked to keep his voice calm. "Well, Ohio is a nice place." He couldn't imagine having Dad back in his life—didn't need more disappointments along that line.

"Your mother and I were hoping for an invitation. You'll be there another year or so, right?"

"As far as I know, but once I destroy that video, anything could happen."

"That's what makes life such an adventure!" Even though his dad's voice came from across a continent and an entire ocean, it contained the power that swallowed lesser men. If he had not lost his fervor, Fletch wondered what was motivating Dad to leave the mission field. "We're looking forward to seeing you. Maybe we can get your sister to come to Ohio for a visit, too."

"I haven't seen her since she got married." The line got quiet. "When will you come?"

"Nothing's definite yet. I'll e-mail you when we know more."

Aha. There was the catch. As usual, Fletch didn't have to wait long for Dad to dash his hopes. As far as he knew, the move to Ohio was all bluster. He took off his cap, ruffled his hair. "Sure. That will be fine. Thanks for the advice."

Dad chuckled. "You already knew what to do."

Fletch felt resentful that Dad found the situation amusing.

"Give Mom my love."

The call was bittersweet, but it helped Fletch move ahead and delete the footage. That night as he pushed levers on the small video camera, he explained to Buddy, "A touch of the button and it's gone. But the consequences, not so easily."

Buddy raised his flabby jowls and howled.

"Well let's hope it's not that bad." Fletch placed the camera on top of the refrigerator, where it would remain until he returned it to Marcus. His friend had returned to Plain City, but Fletch hadn't gotten a chance to ask about his trip yet, and now more than ever dreaded their next encounter.

CHAPTER 26

Fletch drove around a curve just before the farm shelter came into sight and noticed one of the shelter's horses trotting down the center of the road. *What on earth?* He pulled the car over onto the embankment and hopped out. He tried to get the horse to come to him, but it was jittery. Without a halter, it was useless. Fletch hopped back in his car and swept his phone from his pocket. "Marcus! Come quick! One of your horses is out."

Fletch pulled into the farm and met Marcus, and they both ran for the barn. But ten yards from the door, they halted. The door wasn't left open like Fletch expected. It was demolished. Shredded and mutilated.

"Vandals!" Marcus cried bitterly.

Fletch ran into the vacated barn and located the halter and lead and jumped back in his car while Marcus stayed behind to round up the other straying animals.

It was hours before they had all the livestock located and secured again. The horse, Taffy, had reinjured his bad leg, and Fletch couldn't be sure if the recovery would be as swift or as complete as it might have been before the incident.

Weary and dejected, Fletch joined Marcus and Ashley in the office.

"Do you think the vandals will be back?" she asked.

"It depends if they have an issue with the shelter or if it was just a random kid's prank," Marcus replied with a grim countenance.

"What if they harm the animals the next time?"

"They injured Taffy. With the sprain the horse already had, frightening him added to the damage. I administered a cold press. Now he needs total rest. I'll make sure Vic stops in to take a look at him."

Marcus nodded. "I don't suppose the police will do much. This is a tight-knit community. They'll be backing the farmers, some of whom consider us the enemy." He placed his head in his hands and muttered, "With all that's going on with Dad, I almost wish we hadn't started the shelter."

"You must not say that." Ashley rushed over and placed a hand on his taut shoulder. "We're helping a lot of animals. You're just overwhelmed right now."

Fletch wondered if something worse was troubling his friend. "Did Marshall agree to take chemo?"

"He's leaning that way."

"Thank goodness." Fletch was relieved about Marshall but didn't have the heart to hand over the empty video camera now. Not when Marcus seemed so despondent.

—◌—

Later that night on the way home from the shelter, Fletch swung by the doddy house in hopes of catching Lil at home. She was at the kitchen table with her recipe journal and a scattering of recipe cards. Megan lounged on the nearby couch with her pretty nose in a book.

Fletch picked up one of the recipe cards. "Gnocchi?"

Lil snapped it out of his hand. "This is top-secret stuff."

He grinned, harboring his own secrets of the heart variation.

The doddy house was quiet without the hum of television or computer, reminding him how different Lil's life was from his own. His apartment, though sparsely furnished, had both technologies.

"You guys always this quiet?"

"You caught her in a rare moment," Megan called from the adjoining living room.

Lil shrugged. "You look tired."

"A little discouraged."

Lil swept her recipe cards aside and aligned them into a neat stack. "Sit here?"

He pulled out a chair and joined her. "My dad called."

"That's good, right?"

"I guess. He might be quitting his missionary work. Might be moving here."

"Really? It would probably be good for you to spend some time together."

"Maybe. I'm not getting my hopes up."

She nodded, her gaze filling with concern.

"He didn't seem troubled about the possibility of losing Marshall's support."

"I imagine he was sad to hear about his cancer."

"Yes. Anyway, he didn't give me any advice, but after talking to him, I erased the video."

Lil jumped up and threw her arms around his neck. "Oh thank you!"

Her welcome rush of gratitude was a joyful relief, and he pulled her into his lap, holding her tight and stroking her hair. "I'm just sorry for what I did." He touched her cheek.

"I'm still in the room over here," Megan reminded them. "And in case you never noticed, my fair skin blushes easily."

"Oops. Sorry." Lil jumped up, embarrassed.

"Anyway, I went to the shelter to return the camera to Marcus. But I couldn't do it." He saw Lil's expression sag, and quickly explained. "He was still upset about his dad. Besides that, someone vandalized the barn. When I got there, the animals were out. I helped him round them up. Had to treat one of the horses."

Lil's eyes widened with fear. "What about the lambs?"

"They're fine." He smiled. "They didn't get very far."

Lil gave a sigh of relief. "Do you think it was one of my brothers? They made some threats against you."

Fletch rubbed his temples and briefly closed his eyes, hoping that was not the case. When he opened them, he saw Lil's distress mirrored his own.

⌒ఌ

The next day, Fletch and Vic returned to the dairy farm. Vic allowed Fletch to treat a white-faced cow with a cancerous growth by the eye. The cow had already lost the other eye, but they were able to save the second eye by numbing the area and then freezing the cancerous spot with liquid nitrogen.

"The cow will recover. Even after removing the first eye a couple of years ago, its milk production increased, which is a sign of improving health," Vic explained, returning his instruments to his satchel.

"Thanks for letting me do the surgery."

"You're here to learn."

"I know. But I feel like you're giving me a second chance. I appreciate it. And I wanted you to know I deleted that video footage." Thinking of Marcus's condition the last time he'd seen him, Fletch said, "I haven't returned the camera yet, but I will as soon as the Lewises have a break from their string of bad luck."

"The fallout I expected never happened. I guess it's a tribute to the Landis family's integrity that they didn't spread a bunch of gossip about us."

Fletch gave the cow a couple of pats then released the animal. "They're good people." Vic was right. After sleeping on it, Fletch was giving them the benefit of the doubt, assuming they hadn't vandalized the shelter.

"But they still don't want you taking care of their animals."

"How is their herd?"

"They're not isolating the hogs like they should. Until they do, they'll never get the disease under control."

Fletch frowned, wondering if Matt had taken his advice about the hoop barns.

They walked down the row of cattle, doing their routine checks. The herdsman had left them to take a customer on a farm tour, so they were able to discuss private matters.

"This whole thing with Marshall and you has forced me to take a hard look at my life. I shared some things with Britt, and we got in a big fight about finances. I told her we needed to cut back. She pointed out that I was the one driving the newest vehicle."

So Fletch's hunch was right—the vet had been under stress at home. He knew that the vet's truck barely had the dealership's sticker off its windshield, but Britt's car wasn't much older. From everything Vic had previously told him, he didn't think Britt was being very fair about their financial situation.

"I didn't tell her yet, but I'm thinking about trading my truck back in, getting into something older."

—◌◌—

One week later, Fletch drove to Ivan Miller's farm, fiddling with Vic's used-truck accessories. When he pulled up next to the doddy house, Lil stepped out onto the porch.

Her eyes widening, she hurried down the steps and strode to the front of the truck. She turned sideways and bent to examine the emblem on the grill. The white bow tied at the back of her curvy waist made his mouth go dry. With a silent intake of breath, he hopped out of the cab, stifling the urge to clasp his hands around that captivating waist.

She said almost accusingly, "I know what this red contraption is. It's a Dodge Ram." Then she turned and faced him, her hands back on her apron-clad hips. "Is this yours?"

He smiled. "I wish. It's Vic's. He traded down."

"And he's letting you drive it?"

"He was in one of his better moods."

She gave him an impish smile. "The color suits you."

He reached for her hand. "Hop in."

When she grabbed the handrest attached to the truck's ceiling, he assisted her into the cab. He nearly melted when his hands completely swallowed her waist.

Lil settled into the leather seat and gazed down at him adoringly, with her feminine hands gripping the man-sized steering wheel. "You gonna let me drive?"

"Nope," he nearly squeaked, not having actually prepared himself for that idea. He thought she would scoot over to the passenger side, as it had a bench seat, and let him drive. She was, after all, a wrecker of cars.

But she was already fiddling with the gearshift. "It's an automatic? Great!"

He cleared his throat, scrambled up, and tapped her hip. "Move over."

She giggled but hardly budged, obviously intending to drive Vic's truck. But Fletch had other ideas. He squished into the seat beside her and closed the door. Thankfully, he had the keys in his pocket. He was still in control. He started the engine, and a seat belt warning chimed.

"That sounds prettier than most," she remarked. "Jezebel doesn't have one."

"Pretty like you." They sat so close that he took the driver's seat belt and wrapped it around them both. She gave him a saucy grin. He placed his arm around her and put the vehicle in gear.

"We can't go far. I have sauce on the stove."

"Okay. But I kind of like this." If it was any indication of what it was like to blend two lives into one, he could get used to it.

She wiggled her elbow between them, probably to remind him she wasn't easy—as if he hadn't already figured that out—and they merged onto the road. He gunned the engine, and she gave a joyful shriek. The air coming through the vent lifted her hair enough that he caught its tropical scent.

They drove past freshly harvested fields, and for lack of rain, a trail of dust billowed behind them, making a private curtain for them in their red leather cocoon. Fletch could have driven on for miles, for days, but suddenly Lil straightened.

"What was that squeak?"

Being so caught up in the Ram and Lil, he'd forgotten they weren't altogether alone in the cab. He steered the truck to the side of the road. When the dust settled, he unbuckled and jumped out of the cab, ordering, "Stay right there."

She tilted her button-cute, freckled face and studied him curiously while he reached behind the seat into a box on the floorboards. His hand engulfing a tiny fur ball, he laid the mewing kitten on Lil's blue skirt like a love offering. Lil took a sudden intake of breath, but her resistance quickly vanished, as he had hoped it would. He placed his elbows on the seat beside her, watching to see how quickly she'd fall in love with Slinky. Who was he kidding? He hoped she'd fall in love with him.

She brought the tiny kitten up to her face, nuzzling him against her cheek, and Fletch held his breath. Fortunately, Slinky didn't bat or scratch, too busy licking Lil's cheek.

"His tongue is scratchy and tiny," she giggled. Then she turned and gave him an arched look. "Oh, Fletch. What have you done? How will I find time to take care of him?"

That was all he needed to hear. He climbed back up and nestled next to Lil and her kitten. When he closed the door, the interior of the cab seemed cozy, like one happy little family. Only Buddy was missing. "Kittens aren't much trouble. They use a litter box and mostly sleep when their owners are gone. They hunt mice, too."

But this kitten had other ideas. He evidently didn't realize he was on trial and double-crossed Fletch by creating a wet spot on Lil's apron. Her eyes widened and her lips pursed. She made a disgusted face. Fletch waited for the inevitable. He knew the fury that could spew out of his girlfriend's mouth.

Lil clutched her apron with her left hand and stared at the kitten. "Let's go home. Slinky has a lot to learn." But the way she slowly emphasized *has a lot to learn* with a sharp glance Fletch's way, he understood that she was making a valid point about him.

He didn't care. He was content that she hadn't flung the miscreant at him with a quick change of heart. Yes, that was a very good sign. But sadly, Fletch's good fortune lasted only about five minutes longer. For when they pulled into the Millers' driveway, Matt Landis's pickup truck was parked next to the doddy house.

CHAPTER 27

Lil cringed to see her brother's blue truck. As soon as Fletch cut his engine, Matt jumped out of his vehicle. Sporting a ridiculous "Not by the hair of my chinny-chin-chin" T-shirt, her brother planted his feet and slapped his hands on his hips to wait for them.

Beans! She felt her face heat at the humiliation of being caught all cuddled up next to Fletch and even belted in the same seat belt with him. As if Fletch felt the same, he quickly unfastened it and jumped out of the cab.

Lil scrambled after him, accepting his assistance to lift her and the kitten down. Her long skirt caught the truck's seat lever, showing too much leg, which only added to her shame. With her free hand she yanked it loose, though not without a consequent ripping sound.

As soon as her white sneakers hit the gravel drive, however, Matt speared her with a condemning gaze. "Isn't this cozy?"

Lil felt more wounded than angry over her favorite brother's disapproval. It certainly wasn't like it probably appeared to him. She hadn't done anything wrong with Fletch. She took a deep breath and softened her voice. "Did you come to criticize me, or do you want to come inside and discuss this over a plate of pasta?"

She felt Fletch's reassuring touch at her arm.

"No, I don't want pasta," Matt said angrily. "I came to tell you that because of you two, our dad is sleeping in the barn. Without you, Mom has gone completely over the edge."

The news cut deep. Lil feared what her mother might do again. Anything was possible. Once, Lil would never have dreamed her own mother would overdose herself. Mom had never claimed it was an accident. Would her parents be the first and only members in their church to separate or get a divorce, too? Though she felt that she had contributed to the general family upheaval, and her heart clenched with guilt, Lil still couldn't allow Matt to dump all the blame on her. Out of her own pain, she lashed back. "Has she? Or has she finally stood up for what she believes?"

"You know that women are supposed to be submissive. Actually, you don't understand that concept at all." Matt shifted his gaze to glare at Fletch. He thrust his finger, poking it in Fletch's direction. "I did forgive you, but you attract trouble like hogs attract flies."

Fletch touched Lil's waist protectively and jutted his chin. "I don't care if you blame me, but I don't like the tone and insinuations you're using with Lil."

Matt gave a scoffing laugh that turned out more like a snort.

The men's angry expressions ignited the atmosphere with tension. Lil thought they might fly into each other at any moment. She tried to reason. "Matt, you of all my brothers should understand that the old ways aren't necessarily the better ways."

Her logic fell on deaf ears. Matt turned suddenly and stomped back to his truck. He jumped in and slammed the door.

The noise startled Slinky, and the kitten leaped, clawing, from Lil's arms. "Oh no!" she gasped, looking down to see if the poor thing had broken its neck. But it jumped up and darted beneath the doddy house porch.

Behind her, Matt's tires spewed gravel. Fighting back tears of desperation, Lil knelt down to look between the gray step and the porch.

She felt a touch on her shoulder. "Let me."

"I hope Slinky's not injured," she choked out.

"Not on my shift. And certainly not by the hair of my chinny-chin-chin," Fletch joked, his hand probing in the dark crevices as far as he could reach.

Lil let out a nervous giggle even though she knew they shouldn't be taking her brother's angry display so lightly.

"Got him. Ouch!"

The kitten came out batting and struggling in Fletch's hand. Nevertheless, he drew Slinky tenderly up before his face. Turned him this way and that. "I think all he needs is a small bowl of milk and some time back in his box."

Nodding, Lil touched Fletch's arm. "Thanks."

"I'll get his box." He looked at Lil hopefully. "Maybe we can have some of that pasta."

"Sure." She watched him stride to the truck.

He spoke to the kitten, and she knew it was for her benefit. He wanted to take away her pain. "Look, Mr. Slinky, you're not doing a great job of impressing your new mommy. You'd better. . ."

His words drifted off, but Lil was very aware of his presence as she watched him and wondered how she had gotten so attached to somebody who had caused so much havoc in her family. Then looking down at her potty-stained apron and ripped skirt, she made a dash for the doddy house.

A few hours later, Lil stood at the window and gazed under the plain green roller shade to watch Fletch drive away in the flashy red truck. Her blond Rollo and that red truck—even though it went against the prideful image that the Conservative Mennonite Church tried to shun—they both made her heart zip with pleasure.

If her family was already upset with her, maybe it was time to try Fletch's church. She imagined how it would be. Would his congregation take her in as one of their own? Would she be able to release the church restrictions that sometimes felt like a tightening noose around her neck? Or would she still adhere to them? Could she really step over the chasm that separated the Mennonites who didn't wear ties from the ones who did? Once, she thought she could. Now she realized it wasn't an easy thing to do.

She felt God drawing her to trust Him, but she felt impatient, wanting to know what her future held. The lyrics of an old hymn ran through her mind: *"I know whom I have believed and am persuaded that he is able to keep that which I have committed to him against that day."*

She sincerely hoped so. She drew Slinky to her cheek, finding comfort in nestling the kitten that Fletch had gifted her.

———⌒———

"Hello, Mom?" Lil went through the Landises' mudroom and entered the kitchen, which smelled of cooked cabbage and sausage. Mom turned away from the stove and quickly crossed the room to her.

"I miss you. Where have you been?"

"Just getting settled. Working."

"Dating that Stauffer boy?"

Lil nodded.

"I figured."

"I missed you, too. Cabbage from Michelle's garden?" Lil lifted the skillet lid and took the fork her mom had just abandoned to taste it. "Delicious. I wonder if you could switch Dijon mustard for German?"

"Always telling your mother how to cook."

"Sorry. It might make it too sweet, anyway."

Mom urged, "Sit down, and I'll make us a pot of tea."

Lil unconsciously fiddled with the canning jar centerpiece and watched her mom, looking for clues as to her frame of mind.

Mom returned to the table with the tea and some homemade oatmeal cookies. "I suppose you came because you heard your dad was sleeping in the barn."

With shock, Lil worked to keep her composure. "I hope it's not because of me."

"It's about you and everything else that has infuriated me over the last thirty years."

Lil's eyes widened fearfully. "Oh?"

Mom sipped her tea and jutted her chin. "I told your dad that if he'd treated me better I probably wouldn't have gotten so depressed."

Lil's appetite fled. Her dad had enough problems with the farm's failing finances and sick hogs. How could Mom blame her depression on him?

"Then he wanted to know what he'd done. So I told him."

Lil was terrified to ask what Dad had done to ruin Mom's life.

"I told him plenty. That he treated me like a child, never discussing farm business. That all he wanted me around for was to cook and clean and see to his needs. I told him I had a brain, and a heart, too."

Lil imagined herself in Mom's situation. Everything she said held truth, but Lil had never known that her mom hoped for anything more.

"Well! I tell you. Your father went off in a huff. Slept in the barn for two nights. And I felt miserable. Lower than a dirty old rug. So the next night when he was preparing to go out after I had fixed him his supper, I asked him to stay. Told him I was sorry."

Many images passed through Lil's mind. Her mom had still fixed his supper for him while he was sleeping in the barn? She folded her hands, tapped them against her chin, both enraptured and sickened in the details of her parents' big fight. "What happened?"

"He took me in his arms and cried."

Lil felt her own eyes mist. "Dad?"

Mom nodded. "He said some real nice things about us, and since then, he's been talking to me. Really talking. We're not good at it, but it makes me feel better about a lot of things. It could have been different for us if he'd always talked to me like this."

Lil released a loud sigh, grateful they had worked things out between them. "Maybe it can still be different. The way you hoped."

Mom nodded. "Maybe so." She took a sip of her tea. "When Will finds out you came today, he's going to ask me if you're seeing Fletch. And now that we're talking, I can't keep any secrets from him."

"All right. Tell him that Fletch deleted the video footage. That I believe he's sorry about what he did."

"Do you love him?"

"I wish it were that simple."

"Nothing's simple about love. That's for sure. Life either."

"Megan says that the most worthwhile things aren't the easiest." Lil sighed. "Mom, please don't fight with Dad about this."

"It's a touchy subject for your dad. He feels responsible for bringing Fletch to the farm."

"But he didn't really. Bring Fletch. It was Matt who invited him to supper."

"Good news! Matt got his loan from the Plain City Bank! He's ordered some hoop barns."

"That is good news." Lil touched Mom's hand. The hoop barns had been Fletch's idea. She hoped Matt remembered that and dropped his grudge against Fletch.

CHAPTER 28

Fletch was working on a research paper for school, entitled "Obstacles in Obtaining Medical Attention." Across the room in Fletch's apartment, Buddy gnawed on a rawhide bone. Fletch tapped his finger impatiently against his space bar, and Buddy cocked one ear.

"Am I disturbing you?" Fletch asked. The dog lifted his head and panted in his direction.

It was eating away at him that he hadn't talked to Marshall since he'd been diagnosed with cancer. Since he'd deleted the footage. Fletch dreaded hearing the frail voice from the last time they talked, when Marshall had been in the hospital running tests. But he wouldn't be able to move forward, like his dad suggested, until he made the call. Finally, he picked up his phone.

"Hello."

"Hi, Marshall. It's Fletch."

"I may be terminal, but I'm not ignorant," the southerner drawled. "Ya are on my contact list."

Fletch grinned inwardly. "Genius would be more appropriate."

"That's my boy. Ya always know how to compliment me when I'm fishing for one."

"Speaking of fishing. There's a little river here called the Darby. I think you'd enjoy it as much as I do. Wish you were here and could throw in a line. I think you'd like Plain City."

"Actually, I've been thinking of driving over."

"No kidding? I mean, you'd be able to do that?"

"After the chemo is finished. I think Marcus needs my support."

"I'm relieved you're taking the chemo." Fletch swallowed. It sounded as if Marshall wanted to tie up loose ends. "The last time we talked, you asked me to pray for you. I've been doing that."

"Thanks, kid. Marcus tells me you're in the middle of a romance." Fletch didn't miss how Marshall quickly changed the topic away from God. "The little Conservative girl we talked about before? He told me that ya got caught filming at her farm and it caused a big ruckus."

Relieved that Marshall opened the topic he most wanted to talk about, Fletch quickly replied, "That's true. That's one of the reasons I deleted the film."

"What? Marcus didn't mention that!"

"I haven't told him yet."

"Look, the sooner we get what we need, the sooner this shelter can support itself. I'd like to see that happen yet, before I go."

Fletch pressed his eyes closed in pain. When he opened them again, he said, "I don't like to think about that, Marshall. I believe you'll recover or at least go into remission. And I don't mean to be disrespectful, but while we're on the subject, I need to let you know that I don't plan to do any more filming."

"Well I don't know what that is if it's not disrespect. I'm real disappointed in ya, boy."

"I sympathize with your cause. But I'm already in a bind with the farmers, with Vic, and possibly my grades. Client confidentiality is a big thing in a small town like Plain City."

"Ya can twist this around however ya want, but I was counting on ya. Ya let me down. It feels even worse because I'm laid up here."

"I'm sorry, sir. Real sorry about your illness."

"Sounds like it. Sounds more like that little girl has ya wrapped around her fingers."

Fletch felt hurt and confused. Hadn't Marshall urged him to pursue Lil?

"Let me remind ya that your dad depends on my support. I'll tell ya what I'm going to do. I'm going to let ya redeem yourself. I promised one of our big suppliers that we'd do some local veal boycotting. You head that up, and I'll forget about the video. Surely, that's not problematic? Not too much to ask."

Fletch tipped his chair back and stared at the ceiling in disbelief.

"Marcus will set you up."

After the call, Fletch stared numbly at the phone. It felt like he was losing Marshall in more ways than one. The man he had just talked to sounded like a complete stranger.

~ ⌒ ~

As soon as Lil stepped into Volo Italiano, Giovanni motioned her over. He was talking to the owner of the restaurant, an older Italian woman. Although Giovanni ran the place, Camila Battelli was the real heart of the establishment, often chatting with the restaurant's customers. Mrs. Battelli stepped forward in her tight pencil skirt and clingy sweater— both too young for a woman of her age and curves.

"Hello, Lillian." Her accent was thick.

"Mrs. Battelli."

"Call me Camila."

Lil glanced at Giovanni and saw the proud look in his eyes, like her father had looked when his children were old enough to sit on a tractor. "Thank you."

"Let's sit at one of the booths. My feet hurt today," the widow said.

Lil settled into the booth, thinking that the woman should give up wearing heels. When she glanced back at Camila, the older woman was curiously studying her. "So what do you think of my restaurant?"

"Why, I love working here."

"And we love having you here. Every day, Giovanni fills up my head with good things to say about your work."

Lil felt slightly embarrassed and very much aware that something good was happening, perhaps even a raise or a promotion. "I want to succeed."

"And you shall, little one. Giovanni has recommended you as his replacement."

"I wanted to tell you myself." Giovanni shrugged. "Eh. . .but Miss Camila, she has her own ideas."

"I don't understand," Lil fumbled, her heart beating so loudly she felt they must surely hear it. "Why are you leaving?"

"Because as you know, my wife she is pregnant. Eh. . . We can't stand to lose us another baby."

"But I don't understand."

"I am taking my sweetheart back to Italy to be happy with her family. She always wanted me to go into the family business." He shrugged. "Eh. . . I wanted to work here in America. But going home, this brings her much joy. I think it is what she needs to make a healthy baby. And even if it is not, well then, she will need her family, no?"

"But this is a great sacrifice for you," Lil argued, not wanting to lose her boss, even though it was an advancement for her own career. She couldn't understand how going to Italy could help the woman carry the baby to term, but then she knew this wasn't the time to argue the fact.

"Eh. . . It is what I want."

Lil swallowed and looked back at Camila. "But I am not the next in line. Surely you're not serious about me taking Giovanni's place?"

"The others, they do not work for the sheer joy of cooking. They work to feed their families and to pay their house bills."

"But I told you that I needed this job to buy a new car. That is why people work."

Giovanni argued. "You have the dream of a new car. Yes. But you also have the dream of becoming head chef. Eh? Don't deny it. You have the special flair. The potluck genes."

"Well. . ."

"The others, they do not realize they are working at the best restaurant"—Camila snapped her fingers to emphasize—"in Columbus. Do you want this job, or are you afraid, little one?"

Lil drew back her shoulders. "I am not afraid. Giovanni is right. I do covet his job. But I respect him, and I would never have wanted to take it from him."

"Oh, you are too kind," Giovanni exclaimed. "But I see right through you. And I see that you are just like me, no? And I"—he thumped his chest—"have made this place a success, no?" He looked at Camila, and she shrugged. "And you will, too. I give you my blessing."

Lil shot out of her seat and hugged Giovanni around the neck. "Thank you. I will not let you down." He patted her back, then gently drew her away. Lil turned to Camila. "You, either."

"Don't cry." Camila shook her head. "We have plans." She motioned at Giovanni. "Open up the restaurant while Lillian and I chat."

With sadness, Lil watched Giovanni leave them. She knew no matter how much he denied it that it had cost him a great deal to leave his position.

"This is for good business. You need a signature dish." Camila gestured with her ring-clad hands. "We will advertise it in all the right places. It will draw in the new customers and remind the old ones. They come to see what all the hoopla is about." She rubbed her hands together. "I've been thinking all this weekend. I think the perfect dish will be veal. It is something different, and we are known for special entrées. Do you have a specialty with the veal?"

⟞⟝

At the doddy house, Lil bent over the meat grinder, pressing through a chunk of meat and tossing in premeasured amounts of onion and garlic. "Then Marshall asked Fletch to head up a veal boycott."

"Veal?" Megan's eyes widened from the other side of the counter. "Did you invite Fletch to dinner? I hope this isn't how you're going to tell him that veal is going to be your signature dish?"

"I'm not an idiot," Lil replied. "There, that's finished. Next, I. . ." She dumped the contents into a frying pan with sizzling butter and began to stir. "The recipe is up to me, and for Fletch's sake, I thought a veal-and-spinach ravioli was better than a dish where the plate was smothered in veal."

"But Lil, it's still veal. No matter how much you conceal it. It will still be listed on the menu. Fletch doesn't have a personal problem with veal, right?"

Lil turned away from the stove and faced Megan. "No, and I don't think he has any intention of heading up a boycott. But he didn't exactly come out and say that, and I didn't have the heart to ask him. This whole thing with Marshall is a touchy topic."

Megan's slanted brow gave away her displeasure.

"I didn't have any choice. Camila had already decided that the new menu item was going to be veal."

"I think you need to tell Fletch."

Lil blushed, feeling guilty that she hadn't already told him.

"Does he know about your promotion?"

Lil turned back to the skillet and dumped the ground meat mixture into a container that she put into the refrigerator to cool. "No, not yet." She meant to tell him. The last time they were together, he had already been upset over his conversation with Marshall. The timing hadn't been right. Especially since it was a veal dish. But she planned to tell him. She didn't want to keep secrets that strained their relationship. "Camila is nothing like Giovanni. She's pompous and stubborn, and frankly, she scares me a little bit."

"And do you want to work for somebody so scary?"

Turning away from the refrigerator, Lil shot back, "And do you want to work for somebody so charming and handsome?"

Megan colored. "Yes, I'm afraid I do. I like my job."

Lil softened her expression. "Then we're both doomed."

"But I know where I'm going to draw the line," Megan clarified.

"Oh?" Lil replied, pulling a bottle of dry white wine out from a bottom cupboard. "Where?"

But Megan's gaze was riveted on the wine bottle. "Where did you get that?" she gasped.

"From work. I have another bottle under there, too."

Megan shook her head, and her hair fell to the front of her shoulders, shimmering in the afternoon sunlight coming through the doddy house window. "I hope nobody from church sees it. That would not be good."

Lil smiled. "It's good for cooking, not drinking. I have to use it for this dish when I make it at work, but once I get the recipe perfected, I'll experiment with some substitutes for us."

"You must never let Katy find out you brought that into the doddy house. She'll probably disown us."

Lil grabbed the veal mixture out of the fridge and returned it to the skillet, adding the wine and beef broth. "You're right. It probably wasn't the best choice. Have you talked to her lately? I miss them."

"No, they just seem to be in their own little world. Happy just to be together."

Lil and Megan exchanged an envious glance. Then Lil repeated, "Where exactly are you going to draw that line you mentioned?"

"Don't worry. I won't end up like the last girl."

"What do you mean?"

Megan blushed. "Remember she was pregnant? I think they might have had an affair. I believe that's why his wife left him."

"What?" In shock, Lil placed her palms on the counter to think. Things like this weren't supposed to happen to them. Her first impulse was to demand that Megan quit her job. To protect her. But she knew that wouldn't work. She needed to remain calm. "Megan, you must be careful. Please don't go on any of those mission trips with him."

Megan's expression fell. "I hadn't thought about that. You know I wouldn't want to miss an opportunity."

Lil couldn't believe Megan could be so naive. "It might start out businesslike, but once he got you in another country, he might take advantage of the situation. Especially if you spent a lot of time together. Do you spend a lot of time together?"

Megan arched a blond brow. "What are you going to do if Fletch finds out about the veal before you have a chance to tell him? That's more likely to happen than your make-believe scenario about my boss. Who, by the way, has not done anything out of the way toward me."

"I'm going to tell him the truth the next time I see him. He's taking me to the Shekinah Festival on Saturday. Oh, no!" she cried, quickly pulling the skillet off the burner. "Ugh! Now I've got to start all over."

Megan sighed. "Will that be wasted?"

Lil turned away from her roommate, facing the stove and fighting back the tears that burned her eyes. "No. We can eat it. But I have to get it right before I introduce it at the restaurant."

"I'm sorry." Megan moved toward the sink. "Let me clean up for you, at least."

Lil nodded and went to the fridge for another chunk of veal. "I guess Fletch and I got started on the wrong foot from the beginning, but our relationship is moving forward. I just need my dad's approval. You know?" Lil turned the grinder's old-style crank. "Megan? Do you think any of my brothers would vandalize the shelter?"

"No. And I don't think you'd better ask them either."

"I don't intend to." And then Lil realized that Megan had just duped her, using her own tactics of changing the subject when she didn't want to talk about her boss.

CHAPTER 29

Fletch took Lil's hand and started through the parking-lot maze. "This is not your typical festival, is it?"

"The Shekinah Festival is huge. It's been going on for over thirty years. Some day I'm going to go up in one of those hot-air contraptions." Lil's eyes lit up with excitement as she turned her gaze toward the brilliant balloons, all in various stages of flight. "Look at the sky. It's full of giant teardrops turned upside down and made happy."

"What a nice thought." The observation was typical of Lil's general outlook on life. Overhead, the balloons floated in a parade of color, brightening the sky, just as Lil lit up a room and set the tone. She was a born helper who didn't hesitate to take risks if it could turn someone's teardrops upside down and make them happy, too.

"Megan went to the concert last night, held in the big tent over there." She pointed. "It featured a hometown boy who made it big—is actually performing with the big names in the Christian music industry."

As they made their way toward the activity, she took him on a shortcut across the tree-clad lawns. A cluster of teenage girls in plain dress and coverings approached, coming from the other direction. One waved.

"Hi, Anna." Lil waved back. After the greeting, the girls lowered their gazes until they were past. "Anna's mom heads up the quilt part of the auction."

"They seemed shy."

"Because of you. Probably your red shoes," she teased. "Conservative girls don't mix with the world much until they get a job. So seeing us together probably made them feel uneasy. They don't know how to act around a guy like you."

Lil's comment hurt. *Guy like you?* It brought a general concern to his mind. "Do the people at your church know we're dating?"

Lil nodded.

"And is this already causing a problem for you?"

"It's a small community. After today, it will be confirmed. My family is under a microscope right now, anyway. My mom went to church for the first time in months. After the sermon, she stood up and asked for the congregation's forgiveness for not attending church and for disvaluing God's gift of life."

Fletch tried to hide his surprise because he could tell that it was a painful admission for Lil. "She's doing better, then?"

"Yes. She even joined the hostess committee again. And something special happened. Ever since she took the overdose, her ears had been ringing. It bothered her a lot and reminded her of her mistake. She told me that when she confessed on Sunday, her ears quit ringing. She believes it is an affirmation that God forgave her."

"That's amazing." He knew that God was at work in all their lives, but that they needed to settle their church issue soon, before it drove a wedge between Lil and her congregation. "I have an idea. Why don't you come to church with me tomorrow? The next Sunday, I'll go to your church. We can take turns, switching back and forth. It might help us decide where we'll go when. . .you know, help us make some choices."

"And what if my dad and brothers run you off the church property?"

"If we tell them that we're giving both churches an equal chance, won't they want to welcome us, convince us to come to their church?"

"Well, they would if they weren't still mad at you."

"And what kind of forgiveness is that? Maybe we need to help them along. And I have an idea how to do that." He'd been tossing the idea around in his mind, but he didn't want to tell Lil more about it now. He didn't want her worrying that his plan would backfire.

———

"What's your idea?" Lil asked.

Fletch grinned. "It's a surprise."

What kind of surprise would help her family forgive him? Surely he wasn't thinking of proposing, of forcing them to make the choice to accept him or reject him? "Please, tell me what you're up to."

He touched the tip of her nose. "Nosy. My nose smells food. Come, on."

They came to a line of booths selling many tempting delights: apple dumplings, popcorn, funnel cakes, and ice cream. But Lil's senses were only partly engaged, for she couldn't get past Fletch's near slip of the tongue. When he had brought up the question of which church they would attend, he'd almost said *after we get married*. She was sure of it. It still amazed her that Fletch had fallen in love with her—plain Lillian Mae Landis. That he wanted to take her to his church.

"About going to your church. Maybe not tomorrow. But I'll think about your suggestion."

"All right."

She saw his expression sadden and quickly said, "You have to try the homemade ice cream. Roger Headings and his wife, Crystal, always have a booth at local events. And before we leave, you should buy some trail bologna and cheese to take back to your apartment." He chose chocolate, and she ate strawberry.

Since the festival was a school fund-raiser, it featured lots of events for the children, from a petting zoo to a pony ride. "The pedal event is hilarious," Lil told Fletch. "I believe it's getting ready to start."

They found a seat and watched some adults trying to get the little ones lined up and ready to go. It provided the interval she needed to tell him about her promotion and her new signature dish. She had made a vow with herself that she would tell him sometime during the festival. She wanted to get it over with and off her mind so that she could enjoy the rest of the day.

"Fletch? Something happened at work."

He chuckled at a little boy who got out of his car and sat on the ground. Then he turned to give her his full attention. "What?"

"I got a promotion. A big promotion."

"Why that's great."

"To head chef."

"What?" Fletch jumped to his feet. He grabbed her up and hugged her. "That's wonderful! I can't believe it. You just started working there."

She smiled up at him. "I know. Giovanni is moving back to Italy, and he recommended me to the restaurant's owner."

"Sit down!" Somebody from behind them yelled. "The race is starting."

"Not until she does the garbanzo dance!" Fletch yelled back.

Lil laughed, did one little shimmy, then promptly seated herself, pulling Fletch down by the sleeve. He turned and stared at her, still beaming at her accomplishment.

"I'm glad you understand how important this is to me."

"I'm proud of you. I'm speechless."

"Thanks."

Applause sounded as the event began. "Cute," Fletch said. The youngsters peddled every way but straight ahead. He glanced over at Lil. "But I can't believe you didn't call me right away with the big news."

"I had some things to think through first." And it seemed she still did. She had planned to tell him about the veal dish, but now she wasn't so sure. Things were going so great between them. He had destroyed the video for her and her family. And he had a surprise in store for her. Something that would help her family forgive him. Could she ask him not to boycott veal, too? When he gave her another side hug, she knew she couldn't. There would have to be another way. She would try to change her boss's mind instead.

❧

In spite of the fact that Plain City was in the middle of a dry spell, harvest was starting earlier than usual. It stirred up clouds of dust in the corn and soybean fields on either side of the road so that Fletch kept his windows closed. Buddy panted against the glass, seeming to know where they were headed. It was Fletch's night to volunteer at the shelter.

He pulled into the drive, and once he'd parked, he released Buddy for some exercise. He knew the basset's routine of sniffing along the fence row and the strip of bushes on the east side of the drive. It ended by whining or howling at the front door of the farmhouse until Ashley fussed over him. He was smitten with all females.

A sudden noise similar to a creaking branch sent Fletch glancing up into a nearby pine. Curious, he brought his gaze down and extended it out toward the barn. The sun's glare was blinding so he gave his cap a tug to shade his vision. He heard another noise and saw two elongated shadows zip around the far corner of the barn.

Fletch hastened his steps until he broke into a run, chasing after the shadows. When he came around the barn, he saw two men preparing to hurdle the fence to the neighboring pasture. One of them was carrying a small animal.

His heart somersaulted. "Stop!" Not even wanting to think about their intentions for the animal, he sped after the thieves. They had stopped by the fence when one of them got his shirt caught. But by the time Fletch reached the fence, they had both taken off again. The bleating animal was one of the shelter's lambs. Fletch thought he could outrun them if his lungs didn't cave in first.

He hurdled the fence. "Stop!"

The men kept running.

Fletch chased after them. Panting hard, he got within several yards and decided to go after the guy with the lamb. He dove for his legs. The runner stumbled, smacked the ground, and rolled. Meanwhile, the lamb jumped clear. Fletch easily pinned down the intruder.

The guy he'd tackled was only a kid, about high school age. Fletch had the boy's arm pinned, and his knee was on the small of the boy's back. "What's your name?"

The boy grunted. "You're hurting me."

About that time, Marcus ran up to them. Probably given the bodybuilder's enormous physique, the lad was too frightened to try to escape, and he even blurted out his name. But when Fletch looked out over the pasture, he saw the accomplice had gotten away.

The police arrived soon after that. They had picked up the other boy farther down the road. When they saw him dash behind a tree, they hauled him in on suspicion. Both boys were handcuffed and placed in the back of the police car while the officers took Fletch's statement.

When they questioned Marcus about the shelter, Fletch told the officers he needed to get the lamb back to safety and to examine the other animals.

"We'll drive up to the barn before we go to get your report on the other animals."

At the barn, Fletch was relieved to learn that all the animals were unharmed, including Cottonball. He must have startled the intruders before they did damage to the barn again.

Later Marcus was able to explain to Fletch that the vandals were farm boys acting on dares. They claimed they'd gotten the idea listening to their dads speak negatively about the shelter. "Thanks, man, for stopping them."

"No problem, but you showed up at just the right moment. I was still trying to figure out how to call you and keep my hold on the kid."

"Ashley had gone to the door to let Buddy in and saw ya take off around the barn like your pants were on fire. She alerted me. I was pretty much right behind ya, only I couldn't keep up with ya."

Fletch shook his head. "I still have a stitch in my side. I can't remember when I ran that fast. I knew I could catch them as long as I didn't collapse first."

Marcus chuckled. "I owe ya. Thanks for your help, man."

"No problem." Fletch could hardly believe that Marcus thought he owed him, but it made a good opportunity to give him back the camera. He took it from his pocket, hoping he hadn't broken it in the scuffle. After a quick examination, it seemed fine. "I guess your dad told you I deleted that film?"

Marcus accepted the camera with a sigh. "Yeah. He was pretty upset about it. But man, with this arrest, what those boys did, we could get some free publicity. I think I'm going to call the newspaper."

"What if it's not good publicity?"

"They admitted they were the ones who vandalized us before. They injured a horse and stole a lamb. How can that be bad publicity for us? Even if it is, it will still promote awareness." Marcus ran a hand over the top of his shaved head.

"I'm glad the horse is recovering."

"I know. Funny how those kids confessed to everything. I wonder if more kids were involved? The ones who dared them?"

"I suppose the officers will get the entire story out of them."

"Who knows? There might have been other incidents."

"That's true."

Marcus looked at the camera he held. "I guess Dad gave you an ultimatum?"

"The veal boycotting? I won't be doing that either."

"Oh man. Ya sure ya can't humor him?"

Hard as it was to see Marcus's pain, Fletch held firm. "Sorry. Not this time. How's his chemo going?"

"We don't know yet. But at least he's willing to give it a try."

Fletch nodded. "I'm praying for remission."

"Thanks."

"Well, I'm done here. Cottonball's fine. But if this had happened a few weeks earlier, or if they'd taken Flannel, it would have been traumatic, probably life threatening. Anyway, I'm finished with my rounds. Guess I'll go find Buddy and be on my way."

On the drive home, Fletch found it hard to release his anger at the kids' disregard of animal life. He didn't know what their intentions had been with the lamb, but he knew if they'd swiped or hurt Buddy, he'd have had a hard time getting over it.

～⌒～

The next morning at the clinic, Vic greeted Fletch with the *Plain City Advocate*. "Looks like you had some action last night. You made the local news."

"I'll bet it's going to be in the *Columbus Dispatch*, too."

"I don't like your name being listed, being involved with the shelter."

Fletch quickly scanned the article to see what had been written about him:

> *Fletch Stauffer is a veterinary student interning under Vic's Veterinary Clinic. The Plain City Farm Shelter operates mostly with volunteer help, and Stauffer is one of many who donate their time to help abused animals.*

Fletch groaned and continued reading:

> *He was getting ready to do a routine check when he saw two shadows sneaking around the barn.*

"I can't believe you gave them all that information. My name!"

Fletch slapped the paper back down on the waiting room coffee table. "I didn't. Marcus must have."

"Well, let's hope this doesn't cause us to lose any clients."

"You would have done the same thing, if it had been you. The kids were stealing an animal."

"I know. I know. I'll be glad when we don't have to go out there anymore." Vic picked up the newspaper and threw it in the trash. "Don't want anybody seeing that."

But that evening when Fletch had returned to his apartment, he snapped open the newspaper that he had retrieved from the trash on his way out of the clinic. He read the article more thoroughly, considering all the implications for himself, Vic, and the shelter. As his mind worked through the matter, he found himself flipping through the rest of the newspaper.

In the restaurant section, where he usually found some fast-food coupons, something caught his attention. He pulled the paper closer, studying it carefully. Volo Italiano? That was Lil's restaurant. The article was about her! His face broke into a beaming smile. She was making her dream come true. He was so proud of her. So glad he'd dug the paper out of the trash. He continued reading:

> *Volo Italiano is proud to announce its new chef, Lillian Landis. She brings delicious new entrées to the menu. Look for her signature dish, Lily's Veal Ravioli. The first twenty-five customers who order her special entrée will be given a 10 percent discount.*

The paper slipped from his hand, floated to the floor, and hit Buddy on the head. The dog jumped back, startled.

"Sorry, Buddy. It's just that I can't believe she didn't tell me." Fletch shook his head, remembering that she hadn't even told him about the promotion when it first happened. Why would she withhold such great news?

He thought back to their discussion at the Shekinah Festival. She had seemed nervous, but he had taken it as humility over her promotion. He thought she was celebrating, but was she really just relieved that he was happy for her. . .because. . .her signature dish was veal, and she was afraid to tell him?

If she was afraid to tell him, then she thought he was going to boycott veal. She didn't trust him, thought he was still allowing Marshall to call the shots. Not only that, what kind of statement was she trying to make with her signature veal dish? Surely she could have made spinach ravioli her dish. Why the veal? This was disturbing news.

CHAPTER 30

Buddy's tail vigorously thumped the wood flooring of the doddy house porch as Fletch waited for Lil to answer her doorbell. When the door cracked open, it was secured by a safety chain that Jake had added when Katy and Lil first moved into the doddy house.

"Fletch! Hi!"

He waited as she rattled the latch free. Buddy rushed in before Fletch could grab him.

"Uh-oh!"

"Buddy!" Fletch called sternly, embarrassed at the dog's poor manners. The basset obediently returned and gazed up at him.

"Sorry about that. I was going to ask if we could come in first. . . . I. . ."

"It's fine. Buddy just surprised me. He won't hurt Slinky?"

"That's why I brought him. I thought we should introduce them while Slinky's still a kitten. Buddy will accept Slinky because this is not his territory, but if we wait too long, Slinky might not allow a dog in his domain." He gave her a grin. "And I'd hate to think a mere kitten was keeping us apart."

Lil nodded skeptically. "Come in. Slinky's in his bed."

Fletch followed Lil into the living room, where she gently lifted up the kitten into her arms. He was pleased to see the bond that had formed between them. "Where's Megan?"

"At her folks. She misses them. Goes home pretty often."

"That must make it lonely for you."

"Yes. But it's a small sacrifice. I'm relieved to have my own place." She looked at the kitten. "How do we do this?"

"Why don't you pet Buddy and show your acceptance of the dog. Try to keep Slinky out of Buddy's space, or he'll poke his nose up against him and provoke the kitten to scratch. I'll help by holding Buddy's collar."

Lil gave a nervous nod, then knelt. With one hand, she kept Slinky in her lap. The other she extended toward Buddy. He sniffed her hand and leaned into her, his tail wagging. "Good, doggie. You're so cute. I've missed you."

Meanwhile, Slinky squirmed, and Lil wasn't able to restrain the kitten.

Slinky pounced off Lil's lap, gave Buddy's face a swat, and sprang to the floor. Buddy backed up, startled but not aggressive. He placed his face on his front paws, eyeing Slinky from his side vision, while pretending to ignore the kitten.

Lil softly giggled.

"We should probably just let them go. If Buddy gets tired of Slinky, he'll growl, and then we can separate them for a while."

The kitten pounced, swatted the dog, and retreated. Buddy squirmed.

By now both Fletch and Lil had lowered themselves to the oval braided carpet. Fletch moved to get comfortable, resting his arm on a sofa cushion. "How's your job going?" he asked, giving her the opportunity to be open about her veal dish.

"First I have to tell you the good news. Matt's hoop barns are being delivered on Friday. He's so excited. They already poured the cement pads."

"That is great news." Things remained strained between them, but Fletch had talked to Matt at church. At that time, he hadn't had a delivery date yet. This information was vital to the plan he had mentioned to

Lil at the Shekinah Festival. With it, he hoped to win back her family's acceptance and approval.

She reached down to pet the kitten, which had pounced back into her lap. "Matt still needs to procure a contract with an integrator company, but he claims that will be easier done, now that he's getting the barns. He said the procedures are almost like starting up a new farm. And of course he still needs to get the hogs healthy again."

"Yes. He needs to practice isolation before the disease spreads, and the sooner the better," Fletch agreed. "I'm glad things are working out for your family. How's your mom?"

"She's doing so much better." He listened as Lil told him about their recent conversation. She seemed excited that her parents were communicating again. It made him wonder why Lil was not being open with him. Did she want to follow in her parents' footsteps?

His parents had always shared a special intimacy. He wanted that kind of relationship with Lil. When it came to marriage, he wouldn't settle for anything less. He'd been disappointed when Lil turned down his idea of visiting each other's churches. To him, it felt like she wasn't ready to commit to their relationship. As his dad had mentioned, if they weren't moving forward, they were moving backward.

"Lil, how's work? How's the new position going for you?"

Her eyes darted nervously to the animals, avoiding eye contact with him. "It's hard. Real hard."

"Why is that?"

She met his gaze. "Because I have to make all the decisions. Not only that, but we've made some menu changes, and the cooks aren't getting it right. I'm not comfortable critiquing them, but if we don't get it right, Camila will hold me responsible. It's intimidating to be in charge of a kitchen full of outsiders with more seniority. I'm not sure I like being the boss."

"They wouldn't have chosen you for the position if they didn't respect you. Giovanni and Camila are confident you are the best qualified. Instead of trying to please the other cooks or even your boss, you need to focus on the food. You're good at that. They will follow your lead."

"I suppose."

Buddy crowded Fletch, trying to avoid the playful kitten. Absently, he massaged Buddy under the muzzle. "It will get easier. Every job has its less-enjoyable aspects. Tell me about the new items on the menu."

"Oh, look." The kitten had suddenly quit playing and curled up next to Buddy's side. "Isn't that cute? I think they're going to get along fine."

"So we can be one big happy family, right?" He pointed at her and back at himself a few times, hoping to coax a smile out of her, hoping she wanted their relationship to turn into something permanent as much as he did.

"I hope so."

What was with this cautious, hesitant attitude? Normally Lil was out-front with everything. This was a facet of her personality that had drawn him to her. He wondered if it was her means of pulling away from him. Figuring one of them needed to be direct, he finally admitted, "I read the newspaper article about your signature dish."

Her eyes widened, and her face paled. "I'm sorry. I should have told you."

He waited for her to explain, but she didn't. "Why couldn't you talk to me about this?"

Her eyes held remorse. "I thought it would make things more complicated between us."

"Can you tell me why you chose a veal dish?"

"It was Camila's idea. I was going to get her to change it."

"Change it, because?"

Her voice grew exasperated. "Because Marshall asked you to boy-cott veal."

"You think I'm Marshall's puppet?"

"You didn't tell me what your intentions were. And now that Marshall has cancer. . ." Lil shrugged. "You'd already destroyed the video. I didn't want to put more pressure on you."

Her lack of confidence disappointed him.

Buddy yipped, and the kitten jumped up, frightened. Lil scooped it up and cuddled it. "Shh. Shh."

Fletch hardly understood the disappointment and anger rising up to overwhelm him. Sure he'd made a mistake. But it was heartbreaking that nobody saw his good intentions and acknowledged the sacrifices he was willing to make. He was tired of shouldering the blame for everything, being the one who had to apologize over and over again. Sorry she didn't trust him.

Lil had been retreating from his advances from the beginning. He was tired of it. "Look, Lil. I feel as though I'm the only one trying to make us happen. You don't trust me. You throw up your guard at every turn, as if I'm making you choose between your family and me. Your job and me. It's not like that. I'm all about winning them back. I won't quit until that happens. I'm about making you happy. But you're constantly pushing me away."

She pressed her lips into a tight line and made no argument to convince him otherwise. Fletch stood up. "I've got a lot going on in my life, too. I'm tired of being the only one who cares here. And tired of being the community scapegoat."

Lil scrambled to her feet. "But I do care. It's just that. . .things are confusing-crazy right now."

Fletch gentled his tone. "You're judging everything from the outside. Blaming the farm, your family, and even your church for your insecurities. Just be who you are. Either there's a place for me on the inside, or there isn't."

Lil angrily brushed cat hair from her skirt. "I can't believe you are preaching to me."

"Me either. I didn't come to do that. I better go. Come on, Buddy." Fletch made for the door, and Buddy slinked after him as if he knew they were both in trouble. All the way to the door, Fletch longed for her to beg him to stay, to tell him that she wanted him. But she didn't.

⁀ℭ

Lil blotted her eyes with a tissue, "Oh, Megan, I'm so glad you're home."

Megan hurried to the couch. "What's happened? What's wrong? Is it your mom?"

"No. Fletch and I got in a huge argument."

Moving onto the couch next to her, Megan asked with concern, "About the veal?"

"Yes, and don't say you told me so. He saw our ad in the newspaper. He was angry that I hid it from him. Angry I didn't trust him." Lil sniffed. "He said he's tired of being the only one trying to make our relationship work. . .that I'm constantly pushing him away."

"Oh, wow."

"And he's right. He's done all the pursuing." She sniffed. "All I do is throw up red flags." She buried her face in the tissue.

Megan patted her back. "I'm sorry."

"I've never seen him so mad. When he left, he seemed bitter and hurt. I think he's giving up on us. I'm nothing but a thorn in his side, with my family and. . .everything else."

"Maybe this is for the best."

"What!" Lil blinked at Megan. "How can you say that?"

"Well, now you know what his limits are. I mean, it's time you decided if you want him or not. If you're willing to give it your all. If you love him."

"Of course I want him! Where have you been?"

Megan nodded with sympathy. "You're right. He has made all the moves. Now he needs encouragement from you. You'll have to pursue him."

"You're right. I haven't done my part. Our relationship seemed hopeless, and I was waiting for him to do all the changing, make everything right." Lil hiccupped.

"Let me make you some tea. If you're sure you want him, then I'll help you figure out how to win him back."

Lil gave a weak smile, clasping Slinky close. "Thanks." But the kitten squirmed and sprang to the floor, strutting off after Megan.

⸺ ☙

In spite of their argument, Fletch was willing to give it one last try before he gave up on Lil. Winning back her family was paramount in winning her back. If his final plan failed, then he would concede and quit pursuing her and her family.

When Vic heard about Fletch's plan, he thought it was a great idea and offered to help him carry it through. So on the morning that the hoop barn was going up, they drove to the farm well before daylight. The farmers would be early at their chores, intent to make a long day of it. When they arrived, Vic's red Dodge pickup was conspicuous even in the dark, and Matt was the first one out of the barn.

In a nervous leap, Fletch jumped out of the cab.

"What's going on?" Matt asked.

"We know this is a big day for you. We came to help." He gestured to include Vic, who had now joined them.

Matt gave a crooked grin. "The thought's nice, but don't know how it will get received by the others."

Fletch clasped Matt's shoulder. "Please. Just put me to work."

About that time, Will came out of the barn. He strode to them and stopped beside Matt. "Hi, Vic. I thought I told you I didn't want *him* on my property."

"He's not here on my behalf. He's here on his own."

"Mr. Landis, I came to help you put up your hoop barns."

Fletch saw surprise flit across the older man's features, but he quickly hardened his expression. "Well, we don't need your kind of help."

Will's rejection was expected. In fact, Fletch had rehearsed his argument beforehand. "That may be true. I don't mean any disrespect, but I'm here to help, and that's that. If you throw me off your property, I'll crawl back on bloody nubs if I have to, because I *am* helping you today. Now it's going to be a long day, and the way I see it, you don't need to be wasting your time and energy arguing."

Will grunted, turned away, and stalked back into the barn. Fletch hurried after him, with Matt and Vic close at his heels. Inside, it was apparent that Hank and Stephen had gotten a quick rundown of the situation.

Hank looked angry. "Now you see here, Stauffer. We don't want your help."

"I understand. But I'm staying. I need to help."

Stephen turned to his brothers. "What are we going to do?"

"Why can't he help?" Matt heaved a feed bag over his shoulder. "We all know we could use the extra hands. Vic is volunteering, too. It's rude not to accept some neighborly help."

Fletch chewed the side of his cheek, disliking but knowing the best way to proceed with the stubborn bunch was to grovel again and make it real good this time. "It was despicable of me to take pictures of your sick animals. I'm not going to give you any excuses for it." By now they knew the reason. "I'm not naturally a backstabbing jerk. Usually, I'm honest and dependable. What I did was wrong. I'm sorry for betraying your trust and Vic's."

Vic quickly added, "I have to vouch for his good character. He's proved himself since the incident. He really wants to make amends. He needs to help you."

"That's because he wants to date Lil," Hank said distastefully.

"I like your sister, but that's not why I'm here. If I had misrepresented myself to any other farmer and had the opportunity to make amends, I would. It's the Christian thing to do."

Will studied Fletch. "I believe him. Sometimes, we just need to forgive." He offered Fletch a handshake.

Fletch gripped Will's hand as if it was his only lifeline. Fletch figured that whatever was happening between the farmer and his wife must have softened the older man's heart. Fletch determined not to disappoint him but to stick with the work until the last hour or until he was dead, whichever came first.

"He can stay," Hank relented. "But he's not fooling me."

Fletch gave Hank a smile. "Thanks for the chance." But Hank didn't respond. Stephen turned his back and moved to the watering trough. Fletch hadn't expected a homecoming like the one for the prodigal son. He was heartened enough that Hank permitted him to stay.

"While we finish choring, you can go haul a stack of lumber to the barn sites. I'll show you where." Matt led them out of the barn and shined a flashlight in the direction of two new cement pads that would go at either end of the two new barns. The lumber company had dumped the lumber just off the circle drive.

Once Matt had left them and returned to the barn, Fletch grabbed two two-by-fours and threw them over his shoulder. Vic only took one because he had the flashlight and he wasn't trying to impress anybody or earn anybody's forgiveness. By daybreak, the lumber was laid out in smaller stacks in two large, rectangular areas where the barns would be erected.

Over the years of his practice, the veterinarian had acquired a complete set of tools. Taking care of livestock got him into all kinds of situations. Fletch had borrowed a tool belt and a hammer, even though he didn't know anything about carpentry. The first order of business was installing treated posts and tongue and groove to make a four-foot exterior bearing wall.

Once Jake arrived, Fletch felt like he had another ally. Jake schooled him so that he was soon swinging his hammer along with the others, who mostly ignored him. It grated his pride when Hank affirmed the vet and didn't acknowledge Fletch's work.

By nine o'clock, a small crane arrived, and the steel tubular arches were secured to the ground posts and sidewalls. After that, the men climbed up to secure the polypropylene tarps. Fletch wasn't much for heights, so instead of following Jake, he stayed below and did groundwork.

Around noon, Fletch had just raised his arm to swing the hammer, when Lil walked up behind him.

"Hi, Fletch."

His reaction was a moment of hesitation, for he wanted to apologize to her yet needed to disregard her so that Hank didn't throw him off the farm. The second of hesitation broke his concentration and brought the hammer down hard on his thumb.

"Ouch!" He jumped back, tossing the hammer to the ground. He cradled his injured hand with all thoughts of Lil driven out by the explosion of pain. The first thing he focused on beyond the pain was a snicker. He looked over to see Hank's amusement. The second thing he heard was Lil calling everyone in to lunch. He didn't look at her. He couldn't.

Up at the house, several long tables were set up outside. Katy and the Landis women served huge platters of ham, potato salad, and baked beans. Fletch waited in line and washed up at an outdoor faucet, his thumb throbbing in waves of pain. He filled a plate and sat between Matt and Jake.

It was only the second meal Fletch had shared with the Landis family. He noticed with as much amusement as he could muster that Stephen, who sat on the other side of Matt, checked the lid of his saltshaker before using it.

Fletch rose to fill his glass from the water jug and returned to find his chair was missing. How did Matt have the energy to pull jokes? Fletch was tired, thirsty, and hungry, and his thumb felt as though it had an electrical current pulsating through it. It was enough to make a man cranky. And he was, but he tamped down his temper, reminding himself that he had a mission to perform.

With a great deal of self-control, he set his glass down by his plate. He slanted a warning brow at Matt and spied his chair folded up against a tree where several of the sisters-in-law had congregated.

He strode after the chair and tipped his cap to the girls, feeling embarrassed as their giggles followed him back to the table. He unfolded the chair and sat, and looked cautiously at his food to make sure everything was still in order. It seemed to be. He took a swig of his water. Beside him Matt began talking to Stephen. Fletch relaxed.

His stomach growled, and he brought the thick sandwich of ham and swiss cheese to his watering mouth and bit down into the delicious *hot, hot, hot, and more hot*. He jumped up. His chair crashed to the ground. Fletch wheeled from the table and spit. Came back for his water and washed down the fire.

Meanwhile Matt cracked up at his expense. In fact, all the Landis men seemed tickled pink. Fletch glared at Matt. It was obvious now that Hank wasn't the only unforgiving brother. He felt like jerking the young farmer out of his chair by the neck of his "Hog Heaven" T-shirt. But that's what they were all hoping to see, expecting. Provoking.

Just then Lil stepped in between Matt and Stephen with a water pitcher. She reached out and gave Matt's hat a push. He grabbed it before it fell into his food. Fletch didn't need Lil fighting his battle. He rose and went to whisper in Rose's ear. She gave a smiling nod and soon returned with a pitcher of his own water. Fletch carried it back to his seat.

The brothers snickered.

Fletch snapped his chair open and seated himself. Then he began the slow and painful process of finishing every bite of his Tabasco-seasoned sandwich, rinsing every couple of bites with another glass of water.

"At least you won't get dehydrated," Matt joked. His brothers laughed, but Will seemed to look at him with a new respect.

Once the attention was off him, he glanced toward the women again. Lil gave him a smile, then quickly diverted her gaze to talk to Katy. Well, Rome wasn't built in a day.

But to Fletch, it felt like it. Once they got the barn erected, there was the work of hauling bedding to the new structures. Fletch got the worst jobs, and by late afternoon it wasn't only his thumb that throbbed, but every muscle ached and groaned for relief.

Vic left around midafternoon, taking Fletch's only mode of transportation. But Fletch didn't want the brothers to see him as a quitter, so he remained behind. He figured he could hitch a ride with Matt after the evening choring. Fletch didn't know if he would be able to raise himself out of bed the next day, but he didn't regret his decision to show the Landis men he was sorry for his mistake.

It was an experience like none other to watch the barn go up and to feel the satisfaction of knowing that the hoop barn had been his idea. Whether Matt ever realized it or not, they had done the right thing. The hoop barns would help the Landis family fight their way out of debt, if that was possible. And now Fletch's conscience was clear.

He had given them the hoop barn idea and helped them erect the barns. He had erased the video so nobody had received false information about their farm or farming methods. He had given them hours of free veterinary service before they kicked him off the farm. And he had permitted them to belittle him, even make him the object of their jokes.

He'd done his part, and now it was up to the Landis family to accept or reject him. He didn't know Hank and Stephen that well, but he liked Matt, and he respected Will. Because he'd been praying for Rose, he already felt a bond there.

As for Lil, well, he loved her of course, but he didn't know if that was enough. He didn't know if she would use their recent argument as a chance to run in the other direction, or if she would be willing to try again. Either way, he wanted her family to succeed. He was more than happy he had done what he could do make that happen.

The men didn't quit to eat supper until after dark. Chores still waited. Fletch washed up, planning to eat another meal with them and help chore. But Matt stuck his head into the kitchen and asked his mom to make him and Fletch a sandwich for the road.

"I'll take you home now. We can eat on the way."

Fletch, who hadn't even asked him for a ride yet, started to protest. "Are you sure? I'm prepared to stay." He dried his hands on the towel and turned to find Hank staring at him.

"You've done your share," the older, darker son replied. "You don't have to stay till the last chore is done and crawl yourself home on bloody nubs." A smile formed on the corner of Hank's mouth. "We're not that callous."

Even though it was what Fletch had hoped for, now that Hank was actually softening toward him, it felt nothing short of miraculous.

"You didn't have to come today. It took guts to face us like you did and stick with us all day. You and I are good now. Thanks. Your help was appreciated."

"That. . .means a lot to me." Fletch offered his hand, and Hank clasped it. Stephen followed suit.

Will folded the hand towel. "We shouldn't have doubted you. You're welcome here anytime."

Fletch couldn't help but notice that nothing was mentioned about Lil, and she had disappeared. But later he guessed she must have sneaked out the front door, because when he reached Matt's truck, she was waiting for them.

"I need to talk to you."

Matt sighed. "I've got to get back and do chores." Her brother strode around to the other side of the truck and got inside. He turned on the truck and its headlights.

Her lip trembled in the dim light, and Fletch wondered if she was going to break up with him.

"I just wanted to say that. . .well, everything you said the other night was true. I'm sorry. . . ."

For the life of him, exhausted as he was and staring into her distressed eyes, Fletch couldn't remember a thing he had told her. Worse, he couldn't tell if she was trying to break up or trying to apologize.

He knew Matt was antsy inside the truck. "Could you give me a hint? Are you trying to break up here or are you trying to make up?"

"Don't make it so hard. I'm apologizing."

"Then I'm accepting. But I'm too tired to make much sense tonight."

"I know. I'd better go before I'm missed."

Fletch squeezed her hand, then flinched from the pain.

"Thanks for helping my family."

He watched her hurry back toward the house, climbing wearily into the cab.

Matt shook his head. "You just don't know when to quit, do you?"

"It would seem so."

CHAPTER 31

Fletch threw his gloves in the trash, then strode into the clinic's waiting room to call in the next client. "Who's next?"

A couple stood, but he didn't see any pet, and he quickly glanced up, expecting to hear a request for a prescription.

Frank Stauffer grinned at him, at eye level, now. He was still larger than Fletch, broader across the shoulders, and not quite as slim at the waist. The fiftyish eyes sparkled with amusement, but he didn't say anything or move a muscle to advance. Fletch's mother clutched her husband's arm. She was still blond and trim and modestly dressed. Her lips trembled. Tears rolled down her cheeks.

"Mom!" Fletch hurried forward and scooped her into his embrace. She cried and repeated his name over and over. Then she cupped his face with her hands and looked up at him. "You look wonderful. So handsome and tall like your father. How I've missed you."

Fletch struggled to keep his composure. Next, he turned toward his father, instinctively straightening, allowing the other man to examine him. But Frank gripped him hard in the upper arms, and pain from his sore muscles shot through his body. He swallowed. And his dad swept him into a lung-constricting, bear hug.

They separated, and Fletch gasped, "What a surprise." He stared at them with disbelief. He'd never dreamed that they would really come to see him.

"Take these people to lunch or something. You are making a spectacle." Vic's teasing voice came down the hallway.

Fletch turned. "You sure? Two days off in a row?"

"Yes. It's not every day that a man's parents come all the way from Africa to visit. Take the rest of the day off."

Grateful, Fletch made the introductions and even included the farmer with the goat that had gotten its head stuck in the fence, who now stood next to Vic. "Thanks again."

Vic took the farmer and his goat into one of the back rooms, and Fletch turned back to his parents.

"It's too early for lunch. Would you like to go to my apartment?"

"Yes," his mother replied. "This is a very nice clinic. Your boss seems nice, too."

"Vic? We get along now," Fletch replied. "But that's a long story."

"We'll have time," his dad replied.

"Look, I forgot about the time change. Maybe you are hungry? Did you just arrive?"

"Let's pick up some pop at a drive-through and then go to your place," Frank suggested. "I can't get enough pop."

"Sure. How did you get here?"

"Taxi," his mother said. "The driver was so nice."

Fletch had forgotten that about his mom. To her, everybody was so nice. Truth was, everybody loved her, too.

Frank got in the front passenger seat, and Fletch, still reeling from the shock, moved as if he walked inside his own dream. He opened the back door of the Focus for his mom and hurried round to the driver's side.

He pulled into the street and looked in his rearview mirror. "There's a little place called the Eskimo Queen. I can get you some pop there."

"Oh, I'd like a cone, too," Mom piped up.

A pang from some long-forgotten memories shot through him. He'd forgotten what it was like to be out of the country for so long and then wanting to make up for all their deprivations.

Dad thumped the dashboard. "This baby sure has held up."

"Yes. And hopefully it will for a while longer. Till I graduate and get a job."

"Doesn't the vet pay you, dear?"

"Just enough to cover the basics, Mom."

"All that's needed," Dad added. "The Lord supplies."

His dad firmly believed that, which was probably why he hadn't flinched when finding out he could lose Marshall's support. They pulled into the fast-food place, and Fletch picked up the items that would satisfy his parents' cravings, refusing his dad's offer to pay.

"This is wonderful. Thanks, honey," his mom purred from the backseat. "But you didn't get anything, Fletch."

"I'm good." They drove in silence for several moments until he realized that in all the excitement, he'd forgotten Buddy. "I need to backtrack. I forgot my dog. I need to get him because sometimes Vic has to leave in a hurry."

"Oh, you have a dog? That's fine. We like looking around."

"I don't live far, anyways."

Once he'd gotten Buddy, he cracked open the back door. "You want him, Mom, or should I put him in the front with Dad?"

"I'll take him," she replied.

Buddy jumped up on the floorboards. As Fletch had suspected, the basset took to Mom like he did all females, and she seemed to like him, too, but moments later, he heard her admonish Buddy to keep away from her ice-cream cone. His heart ached to think that his parents had swept into his life to touch his heart and flirt with his emotions only to leave him again. For regardless of what his dad had said about quitting mission work, Fletch wouldn't allow himself to believe they would stay long. Africa was their life. He was sure they would never leave it.

Inside his apartment, he motioned for them to sit, at the same time sweeping up a pair of underwear, socks, and a T-shirt and tossing them into a clothesbasket in his closet. "Sorry about that."

"Bachelors." His mom smiled. "Do you have any girlfriends?"

Fletch sat on the edge of his bed, allowing his parents to have the two chairs at the table. He didn't want to talk about himself, especially something so personal as his love life, but he didn't want to disappoint his mother's concerned curiosity. He'd never been able to figure out how she remained so upbeat and sweet, given their exposure to hardships, and the difficulty of living with Dad.

"I think so."

Dad found that amusing. "If you're in a state of confusion, then you're probably in love. Oh wonderful, hopeless love."

"Now Frank, let the boy speak for himself."

Dad deferred to Mom, probably wanting to watch Fletch squirm.

Fletch figured that if he started at the beginning, by the time he got to the end of his story, he might have figured out how to explain Lil. "Last summer I met a Conservative Mennonite girl. Her name is Lil." He saw his parents' surprise and continued, "She's a feisty little thing, not your typical. . . . Well, I never knew another Conservative girl. Anyway, we've been dating, but there've been some outside problems, so it's not been smooth sailing."

Dad slapped his knee. "What did I tell you?"

"Problems with her family?" Mom gently probed.

"Yes." Fletch got up to refill Buddy's water dish. "Actually the video I told you about, Dad? It was her farm. Her dad and brothers took a disliking to me after that." He rubbed his shoulder as he went back to the edge of his bed. "I'm still sore from spending all day Friday helping them erect two hoop barns. Figured I needed to make amends."

"Did you?" she asked.

"Yes. But there's still the issue of whose church we'll attend." He sighed. "And my uncertain future, her career. . ."

"Career?" Dad asked.

"She's head chef at a reputable restaurant, and she's very into it."

"Oh, a wonderful cook. Lucky boy." That was his mom again, looking on the bright side. "Can we meet her?"

"Well sure. How long are you going to be here? Do you have a place to stay? I can sleep on the floor if you need a place."

"Thanks, son. We'd be happy to take you up on that. Long as your boss doesn't mind."

Fletch couldn't believe they actually intended to move in with him, but then he realized that's what always happened with them. How many times had they stayed with friends, moving from place to place? "You saw for yourself that Vic was happy to see you."

"Tell him he doesn't have to pay us, too," Dad joked.

"It will be so wonderful to catch up, won't it?" Mom added.

"Yes. It's good to have you."

"It feels so right," she added. "But of course we'll find a place of our own as soon as we find some work."

"You're going to spend your entire furlough here?" Fletch asked tentatively.

The straw in Dad's super-sized drink hit air, and he set his cup aside. "I thought I explained that over the phone. We aren't going back to Africa."

Fletch's heart flopped like a bass in a net. "I thought you were. . . just dreaming."

"No dear," Mom tried to explain. "We grew restless there. It was as if God was prompting us to come home. To get to know you again. And then God supplied the mission with a young, eager couple to replace us."

Home? Get to know him? Ohio wasn't their real home, but Fletch let out a sputtering laugh. "Well then, welcome to Plain City, Ohio."

❧

That evening, Fletch grilled hamburgers while Dad watched, cola in one hand, the other scratching the basset. Inside, Mom was cooking potatoes in the microwave.

When he had apologized for not having a real kitchen, she cheerfully replied, "I've cooked with less."

He supposed that was why they didn't think his studio apartment was too small for the three of them. When a text message came through on his phone, he was happy for the diversion, even though it was from Marcus. Until he read the message: DAD'S IN TOWN. HE WANTS TO TAKE US TO DINNER TOMORROW NIGHT.

Fletch released a sarcastic laugh. "You aren't going to believe this. I just got a text from Marcus. Marshall's in town. He wants to take me to dinner tomorrow night."

"I want to see him. See if we can all go."

Fletch nodded and replied:

> GREAT. MY PARENTS ARE HERE, STAYING WITH ME.
> BRING THEM ALONG. BE HERE AROUND SIX?
> CAN WE JUST MEET AT THE RESTAURANT?

Fletch flipped the burgers and added cheese, waiting for a reply. Finally Marcus sent him the name of a restaurant.

"This should be interesting," Dad remarked.

"He's mad at me, you know."

"Marshall should be worrying about his soul."

"He's such a nice man."

Fletch started. Mom stood on the tiny patio with them. She moved quiet as a mouse. He'd forgotten that, too.

"Invite your Lil to come. The potatoes are done."

Lil. He'd forgotten all about her. She probably wondered why he hadn't stopped in to talk after her apology. He'd go over after church—that is, if he could get a moment away from his parents.

CHAPTER 32

Lil blinked back tears and tried hard to remember why she had wanted to become a head chef, for there wasn't any glory in having to apologize to a customer for finding a hair in his meal. Why, he'd stared at her head as if it had been hers! Before that, there had been a commotion in the hostess area. A young man had been handing out flyers and boycotting her veal. She wondered if it was one of the volunteers from the shelter. Surely Ashley wouldn't do that to her. Or would they? To get revenge on Fletch?

And Fletch. . .she hadn't heard from him since the day he helped with the hoop barns. He had admitted he was too tired to think. Now he was probably wishing he had broken up with her on the spot, maybe that was even what he had been trying to do. The very thought made pain flash through her heart.

"Miss Landis! Lily!"

She swiped her arm across her eyes and wheeled about. "Yes?"

"Thomas burned his hand in a grease fire. Should he drive himself to the hospital?"

With a gasp of disbelief, she clattered through the kitchen to his station, pushing through the huddling cooks. "Move, please. Let me see."

Thomas held his arms out, and Lil felt sick to her stomach to see the large patches of reddened, blistering skin. "Elaine! You take him."

Quickly washing her hands and pulling on some gloves, Lil intended to take over both their places. She saw that the fire had been put out, but the work area needed to be cleaned. With a sinking heart, she realized she couldn't do everything. Tearing off her gloves, again, she went to the house phone and tried to recruit some workers because it was Saturday, their busiest night.

By the end of the evening, Lil's nerves were completely frazzled. Her legs hurt and her feet burned. At least Elaine had returned with a good report on Thomas. When the last customer departed and everything was finally put back in order, she called Camila to report the injury. The Italian matron told Lil she needed to keep all her tomatoes on the counter before they were all swimming in sauce. Because tomato sauce wasn't made for drowning people but for the taste buds, and did she understand that? Or did she need to come to the restaurant and explain it to her?

Lillian apologized and promised it wouldn't happen again. But she had wanted to shout, "Now I know why Giovanni went to Italy!"

⁓⌒

On Sunday afternoon while Fletch's parents enjoyed a siesta, he went to the doddy house. To his pleased surprise, Lil came to the door.

"Hi. Would you like to go for a walk? Sometimes I can think better when I'm doing something."

"Will swinging work?"

He thought about the cottonwood tree at the Landis farm. About their first kiss. "You have a swing here?"

"Yep." She led him around to the back of the doddy house. A swing wide enough for two was suspended from a spreading oak tree.

"I didn't know this was back here. M'Lil, first." He gave a mock bow, gesturing for her to be seated.

"That's because Megan's dad just put it up yesterday. You should have dated her when you had the chance. Her parents are supportive, and she doesn't have a dozen stubborn brothers."

He settled in next to her. "Megan's a nice girl"—he heard his mother's voice horning in on his date—"but it was you I wanted to date."

Lil glanced up at him and smiled. "Are you saying you still want to?"

"I'd like nothing more."

"Me, too. I'm sorry that I pushed you away."

He took her hand. "You'll try to trust me?"

She nodded. "Yes."

"Thank you." She looked so lost and vulnerable, and he longed to kiss away her misgivings. But if he did that, he'd forget all the important things he wanted her to know about him.

"I believe I've made amends with your family. Do you feel like I have?"

"Oh yes. Everyone's forgiven you. You've helped them, and the offense is all in the past now."

"Good. I know we still don't agree on which church we'll attend and that serving the Lord is important to both of us. You're just getting settled in your career, and I don't even know if I'm staying in Plain City. But"—he saw her brows crease with worry and continued—"we'll get to those things, if you still want to date me after you've met my parents."

Her face lit up with surprise. "They're here?"

"The three of us are squeezed into my studio apartment."

Her hand flew out of his, and she grasped his sore arm. "When did they come? How long will they stay? When can I meet them? What if they don't like me?"

"Whoa, whoa. Lily? You want to meet them?"

"Yes, but what if they think I'm too plain for you?"

Fletch chuckled. "That's the least of our worries. They'll adore you. But it's not going to be the most conducive atmosphere for a first meeting."

He saw her growing confusion and anxiety. "I'm trying to trust you."

"Marshall's also in town. He's taking me and my parents to dinner tonight, and my mom insists you come, too. You can refuse if it's too much."

"She insisted? Why? Is she worried I won't be right for you?"

"No. She's excited to meet you."

Lil fidgeted with her skirt. "What time?"

"Six." Fletch glanced at his watch. "It's 3:30 now. I can come pick you up on our way to the restaurant, or else you can come with me when I leave, which would give you some time to meet my parents before we meet Marshall. I'll let you decide."

"Oh." Lil sucked in her bottom lip and glanced at the oak's canopy. "I think either would work. What do you think would be best?"

"I'd like you to come back with me now."

"All right!" she said, jumping up.

Fletch reached out and caught her by the arm. "Not now! I just got here. And we have some making up to do."

She tilted her face. "I thought we just did that."

"You're right, we did." He gave her his most persuasive smile. "But I thought we might work on our tradition." Slowly he pulled her closer.

"I don't know what you mean," she teased.

"I think your meeting my parents calls for a good-luck kiss."

"Or two, if I recall."

He'd just pulled her into his lap, when Megan called, "There you two are. My dad's here to put sealer on the swing."

Lil fairly flew out of his arms, and he felt his own cheeks sting as he rose to meet Megan's dad for the first time. Fletch wondered if Lil really knew Megan's parents at all, because Mr. Weaver didn't seem all that friendly or lenient. And then he remembered Lil saying that he was an elder at their church.

CHAPTER 33

And so a monkey was the culprit after all," Bonnie exclaimed.

Lil's eyes widened as she followed the graceful movements of the amazing woman wearing a flowered shirtdress. "And if I could have caught that miscreant, at that moment, he would have landed in the stewpot. After that, Frank fixed the window, and the creature never ventured inside again."

Bonnie's story captured Lil's imagination as much as the floor's old-world Saltillo tile and the bright blue-and-orange tiles that graced the walls around them with painted images of birds and flowers. The Mexican restaurant's huge potted plants easily swept Lil into the jungle mood.

"Oh, it was Bonnie's scream that scared it away, but she softened over the years. She even fed an orphan vervet two years ago."

"Yes. I suppose I did. But enough talk about us. Lil, I hear you love to cook?"

"Never tried monkey stew, but I have ventured out a bit from the traditional Mennonite fare."

"I like that." Frank sent Fletch a look that Lil translated as positive. But the atmosphere changed immensely when moments later,

Marshall, Marcus, and Ashley joined them. The other girl was dressed in tight black slacks and a glittery beaded top that once might have made Lil feel plain. But oddly, she didn't feel any barriers between them. She greeted her with enthusiasm.

Fletch jumped to his feet to greet Marshall. By their emotional embrace, Lil could see that whatever their differences, the reunion touched them both.

Marshall also greeted Fletch's parents warmly. Next, he came to Lil's chair with a tight smile. "And this must be the girl."

The words could have been meant for a compliment, implying she was special, but the way he said *the* made it seem like just the opposite. Lil interpreted it as "the girl who interfered with my plans for you."

She glanced at Fletch and saw a flicker of pain cross his eyes, but he didn't respond as if he had been offended. "Yes, Lillian Landis. May I introduce my special friend, Marshall Lewis."

"I've never met anyone from Texas before. I wish I had a poem or something for you to read. I love listening to your voice."

"He could read us the menu," Frank suggested, causing everyone to laugh.

"And ya have an accent as well. What is it?"

"Dutch, I suppose. My grandparents spoke a form of German that our people refer to as Dutch."

He glanced at her covering. "I see. Charmed to meet ya."

When everyone was seated, Fletch gave her hand a squeeze from under the table.

Lil quietly sized up the situation. Marshall, who was footing the bill, had called the group together and was the man in charge. Frank, who had a commanding presence, seemed the most at ease. Conversation lulled in an almost awkward silence as they looked over the menu, which Marshall chose not to read to the others.

After the orders were taken, bowls of chips and salsa appeared.

With the lively background music, Lil couldn't catch all of the conversation, but she had just raised her water to her lips when she clearly heard, "I guess ya'll know about my absurd situation?"

Peering over the rim of her glass, she saw that Marshall had directed

605

his gaze at Frank.

"It is tragic. I suppose it's those nasty cigars."

Lil choked, and quickly brought her napkin to cover her mouth.

"That's the spirit. I hate when ya'll gush over me. Just wanted to get it out in the open and over with. Now we can enjoy ourselves."

Lil dipped a chip in the small bowl of salsa she was sharing with Fletch, who at best looked dismayed.

"It is wonderful to see ya'll again." Marshall was talking to Fletch's parents. "But it is for Fletch's sake that I called this little rendezvous." He tapped a chip with a ringed finger, then brought it to his mouth. She got a flash of his watch, its face encircled in clear jewels, and Lil guessed that they were real diamonds.

"For me?" Fletch asked.

"Yes, I know we've been playing a little cat and mouse lately, but let's just say I have a new perspective. Cancer does that. I want to offer ya a real job."

Lil joined the others in staring at Fletch. She saw his jaw clench and knew that he was bracing himself for yet another of Marshall's schemes.

"You've already done more for our family than we can ever repay. Perhaps we've. . .I've leaned too heavily on your generosity. I need to learn to. . .make my own way."

"Of course. Ya want to prove your manhood. Maturity includes the ability to recognize opportunities. Life-changing opportunities."

Lil clasped her hands in her lap, her face on fire in embarrassment for Fletch. How could he have been so enamored and under the spell of this condescending man? If not for Fletch's parents and Marshall's cancer, she might not have been able to hold her tongue.

Beside her, Fletch said, "I'm listening."

"I'm going to set ya up at the shelter. The shelter of your choice. If you're not happy at the Plain City Shelter here with my Marcus, there's the farm in Indiana. I believe we need a full-time veterinarian on staff." He waved a flash of diamonds. "Take your time to decide." He ran a warning gaze over Lil, and it sent a chill down her spine. She jutted her chin and met his disdainful gaze, but beneath the table, she twisted her napkin.

"It's a generous offer."

And it was, because Fletch had told her that getting started wasn't easy.

"But the shelter is not my cause."

Lil felt relief flood over her. She'd never felt as attracted to Fletch as she did at that moment.

"I'll probably take an internship after I graduate. I'm sure the school will have some recommendations."

"I find your rejection quite disrespectful."

"Now wait a minute," Frank interrupted. "You don't own my son."

Marshall set down his water glass so forcefully that it spilled onto the table. "I've been more of a father to him than ya have."

"Gentlemen," Bonnie said, "please, calm yourselves."

"And lower your voices," Marcus added. "People are staring."

"Let them stare! I'll buy this restaurant," Marshall cursed. "See if I care about gawkers!"

Lil's family may have had their share of arguments around the kitchen table, but they never had made themselves a public spectacle.

Marshall glared at Frank. "I've a mind to withdraw my support."

Frank replied calmly, "Marshall, that is not the important thing here. Nor any of your charitable causes, commendable as your life has been in that area and appreciative as I am for your support over the years. But now is the time for you to search your soul. You don't have time for anything less."

"I don't want to hear ya'll—"Marshall suddenly coughed and lost his voice. The southerner slumped, took several deep wheezing breaths.

"Dad?"

"This isn't finished," he gasped, standing up. He clenched his fists, then turned abruptly and left the dining room.

Marcus slapped a couple of large bills on the table and hurried after his dad.

"Sorry, everybody," Ashley mumbled, then scurried to catch up with the Lewis men.

They could hear Marshall coughing as he left the restaurant.

"He's a changed man," Bonnie gasped. "I don't even recognize him."

Fletch turned to Lil. "He wasn't like this before."

"Are you sure you just never crossed his purposes before?"

"No, he and Frank have had a few differences," Bonnie explained. "It must be the cancer."

"He's a desperate man," Frank observed. "He's worked hard to buy his way into heaven. And he's afraid he hasn't done enough."

After Marshall left, everyone was subdued. Frank made an attempt to praise his son for holding his ground, but Fletch simply withdrew. And when he dropped Lil back off at the doddy house, he was still restless, as if the argument was working on him.

They stood on the doddy house porch while Lil looked for her keys.

"Sorry for a terrible evening."

"Almost made me feel at home."

"Hardly."

"I like your parents, but your dad isn't the way I had him pictured." Fletch gave a bitter laugh. "How's that?"

"I expected a missionary to be gentle, but he's so bold."

She saw Fletch flinch and wished she'd kept her observation to herself. He didn't need more ammunition against his father.

"Domineering. And I need to get him out of my house before he drives me crazy."

"Your mom is sweet."

"Yes, but she's spunky. She has to be to live with him."

"Are you worried about Marshall?"

"Of course I am," he snapped. "The man's dying. He's trying to tie up loose ends, and we picked a fight with him. He's always been there for me. Now when he needs me. . .I'm rejecting him."

"It was almost like he came trying to pick a fight."

Fletch narrowed his eyes. "We told you, he's changed. That's the whole point. He's struggling right now. What if that whole scene was a struggle of wills. And the only reason my dad came was to win?"

"Win what?"

"Me. You heard what Marshall told him. That he was more of a father than my dad had ever been."

"Well if he came to win you back, then that's a good thing, isn't it?

That he realizes he made a mistake and—"

"Not to win my affection. Just to win out over Marshall."

"Oh, Fletch. I don't know, I—"

"I don't expect you to understand any of this. Look. I need some time to sort through all this. I need to go. I'll be in touch."

"In touch?" Lil felt her stomach knot with confusion and dread. "Fletch, what are you saying?"

"Don't try to put words in my mouth."

"I'm not."

"Good." He reached up and touched her chin, stared into her eyes, but she felt like his soul was miles away, perhaps back at the restaurant or even traveling out to the shelter where Marshall was staying. Would he go out to see him once he left her? Or would he go back to his apartment to his sleeping bag on the floor?

His caress on her chin was a far cry from the good-luck kiss he had promised earlier in the day, the one Megan's dad had spoiled for them. She nodded, leaned her cheek into his hand, hoping he would understand her need. But he pulled away and strode silently to his car.

Lil sank to the stoop in despair, silent tears rolling down her cheeks. Just when she'd decided to give her all to this relationship, he'd pulled away. She wondered if this was how miserable he'd been feeling when she was the one dragging her feet. But then she remembered the promise she had made him. *I trust you, Fletch Stauffer. You may not believe in yourself right now, but I do.*

She gazed up at the expanse of glittering September stars and realized that she hadn't spoken to God for a while. She dipped her face in the crook of her arms and apologized to the One who had formed both their souls. Marshall's face popped into her mind, and she wanted to squirm out of praying for the man whose cold eyes had warned her to stay away from Fletch. Or were they daring her to pray for him?

—◡—

"You didn't have to wait up." Fletch patted Buddy on the head and put his car keys on a small hook.

"This is close quarters, dear. We are rather in this all together," Mom replied. "We've been sitting on the patio. But it got chilly so I made us some decaf coffee. Would you like a cup?"

"Sure."

Fletch slipped to the floor, careful not to spill his coffee, and leaned his back against his bed.

"That's a lot of sighing going on down there," she said from her seat at the table.

"It just feels like we've used Marshall for his money, and now that he needs us to walk with him, we're tossing him aside."

"If that were the case," Dad replied, "we would be staying all the more in his good graces in hopes of getting something out of his will. A friend tells the truth, even when it hurts."

"But does it have to be so harsh?" Fletch asked, which really was a major issue he had with his dad.

"I was proud of your firmness with Marshall."

"He called it disrespect."

"No, you weren't disrespectful, dear. It's just that Marshall wanted you to accept so badly that he lashed out. And Frank, put some sugar in your coffee beans."

"So you both think I came across too strong."

"He could be the apostle Paul's twin," Mom observed.

Dad ignored her comment. "What I told him, about searching his soul? That goes for you, too, son."

"What's that supposed to mean?"

"I sense restlessness in you."

Not until you came.

"Just make sure you're following your calling, not man's."

"Marshall was there for me when I didn't know what classes to take. He pointed out my natural gifts and talents when I didn't think I had any."

"There's more than one reason your mother calls me the apostle Paul. When I was young, I resisted God's call. I was a rebel. My dad forced me into a box so I fled. I'd turned my back on God altogether until I was in a motorcycle accident and fell in love with my nurse. But she wouldn't have anything to do with me. That's when I looked inside.

Tried to figure out why."

He chuckled. "And there it was all the time, the call to adventure. Only not motorcycles, but Africa. I guess that's why I never tried to interfere with your life. I didn't want to push you to rebel, like my dad did me." Sadly, Dad swirled the shallow contents of his cup. "I guess I gave you too long of a leash. And I certainly didn't expect a stranger to step in and do what I tried not to do."

"I guess the leash was so long I didn't realize it existed. I felt alone in a big world. Bigger than most kids'. I didn't have a backyard to play in. I had a jungle. You know?"

Mom stared into her cup.

"Just don't make the same mistake I did," Dad replied, "and run from your calling just because your father didn't do his job right."

"And. . ." Mom shot Dad a stern look.

"And. . . God's been nudging me to come to you. I didn't know why until I got here. But now I understand. I need your forgiveness for how I've treated you."

Fletch hadn't hoped for affection from the man who never showed him the acceptance he craved. But when it came, it deeply moved him. It carried something divine in it that couldn't be denied. He was ready to forgive. Ready to find healing. He went to his dad. Opened his arms.

Dad gripped him in an ironlike embrace.

Fletch whispered, "I forgive you."

"I love you," Dad said, releasing him and clapping his shoulders.

There was more shoulder clapping and bear hugs and manly sniffles, and finally Fletch realized that some of them were feminine, too. He went to his mom and gently embraced her.

"Love you, Mom."

When they'd finished, Fletch sank back to the floor, clasping his bent knees and swiping his arm across his eyes. "Thanks for coming home."

"Well!" Mom exclaimed. "Tomorrow is job hunting. Won't that be fun!" And with that, they all fell to laughing and yawning and getting their beds in order.

But Fletch couldn't fall asleep. First of all, Dad snored. Secondly, if

God had blessed him by healing the rift he'd always felt toward his dad, then maybe he needed to take what his dad had told him to heart. The part about searching his soul and hearing his calling.

Had he ever really done that, or had he just assumed Marshall's guidance was right for him? He had never questioned Marshall until lately. Had he been rejecting his dad, or had he been rejecting God's calling? He plumped his pillow and turned to his side. And what about Lil? Would she be patient while he sorted through this? She was a girl who'd always known what she wanted. What would she think of his uncertainty?

CHAPTER 34

Lil blew her bangs out of her eyes, not wanting to reposition her bobby pins, because then she'd have to wash her hands again. The pins were no good, too loose. She might as well toss them in the trash. She was going over her supply list one final time because yesterday they'd run low on mozzarella cheese and had to skimp.

"Hi, Lil." Megan now had the run of the restaurant, being given the VIP treatment every time she popped over from nearby Char Air.

Lil looked up. "Is it one o'clock already?"

"Yep. I just have five minutes though, because I have to run some errands for the boss."

Lil glanced up, forever searching her friend's expression at the mention of her good-looking, off-limits boss. But Megan had become good at concealing her feelings about him.

Megan sniffed with pleasure. "Got a doggie bag for me?"

Lil yelled over her shoulder, "Elaine! Bag some spaghetti for me?"

"What time will you be home tonight?"

"I'll be late. Fletch came over last night and invited me to go to dinner at his boss's."

Megan made an ugly face. "Another dinner? The last one had you in a funk for over a week."

"I know. But Vic's never asked him before. And Fletch wants to talk to me about something. I'm thinking it must be something good. He wouldn't take me to his boss's to break up with me, right?"

Megan leaned on the counter. "He's not going to break up. He loves you."

"It's rocky right now. You know that."

Elaine brought the doggie bag, and Megan thanked her. "He's probably going to apologize for his behavior the last couple of weeks. Sorry. I've gotta go."

Lil had just started concentrating on her list again when she heard the hostess take a reservation for a large party of Ranco customers. The back room would have to be prepared. She was going to have to hustle to make her date.

—⁄⁀⁄—

Lil felt dazzled from the moment she stepped into the softly lit foyer of the Fullers' two-story, track home and handed her coat to Britt. The other woman wore a jean skirt that skimmed her knees and a pink sweater set. She had silver hoop earrings that flashed in and out of her dark bob. Soft, side-swept bangs fringed expressive brown eyes. She still carried some of her baby fat from her last child, but it softened her in a pleasing way, as did her generous smile. "Come into the kitchen. I have some appetizers. If we don't get to them soon, the kids will."

They moved past a magazine-worthy living room and stepped into a tiled, open area that served as kitchen, breakfast nook, and family room. Vic motioned Fletch to a sectional where he was watching a sports game on the television.

Fletch squeezed Lil's hand, and she whispered, "Go ahead. I'm fine."

Britt called to her husband, "Vic! Why don't you turn the TV off?"

"Oh." The thin, redheaded vet shot Lil a contrite expression and reached for the remote. "Sorry."

"You don't have to do that on my account," Lil said. "But thanks for the offer."

"You sure?" he asked, looking to his wife for validation.

Britt shrugged, and Vic returned the remote to the side table.

"Can I help with anything?"

"No, just pull up a barstool. Only, I can't believe I'm cooking for you. Vic told me you're head chef at Volo Italiano."

Lil shifted in the stool. "Where I was on my feet all day. But then, I suppose you were, too."

Taking the sour cream container from the refrigerator, Britt replied, "Not all day. I shuffled the boys off to school, did two loads of laundry, and some dinner preparations. But before I had to pick them up again, I watched my favorite reality show. I tape it and treat myself each—I'm sorry." She dropped the sour cream lid on the counter and shook her head. "I'm as bad as Vic. Watching television isn't all we do. I mean—"

"Please," Lil interrupted. "I'm in your home. I understand that most people watch television. In fact, a lot of restaurants have them, too. Although the church I attend doesn't allow them, I've broken the rules a few times."

Britt added the sour cream to her stroganoff, turned off the burner, and stirred the sauce until it was blended. She whispered, "Don't tell the kids, but I've been known to bend a few, too."

"Oops. Sorry," Lil said, looking to see if any of the boys had overheard their conversation, but Fletch was showing them how to build a truck with their plastic building blocks.

Lil took a bite of the cracker appetizers, swallowed, and ventured, "Can I ask you a personal question?"

"Of course."

"How do you get your bangs to do that? Mine are about that length, and all they ever do is fall in my eyes."

Britt carried her skillet to the counter with a stack of plates, glancing at Lil's hair. "I can help you with that. After dinner, I'll get out my straight iron."

Lil moved to hand her plates as Britt served up their dinner. "You can do that with a straight iron?"

"Yep. I can finish here if you want to call the guys."

Lil strolled across the sparkling tile to the family room and placed a hand on Fletch's shoulder. "Britt wants us to come eat."

Vic flicked off his show and gathered up his boys. Lil was glad Britt was keeping it casual, the adults dining at the kitchen table while the boys ate at the kitchen island.

Vic cleared his throat. "Fletch, you want to pray?"

"Wait, boys," Britt told her sons, who had already started eating.

Lil bit back a smile as the youngsters' forks clanged onto the granite countertop. Fletch took her hand.

"Lord, I thank You for this home and for providing me with such a generous employer. Bless Britt for making this meal, and bless the boys in all they do. I thank You for this food. Amen."

"That was nice," Britt said. "But you do realize that since you two got involved in my husband's life, our world has turned topsy-turvy."

Fletch's fork stopped halfway to his mouth. "Just for the record, it was really Lil who wrecked your car."

Lil grimaced. "Sorry about that. It was how we met."

"Tell us what really happened that day, Lil," Vic urged.

When the story had been told, the couple agreed with Fletch that it was Lil's fault, after all. But the dinner turned out to be nothing like the meal with Marshall. This one was warm and personal, and Lil felt as though she'd made friends with Vic and Britt.

On the ride home, Fletch reached across the console and touched her hand. "I like your hair."

She gave her bangs a puff. "These? Thanks. Britt has a knack. She's pretty and sweet. But I was kind of surprised that she doesn't work. She really had her house in order."

"She's a stay-at-home mom."

Lil watched the moonlit trees moving past her window. "In the Conservative Church, we don't even use that expression. It's taken for granted. It's just what women do."

"Not all of them," Fletch observed.

Lil ignored his reference to her own career. "Britt seems to be a good mother. I mean, it would be better if she took the boys to church, but. . .I liked her."

"Vic claims she's great with the boys. He just wishes she didn't like to spend money."

Lil laughed. "Ugh, money. I don't even have time to spend mine anymore."

Fletch fell into a contemplative mood until they reached the doddy house. "Can we sit in the car and talk?"

When he had picked her up that evening, he had given her a quick apology about being in a bad mood the last time they were together. She assumed that was their talk. Now, her apprehension returned. "Sure."

He turned to face her. "Let me start by telling you that my dad and I worked some things out, and things are better between us. But he said some things that got me to thinking. He asked me if I was running from God's calling."

"Isn't your veterinary career your calling?"

"I thought so, but I've been praying, and now I see there's more to it. I don't know how to tell you—I know that your career is important to you, and I don't know how this will affect our relationship."

"What is it?" she asked nervously.

"You know how I've always vowed that I would never go into missionary work?"

Lil felt her heart sinking into despair. She blurted out, "You want to be a missionary?"

Fletch sighed. Became stone still.

"I mean, is that it?" Lil urged, seeing she'd frustrated him.

"I was afraid that would be your response. I had hoped you'd be willing to at least consider. . ." His voice faltered.

"It's just that I didn't see this coming. It's out of the blue. Are your parents going back to Africa? Are you going with them?"

"No. But there's a program at OSU. It's available for veterinary students. They go to other countries to treat and train others regarding the care of their farm animals. It's called Christian Veterinary Mission. I want to check it out. Try to understand. All this time I thought I was rejecting my dad. Now I wonder if I was rejecting God's calling. I need to find out."

"I don't know what to say. This is so unexpected." Lil shook her head and stared straight ahead, unable to meet his gaze given the way he was breaking her heart.

"Lily," he pleaded. "Look at me."

She turned, fighting back tears of resentment that he would come into her life and make her fall for him. He had persuaded her to trust him. Just when she was willing to give their relationship her all, he got restless on her. And now he wanted to run off and find himself doing missionary work. As if their church predicament wasn't bad enough.

"Lil?"

At his request, she stared into his pleading brown eyes, knowing that she would never recover from loving him. "What?"

"I want you to know I love you."

She shook her head. "Why would you tell me that now?"

"Because I'm asking you to wait."

"What?"

"A little while. Give me time to talk to my professor and find out more. Time to pray. I need to spend time with my dad. If God wants us together, He's going to make a way for us. Right now, if I asked you to marry me, I wouldn't even know what I was offering you."

"Have you heard me asking for a marriage proposal?" Why couldn't they just go on dating. Let things work out?

"Isn't that where we're headed?"

She bit her lip to keep from saying something that would ruin all her chances with him. "If you love me at all, will you wait and pray? For us?"

"Let me get this straight. We're not exactly breaking up, just taking a break? And am I supposed to be trusting you during this little interval?"

"I think it would be better if we both trusted God right now."

"Whew!" She puffed her bangs again. That clarified things.

⁓

Furious, Lil slammed the door and marched through the doddy house. "Megan!"

Peeking over the arm of the sofa and looking at her with one eye, for the other was covered with a waterfall of hair, Megan replied, "What?"

Lil sank to the sofa.

Megan snatched up her legs to keep them from getting crushed.

Lil tossed Megan's Christian novel onto the coffee table.

"You just lost my page." Megan ran a hand up the side of her face, further ruffling her hair. "You crying?"

"I just got dumped."

"He didn't!"

"He's dumping me to become a missionary."

Megan suddenly perked up. "What? Did he ask you to go with him? Did you even give it any thought?"

Lil's mouth flopped open. "I shouldn't have expected you to understand. And no, he didn't ask me." She stopped, thought back to make sure that he hadn't. She was unsure. "He wants me to wait for him while he figures out his future. Later, if I fit into his plans, he might be back. I don't think he's willing to make compromises anymore. He's taking charge. He's changing."

"That all sounds pretty iffy," Megan said with disappointment.

"I didn't see this coming. I thought our last hurdle was deciding which church to attend."

Megan wrapped an arm around Lil. "I'm so sorry. I don't suppose there're any Italian restaurants in Africa?" But then her friend turned thoughtful. "Well we don't know that for a fact, do we?"

"It's not about me. I'm not the barrier. I don't even like my stupid job."

Her face twisting in horrific disbelief, Megan blinked. "You don't?"

"It's not as glamorous as I thought it would be. It's glorified slavery. The higher up you go, the harder the work."

"Really?"

"Trust me. Tonight when we were at Britt and Vic's, I envied her for her little homemaking life."

"Has your face been too close to the gas burner all day?"

"I've been trying to tell you. And Fletch, too. Except, I haven't seen him that much lately. And nobody's listening. Maybe I need to do like he's doing and go find myself."

"That's kinda scary, because you always knew what you wanted."

"I thought I knew what I wanted." Slinky rubbed against Lil's ankles. She swept the purring kitten up against her cheek then settled him on her lap.

"Let's back up. Fletch wants to find himself?"

"Yes, but he didn't put it that way. He said we needed to pray. He told me not to trust him, but to trust God."

Megan tilted her head thoughtfully. "There's nothing wrong with that advice. For any of us."

Lil gave Megan a sideways glance. "Your boss isn't bothering you, is he?"

"No, but something's bothering him, and of course, that affects me, but I do like my job. I'm sorry you don't."

Lil felt suddenly weary. It felt like they were talking in circles, and it had already been such a trying day for her. There had been too many trying days in a row. She was exhausted. "Thanks for being here for me. I don't know what I'd do without you."

CHAPTER 35

Rolling the kinks out of his shoulders, Fletch climbed out of Vic's pickup and followed the vet into the clinic. Successive nights of camping out in a sleeping bag on the floor of his apartment was taking its toll. Make that half a sleeping bag. Buddy assumed the floor pallet was an invitation for him. The dog's dead weight wouldn't budge. His breath wasn't that appealing either.

He opened the clinic's back door for the guilty party to use the dog walk. When he went back inside, Vic asked him to go fetch an extra cage from the truck.

Fletch stepped back outside, and a swirl of brown leaves skittered across his red sneakers and down the sidewalk.

"It only takes one hard freeze. Soon they'll all be dead. All gone."

He halted. Turned. "Marshall?"

The older man raised a gloved hand. "I came to apologize. Your dad was right. I've been manipulating ya, and that was wrong." He sighed deeply and cleared his throat. "I didn't do it on purpose. There's so little time, and in my mind I thought I knew what would be best for everybody. But I can't make the world a perfect place."

"I understand. Earth's far from perfect. Or fair. It hurt, bad, to hear about your cancer. But there are survivors."

"I won't be one of them. The most we can do is slow it down." He squatted and picked up a leaf. Crumbled it. Scattered it on the sidewalk. "It's only a matter of time."

There was no changing that, Fletch thought glumly.

The southerner stood. "On the bright side, I'm taking your dad to lunch tomorrow."

Giving Marshall a wry smile, Fletch said, "Now that's a scary thought." Although Marshall's anger had dissipated and he was releasing his control over Fletch, this still wasn't the friend that Fletch had known all his life. This was a grieving man.

He was thrilled Marshall was having lunch with his dad. But after the scene at the restaurant, the image that shot in his mind—of Frank and Marshall chatting together—was that of a pile of leaves and a match.

"I'm going to give him one shot to preach to me."

"You are?" Fletch had to chuckle now. "I mean, that's great." God did have a sense of humor to orchestrate this—Marshall's most important moment on earth. But after all those years of Marshall supporting Dad's ministry, it was the perfect plan. Fletch's admiration for both men grew considerably. For his dad, because he'd been tough but said just the right thing to set Marshall thinking. For Marshall, because he wasn't bowing to his pride.

And if God could set Marshall's mind at peace, then Fletch should be able to trust Him with his own future.

Marshall reached into his coat pocket and pulled out an envelope. "Ya know how I like to give gifts?"

"Oh no, Marshall. Please don't—"

"It's for Lily. I think I offended her."

Join the club, Fletch thought, remembering how she flew out of his car in a tiff on their last date. He took the paper that Marshall offered. "What's this?"

"It's a phone number of a Mexican restaurant chain that will give the Landis family a contract if they agree to certain organic methods."

Shaking his head, Fletch stared at the paper. "I don't know how to thank you. It's too much."

"I think Lily's perfect for you. She was delightful, by the way. Makes me think of my Barbara. She passed long ago. Now she was a fine Christian woman."

"I wish I could have met her." He would give the information to Matt. His friend was supporting him in his decision to take a break from Lil. To figure out what he really wanted to do with his future. A lump formed in his throat at Marshall's generosity. "Lil's friend Megan loves her job."

"Good. Good."

Fletch stepped forward. "Thank you for everything. You've been such a blessing in my life."

Marshall studied him with a smile.

After this, they would drift apart. They both knew it. Marshall would draw strength from Marcus. Fletch and his dad would enjoy the relationship they had never known. "I really needed you."

"Our friendship was no accident."

Fletch thought they must both be thinking about the next day's lunch.

"Are ya on your way—" Marshall's words cut off with a sudden cough.

"No. Vic sent me to fetch something off his truck." He watched the man wheeze and fight for control of his breathing.

When he was able to speak, Marshall said, "Well, stop by the shelter if ya have time. I'm headed home on Friday."

"Thanks." Neither Fletch nor Vic had been at the shelter in days. Fletch felt as though his time there was finished. But he did want to see Marshall again, hoped to see how the lunch went. "I'll try."

⁓

It was embarrassing that Lil hadn't been to Katy's new house yet. She and Jake had dropped by the doddy house a few times since the move, but the weeks had flown by with new jobs and everybody settling in. One October Saturday, however, Katy invited Lil and Megan for tea. Lil made some oatmeal raisin cookies and Megan took a stack of Christian novels she wanted to share.

They walked up the pristine, perennial-lined sidewalk that led to the front door. Lil rang the doorbell. "This is nice."

Megan shifted her novels to the other arm. "I like the gray siding. It's one of my favorites."

Katy opened the door and pulled them inside. "I've missed you."

"Yeah, but you've got the chump to keep you company," Lil teased.

"He's off playing basketball with Chad. I usually go along, but today I needed to see my friends."

Katy gave them a quick tour of the house. Though small, it had high ceilings and three bedrooms. One of them was made into Jake's home office. The other one remained empty. When Lil stepped into the kitchen, she froze. "Granite countertops?"

"They came with the house. You know it was a model, so they had it fixed up nice." Katy filled the teapot with water and turned on the burner. She was all smiles. "I have to admit, it's really fun to clean our new home."

Lil unwrapped the plastic that covered the cookies and set them on the table. "We have played musical chairs. I never pictured it would be like this. I always thought we'd all three live together."

"We don't have to live together to be best friends. Where do you want these books?"

Katy took them to the living room and returned just as the teakettle whistled. She served them their chamomile along with Lil's cookies. She'd been sporting a smile ever since they arrived. At first Lil thought it was just the joy of showing them her home, but now her friend's smile deepened, spread across her face, and lit up her eyes.

"I have something to tell you both. Aside from Jake, you're the first to know."

A sweet inkling blossomed inside Lil. "Yes?"

"We're going to have a baby."

Megan and Lil squealed, jumping up to hug Katy.

"This is wonderful. How do you feel?"

"I'm not even sick. Just a little tired."

"When's it due? What does Jake say?"

"The baby is due the end of April. Will you help me prepare the nursery?"

"Of course!" Lil touched Katy's arm, thinking about the empty bedroom. "We'll give you a shower, too."

"That would be nice. Maybe after Christmas."

"Perfect."

"Are you going to keep working?" Megan asked.

"Probably until the baby comes. Then I guess we'll see how it goes. If I do, I'm sure I won't work as much."

"I imagine the chump's excited?"

"He's been wonderful, doting on me. But we've only known a few days. I suppose that will wear off soon."

Lil clasped her cup with both hands. "Your baby will be born right after Michelle's. Maybe they'll play together."

"I hope so." Katy talked happily about her baby, and they emptied the teapot.

Lil hadn't known there were so many things to say about an unborn child, but Katy already seemed to be well informed. She'd picked up some library books on the subject.

Katy gave a happy sigh. "Enough about me. What's going on in your lives?"

Lil crossed her legs and swung her foot in tiny circles. "I haven't heard anything from Fletch since he asked me to wait for him. But Matt says he's still in town. That's something. Matt doesn't really want to talk about Fletch. He feels like he's squealing on his friend."

Megan went to refill her cup, but the pot was empty. "I see his point, but the brother–sister bond should be stronger."

"It's frustrating."

Katy refilled the teapot and set it on the stove. During the second pot of tea, Lil told them about her frustrations at work. When she was finished, she glanced at Megan. "Tell Katy what you found out yesterday."

Megan turned pink. "My boss is getting back together with his wife. It's a good thing. He is taking an extended leave of absence. In the meantime, his brother is taking his place. He worked in the field before."

"How will this affect you?" Katy asked. "Should we make a third pot for you?"

"I'll tell you the story, Katy. But please, no more tea."

⁓

The baby's due in April. Jake is wonderful, doting on me. Lil remembered their earlier conversation. The words kept swirling in her mind, long after she and Megan left Katy's home.

Why wasn't she happier? Sure, she'd done the garbanzo dance at the time, but now she felt bereft. Lil glided slowly on the swing, remembering the Sunday when Fletch sat next to her, swinging and talking optimistically about their relationship. She sighed. That was before he realized he wasn't happy with his life. She bit her lower lip, wondering if he had felt as miserable as she now did.

She wasn't even happy with her job. It wasn't the hard work—she'd never been afraid of work. It just didn't fulfill her like she had hoped.

Her Bible lay open on her lap. She had been fighting against Fletch's request to trust God with their relationship. Instead, she'd pleaded with God to bring Fletch back to her.

She gazed up at the canopy of brittle oak leaves and followed the trail of one to the ground. Her hopes and dreams were like those leaves. *Lord, what are You trying to tell me? Have I been following the wrong dream all along? Fletch claims he had. Have I, too?*

She stared at her Bible. Everything had pivoted around her goals for so long she didn't know how else to live. Then her eyes fell upon a passage she had never read or heard before. She glanced at the header and thought grimly, *I'm in the book of Job. How fitting, for of all Bible characters, Job's life was one of affliction.*

Starting at Job 8:12, she read a few verses: "Whilst it is yet in his greenness, and not cut down, it withereth before any other herb. So are the paths of all that forget God; and the hypocrite's hope shall perish: whose hope shall be cut off, and whose trust shall be a spider's web. He shall lean upon his house, but it shall not stand: he shall hold it fast, but it shall not endure."

Lil gasped. She understood what the writer meant. Without God, her dreams were fragile and unable to hold up to life's pressures. Like a spider's web. Like brittle leaves. Her motives had been full of selfish ambition, always yearning for the spotlight. Just like those circus performers so long ago. Her dreams were never about God's will. She was supposed to give the glory to God, but she'd fought all these years to claim it for herself.

She began to pant, *Oh no. Oh no.*

She'd been chasing something that was as foolish as a circus performer using a spider's web for a net. "Foolish, foolish, foolish," she gasped. She'd been just like her mom.

I'm so sorry, Lord. So ashamed. She put her face in her hands and cried out to God in waves of repentance until she had laid out all the ugliness. All her selfish whims and desires. Even rejecting the farm, hating it when it had been God's gift to provide for her family. It had been a generational gift. A gift that had given her a pleasant childhood. Living on the farm, she had been able to enjoy nature, good food, and animals. He'd given her many friends and a loving family who stuck together no matter how much they disagreed.

I'm so sorry. I admit I'm caught in a sticky spider's web. What now, Lord? Can You change my heart? I need firm ground for my feet and clear direction because I haven't learned how to hear Your voice or appreciate Your gifts.

⌒

Two weeks passed. Peace settled over Lil. She still held the same job, but she went to work with a renewed bounce in her step. She was naturally a bouncy-step-type person, but she'd discovered the source of joy. It came from a continual, silent conversation with God. Telling Him her thoughts. Listening for those impressions He placed in her heart. Making Him a part of her day.

She couldn't disregard a strong yearning for Fletch and wished she didn't have to wait, that she could find out what was on his mind.

She hoped someday she would get the chance to tell Fletch how she'd changed. If she got another chance with him, she would be open to consider all the options for their future. She couldn't picture herself as a missionary, and every time she tried to, she was impressed not to worry, to just trust God.

She spent her evenings searching scripture and allowing God's powerful words to penetrate her spirit. Her resentment toward the rules and regulations of the church disappeared when her studies revealed the reasons behind them.

She'd had a long talk with her mom about the situation and discovered they were at similar places in their lives. It was heartening to think she didn't have to wait forty years but could learn it now alongside her mom.

The goals no longer seemed as important as the journey itself.

CHAPTER 36

One day in early November, Lil stood in the vestibule speaking to Brother Troyer. "So I've been thinking about the spider web analogy in Job, and. . ." Brother Troyer's gaze went spacey as if trying to recall her particular analogy, and he gave her a patient nod. "You know how spiders' webs are all sticky and gross and once you get them on you, you can't get them off?" His mouth twitched on the left. "And sometimes they're so invisible you don't see them and walk right into them. Other times they're beautiful and useful to the spider, too. I mean without them, spiders wouldn't eat, and I suppose spiders are good for something or God wouldn't have created them. Anyway, I'm thinking of. . .say, television. Do you think it's like that?"

Brother Troyer coughed. "Yes, I can see the similarities, but what is the question, exactly?"

In the many discussions they'd had since Lil had been reading her Bible and praying, she sometimes thought the preacher could be so dense. She opened her mouth to go at it from a different angle but snapped it closed again when every muscle in her body tensed. For somebody much more interesting than Brother Troyer had just stepped through the church doors and hesitated in the foyer.

Fletch? He looked taller, more wonderful. His jean-clad legs were planted purposefully, and somewhere beneath that button-down dress shirt was a heart that had surely stolen hers. His gaze swept over his surroundings. His hand went up to smooth his wind-tousled hair. It had been so long since she'd seen him that she'd forgotten how much the sight of him could send her heart racing and turn her brain to mush. And then his soft brown gaze rested on her.

"I. . ." Lil couldn't remember what she and the preacher had been speaking about. "Excuse me." She took a few steps toward Fletch and stopped.

Why was he here? To break up for good? To confess his love? She swallowed. Was she ready to accept his decision, or should she scram out the back door? She couldn't move. He started toward her. And when he was so close she could have reached up and brushed his hair in place, he stopped. "Hi. I'd hoped you hadn't forgotten me."

Lil gave a nervous little laugh. "If I had, my memory is jogged now."

"I came, Lily, to make my offer."

Her heart did the complete somersault. "Here? Now?"

Then he smiled. "I thought it was the perfect place. If you're willing, I'd like to be your guest this morning. See what your church is like. Do you think they'll kick me out?"

She glanced down and couldn't believe he'd worn his red tennis shoes. It was as if he had done it on purpose, because they didn't even match his shirt. She looked back at him with confusion.

He shrugged and gave her a disarming, yet boyish smile. "If they'll accept me, they need to know who I am. That's not to say I won't change."

Her congregation already knew all about him. There were no secrets in this church. She nodded, wet her lips. The service was ready to begin, and they were the last ones in the vestibule. She wanted to tell him how she'd changed and pour out her heart about how she'd found God, but she was curious about his offer.

"Mmm, you mentioned an offer?"

"Another reason I wore these shoes. To barter. I'll give up my shoes or whatever else you or your elders require if you'll let me pursue that mission opportunity I told you about. I went to some of their campus meetings. They have lots of short trips to other countries. I could go on those for now, and after I have my own practice and we have children"— he grinned mischievously—"there are other ways that veterinarians can support the work without actually traveling."

"Children? I think your plan skips an important step."

"No, I didn't forget it. It's all I can think about. But let me finish my offer. In return, I'd let you pursue your career."

"You're staying in Plain City?"

"If you'll have me. Vic has offered me a job. I know what I want, Lil. I want you. I've already talked to your father. He gave me permission to date you with intentions toward marriage. Will you give me another chance?"

Lil reached up to touch his cheek. "Yes, I will. But I have one condition."

"All right."

"You'll let me visit your church, too. And I have so much to tell you."

"I'd like to kiss you right now, but I think that will have to wait until after the service."

"I'm going to claim that kiss today. But right now you'd better hold my hand real tight or I'm going to embarrass both of us by doing the garbanzo dance down the aisle."

⎯⎯ꕥ

Flowers were strewn down the center aisle of Fletch's church, ribbons tied on the oak pews. After months of preparations, the day to unite their dreams and lives had finally arrived. Outside the church, dogwoods were making a showy splash of white and pink. May brought newness to Plain City and to Lil's heart.

She examined herself in the mirror, still surprised every time she saw her reflection since Britt had taken her to a hairstylist. Lil had gotten her bangs professionally trimmed and her hair styled to wear straight just below her shoulders. She'd wanted something easy to care for when she went with Fletch on his upcoming mission trip to Vinces, Ecuador.

Michelle helped her position her veil, a traditional style that hung long down her back.

"Mommy, when I grow up, can I wear a covering like that?" little Tate asked. She held her yellow flower girl skirt out, posing in front of the mirror.

"When you're older, we'll see."

Lil's elegant dress was a slim, A-line style. Beaded lace adorned the bust and sleeves and ruched charmeuse accented her waist. She'd doubled her sit-up regimen. The plain satin skirt had a scallope lace hem.

Megan popped her head into the dressing room. "Katy's feeding the baby; then Marie will take little Jacob, and Katy will join us."

"Perfect."

Megan fluttered over her, tugging here and moving there. "You look beautiful." Together, they had shopped to find the perfect combination of elegant and modest. Not only in her wedding dress, but in her new wardrobe items.

No longer did Lil feel plain and restricted, but her clothes reflected her heart, modest in cut and cheery in color. She and Megan had grown close over the months they had shared the doddy house. There had been a time when Megan seemed sad, and Lil knew it had something to do with falling for a man she couldn't have, but Megan had found her peace. The experience had given her an even lovelier spirit than before.

Dressed in a yellow bridesmaid dress, Megan reflected Lil's joy. Her friend had been eager to move home again so the doddy house would become a honeymoon shack for the second time.

Lil clutched Megan's hand. "I'm nervous. I need to see him."

"You will soon enough."

Katy opened the door and stepped into the room with Lil's mom, who carried Michelle's baby boy. "Jake said Fletch is ready. But you'll never guess what your brothers did to him."

"Oh no," Lil groaned.

"They changed his real tux jacket out for one that was two sizes too small."

"Oh, that's going to ruin the wedding!"

"No. They had the right size, too. They just wanted to see Fletch squirm."

Mom handed the baby to Michelle. "I'm sure Matt was the genius behind it. But I have a surprise for him."

"You do?" Lil asked.

"I was thinking a squirt of hot sauce on his cake would be the perfect payback."

Lil giggled, relieved her mom's sense of humor had returned. "The cake is so lovely." She took her mom's hand. "Thank you for everything. You've taught me so much."

Mom squeezed her hand. "Now stop, or we'll have to cry. Anyway, the church is filled. I'm going to go ahead and get seated. Your dad is waiting in the foyer."

Lil found him there, and together they watched Lil's bridesmaids take their turns walking up the aisle. "I'm so happy," she told him.

He patted her hand. "It all turned out good."

Remembering that morning so long ago when her dad had first confided that the farm was in trouble, she knew his words held plenty of meaning. They expressed happiness over the farm's financial breakthrough. Matt had signed the contract with the Mexican restaurant chain, and the herd's disease was on the decline. But her dad also referred to the way the family had accepted Fletch and then agreed with Lil's decision to attend a different church. The family was united and stronger than ever for working through their differences.

"It's time, honey."

Lil gripped Dad's arm and floated down the aisle toward the blond groom in a perfect-fitting black tuxedo. Ever since their accidental meeting, he was all she had wanted in a man. His looks and charm first attracted her, but she'd fallen in love with his gentle strength.

Fletch's sister, Erica, all the way in from Canada, sat at the piano and played the bridal procession. At rehearsal, Fletch had helped her position the piano bench just right so that she could reach across her pregnant belly. And Lil loved the French accent of Erica's husband.

Her groom's gaze, so full of reassurance and a dash of daring, drew her toward the altar where they would exchange their vows before

God, family, and friends.

When at last the preacher said, "I pronounce you husband and wife; you may kiss your bride," Lil melted into her groom's embrace.

"For luck for the rest of our lives," he whispered.

"And love!" she added breathlessly.

His sister started the music again, and together they swept down the aisle. About halfway, Lil couldn't resist a few steps of the garbanzo dance. Laughing, Fletch clasped his hand around her waist and rushed her out of the sanctuary.

In the lobby, he drew her close for a real marriage kiss. She closed her eyes and cherished her husband's eager embrace. Afterward, she looked into his tender gaze, so glad that she had dared to let go of old dreams and embrace something new.

At their reception, each person they greeted reinforced the Lord's blessings along their journey. There was Giovanni waving them over to meet his wife and baby.

"This. . .eh. . .reminds us of our own wedding. In Italy. What can I say? It is spring and love is in the air."

Lil asked if she could hold the little one. "Here," Giovanni's wife placed a cloth over Lil's shoulder. "You must protect your pretty dress." But she beamed to share her little one. "We are happy to be back in the States. Thank you for giving Giovanni his job back."

"I was happy to fill in for him," Lil replied, giving the baby a final kiss and returning her to her mama. She had never felt as relieved as when Giovanni returned and reapplied for a cooking position.

She smiled at Giovanni. "Remember your promise to give me time off when Fletch has his mission trips."

"You already have the time off for your honeymoon. Eh! You are so demanding of Giovanni."

Next, Fletch shook hands with Vic, and Britt hugged Lil. "Come for dinner when you get back from your honeymoon. I want to hear everything."

"All right. But after that, it'll be my turn to cook."

~ప~

Fletch and Lil paused in the vestibule before they made a dash for the limousine Marshall had insisted on renting. Marshall's remission had been the only wedding gift Fletch had desired from his longtime friend.

Outside the doors, two long lines had formed, and they were to make a pass through the middle. It wouldn't have been so bad if Lil's brothers didn't form one long, intimidating stretch of that line. His parents were first, clutching birdseed Dad had supplied from his job at the discount pet store. Mom had spent the winter editing her journals into a devotional for publication with a Christian publishing house. She was encouraging Lil to get started on her cookbook.

"Why are we waiting, Fletch? Are you getting cold feet?"

Fletch smiled at his adorable bride. "Not on your life. It's not that I don't want to get to the limo or start our new life together, but did you notice that long row of Landis men?"

"I'll protect you," she teased, grabbing up her gown's hem in readiness. "Anyway, you might as well get used to it."

"You're right about that." Fletch loosened his necktie. "Ready. Set. Go!"

Laughing, they ran through the line, spitting birdseed and making it without incident to the limo. The driver opened the door and waited until they were inside. Fletch wanted to steal another kiss, but Lil was waving madly at their family and friends.

The chauffer started the engine. When he did, the car came alive. Really alive! Turn signals blinked, lights glared, window wipers swished, and the radio blared. Every accessory had been turned on.

They burst into laughter as the chauffer struggled to get everything back in order.

"How did they manage that?" Fletch asked.

"I saw Hank talking to the driver."

"Ah, the diversion tactic."

As the limo eased into the street and left the church behind, they relaxed into the plush seating.

Lil squeezed his hand. "That was amazing."

"You're amazing. I have a gift for you." Fletch leaned forward and reached under the seat. He placed the gift box on her satin skirt.

She bit her bottom lip. "But I don't have anything for you."

He touched those lips. "Oh, but you do, and I can't wait to—"

She gave him a playful shove. "Shush. The driver might hear us."

"He can't. The sliding window is closed."

She gingerly untied the ribbons. The box had a lid, and she removed it. "For me?" Grinning, she pulled out a pair of red tennis shoes, almost a perfect match for the ones he owned. Those had become a commonplace sight in the Landis mudroom over the past couple of months. "I love them!" Then she noticed what he had attached to one of the shoestrings. "What's this?"

Fletch helped her remove it then held the golden circle between his fingers. "It's your wedding band." He knew that Conservative Mennonites didn't wear rings. Some people in the church they now attended did. He watched her eyes soften. "You don't have to wear it, but I wanted you to have one. I didn't want to offend anyone who might be attending the wedding."

"That's so thoughtful."

"I hope it's not too plain." He searched her expression hopefully.

"How could it be plain? When it belongs to you?"

LIL'S RECIPE JOURNAL

THREE BEAN SALAD

¾ cup red wine vinegar
¾ cup sugar
¾ cup vegetable oil
Dash dry mustard
½ teaspoon dried tarragon
1½ teaspoons dried cilantro
1 (16 ounce) can green beans, drained
1 (16 ounce) can garbanzo beans, drained
1 (16 ounce) can kidney beans, rinsed and drained
1 red onion, diced
1 red bell pepper, chopped

In small saucepan or microwave heat vinegar, sugar, oil, and seasonings until sugar dissolves. Pour over remaining ingredients. Stir and chill.

LIL'S SUMMER CHILI

1 pound ground pork
1 onion, diced
1 green bell pepper, chopped
2 teaspoons chili powder
2 cloves garlic, pressed
1 teaspoon pepper

5 cups diced tomatoes
2 (16 ounce) cans kidney beans (or any other kind)
½ cup water
¼ cup chopped cilantro
1 cup corn

Brown pork, onion, and pepper together. Drain off fat. Mix in all other ingredients and simmer for at least a half hour. May serve cold.

ZUCCHINI RELISH

10 cups chopped, unpeeled zucchini
4 cups chopped onions
5 tablespoons salt
2¼ cups cider vinegar
5 cups sugar
½ teaspoon pepper

2 teaspoons celery seed
¾ tablespoon nutmeg
¾ tablespoon turmeric
1 tablespoon dry mustard
1 tablespoon cornstarch
1 green bell pepper, chopped
1 red bell pepper, chopped

Mix together zucchini, onions, and salt, and let stand overnight. Rinse and drain.

Place vinegar and sugar in large pot. Stir in pepper, celery seed, nutmeg, turmeric, dry mustard, and cornstarch. Bring to boil. Remove from heat and add drained zucchini mixture and peppers. Return to heat and simmer, uncovered, stirring occasionally for 30 minutes. Pour into canning jars. Cover with lids and rings according to manufacturer's instructions. Process in hot water bath according to recommendations of local extension service.

CHOCOLATE ZUCCHINI CAKE

2 cups flour
1 cup sugar
¾ cup unsweetened cocoa powder
2 teaspoons baking soda
1 teaspoon baking powder
½ teaspoon salt
1 teaspoon cinnamon

4 eggs
¾ cup vegetable oil
¾ cup applesauce
3 cups grated zucchini
½ cup walnuts, chopped
½ cup chocolate chips

Preheat oven to 350 degrees. Grease and flour a 9 x 13 oblong pan.

In large bowl, mix together dry ingredients. Stir in eggs, oil, and applesauce. Mix well. Fold in zucchini, walnuts, and chocolate chips. Pour into baking pan. Bake 50 to 60 minutes. Frost with favorite frosting or dust with powdered sugar.

VEAL AND SPINACH RAVIOLI

1½ pounds veal
1 onion, diced
3 cloves garlic
2 tablespoons butter
1 teaspoon salt
½ teaspoon pepper
1 cup dry white wine (ginger ale can be substituted)
1½ cups beef broth
6 ounces Parmesan cheese, grated
2 eggs
4 ounces fresh spinach, chopped
40 pasta squares
1 egg white

Grind veal, onion, and garlic. Brown in butter. Add seasonings and wine. Sauté until dry. Add beef broth and simmer until dry. Cool. Add Parmesan, eggs, and spinach. Mix well. Coat pasta squares with egg white, fill and fold. Seal. Boil ravioli for 7 minutes. Serve with Lil's special sauce.

LIL'S SPECIAL SAUCE

½ cup mushrooms
6 tablespoons butter
4 cloves garlic, pressed
1 cup grated Parmesan cheese
1 teaspoon basil
2 cups heavy cream or to taste

Sauté mushrooms in butter. Add garlic, cheese, and basil. Blend until heated. Stir in cream.

Herb Chart

Basil: Meat, pesto, salads, soups, stews, tomato dishes
Bay leaves: Meats, sauces, soups, stews, vegetables
Borage: Salads
Catnip: Tea
Chervil: Fish, salads, sauces, soups, stuffing
Chives: Appetizers, cream soups, eggs, garnish, salads
Coriander: Confections, salads, Asian foods
Dill: Bread, fish, salads, sauces, vegetables
Marjoram: Fish, poultry, soups, stews, stuffing, vegetables
Mint: Beverages, desserts, fish, sauces, soups
Oregano: Fish, Italian dishes, meats, sauces, soups, vegetables
Parsley: Garnishes, sauces, soups, stews
Rosemary: Casseroles, fish, salads, soups, vegetables
Sage: Fish, meat, poultry, soups, stuffing
Savory: Poultry, meat, salads, sauces, soups, stuffing, vegetables
Tarragon: Eggs, meats, poultry, salads, sauces, tomatoes
Thyme: Fish, meats, poultry, stews, stuffing, tomato dishes

SOMETHING BLUE

DEDICATION

Many things I love are blue:
beach vacations, sunny skies, faded jeans, my computer
background, and the color of my husband's eyes.
Happy fortieth anniversary, sweetheart!

CHAPTER 1

Brother Eli Troyer groaned and clutched a hand over his heart. The fast, strange sensations escalated as he weeded his wife's vegetable patch. But it wasn't the first time this had happened. Always before, the frightening condition went away on its own. If he told his wife, Barbara, she'd shoo him off to the doctor. He was long overdue for any kind of medical checkup.

He groped for the blue handkerchief in his pocket and mopped his damp brow. He glanced up at the June sun then replaced his straw hat. There were more important things to do than go see a doctor. He couldn't let up when he needed to visit folks who were actually sick. It took time to plan his sermons. Preaching and residing over his little Conservative Mennonite flock was a full-time responsibility, almost becoming too much for him as his energy waned. Why, he would be seventy on his next birthday.

He slowly bent for his red-handled hoe and continued to work his way down a garden row of bushy green beans, fighting against his increasing exhaustion. But he'd promised Barbara that he'd finish the weeding before she returned from her outing, with two other sisters from the congregation, to the discount fabric store in Columbus. Those sisters made up the core of the quilting group, and Barbara was going with them to show her support for their latest project.

Less than ten minutes passed, and he heard the sweet gurgling whistle of a bluebird. He paused to gaze up into the nearby evergreen. Barbara had suggested he put up one of those nesting houses on a pole this spring, the kind that attracted bluebirds. But he hadn't gotten it accomplished. Probably too late for occupancy this year, he decided with regret. The bluebirds would stay around anyway, at least until the blueberries ripened later in the summer. Barbara always planted sunflowers for the birds. And she already had several birdhouses strewn around the yard. She had been a good helpmeet to him over the years, and he now wished he had made that birdhouse for her this spring.

The chest pain returned, harder than before. Maybe it was stress. The last couple of years had taken a toll on him, with some younger members of the congregation pushing for changes. Such notions filled their heads these days. The latest upheaval ended with the men and women sitting together during services. That came after years of segregated seating. He shook his head. Before that, they'd changed the ordinance on the women's prayer covering, allowing women to make up their own minds whether they wore them outside of prayer and worship. But changing the ordinance had kept the congregation from splitting. Thanks be to God for that. He knew it was part of his job to try and understand the younger generation. Sometimes that was hard because he and Barbara had never had any children of their own.

Feeling lightheaded, he decided to call it a day, put away the tools, and head for the house for some of Barbara's homemade lemonade. He started toward the tool shed but only got a few steps when an immobilizing pain seized the center of his chest. He reeled forward, his palms and knees slamming, then sank down to the rich garden soil. Panting, he clutched his heart. What was this? Surely he wasn't having an actual heart attack?

With no one home to help, he wasn't sure if he could make it to the house to use the phone. He crawled a short ways, but the pain was unbearable, making it impossible to draw a breath. He clutched his heart again, realizing his life was in the Lord's hands.

As the painful attack increased, he curled up on his right side, his right hand clawing the soil and dirtying his fingernails. A sudden gust of wind blew off his straw hat, and it tumbled down the garden row and caught on a green bean bush, leaving Brother Troyer's balding head and face exposed to the sun.

Just before the preacher blacked out, he thought, *I'm dying. And I've left a few things undone.* He had no real regrets where his wife was concerned, other than the shock and pain it would cause Barbara to find him this way. But it was a church matter that bothered him most. Had been bothering him for some time. "I shouldn't have put off talking to widow Schlagel. I should have dealt with that." He tried to pray, but his thoughts convoluted, and he forgot all about widow Schlagel, sensing something faint, sweet, and wonderful drawing him. His fingers relaxed in the dirt, and he closed his eyes for the last time on earth.

———

"Glory be!" Megan Weaver's black oxfords pitter-pattered lightly across the firm's ceramic tile flooring. She sometimes left off the *to God* in her exclamations, because the rest of the staff at Char Air all knew whom she praised for all the good things that came into her life. Only a few of the employees of the small company she worked for shared her Christian— though not Mennonite—sentiments. She came to a halt and waved a photograph before the face of a middle-aged brunette woman in a beige suit. "Look at this, Paige."

The manager of finance looked up from her computer screen and squinted through her new bifocal contact lenses. "What is it?"

"Remember those bicycles the company flew to Haiti last month? This came with a letter from a missionary near Port-au-Prince. It's a girl with a clubfoot posing with her new bike. This letter says she lives in a remote village and has been walking over two miles to school. Now she can ride a bicycle." Megan studied the girl in the photo. "Isn't that an amazing story? Can you use it in our newsletter?"

"Sure. It's perfect. Thanks." The woman who was in charge of recruiting donations stood up from her desk, which was surrounded on three sides with sleek, chrome-and-gray partitions. Paige stretched then examined the photograph and letter. "I love it. These stories never get old, do they?" She blinked profusely and scanned the letter while Megan pushed a stray blond hair back beneath her prayer covering and waited. Paige placed the items on her file-cluttered desk. "You've sure been busy today."

Megan briefly rested her hands on the waist of her midi-length skirt. "That's because Randy is trying to get caught up before he leaves." As Randy Campbell's assistant, Megan had been careful never to discuss the particulars of her boss's delicate situation with others in the office. Yet everybody knew that the president of Char Air was taking a two-month leave of absence to spend time with his wife in a scrambled effort to save his marriage. Whispered rumors, along with the few details Randy had supplied Megan, led her to believe that his wife would have good cause to leave him but was allowing him one last chance to persuade her to stay.

Paige poked at the watery corner of her left eye. "I hear his brother, Chance, is going to fill in for him. Now he's a feast for the eyes. Too bad I'm happily married."

"I've never met him." Good looking? When she'd first started her job, it had been hard to keep her mind pure while working so close to her handsome, married boss. If his brother looked anything like him, Megan would be spending a lot of time staring at the floor and praying for guidance. As it was, she had already memorized the office floor's herringbone pattern. But now her gaze was on Paige. "I see you're having trouble adjusting to your new contacts. Is it painful?"

"Just bothersome. I'm giving it the rest of the week before I break down and wear my old frames."

Megan nodded, disappointed at Paige's obsession with outward appearance. The other woman was always trying something to beautify herself. Although friendly, Paige wasn't open to any of Megan's advice on that topic. It was obvious from past discussions, Paige considered Megan, with her plain garb and cosmetic-free skin, inept in topics pertaining to fashion and style.

Paige purposefully drew her hand away from her face and straightened her pencil skirt. "He used to work here. He's a pilot, you know. But he's been overseas."

"Really? Doing what?"

"He's a missionary pilot."

Megan's interest piqued as her heart sank. This made the newcomer all the more fascinating. She glanced out the glass wall and watched a flight line technician walk from the company hangar toward a Learjet that was going to transport a local sports team to Atlanta. "Sounds like a nice man." However, she knew that if he was Randy's brother, he was not a Mennonite man. That meant, romantically speaking, she needed to keep up her guard.

Her friend Katy had repeatedly pointed out that working for outsiders was treading a slippery slope. But Megan found her job interesting. If Randy took away her meager paycheck, she'd probably work for free. Not that her job was easy or undemanding. It entailed plenty of patience, making phone calls to smooth over problems with dissatisfied customers, and the constant struggle to find and keep volunteers for the nonprofit flights. Even keeping her hyperactive boss on schedule wasn't a simple task.

"Randy's convinced that Chance can do the job, but I have a hunch our lives won't get any easier the next couple of months." Megan sighed. "But we'll make do."

"I love your attitude." Paige turned toward her cubby. "If you do get any free time, you can help me."

"I thought that's what I just did."

"Oh yeah. Thanks for the photo. And the story."

Megan smiled and went to her desk, a modern cubical identical to Paige's, only located adjacent to Randy's plush, private office. She settled into her wheeled, black leather chair, both anticipating and dreading the arrival of her handsome, temporary boss. Of all things, Chance Campbell was a missionary pilot. *Aye, yi, yi.*

Megan entered her mom's kitchen and donned a blue-striped ticking apron while following a sweet aroma to the black iron kettle, where Mom prepared their first batch of garden sweet corn. Megan's mouth watered. She loved summer nights when their meals consisted entirely of fresh garden vegetables and large slabs of warm, homemade bread and melting butter.

"I'll do the vegetables."

"Slice tomatoes and cucumbers. We're eating early. Your dad has an elders meeting tonight."

"Good because I'm starved. I only had time to eat half my lunch."

She warmed under Mom's approving gaze. Mom placed much stock in hard work, as evidenced by her tidy home and neat garden. But she didn't understand what Megan's job really entailed. Lenient as her parents were, it was probably better that way. She didn't want to worry them about the modern technology and worldly coworkers who surrounded her on a daily basis. Working at Char Air was Megan's first real job since graduating from Rosedale Bible College. Although it might seem like a strange job for a Conservative Mennonite woman, it was the connection with missionary and charity flights that had drawn her. Service and ministry jobs had always sparked her interest.

The house phone rang. Mom wiped her hands and rushed toward the counter. "Hello?"

Megan glanced over, curious, and froze at her mom's growing expression of alarm.

"Oh no. Oh no," Mom repeated, then quietly listened while snatching up a tissue from a blue-flowered box and blotting her eyes with it.

Hurrying across the kitchen, Megan felt her heart pound. "What? What's wrong?"

"Just a minute, Vernon." Mom lowered the phone and whispered, "It's about Brother Troyer. He went into sudden cardiac arrest."

"Will he be all right?"

Mom shook her head and dabbed her eyes again then returned to her phone conversation. Stunned, Megan dropped into the closest chair. Her mom ended the call by saying, "Such a shock. Yes, I'll tell Bill the meeting is cancelled." Mom stepped away from the phone toward Megan. "Barbara went with the quilters to buy some fabric, and when she came home, she found him. I just can't believe it. He died weeding their garden."

"How awful." Megan rose and slipped her arms around her mom's waist. Tears stung her eyes. The last time she'd seen Brother Troyer was at the Memorial Day potluck. He'd told Megan he was going fishing on the Big Darby the next day. He'd seemed cheerful and spry. Normal.

"It's shocking. Poor Barbara. No one suspected anything like this," Mom whispered.

Megan stepped away. "What will we do? Surely Dad won't have to preach?"

Mom's red-rimmed eyes widened.

CHAPTER 2

Megan stood next to her mom. Her nostrils filled with the pungent aroma of mowed grass as she stared at the brown mound of dirt and the freshly dug hole, trying to imagine her life-long preacher actually being laid to rest in it. The grim thought was paradoxical, with his soul alive in heaven. Megan found it hard to release him to God. Her thoughts and prayers remained argumentative, reminding God that they still needed Brother Troyer on earth.

Beyond the road across the pristine, rolling, cemetery lawn studded with neat rows of plain gray headstones—some adorned with flowers—a tributary of the Big Darby gently swirled and cut through the Plain City farmlands. Brother Troyer had spent a lot of time on that river. She tried to picture him fishing in heaven, but it was hard with that pile of dirt and rectangular hole. Yet Christian faith was all about eternal life. That's what Brother Troyer spent his life proclaiming to his humble followers.

The preacher had often turned soil in search of worms for his bait bucket. Megan's mind turned hard ground, poking at this death-life issue, but there was nothing under the clods of her mind besides the image of dead bones and the stark call to *faith* regarding things unseen.

The soft, even whir of the hearse's engine drew her attention, and she saw it park near the grave.

"They're here," Mom whispered.

Megan watched Dad join the pallbearers and carry the plain casket. Off to her left, she heard Barbara's soft gasp and faint whisper, though it was only meant for Barbara's sister. Megan strained to catch the widow's painful words.

"I'll never let the weeds grow on his grave. . .the least I can do. Eli hated weeding. If only I'd not been so proud of my garden." Her voice broke. "He might still be alive."

Megan dipped her head and stared at the ground. By her mom's flinch, she'd caught the pitiful conversation, too.

Barbara's sister, who'd driven in from Indiana, softly replied, "You did for him, too. That's how love is. God must've planned it this way. Eli met his maker in a beautiful garden. Quickly. With no lingering sickness."

Megan was grateful for Clara's calm reassurance, but aye, yi, yi, surely the bean patch wasn't Eli's place of choice. It would've been the riverbank or even the pulpit. Yet he was a kind leader. Devoted husband. Maybe Clara was right.

This was hard. Way too hard to think about. Nothing like when Jake Byler's grandma passed away last winter. Everybody called that a blessing because she was in the last throes of Alzheimer's, not even recognizing her family. But Eli had been so alive. Vital and needed. Megan's heart rebelled against the death and the changes it would bring.

At least Barbara had one living sister who was able to come and be with her during her grief. Mom had pointed out that some elderly people didn't have living siblings. Megan wondered how she could support Barbara in her journey of loneliness. She wished she could weed her garden, but weeds were Megan's dire enemies. Her allergies would never permit it.

"Friends and family. We are here to remember Brother Troyer."

Bishop Heinlein, an overseer of several Ohio churches, had come to help the congregation. Standing between the grave and those gathered, he wore a plain, black, collarless coat. His head was hatless, as was the custom of Mennonite men during worship. In his right hand he held a large black Bible. He cleared his throat and looked out over the mourners, a mixture of black coats and caped dresses. But Megan noticed that prayer coverings and doilies were intermixed with ties and high heels. Amish people and even some outsiders gathered because Brother Troyer was loved and known in the community.

"Psalm forty-six reminds us that God is our refuge and strength."

Earlier at the funeral held inside the meetinghouse, Bishop Heinlein had preached a somber message on righteous living, making the point that nobody knows the hour when they will be called home. But thankfully, now at the graveside, the bishop was quoting a scripture about seeking comfort in the Lord's arms.

"When he will wipe every tear from our eyes. Death will be no more. . . ."

A huge flock of starlings fluttered in and landed nearby, hunting insects in the graveyard's lush lawn. Ugly birds. Megan had a sudden image of rotting flesh and birds pecking Brother Troyer's eyes. She quickly quelled the image.

The bishop didn't heed the birds. "But thanks to God who gives us victory."

The burial ground was just down the road from the church. It was purchased after the original cemetery, adjacent to the church property, had been filled. This one was spacious enough to provide the resting place for several future generations. Megan watched the flock of speckled scavengers. Nobody liked starlings. And she was discovering she didn't like graveyards much, either.

"It's still lonely." The comment drifted to Megan, and she glanced at the quilters to her right. Their group numbered three to ten and included some widows. The core members were Susanna, Mae Delegrange, and Ann Byler. Although her comment had sounded sympathetic, Susanna Schlagel had her brown, hawk-like gaze riveted on Barbara's back. No doubt the young widow planned to swoop down and snatch Barbara into their group, befriend her as only another widow could. But something about the thought of those two women together made a hard lump in Megan's stomach, about the size of one of their thimbles.

Beyond the quilters stood the young single women. As Megan watched Ruthie Ropp, Lori Longacre, and Joy Ann Beitzel, her thoughts continued on the dark side, wondering how long it would be until she'd wind up in their group. Her two best friends, Katy and Lil, were both married now. And Megan didn't even have a boyfriend. Never had, really. Would there come a time when she would be considered an old maid like Lori, the church librarian who wore too much perfume?

Bishop Heinlein prayed; then Ray Eversole stepped to the front of the mourners and passed out hymnals.

Mom took one to share with Megan. "Surely, we don't need these?"

"It's something to do," Megan whispered. "There's a few outsiders here."

"Then let's pass our book back to them." Mom snatched the book away and turned, motioning for it to be passed back to the visitors.

Frowning at her mom, Megan rubbed her thumb.

The song leader led them in a cappella, four-part singing. And Mom was right—they did know all the words. A beautiful song, surely an angel's song, sweet and melodious. She felt her spirit lift. She'd always felt as if congregational singing was a hug or the Holy Spirit's wings around her. A safe place where she was loved.

> *"When we all get to heaven,*
> *What a day of rejoicing that will be!*
> *When we all see Jesus,*
> *We'll sing and shout the victory!"*

While the message was amazing and stirring, so was Megan's visual. The casket was lowered into the hole. Several strong men discarded their Sunday coats and picked up shovels. Dad helped. Her friend Katy's dad, Vernon Yoder, too. Wrong, somehow, to see them sweat and bunch their muscles in their white dress shirts. They went about their task with somber reverence. As they worked, dust tickled Megan's nose and filled her sinus cavity. With the singing, she couldn't actually hear the dirt hitting the casket.

Each shovelful added to Megan's concern. What would the congregation do without their leader? Would everybody work together, or would this cause the type of conflict that soured Megan's stomach? How would it affect her dad and the rest of her family? Brother Troyer had been the one who united his flock, especially over the past three years when they had experienced so many changes—the seating issue, the revision of the prayer-covering ordinance. And more issues were brewing. She'd overheard Dad talk to Mom after elders meetings. What would happen once the funeral was over?

Megan swiped her wet cheeks. Sniffing, she thankfully accepted the tissue Mom pressed into her hand.

They sang "Amazing Grace." A breeze soughed through the hickory trees that graced the cemetery and lifted the corner of Ruthie's covering. The thin, single brunette reached up a hand to secure her straight pins. The singing waned, and a red-tailed hawk gave a raspy cry and circled above the mourners. Megan wished, like that bird, she could board one of her company's planes and rise above the grief and confusion surrounding her.

Getting a hold of herself, she thought, *Up there somewhere is God. He will see us through this. Bishop Heinlein just preached it.*

The bishop said, "The women have prepared a dinner back at the church. Sister Barbara thanks you for coming. You're all invited to the meal."

Food. What else could take their minds off their despair and the thin veil separating heaven and earth? The men quit shoveling. They weren't finished with the task, but it was time to end the service and escort Barbara and the women back to the church.

"Let's go," Mom whispered, her voice holding the same desire as Megan's.

Megan took a final look at the partly filled hole that reminded them all of their own mortality. They started toward the car. "That was hard. Poor Dad."

"He wanted to do it for Brother Troyer. Helps him deal with it."

"I don't like cemeteries much."

"Yeah well, Brother Troyer's in heaven now. That's just his body's resting place. Until he gets a new one."

Megan's gaze shifted from the grass, where she had been taking care not to walk across any other graves, to the road. Buggies, black cars, and colorful cars made a parade along the narrow country road. Her next inhale was wheezy, probably from the pollen of the tansy and reeds that grew along the creek on the far side of the road. She coughed, trying to clear her throat.

"You all right?"

Megan nodded as she withdrew an inhaler from her black purse. She released medicine twice then returned it to its silky pocket. After several breaths, she replied, "Better."

"That's good."

They neared their car, and Megan heard her name. "It's Katy. I'll just be a moment."

"Take your time."

Megan nodded and turned to wait for her friend.

"Where's little Jacob?"

Katy smiled, and her large, dark eyes lit. "Oh, my mom has him. She's helping to set up the meal." She pursed her full lips. "I hope he's napping for her. He's such a *nix nootz* right now, always squirming to get out of our arms. There's no way we could have kept him quiet."

Megan thought that if Jacob had his dad's ornery ways and was a handful at two months, Katy was in real trouble.

"I'm sure Lil's helping with the meal, too." The third friend in their tight trio attended a different Mennonite church now but had grown up under Brother Troyer's preaching. She was a chef by occupation. Katy was a housecleaner, but wasn't working outside the home since Jacob had been born. Jake's carpentry business was prosperous, and they had settled into a happy marriage.

"I'm sure she is. This is so sad." Katy lowered her voice to a whisper. "I hope working with the search committee won't be too hard on our dads. Mine's still adjusting to his insulin shots."

Megan touched Katy's arm. "I didn't hear about a search committee."

"Mom told me they have no choice but to find somebody quick."

"How?"

"The way she explained it, first the elders elect people to serve on the committee. Then the committee takes suggestions from the congregation and the bishop. Once they narrow down the candidates, they invite them to come and meet the congregation."

"So much is happening. I've spent too much time in my room this week or I would have heard about this sooner." At Katy's curious expression, Megan reminded her, "My boss is getting ready to go on a leave of absence." Katy nodded, her expression filled with concern. "There's been so much to do, that I brought some work home."

"I worry about you."

Katy had always disapproved of Megan's attraction for her boss. Her friend had some bad experiences working for outsiders, and although she'd become more tolerant, she was still skeptical of Megan's position.

"Don't worry. I'm fine."

Jake stepped up and touched Katy's elbow. Ever since Megan had known them—for Jake had been chasing Katy since they were kids— he'd pulled Katy's black ponytail. But after Jacob had been born, Katy started wearing her hair up. Subtle changes, him touching her elbow, them acting like a married couple. "You 'bout ready, Cinderella?"

As she watched her friends head to their vehicle, Megan wished she could have told Katy the truth, that she didn't feel like anything was fine. But she'd always made it her job to make life easier for everybody around her, and she didn't have the heart to trouble Katy now that she'd found her fairytale life.

─◌

That night in her room, Megan grew nostalgic, thinking about life and friendships. She even found herself on her knees at the foot end of her bed, digging through her hope chest, looking for an old journal. That first one she'd gotten on her tenth birthday. Standing, she wiped her hand across the solid blue cover, though it bore no dust. Her first journal was actually a diary with a key. She lowered the lid to her hope chest and sat on it, leafing through the small book, reading bits of entries long forgotten. Her mouth curved into a smile, and she laughed once until she cried. She paused to read an entry from summer camp:

Dear Journal,
Alone in the cabin, but I gotta write quick before the others come back. They're busy for a few minutes because a spark from the campfire burned a hole in Lil's jeans, and our camp counselor

is outside trying to patch things up with the girl who loaned them to her in the first place. Katy told Lil that the spark probably came from hell because she's sneaking and wearing those jeans. That's what made Lil cry in the first place.

At the campfire, we made a vow. Now I'm sorry I made it. I only did it to keep peace. Lil wanted us to move in together when we grow up and to vow to be each other's bridesmaids. Katy said Mennonites don't make vows, and they don't. But it made Lil sad, so I smoothed it over and got them to agree. That's how I ended up being part of the vow.

Katy wants to marry Jake Byler. Yuck. If I get married, at least, it will be to a missionary or a preacher. Not Lil's cousin!

By the way, I'm going to name you, so you don't have to be a plain old, dear journal anymore. I got the idea when our counselor made us name our group. We call it Three Bean Salad. Katy's the kidney bean, I'm the green bean, and Lil is the garbanzo bean. Lil even made up a garbanzo dance to go with it. But Mennonites don't dance. Maybe Katy's right and that spark was from hell. I hope not.

Here's the names I've thought up so far:

Jo. That's short for journal. It was Katy's idea. Lil thinks I should make up a name that nobody ever heard of before, but it's hard enough to think of ones I have heard of.

Sharon. Because I share stuff with you.

Djibouti. That's a place in Africa. It's fun to say, and I think it would be fun to write.

Maisy. It was my doll's name, but I don't play with her anymore because I'm ten.

Hope Marie. But I really should save that name because it's my favorite.

Phooey, here they come!

CHAPTER 3

Chance Campbell was better at steering the nose of a Cessna through mountains and thunderstorms at zero visibility and landing safely on a runway carved out of the jungle than he was at sitting in a plush leather office chair and pushing a Char Air pencil. He stared at his computer screen with bored eyes, and he'd only been at it a couple of hours.

He'd arrived early, hoping to get in before the other employees arrived since it was his first day filling in for Randy. Only two hours into the job, and he was regretting being persuaded to do his brother this favor. He glanced at the calendar pad that took up the center of his desk. Sixty days. He'd just have to make the best of it. And if he was lucky, Randy would get his act together and return sooner.

But his big brother, normally the reliable one, had gotten himself into trouble and needed rescuing. Usually Chance was the one who took risks and got into scrapes. He hadn't been able to turn down the opportunity to pay his brother back for all the help he'd received from him over the years. Mostly his teen years, but help was help. Randy had intervened many times to keep their dad from finding out about his misdemeanors, even took the rap for him occasionally.

Chance gloated inwardly. It felt satisfying to be the good one for a change. And for the sake of his nephews, he wanted Randy to save his marriage. He was especially partial to the youngest.

A younger brother was in constant competition. Sometimes it took manhood to finally catch up. Chance had. He'd found his glory in the air force. He had even been awarded the Distinguished Flying Cross. But that mission in Iraq, back in 2003, had also been the one that changed his career direction—piercing his heart and bringing his fighter pilot days to a sputter. After that, he had not reenlisted.

Flying was in the family genes, and he could get the same adrenaline high working as a mission pilot. His job, with its life-and-death situations, provided the adventure he relished; only he was helping people instead of killing them. Not that he regretted what he'd done in the air force, because somebody had to do it for the sake of the country. He'd had his personal fill of it and gotten out of it before it resulted in nightmares and a need for counseling. He'd done his part for the country, and now he wanted to invest his talents in something that brought instant gratification—relief and healing for hurting people.

He rose to head for the coffeepot. He hoped that back in Ecuador, the rookie who was taking his place for the next sixty days—mostly to rack up some flying hours for his résumé—wouldn't make too many mistakes. Outside his office, his thoughts and steps came to a screeching halt.

Whoa! Chance slackened his jaw and riveted his gaze on the female headed his way. Who was that babe? As he stood and gawked at the lovely creature, his gaze moved in confusion from the little net cap to her boyish shoes. Why the odd getup? The baggy clothing? It wasn't black or gothic, exactly. His mind scrambled to sift it out, quickly going over his conversations with Randy until it clicked. He remembered, with disappointment, that she must be the chick who Randy had warned him not to touch. The one who was off-limits because she was Conservative Mennonite.

Chance had hardly paid any attention—conjuring up a vision of staid homeliness, similar to an old maid stereotype—even though Randy had been adamant and even made him swear on the Cessna's name that he would leave her alone. At the time, he thought it was just a joke, a jab at his bachelorhood. He'd passed it off without a second thought, assuming the obvious; he wouldn't pursue a Mennonite woman. Not that he knew anything about them.

But *now* he understood why Randy had pushed the issue. If Chance recalled correctly, he and this woman would be working closely together. And Randy had known that this woman's face and figure would rev Chance's engine.

Tall, check. Thin, check. Blond, check. Definitely his type. Only something else was striking about her. An aura of purity. Too much so, for his taste.

His mind backtracked. This wasn't the woman who had gotten Randy's life all entangled? No, that was his previous assistant. But Randy obviously regretted what he had done and was worried, not wanting Chance to make the same mistake that he'd made. But why on earth would he have hired a gorgeous replacement after he'd just succumbed to temptation? The only explanation was their Campbell genes. His father's fault. Women and planes.

The pretty face suddenly reddened. The slim shoulders squared, and the angel started toward him. His mouth went dry.

"I'm Megan Weaver. You must be Mr. Campbell?"

He reached for the feminine hand that was extended toward him. Her touch affected him. "In the flesh," he blurted out, letting his hormones speak for him. And he shouldn't be joking with this type of woman.

She pulled her hand away with understanding and frowned. "Nice to meet you. I am your assistant. My station is right here outside your office." She watched him warily and moved toward it. He followed her, rested his hand on her desk as she placed her purse in her right-hand drawer then looked up at him again.

"Yes, Randy warned—told me," he quickly corrected, "about you."

"Oh?" She straightened her mouse pad and didn't look happy.

"No worries. He said you're very. . .qualified. That you'd be a big help." He was acting like a brainless idiot. Giving a terrible first impression. He took a deep, steadying breath, whipped his hand off her desk and into his pocket. At the same time, he gave her a practiced and usually foolproof smile. "I'll need it, you see. I'm at home in the sky." He shrugged. "Not so much here."

He watched her face. Her cheeks were pale, pale peach with no makeup. They looked soft and fresh, like a child's. Her eyes studied him, unlined, blue, and vulnerable. The way she wore her white-blond hair up in that bun-thing exposed a delicate, tempting neck that definitely didn't belong to a child. That neck would surely provoke him for the next sixty days, but the silly net cap that perched on top of her head gave her a standoffish appearance. Too pious. It was an off-limits warning and would definitely keep her safe from his advances.

She smiled back. "I'm sure you'll do fine. What can happen in eight weeks?"

He knew what he wished could happen. He'd like to see that net cap removed. See what happened then. But he had too much honor to act on that. No, God wouldn't want him messing with His Mennonites. "I was browsing through the mountain of instructions Randy left me, and saw that on Mondays he meets with Tate in Operations. Do you have anything on your calendar for me?"

"On Friday there was a dispute between Jon, director of maintenance, and some of his flight line technicians. You should probably make sure that got resolved. Usually Jon can manage them, but sometimes Randy. . ." He nodded, so she moved on. "I've got some PR calls to make. From there, as Randy says, we wing it." She talked like a businesswoman, only her voice carried a husky accent that he couldn't identify. Possibly a touch of German?

"Great. Do you sit in on the meetings?"

"No. Randy gives me instructions afterward."

"Well today, I'd like you to join us. The two-ears-better-than-one thing. You have time?"

"I'll make do."

"Great. I was headed for coffee. Can I get you a cup? Though I gotta warn you, I made it. It's probably plenty strong for a sweet thing like you." He suddenly stopped, and this time, good grief, he felt his cheeks heat. He was asking a Mennonite about coffee? Calling her a sweet thing? "I'm sorry. Do you drink coffee?"

She arched a blond brow at him. "Yes. And I drive a car, too."

Her tone carried a disapproving sting. Up to this point, she'd been tolerant of his blunderings and his roving, staring eyes. So she was touchy about her religion. "Look. I don't mean to offend you. Why don't you just make me a list, whatever I need to know about you. . .with your"—he glanced up at her net cap.

She tilted her head, studying him as if he were a bug splatter on a clean Cessna windshield then lifted her chin. "My beliefs haven't interfered with my job so far. They won't while you're here, either. But you're welcome to examine my employment application. It has everything personal you need to know. Summer's our accountant. She keeps employee records, too."

Now she was ticked. Women. He raised his palms. "Whoa. I didn't mean to make you mad. That's what I'm trying to avoid, here. We're gonna be working close. I'll need your cooperation, and I'm not the type who even knows *how* to walk on eggshells." He pointed at his shoes. "Big feet." He gave her his smile again, coaxing her to forgive him and get with the program.

Her expression instantly softened, but she didn't smile. "Just treat me normally. Like all the other employees. Really, I don't get my feelings hurt easily. That is, as long as you don't forget the creamer and sugar in my coffee."

"You got it." He winked then turned on his heels, glad to escape to the coffee bar. Just like in the fighter plane's cockpit, it was better to make a hit then zoom it out of there. He needed to regroup was all. She'd caught him off guard. All he'd wanted when he stepped out of his office was a lousy cup of coffee, and then bam, there she stood, looking all pretty and vulnerable and catching him unawares. But that wouldn't happen again. Anyway, there was nothing he liked better than a good challenge. Especially a pretty one.

_____

Megan glanced at the clock and realized she'd been staring at the speckled texture of her bedroom ceiling for twenty minutes, unseeing and going over every exchange she'd had at work with Chance Campbell. She rolled onto her stomach and retrieved her pen and journal from the top drawer of her nightstand, and started writing:

Jo,

Chance Campbell has curly, sandy hair, broad shoulders, and a disarming, if not conceited, smile. He's older than I am. Early to midthirties. He looks a lot like Randy. Of course, I won't give in to the attraction.

I don't have him figured out yet. He's harsh and sweet at the same time. It's sadly amusing, the way he flounders around the office. I can't help but jump in to keep him out of trouble.

Today I made peace between him and Tate, when Chance wanted him to reserve more planes for the charity flights. Everybody at Char Air knows that although the charity flights are important to the company, they use volunteer pilots and aren't profitable. We need all our charter flights. But I could have hugged Chance, with his love for missions.

Something underlies his smile and clear blue gaze that makes me scared. It seems to imply that he gets what he goes after. He won't go after me. He treats me with caution, like I'll set off an allergic reaction.

That first day when he asked me to make him a list, I almost slapped his face. My anger shocked me more than him. I've never felt that way about an outsider's curiosity. For once, I could relate to Lil. When I snapped at him that I drive a car and he could get anything more personal off my employment application, that was straight outta Lil's mouth.

Megan stopped writing when a classroom discussion from her psychology class at Rosedale Bible College came to mind. *Angry because I'm fighting the attraction.* She felt her face heat with the realization that she might be in real trouble. *Aye, yi, yi.* Her pulse quickening, she tore a page out of the back of her journal and tossed the journal in her drawer. She grabbed her Bible. Where was that verse? Then she remembered she'd penned it inside the back cover. It had been special at the time because her dad had been so sweet when he gave it to her. There: *"Be ye not unequally yoked together with unbelievers: for what fellowship hath righteousness with unrighteousness? and what communion hath light with darkness?" 2 Corinthians 6:14.*

It referred to oxen, but she'd been to some Amish pulls. Seen a team of draft horses yoked together. They made a beautiful sight, working together. Her dad had talked to her about it and quoted that verse right before she started college. He had explained that even getting involved with a man from a more liberal Mennonite church would be problematic. She'd taken it to heart. She'd witnessed that with Lil and Fletch. Eventually Lil left the Conservative church.

Chance was a Christian, but he wasn't a Mennonite. That was even worse than Lil's situation. This verse definitely applied. At least, the way her dad had explained it. She thought sarcastically she should make it into a poster and pin it to her wall. Her ceiling. But seriously, she needed a reminder that wouldn't give away her attraction. She tapped her pen against her lips. She needed a place where she could see it every day. On her car's visor!

With summer's glare, she usually flipped it down every time she drove. It would remind her on the way to work when she most needed it. She would meditate on it on the way home from work, too. She would not be unequally yoked, even with a handsome missionary pilot with sandy, wavy hair and gentle blue eyes. Even if he pursued her. Which he wouldn't.

After copying the verse to paper, she jumped up to take it to her car. Gliding her hand along the freshly waxed stair rail, she paused when her feet hit the bottom landing and she heard her dad say, "The professor had a recommendation for a preacher candidate."

Megan knew the professor in question was Noah Maust, a member of their congregation who taught Old Testament at Rosedale Bible College. She crossed the hand-braided rug and quickened her steps. On her way back in from the garage, she'd join her parents and catch up on what all was happening with the search committee.

CHAPTER 4

On Thursday Megan hurried across the hot, sticky asphalt of Volo Italiano's parking lot. It was the swanky Italian restaurant where Lil worked. The establishment was on the airpark outskirts, practically across the street from Char Air. About once a week, Megan got a take-out lunch, always calling first to be sure Lil had time for a quick chat. Time spent with Lil was never dull. She faced issues head on, presenting her opinions quickly and openly. The best part was that Lil was not judgmental.

As soon as the hostess recognized Megan, she went to the kitchen after Lil. Appearing almost breathless in a white chef's uniform, Lil gave her a quick hug and shoved a Styrofoam take-out container in her hands. They went to their usual corner in the foyer, settling in on an imitation stone bench next to the window.

"Hi, Green Bean. How's it going with your new boss? Spill it. You have exactly eight minutes."

Megan giggled, knowing they could cover a lot of ground in eight minutes. "It's been quite the week. I'm exhausted."

"I suppose he's gorgeous?"

"Aye, yi, yi. One of God's masterpieces."

"You're right to say *one* of. You haven't met *your* masterpiece yet."

"I suppose so. But if Chance was Mennonite"—Megan released a dreamy sigh—"I'd snap him up. He's perfect, otherwise."

"Chance? That's an unusual name."

"Suits him though." Megan shrugged. "Work-wise, it was hard at first. It would be easier to do the work myself rather than explain everything to him. But it's getting better. I'm making do." She leaned toward Lil. "He's full of interesting stories about Ecuador. But for that, we need more than eight minutes. We need to get together soon."

"Ecuador! We should swap stories. I'll have you over for dinner before Fletch and I go on our mission trip at the end of the month."

Megan gave a mildly envious sigh, remembering her childhood diary entry that she'd recently read. It hardly seemed fair. She was the one who was supposed to marry a missionary or preacher. Lil hadn't even been interested in such things until she met Fletch. In fact, for a while they'd even broken up over his interest in missions. Lil was into cooking and working at the restaurant. But she'd fallen hard for Fletch.

He was a veterinarian, now involved with an organization of vets who went on worldwide mission trips to teach people how to care for their livestock. So far, Lil had been able to go along. She had made such a favorable impression at the restaurant, that the owner, Camila Battelli, had given Lil permission to take leaves of absence as long as she plugged them into the calendar at least six weeks in advance. The head chef, Giovanni, had a good working relationship with Lil, too.

"I'll miss you."

"I know. I guess there could be a lot of changes while I'm gone. Have you heard anything new about the search committee?" Even though Lil attended another church, most of her family remained at Big Darby Conservative Mennonite.

"They have two candidates. Actually, they'll stay at our house." It didn't bother Megan that she still lived with her parents. It was the norm for an unmarried Conservative woman. She had been fortunate to have gone to Rosedale Bible College, and she had even lived a few months with Lil in a doddy house that they had renovated. But once Lil married, Megan was content to move back home. Being an only child, she'd always had plenty of space and privacy; in fact, right now she had the entire upstairs. And Char Air kept her occupied.

Lil wrinkled her nose. "You poor thing. A preacher at your house?"

"Two. Maybe more." A sudden image of the graveside service shot through Megan's mind, bringing a pang of sadness over losing Brother Troyer and talking about his replacement.

"I'll invite Katy and Jake, too." Lil glanced through some Roman-style pillars and urns filled with artificial greenery toward the back of the restaurant. "I'd better get back to work. I'll see you soon. Thanks for stopping in to see me."

Megan nodded and looked at her food container. "What's in here?"

"Lasagna."

"Yum. Did you talk to your boss yet about not using Styrofoam?"

Already disappearing around the corner, Lil chirped, "She claims it's cheaper. I'll keep trying."

Regardless that promoting the use of Styrofoam made her a poor steward of God's creation, Megan lifted the container to her nose and smiled. She needed to get back to work before Chance got himself in trouble. Her steps faltered. Should she have gotten him something? He usually left the office each day at lunchtime. He might already be gone. This was the first time she hadn't packed her lunch. She shook her head. No. Absolutely not. She wasn't starting that.

―❦―

Back at the office, Megan barely made it to her desk before Chance's tan, rugged face popped around the corner. "That was fast. Oh. You brought lunch back." He sauntered to her desk, uninvited, and she felt a lump in her throat. Surely, he wasn't going to stand there and watch her eat? If she'd brought him back something, maybe he would have taken it into his office.

"Did you eat?"

"Not yet. I was just heading out. What do you have there?"

"Lasagna from Volo Italiano. My friend's a chef there. You should try it. She's there now. Tell the hostess I sent you, and Lil will give you something special." And she'll get to sneak a look at you.

"I'll do that. As fast as you got back, it must be close?"

Megan scribbled the address on a yellow sticky note, hoping he'd hurry and leave before her own lunch grew cold. Instead, he perched one hip on the corner of her desk. "I'll probably get fat working here. At my real job, I don't eat much. There are usually so many emergencies, I don't get time to eat. He touched his belly. But I guess I make up for it on rainy days. Sometimes I eat at the villages to be polite. If there's time. . ."

He looked trim enough. Not that she'd looked too closely. Most of her evaluations had been snatched while he walked away from her desk. But usually she tried not to watch him at all. She should have read her Bible verse on the way back from the restaurant. She tried to recall it from memory, but her mind wouldn't focus.

". . .But the missionary wives, they cook the best. Whoa. You aren't even listening to me."

"I'm sorry. I like your stories. I've always been interested in the mission field, even though I haven't had many opportunities to participate." She didn't add that she had hoped this job would provide such opportunities, for that wasn't really his problem. It was Randy's, but he had changed since he'd hired her. The promised opportunities hadn't developed yet. She looked up. Chance was studying her intently. "I did go to Bangladesh right after I graduated from Rosedale Bible College."

He questioned her further, and she got swept up in the memories, telling him about the prayer walks through the village. When she finished, he stood, quietly staring at her. She couldn't tell what he was thinking, but he was lost in his thoughts. She fiddled with her Styrofoam container then remembered the sticky note. She tore it off the yellow pad and handed it to him. "I wrote my friend's name, Lil Landis—I mean Stauffer. She's a newlywed."

"You want me to bring you back a replacement? That probably got cold."

"No. It's fine."

"Hold my calls then," he joked, because she fielded all his calls and was handling a fair share of them these days. She heard his departing footsteps and refused to watch him leave.

Megan had only taken two bites when Paige rounded the corner of her wall. "Holding your own, sweetie?"

"Of course."

"Good. Because I came to vent. We just lost a major donor. They said the economy has forced them to cut back. And you know what that means?"

"You have to make a hundred calls? That why you're only wearing one earring?" Megan found it amusing how Paige wore the most unpractical clothing and contraptions.

"Yep."

"Had lunch? I'll share."

"I'm headed to the break room now. I have a sandwich in the frig. I have to work through lunch."

"At least you got used to your contacts."

Paige blinked. "Oh honey, you shouldn't have reminded me. That'll be the next thing. But my eyes are doing better."

She gave her tight suit skirt a twist. "Anything I can get you? Although in my opinion, you've got the advantage, over on this side of the office. Didn't I tell you he's a charmer?"

Megan leaned to whisper. "He's a gentleman, but my workload has doubled again."

"So no ideas on donors?"

"You ask me this every week."

"I know, and you'll keep your ears open, like always?"

Megan shrugged and watched Paige prance away, perfectly poised on three-inch heels. She took a forkful of lasagna. Sure, Paige joked about Chance, and even some of the younger flight line technicians, but she was dedicated to her husband. And as far as Megan could tell, there hadn't been any inter-office flirting. If anything, Paige seemed to watch out for her. Megan didn't like the way men consumed her thinking, these days.

Her friends sensed it, too. Katy and Lil had both told her she needed a boyfriend. The handful of single guys at church had all pursued her at one time or another. She'd had guys interested in her at college, too. But nobody had caught her attention. Except the ones who shouldn't. She put her half-empty container in the wastebasket and picked up her phone. She had calls to make, too. Today she was following up on the corporations who had recently chartered flights. She punched in a number then looked up as Chance breezed back into the office.

"Lil's quite the gal. We hit it off."

Her phone still to her ear, Megan replied, "Great." She couldn't wait to talk to Lil again.

"She told me to keep my hands off you."

"What!" When Megan realized she had blurted *What!* into a customer's ear, she motioned to her phone and turned her gaze away from Chance. *What on earth was Lil thinking?* "Hello. This is Megan at Char Air. I see you flew with us on. . ."

In the background, she heard Chance chuckle. "She also gave away your strategic vulnerability."

Megan glanced back at Chance with narrowed eyes and continued speaking to her customer. "And I wanted to make sure your experience was a pleasant one."

—⟳—

Very pleasant, Chance thought, still chuckling and walking into his office. He'd never known that Conservative girls could be so much fun. Lil was outspoken and delightful. Easy on the eyes, too. She'd come straight to the point, warning him away from Megan. But she'd given away enough about Megan for him to realize that there must be some interest in him on her part, or else Lil wouldn't even have heard about him. And the feisty chef had confirmed his hunches about his assistant. Megan was fascinated with the mission field, longing to see other countries and help people.

It gladdened him, because there was nothing he liked better than sharing stories with interested parties. He'd thought Megan was interested, until this morning when she'd tuned him out. But maybe she was just hungry. It would certainly help him to pass the time if he would find in her a willing ear.

And there was nothing he would love more than to show her around Ecuador. As friends, of course. But if he could do something to make those blues of hers light up, he would. For sure, when his two months were over, he would set up a trip for her to visit the mission station in the village of Shell, take her on a couple flights into the rain forest.

He took a taste of his lasagna and figured he'd found his local lunch hangout. There was a sudden rap on his door, and without waiting for him to answer, Paige stuck her brunette head inside.

"Interrupting you? I couldn't help it. I just landed us a huge donor!" She did a little cha-cha shuffle.

He couldn't help but grin at her enthusiasm. "To make up for the one we lost today?"

"Yep, and now I can breathe again. So, I'm headed to the bank. You need anything while I'm out?"

"Nope. But congratulations!"

Just as quickly as she'd popped in, Paige disappeared. The news gladdened him, because his personal goal while working at Char Air was to promote Randy's charity flights. Next he heard Megan's squeal and assumed Paige was passing along the good news. This definitely wasn't South America, but he had to admit, Ohio was growing on him. So was his respect for what his brother had done to promote the charity flights.

CHAPTER 5

On Saturday Megan and her mom went to visit Barbara Troyer. They wanted to help her put up green beans, figuring that since Barbara had found Eli dead in the bean patch, it would be a trying chore for her.

For a parsonage, Barbara's home was pleasant sized with a large yard. Thankfully with Megan's allergies, Barbara set them up in the summer kitchen, which wasn't really a kitchen but a glassed-in porch. Under normal circumstances, it would have been idyllic, the way it looked out over the lawn and garden, edged with tall purple foxglove and a shorter row of yellow snapdragons. The garden contained rows of well-tended vegetables, and a sentry of sunflowers guarded the far end. The view was both beautiful and heartbreaking, given Brother Troyer's demise. Poor Barbara. Megan remembered what she'd overheard at the funeral, how Barbara wished she hadn't asked him to weed the garden that day.

They sat on rush-seated, white folding chairs. The summer porch had slick cement flooring, with only two colorful rugs for covering, one at the door going into the house and one at the outside door. It was the perfect place for messy projects. Each woman had half a bucket of beans—the first crop. It wouldn't take them long to snap off the tips.

"I picked these this morning." Barbara's gray-blue eyes saddened, but

Megan noticed with relief that they weren't misty. "The first thing I did was take the rake and. . .rake the ground where. . .you know."

"Somebody should have thought to do that for you," Mom said.

"No. I needed to do it. It's just that everything reminds me of Eli. The shed, the house. . ."

Poor thing. Megan's throat tightened, glad they'd come.

Mom reached into her pail, drew out a handful of beans, and started snapping. "When did your sister go home?"

"Thursday. Lots of church people have come to see me. I'm blessed with friends. I have enough food to last me for an entire month. Maybe longer. I probably should share it. Must be someone who needs it more than me."

"Don't worry about that," Megan urged. "You going to freeze these?"

"I usually do."

"Ever make three bean salad? Lil has the best recipe."

"Oh?"

Mom laughed. "It's a thing with Megan and her friends. Katy and Lil call Megan *Green Bean*."

Barbara's expression grew animated. "I didn't know that. There must be a good story behind that nickname."

Happy to see a bit of the old Barbara, Megan explained the story. She was ten. They had gone to church camp, and their counselor made them name their group. Lil had insisted they call themselves *Three Bean Salad*. "Katy was furious because she had to be the kidney bean."

Barbara laughed. "I can just picture her."

"I was the green bean because they think Mom stresses good steward-ship a little too much. And me, too."

"Nothing wrong with that," Barbara insisted.

"Exactly!" Mom agreed.

Megan knew Mom had gotten over that insult years earlier, because sometimes her friends still called her *Mrs. Green Bean*. They called Dad *The Blues Man* because his hobby was fixing up old Novas, preferably blue. And because there was nothing dismal or blue about Bill Weaver's personality.

"So Lil was cooking way back then. I'd forgotten that. I should do something different this year. Think I could get Lil's bean salad recipe?"

Barbara's buoyancy impressed Megan. "I'll get it for you. I'll even help you make it."

"How fun. Let's do it in a couple of weeks, when the beans really come in."

After exchanging a smile with Mom, Megan agreed.

They snapped in silence for a while, and Megan gazed out across the peaceful setting. A hummingbird flitted around some pink tubular flowers then zipped into a dogwood tree. Her gaze following it, she was the first to see the widow Schlagel dart past the pink carnations that lined the short sidewalk curving from the driveway. The woman was a bundle of energy who gave out an aura of constant unease and discontent. When Susanna noticed Megan, she gave a jerky wave.

"Susanna's here." Barbara went to the door. "Come in."

Susanna's hand flitted to her upswept chestnut brown hair. "What's going on here?"

"I've put them to work." Barbara unfolded another chair. "Join us?"

"Oh, just for a minute. Can I help?"

"We're almost done. No need to dirty your hands," Barbara gestured at the empty chair. "But sit and visit with us."

Susanna perched with a deep sigh. "This is nice. I miss my garden. Never thought I would. But this time a year, I do. If I could get one of my boys to help in the spring, I'd put one in. But they're all busy with their own lives."

"If you really want one, I'm sure we could get someone from church to help you," Barbara offered.

"Maybe someday." The lovely widow opened her purse and pulled out a small softcover. "Here's the book I was telling you about."

Barbara rose and took the book. "Thanks. I'll just put it by the door and look at it later."

Megan couldn't read the title, but when Barbara turned her back, Susanna exchanged a glance with Megan, causing her spirit to bristle much like it had at the cemetery. She wondered if Mom, who was naturally discerning, felt it, too.

Susanna softened her expression and shifted her brown gaze to Barbara. "I marked the portions we talked about." Abruptly she stood and folded her chair, resting it against the wall. "I need to go, but would you mind walking me to my car?"

"Sure," Barbara said, setting her beans to the side and wiping her hands on her apron.

"G'day." Susanna started to the door and tripped on the throw rug. She righted herself and went outside with Barbara, casting Megan a sour look through the window.

"Did you see that?"

"What?"

"Never mind." How could she explain to Mom how the beautiful widow in all her red plumage reminded Megan of a hawk hovering over its prey?

Barbara returned, slightly out of breath. "Out at the car, Susanna offered to stay nights with me."

"Oh?" Mom replied.

"That's why she dropped by. Well that and the book. But I turned down the offer. It was thoughtful but not what I'm looking for. I can't imagine myself in the widows' group. I've always spent some time with the quilters, but you know that widows' group is a tight circle." She spoke as if she were sorting out the matter. "I do get along well with Ann Byler. She always sees the best in everybody."

And tries to quell Susanna's bitter remarks. Megan couldn't forget Susanna's parting look. The woman was recently widowed, younger than the other widows. Only in her forties. Mom had gleaned from Dad's elders meetings that the woman was bitter and had started several hurtful rumors. Mom felt sorry for her. As a preacher's wife, Barbara must be aware of Susanna's actions, too.

It was kind of her not to mention how Susanna started things, told them to Mae, who spread it around. Mae got the blame for being the gossip. This put the third woman in the widow triangle in an uncomfortable position. Ann Byler tried to squelch gossip. She was on the timid side, so the other two pretty much ran over her. If Barbara entered the group, it would change the schematics. Barbara wouldn't tolerate gossip. But Barbara wasn't ready to join their group.

Megan kept her thoughts to herself. Although Mom occasionally told her about church matters, both of them kept such things confidential. What Dad brought home from elders meetings stayed within the Weaver household. Unless Katy brought up a matter. Since her dad was also an elder, sometimes they discussed things together. It was a small community. News got around quickly, even with the best intentions. But that was different than initiating spiteful rumors.

A clock inside the house chimed twelve times, drawing Megan's attention away from her thoughts.

"Noon. And we just finished. I guess we can go blanch these and get them in containers. Then I'll fix us some lunch from my plentiful donations." Barbara grinned. "Coming, Green Bean?"

Megan smiled back and stood. Moving to the door, she cast a final glance out the window. The lawn needed mowing. She'd mention it to Dad. He could set up something with the churchmen to take turns mowing. The parsonage would need a man's upkeep. Maybe Dad had already handled the situation. But what would happen when they got a new preacher? Surely they wouldn't make Barbara move? Would she even have a garden next year?

~ ⌒ ~

Megan handed her dad a wrench and stepped back from the open hood of the classic Nova she drove.

"So what kind of noise was it making again?" he asked.

"I don't know. Just different. Rough."

She fetched a bucket, upturned it for a seat, and watched him work. Knowing that he'd gotten home late the night before from one of his church meetings, she asked, "How's it going with the search committee?" The last she'd heard, in the three weeks since Brother Troyer's funeral, the search committee had gotten a lot accomplished.

"We got it narrowed down to two candidates."

"Really?"

"Yep. The first one is coming to meet the congregation. He arrives this Friday night."

"And he's staying with us?"

"Umm-hm."

"Where's he from? Is he your favorite, since he's coming first?"

"I'm trying to keep an open mind, and if I tell you too much, it'll spoil it for you."

"Not really."

"His name's Joe Zimmerman. He's the professor's suggestion."

"Oh." Megan figured if her stuffy Bible professor recommended him, he'd be. . .well, like the professor. "And the other one?"

"Ben Detweiler's one of the bishop's recommendations."

Both men sounded old. She didn't know what she'd been expecting until she'd felt disappointed. Restless. That's how she felt.

Dad drew his head out from under the hood, sporting a twinkle in his eyes. He was up to something, but Megan had no idea what. "Start the engine for me, will you, honey?"

She climbed into the bench seat and turned the ignition key.

"Purring like a kitten now," Dad boasted. "How's work?"

"Fine." She had no intention of giving him any personal details.

"I suppose it would be fun to work on airplanes. Scoot over and let me in. How about we pick up your mom and go to the Dairy Queen? So I can see how it runs."

Megan quickly moved over. The Nova rumbled out of the garage, and Dad parked it in front of the house. He hit the horn. Soon Mom appeared at the screen door. She placed her hands on her hips.

"What are you two up to?"

"Going to the Dairy Queen." Megan motioned. "Come with us?"

"Oh!" Mom hurried out then turned back and shut the door. "What's the occasion?"

"We're just taking the car on a test run."

When Megan opened her door, her mom waved her hand. "Stay there. I'll just hop in the backseat."

While Dad drove the car, he checked every working part within reach. When he flipped down the sun visor, the Bible verse fell onto his lap. "What's this?" He picked it up and gave it a glance.

"Nothing." Megan snatched it away and shoved it into her pocket. In the future, she needed to learn to do her own tune-ups.

"You got a boyfriend?" The question jolted Megan from her paperwork.

She looked at Chance with contrived annoyance. "Check out my personnel files."

Chance burst into laughter. "Where have I heard that before?"

Her hand involuntarily moved to twist her hair, a habit from years of wearing it long and free. But she'd started wearing it up in a bun at work, so her hand moved through thin air then rested on her skirt. "Why?"

"Just curious. That why your friend Lil warned me off?"

It had been three weeks since they'd started working together and since Lil had warned him to stay away from Megan. He'd never brought it up again. Until now. They had fallen into an amiable work relationship and routine of sorts. At first, she had meditated on her "don't be yoked" Bible verse daily. But after it had fallen from her visor, she'd forgotten to replace it.

"No boyfriend."

"If you did, what would he be like?" He glanced at her prayer covering, a reminder of the dos and don'ts of her religion. "I'm sure he'd drive a car," Chance teased.

"He'd be a Conservative Mennonite guy, if that's what you're asking." This was her opportunity to make him aware that she was unavailable to guys like him.

"He couldn't just be a Christian? Is that why you wear that net cap? To set your boundaries?"

"No." The covering was an object of curiosity for outsiders, but a topic that couldn't be explained without getting into scriptures and deeper Mennonite theology. She didn't think he was after that.

Chance perched on the edge of her desk, in the place that she had intentionally cleared for him after he'd knocked her stapler and plastic inbox on the floor way too many times. "I ever tell you what happened to the first Christian men who visited the Auca Indians?"

With hesitance, Megan repeated, "No."

"The Aucas have been called the worst people on earth. They hated all strangers, lived to hunt, fight, and kill. Even their neighbors—the Jivaros, who were famous for shrinking human heads—feared them. They buried alive their old and sick. Strangled babies with vines—"

Megan threw up her palms. "Please stop. I understand. The worst people on earth."

"Sorry. Anyway, they were territorial and didn't like strangers or intruders. Five men from different mission groups all got the calling to take them the Gospel. They teamed together and studied the language; then they flew over the tribe and made air drops of gifts useful to the Aucas. The Indians knew the gifts came from the men in the planes, who shouted down at them in their own language, 'We like you. We are friends.' The Indians accepted the gifts. So one day the Christians landed. But the Indians viciously killed them and vandalized their plane then ran for the jungle, waiting for other strangers to come and retaliate. But of course, they didn't, and missionaries continued to pursue them for the Gospel. Today about a third of the tribe is believers, and they are more commonly called the Waorani."

"That's a touching story." Megan considered the costs of the missionaries and their families, wondering how she would have responded.

"Don't be an Auca, Megan." Having just searched her soul, she narrowed her eyes and tried to follow his line of reasoning—comparing her to the most awful people on earth instead of the Christian missionaries. "I'm harmless. Please, don't shoot me out of the sky."

"They didn't shoot the plane out of the sky. They had spears and had to wait until it landed."

"That's what I'm saying. I landed on your turf. But I'm not the enemy. Especially if there's no boyfriend itching to pick a fight with me."

How quickly he could twist a story for personal conquest. "Conservative men don't fight." She wasn't giving him the green light, just correcting his understanding of Mennonite men.

"They don't stand up for their women?"

"We are nonresistant."

Chance scowled. "Pacifists?"

Feeling his disapproval, she tried to explain. "Sort of. There's a difference. Pacifists use political means to gain their end."

"You're referring to activists?"

Megan nodded. "They would defend themselves in a lawsuit.

Nonresistance is a submissive term. It stems from peace with God. Pacifists aren't necessarily Christians. While both groups abhor violence, pacifists think more about war and human rights. We would give up our rights to help a neighbor. We are mostly concerned about his soul. There's a big difference."

Chance looked concerned. "Your men don't go into the military, either?"

Megan shook her head. "But during the draft, they served in other ways. Like medical workers and firefighters. And we still help our country by volunteering after natural disasters." She tilted her head, studying him. "What about you? Are you a pacifist?"

"I'd rather be a lover than a fighter." He raised a sandy eyebrow. "Hypothetically speaking, what would a jealous Mennonite man do? Or a protective father?"

She didn't appreciate his menacing question, especially after her lengthy explanation. "Why does it matter? It doesn't pertain. You're not an enemy."

"Then we can be friends?"

"That's not a good idea. You're my boss, and we work together."

"You're friends with Paige."

"Only here at the office."

He gave her a sly smile. "You're forgetting something important. I'm not *really* your boss." He shifted off her desk, and she gave an inward sigh of relief. "Who needs to get back to work. But sometime we should go to lunch. Or let me take you out to dinner. You can tell me why you wear that net cap. I'm really interested in that."

"It's called a prayer covering." She clamped her lips, aggravated that he could easily bait her.

"Even more intimidating. But keep in mind that the Aucas couldn't hold off the Christians forever."

He strode into his office, and Megan stared after him with a heart full of concern. She figured she'd better copy that Bible verse again and tape it inside her desk drawer this time.

CHAPTER 6

By Friday Megan was exhausted and confused from a week of having to fend off Chance's advances. Ever since he had told her the story of the Aucas, he had initiated a campaign to break down her personal boundaries. She had purposefully taken great pains to establish lines that would help her fend off his charms.

Sure her workload had lightened a bit as Chance had become accustomed to the office routine, but not enough to make up for the time he spent perched on her desk or interrupting her for no good reason.

She turned the Nova onto her road, stirring up a trail of billowing dust when she hit a patch of loose gravel. The heat sapped energy from her, too, and she swiped her hand across her forehead. While driving the old car was fun, it had summer drawbacks, such as its lack of air-conditioning.

Weary, she whipped the Chevy into the front circle drive. No need to put it away when she was going over to Lil's for supper. She had looked forward to spending time with her friends all week. Finally she could unwind. It was even a holiday weekend. There were festivities in Plain City, celebrating the Fourth of July.

Chance had tried to worm his way into an invitation to attend some of those events with her, but she'd been able to make valid excuses, until finally, he'd relented. Now she took a satisfied breath, looking forward to a sweet snack and a cool shower. Snatching her purse off the seat next to her, she got out of the car, moved up the steps to the country-style porch, and reached for the screen door. Her hand was already on the doorknob when she heard a familiar creaking sound.

Thinking it was Mom, but surprised that Mom would be swinging this time of day instead of preparing dinner, Megan glanced at the white porch swing. Instead of Mom, a male figure lounged on their porch. She felt a moment of alarm until she remembered the preacher candidate. "Hello?"

"Hi. Hope I didn't startle you." He had a deep-timbered voice.

"A bit." The buckeye tree next to the porch set a deep shadow across his face. She stepped closer and realized that she was speaking to a much younger man than she had expected. "I'm Megan Weaver."

"I know." His voice held amusement laced with triumph. "We've met before."

Something familiar about the voice niggled at her. Confused, Megan took a few steps closer and halted. Her eyes widened when she recognized him. She felt as though she'd walked straight into a living nightmare.

"Micah?" *Aye, yi, yi. Skinny Man?* At college, the name had been a play on *Zimmerman*, and she'd also thought of him as stick man. "You're here about the preacher's position?" Her question came out more disdainful than polite.

He chuckled. "I guess you're not the welcoming committee."

She scowled, having no intention of welcoming *him* into her community or her life. "That would be Mom and Dad. I wasn't expecting you. I was expecting some old Joe Zimmerman."

He grinned. "Sorry to disappoint you."

"Oh no. You didn't." If he was Dad's candidate, she needed to show him some respect. Anyway, disappointment was far too weak for the emotion she was feeling about him. Outrage? But now it made sense that this former Rosedale Bible student would be the professor's recommendation. She hadn't considered one of the professor's students. Dumb. Well, if it had shocked her, his age would be a shock to the rest of the congregation, too.

She recalled the mischievous glint in Dad's eyes when he'd worked over her Nova and discussed the candidates. Bill Weaver probably thought bringing in a younger man was going to be a wonderful surprise for her. He had no idea what he'd set into motion, inviting this man into their home, because he did not know that she had spent her entire first semester fending off his clumsy and dogged pursuit, which had made her skin crawl every time they'd been in the same room.

She forced away the image of him trying to give her a tiny stuffed bear after she'd refused to go to the Columbus zoo with him. The thought of him mooning over her the whole day at the zoo and even bringing her back a souvenir had almost given her the feeling of being stalked. That was when she'd determined to make it clear to him that she wasn't interested. That was right before she'd hurt his feelings.

He stood now, and his smile faded. He towered over her, a Mennonite Ichabod Crane. His brown eyes scrutinized her, not in a suggestive way, but as if trying to pull something out of her soul that wasn't there to give. It had always been that way with him. It gave her the shivers. She'd never been able to understand why his actions disturbed her so deeply.

"As I remember, there was plenty of disappointment. But I'm hoping we can put that behind us."

"Oh that." She lowered her lashes in embarrassment then glanced back up at him. "Sure." As long as he didn't start it up again. He had been a piece of double-stick tape that was impossible to remove, and she didn't want to find herself back in that predicament.

"Good. I—" He sneezed midsentence.

"Bless you," Megan said, and then, her eyes widening, she pressed her finger to her upper lip, trying to ward off a similar impulse. She saw the branches over the swing fluttering and knew that the breeze would bring in more pollen, that she needed to get inside, but her sneeze wouldn't be denied, either.

"And to you," he said softly.

"Allergies. I'd better get inside."

"Wait. Me, too."

Dread engulfed her. So it was already beginning. His trailing her around. Was there to be no peace at home this entire weekend? She'd looked forward to relaxing and having fun. She strode into the kitchen,

Skinny Man at her heels. "Hi, Mom."

"So you've met." Mom beamed and wiped her hands on her apron.

Megan smelled meatloaf baking, which meant her mom was going all out, heating up the kitchen in the summer. She was preparing to cook a big kettle of corn on the cob, too. "Yes." Wanting nothing more than to escape to her room and take a shower, and not get forced into a polite conversation that Mom would initiate with the candidate, Megan quickly added, "You remember I'm going to Lil's for supper?"

"No." Mom looked disappointed. "I'd forgotten."

"You need some help?"

Mom's gaze held a yearning for Megan to stay, but she waved her away, "No, I've got it covered here. Your dad will be in soon. Some others from the committee are coming over after supper to get to know Joe."

Joe. Even his name provoked Megan. Imposter. She didn't want to hear why he was Joe now and Micah at school.

"Thanks, Mom." She glanced at Micah. "See you later."

"I believe I'll freshen up before supper." He followed her to the stairway. She cringed. As they climbed to the second story, he said, "I like your mother. What's your dad like?"

"His nickname is Blues Man." Let him fret over that. Think he was gloomy and mean. It was the only thing she could think of that might give Micah a little anguish before he found out how friendly and good-natured her dad really was.

In the hallway, Micah stopped at the first door. "Megan. Can I call you that?"

Her neck bristled. "Sure."

"What happened at school. . .can we keep that confidential?"

She braced her back against the cream-colored wall with dark-stained moldings. His question carried a lot of weight because she was ready to explode, had already envisioned venting to her friends. "I have to tell Mom and Dad. Otherwise, I'd feel uneasy with you staying two doors down from me." When she saw his expression fall, she tried to soften her words. "Not that I don't trust you."

He glanced down the hall and bit his lip. "I understand."

"To be honest, I'll probably tell my best friends, Lil and Katy, too. But they'll keep it confidential. So, yeah, your secret's pretty safe."

He looked at her with resignation. "Thanks for the honesty. This position means a lot to me. It's important that I find a church. Start a ministry."

She nodded. "I understand. But just so you know, Brother Troyer's shoes will be hard to fill. I'm not sure how this will go for you."

Micah softly chuckled. "I know. Nothing like a pair of broke-in shoes for comfort. Thanks for the warning."

She didn't like his flippant reference to Brother Troyer. "I miss him. He's not an old pair of shoes."

"I'm sorry. That was thoughtless."

Realizing she'd snapped when she was the one who'd brought up Brother Troyer's shoes in the first place, she replied, "God's will be done." Inside her room, she leaned against the smooth surface of the door. *Aye, yi, yi!*

────⟶ 🜚

Micah Zimmerman watched Megan disappear, regretting his stupid blunder. Frowning at the awkward incident, he went into the Weavers' pale yellow guest room that Anita had offered him earlier. Megan hadn't changed much, unless she'd grown lovelier. She'd taken the shock of his appearance gracefully, but he'd felt her resistance as strongly as he had that time he'd asked her to the talent show back at Rosedale. He'd quickly discovered her talent was evasion. She did this constant magical act of vanishing into thin air.

She'd refused to accept any goodies from him at the coffee shop, and she hadn't been interested in his disc golf skills either. Her disinterest wasn't merely indifference. She'd been passionate and creative in her snubs and rebuffs. And foolish as it seemed to him now, he'd been just as zealous to change her mind. Only she hadn't given him a chance.

But he hadn't returned to Plain City because of her. It was just the way things had fallen into place. Micah sank onto the yellow-and-blue star quilt, but the soft bedding didn't comfort its guest. He couldn't forget the blond woman who'd given him such a frosty look in the hall, made him feel like an intruder. One whom she feared and disliked. But he wasn't intruding. He'd been invited by Bill Weaver, her own dad, to come to Plain

City for an interview. To stay at this house. Her house.

He'd been looking for a church and praying about his future, and the Big Darby Conservative Mennonite church was the only offer he'd gotten. The recommendation had come from Professor Maust, a man who had been influential in his spiritual growth and education. The offer had both excited him and set his neck hairs on edge. He loved Plain City, Ohio. When he'd gone to Rosedale, he'd enjoyed the area. But he hadn't forgotten that Megan resided in Plain City.

It wasn't like he still mooned over her, but he did remember her on occasion. In fact, to receive the letter from her father had been a shock. He hadn't been positive it was her family, but he certainly hadn't been surprised when she stepped onto the porch, either. Now that he knew her dad had invited him, he wondered if she planned to ruin his chances. He didn't know if he could face yet another humbling lesson. Unless God meant to give him another chance with her.

He leaned back on one of the freshly ironed pillowcases. He couldn't allow that far-fetched hope to niggle away his peace of mind. Perhaps it would be a lesson on denial. He imagined shepherding the Big Darby flock and being forced to stuff his attraction for Megan. To do that would be to give God everything.

When he'd accepted the invitation, he'd determined to do exactly that. It didn't seem impossible at the time. He hadn't seen Megan for more than three years. During that time, his grandmother had died, and his brother had moved away. Megan's rejection was just another major disappointment to add to his string of losses. But he'd survived.

As he considered all this, he realized he was rubbing his eyes. They itched. His throat burned, too. He sat upright and examined the pillows. Down. He wouldn't be able to sleep on them. In fact, he would have to act quickly to ward off a more serious allergic reaction, one that would spoil his evening or even his entire weekend. He rose and fumbled through the zipped linings of his suitcase for his allergy pills. He stuck his head in the hall, figuring he needed to get water from the bathroom. The only thing moving was the floor-length sheer panels from the window at the end of the hall. The bathroom was positioned between his room and Megan's.

The handle turned freely, and he entered, closing the door behind him. Inside he caught a citrus scent. Her scent. He realized she must have recently been in the room. Frustrated in more ways than one, he clutched his collar and wiggled it, unable to resist clawing at his neck a few times. But he didn't want red scratches when he needed to make a favorable impression. Micah willed himself to quit. He popped the pill into his mouth and leaned over the faucet, taking just enough tap water to swallow the pill. He needed about twenty minutes for the medicine to kick in and work. He didn't want to trouble Mrs. Weaver about the pillows and risk coming across as a wimp. If he could get them out of his room, he'd make do without them.

Next he used an inhaler and coughed, waiting a moment for the wheezing to quit. Megan's bathroom was neat. He liked that. Maybe they'd put her belongings away because of his visit. Curious, he opened the medicine cabinet. Inside were some body lotions, a can of hair spray, a bottle of face wash, toothpaste, and her toothbrush. Feeling ashamed that he was privy to the brands she used, he quickly closed it.

Tentatively moving back into the hall, he saw a wide linen closet that he'd missed before. He opened it and peered inside. Mrs. Weaver had told him to help himself to linens. If he removed that one stack of towels, he could store those in his closet and replace them with the offensive pillows. He took the stack of four towels, two hand towels and six wash cloths and turned.

"You giving away souvenirs?"

He froze. Megan stood leaning against the wall with her arms crossed, watching him hauling *all* their linens off to his room. He sought for a witty response, but his brain was feather-deadened, consumed with the fire ants crawling up his neck, and nothing came to mind. Then he remembered that out on the porch, she'd admitted she had allergies, too. Maybe she could sympathize without thinking he was a wimp. How else could he explain toting off all the towels in the entire linen closet?

"Keep another secret?"

She arched a brow. "You're making up a missions packet in there? You just moved into an apartment and have no money for towels?"

"I'm allergic to the pillows. Thought I'd store them in the linen closet. Anita said to make myself at home."

Megan's arms relaxed. "You have down pillows in there? I didn't know we even had any of those left in the house. I'll go tell Mom to get you some others."

"No. Please. I don't want to bother her."

"Oh." She let out an indecisive sigh then admitted, "I'd probably do the same thing. I'm sorry about all the open windows. We don't have air-conditioning." She glanced back at her room, and for one horrible instant he thought she was going to offer one of her own pillows. Thankfully, she didn't.

"I'll be fine."

Her face relaxed. "Good. I'm off to Lil's." She started down the hall then looked back and caught him watching her. "By the way, Dad's nice."

She felt sorry for him. Not the emotion he'd prefer, but he guessed her sympathy was better than loath or repulsion. "Thanks. Have fun with your friends."

She gave him a nod then hurried away.

As he carried the pillows to the linen closet, he told himself it didn't matter what Megan thought about him. But he knew it did. He knew how these small churches worked. Everybody needed to be in agreement for him to take the job. He hadn't been able to elevate her opinion of him at school, and here he was stuck with the same problem.

Her approval mattered to him. When she had stepped onto the porch, every masculine and fleshly desire had been awakened. The attraction was annoying. He'd observed her enough back at Rosedale to discover her weaknesses. She was naive and headstrong. Not exactly the ideal combination for a preacher's wife. He needed a compassionate woman who related to the hurts of others, a woman who was caring and giving. Megan had plenty of passion, but she'd always used it to resist him.

His throat relaxed again, but the rest of his body remained uptight. Megan had made it plain that she didn't want him in her home. And under those circumstances, he didn't want to be in her home, either. Sharing a bathroom with her, for pity's sake. Seeing her pink toothbrush was more than he could handle. And no matter how nice her dad was, once she told her parents how he'd dogged her at school, as if she were a lab specimen, they wouldn't want him as a guest, either. If they moved him to the home of another person in their congregation, questions would arise. In this small congregation, news would spread quickly. It wouldn't be good for his chances. Megan had put him in a difficult and awkward situation. No, he'd put himself there.

Confused and irritated, Micah sank to his knees, clasped his hands together, and rested his forehead against the quilt. *Lord, I'm sorry I allowed my eyes and attention to stray to Megan. Again. She's not my goal here. But You drew me here, so there must be a reason. Something I need to learn that will aid me in my work? Or is this place going to be my calling? My home? Please direct my steps, according to Your will. And help me keep my eyes focused on You. Only You.*

The thought popped into his mind that if his history with Megan became public, it would create a good test, give him a feel for how the people in the congregation interacted. This interview wasn't only about the congregation accepting him. This weekend was about his decision, too. He was suddenly very interested to see what the Lord had in store.

CHAPTER 7

D o you tell Fletch everything?" Megan squirted a drop of detergent in a kettle and ran some water in it while Lil arranged their dinner on serving platters.

"I don't know, why?"

Megan placed a few dirty utensils inside the kettle to soak then turned away from the sink. "I'm still single. I don't know how this works. When I confide in you, am I also confiding in Fletch?"

"Oh. I suppose if it came up, I'd tell him. But he's not all that interested in girl stuff." She eyed Megan carefully. "But if I told him it was confidential, you could count on him."

"So if I don't want Fletch knowing certain things about me, even if I asked you to keep it confidential, you might tell him?"

"Let me assure you. All Fletch can think about right now is his trip to Ethiopia. He can't even remember to take out the trash. I don't think you have to worry about him asking about you. It's not that he doesn't like you. He's just got his own things going on right now. Sometimes he barely pays attention to me."

Megan was shocked at the frustration in Lil's comment. "What do you mean? You're not having problems?"

"No," Lil shooed the comment away with a flick of her wrist. "Is this about Chance? Is he trifling with you?"

"Yes, but it's not about him."

Confused, Lil placed her hands on her apron's waistband. "Spill the beans."

"This is one of those confidential things," Megan started, but just then Katy and Jake arrived.

"This isn't finished," Lil warned, then went across the room to greet the newcomers.

Megan followed her and reached for Jacob. "Hey, sweet boy."

The baby stared at her with bright eyes and responded with gurgling noises. Megan nestled her face into the tiny chest. When she drew away, Jacob's arms flew in the air. "I didn't mean to scare you," she cooed.

As the men conversed, Lil drew Katy to a safe distance. "Megan's going to tell us a secret. And she doesn't want the chump to hear."

Katy didn't flinch at Lil's pet name for her husband, who was also Lil's cousin. And Megan didn't blink when Lil invited Katy into the conversation. "It's just that I made a promise that this wouldn't get around in church, but I'm exploding inside."

Katy's dark, almond-shaped eyes speared Megan. "It's about the preacher candidate, isn't it?"

"Who's staying at your house?" Lil clarified.

"Yeah. Old Joe Zimmerman."

"Dad's meeting him tonight." Katy looked disappointed. "How old?"

"That's my point. He's young. And I know him."

"He's a relative?" Lil asked with confusion.

"No. He's from Rosedale."

Lil untied her apron and slung it across a chair. "That's interesting."

"It's a nightmare." Having their full attention, Megan shifted Jacob to her opposite arm. "It's Micah Zimmerman, the guy who I couldn't get rid of. Remember that first semester?"

Katy folded the apron and replaced it. "Skinny Man?"

"The stick man." Lil covered her giggle.

"It's not funny. Don't you remember how hard it was to get him to leave me alone? Now he's just down the hall. In my own house. What'll I do?"

"You poor thing." Lil tilted her head. "Remember how he slid a poem inside your math book? And didn't he take you to the zoo?"

"No! But he tried."

Katy nibbled her lower lip thoughtfully, "You think he's here because of you?"

Megan shrugged and ran a finger across Jacob's soft cheek. "Professor Maust recommended him. Dad wrote the letter inviting him. But even if he isn't interested in me anymore, it'll be awkward if he gets the job. Worse, if he starts asking me out again." As her voice escalated, Jacob made a pout. Megan attempted to rock him with his arms, but he let out a howl.

Katy reached for him. "If he's staying at your house, you'll get past the awkward part."

"Unless I have to give him another set down."

Lil frowned. "Do your parents know?"

Megan shook her head. "This just happened a few hours ago. Micah asked me not to tell anyone about what happened between us at Rosedale."

"Or didn't happen," Lil corrected.

"I told Micah I was going to tell my parents. He said he understood. But I could tell he didn't like it."

"If this gets around your church, folks'll make a big deal about it."

"I know. It'll be humiliating."

"They won't hear it from me. We're going to be out of the country anyways."

"Me either," Katy promised. "So besides your history, do you think he'd make a good preacher?" Her dark eyes teased. "We already know he's persevering."

Megan rolled her gaze toward the ceiling. "I have no idea."

"And now you have to fend off two guys," Lil remarked caustically.

Hoisting the squirmy baby up on her shoulder and patting his back, Katy demanded, "That Campbell man is still after you?"

"Yeah. He even invited himself to the Fourth of July events."

"Ugh!" Katy scoffed, giving her opinion of the matter. "What did you tell him?"

"I turned him down. Chance Campbell will soon be gone," Megan reminded them. "But what if I have to live the rest of my life with Micah's ogling?"

Katy shook her head. "I don't think preachers ogle, do they?"

"You need some help in there, honey?" Fletch called from the table, where he could see they were merely visiting and not paying attention to his hunger needs.

"No thanks." Lil handed Megan a platter and took one for herself. "Let's go eat. If you want, we'll talk more later."

Megan nodded. Lil was more worried about Chance and wasn't taking the situation with Micah seriously. Anyway, she was going to be out of the country. And Katy wanted her to give Micah a chance just because he was Mennonite. Well, it wasn't like she wanted to intentionally thwart his career.

Using Lil and Katy as a sounding board had sorted out her thinking: The real issue wasn't about how to fend Micah off for a weekend. It was figuring out if they could get along as preacher and parishioner. To find the answer to that question, she needed to get more involved in the process. As much as she dreaded it, she needed to use her influence to sway Micah's decision. If she ran from the situation now, she'd surely regret it later.

———ᏻ———

Micah—Joe to everyone in the room except Professor Maust—shifted uneasily in his chair and tried to answer the question that had just been fielded at him. *What have you been doing since school?*

The reference to his seminary training as *school* didn't show much respect for his degree and made him feel less than mature around a room full of people two decades older than himself. But he smiled and discussed his work in Allentown with some inner-city kids through a program at his home church. He explained how his love for sports made it a natural fit. He mentioned he'd been given opportunities to preach numerous times. He'd written several articles for *The Mennonite*, a church magazine.

"How long have you been trying to find a church?"

"Not long. I thought it was better to get practical experience first. Also, my grandmother was sick. I lived with her. When she died, it took awhile to settle some family business."

"I'm sorry."

"Thanks."

An awkward silence filled the room, and then Vernon Yoder recapped Micah's past experience. "Since school, you served at your local congregation and did some preaching."

"Yes, sir. I was waiting for God's leading to move forward."

"And you sense that now?"

"Yes. I felt a strong call to come for this interview. But I have to be honest, I don't know if it's a match or not. I want to follow God's will. I'm as interested as you are to see where this goes."

Anita quietly left the room and returned with a tray of desserts. As she passed them out, her husband asked, "Did you know our Megan at Rosedale?"

Micah cleared his throat. "Yes. I met her during my last semester."

The professor quirked an eyebrow, and Micah sensed that his former teacher knew something about their relationship or lack of it. He met Noah Maust's gaze, and there was a definite twinkle in the older man's eyes. Micah redirected his gaze back to Bill. "Your daughter's very charming. I suppose everybody noticed her."

Bill seemed pleased with his comment, but that would probably change once Megan spoke to him and he learned the entire truth.

"Do you have a special woman in your life?" Anita asked, settling into the chair beside her husband.

"No. Honestly, at this point, I'm more interested in my work. I figure if I focus on the Lord, all the other things will fall into place." He could have quoted Luke 12:31—*"But rather seek ye the kingdom of God; and all these things shall be added unto you"*—because he'd memorized it shortly after Megan's rejection. It had become his anchor verse. But he didn't want to come across as overly pious.

"You've plenty of time for that," Bill agreed.

"But you hope to one day marry?" Mrs. Yoder asked. "A wife would be a good asset for a preacher. Help him in his ministry. Our Barbara is a saint."

Micah adjusted his collar, but not from an allergic irritant this time. "I'm sure that's true. When I feel it's in God's plan, I'll consider marriage."

The woman got a glint in her eyes. "Those things just happen sometimes."

Everybody in the room chuckled at Micah's inexperience. He hadn't meant to sound self-righteous. He supposed they'd feel more comfortable with a married preacher residing over them, but they'd known he was single when they invited him. "No girl. No marriage on the immediate horizon."

"We've hounded Joe enough for one evening. We should let him eat his cake now," Noah Maust said.

Though relieved, Micah still needed to clarify one thing. He cleared his throat. "There's something I should probably tell you. Before this goes any further."

Instantly, every eye riveted on him.

"I don't go by Joe. It's Micah." So it was his own fault that he didn't get to eat his dessert, but he hadn't the appetite for it anyways. Next, he found himself telling the story of how he became known as Micah. "So sometimes it doesn't pay to get named after a relative. It's too confusing. After Grandpa died, it seemed disrespectful to take his name."

The conversation shifted to the committee's itinerary for Micah. Being a holiday weekend, the town festivities were mentioned. "When Brother Troyer was here, we had a church picnic every July Fourth to celebrate our religious freedom. What's your opinion on it?"

"While I can't rejoice about bombs bursting in air, I see nothing wrong with attending some festivities. I agree with Brother Troyer's philosophy. We should be thankful for our freedoms. Honor those who died for freedom."

Soon after the cake had been served, people began to leave, making sure to give Micah a personal farewell. When the last visitor had gone, Bill exhaled a deep sigh, and for the first, Micah realized that the man was under a great deal of strain.

"Let me help." Micah straightened some throw pillows and found a cup that Anita had missed and headed for the kitchen.

"Oh, you don't have to do that," she protested.

Bill grabbed the trash and headed out the back door.

"I want to. I always dried dishes for Grandma."

Anita eyed him kindly. "We've peppered you with lots of questions. Enough for one night. But someday I'd like to hear more about your family."

"That's why I'm here."

Anita handed him a dish towel. "You want to go to the Fourth of July parade with us tomorrow morning?"

"I'd like that." But immediately, he wondered who all Anita was including in the *us*.

CHAPTER 8

Megan sidestepped around a family with a child in a red wagon and felt her arm brush against the preacher's. In her mind, she'd started calling him *Preacher*. Her previous nicknames no longer fit him or gave her any pleasure. Instinctively she pulled back and glanced up at him, but his gaze was roving both sides of the street, taking in the small-town, pre-parade activity.

She stole another glance. Micah wasn't as gangly as she remembered him from college. He'd changed. He'd gained some weight so that the sharp planes of his face had softened. His nose fit his face now. Everything about him seemed more solid, even his mannerisms. And he didn't stare at her all the time and make her feel uncomfortable. He seemed almost human. Normal. Still she shouldn't let her guard down.

Or had she magnified her memories of everything that had happened between them at college? She thought about that first day they'd met. He'd been climbing some exterior steps and had actually stopped midflight, turned around, and asked her if he could carry her books. And she had been going in the opposite direction! At that first encounter, she'd been flattered. Who wouldn't have been? At the time, she hadn't taken him seriously. She'd thought he was just clowning around. She'd grinned, shaken her head, and hurried away.

"How's this?" Dad asked. Mom glanced over at them.

"Fine," Megan murmured, feeling almost guilty for where her thoughts had taken her. Was Micah doing the same thing, remembering all their encounters, perhaps even chiding himself? They were both so much younger at the time. Megan lowered her voice and asked Micah, "So how did it go last night, meeting the committee members and their wives?"

"Okay. You missed a good supper. I guess you know your mom's a good cook?"

"Yeah, but so is my friend Lil. She's a chef, was head chef until she got married and stepped down."

He shrugged. "The committee members and their wives were friendly, but it felt a little bit like being in a dunk tank."

Megan smiled. "Are you still interested in the position?"

"I'm more curious about it than ever."

"So what's your plan?"

"Let's see. It goes something like this. Parade. Eat. Meeting. Eat. Meeting. Eat. Preach. Potluck. Preach. Eat."

Megan giggled. "Yes, that's the Mennonite way, all right."

"Oh, and there's a tour of the church in there someplace. Then Monday I leave, and you can breathe easy again."

"Can I?"

His expression grew serious, and he quietly studied her. They both knew that if he got the position, it didn't end on Monday. She tore her gaze away, toward the street. "It's starting now. The children's parade is first. Here comes the baby float now. There's a baby contest, and they even dub a Little Lady and Little Knight."

Megan hoped that sometime during his eat-meeting-eat-meeting-eat stay, she'd be able to figure out what he was really pursuing. If it was her, she'd put an end to it. If it was the job, the situation was more complex.

At this point, the invitation to actually take the job hadn't been extended. But this weekend wouldn't be the end of it. There was another candidate to interview. No matter what happened, the parade might be her only opportunity to find out more about Micah and to get the answers to some of her niggling questions.

A row of four- to six-year-olds twirling batons led a small marching band that was followed by a preschool float. Then a colorful mishmash of decorated bicycles, tricycles, wagons, and floats were followed by a children's choir.

In the short interval after the children's parade, Micah drew his gaze from the street to Megan. "The other afternoon when I first saw you, I assumed you were coming home from work. What are you doing these days?"

"I work at a charter air company as assistant to the owner and also do some customer relations."

"No kidding?" He glanced at her. "That sounds interesting."

She nodded. "It is. Char Air does a lot of charity flights. I've always liked missions, and my boss pretty much promised me there'd be some travel involved."

"How long have you been there?"

Megan glanced across the street at a row of two-stories. Directly across sat a pretty house with yellow siding and an expansive front porch. Next to it stood a neat, brown brick commercial shop. The narrow sidewalk was crammed with onlookers. "Less than a year. I was just getting started in school when you were finishing."

Music drew her gaze farther down the road, where the shops out-numbered the homes. "Here comes the high school marching band." Following that chugged a string of antique tractors and cars. "My dad's not happy about missing the car show for your meetings."

"Does he usually participate in it?"

"Are you asking that question as a preacher, or are you just curious?" she teased.

"Just curious."

"He doesn't participate because he thinks it would be prideful. I'm sure Brother Troyer and the other elders feel the same. But sometimes the show includes cars that he's restored for someone else. He does that as a sideline, makes extra money that way." She drew close and whispered, "He's well known in the entire Columbus area."

"You're proud of him."

She nodded.

A woman leading a pony with a flag-blanket passed them. A dune buggy followed, and someone threw candy into the crowd. Until the next float appeared, all along the sidelines children with plastic grocery bags scuttled to gather the candy.

"I don't know if our congregation's ready for you. I think your age will be shocking."

He looked startled. "Aren't there very many young people in the church?"

"No, there are." She tore her gaze from a Jeep pulling a float of soldiers. "Was it hard to choose a sermon?"

"Not really. Your dad gave me a choice of three topics."

"He did? I didn't know that. What are they?"

" 'Set Not Your Heart on Earthly Things,' 'Going Forward with Unity,' or 'How to Check a Heart against Pride.'"

Megan widened her eyes. Not because of their earlier conversation about pride, but because she remembered Brother Troyer preaching those exact sermons. "I don't understand. Those were Brother Troyer's last three sermon titles."

Micah frowned and glanced at Bill Weaver, whose gaze was riveted to the street festivities. He shook his head. "I wonder why the committee did that? It'll provoke an emotional reaction from the congregation."

Megan understood his frustration and even felt a twinge of righteous anger toward the search committee. Didn't they see that the first candidate would be put at a disadvantage? She wondered if Micah even knew that they were choosing between two men or more for the position.

Most likely, they'd give them all the same sermon choices. But it still wouldn't be fair. The first candidate would be judged the harshest. She glanced at her dad, who was watching the pizza restaurant's float, then back at Micah. "I'm sorry they did that to you."

He gave a broad-shouldered shrug. "Hopefully the other candidates will have the same list. But thanks to you, I'm forewarned."

So he did know that he wasn't the only candidate. "Which sermon did you choose?"

"The first. I figured the older members would be interested to get my opinion of what was worldly and what wasn't. As you mentioned, I'm a young candidate. Obviously, it'll be hardest to gain their acceptance."

She sympathized with him and had half a notion to pay Barbara a call and ask for Brother Troyer's sermon notes. Barbara would understand. Any woman would understand the emotional dimension involved. "That's smart. You're right about that. And that sermon is the oldest of the three, too. Maybe nobody will remember it."

The fire trucks drove past them, drowning out her voice with their flashing lights, firemen, and sirens. A dog rode in the first truck. She felt a hand on her shoulder and turned just as Micah went to whisper in her ear, causing his lips to brush her face. Shocked at the intimate touch, she jerked away and looked at him with confusion.

But he seemed unaffected. "What did you say?"

Micah's question hung in the air, as her gaze took in something even more alarming than Micah's mistaken kiss. "Chance?"

"Huh?" Micah tilted his head and stared at her lips.

Megan felt her face heat as her temporary boss squeezed in beside her, placing a hand at the small of her back. She sensed Micah stepping away, Chance moving closer. The sirens added to her confusion.

Micah was crushed from the velocity of new information and the sudden turn of events. There was nothing fair about what the search committee had done to him, and most likely he would be up all night reworking his sermon. It was reassuring that Megan sympathized with his plight. She'd tried to tell him something just as the sirens blared.

Then he'd leaned forward because he'd missed her last comment, and she'd moved. His lips had touched her face. She'd jerked away as though he'd done it deliberately. It happened just when she'd started to relax around him; the timing couldn't have been worse. Nearly kissing her was an accident, the least of his intentions. About now he could use the hoses attached to that screaming fire truck to put out the blaze that she'd just ignited in him.

And who on earth was the man who had shoved in right after that and wedged his way between him and Megan? The intruder had possessively placed his hand at her waist. But Megan had turned pale as paste. Whatever was going on between them, Micah could tell the outsider was attracted to her.

One good thing, Megan had shrugged away from the intruder's touch. Watching them closely, Micah tried to determine what kind of relationship they shared. The intruder dropped his hands from her waist and jammed them into his jeans pockets. He leaned close to Megan and whispered something. She shook her head, giving him an arched look.

Micah wondered if she was disagreeing with him or refusing him. At least at school it hadn't been necessary for Micah to watch her interact with other guys. To his knowledge, she hadn't shown interest in any of the other students. The flash of jealousy that he felt wasn't a welcome emotion. Especially not now. Not this weekend.

"That's it!" Anita's voice bellowed. She spoke at the exact moment that the fire trucks turned off their sirens. "Well." She lowered her volume. "The best parade yet, don't you think?"

"A beauty." Micah smiled weakly, unable to share her enthusiasm since his mind was on Megan and the stranger. Anita flinched, and Micah knew she'd just noticed the man speaking to her daughter.

"Megan?" Anita stepped onto the street so that she could face Megan and get a good look at the stranger. "Who's your friend?"

"This is Chance Campbell. He's my boss's brother. He's filling in for him right now."

"Oh." Anita's voice carried resignation.

Chance stepped forward and put on the charm, garnering Micah's disapproval. He watched Anita, knowing most Conservative women weren't taken in by showy pretense. He could hardly bite back a smile when Bill Weaver caught on and strode over to get in on the introductions. He was easy to read: *My daughter's a catch, but you better keep your distance.*

Megan's hand flitted to Chance's arm. "It was fun to run into you. But we only came for the parade. I'm afraid we can't stay. But there's more entertainment. You won't want to miss the hot air balloons. There're some sports events planned, too." Her hand fell away, and she gave him a parting wave. "Enjoy yourself."

The stranger's gaze suddenly shifted up to Micah's, as if he was responsible for her swift and unexpected departure.

Micah stepped forward and introduced himself as a guest of the Weavers.

Anita fanned her face. "It's going to be a hot one today. Better find yourself a tall, cold drink, Mr. Campbell. Ready to go, Bill?" She nudged her husband and started in the direction of their car.

"I'll do that. Nice to meet you."

Micah wanted to wait for Megan but knew he had no business doing so and followed the Weavers instead. Before he was out of ear shot, however, he heard some bits of conversation ensuing between Campbell and Megan.

"I thought you were kidding when you said you had plans. I thought you were only trying to ditch me."

"I always mean what I say, Chance. Enjoy your day. And I'll see you Tuesday."

A lot of information was packed in those short sentences. They were on first-name basis. Megan didn't have to work on Monday. It was important to her for Campbell to understand that she always meant what she said. The statement included a warning. The type of knowledge that would have saved Micah a lot of trouble back at Rosedale.

"Is the barn on fire or what?" Megan asked, catching up with Micah and her parents.

Anita shot back, "Sorry, honey. But that man looked like he wanted to settle in and stay awhile. And your dad has a busy day planned. The parade went longer than we thought. It was bigger this year, don't you think?"

Micah liked Anita better all the time. They walked in silence for a while, and when they'd finally moved out of the general crush of bodies, he glanced over at Megan. She seemed lost in her thoughts.

"You said Campbell's filling in for your real boss?"

"Yeah, my boss is on a leave of absence."

Trying to sound nonchalant, he asked, "How long will he be gone?"

"Eight weeks altogether. Five more. I really shouldn't be taking Monday off with all the work I have on my desk, but Chance insisted that I treat myself. Our work routine is finally settling in, but. . ." Her voice died away.

"You're keeping track of the weeks?" Micah gave a contrived laugh. She'd almost said something negative about the situation.

"It's hard not to do. Every time I go into his office, I see a row of big red x's on Randy's calendar. Chance is a missionary pilot. He's anxious to get back to the action."

Their relationship seemed personal, but maybe that was because it was a small, intimate workplace. She'd called her real boss by his first name, too. Micah had no right to concern himself with Megan's relationships. His time with her was limited, and he needed to concentrate on the more important reasons for his stay.

"Megan?"

She looked over, tilted her face with skepticism. "What?"

"You've been a good sport, keeping our secrets. But I've got another favor to ask you." He thought he saw her shoulders sag the tiniest bit.

"Yeah, what?"

"Regarding Brother Troyer's sermon—the one I'm going to preach. Do you remember much about it?"

Given her brief blank expression, she'd forgotten all about it. As their previous conversation came back to her, however, she relaxed. "Sure. If I thought about it long enough, it'd probably all come back to me." Her eyes took on a glint of mischief. "And you want me to tell you about it."

Encouraged by her insight, he confided, "Now that I know what I'm up against, I'll probably be up all night working on my sermon. Do you think we could find some time to talk about it? I could jot down some notes and try to figure out my approach."

"Sure, Micah. I should be home when you get back from your meetings. Just let me know when you want to talk."

"Thanks." Having the promise of her help made the pill easier to swallow. Gave him something to anticipate while he was closeted up with the search committee. He couldn't help but wonder what other surprises they had in store for him.

CHAPTER 9

Jo,

What an awkward day! The preacher tagged along with our family to the Fourth of July parade. I guess I should have expected Mom to invite him. Anyway, I took advantage of the situation. Given our history at Rosedale, I was worried that Micah came to Plain City for more than a job. But after spending the morning around him, I think his motives are good, that he's mostly interested in the job.

Although I never entirely let down my guard, I did relax around him. I actually felt sorry for him when I found out he has to preach Brother Troyer's sermon. And I even agreed to help him. Now I'm dreading it. What was I thinking?

Even more awkward, Chance showed up at the parade. That man's motives are easy to read. He's driving me crazy. The next few weeks are going to be hard because I don't really want to resist him. But I must. The man is off-limits to me. Handsome, charming, fascinating, and definitely off-limits.

Megan heard a door close, which meant that Micah had returned. He'd be looking for her so that they could talk about Brother Troyer's sermon.

With resignation, she slipped her journal into her nightstand drawer and glanced in the mirror over her dresser. She straightened her hair and covering then moved to her door. Hesitantly, she opened it and stepped into the hall. It was empty. The door to the guest room was closed. But a light shone from under the bathroom door. This was crazy. She felt like she was spying on him. She turned and started back to her room. A door creaked behind her.

"Megan!"

Her back tensed at the masculine whisper, and she pivoted. "I thought I heard you."

He ran a hand through his hair. It hit her that he parted it way too deep on the side for her liking. Was that what had always repulsed her? She stared at the part that was at least a whole inch too low. It almost gave him the comb-over effect. Other than that, his hair was normal, or even better than normal. It was about two or three inches long on top. Thick and dark brown. The coloring matched his eyes perfectly. The sides of his hair were short and neatly trimmed around his ears, giving him a boyish appearance. A slight curl or cowlick made his bangs wavy. Probably rebelling from the ridiculous part, they swept across his forehead. He'd need to do something with his hair before Sunday's sermon. When she realized she'd been staring at him, she blurted the obvious. "You look beat."

"A rough day." He glanced at his room and back. "Where's a good place for us to talk?"

Funny. Everybody had been so busy that the opportunity hadn't arisen for her to tell her parents about what had happened between them at Rosedale. Or maybe the threat had lessened somewhat as she'd observed him and realized he'd changed over the past three years. But the prospect of telling her parents was a trump card that could be played at any time. "How about the kitchen table?"

"All right. I have some stuff to do. Fifteen minutes?"

"Sure. See you then."

With relief she watched Micah disappear into his room. He wasn't interested in her at all, just his sermon. And that suited her fine.

The downstairs lighting was dim, and some clattering noises led Micah to the kitchen, where he found Megan standing at the counter with her back to him. She had two empty plates and was scooping a piece of oatmeal cake on one of them.

"Uh, oh."

Startled, she gasped and turned. "I didn't hear you come down. Do you always go around sneaking up on people?"

"Feeling guilty, are you? You one of those middle-of-the-night eaters?"

"No. On both accounts. But I do have a sweet tooth."

"I hope one of those isn't for me." He raised his left hand and started counting off his fingers. "Eat, meeting, eat, meeting. Yeah, I thought so. This is meeting."

The corner of her mouth tilted. "Suit yourself. Mom and Dad are outside on the porch swing. The kitchen seems to be the hub of our house. They'll probably gravitate through here in a few minutes."

Since their initial encounter on the porch, she'd sent prickly warning signals of her distrust, and his radar told him he needed to change that. One way to convince her that she had nothing to fear from him was to keep their interactions impersonal. He'd focus on the real reason he'd come to Plain City. Hopefully she'd see how he'd changed.

Fishing out his sermon notes, he also took a notepad from his briefcase and started a clean sheet. On the header, he wrote his topic-sensitive title: Set Not Your Heart on Earthly Things. He waited for her to settle in at the table with her cake.

"So did you survive the dunk tank today?" she asked.

"Barely."

"Can you swim?"

He needed her to realize that she wouldn't be chasing him away with her subtle threats. "Yes. I swim with the sharks."

Her hand stopped partway to her mouth. "I should have known."

"It's only three hours to the beach. We go to Sandy Hook in New Jersey."

"Who's we?"

"Our family, when we were kids. After my folks died, I went with my brother and some of my friends."

"And the sharks."

"Right. Those, too."

He noticed she'd hardly touched her dessert. "You want to finish your cake first?"

"No, I can talk and eat. Just think how much more you'd accomplish if you didn't have to separate your meetings from your eatings." She scraped her fork clean to emphasize her point.

He looked away from her lips. "Yeah, but I lose my appetite when people ask me questions."

"Lucky for you, I don't." She studied him. "You can't afford to lose any weight."

Her concern amused him. "That why you tried to feed me cake? To make me easier on the eyes?"

She rolled her gaze toward the ceiling. "Sorry. I didn't mean to be rude."

He'd always been thin, even though he ate constantly. Genes, he guessed. And his height. But the last couple of years, he'd had to buy larger clothes. He was comfortable with himself—or had been until she'd brought it up just now. He realized he'd allowed their conversation to veer off course. "So why don't you just tell me what you remember from that sermon. I'll take some notes."

She gave him the high points of the sermon, as she remembered them, and this led to a general discussion about the Big Darby congregation, especially the recent changes.

"I had mixed feelings over the prayer-covering debate. My concern was that the church would split over it."

Grateful to discover that Megan was more open-minded than dogmatic, he asked, "Do you think there're any hard feelings about it?"

"Oh no."

Rosedale represented the Conservative Mennonite Conference at large, and at Rosedale, most of the women didn't wear prayer coverings except to worship. That helped him understand that this congregation was very conservative, yet open to change. He liked that.

He thought his biggest obstacle might be the congregation's longtime attachment to their previous preacher. The position at Big Darby might be a rebound term, bearing the brunt of the congregation's confusion and grief. But most congregations seeking a new preacher would be in some sort of transition.

"Sounds like Brother Troyer was a good preacher."

Megan tilted her face to the side, resting her chin on her hand. "I've been a bit angry that the Lord took him. It's hard to accept."

He thought about his own losses. "These things take time." There was much he could share on the subject, but he remembered his resolve to keep their conversation impersonal.

"You mentioned that you lost your parents. Were you young?"

"Yes. A teenager. I lost them in a car crash. My brother and I moved in with my grandparents. Next my grandpa died. My brother got married and moved away. I took care of Grandma toward the end. Then I lost her, too."

"I'm sorry."

"After Grandma died, my brother wanted me to keep the house. But if I take a post someplace, I'll have to do something with it. And it holds a lot of memories."

"You have a lot of decisions ahead of you—no matter what happens this weekend." She fiddled with her half-empty plate. "Did you feel some kind of call to come here? Besides my dad's letter?"

"A strong call. But just between you and me, I'm not sure if this weekend will lead to a position or if there's just a lesson to be learned through it." He found it impossible to steer away from the personal. Maybe he just needed to be direct. "Even some closure."

She swallowed. "I haven't told my parents that we met at Rosedale. Since you came, there hasn't been time. I don't know if it'll even come up. I guess that depends on you."

Her warning gave indication she wasn't sharing his need for closure. "Thanks for helping me, even though you still have reservations about me. The only explanation I have for what happened at school is—"

Megan's hands flew up. "You don't have to explain anything."

"Please. Let me try."

She nodded.

"When I first saw you, you awakened something inside me. An awareness that you would be significant in my life. I was curious about you. I interpreted it as attraction. I couldn't understand why you didn't feel it, too." He scooted closer to her and leaned forward, lowering his voice. "What if it was a strong premonition? Given your connection with this congregation. Like an affirmation, even before the call?"

Megan's eyes widened.

He feared he was frightening her more than ever and shook his head. "I suppose you think that's dumb."

"No." Her eyes held wonderment. "I'm glad you shared that. I—"

"I saw the kitchen light on." Anita entered the room. She smiled at Micah. "You working on your sermon?"

"A bit." He glanced at Megan with regret. "If you're closing up down here, I can go to my room and finish it."

"We are turning in. But don't move. There's not even a desk in your room. Please stay and use the table. Just shut off the light when you're finished." She tilted her face and studied her daughter.

Megan rose. "I'm going up, too."

Micah watched her go to the sink, where she rinsed her plate and put it in a dish drainer. As she passed him, she said, "I look forward to your sermon tomorrow." She frowned. "You better do something with your hair, though."

Startled, he pushed his hand through his hair.

"For tomorrow."

"Megan!" Anita chided.

He bit back a smile. "Thanks for the advice. Night."

The two women left him, with Anita scolding her daughter as they went up the stairway.

Do something with his hair? For pity's sake, what kind of encouragement was that? Megan was a confusing woman. Trying not to let his mind get distracted, he glanced back at his notes. He'd let Megan get settled then go up and get the rest of his paperwork. He glanced at the coffeepot, wondering if he'd need to make himself a pot. Although Megan's help had given him an idea of how to approach his sermon, he knew he was in for a night of it.

CHAPTER 10

Once Big Darby abandoned segregated seating and incorporated the new custom of families sitting together, Megan had felt like a third wheel if she sat next to Katy. Since then, she'd drifted to the singles section, where she now found her place on their designated pew.

Joy Beitzel shifted beside her. "Isn't this exciting? A young candidate?"

Megan glanced at the woman, dressed in a crisply ironed cape dress. Although Joy's freckles and exuberance gave her a youthful air, she was four years Megan's senior. She gave Joy an unfelt smile. "He's not the only candidate."

Joy waved her hand. "Bosh, I know that. I type the search committee's minutes."

"Yeah, it's exciting." Or nerve-racking. Megan felt almost as anxious as if she were going to deliver the sermon.

She recalled Micah's story of the previous night, about losing his parents and living with his grandma. The sad determination in his eyes had strummed her heartstrings. The most humbling moment for both of them was when he'd admitted that he might have gotten the wrong message about Megan. Although their conversation had been interrupted, she came away from it with a better understanding. Micah was merely trying to follow God's call. He wasn't a timid man, afraid to admit his mistakes. He swam with sharks.

Afterward she'd felt sorry that she'd treated him so poorly at school. Perhaps if she hadn't been so set against him, they could have fostered a friendship.

"I hear he's from Rosedale," Joy Ann whispered.

Megan nodded. But he hadn't been after friendship at Rosedale. She'd had no choice but to give him that set down. Ludicrous as her silly threats seemed now, it had worked at the time. It had been Lil's idea.

In hindsight, maybe Micah was right about their relationship, that it'd all been orchestrated to help him through this sermon, this moment. The idea sent a thrill through her. Maybe God wanted Micah here. She found herself hoping so, even though she hadn't met the other candidate yet.

Her fingers involuntarily fidgeted with her skirt. She glanced around the room. It was no ordinary Sunday. Excitement filled the air. She and Joy Ann weren't the only ones anticipating Micah's sermon.

Joy Ann nudged her shoulder. "There he is."

Megan's eyes went to the pulpit, where her dad introduced Micah. Her heart leaped with delight to see that the preacher had taken her advice. Somehow he'd managed to control his hair. His bangs glistened, not plastered exactly, but sufficiently tamed for the occasion. Her interest in his makeover caused her to miss the introduction. But when her dad left Micah's side, it pleased her that he didn't seem as vulnerable as she last remembered him. Gone was the sad expression. He stood straight with squared shoulders, and his height gave him an air of authority.

Micah cleared his throat. "The Lord is good. Merciful and loving. As I hope you will be with me." There was a titter of laughter. "I was given a choice of three sermon topics: 'Set Not Your Heart on Earthly Things,' 'Going Forward with Unity,' or 'How to Check a Heart against Pride.' I chose the first one."

Good for you, Micah Zimmerman, letting them know. Megan hoped it would affect others as it had her, making them more sympathetic to his plight. Even now she saw folks whispering throughout the room.

"If I were to name this sermon, however, I would've called it, 'What Does it Mean to Set Our Hearts, and How Do We Do It?' The heart is the seat of our affection. It refers to our worldview or beliefs about life. How we set our hearts determines our future actions. Especially in those instances when we don't have time to think about our actions. The trick is to align our hearts with God's heart before we are faced with choices and temptations."

This was new information, something Brother Troyer had not touched upon in his sermon, Megan thought. Joy Ann's eyes remained riveted to the front of the room, as did many others.

Micah lifted his big black Bible with his right hand. "First from Colossians three, verses one and two, 'If ye then be risen with Christ, seek those things which are above, where Christ sitteth on the right hand of God. Set your affection on things above, not on things on the earth.'"

His Bible remained lifted because he quoted the verses from memory. "To better understand what is meant by earthly, we go to Luke twelve, verses twenty-nine through thirty-one. 'And seek not ye what ye shall eat, or what ye shall drink, neither be ye of doubtful mind. For all these things do the nations of the world seek after: and your Father knoweth that ye have need of these things. But rather seek ye the kingdom of God; and all these things shall be added unto you.'"

He set the Bible on the pulpit and stepped slightly to the side. "Of all the things that the Mennonite church has deemed evil, food isn't one of them. Without food, we can't survive. Food isn't the real issue. Jesus participated in many meals while He lived on earth. I've enjoyed lots of good food this weekend. And I understand there's going to be a potluck after the sermon. Some of you are farmers who produce food. Some of you have beautiful vegetable gardens. If Jesus didn't really mean food and drink, what did He mean?"

Megan sucked in her breath. The garden reference reminded her of Brother Troyer's death in the bean patch. Wondering how many minds had drifted to that memory, she glanced at Joy Ann. But the young woman's expression remained griefless. She was mesmerized by Micah.

"We must not set our hearts on our crops or our doctor bills or our accumulating gray hair. If our crops are good, we can fall under the pride that we're able to provide for ourselves. That we don't need God. When our circumstances are bad, if we don't look to God, our faith weakens.

He's telling us that we need to set our hearts to trust in Him and not our circumstances."

Micah stepped back behind the pulpit, which was on the same level as the seating for the congregation. As he moved, the congregation also shifted, many leaning to one side, looking through a gap, attesting to the fact that he had their full attention.

"But how do we set our hearts? Did any of you make Jell-O for today's potluck?"

A few timid hands raised.

"You ladies had to put it in the refrigerator to set it, didn't you?" There were several nods. "Brothers, when you go fishing, you have to jerk your line at just the right moment to catch a fish. It's the same with your heart. God provides the ingredients and the tackle. He gives the Bible and opportunities. But we have to set the hook ourselves. Jesus tells us to set our hearts on Him, beforehand."

Megan related it to Chance. At first, she'd set her heart against dating him. Lately, her heart had become infatuated with him. Chance was increasingly attractive to her. She focused back on Micah's sermon.

"Setting the hook is agreeing with God, with His truth as it is revealed to us. If you don't set your heart beforehand, you will find yourself more receptive to the circumstances instead of the God of the circumstances. It is also a continual thing."

Megan allowed the seed to sink into her spirit, again applying it to her situation with Chance.

"I hope you don't think I've been too vague. It would take many sermons to cover what the Mennonite church calls the doctrine of nonconformity, all the ways we keep ourselves separate from the world. This is a very hot topic. There are more than twenty sects of Mennonites because of various interpretations of this topic. It affects our daily life, business, speech, and our recreation. As the world continues to change, we need to distinguish between the essential and inessential beliefs. I have no doubt that in the years ahead this congregation will face many hard decisions."

Micah looked earnestly over the believers gathered before him. "I know that I can never fill Brother Troyer's shoes. But I am young and enthusiastic. My heart is set to follow the Lord. And just as He is merciful and loving, I felt that from you this morning. Thank you." He stepped away from the pulpit and took a seat in the vacant front row.

⸻

Megan followed Joy Ann into Big Darby's new fellowship hall, her gaze searching for Katy. But her friend wasn't in sight, probably caught behind the crush of those welcoming Micah, or possibly having to change Jacob's diaper. She moved alongside the tables laden with potluck dishes and took some cookies from the dessert table. She quietly surveyed the room.

"Meg! Over here." Joy Ann motioned. They'd barely gotten seated when Joy Ann nudged her. "There he is."

Megan glanced up to see hospitable hands urging Micah to the front of the line. She couldn't help but remember their private joke. *Meeting, eat, sermon, eat.* There was even more food than usual, for everyone was trying to impress him with their generosity.

"I'm not even hungry." With surprise, Megan glanced at Joy Ann's plate, which was at least as heaping as her own. "I just feel jittery inside."

"Why? Didn't you like his sermon? I thought he did a great job."

"Because Brother Zimmerman's so handsome. I don't even know if I can do my job if he becomes our preacher."

The comment shocked Megan on several accounts. First, that was exactly how she felt about Chance. Secondly, she'd better quit calling Micah by his first name and remember to call him Brother Zimmerman, like everybody else did. Until today, it was hard to think of him that way. And thirdly, handsome? Had that been the reason why Joy Ann had stared at him all through the sermon? Megan tried to school her features from her amusement. "Handsome? You think so?"

"You don't?"

Megan shrugged, imagining the petite woman with Micah. She turned to one of the other singles. "Ruthie? What about you?"

The heavyset younger woman wore her black hair in a bun and covered it with a doily. She unconsciously wiped her hands on her denim skirt and nodded. "Yeah, he's cute."

Lori Longacre, the church librarian, leaned forward, her perfume tickling Megan's nose. "Well, I wasn't thinking about his good looks.

But I'm impressed that he's our age. Just think how that could affect the congregation." Megan had to hide her mirth, because Lori was definitely older than Micah or anyone else in their group, nearing thirty at least. She tilted her pretty head. She had a mole on the flange of her nose that resembled one of those studs outsiders wore on purpose. The only time it was noticeable was when she got excited and flared her nostrils. Like now. "So, Megan, he's staying at your place. What do you think?"

Megan tapped her fork on her napkin, while her friends waited for her to reveal something wonderful about Micah. "From what I can tell, Brother Zimmerman's a nice man. He's been through some hard times. I think he's seeking God's will for himself and for us."

"Oh posh." Joy Ann frowned. "You're holding back. You went to Rosedale with him."

Megan didn't know how Joy Ann had obtained that information, but she quickly recovered. "Only one semester. I didn't really know him. I mean, of course, I recognized him." She waved her fork. "Let me tell you something funny. I'd heard a Joe Zimmerman would be staying at our house, and he went by Micah at school so I wasn't even expecting him. It was a total surprise."

"A nice surprise." Joy Ann twirled one of the strings on her covering. "He told the committee pretty much the same thing: you weren't friends, but he'd noticed you. He told your dad that most people noticed you."

"He did?" Megan wondered why Micah hadn't told her about that conversation.

Lori pointed. "Look. Something's going on over there with Brother Zimmerman. I think your dad's trying to get your attention."

Megan tensed at her dad's frantic wave. One glance at Micah, and the way he was clutching his neck and bending over his plate, assured her he was definitely in some kind of trouble. Quickly scooting out of her chair, she hurried to their table. "What's wrong?"

Dad said, "I don't know, but he's wheezing like you do sometimes. It came on him suddenly. I thought you'd know what to do."

Placing a palm on the table, she bent to look into Micah's face. "Are you choking?" He shook his head. "Is it something you ate?" He nodded, gasping and unable to speak.

Megan slammed her purse on the table and rifled through it. Her pulse quickened with alarm, making her all thumbs. Beside her, she heard his short gasps as he struggled for air through restricted breathing passages. Frightened, she tossed out the contents of her purse. The EpiPen rolled onto the tablecloth, and she swiped it up. "Don't worry. This will help you." Her hands shaking, she worked to set it. She placed her left hand on his shoulder to steady herself and knelt down beside him.

His frantic gaze met hers and went to the EpiPen.

"This will hurt. All right?"

He nodded.

"Hurry, Megan," Dad urged.

"I've never done this to someone else." But another glance at Micah's face told her she couldn't procrastinate. "I have to do this right. I only get one try."

Micah looked away, concentrating on sucking in fresh air.

She'd have to penetrate both his clothing and his skin. Setting her teeth, she glanced at him one last time then placed both hands over the needle, positioned it above his thigh, and jabbed hard. Micah's leg jerked up from his chair, but the needle felt solid. "Don't move." She finished the injection, hesitating and examining it closely before she removed it.

Her own legs went weak, and she was appreciative when her dad reached down to help her stand.

Micah placed his elbows on the table, slumped forward, and waited. As they all did, watching the back of his suit jacket heave with each struggle for a breath.

"Do you think we should take him to the emergency room?" Dad asked.

Micah shook his head but still couldn't talk.

"Let's wait a bit," Megan recommended, holding tight onto the back of the chair her dad had vacated. Time had never moved so slowly until finally Micah straightened a bit, his breathing much improved. When she saw that his normal coloring was returning, she asked, "What are you allergic to?"

"Sesame seeds," he slurred, "I didn't see it in my food."

"Oh, that's Inez's famous Chinese Chicken Salad."

Micah took several deep breaths. His speech improved. "Thanks. I don't know what would've happened if you weren't here."

"I was. That's all that matters. But in the future, you should carry one of these." Megan waved the EpiPen and dropped it into her purse.

Micah's hand moved to help her pick up the rest of her strewn items. "I'll reimburse you for your medicine."

"That won't be necessary." She quickly scooped up her billfold, and glancing up at the cluster of observers, snatched her cherry lip balm out of Micah's hand.

"You saved my life," he croaked. And the admiration on his face frightened her more than when she'd first found him sitting on her porch swing.

CHAPTER 11

On Monday after lunch, Micah went to the guest room to clear out his things, but his bag was already packed and waiting. He opened up his briefcase and got out the cheat sheet that he'd been creating to remember Big Darby's members. Not that he'd probably be asked back after his embarrassing allergic reaction. But he needed something to fill in the minutes until his humiliation took him back home to Pennsylvania. He looked over his sketchy notes, jotting down anything new that came to mind:

> *Big Darby Conservative Mennonite Members*
> *Bill and Anita Weaver—Elder. Search committee.*
> *Nova blues man, mechanic. Hosts.*
> *Megan Weaver—*
> *Barbara Troyer—Last preacher's widow, no children.*
> *Leon and Inez Beachy—Search committee, painter, sixties. Feisty wife, hostess committee.*
> *Ray and Emily Eversole—Search committee, song leader. Quiet wife.*
> *Noah Maust—Search committee. Rosedale professor.*

Vernon and Marie Yoder—Elder. Search committee. Middle-aged cabinetmaker. Kids.

Jake and Katy Yoder—Carpenter. Vernon's daughter is Megan's friend. Baby boy.

David and Erin Miller—Farmer with shiny black truck. Married to Jake's sister.

Will and Rose Landis—Farmer. Rose on hostess committee.

Hank and Sara Landis—Farmer. Oldest Landis son. John Deere coffee cup. Little boys.

Stephen and Lisa Landis—Farmer. Youngest Landis son. Curly haired wife. Red-haired baby.

Tom and Michelle Becker—Farmer. Michelle is a Landis daughter with four little girls.

Ivan and Elizabeth Miller—Farmer. Toddler.

Chad and Mandy Penner—Farmer. Easygoing guy. Toddler

Mark and Lanie Kraybill—Sunday school superintendent, carpenter. Wife is taller. Little boys.

Phil and Terri Yutzy—Tall, thin, church groundskeeper. Wife a fancy dresser.

Susanna Schlagel—Widow. Pretty redhead. Inquisitive. Leader of the widows.

Mae Delegrange—Widow. Heavyset with asthma. Talkative.

Barry and Linda Beitzel—Tax accountant with thick glasses. Joy Ann, church secretary

Ralph and Mary Ropp—Builder Supply Company. His shirts match her dresses.

Ruthie—Single, plumpish daughter.

Lori Longacre—Librarian, single, strong perfume.

If nothing else, the cheat sheet would serve as a memory. Someday, he could look back and remember his first interview, his first love.

Megan dipped her hands in hot soapy water, doing the lunch dishes, while next to her Mom lifted the lid to a tin bread box that she'd recently purchased at a garage sale. She removed a loaf of homemade wheat bread and took a serrated knife from the drawer. "Can you get me the cheese from the refrigerator? I want to send a care package along with Micah."

Knowing it would be useless to point out that they'd just risen from the lunch table, Megan quickly dried her hands on her apron and got the cheese. In the meantime, she heard the *plop* she'd been waiting for, coming from the bottom of the steps.

"Please tell him to wait a minute." Mom scrambled to finish the sandwich.

Megan went out of the kitchen and around the corner. Sure enough, Micah stood at the foot of the stairway, his suitcase at his feet.

"Your dad went after the car."

"Mom's fixing you a snack for the road."

Their smiling gazes met. "That's kind. Look, Megan, I don't know how to thank you for everything." He glanced toward the stairway. "Giving up your privacy, helping me with my sermon. But mostly giving me that EpiPen shot. That took a lot of courage. You saved my life."

"I only did what I'd do for myself. I know what it's like. I've had some asthma attacks. But you've got to start carrying an EpiPen for emergencies, Micah. Especially if you end up moving here and everybody keeps feeding you."

He smiled. "I won't forget your kindness." He dug in his pocket and handed her a little card that he had prepared beforehand. "My phone number. If you ever need anything, call me."

She took the card, staring at it as if it were a piece of double-sided tape. She gave a nervous laugh. "Really, you're making too much of it."

"You were my guardian angel. This entire weekend."

She wet her lips then studied him. "I'm glad I got to know you better."

A breeze fluttered in through the open screen door. Micah sneezed. "Excuse me."

Mom burst into the room. "Oh good. You're still here. I packed you a snack."

Megan unsuccessfully tried to resist the tickling sensation that irritated her own nose. Afterward she glanced up at Micah, embarrassed by their allergy association.

But he'd already turned his attention to her mom. "I appreciate that. As a bachelor I feel like a bear that's stored about a month's worth of food this past weekend."

"I promise you: if you come back, you'll never go hungry again." Mom beamed with assurance.

Megan's dad sounded his horn.

"My call." Micah leaned and gave Mom a gentle hug around her shoulders. "Thanks for everything, Mrs. Weaver. You're one special lady."

"I hope you come back," Mom half whispered.

He turned to Megan and clasped her hand, gently yet assuredly, like something a fond uncle would do. "Good to see you again." He picked up his suitcase and started for the door. Just before he stepped through, he added with a sly grin, "Thanks for the use of your hairspray."

The screen door slammed behind him, and Megan broke into laughter. "So that's how he accomplished the impossible."

"Serves you right. I still can't believe you told him to fix his hair," Mom scolded. "Why he could be our next preacher. But I guess you were friends from school."

Megan remembered Joy Ann's comment, that Micah had shared a little about Rosedale with the search committee. She figured it was time to fill Mom in on all the facts. "If you like while we finish the dishes, I'll tell you about the Micah I knew at school."

"Oh, I'd like that. I don't see how the next candidate could be any nicer. Do you?" They went back to the kitchen, and Mom freshened the dishwater.

Taking up the white linen drying cloth, Megan confided, "Micah Zimmerman was my biggest nightmare at school. The only way I finally got rid of him was by threatening to tell my professor, the church elders, or the law if he didn't stay away from me."

"What!" Mom clutched the countertop. "Oh, Megan."

⌒⌒

"I thought you said you didn't have a boyfriend?" Chance speared Megan with a glittering, blue gaze.

She picked up a stack of paperwork and tapped it against her desk to align the uneven edges. "I don't. I told you that I don't lie."

The creases around his eyes relaxed. "Then who was that guy with you at the parade? He said he was your guest?"

Megan sighed. "Remember I told you that our preacher died?"

Chance perched on the edge of her desk, knocking a pencil onto the floor. He quickly moved to retrieve it, handing it to Megan. "Yeah."

She pulled her hand away from his touch, stuck the pencil inside her drawer. "Micah is a candidate for the position."

Chance's brows furrowed. "And he's staying at your house?"

"That's right. My dad's an elder. Micah left yesterday. I don't know if he'll be back. There's supposed to be one other candidate."

Chance's left cheek twitched. "Whoa, no kidding? Your dad's an elder?"

"And he's the elder who's also on the search committee, and we've got plenty of room at our house, so he volunteered our place." She didn't know why she found herself confiding in Chance, but she added, "As it turns out, I knew Micah from Rosedale Bible College."

He narrowed his left eye. "So that's why you looked so cozy at the parade."

Megan dropped her paperwork and steeled her own gaze. "Why does it matter? I don't like to bring my personal life to work."

He leaned close. "I've noticed. You purposely push me away. Why do you do that? It's not like I'm not a Christian."

Squaring her shoulders, Megan gave him an honest reply. "I'm just setting my heart."

"What?"

She hoped that if she explained her feelings and convictions to her temporary boss, that God's blessings would surpass her disappointment over slamming the door in Chance's face. "Micah preached about it Sunday. Christians need to set their hearts intentionally, so that when things come up, they respond the way they should."

He stood, squinted at her, and placed his hands on his hips. "You're telling me you're purposely setting your heart against me? And that guy told you to do that?"

"No." Megan blushed. "Not against you. And he wasn't specifically talking to me, but to the entire congregation. You've been to church. You know what I mean."

"Not your church. I don't understand you much at all."

Megan wet her lips. "I'm setting my heart to honor what I've been taught about relationships."

"You're rejecting me because I'm not a Mennonite?"

"Yes," she finally relented.

His face broke into a slow smile. "So you're setting your heart against me because you're attracted to me?"

"Shh! I can't believe you're talking like this. What if somebody hears you?"

He turned and tossed over his shoulder. "Come into my office."

"No." Megan shook her head, just wanting him to go away and leave her alone. "I have a ton of work to do."

He pivoted and hardened his tone. "I'm not asking you, Megan. I'm telling you."

Angrily shoving back her chair, she strode into his office, casting a wary look behind her to make sure no one had overheard them. He reached around her and shut the door then remained standing next to her.

"Do you think this is wise? I don't feel comfortable coming in here to talk about something personal."

"But you don't want everybody at Char Air overhearing our conversation, either. Just relax."

After his showing up at the parade and now his direct questioning, Megan couldn't ignore his personal interest. He wasn't relenting, and they needed to address it. "Fine. But I feel like you're pushing me to go out with you. And I want you to stop."

"It's nice to know I haven't been talking to a wall. Why won't you go out with me?"

She tilted her head with an exasperated sigh.

"We can just go out as friends, if that's what you want. I'll let you set the parameters. Since you're an expert at setting things."

"It's nothing against you personally. I'm not going to date somebody who's not a Mennonite. And going out with you would just encourage you to hope for more than I can offer."

Chance leaned against his desk and crossed his arms. "Why can't you go out with me as a friend? I'm a Christian. I'm a fun guy. And I'm not asking you to marry me."

His comment brought heat to her face. In her thinking, marriage was the object of dating, not friendship. She'd been brought up to believe that intimacies were saved for marriage. Their thinking was miles apart. Conservative Mennonite couples used dating to test for compatibility because marriage was geared to last a lifetime. The more differences, the less compatible, according to her dad and the Bible verse that was once taped to her visor. Swallowing her embarrassment, she asked, "What if I grew to like you and wanted to marry you?"

He grinned. "I suppose that depended on how nicely you asked me." Instantly angry that he mocked her, Megan wheeled and started toward the door. Chance sprinted after her and snatched her arm. "Wait. I'm sorry. I was just teasing. Why are you a good sport about every other topic, but such a gloom and doom about dating? You're the sunshine of this office. What is it about me that scares you?"

Taking a deep breath, she closed her eyes. When she opened them again, he was staring at her and waiting. "Just you. You frighten me."

"Why?"

"Because I like you. And my only defense against you is myself. You're making this hard for me. I wish you'd just forget about me."

"Look, I give you my word that I won't push you into anything serious. I understand about our differences. Just think how we can learn from each other. Become better people for it. I know you're interested in missions. I could take you to Ecuador. Show you my work there. Maybe we were supposed to meet for a reason. Did you ever think about that? Maybe God wants you to see Ecuador."

His reasoning caught her off guard. It sounded similar to what had just transpired between her and Micah. Was there more to Chance than she had imagined? Was he her door to Ecuador? Had she actually been working against God's will? "That's an interesting idea," she admitted.

"Good." Chance smiled. "So let me take you to lunch. Let's go to your friend's restaurant, and we'll talk more about this."

Megan knew that Lil wouldn't be at Volo Italiano. Chance knew it, too. She considered having lunch with him there. It was private and just around the corner. Maybe if she went with him, he'd quit pressuring her. Maybe he wouldn't even like her. But if they left together and returned together, it would start office talk. "No, not lunch."

"Mr. Campbell?" Megan jolted at the voice that blared over the office intercom and interrupted their conversation.

With an angry huff, Chance stepped to his desk and replied, "Yes?"

Megan recognized the voice of the flight technician and turned to go.

"Whoa," Chance ordered her with an upturned palm. Then to the technician, he replied, "I'll be right there." When he returned to Megan, he softened his voice. "You think about it. Give me a place and a time before you leave the office today. We need to get some things straightened out between us. Otherwise, I don't know how we're going to continue working together." He glanced at his desk calendar, with several rows of large red x's. "We've got more than a month."

Megan's heart tripped. Was he threatening her? Could he even fire her? With an abrupt nod, she left his office. How dare he insinuate that she had to go out with him or else? Paige had jokingly mentioned that if he bothered her it was sexual harassment. Or maybe she had been serious. Had Paige noticed what was happening? And now that Chance knew she believed in nonresistance, he assumed she would never press charges against him. She'd opened herself up to his harassment. Or was it harassment, when he knew how much she liked him?

She stared at her computer screen, wishing Lil wasn't out of the country. If she went to Katy with her concerns, she'd probably advise her to quit her job. Although it might be the advice she needed to hear, Megan wasn't willing to do that.

She considered Randy. Upon his return, he'd set everything right again. But as Chance had reminded her, that was more than a month away. The more she thought about Chance's coercive behavior and his ultimatum, the more determined she was not to go out with him at all. She didn't have to date him. She wouldn't.

If he pressed it, she'd tell Paige. She hated the thought of going to an outsider with her problems, but she didn't think she could admit to her family or friends just how much she was attracted to Chance. And without that information, they wouldn't really understand her dilemma. If they knew the pressure he was exerting on her, they'd be furious. She'd never met anyone as determined as Chance. Except for Micah.

CHAPTER 12

Megan filled canning jars with Lil's three bean salad recipe, while Barbara Troyer fastened lids and placed the jars inside her seven-quart canner. When the second and final batch was cooking, Barbara invited Megan to sit a spell.

Swiping her forehead, Megan eased into the kitchen chair. "That was fun. The bright colors will look pretty on your pantry shelf."

"What's really fun is that every time I open a jar, I'll remember this morning." Barbara went to her cookie jar and came back with a strawberry-shaped plate containing two peanut butter cookies. "Your mom is blessed. For years I longed for a child." She sighed, going to the refrigerator and returning to the table with two tall glasses of milk. "But it wasn't in God's plan."

"I'm sorry. But maybe that's why you made such a wonderful Bible school teacher."

"We must make the best of our journey."

Megan nibbled on a cookie, savoring the sweetness. "Do you think people's paths cross for specific reasons? Even in one-time situations?" Megan was aware that Barbara possessed a wealth of wisdom where practical life was concerned. And she probably wouldn't ask as many questions as Mom before dishing out advice.

"Proverbs twenty, verse twenty-four says, 'Man's goings are of the Lord.'" Barbara nodded. "I believe God's all knowing and enjoys watching His people interact. There are no accidents with Him. But we can miss opportunities. He certainly doesn't twist our arms."

"Do you think that includes relationships with outsiders?"

"Sure. Remember your friend Katy? Her employer had a big influence on her."

"You're right." Megan knew that Katy's struggle with seeing things as black and white had changed when she found out that God used hymns to bless her employer, the same way He did to bless Katy. It had been eye-opening for Katy to realize that outsiders could be Christians. Chance claimed he was a Christian.

Barbara leaned forward, her eyes lighting with excitement. "It's interesting that you brought up the topic of personal journeys. My sister's into genealogy, and while she was here, she got me interested in it, too. For years she's been doing research about our family roots. Did you know that there's a lot of information in the *Mennonite Encyclopedia*? She also has a Mennonite friend with access to a computer."

Barbara's aged hand whipped through the air. "I don't understand it, but she's able to dig into records. She just mailed me a large envelope full of good information. There are photocopies from family trees that relatives wrote inside their Bibles. There're some wonderful faith stories. And these people were our ancestors. It's humbling and wonderful to think how God works down through the ages. I suppose it's a blink of an eye to Him."

Barbara brushed some crumbs into a neat pile on her tablecloth. "I guess when you get to be my age it's natural to wonder if you fulfilled your life's purpose. It's amazing to read some of the stories of my relatives. How they passed their faith on to the next generation. Someday I'll meet them in heaven. Eli might already have met them. But this must be boring for you."

"Are you kidding? I find it fascinating. And I think it's wonderful that you're doing something new. I'm in a bit of transition myself. And I don't have your experience to lean on."

"Oh?"

"As you know, my two best friends just got married. I'm discovering that what I used to share in confidence now gets passed along to their husbands."

Barbara smiled. "That's true. You're smart to realize it. Discretion is important. There should be a sermon on that." She shook her head. "But I interrupted you. Go on."

Megan sighed, glanced at the hummingbird feeder outside the kitchen window. "Lil's out of the country right now, still adjusting to married life. And Katy's busy with little Jacob. And since I started working, I've got this whole new life and nobody to talk to about it. Of course, I'm the only Mennonite in the whole company. I used to tell my mom everything, but suddenly I find myself holding back, not wanting to worry her. I guess I'm afraid she might be overprotective and want me to quit. But I like my job."

"You can always talk to me. It won't go any farther than these walls."

Barbara's walls were a cheery yellow, a reflection of her personality, and Megan trusted her. Chance's remark popped into her mind, too. *It's nice to know I haven't been talking to a wall.*

"What's your job like?"

Megan told her about the charter flights and described her job. She explained how her boss was on a leave of absence and how her temporary boss had generally upset her job and her life.

"Why is your boss on a leave of absence?"

"See, this is the kind of stuff that would upset Mom. Randy was unfaithful to his wife, and they're trying to work through it, trying to keep their marriage together."

Barbara's eyes widened. "That's a big burden for you to carry. It's hard to be thrust into an outsider's world."

"Katy and Lil know about it, but they don't really understand what I'm going through."

"So you're wondering if God wants you at this job? But you don't really want to hear that He doesn't?"

"No, I'm not questioning my job. I guess I'm struggling with how close to get to my coworkers."

"Aha." Just then the stove's timer went off. "I'm sorry. I need to get that. But I've learned that most often, the answer is inside you; confiding in someone just helps you sort it out." Barbara lifted the cage out of the canner and placed it on a cooling rack. "Beautiful!" she exclaimed.

⌒

That night for supper, Mom served bean salad that Barbara had sent home with Megan. "My mouth's been watering for that all day."

"It was nice of you to spend time with Barbara," Dad noted.

"I like her. Did you know that she's interested in genealogy?"

Dad cut into his savory round steak, browned and simmered in the skillet, just the way he liked it. "No."

"Her sister got her going on it. I think it's a good thing. Like a puzzle, something to occupy her mind. Do you know much about your ancestry, Dad?"

He glanced across the table at Mom and hesitated. Megan noted that he waited for Mom's nod before he continued. "I do. Some of the relatives have traced our roots all the way back to the old country. In fact, we have a few heroes in our line."

Leaning forward, Megan asked, "What do you mean?"

Dad placed his knife on the edge of the bone-colored dinnerware. "You know the story of Dirk Willems?"

"Sure. I learned about him in college." His story had been documented in *The Martyrs Mirror*. He had been fleeing his pursuers when a beadle fell through a frozen river and was in trouble. Dirk Willems had turned back and saved his persecutor. But the beadle had still taken him into custody, and Dirk was killed for his faith. He was a Mennonite hero. "You're not saying *he's* our relative?" Megan looked from Dad to Mom, who focused more on her meal than the information.

"Yep. It's not the Weavers, but through one of the wives, and his blood is definitely in our line."

"But how can that be if he was martyred?"

Dad chuckled. "You're right. Not his. But the same bloodline."

"I can't believe you never told me this before."

Mom got up to take her plate to the sink. While she had her back turned, Dad jerked his gaze in her direction, and Megan realized that he hadn't talked about it for her mom's sake. Mom was adopted. Dad had been protecting her feelings. Mom never talked much about it. In fact, the times Megan had questioned her, she usually closed the topic swiftly.

Feeling sad that her mom had blanks in her past, Megan gave her dad an understanding nod. She'd always wanted to know more about her roots, even before she knew that Dirk Willems was her ancestor. Just hearing his story bolstered her faith. It was a lot like the missionary stories she loved. But she could tell that her dad had closed the topic. If she wanted to know more, she'd need to ask him in private.

Mom returned to the table. "Dessert? Micah's sermon made me hungry for Jell-O."

"Yes," Dad said. "Speaking of Micah, I have news."

Megan dipped up some of the Jell-O, wishing they'd had cookies instead. She'd need a dollop of whipping cream on hers.

"Our second candidate has declined the invitation to come and check out Big Darby."

"Why?" Mom asked, posing her fork midair.

"He felt God wasn't in it."

Megan's mind raced, wondering what this would mean for Micah. "What now?"

Dad took a drink of water then replied, "The committee talked about going to the third person on our list, but then we changed our minds. Instead, we decided to invite Micah back for a three-month trial."

"How would that work?" Mom asked, glancing nervously at Megan.

"He comes as an interim preacher, and at the end of the three months, the congregation takes a vote to decide if they want him to stay permanently. After the vote, he's given the opportunity to accept or decline."

"So the vote itself, whether it's a strong one or not, could influence his decision?"

"Yes."

Mom fiddled with her Jell-O. "I never thought about the candidates turning us down."

With growing alarm, Megan asked, "Where will he stay?" Although she hoped Micah would get the invitation, she didn't want him living just down her hallway for three entire months.

"The committee assumes he'll stay here."

In frustration, Megan blew air between her lips.

"But your mom told me how he pursued you in college. So I'm not happy about him staying with us."

Megan nodded in agreement. "You didn't tell the committee about it?"

"No. I didn't want to bring that to anybody's attention."

She sank with relief. "Isn't there somebody else on the committee who can house him?"

"Unfortunately not. We haven't discussed it recently, but back at the beginning of our search, our home seemed like the only viable option. Unless we rented a place for him. But I came up with an alternative, if your mother and you agree." He leaned forward, and Megan could read the excitement in his eyes. "You know my shop room? We could fix it up for him. I'm sure we could get some folks to help. It wouldn't need much work. I could suggest it to the committee, saying he might feel more comfortable having his own space for that long of a time."

The room was part of her dad's home mechanic shop. But it was separate from his work area. He used it for storage, and it had plumbing.

Megan made a face. "But it's dirty and gross."

"But we could fix it up." Mom caught the vision. "And afterward, it would be a little guest cottage."

"Have you contacted him?"

"No. I'm going to call him tomorrow. I wanted to check with you both before I took the shop idea back to the committee. So what do my girls think?"

"I'm for it. If Megan doesn't care."

"He gave you no indication that he's still interested in you, right?" Dad asked. "Because if he is, then I'm putting my foot down about him staying here."

"No. He's changed. I'm not afraid of him or anything. I guess it would be all right."

"You'll tell us if he does anything out of line? If it's not working out for you?"

"Of course." She shifted her gaze nervously. She hadn't done that with Chance.

"I want to keep my eye on him," Dad said. "I won't let him bother you."

"Thanks. But what's going to happen with Barbara? Is she going to be able to keep her home?"

"We haven't decided what to do about that yet. The church owns the property, but Brother Troyer always paid his rent on time. If she wants to stay there for a while, it seems sad to remove her."

"Especially for a bachelor," Mom observed. "Micah probably wouldn't be interested in keeping up that big garden." She looked at Megan. "Do you think?"

"I don't know much about his interests. I just hope he doesn't live with us forever."

Dad chuckled. "Don't worry. It won't be forever."

"It'll just seem like it." Mom laughed.

A loud bang interrupted their conversation, causing Megan to flinch and look down the hall. The entry door had blown shut.

"There's a storm coming through. I heard on the prayer chain that the Millers have relatives in Indiana, where there've been some tornado warnings." Mom jumped up. "I'd better close the windows. Even if it doesn't rain, I don't want all that dust blowing in."

Dad stood. "I'll help you, honey."

"I'll get the dishes." Megan cast a worried glance out the kitchen window at a menacing sky, glad they hadn't been forced to the unpleasant storm cellar. She stared at her dad's shop, wondering how Micah's presence would change their lives. Would he take all his meals with them? Be constantly underfoot? She hoped it wasn't a big mistake.

A sudden crack of thunder shook the house, and with it came a sense of foreboding. Strange how two men had invaded her life. The look Chance had given her when she left work on Friday still sent chills down her spine. He'd stopped by her desk to make plans, but she'd grabbed her purse and left him standing there. She'd half expected him to follow her to her car, but he hadn't. Would he seek revenge, or find a new way to wear down her resistance?

CHAPTER 13

When Megan returned to the office Monday morning, she put her purse in her drawer and froze. Resting on top of a stack of paperwork was a two-inch rock that she hadn't put there. And it was heart shaped. She glanced at the door to Chance's office. It was closed. But who else would have put it there?

"Morning," Paige chirped, stopping in front of her desk. "That was some storm on Saturday, wasn't it?"

"I know. It took me a long time to get to sleep."

"The wind knocked down several trees on our street, but our property's fine."

"I don't think it did any damage around us either."

Dangling her empty coffee cup, Paige said, "I guess Indiana had some bad tornados."

"Is there a good kind?" Chance asked, stepping into view. He perched on Megan's desk. "You told me that your church helps out after natural disasters. Will they be going to Indiana?"

"I'm sure MDS will send someone."

"What's MDS, honey?" Paige asked, running her finger over the smooth surface of the mysterious heart rock on Megan's desk.

Feeling the heat rise to her face, Megan replied, "Mennonite Disaster Service. They organize volunteers to go in after natural disasters and clean up, repair, and rebuild."

Then Paige asked Chance, "You think this will affect us?"

"Let's make it affect us. I'll get on the phone and see what I can find out. You have time to drum up some donations if I can put together some extra flights?"

"I'll make time just as soon as I get my coffee." Paige gave Megan a wink and started toward the coffee room.

"You have the number for MDS?" Chance asked Megan.

"I'll find it. I know a little about them. I considered applying for a job there, but there wasn't anything local." Randy had never gotten involved with them, but then he hadn't been as motivated in that area as Chance. Mostly Randy handled what charitable opportunities came to him without seeking anything out. But since Chance had arrived, the entire staff had become more charity-minded. Even Paige's enthusiasm was contagious.

"They don't have anything local?"

"Oh, they do. But they work out of Pennsylvania and cover the country in zones." She waved her hand. "It doesn't matter. I'll find the number."

"Good." Chance rose and started toward the door that led out to the hangars.

Megan hesitated, then asked softly, "Chance?"

He paused. "Yeah?"

"Did you put this rock on my desk?"

He came back and whispered, "I can set my heart, too. I put it on your desk. It's to remind you that I won't ask for more than you can give. Just friendship."

As he walked away, Megan felt a lump in her throat. How sweet. He was definitely not firing her. She booted her computer to search for a phone number for MDS at its headquarters in Lititz, Pennsylvania.

Before the office closed at five, Chance had set up three flights that would help with the Indiana tornado disaster. Two would carry MDS volunteers and a third would take in supplies that Paige was rounding up from their own donors. They had also arranged for a press team that would help promote Char Air. And by Friday, two more flights had been arranged. One carrying supplies was scheduled for Saturday, and Chance was going to pilot it.

"I wish you'd go along, Megan. It's your people. And the invitation was given to everyone in the office. Since it's a weekend flight, nobody sees this as a personal thing. It's been a group effort."

But Megan sensed that it was personal. She knew that Chance was motivated to help others, but he'd also made it personal by contacting MDS. He'd opened the door for her, given her a perfect opportunity to get involved, and she wanted to be on that Saturday flight. But she'd had to turn it down because of what was going to happen at her house over the weekend.

"I'd really like to go; it's just that I have an obligation this weekend. I'm expected to do my part because other members of the congregation are coming to help. It wouldn't look good, if all the family wasn't there pitching in with the others."

"But he's not just your preacher. The congregation should do the work. He'll be staying at your house, after all."

"Yes, but it's our property that's getting remodeled. We will benefit from it in the long run, after Micah's gone. It's hard. They're both good projects. But my dad always says God wants you to take care of your family and your own obligations first, and then you reach out generously to others."

Chance arched his brow in disapproval. It sounded rather selfish in Megan's own ears, something was missing from the way her dad always said it. "It's like a circle. You start giving in the core, your family and church, and then it ripples outward."

"That's a different concept for me. My job puts me in direct contact with strangers, one on one, helping the least likely."

"But you came to Ohio to help your brother."

Chance shrugged in acquiescence.

"Now that we have this connection with MDS, I'm sure I'll have other opportunities. But I'm glad that you get to take a plane up on Saturday. I know how you've been missing it. You must be excited."

"I am, and it's your loss, Megan. Just like the Aucas."

Straightening her desk to leave for the day, she ignored his dig because she'd come to realize that he would say anything, no matter how hurtful, if he thought it would persuade her to act according to his wishes. "I admire what you're doing for Char Air." Picking up her purse, she asked, "Have you heard from Randy? How it's going for him?"

"At this point, he still doesn't know if his marriage is salvageable. Tina is bitter. They're having a rough time of it. I hope for the boys' sake that they don't give up."

"I'm sorry to hear that. Have a good trip. I'll see you on Monday."

⌒

Chance watched Megan depart then went to his office and shut the door, sinking into his chair with frustration. The woman's will was indomitable. An admirable trait when pressing through a jungle trail, not so excellent when she used it against his advances. Everything he had tried to win her over had failed. She was even becoming immune to his stories, had hardly flinched when he'd told her about the time that he'd spent the night in a tree fending off some crocodiles. And when he'd told her that the green anaconda could reach twenty-nine feet and weigh five hundred pounds and that they had eyes on the top of their heads so they could hunt submerged, she'd asked him if he thought they might be the leviathan sea monster mentioned in the Bible. He'd told her that he wasn't making up some Loch Ness monster, that they were real and sometimes they even ate jaguars. But that hadn't impressed her, either. She'd shaken her head as if she didn't believe him.

It was driving him bananas, and he couldn't get her out of his mind. She'd ruined him now because he didn't even look forward to returning to Ecuador if he had to return without her.

He'd gotten so used to her assistance, her companionship, her sunny smile, and especially her throaty accent. And even though she kept rejecting his overtures, he knew that she possessed a heart that yearned for adventure. He was the man to help her with that.

Chance spent more hours than he cared to admit daydreaming about her being beside him as he flew the sick to Hospital Vozandeson, befriending the missionaries that he transported, making his hovel a home. He could envision her grabbing hold of that life. She'd be wonderful in the field.

If only her family hadn't been occupied with their renovations for that preacher candidate, he was sure she would have gone with him on Saturday. The trip involved her people. And once he got her up in the air and she experienced the satisfaction that came from helping others and the camaraderie of working together, she would understand what motivated him. Realize that he was the man for her. How could anyone recognize the call and not give in to it? It was the fuel in his veins. And he believed that Megan had the same desire for the adventuresome yet simple and practical lifestyle.

Chance had always done what he thought was right. He'd helped his country, and now he was helping others. Surely God had fashioned Megan just for him. Although he'd been a bit of a womanizer, he'd settled down some. He even saw God's sense of humor in handpicking a little Mennonite maiden, prim and proper. But he loved the idea. He didn't care if she wore that net cap. Missionaries came in all flavors. Nothing seemed peculiar in the field where the cosmetics were most often left behind, anyway. In the field, things got real. He was willing to let her keep her identify. He just needed to prove himself to her.

He picked up his stapler, felt the instrument's prickly edge. And if he was willing to accept her, then surely she'd accept him even though they had a few minor differences. Well, major. Especially the one he'd been hiding. Ever since she told him that Mennonites were nonresistant, he'd done some research. He'd discovered that they were adamant against war. If Megan knew that he'd been a fighter pilot, he wouldn't stand a chance with her. If she knew about that mission that earned him a medal, it would be over. That's why he hadn't told her. That was better left concealed until the past was so far behind them that it didn't matter.

But the hourglass was losing sand. If she didn't spend time with him soon, she'd never see his heart, and if she didn't understand his motivations, she would never give him a chance. He replaced the stapler and pulled the red marker out of his drawer. He drew a big red x over the day's date. Only now, he wasn't marking off the time from boredom, but from worrying about the remaining days. So little time was left.

CHAPTER 14

At 6:00 a.m. the sound of Jake Byler's hammer resounded through the air, and the workday began. As Megan set up the coffee table near her dad's shop, she quietly observed the man who had captured her friend Katy's heart, long before Katy had even been old enough to date. The way he handled his tools made them appear to be an extension of his body, all performing together like a well-oiled machine.

"Katy said to tell you that she'll be over after Jacob's breakfast."

"Good. Help yourself to some coffee, and tell the others."

Dad passed by her with a two-by-four slung over his shoulder. "I'm too old for this." He grinned.

"Hardly," Megan replied. "But you might be sore tomorrow."

"Mark's here," Dad told Jake.

Mark Kraybill worked for Jake in the carpentry business. He had a wife and a young son. Megan watched him get out of his truck and don his tool bag. Next he grabbed a tray and headed toward her. "Lanie didn't think she'd be much use today, with running after the baby, but she sent these."

Megan's sweet tooth drooled as she carried the tray of pastries laden with thick penuche frosting. As she placed them beside the coffee, her mom pointed at the sky.

"I don't like the looks of this."

"You think we should set up the coffee inside?"

"Nobody will quit their work to come inside the house for breakfast, especially if rain cuts them off from the house."

Megan glanced toward Dad's shop. But they'd already discussed that option and decided there wasn't enough room inside it to set up the food table.

"No. I don't think it will rain that soon. But from what I understand, lots of donations and furniture will be arriving. We can't just set them around on the lawn and let them get ruined."

"But Dad's got a car inside, and you know how fussy he is about people getting too close to his cars."

"Bill!" Mom called as he made another pass with some lumber. "We need to talk."

"Let me take this to Jake. I'll be right back." But Mom trailed him to the shop's open garage door. He laid the lumber on top of a growing pile. "Something wrong?"

"It's going to rain. My arthritis is acting up. I'm sure of it."

Dad sighed, looked around his shop, his gaze lingering over Chuck Benedict's Nova. While Dad worked on various models at a Chevrolet dealership, on the side he restored only Novas. It was something he did for fun. "I don't like the idea of parking Chuck's car out front. I promised him it would always be protected inside. Anyway, we're going to need our entire driveway for parking." Torn, he looked at the Nova with concern. "It's Chuck's pride and joy, Anita."

"It's drivable?" Megan asked.

Dad nodded.

"Let's take it over to the doddy house. Lil and Fletch are gone, and the Millers have that new carport. It's big enough, and I'm sure they won't mind."

"All right. Let me get a car cover, too. Anita, tell Jake I'll be right back. Megan, run me over?"

"Sure, Dad."

By the time they had returned from the doddy house, Dad's shop looked like one of those garage sales Mom loved, or even a mini relief sale that the Mennonites were always holding. This one would contain mechanic tools and country furnishings. Mom gave Dad a quick hug, assuring him they had done the right thing.

"This is a lot of stuff," Megan said with disbelief. "And it's still early. Don't you think we should leave Micah some space for his own belongings? His room's not very big. If he's going to be here for three months, won't he bring his own things?"

"He'll just have to make do. There's no telling what he'll need. We can't turn down some donations and not others."

"But he owns a house. His grandmother's house, where he's lived for years. Surely he has everything he'll need. And he's driving so he can bring his own stuff."

"But everybody wants to chip in, so. . ." Mom shrugged. "Wait and see. It will work out."

"I guess." Megan wasn't sure why she was objecting to the congregation's generosity. She lowered her voice. "But what about afterward? Will we keep all this stuff?"

Once again, Mom shrugged. "Look. There's Katy. Why don't you bring her inside, and we'll start working on lunch? Yesterday Rose Landis brought over a pork roast, and I need to get it into the oven. The men will be hungry by noon."

Megan helped Katy get Jacob out of the car.

"I think the little outside apartment is a great idea." Katy grabbed her diaper bag. "Are your folks doing that because of, you know?"

Megan nodded. "I'm embarrassed. I'm sure I overreacted. From what I could tell while he was here, Micah's not as awful as I remembered him."

Katy chuckled. "I hope not. He's going to be our preacher. When he preached the other Sunday, I couldn't figure out why you called him Stick Man. He's not much thinner than Jake." She tilted her head. "Probably taller though."

Megan felt her cheeks heat. "He's put on weight since college."

"I think you're off the hook anyway, because from what I heard, it was Joy Ann Beitzel's dad who insisted the committee give him a chance instead of going down the list to the next candidate."

"But Barry Beitzel's not even on the committee. How did he know that the other candidate had backed out?"

"Because Joy Ann's the church secretary. And without a preacher, she's handling some of the paperwork for the committee."

"That's right. She told me she thought he was cute, but that takes some nerve to get her dad to go to the committee and make a request like that."

"Exactly. But from what I hear, she's not the only one interested in your castoff."

"Shh!" Megan reached for Jacob. "Watch what you say."

Katy handed her the baby and lowered her voice. "He's got the attention of every other single woman in the congregation."

"Even after his allergy attack?"

"Yep. So like I said, you're off the hook."

"I have a feeling things are going to get interesting around here."

Before Katy left for little Jacob's nap, Jake and a few helpers had installed a door that would keep the shop's gas fumes out of the new room. They also erected some walls: one partitioned off a bathroom, and one formed a closet. The carpenters had even cut a hole in an exterior wall for a new window. They'd sent one of the men to purchase a window after Jake claimed they needed to be up to code, since there was no exterior door. The fire that broke out in the fellowship hall a few years earlier was still fresh on everybody's mind.

Megan stood at Katy's car. "That window was a good idea. It makes it more like a home. You gotta be proud of Jake."

Katy winked. "More than proud. Can you believe that Jake's general contractor, who doesn't even go to church, donated the insulation and dry wall?"

"He must think a lot of Jake." Megan looked at the sky. "You'd better scat before the storm hits."

Afterward Megan didn't think Katy could have made it home in time, because soon after her departure, the sky opened and the clouds dumped their rain. The yard became soup, and everybody started looking like wet noodles. Especially the women. Susanna burst into the house all aghast and shaking the rain off her clothing while deeming Megan her messenger and errand girl.

Sometime during the day, Mom started calling the new room the blue cottage, and it caught on. At first Megan figured it had something to do with her dad's nickname. But when Susanna sent her out into the storm to find a man to move Mom's sewing machine into the living room, Megan got her first look at the brightly colored walls. The hideous blue paint was leftover from Leon Beachy's latest job. He had admitted, sheepishly, that after he'd bought the paint and done a three-foot wall sample, the customer had changed their mind. He'd laughed, saying he hoped it didn't make the preacher change his mind, too. But it was free. Megan was learning a lot about accepting donations with a grateful heart.

Besides Mom's sewing machine, the quilters brought portable ones that Leon Beachy toted through the storm and set up in the Weavers' living room.

Susanna seemed pleased. She tilted her pretty face with its beak-shaped nose. "Now Megan, don't you just love this material? We're gonna make Brother Zimmerman's curtains. It's the fabric we bought the day that Barbara went with us, the day Brother Troyer passed away in the bean patch. Don't you think that's fitting?"

Megan thought it more ironic than fitting. "It's very nice. I'll just go after that thread you need."

By the end of the afternoon, Susanna had frustrated everyone with her flapping, controlling ways, and Megan vowed never to become a quilter. Susanna had even aggravated Jake when she'd made him lower the curtain rod an inch and a half after he'd used a tape and level.

The singles had shown up and were mostly underfoot as Megan tried to keep everybody happy. Lori Longacre, the librarian with the cute mole on her nose, had brought a few books that she thought would add a welcoming touch. There was personal flowery stationery with it.

"Just a note that explains when the books need to be returned to the library," Lori insisted.

But when Lori took her umbrella and headed outside to see the blue cottage, Megan sneaked a look inside the pretty folded stationery:

I hope I can help you, when it comes to reading material and research books for your sermons. I'm friends with the Plain City librarian, too. Just give me a topic, and I'll be happy to give you a hand. Really, it's no trouble. I look forward to it. Here's my phone number.

"Denim's on sale at the discount fabric store."

Megan jerked her hand away from the stationery and wheeled around. Ruthie Ropp stood watching her. "It is?"

Ruthie eyed her curiously. "Yes. At $3.99 a yard, that's a steal."

"Maybe you should tell Barbara."

"I'll do that." Ruthie left, but she gave Megan a look that let her know she'd caught her reading Lori's note. Ruthie was an expert on denim, owned an entire wardrobe of jean skirts made from the same pattern. She used her sewing expertise to make each one appear a little different. Ruthie had brought a hand-sewn comforter for the preacher's twin bed.

Back at the sewing machines, Ruthie joked that it was out of her hope chest, but since there wasn't much hope left in it, she was ready to part with it.

But Ruthie's friend Joy Ann, the church secretary who was ultimately responsible for Micah's internship, scoffed, "You couldn't get the lid closed on your hope chest anymore. Now that you're such an expert seamstress, you wanted to replace some of the older stuff with new."

Ruthie met Joy Ann's gaze with defiance. "I wouldn't dream of giving the preacher an inferior item."

But all three of the singles had been able to agree on one important factor. They'd been adamant about the need to put a small refrigerator in the preacher's apartment.

At first Mom objected, claiming he'd be welcome to join them at their family meals. That had agitated the singles, giving Megan her first real indication that she'd need to be very careful not to provoke jealousy. They already assumed she'd have certain privileges that they didn't share.

Mom insisted, "I always cook anyways, and I don't intend to banish Brother Micah from the house."

Megan gave her mom the gentle elbow, their signal that Mom was missing something.

She let it go. "I suppose you're right. Folks will want to gift the preacher with food to show their hospitality. I shouldn't be the only one who gets the pleasure of cooking for him." Later she whispered to Megan, "From the looks of things, it's good you didn't set your cap for the preacher. Not that you wouldn't stand a chance, but because you might lose a few friends."

Although watching the singles had been amusing, Megan knew her mom was joking, stretching the matter out of proportion. There was no way that Micah could initiate such a stir. "That's the least of your worries, Mom."

"I don't know. He's a good catch."

Megan glanced at her mom skeptically. "But you hardly know him."

"Maybe not, but I know men like him. Good men."

The singles agreed with Mom because once they were gone, Ruthie's dad returned with a tiny used refrigerator strapped in the bed of his 1980 Ford truck. It almost made Megan feel sorry for Micah. *When a girl's dad got involved*— But Megan broke off her thought. Maybe Micah would be open to the local girls. Maybe he'd be ready to settle down and take a wife. It would be interesting to watch, only she had this awful feeling that just like Susanna was moving in on Barbara, the singles were going to move in on her space. They'd want to include Megan in their circle so that they could find out more about Micah, even control her a bit. And while Megan sat with them in church, she wasn't ready to officially join the group.

At the end of the day when Megan and her parents stood and looked over the work, they were satisfied. The blue cottage was packed with furniture and extra linens and toiletries. Noah Maust, the professor, had furnished a desk and a lamp.

"I guess it's the Lord's room now," Dad said.

Mom sighed. "It's exciting to think about the guests He might send our way."

Megan glanced at her dad. "It's still your room, too."

"I know. I'm all right with it. It was my idea." He smiled. "I guess if the Lord sees fit to keep it filled with guests, to give it another purpose, then maybe I'll have to add on the back of the shop."

Mom smiled. "Yes, you can always do that, honey. There's leftover cake inside that Inez Beachy sent. Anyone hungry?"

"I'm always hungry." Dad moved to shut off the professor's lamp.

CHAPTER 15

He's here!" Mom exclaimed just before the sound of cracking gravel wafted through the open living room window.

Megan set her Christian novel aside on the garage-sale coffee table and followed her mom to the window, keeping discreetly to the shadows of the opened drapery.

The grandfather clock, one of Dad's family heirlooms, chimed twice, and he chuckled. "Good. He's punctual. When I called to tell him about the blue cottage and its furnishings, he calculated that he'd arrive mid-afternoon.

But Mom wasn't listening to him. She'd already opened the screen door and stepped onto the front porch.

"She's in her heights of glory," Dad told Megan with a chuckle. "Loves to entertain."

Megan and her dad followed Mom outside, where the tall, lanky guest was unfolding himself from a dark blue Honda Civic. She exchanged a smile with Dad, who appreciated the irony of such a big man in a small car. That was probably a strike against him in Dad's estimation, but then Micah had surely gained it back when he'd gotten the color right.

Micah's eyes looked a tad road weary, yet radiant. Excited. And Megan felt a tug of happiness for him and his adventure. She believed her mom was feeling the thrill of his adventure, too. Mom gave him a hug, and Megan watched Micah's forearm harden when Dad grasped his hand and cranked it like a wrench.

"Hi." Megan stood back, keeping her hands to her side, and gave him a warm smile.

He held her smile a moment with a matching one. "I can't wait to see the little cottage."

"We call it the blue cottage. You'll soon see why. Come." Mom motioned.

"I should get Miss Purrty out of the car first." Micah's voice trailed off as if speaking to himself. "I hope she doesn't take a notion to run away."

Many things ran through Megan's mind, and she was positive her parents were just as surprised and confused to discover that Micah had a Miss Purrty with him. The three of them instinctively backed away from the car as Micah strode around the back and lifted the hatchback. With a few grunts and some shuffling of belongings, he soon backed out, holding a small, gray animal crate in his hand.

Curious, Megan tried without success to see through the air slats. Micah turned, looking sheepish. "I didn't have any place to keep her. I inherited her. She was my grandmother's favorite cat." Though his face reddened slightly, his voice never wavered, giving the impression that the cat was not an option.

The look on Mom's face indicated that she hoped the cat would wander off and get lost. Mom was pretty persnickety with keeping the house and yard clean. They'd never had any pets, mostly because of Megan's allergies. But now Megan was thankful they'd fixed up the room for the new preacher, because honestly, the last thing she needed in the house was a cat. Of all things.

She wouldn't bring up her objections, though, because she sensed that her parents both harbored plenty of their own. Dad didn't like cats because they jumped up on cars and scratched the paint. And he was into restoring, not scratching. She cast him a tentative glance and saw his eyes widening in undisguised disapproval.

She was sure that Micah saw it, too, because she caught a glimpse of the preacher's doggedness that he had employed so readily at college. Something in the set of his chin and the way he straightened his shoulders.

"Go ahead. Lead the way." His voice was set in defiance, as if there wasn't anything unusual about showing up with an uninvited pet. The way he urged them to lead the way made it sound as if he was inviting them to join him on his great adventure.

When nobody moved, Megan stepped forward. "This way. It's attached to the shop, but you have to go inside the shop to get to it." She found herself babbling, trying to cover the noise of her mom whispering to her dad, most likely trying to calm him from the terrible news that a cat would be prowling around in his sacred shop.

But when she ran out of small talk, her dad's comment was easily heard. "I wonder if Barbara likes cats?"

"Who's Barbara?" Micah whispered through the side of his mouth.

"Brother Troyer's widow," Megan replied.

She saw Micah's shoulders grow more rigid, but he didn't back down, just kept carrying his grandma's cat toward the cottage. Somehow Megan knew that once that carrier was inside the blue cottage, they'd all be bested. There'd be no way Micah was going to budge.

When they reached the shop, Dad riffled through his pockets and came out with a key. "You'll need this. I made an extra. Here's a church key, too." It also worked the lock of a side door, several feet from the overhead garage door that worked with an automatic opener. "Sorry, but there probably won't be any room inside for your car."

"That's not a problem," Micah assured him, accepting the keys and placing them in his pants pocket, while with the other hand, he clamped tight to the pet carrier's handle.

Dad opened the door for them and flipped the switch. A blast of overhead light from the rows of fluorescents filled the room.

"Too bad we don't have a dimmer light of some sort for Micah to use before he gets to his cottage. That could be quite startling at night," Mom noted.

Dad sent her an undeniable dirty look, obviously having reached his limits. "It hasn't blinded me yet."

"It's just temporary," Micah quickly reminded Mom.

She gave a reluctant nod and motioned him to enter the room first.

The moment Micah stepped into the blue room, his face lit with delight. Then a low chuckle rumbled his throat. "Now I know why you call it the blue cottage."

"Leon Beachy's a painter by trade," Megan explained. "He showed up with the paint. Said it's called Something Blue. I'm not sure what the *something* stands for, 'cause I can't think of another thing this color. Hopefully, you can get used to it."

"Actually, it's perfect. It will keep me awake when I need to work on my sermons." Micah placed the crate in the middle of the room. The cat had yet to make a sound or make any kind of an appearance. But Megan thought she caught a glimpse of yellow. Then he turned and gripped Dad's arm. "I won't forget your kindness. I'll do my best to be a good neighbor."

"I'm sure you will," Dad replied, the annoyance already gone from his voice, and his natural good humor returning. "I hope you can work us up some good sermons in here. I, for one, need them."

Megan saw Dad relax a bit and held her breath, wondering if he was going to let Micah get away without setting some boundaries for the cat. Wondering if she should forewarn Micah if he didn't.

"Are you hungry or thirsty?" Mom asked. She also had let go of any irritation toward the cat. "There's some iced tea in your little refrigerator. We expect you to take your meals with us, but the congregation insisted you own a refrigerator so that they could gift you with food, too. I told you that you'd never go hungry."

Micah glanced at the little white frig and the tray of dishes and glasses on top of it. "I remember. I picked up a water bottle in Plain City, though, so I'm fine. I'd like to get the unpacking done and then spend some time on tomorrow's sermon."

"Of course. We'll help you bring things in from the car," she insisted.

At the Honda, he handed some clothing to Mom and a taped cardboard box to Dad. As soon as they were out of earshot, he turned to Megan. "Can you do me a favor?"

"Sure."

"There's a leash on top of Miss Purrty's cage. Can you attach it to her collar and walk her out back some place away from your parents? I don't think I can let her loose yet, and she probably needs to, you know."

Megan stifled her surprise that he'd drawn her into his predicament as an accomplice again. So quickly, he depended on her. Only, she was allergic to cats. Actually, she couldn't believe that Micah wasn't also. But she saw a glint of desperation in his eyes and agreed, this one time. "She won't scratch me then?"

"She's really old. You'll be fine."

Megan grabbed some dress shirts on hangers, feeling a little strange to be carrying his personal items, and headed back to the blue cottage. Micah followed her with what appeared to be a small, wheeled file cabinet. It didn't roll in the gravel, and he ended up carrying the awkward piece. Inside the blue cottage, she fiddled with the clothes in his closet until her parents left to get another armful from the car.

Quickly, she attached the leash to Miss Purrty's collar. She'd never seen a cat walked on a leash before. She soon discovered she wouldn't see it then, either, because the large golden cat balked the moment she got her freedom. Miss Purrty gave a soft hiss and lay down, whipping her tail from side to side.

"Oh, no you don't, missy." Megan gave the leash a tug. The cat gave a sharp mew and looked at her through dark-slit pupils but didn't move. With a sigh, she petted the cat on the head, scratched behind the ears long enough to make friends, then scooped Miss Purrty up and made a dash through the shop toward the back of the property.

Megan looked around their property, figuring the cat would need a place to dig and bury. She didn't want to train her to dig up her mom's flower beds or small vegetable garden. She decided for the old buckeye tree. Nothing grew beneath it except weeds and mushrooms. It was the only bad spot on the property. Mom couldn't even get bulbs to live under that tree.

Megan set Miss Purrty down, and the old cat arched her back and stretched; then in her own timing, Miss Purrty started to sniff and explore. She turned and batted at the leash once, then made the right decision to just ignore it. By the time the cat was finished, Megan had determined that Miss Purrty no longer possessed good digging skills and hoped Micah would clean up after her. Suddenly the cat loped back toward the shop. Pulling against the leash, she continued past the shop toward Micah. Since Megan didn't want to break the cat's neck or get scratched trying to pick her up again, she allowed the behavior.

Micah stopped, and Miss Purrty leaned against his legs, weaving in and out and mewing. He reached down and tickled the white fluff of her neck. "Thanks. If you don't mind, just put her back in her crate for now."

Megan nodded and took the pacified cat, who stared at her with green eyes. By the time she had finished her task, the last of Micah's belongings had been deposited inside the room.

"Well," Mom said with satisfaction, "supper will be at six. Just come on up to the house when you're ready."

"Thanks."

"I'm grilling hamburgers, and Anita makes a fierce potato salad," Dad said, giving Mom an appreciate gaze.

"Great."

And then Megan began her sneezing spree. She gave a little wave and joined her parents, brushing cat hair off her blouse as she went.

—⟶

"Whew." Micah blew out a relieved sigh. "That was tense." He released Miss Purrty from her crate. She walked stiffly and held her head as if miffed. "You didn't make a real good first impression, missy. But they didn't kick you out. Not yet anyway. And lucky for you, I don't believe they have any dogs around the place."

Miss Purrty was not Micah's idea of a pet; he'd never liked cats because he was allergic to them. But this big yellow tabby had been his grandma's baby. And when she had died, she had made him promise to take care of her cat. Just as he'd insinuated to Bill, Micah did it for her. The cat wasn't debatable.

But the cat was a bother because Micah had to bathe her weekly in order to survive around her. To him, washing the cat was like foot washing, a humbling thing you did—not because you enjoyed it, but because Jesus had set the example when He had washed his disciples' feet at the Last Supper. It was something he could do in remembrance of his sweet grandma.

And he'd given the cat a bath right before he'd left, but Megan had still sneezed. Maybe he was getting some kind of immunity to the cat, because the last time he'd been here, he'd discovered that he and Megan were pretty much on the same page—when it came to allergies. That fact and the memory of how she'd whipped out her EpiPen to save his life when nobody else knew what to do formed a sense of solidarity between them.

He moved around, inspecting the small cottage that would be his home for the next three months. He'd been speaking his mind when he told Bill it was perfect. The three-month interim had been an unexpected offer. At first it was less than he'd hoped for, but given the circumstances, it was an appropriate step. Even if he didn't get a permanent position, it would be a learning experience.

And he'd been exceptionally grateful to hear about the little cottage. He wouldn't want to continue on as a guest inside Megan's home, sharing her hairspray for pity's sake. But thanks to her goading, he had learned how to master his hair. He'd used her hairspray mostly to spite her, but it had proved useful.

He stuck his head inside the bathroom and drew back the glass shower door that appeared to be brand new. He grinned, thinking how nice it would work when he gave Miss Purrty a bath. A shower curtain wouldn't have been able to contain her. Bath time was when she recouped all her youthful vigor and ricocheted off the walls like a wet cat-ball. It took her the rest of the week to recover from the ordeal, and by then it was time to repeat the dreaded process all over again.

He opened the medicine cabinet and noticed more storage beneath the sink beside a stack of Anita's fluffy white towels. It reminded him of the pillow incident the last time, the incident that had finally broken the ice with Megan. Yep, he had a great setup with this little cottage. It afforded privacy while he could still take his meals inside and explore whatever it was he felt for Megan.

He went back into the main room. His gaze shifted to the door, which also appeared to be brand new. Just to the right of the door was a beautiful rolltop desk and a lamp with a beaded string. He dragged his wheeled, plastic file cabinet over and found it fit in the corner next to the desk.

The adjacent wall had a twin bed with a spindled wood headboard. He was pleased with the simple, utilitarian style. Although the room carried obvious feminine touches, it wasn't filled with dried flowers and doilies like his own home had been. After his grandma's death, he'd hauled most of that old-fashioned feminine stuff to store in her bedroom, never taking over the master for himself.

Unmatched, medium-sized dressers flanked either side of the small bed instead of nightstands and covered the expanse of the wall. It was disproportionate but practical, yet he would have been willing to give up some storage in exchange for a larger bed. His gaze traveled back to the dresser on the left, which had raised panel drawers with loop bail handles on back plates. The dresser on the right was more decorative with an attached mirror.

Turning the corner brought him to the closet. Its sliding doors glided almost effortlessly. One half of the closet had high-low rods for clothing and was already holding his dress clothes, and the other half had built-in shelving. Nice. Beside it was the entrance to the bathroom, which he'd already explored. And in the small wall in the corner was the little refrigerator. Above it was a hat rack. He smiled to see that it already held a checkered tea towel and a black umbrella with a wooden handle.

Pivoting on his heels, he noticed that the wall opposite the bed had a window with brown paisley curtains. A small table stood directly beneath the window. On top of it were several books. Two small, stenciled, Pennsylvania Dutch chests served as bookends. They felt heavy. Then he saw the flowery stationery. He read the message with a smile, unable to place the librarian from his last visit. He'd have to get out his cheat sheet. He wondered if the tiny chests came from her home.

He carried the pet carrier over and stashed it neatly beneath the library table. "Good fit. There's your bed. And when you aren't sleeping, you can sit up here and look out the window." He cleared a space by moving the books to the dresser closest to the desk. Looking out the window was Miss Purrty's favorite pastime.

On either side of her new nest were mismatched, upholstered wing chairs. The more comfortable-looking one had a matching footstool. A floor lamp stood between the comfortable chair and the door. That would be the light he used when he entered the cottage. He couldn't think of a thing that was missing. Unless. . . His eyes scanned the room again, and he found what he was looking for on the dresser with the mirror. Five o'clock already. He needed to quit dawdling.

Grabbing a stack of clothing and heading for the closet, he said, "We can be comfortable here, missy, so don't get your dander up and get us in any trouble."

The cat walked over to her crate, poked her head beneath the table, and sniffed. Then she lifted her queenly head and jumped up onto the chair without the stool. She curled into a ball and started her motor.

"Well, at least you didn't pick the chair I wanted," Micah said, knowing from experience that aside from the weekly bath, that cat always got her way.

CHAPTER 16

After dressing in a pink shirtdress with tiny pale flowers and donning a new pair of black stockings and her Sunday shoes, Megan took pains with her hair, making sure it was smooth and tidy. She got a freshly ironed covering that she hadn't worn before, even on Sundays. She wasn't doing it for Micah, exactly. But she knew that people would be paying more attention to her family just because the preacher was staying at their place. This wouldn't be one of those Sundays when you slipped in and out without any notice. The congregation would be expecting the Weavers to make a good representation of the entire body of worshippers. Everybody would probably try to put their best foot forward.

She hadn't seen anything more of Micah since their quick supper. He'd been in a hurry to get back to his room, settle in, and work on his sermon. Mom had sent him a plate of leftover pastries that she'd frozen after the workday, and his Honda was already gone by the time the Weavers left for church.

Inside the Big Darby church, Megan stepped into the lobby, jammed full because Micah stood at the entrance to the auditorium. The line to greet him moved slowly, backing up into the lobby. She wondered if church would even start on time. Their congregation was used to Brother Troyer's ability to watch the clock and keep to the required schedule. Running overtime could burn roasts and cut into afternoon naps.

Inez Beachy placed a hand on Megan's shoulder. "Good morning. I hear the preacher's apartment turned out real good."

"Yes, and your husband's paint sure brightened up the place."

Inez chuckled. "He said it was awful—not befitting a preacher—but that it would have to do."

"Brother Micah didn't mind. He said it would keep him awake while he worked on his sermons."

Laughing, Inez replied, "Sounds like he's a man with a thankful heart." Megan took a few steps forward. "I would have come to help, but my arthritis rears up when it rains."

"I'm sorry to hear that. My mom's does that, too."

"She's too young to suffer like that, poor dear."

Megan found herself suddenly facing Micah. She placed her hand in his, and he gave it a firm but clammy handshake, then released it and ran a finger along the inside of his white shirt collar which stood above his dark collarless suit coat. "Megan. Nice to see a familiar face."

Noticing the red welts on his neck, she whispered, "You all right?"

He leaned close, "Just a little itchy."

"You ever get an EpiPen?"

"No. And don't get any ideas. Those things cause a terrible headache."

"All right. But just say the word."

"Now don't go telling this good man how to preach his sermons," Inez chided good-naturedly. "And move along, dear. You're holding up the line."

Megan buttoned her lips and stepped into the main auditorium. As she moved down the center aisle, Joy Ann waved. Cringing, Megan didn't like that Joy Ann was sitting fourth row from the front, up several rows from their normal pew. Instinctively, she shied away from the front pew; being toward the back of a line was the neighborly thing to do. But if Megan didn't go and sit with her, Joy Ann would keep waving and draw everybody's attention. Megan saw her life transitioning in ways she didn't like. She didn't want Micah to think she was a permanent member of the singles' group.

On the other hand, if he did require a shot from her EpiPen, she'd be close enough to pass it up to him. Hopefully he could administer it himself. If he didn't allow himself to get so far gone, and surely he wouldn't if he was standing in front of the entire congregation.

Settling her mind, she lifted her chin to a royal position and moved quickly down the center aisle. The women had spruced up their men, and Megan caught distinct whiffs of shoe polish and discount store aftershave.

She could understand how, as church secretary, Joy Ann would be inquisitive about the preacher. Megan certainly knew what it was like to have a new boss. She probably wouldn't have thought twice about it if Joy Ann hadn't asked her dad to persuade the search committee to give Micah this opportunity.

"Hi." Megan sat and smoothed her skirt. "Why so close to the front?"

"Are you kidding? Without a platform, I have to sit close to see." Joy was a short woman. Brother Troyer never wanted to elevate himself above his parishioners. It was true that sometimes it was hard for everyone to see the preacher.

"But"—Megan caught herself almost calling Micah by his first name, a practice she would have to amend—"Brother Micah's pretty tall. I think everybody will be able to see him."

Just as the minute hand reached the top of the hour, Micah strode past Megan's left side to the front of the congregation. "Good morning," he said and gave his collar a tug. "It's my fault we still have people in the vestibule. Just goes to show how friendly this church is. Let's have a song while everybody gets settled." Micah sat down on the front pew, and a red-faced song leader hurried to the front. It was obvious he hadn't prepared for the extra song and didn't appreciate being put on the spot.

They sang a hymn from memory, and then the service took the usual order of things. When Micah moved behind the pulpit again, the congregation hushed. He cleared his blotchy throat. "First, I want to thank everybody for inviting me to be your interim preacher and for allowing us time to get to know each other. I think it's a perfect plan. And I also thank you for the little cottage at the Weavers' place. I hear that a lot of people chipped in and made donations. It'll make a wonderful home for me and Miss Purrty."

That brought a soft rumble over the people. "The cat I inherited from my grandma at her passing."

Smart, Megan thought. He'd just made his stance about the cat. Surely there were as many cat lovers as haters in the congregation. But his statement brought more murmurs because everyone knew about Dad's penchant for restoring cars and understood his sacrifice.

"This is a generous congregation. It's been brought to my attention that July has brought Ohio and Indiana some storms, and since I know you're going through your own storm of changes, my sermon's entitled, 'Weathering Unexpected Storms.'"

He thumbed through his Bible and read a verse about God's protection. "Though I'm young to some of you, I've experienced some storms of my own."

Megan noticed that everyone settled in and really listened to his story. He told them the same story he'd shared with her. As he spoke, his hands flitted occasionally to his throat or his eyes, and she could tell that he was really struggling with an allergic reaction.

Soon, his eyes became mere slits in puffy sockets. She squirmed, wishing there was something she could do.

"What's wrong with him?" Joy Ann whispered.

"Allergies."

"Is he going to need your shot thing again?"

"Not as long as he can breathe."

"The poor man. What a hard life. And now he's broken out in hives. How's he going to make it through the potluck? I really wanted him to taste my lemon meringue pie. You know I have the knack for meringue. You think we need to get a list of the foods he's allergic to?"

It was true that if anybody could give Lil some competition in the food department, it was Joy Ann. "I don't know," Megan whispered, keeping a close eye on his face and breathing. Though he wasn't struggling in that area, she knew he was terribly itchy.

Micah, however, continued through his sermon, using his doggedness to prevail, and didn't cut it a minute short either, from the sound of it. Her heart warmed with sympathy and admiration.

As soon as the service ended, he strode straight to Megan.

"That was a comforting sermon." Joy Ann stepped in, causing Megan to squirm uncomfortably.

"Thank you." He turned to Megan. "Could you tell your dad I have hives and ask him to go to my apartment and find my antihistamine? It's in the medicine cabinet."

"Of course. I'll go right away."

Joy Ann offered, "I'll be sure to pick up an extra bottle to keep at the church. What brand do you use?"

"That won't be necessary. . . ."

Megan left them and hurried to find her dad but didn't see him anywhere. Making a spur-of-the-moment decision, she thought it would be faster if she just went after the medicine herself. As she hurried over the gravel roads at just a few miles over the speed limit, she wondered what set off Micah's hives, but nothing came to mind. A pothole made the car shudder.

At home she got her dad's shop key off the hook by the kitchen door and ran across the lawn, hurrying through the shop and into Micah's cottage. She opened the door and let out a shriek when the forgotten cat leaped across her path. Placing her hand over her heart, she wondered where the cat had been. Miss Purrty had flown across the room airborne. Megan hurried past the animal and into the bathroom, found the right bottle, and started back out. But the cat had situated herself in front of the door and was now taking a spit bath.

Megan hesitated, wondering if she should get the leash and put Miss Purrty in the cage lest she take another unexpected flight and escape through the open door. Since Micah had given his pet the run of the cottage, Megan opted to do that only as a last resort. Tentatively, she grabbed the door handle and tried to move the cat with her foot. The cat swatted her leg, catching a claw in Megan's new black stockings.

With a gasp, she tried to shake the cat off her leg. At the same time, Miss Purrty tried to back away, but her claw caught and put a run in Megan's stocking.

"No! Stop!" Megan squatted down and caught the cat by the collar and then tried to untangle the claw. By the time she'd finished, the cat had ruined her stocking. "Now look what you've done. Phooey! You naughty, naughty thing!"

The cat hissed and backed away, whipping her tail.

"Now I've got to change my stockings," Megan huffed, as she opened the door.

But the moment the door opened, the cat leaped past Megan into the shop. With a shriek, Megan flew after the cat. Miss Purrty disappeared under Chuck Benedict's Nova.

"Aye, yi, yi," Megan bemoaned. She stomped back into the cottage after the leash, wishing she'd listened to her intuition and caged the animal from the beginning. *Next time I won't feel sorry for the dumb thing.* She returned to the shop and gasped. The cat had jumped on top of the Nova's hood, the very thing they'd all wanted to avoid. "Don't move. Oh please, don't move."

Megan tried to think what to do. What would create the fewest number of scratches on the Nova's shiny paint? She started by lowering her voice and going for a soothing tone. "You are a nuisance. Nice kitty. Nice kitty." She took a step closer. The cat stood, made a complete circle, and slightly arched its back.

With each feline footstep, Megan flinched. Yet she continued to woo the cat in a singsong voice. "I can't believe you're doing this, Miss Purrty. Don't you know this is the worst thing you can do for yourself. For Micah?" When Megan got close enough to touch the little imp, she warned, "I'm just going to pet you behind your ear." She reached out slowly. The feline accepted her touch and pressed its yellow head into Megan's hand. "You're an unpredictable creature. Nice kitty."

The cat took cautious steps across the hood of the car toward Megan. "If you're going to live here, I think you may have to get declawed. Nice kitty, kitty." The cat reached the edge of the hood and leaned into her. Megan lifted Miss Purrty by her tummy and snapped on the leash. At the sound, the cat stiffened. Megan hurried back into Micah's apartment.

"Sorry, kitty." Megan tossed the cat into its cage. When she reached inside to remove the leash, Miss Purrty bit her hand.

"Ouch!" Megan jerked away, banging her hand on the inside of the cage. When she examined it, she saw no blood. It was more of a feline warning. "Fine. Keep it on then."

Megan secured the cage door and hurried out of the cottage, running toward the house. She ran upstairs and changed her stockings. Tried to brush cat hair off her dress, and then hurried back to the car. Inside she checked to make sure she had remembered Micah's medicine. Thankfully she had it, so she steered the car back onto the gravel road.

As she drove, she thought about the cat's claws on the Nova's hood, wondering if her dad would be able to spot any damage. If he did, she would need to take the blame.

When she reached the church, the fellowship hall was bustling with voices and activity, and it took her awhile to spot the preacher. He was seated at a table with Jake's sister, Erin, and her husband, David Miller. Megan greeted the younger couple and, as discreetly as possible, handed the medicine to Micah. She noticed his face was blotchy and his eyes had narrowed into even thinner slits.

"Oh good," Erin said. "It's getting worse."

"Where's your dad?" Micah asked, gulping down two pills and some water.

Megan sensed a hard edge to the question. "I couldn't find him, so I went after your medicine."

"You've been gone at least an hour."

She didn't think she'd been gone that long, but it probably seemed like an eternity to Micah. She sympathized with his agony and felt some admiration that he'd been able to keep his hands away from his face.

"I need to talk later, about your cat."

"Miss Purrty?" His eyes widened every so minutely.

"She's fine. We'll talk later." Megan turned away and asked Erin, "Is there any food left?" But in reality, she'd lost her appetite.

⁓

Micah gazed around his cottage through slotted eyelids and didn't see anything amiss. Then Miss Purrty mewed, and with surprise he saw she was inside her cage. Probably what Megan wanted to explain. He bent to let her out and was irritated to see her leash twisted around one of her legs. When the cat favored the leg, anger flared up at Megan. Why would she leave Miss Purrty unattended with a leash that could have wrapped around her neck? What sort of trouble could an old cat make, anyway?

All he'd wanted, those agonizing hours of the potluck, was to kick off his shoes and flop onto his tiny bed. But first, he needed to take out the cat. Monday he'd get a litter box. He picked up Miss Purrty and started toward the back of the property. Irritably, he scratched at his neck and set the cat down. It walked over to a nicely turned flower bed and made itself busy.

"Micah? You feeling better?"

Flinching, he turned. "Nope."

"I'm sorry."

"When I got home, my cat had its leash knotted around its paw. Why did you cage her? And why did you leave her leash on?"

Megan took a deep breath, allowing for the fact that Micah wasn't at his best.

"Because your cat dashed into the shop and ran under the Nova. So I went for the leash, and when I returned, it was on top of the hood. Dad will have a fit when he finds out, especially if there are any scratches on it. He restores cars, Micah. He sees every little mark. Maybe you need to get Miss Purrty declawed."

"She's too old to go through that. Why didn't you send him after the medicine like I asked? The way he protects his cars, he wouldn't have let the cat out."

"I was only trying to help."

"Now Erin and David Miller think that you go in and out of my cottage. I don't know them. Will they spread gossip? As a bachelor, I can't have you going into my room, Megan. I thought that's what the cottage was all about." Megan clenched her jaw. He made it sound as if she were some tramp. "I have just two things to say to you, Brother Zimmerman. First, quit expecting me to get you out of your scrapes. Secondly, Mom won't be happy that your cat just uprooted one of her pansies." Looking furious, Megan turned on her heels and started to the house. But then she stopped, wheeled back, and said, "Actually, there's one more thing. You owe me a pair of stockings."

His gaze naturally dropped to her legs. They looked fine to him. When he raised his gaze again, her face had reddened. "Just so you know, buying women's stockings does not come under the definition of discreet." He reached in his pocket and pulled out his billfold. "How much do I owe you?"

"Oh, phooey. Just forget it." She stomped away.

The only good that came out of it was that sometime during their heated conversation, the cat's leash had fallen away. The feline had curled up in the pansies. It appeared Miss Purrty had no intention of running away. But Micah just might.

CHAPTER 17

Megan sliced cold meatloaf, feeling miserable and wondering if Micah would make an appearance for supper. No routine had been established, and she noticed her mom casting nervous glances out the kitchen window, which was in a direct line with the cottage.

"I hope he's doing all right. I wonder how long it takes to get rid of hives?"

Megan shrugged. Thankfully it'd never been a condition she'd experienced. She hadn't told her parents about their altercation. "I imagine he's sleeping it off." Hopefully his foul mood, too.

"If he doesn't come in, I'll send Bill out to him with a sandwich."

Megan doubted Micah needed food, doubted he wanted to see any of them about now, especially her. At least he hadn't been required to preach that evening. She felt miserable for snapping at him. It was not like her, and she needed to apologize. Only the matter about the cat and the car still bothered her. If Micah didn't tell Dad, she'd need to do it. It was her fault.

The Weavers had just sat down to their meal when Micah tapped on the kitchen screen door.

Mom shot out of her chair. "Oh, you don't need to knock at mealtime.

Just come in. I hoped you join us, but I didn't want to bother you."

He took an empty seat and waited while Mom brought a fourth plate and set it in front of him. Micah dipped his head in silent prayer.

When he was finished, Mom asked, "Are you feeling better?"

"Some." It was easy to see that the symptoms hadn't completely vanished. Micah started to make a sandwich.

Megan felt her face heat, not sure if she should apologize in front of her parents or hope for an opportunity in private.

From the corner of her eye, Megan watched Micah fork out one of Mom's homemade dill pickles and cut his sandwich in half. But instead of eating it, he placed his hands on his lap. He seemed to be struggling about the incident. "I need to apologize for some things that happened today."

"No, I do," Megan quickly objected.

She felt her parents' surprised gazes darting between them.

Micah gave her a smile. "Please, let me go first."

She nodded.

"Bill. Anita. I'm sorry about my grandma's cat. It was not part of our bargain. And today there was an incident. Well, two. She got into the shop and jumped up on the Nova. And later she messed up the flower bed."

Dad's fork clattered to the table and his gaze went to the screen door. The color drained from Mom's face, whether from the news of her flower bed or the scene that was playing out, Megan couldn't tell.

To Dad's credit, he didn't run out to the shop to check on his baby but remained to face the discussion. "It's not my car. Usually the Novas out there belong to owners who trust me to keep their cars in mint condition."

"I understand that."

"It was my fault," Megan blurted, unable to allow Micah to shoulder the blame. "I let the cat out of the cottage when I went after Micah's pills. I shouldn't have been out there in the first place. He asked me to get you, Dad. Instead I went myself. I didn't think about how it would look to the church members." She saw her dad's shoulders sag.

"Maybe I need to find an apartment someplace else. Is there anything in Plain City for cheap?" Micah asked, looking extremely sheepish. "I don't suppose Barbara has an extra room? Maybe I could help her out?"

"No!" Mom lifted her chin. "Everybody pitched in to fix up the Blue

Cottage. It's better not to stir things up. We will work this out on our own." She turned her gaze to Dad. "Bill?"

Dad clasped and kneaded his hands. He swallowed. "I appreciate your honesty. It's no secret. I don't like cats. We will all have to be more careful. We're just getting started, and we've got three long months ahead of us. But I'm sure we'll work this out."

Megan felt a rush of relief that Dad forgave them.

"The congregation's watching us," Micah replied.

Mom nodded. "My point, exactly."

"It was my fault. I went to Megan instead of coming directly to you, Bill. I could've gone home myself or carried pills in my car. The hives were unexpected." Now he turned his gaze toward Megan. "When we talked earlier, I shouldn't have put the blame on you. It's just that I didn't think you understood my situation. Being single, I have to be careful how I interact with women." He shrugged. "But I shouldn't have expected you to think about that. This is your home, and you're used to having the run of the place."

Dad turned to Megan. "He's right. Even though we all know that you and Micah are only friends, you can't be going into his cottage."

"I understand. I'm sorry. But surely with time, everyone will figure out that we're not interested in each other. That we're only friends."

Micah nodded with clenched jaw. "I'll get a litter box and try to keep Miss Purrty out of your flowers, Anita. I replanted the one she tore out, but I don't know if it'll survive."

Mom gave a nervous laugh. "How much damage can one cat do?" Dad quirked his eyebrow, and she quickly amended, "I mean in the yard? Now everybody, the food will get cold."

"It's cold meatloaf, Mom." Megan grinned.

"Oh, right." Mom was clearly flustered. Megan knew Mom wanted to be the perfect hostess for their important guest and felt uncomfortable caught between pleasing him or her husband.

After the meal, Micah passed on dessert and excused himself, starting to his apartment. Megan jumped up and fled after him. "Wait, Micah. I know you don't want to be alone with me, but I need to tell you I'm sorry I snapped at you. Everything you said was right."

Micah smiled. "I started it."

"Only because you were in pain, feeling miserable."

His expression saddened. "Today was a poor start. The entire congregation saw my weakness. I guess God wanted to humble me."

"You're not weak at all." Even at Rosedale, she'd seen his strength, his ability to persevere. "If God wanted to humble you, then He must have big plans for you."

He nodded. "You're right. Good night, Megan."

She watched him turn and walk toward his cottage, wishing there was more that she could do to encourage him. But today, she'd hindered him. When she stepped into the kitchen, both her parents stared at her.

"I just needed to apologize."

Dad reached out and took Megan's hand. "I still don't like the idea of having a cat in my shop, but I'm glad he came to us with the truth."

"The windows are open," Mom reminded them. She whispered, "He had a rough day."

"We all did." Megan squeezed her dad's hand and released it, taking their plates to the kitchen sink.

$\sim_\mathcal{C}$

Megan watched a plane roll up to the hangar then brought her gaze from the glass window behind Chance and focused on their conversation.

"Randy had a rough weekend. He got in a big fight with Tina." Chance kept his voice low. "He came to my apartment, ready to leave her."

Megan was sorry to hear it. "What did you do?"

"I persuaded him to give it another try. He texted me a little while ago that they're going to book a cruise if I'll stay longer."

This news brought Megan conflicting emotions. "Longer?"

Chance laughed. "Don't look so mortified. Yes, you're stuck with me two extra weeks."

Two weeks wasn't so long. "We'll make do."

"That's the spirit," Paige said, stepping into view from somewhere behind Megan. "I swear, she's the most positive person I know. But one of these days, her desk is going to sprout wings on it, the way you always perch here like it's your personal cockpit."

Megan felt her face heat as Chance stood. "You're right." He leaned close to Paige's ear, but Megan could hear his rebuff. "I don't like being cooped up in there."

"Just two more weeks," Paige said.

"You keeping count?" Chance appeared insulted.

Paige shifted her files to her other arm. "It's not hard. Every time I put invoices on your desk, I see those big red x's, and the yellow highlighted square that is your last day."

Megan rubbed the side of her head with the end of her pencil then got it caught in her hair. Working to free it, she pointed out, "That yellow square has changed. He's staying two extra weeks."

"You are?" Paige laid her files on Megan's desk and moved to help her, then handed Megan back her pencil. "I guess we can carry him for two more weeks, right honey?"

Rubbing the sore spot on her head, Megan nodded. "That's just what I was saying when you walked up. We'll make do."

Paige picked up her files and parceled them out. "One for you, honey, and two for you Mr. Campbell." Then she strode back toward her desk.

Chance tucked the files beneath his arm. "I love to irritate that woman."

"Love to irritate women, period," Megan corrected, but then when he turned back and perched on her desk again, she wished she'd kept quiet and let him have the last word.

"Speaking of, I'm taking the Cessna back to Indiana on Saturday. Want to go along?"

Her heart raced. After the last trip and Chance's report of actually getting involved with a rescue, she'd regretted missing it. She glanced at her desk. Interesting as the man was, she had a list of calls to make. She didn't want to waste another half hour arguing about his question. "I'll think about it. When do you need to know?"

With surprise, he stood. "Thursday or Friday."

"Thanks for the offer."

With an expression much too hopeful, Chance smiled. "You're welcome." Finally he strode back to his office.

Megan glanced out the huge glass windows, watched a plane gliding out toward the runway. This was the opportunity she'd been waiting for.

It wasn't Ecuador or Djibouti, but it was going up in a plane, helping with MDS. She really wanted to go. But would Chance misinterpret her actions if she agreed?

⸺ ☙ ⸺

That afternoon when Megan pulled her Nova into the driveway, she noticed Micah sitting on the porch swing. Parking next to his Honda, she followed the shrubbery then clipped the corner of the lawn to the front sidewalk. She was already climbing the steps when she remembered she was not supposed to be hanging out alone with him. She hesitated.

He waved her forward, as if he'd forgotten, too.

Megan plopped her purse next to the screen door. "Hi."

Micah laid his Bible beside him on the swing. She wondered if it was intentional, to keep her from sitting beside him. She eyed it. "It's kinda funny. I used to be the one fending you off, now you're trying to keep your distance from me."

He looked stricken. "That's not true."

She waved a hand, "It's all right. Makes me kinda relieved. At least at home, I can drop my guard. Let you worry about that."

"Oh? But at work, it's different?"

"You're perceptive." At least he was perceptive when he didn't play dumb, like he had back in college. Or when he'd muscled the cat in, despite the disapproval he felt from her dad.

"Part of the job, I guess," he said.

"No, I think it's a gift. Mom has it, too."

"So what's going on at work?"

"Oh, Chance asked me to fly with him on Saturday. He's working with MDS, taking supplies to Indiana for victims of the recent tornado. Char Air does a lot of charity flights. And I've always wanted to go on some of these flights. I just don't want to give him the wrong impression."

Micah ran a hand through his hair, started to say something, then refrained, his expression looking pained as if it was hard to remain silent.

She glanced at the buckeye tree then at Micah's Bible. "I told him I'd let him know at the end of the week." She saw Micah's jaw twitch. He probably didn't realize he was tapping his leg. "Any advice, Brother Micah?"

"You asking me as your preacher?"

"Sure."

"It's a good cause. MDS wouldn't be able to keep going without volunteers."

She picked up his Bible, scooted in beside him, and dropped it on her lap, careful not to move his marker. She sank back against the swing's back, allowing the slight movement to ease away the day's stress. "Would you give me the same advice as a friend?"

She heard him sigh. "I'd agree that you needed to be careful not to give him the wrong impression. All men are easily encouraged."

She fondled the soft leather cover. "As a preacher, you say yes, but as a friend, you say no? That leaves me without any clear direction."

The swing creaked, filling in the comfortable silence. She wondered if this was what it was like to have a brother. Heaven knew she needed another friend, what with Lil gone and Katy busy with her little family.

"Some things you have to decide for yourself."

Her legs gave in to the soft swaying movement of the swing. "That's exactly what Barbara told me."

"You talked to her about this?"

"No. But I talked to her about Chance."

"I'd like to get to know her."

They fell into silence except for the rhythmic creaking. "I see you got rid of your hives."

"Yes. I went into the office today. Joy Ann says she needs a witness to count the offering. But I don't think the preacher should see the checks. I'd rather not fall in a trap of judging people by their donations. I'm going to suggest that a treasurer assist her with that."

"Good idea. How often will you go to the office?"

"Joy Ann says Brother Troyer went in every morning. I'll try that. She only comes on Mondays and Fridays. She cleans house the other days. Joy Ann told me you're friends."

"Yes, but not close friends. I think she's trying to impress you."

He sighed. "I was afraid of that. Guess I better talk to your dad about not being at the office alone with her. I suppose it wasn't an issue with Brother Troyer. But things are different these days." He continued telling her about his day. "On my way home, I picked up a litter box. And when you pulled up, I was thinking about next week's sermon topic."

"What is it?"

"I don't know yet."

Megan patted his arm and rose. "How about something like 'How to Hear God's Voice' or 'How to Follow God's Leading'?"

He laughed. "You'll have to make up your mind about the flight before Sunday's sermon."

"True, but there's always next week and next week's problems."

"You're right, Megan. There's always that."

CHAPTER 18

"**D**o you know how to make hot dogs?"

Megan looked up, her gaze following the aroma of french fries and the masculine voice that was hard to resist. She laughed at Chance's serious expression. "Sure. That's not hard. They're not healthy, though."

He shoved a red fast-food container toward her. "Want one?"

She looked at the fries. "No thanks."

"Hard to eat these without the hot dogs. In Ecuador, they have what's called *salchipapas*, french fries with little hot dogs on top."

"Can't you make hot dogs?"

"I could if I had a grill. But I'm not staying in the States long enough to buy one."

"You can boil them in water."

"I tried microwaving one, but it blew up. The woes of being a bachelor." He wagged his eyebrows at her.

"Now that's the way to charm a woman." Megan mimicked his voice, "Come make me some hot dogs."

"Yeah? Nothing else is working. And it's really too bad, because you would love Ecuador. It's beautiful from its sky to its jungles. It has cliffs and waterfalls. And the weather is perfect. Always in the seventies, perpetual spring. I'm telling you, Megan, it's the life. Sure beats asphalt and high-rises."

"Plain City doesn't have any high-rises. And I thought you said it rained a lot and the runways were gooey."

"But that's what makes it the rain forest. Gorgeous."

"You miss it."

"Yes, but I'm going back. You, on the other hand, will miss out altogether unless you let me take you over." He opened a ketchup packet and squirted it inside his cardboard container. "You should go before all your shots expire."

Megan smiled. "What kind of work would I do? I'm not a nurse."

"The hospitals need employees to keep records, too."

"Tell me about the hospital."

"There's more than one. The Hospital Vozandeson is on the edge of the Amazon rain forest and has twenty-eight beds. They do surgery and treat snakebites and tropical diseases. Oh, and they deliver babies. There're a couple of houses in Shell, mission hubs for missionaries, translators, supplies, pilots. I'm sure they need help running those places, too. I don't suppose you'd want to get your pilot's license?"

"Hardly. What you just described, are these voluntary positions?"

"Most. But not all. I'm telling you, once you visit, you'll fall in love."

Megan smiled. Yes, she would. She'd already fallen in love with his irresistible smile. It was hard enough in a sterile chrome and glass office not to give in to his charms. What would it be like to be with him in his Garden of Eden?

"But first, you should go with me on the MDS drop on Saturday. See what a safe pilot I am, build a little trust that I can deliver what I promise." It was certainly tempting. He'd promised that if she claimed his friendship, he wouldn't press her for more. But he hadn't promised to protect her from her own feelings and desires.

Just then Paige and Tate entered the office. "It's nonstop lunch and break time with you two, isn't it?" Paige plucked the last french fry out of Chance's hand, stuck it in her mouth, then smacked her red lips. "Too much ketchup."

Chance shook his head, handed Megan the empty carton, and fell into step with Tate. "What's the story on that cargo plane?"

But Paige lingered at Megan's desk. "The only thing that man understands is power. He respects it. That's why I boss him around. Keeps him from bossing me around."

Megan rolled her gaze to the ceiling at Paige's weird philosophy and tossed the french fry carton into her trash. Brushing her hands, she looked Paige in her contact-covered pupils. "I'm not after his respect; I'm trying to repel him."

"I knew it." Paige hit the desk with her fist then leaned close. "Don't give in. Not a sweet thing like you. I can give you some tips."

"That's what I'd hoped."

"Over-laugh at everything he says."

Megan snickered. "That's your advice?"

"No, seriously. I just read this article about the best ways to repel a man. When you said repel just now, it reminded me of the article."

"Why were you reading that kind of article?"

"Getting my hair done and it sounded interesting."

Megan could see how a laughing hyena might deter a man. "What else?"

"When you're not laughing, cry for no reason. Talk loud. Nag him." She stood, straightened her pencil skirt. "If those don't work, then don't wash your hair. Got it?"

"Sure. Just be generally obnoxious?"

"You have any better ideas?"

Megan shook her head.

Paige shrugged. "Then try obnoxious. And if that doesn't work and you get yourself in a pickle, just scream. I'll be across this room in a flash. He'll never know what hit him."

"Thanks, Paige. If nothing else, you know how to lift my spirits."

After that, Megan buried herself in her work, which must have been why she didn't notice how the sky had darkened until Chance strode through her office. "Look outside!"

Megan lifted her eyes and saw an ominous sky. "Aye, yi, yi."

Chance's mouth quirked, but his smile didn't reach his eyes. "There's a storm heading in. And now there're tornado warnings. I'm closing up shop. Everybody goes home early."

Tornado warnings! Megan leaned over her steering wheel and squinted between strokes of the windshield wiper for a better look at the sky, scanning for any indication of funnel clouds. It was too dark to tell. Plain City didn't usually get tornados, but she couldn't dismiss the severity of the storms that had recently ravaged Indiana. She fiddled with the radio, but the antique only hissed static.

Sheets of rain blurred her vision. Wind whipped the car, and she fought the steering wheel to keep it in its proper lane. By the time she'd taken her exit on the down ramp, her nerves were fraught. Between blinding bursts of rain, visibility cleared enough to reveal some new obstacles. Her eyes widened at a row of telephone poles that had been snapped like matchsticks. "Aye, yi, yi."

She clamped the steering wheel and drove another mile, and then the wind suddenly quieted. The rain quit. The wipers screeched against the windshield, but she didn't have faith to turn them off. Drawing in a breath of relief, she searched the sky to see if it was just a lapse between storms. It looked like she'd have a clear road now, and she was almost home. The worst was over. Still thinking about the telephone poles, she glanced in her rearview mirror.

Back in the distance, a swirl of dust moved across a field. How could it be dusty after the downpour she'd just driven in? She glanced in her rearview mirror again, unable to take her eyes off the peculiar squall. It bounced. . .and spewed things!

Frantic again, Megan rolled down her window and jerked her side mirror. Then she saw what was feeding the whirlwind. A small funnel cloud hovered over the field, touching the ground, scraping it, and sending splatters of destruction back into the sky. Oh no!

With a groan, she stomped on the gas pedal and held it to the floor. The car bucked and slid. She whipped the steering wheel and the tires straightened and gripped the road. It took all her concentration to keep the Nova on the road, and she couldn't see much out the rearview mirror except that the tornado was gaining on her.

With a prayer of relief, she braked just enough to make the drive, spitting gravel and hitting the brakes. Her car slid sideways and barely missed Micah's Honda. Her hands trembled so bad she couldn't get her car door open. But it suddenly burst open. Micah grabbed her arm.

"Hurry!"

"There's a tornado!" she cried.

"I know. I've been out at the road watching for you."

She must have driven right past him. Clutching her arm, he dragged her toward his cottage. She stopped and shrugged him away. "No. We have to go to the root cellar. This way."

She broke into a run, assuming Micah was behind her, and yelled over her shoulder. "What about Mom?"

"They're at your grandparents. Hurry."

They'd reached the corner of the house, and she led him past the kitchen door to a smaller one with a wooden bar. A downburst drenched her in seconds, and she fumbled with the bar.

A hand clamped on her shoulder. "Let me."

Megan danced to the side, and Micah jerked the door open, revealing a dark, cavernous hole. She'd never liked the root cellar, hated when Mom sent her after canned goods. It was smelly and full of spiders. Once they'd even had a snake.

A roar filled Megan's ears, and her heart lurched in fear. "It's coming."

"Are there steps?"

"Yes."

He nudged her. "Hurry, Meg."

She jerked the string that dangled from the ceiling. A light switched on. She started down. "Can you close the door?"

"Yes, I've already got it bolted."

She'd hit the bottom landing and swung around. She grabbed his shirt. "What about the cat?"

He placed his hand over hers and squeezed. "It'll be fine."

She looked into his eyes. They brooked no argument, so she nodded.

He gave her a grim smile. "We will be, too." His gaze swept over the small cellar.

As the roaring sound grew louder, the electricity flashed off, pitching them into complete darkness. Megan gasped and clutched Micah's shirt tighter.

He drew her close against him. "Let's go beneath the stairs. It's the safest place."

They couldn't move unless she released her hold on him. He was right about moving under the stairway. Reluctantly she eased out of his arms, and they felt their way around the stairway.

"Let's sit down." His calm voice was an anchor in the storm.

"All right, but it's dirty."

He laughed. "The least of our worries."

They eased down and braced their backs against a wall that probably had spiderwebs. She hated the brown recluse that occupied dark corners. When Micah's arm slipped around her, pulling her close, she burrowed into his protection. The winds howled, and he softly prayed something out of the Psalms. Her fingers curled around the front of his damp shirt.

A loud crash rattled the wall near the entrance. He patted her hand. "Shh."

She hadn't realized she was crying. She gulped, embarrassed. "It was an awful drive home. The funnel cloud chased me. I didn't know if I could outrun it."

Beneath her hand, his chest rumbled with low laughter. "I saw you coming down the road. It was amazing the way you handled your car."

"I couldn't even get out of my car. Thank God you came for me." He'd been the best sight of her life.

"I've got you now."

She hiccupped. "After all your blabbering about being discreet, here we are alone together. In the dark."

" 'When it is dark enough, you can see the stars.' "

"What?"

"Ralph Waldo Emerson."

"I don't see any stars. I highly doubt stars are out there tonight."

"Maybe not tonight, but tomorrow."

"But—"

"Listen! Hear that? It's letting up."

She let out a nervous laugh, grasping at the hope that the nightmare was ending. "My grandparents have a basement. Is that why Mom went over there?"

"She was visiting them when your dad came home. He wanted to go over and help your grandfather get ready for the storm."

"He doesn't get around so good anymore."

"Your dad was worried Anita might get caught on the road in the storm. He was worried about you, too, but I told him I'd keep you safe." He relaxed his hold on her. "Maybe I should go up and look around. Where do you keep a flashlight?"

She hated to be in the dark cellar alone. "In the junk drawer in the kitchen, but I want to come with you."

"Wait here for now." He disengaged himself from her, and she heard his footfall on the steps. She heard scraping, a thump, and a groan.

"What's wrong?"

"The door won't budge. It's probably that loud noise we heard. Something's blocking it. There's a hole and water leaking in, too."

Panic tamped up her spine. "But we can't stay down here."

Several stair steps creaked, and he sidled in beside her again. "We have no other choice. We'll just have to make the best of it."

"How?"

He stroked her cheek. "If you don't think of something, I will."

He meant to kiss her! For an instant, she wanted it, too. But then she came to her senses. "I guess you could practice next week's sermon on me."

His touch fell away, and his laughter rumbled through the darkness. "That would be my second-best idea."

She tried to straighten against the wall and not humiliate herself by clutching him like a frightened bird again, but it wasn't nearly as comforting. Especially when the storm continued to brew overhead. He mumbled something about dealing with pain. His sermon did little to warm her, and she shivered. He moved closer. She felt the hard planes of his side and leaned against his strength.

⟶ ⟜

Megan awoke with a start, stiff and hazy-minded. Her face was pressed against a beating heart. She went rigid as the night's events came back to her. Lifting her head, she gently pushed away and swiped at her hair.

"Your dad's back. But he had to go after help."

"What time is it?"

"Still the middle of the night, I think." Micah pushed up and started up the creaky stairway.

"He was here earlier?"

His voice grew more distant, coming from overhead. "Yeah, you were sleeping."

She didn't want him to leave her alone in the dark. "Is everybody all right?"

"Yes."

Megan stood and bumped her head on a step. With a groan, she rubbed it. The cellar was too dark to see much until her eyes adjusted. She swiped at her clothing and moved to the bottom of the stairway.

"Stay put for now, Megan. When they remove the structure, there could be a cave in."

"Cave in?" She backed into a row of canned goods.

"Micah! I'm back."

"I'm here." Micah returned her dad's shout.

How had she slept through his first visit? The floor was flooded. Had Micah kept them dry? She was embarrassed that she'd slept while he kept vigil.

Dad gave Micah instructions, and Micah backed partway down the steps again. There was a big commotion, and suddenly, the door burst open. Megan scurried up the steps behind Micah, and he helped her out the splintered opening.

Dad pulled her into the safety of his arms. "Thank the Lord you're safe."

"I'm fine. Where's Mom?"

"I made her stay inside. She's worried. Better go in to her."

Megan stepped out of his embrace and into the predawn. She swept her gaze over the property, portions dimly lit by the headlights of Will Landis's tractor. The only major damage she saw was the tree that had smashed into the cellar door.

Will grunted, pushing debris out of her path.

"Everybody all right at your place?" she asked the farmer.

"Yep. We won't be able to tell what's happened till morning, but I haven't gotten any calls that anyone's in trouble. 'Cept you."

Micah stepped up beside her. "Looks like we picked the most dangerous spot on the property."

Bill tugged his dripping ball cap. "You did the right thing."

Megan looked up at Micah, who'd been her mainstay. She couldn't think of words to express her deep thankfulness. Awareness of their intimacies burned between them. "You coming?"

"In a minute. I'm going to check on the cat."

Almost relieved, she rounded the house to the kitchen. While Micah's embrace meant everything in that dark, dank hole, she feared once the sun broke, matters would take a different spin.

CHAPTER 19

Bill used the chainsaw, and Micah dragged away limbs and tossed debris into a trailer that Will Landis had loaned them. Bill hadn't said much, other than to thank him for keeping Megan safe. The night spent in the pitch-black root cellar with Megan dominated Micah's thoughts. The way she'd clung to him for protection had crashed his defenses so that all he had been able to think about was shielding her from harm.

When he'd seen the funnel cloud chasing her car and met the desperation in her eyes as she drove unseeing past him, instinct launched him to her side. He'd every heroic intention to sweep her up into his arms and to the shelter of his cottage. But she'd summoned her wit for the both of them and run toward the root cellar instead.

That night, the cellar became a world within a world, a journey to a place where time fell apart and set them on the cusp of reality. Everything material and inconsequential fell away. Everything dear and true became monumental. All that mattered in the darkness of the storm was Megan and God.

When she'd quieted in his arms, everything was pure and right. There with Megan and God, he had been satisfied and fulfilled. But then the storm ended, and Bill's voice from the other side of the trappings thrust him back into the harsher, outside world.

Micah heaved an armload of debris. It thudded into the trailer. He pulled himself up over the side rails and stomped down the trash, oblivious to the pain of sharp branches and prickly brush. He hopped out again and strode toward Bill.

The kitchen door opened, and Megan stepped into Micah's view. She looked pretty and fresh, calm and collected as if it were any other normal day. She stopped beside her dad and commented on the damage. "We'll miss that tree, won't we?"

"Yep. It's going to expose your Mom's garden now. Coulda been worse, though."

She looked at Micah with a heated gaze that validated his own feelings. For them, normal had evaporated and rolled away with the clouds. They would have to redefine their relationship.

She looked away. "I gotta go."

"Micah and I are going to Barbara's and the other widows' after we're done here."

"Good. I'll see you both tonight." She started toward her car, off to the pilot and everything that drew her away from him.

⸻

That afternoon Megan drove home, sadly observing the tornado's hit-and-miss destruction. Some barns had been damaged and trees downed. The road was washed away in places, but from all she'd heard, Plain City had missed the brunt of the storm. Still, she found it hard to shake off the vivid memories of the funnel cloud and the terror that had clamped her chest and stolen her wits. Through it all, Micah had been solid and strong, tender and reassuring.

She flicked down her visor to ward off the afternoon's glare and flinched. The paper with the words *Do not be unequally yoked* was pinned to her visor with a prayer-covering pin!

Her mom must have found it in her skirt pocket. A pang of guilt struck her that she'd completely forgotten about it. Her conscience recalled how she'd earlier memorized it and meditated on it throughout her workday. But Chance had broken down her guard with his constant presence. It was hard to think about Bible verses when he was perched on her desk, painting her pictures of his jungle paradise.

She removed a sticky note from her steering wheel and stuck in on top of the verse then glanced back at the road. Just before she'd left the office, she'd returned to her desk from the ladies room. That's when she'd discovered the sticky note. Chance had placed it on her computer screen. It read:

MDS needs you. So do I. No hot dog making required.

She remembered snippets of their conversation, his concern for her well-being during the storm. Tomorrow was Friday, and she still hadn't given him her answer about the flight to Indiana. She needed to make her decision tonight. She had thought up an excuse she could use, flimsy as it was. Lil and Fletch were returning tomorrow, and she was anxious to see them again. Chance would know it was the truth, since he still dropped in at the restaurant, but there was no reason Megan had to see them on Saturday. Flimsy.

She pulled into the drive and noticed that Will Landis's tractor and trailer were gone. Aside from the ugly gap where the tree once stood, things looked pretty normal. Her gaze swept across the garden and froze when it found Micah. He stood with his back to her and his shoulder pressed against the scaly trunk of a surviving hickory tree. She should talk to him and get it over with before things got more awkward. Slinging her purse over her shoulder, she shut her car door.

Micah startled and looked over his shoulder. "It's that late already?"

Starting toward him, she replied, "It's been a long day for me."

He kneaded his arm muscles. "Couldn't be as rough as mine."

She shrugged. "I kept thinking about the storm. How's Barbara?"

"She's fine. Nobody got hurt. The men have been cleaning up all day. I helped out at Lori Longacre's this afternoon." He touched the back of his neck. "Did I mention how sore I am?"

"I took the hint." The muscle flexing was hard to ignore. She tried by fixing her gaze on Miss Purrty. The cat rolled in the litter at the edge of the woods. But when silence prevailed, Megan's thoughts rushed out. "Thanks for everything last night."

The rascal's mouth quirked up in the corner. "It was my pleasure."

Hers, too, but she wouldn't admit it. Now in the daylight, the way she'd clung to him was pitiful. But her embarrassment clearly amused him.

"I thought if I was going to meet my Maker, hanging onto the preacher's coattail was the smartest thing to do."

He arched an eyebrow. "I did notice your attachment to my shirt."

She smiled. "Your sermon was good, too."

"Just doing my duty. Protecting Bill's little girl."

She felt her face burn.

Micah bent his knee and propped one foot behind him on the tree, studying her, trying to draw something from her that she wasn't willing to reveal.

"So Lori had some damage at her place?"

"She lost a tree. She wants to pay me back by helping me with my research." He scratched his head and brushed away bits of bark. "Usually librarians are sweet old widows. But Lori's young and smells good. I like her. But I don't know if I should take her up on the offer."

It galled her that his statement was worded like a question, seeking her permission. Was he talking about Lori so Megan wouldn't consider the root cellar incident anything more than a man doing his duty? It irritated her how swiftly he went from helping one woman to the next. Their night together obviously hadn't affected him like it had her. She hadn't been able to work through it yet, but this conversation was adding clarity.

She kept her voice nonchalant. "I can tell you what I know about her. Normally she doesn't chase men. I don't recall her helping Brother Troyer. But maybe I just didn't know about it. Although she's not old-old, she's older than you. So maybe she's just trying to be helpful."

Micah laughed sarcastically. "She's not old. And I don't want to give her the wrong idea. I need to stay focused on my goals."

Megan couldn't tell if he was warning her off or if he was only talking about Lori. She knew what it was like to fixate on the wrong person. But Lori was a good Mennonite woman. "She's smart, even progressive in her thinking. Maybe you should just give her the I-have-to-be-discreet speech you gave me. Tell her the truth."

He looked out across the garden and fell quiet. Megan was just ready to end their conversation and go inside when he asked, "Did you know that church secretary is a volunteer position?"

Confused, she replied, "Sure."

"The elders told Joy Ann they're getting somebody to help her."

Why was he dragging all his female admirers into their conversation? "Safety in numbers?"

"Right. Anyway, when they told Joy Ann, she didn't bat an eye and recommended her friend Ruthie Ropp."

"That's surprising. I figured Ruthie would be her competition, interested in you herself."

"No. Ruthie's not interested."

So there was one woman he hadn't smitten with his Ichabod charms? Megan saw her chance to get under his skin. "Maybe I can help. I can give you Paige's sure-fire ways to repel a man. Maybe they work for women, too."

His lip twitched. "Repellents? Are these the tactics you used on me at college?"

"Hardly. I didn't even know Paige then. I work with her. She recommends over-laughing at everything. She read this article. It also recommends nagging."

"Men don't nag." He lowered himself to the base of the tree, placed his back against its trunk, and motioned for her to join him. "But this is amusing. So your friend Paige does these things to fend off men?"

Megan set her purse on the damp ground and joined him, tucking her skirt around her bent knees. "She's happily married, and if anybody gets out of line with her, she clobbers them with her list of donors. She employs power and conquest. And perhaps the element of surprise. Oh wait"—her hand flew to his arm—"I remember another one." She glanced at his wind-tousled hair. "Don't wash your hair. Leave it all *stroobly*."

His hand instinctively went up to his hair. He brushed it off his forehead and asked, "Or use hairspray?" Then he laid his head back against the tree. "No. I won't do anything that puts me in a bad light."

"But according to Paige, you have to make yourself less attractive."

He leaned forward and scratched his head. More bark chips showered down his back. "That won't be hard for me."

Megan thought she'd teased him long enough. "My mom says you're a real prize."

He burst out laughing. "I'm sure you set her straight."

"Just because I don't want to date you, doesn't mean I don't think you're a prize. You were there for me last night. If I'd had a brother, I'd have wanted him to be just like you."

He picked up a piece of bark and tossed it in front of the cat. It switched its tail. "But when it comes to the romance department, you're looking for somebody more like Chance?"

She draped her arms across her skirt and shrugged. "Maybe."

"What's he got over the rest of us?"

"You've seen him. He's fun. Likeable. Has this vulnerable side to him. Kinda like a teddy bear."

Micah made a disgusted face. "I thought he seemed aggressive. Arrogant. More grizzly than teddy."

She tilted her head thoughtfully. "He's sure of himself, all right. There was something in his confidence that scared me at first. Not anymore." Megan narrowed her gaze, followed the cat's movements as it stalked a sparrow.

"If he's like every other air-breathing man, you'll have to draw him a line in the sand. He won't stop until you show him that line."

Megan smiled at him. "I can't wait for you to meet my friend Lil. She'd tell you that's a good thing. Lil's draws her own lines."

"Maybe. When does she get back?"

"This weekend." The cat gave up on the bird and inched across the lawn toward them. She strode snootily past Megan and stepped possessively, one foot at a time, into Micah's lap.

"Maybe I'll take your advice. I'll go on that MDS flight and set some boundaries."

"If you're not too swept away by the entire experience that you forget to do that."

Megan grew weary of the topic. She reached out and touched the purring cat's head, scratching her behind the ears. "So are you still worried Miss Purrty might run away?"

"Not really. I was worried about her getting lost in the woods at first. But she doesn't seem to want to get too far away from me. And now she knows that the cottage is our home. I think she's adjusting."

"I guess if Miss Purrty's so attached to you, she's got her competition cut out for her," Megan said, rising and brushing off her skirt.

"Nope, she's the only female for me."

Laughing, Megan picked up her purse and left him to go into the house.

Micah scooped up the tabby and headed for the cottage, watching Megan retreat to the house. He wished he could tell her how foolish she would be to go on that plane ride with a conceited outsider who wanted to despoil her. What else could the man be after? At the least, he wanted to despoil her soul, wanted her to give up her religion for him. It made Micah's blood boil, made him want to drive over to Char Air and spin the man's propeller.

But if he did that, he might drive Megan away forever. And probably drive her right into Campbell's undeserving arms. He tossed Miss Purrty onto the floor, and she instantly leaped up onto her favorite chair, settling herself in for another spit bath. Micah slumped in the chair on the other side of the table and crossed his long legs on the footstool, his insides jumping more than they'd been during the storm.

It irked him that Megan would choose a man like Chance over himself or another good-hearted Mennonite man. He'd been foolish to attribute her actions in the root cellar to anything other than fear.

If he'd never chased Megan in school, would she look at him differently now? The question had little bearing on Megan's infatuation with her boss. He'd just have to trust that she'd remain faithful to her convictions. Even though she'd spurned his own advances, he wanted the best for her. Chance Campbell was not the best.

Megan knew the right thing to do. But people made foolish decisions all the time. He went over their conversation again, and then he remembered something she'd told him. *"If I'd had a brother, I'd have wanted him to be just like you."* He snarled his lip. She thought of him as a brother. He liked the idea of Lori and Joy Ann, or even Ruthie, thinking of him as a brother. It was the exact image he'd hoped to create. But Megan feeling that way made his heart sink into gloom. Before a day had passed, their relationship had been redefined.

CHAPTER 20

As Megan approached the white-and-green-striped Cessna Caravan waiting on the tarmac, excitement tramped up her spine. Chance guided her to a right rear air stair, and soon she was inside the small cargo plane. She leisurely took in the plush cockpit then glanced back at the cavernous cabin, the exterior of which was now partly filled with boxes of supplies. She knew some had also been stored underneath the cabin.

"Make yourself comfortable while I do a few last minute things," Chance said with a smile and eyes that mirrored the excitement churning in the pit of her stomach.

"Sure." Her eyes traversed the plane's features, ten times more luxurious than her Nova. As she waited for her pilot, she gazed out at the familiar tarmac, easily visible because of the plane's high wing position, and reassured herself about her decision. She worked for a charter flight company. It made her a better employee to experience a real flight. It would be foolish to turn down the opportunity when it was the reason that she took the job with Char Air. Barbara claimed that paths cross for a reason. She couldn't be obstinate just because her pilot was attractive.

She'd done everything to persuade him that she wouldn't veer from her convictions. Now she needed to give God the opportunity to show her why their paths had crossed. She was merely taking supplies to MDS volunteers. And she would do her share of the workload. It was more worthwhile than anything else she could have done with her time.

"All set." Chance moved into a plush beige leather seat and touched the W-shaped yoke.

Megan glanced at the control columns on her side of the plane, amazed at all the dials, levers, and the three large screens. As Chance did his job to prepare to taxi and take off, she fastened her restraints. She watched through the tinted glass cockpit as they moved down a taxiway and then sped down a runway. When they lifted into the sky, her stomach did a little flip, but she gave Chance a huge grin.

"You're a natural." He smiled at her then gave his attention to piloting.

She glanced at his headgear. After all the stories she had heard about surviving impossible landing scenarios and storms and near misses, she now felt confident to have the plane in his competent hands. "Don't you think it's a little early to tell?"

"I can tell."

She relaxed and settled in for the flight. The cabin was quieter than she had expected, but Chance wasn't all that talkative while he worked. He did point out various landmarks such as the Wabash River that wound through square quarter sections of farmland. The time went so quickly that she could hardly believe it when he was pointing out the recent tornado's destructive pathway.

"Looks like someone ran their finger through the sand," he said.

From the air, that's exactly what it resembled, only instead of sand, it was housing communities and forests and fields. Looking at the destructive power of nature brought back the terror of trying to outdrive the funnel cloud. What would she have done if she'd had to spend the night alone in the root cellar? Her heart clenched with fear, even though the incident was behind her. She tried to hide her anxiety from Chance. She hadn't told him the entirety of what had happened. She knew he wouldn't approve of her time alone with Micah.

She looked down, took some deep breaths, and tried to focus on God's creative and sustaining power. When they dropped to a lower elevation, she was able to peer into homes as if they were dollhouses without roofs, their contents strewn and trees uprooted. Her heart instantly filled with compassion for the people who had not been as fortunate as she had. They had lost so much. "It still looks bad. As if it just happened."

"They work first to set up temporary housing, do the search and rescue. But now they're ready to start cleanup and rebuilding. It all takes time. There used to be a trailer park down there." He pointed. "I saw a lot of devastation the last time I was here."

Now the stripped lot with twisted metal looked more like a junkyard. Megan tried not to imagine what the occupants had experienced. Chance spoke to the control tower and turned the plane. "Prepare for landing, Megan."

She glanced over at him, wondering what it would be like to join him for a day in Ecuador. In his paradise, there would be mountains and rain forest instead of corn and soybean fields and cities. The plane gave a little bounce, but mostly it was a smooth landing; then Chance steered the Cessna to a specified taxiway. At the ramp, they were immediately met by a handful of MDS volunteers.

The married couple in charge stepped forward and introduced themselves. Danny was a retired farmer, and his wife, Cindy, was a friendly woman who told Megan, "The UPS driver should be here anytime. That company's been a Godsend the way they activated an action team and provided trucks and services."

"Whoa. There he is now." Danny waved the driver over.

Chance quickly raised the cargo doors on either side of the plane and pointed out which were the lighter boxes. They lifted the boxes out of the plane and dollied them to the van. The group worked for a good hour moving boxes of gloves, first-aid kits, bleach, shovels and rakes, trash bags, tarps, and food and water. Perspiration had collected on Megan's brow by the time the last box had been loaded inside the brown truck.

Cindy thanked them and hugged Megan. "We can give you a ride to the shelter, where they divvy out the supplies."

Chance thanked her. "We need to get the plane back this afternoon so that it can get serviced. It's booked for another flight. This one was barely squeezed in."

"Well, it's much appreciated."

Megan watched the older couple and other volunteers get into a white van and drive away.

"We do have time for a bite to eat," Chance said. "There's a restaurant within walking. Nothing fancy like Lil's place."

"Sure."

He locked things up, talked to some flight techs, and led Megan through a side door. The restaurant was more of a fast-food cafeteria for the working crews.

"All this just to get your hot dog?" Megan teased.

Chance laughed. "They have some deli sandwiches and salads."

"I'll have whatever you have. Hold the onions."

"You got it."

Megan found a small booth by a huge window that looked out over the airport apron. When Chance returned, she took a long drink from the soda he had provided. "Seems even hotter here," she remarked.

"Farther south." He gave her a look of admiration. "You worked hard today."

"You worked harder."

He shrugged, took a bite of his hot dog. He swallowed. "All day, I kept seeing you with me in Ecuador."

She felt a sharp intake of breath. "I thought about it, too. What it would be like to drop down into the jungle instead of an airport."

"It's not Indiana. It's dangerous. There are no UPS trucks with helpful drivers."

"Just the other day I learned that one of my ancestors was a hero."

"I'd love to hear the story."

"His name was Dirk Willems. He was a Dutch Anabaptist, before we were called Mennonites, who had been imprisoned during the Reformation."

"The 1600s?"

"Yes. Many were getting burned at the stake for their beliefs. Anabaptists believed in baptism for adults instead of infants, and the state church called them heretics. Anyway, Dirk tied strips of cloth to make a rope and escaped from a prison tower. As he ran across the countryside, a guard chased after him. They came to pond covered in ice, and Dirk took the risk and crossed it safely. But his pursuer broke through the ice and was doomed. Dirk had to decide if God was securing his escape or if he should go back and help the man. He decided to go back. But the guard took him back to the prison, and Dirk was later burned at the stake."

"It sounds like the missionaries who helped the Aucas."

"Yes."

"And he's your ancestor?"

Megan leaned forward. "I just found out from my dad. He doesn't talk much about these things because it troubles Mom. She's adopted, and I guess she has some blank spots in her background."

"But she's Mennonite?"

"Of course." Megan took a sip of her drink and hit bottom. Then she pushed it away. "The point of the story is that I read about Dirk Willems in college. His story is in a huge book of Anabaptist martyrs called *The Martyrs Mirror*. These stories always stir up my faith. And now to find out that this man I always admired is a relative just makes me a stronger person. I have to wonder if his mother prayed for her descendants, what ties connect us."

"But if he died, then how—"

She laughed. "That's the same thing I asked. Not him, per say, but his bloodline."

"I see." Chance glanced at his watch. "Maybe this stirring in you is a calling. Think seriously about Ecuador. It could be the reason we met."

Megan's pulse raced, and she wondered if it was true. She wouldn't have to marry Chance to go to Ecuador.

"I have a DVD at home I'd like you to see."

"I don't watch television or movies," she objected, reminded of her conversation with Micah. She had told him that she could use this trip to draw the lines in her relationship with Chance.

"I think you could make an exception for this one. It's called *The End of the Spear*. It's the story of the missionaries who were killed by the Aucas. And the scenery is representative of Ecuador."

"It wasn't filmed in Ecuador?"

"No. Colón, Panama. On the Panama Canal much farther north. It's more touristy, but the movie gives a true picture of what it's like."

"I'll think about it. Maybe I should ask our preacher if this would make a good exception."

Chance bristled. "Preacher? As in the guy staying with you? Are you two getting chummier?"

Embarrassment fell over her to think of the night she spent with him in the root cellar. Chance would definitely consider that chummier. "We're friends. Having him around is like having a big brother."

"Just because you view him as a brother doesn't mean he sees you as a sister. Better watch how chummy you get with him, unless you want to be a preacher's wife." Then he finished off his hot dog and glanced at her paper cup. "You want a drink for the sky?"

"No. I'm fine." She wished she hadn't brought up Micah. Just when she'd thought that Chance was acting reasonably, he'd gotten jealous. She mulled this over as they returned to the plane. She might not get another opportunity alone with him to draw the line in the sand.

Just before takeoff, she turned to Chance. "Are you jealous of Micah because I said he's my friend and because I'm cautious about my relationship with you?"

"Do you blame me?"

"Micah's a Mennonite preacher. Even if a friendship with him deepened, it would be acceptable."

"So you're considering a relationship with him?"

"No. That's not what I'm saying."

He nodded. "Fasten your seat belt, Megan."

Frustrated, she prepared for takeoff.

As the flight progressed, his irritation vanished. Megan was able to relax and enjoy the trip. Once she looked over and caught his gaze. "Thanks for today. You kept your promise. And I appreciate that."

He knew exactly what she meant. "I'd keep my promise if you stopped by my place and watch that movie with me, too. I'd be a perfect gentleman."

Megan nodded. "I'll think about it. Right now, I just want to enjoy this plane, the flight."

"I get that. This baby is sweet from spinner to rudder. A little bigger than my Cessna in Ecuador, but sweet just the same."

"Very sweet," Megan agreed.

꠲

"How was your flight?"

Startled, Megan whirled and whipped her hand to her pounding chest. Her purse dropped back onto her car seat. Micah stepped out of the growing shadows, his brow creased in apparent worry. "Great. It was very exciting."

"No regrets?" he pressed, studying her carefully.

"No. Chance was a perfect gentleman. Actually, he doesn't talk much while he works." The observation suddenly hit her as amusing. He must not consider the office work, the way he talked nonstop there. Smiling, she determined to tease him about it.

Micah shook his head. "Your dreamy smile is not a good sign."

"No." She waved her hand through the air. "I was just thinking something about work."

"No doubt. And MDS? Were you impressed with them, too?"

"Yes. We actually never left the airport. They came to us with a UPS van. But we worked hard to get everything unloaded and into the van. They were appreciative for all the supplies." Megan reached back inside the car for her purse and inclined her head toward the house. They started walking. "I was able to see the devastation from the sky. It's really unbelievable. It lifted houses off their foundations."

Micah fell into step with her. "I was on a volunteer team once. Pretty heart wrenching."

"Exactly." She glanced over. "You have your sermon ready?"

"Yep. I was just putting an antihistamine in my glove box for tomorrow when I heard you drive in."

"I hope you don't need it."

"It's good to be prepared. My day was more boring than yours, so bear with me if I ask too many questions. What kind of a plane was it?"

"A Cessna Caravan, single engine. The Caravans are cargo planes. They can even put those floatie things on them for landing in water. I learned quite a bit about planes today. That can't hurt my job. I'm glad I went."

Micah grinned. "You learned about 'floatie things'?"

"Fine. Pontoons. But we didn't need them."

"Never been in a small plane."

She glanced at him. "You'd like to?"

He shrugged. "Wouldn't turn down the chance."

She stopped walking. "How thoughtless. I should have invited you along today. Would you have gone?"

"Probably."

"I'm sorry. Next time just tell me."

"All right. But my curiosity's not satisfied."

Megan started walking again. "Yes?"

"What I'm wondering is what did Chance do after you drew the line in the sand?"

"He was a perfect gentleman." Reaching for the screen door, she asked, "Any more questions?"

"What's for dinner?"

"Taco salad," a voice chirped from inside the kitchen.

Megan jumped. "Aye, yi, yi! Mom, you scared me." She frowned at Micah. "You two in cahoots or what?"

Micah threw up his arms in a gesture of denial.

"What do you mean?" Mom asked.

"Oh nothing. It's just that Micah scared me, too, out by the car."

"Maybe you're just jumpy." Mom's piercing gaze held a strange glint, causing Megan to wonder how much her mother had heard of their conversation about Chance.

Jo,

My heart's full of hopes and dreams and questions. Barbara claims nothing is an accident with God, that people's paths cross for a reason. Chance wants me to take a trip to Ecuador. I have no idea how this would be arranged. But Randy will owe Chance a big favor, and Chance could probably make this happen for me.

I know flying is not a Conservative thing. But on the mission field, it's necessary. Chance understands me, the stirring I feel.

Then there's Micah. He's become like a big brother protector. The night spent in the cellar with him was confusing and special,

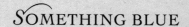

bringing us close. Though we both continue to make light of it, I think he feels it, too. It's nice to know I have a friend. I don't blame Lil and Katy for being busy with their own lives.

CHAPTER 21

On Sunday after his sermon, Micah tried to figure out why he'd gotten hives again. Speaking in front of a group didn't make him nervous. He'd earned As in speech class. He liked research and Bible study. Loved the writing process and hoped to branch out in that area.

Micah savored the intimacy that his sermon preparation created with God. All week long, the Lord gave him spiritual insights and affirmations. He even relished the times when God convicted him of sin.

But the ultimate fulfillment came during his sermon and afterward, when he saw how the message touched people. Eyes shone with revelation. Faces softened and sometimes sorrowed with repentance. All in all, it blessed him to shepherd a soul into God's truth. He knew he'd never tire of it.

So why when he was doing what he loved did he get hives again? Was it some allergy that had nothing to do with his spiritual growth? Or was it God speaking to him? He supposed a man could learn from every experience. But how could he do his job when all he could think about was clawing his face and throat? And it was becoming more difficult to concentrate on his conversation with the librarian when his mind was fixated on the antihistamine bottle in his glove box. He thought grimly that he should have put a capsule in his pocket for good measure.

"I love the quote you used in your sermon from *The Problem of Pain*. 'Pain provides opportunity for heroism; the opportunity is seized with surprising frequency.'"

"Yes, thanks for the book. C. S. Lewis is one of my favorite writers."

Lori smiled. "You're welcome. I also liked the part that age has nothing to do with pain. I know I've had my share."

Micah scratched the side of his neck, and his nose started tickling from her perfume. "I'm sorry. Glad you found comfort in the sermon."

"Oh, I did."

Across the vestibule, he saw Megan speaking to a petite brunette and wondered if it was her friend Lil. When Lori moved on, he went over to introduce himself.

"Fletch Stauffer." The brunette's husband offered a handshake. "I'm sorry we haven't met earlier, but we've been out of the country."

"So I heard. Where did you go, again?"

"Ethiopia. Taught some classes at the university."

"I'll bet you came back with some great stories."

"Lil invited some people for lunch today. Can you come?"

Micah didn't miss the frantic note in Lil's glance, though her smile affirmed her husband's invitation. The guest list had to include Megan, but he didn't want to push his way into her circle of friends.

She touched Lil's arm. "Micah and I've become good friends."

"Oh. We'd love to have you, Micah."

Fletch gave some quick directions to the doddy house; then the couple departed.

"You have hives again." Megan made it sound like he'd done it purposely.

"Yes, but I have medicine in my car. I'm headed there now. I'm going to swing by my cottage and make sure it settles down first."

"Take your time. Lil won't have the meal ready for at least half an hour. I'll see you there."

"Oh, Brother Zimmerman?"

Micah pivoted, colliding with Joy Ann's smile. "Mom wants me to invite you to dinner if you don't have plans."

"I'm sorry. I just accepted another invitation."

She furrowed her brow. "From Megan? But you eat with her every day."

Micah bristled at her resentful tone. "Fletch Stauffer just returned from a mission trip. I'd like to get to know him." He tried not to sound defensive, but he shouldn't have to explain his actions.

"But they don't even go to our church anymore. Not since they got married."

He hadn't remembered that. "Will you give your mom my apologies? Maybe I can take a rain check."

"Put us on the waiting list then." She gave him a flirtatious smile. "Hopefully we're at the top."

"Yes. You are." Now would be the perfect time to employ some of Megan's woman repellants, only he couldn't drum up so much as a solitary chuckle. It erupted into an impatient cough. He had a growing inkling that he would end up hurting Joy Ann's feelings.

"I'll see you tomorrow when we count the offering."

He needed to tell her that the elders had taken his advice, and a treasurer would be helping her with the offering in the future, but he didn't want to detain her any longer. He was one-tracked, needing to get to his car and get relief for the fire ants that marched up and down his neck.

⁓

Megan folded the quilt they would use for the picnic while watching Lil's animated expression.

"The trip was so good for our marriage. We'd gotten off track, you know." Lil placed dinnerware in the picnic basket that had once been her grandma's. "Just a lot of adjustments, and with both of us working, we were getting snappy. So on the long plane ride, we came up with a plan to keep our relationship exciting. Romantic picnics. Our first date was a picnic. So we're going to plan them around our work schedules."

"Nobody said anything about this being a *romantic* picnic."

Lil waved her gloved hand then took the ham out of the oven. "Silly. This is just a fun day with friends." She shook her head. "I've missed you."

"Chance goes to Volo Italiano all the time now."

"How's it going with him?"

"He took me up in a Cessna, yesterday."

Lil momentarily froze. "You're kidding. Why?"

"While you were gone, Indiana had some tornados. MDS went in to help. We flew in some supplies. I didn't help with tornado cleanup, just helped unload the supplies. But the plane ride was amazing."

"Wow." Lil eyed her with skepticism. "I didn't really like flying over the ocean." She got a knife and carved the meat.

Megan made sandwiches. "So what was Ethiopia like?"

"It's in the Horn of Africa. Mekelle's one of its largest cities. The market had rows of palm trees. I got some recipes from the locals. You know the recipe book I'm working on?"

"Yeah?"

"Since I'm going to be traipsing around the world with Fletch, I thought I'd add an ethnic section. It'll give me something to focus on while he's doing his thing."

"What was his thing?"

"He lectured at the university about gross parasites. The place is known for their cows and honey. I brought you back some."

Megan shivered. "I hope you mean honey and not parasites."

Giggling, Lil touched her arm. "I'm glad to be home, Green Bean. Did I tell you I invited Ivan and Elizabeth? The babies are close in age, and I thought it would be nice."

The doddy house was on Elizabeth and Ivan Miller's property. The young married couple occupied the big house. "Our lives are branching out, aren't they?" Megan smiled. "Soon you'll have children, too."

Lil leaned close. "I wonder. I thought by now. . ." She sighed. "It's all right. I'm enjoying the restaurant, but watching Katy and Elizabeth, the idea of becoming a mom is growing on me."

"Katy seems very busy."

"But I've never known her to be happier. She makes it look easy. Back to Chance. So the flight was strictly work related?"

"Yeah, but he wants me to go to Ecuador next. Thinks I can find a job there."

"What?" Lil looked stricken.

"It's just an idea."

"I'd hoped to keep you here. But after Ethiopia, I understand you a little better."

Katy stepped into the doddy house and hugged Lil's shoulders. "This is so fun. What can I do to help?"

"Did you see if Elizabeth had the table set up yet?"

"She does."

Lil closed a plastic container that held the sandwiches they'd just prepared. "Let's start carrying the food out."

As they moved onto the porch, they saw Micah drive in. "So you and Micah are friends now, too?"

"Yeah, the night we spent together in the storm cellar pretty much cemented our friendship."

Katy's eyes widened. "You what?"

"When the tornado came through. We got trapped in there when the tree fell on the house."

"Dad told me about rescuing you guys," Lil admitted. "Said Bill wants to keep it quiet."

"What happened?" Katy asked.

"I was so scared, but Micah protected me. He's like a big brother."

"If you're looking for a brother, you can have one of mine," Lil scoffed.

As Megan helped spread the quilts on the ground, she saw Elizabeth leading Fletch their way. "Let's drop it for now."

Fletch clamped Micah's shoulder. "You're just in time to say grace."

During the meal, Fletch shared stories about his work in Ethiopia. Lil kept an adoring eye on him and interjected colorful tidbits. Megan nibbled one of Lil's cookies and rubbed little Jacob's back until he drifted asleep on the quilt.

When Micah finished eating, he swept up Elizabeth's fussing toddler and took him a safe distance from the sleeping baby. He tossed the child in the air until he giggled.

Katy watched him. "You've missed it, Lil. Regardless how brother-like he is, Micah's caused quite a stir in the community."

Lil glanced at Megan as if she'd been holding back on her. "He's single." Megan shrugged, as if that explained everything to Lil.

Katy traced a finger across the back of sleeping Jacob's neck. "I believe Joy Ann has set her cap for him."

Lil pierced Megan with a gaze that demanded honesty. "But you're not interested in him?"

"I'm very interested in him. As our next preacher. I'm probably his biggest supporter."

Lil's gaze swept back to Micah. "From what I see, I like him."

"We like him, too," Elizabeth chimed in. "It's time for somebody younger to take over the reins at Big Darby."

Jacob stirred, and Katy withdrew her hand. "When we were kids, you always said you wanted to marry a preacher."

"Or a missionary," Megan reminded her friend.

"Lil got the missionary. But there's an available preacher who's watching you with interest."

"Elizabeth, don't pay any attention to these two."

The other woman grinned. "Here he comes now."

"Shh!" Megan warned them.

"The little guy's strong." Micah lowered the toddler and watched him run to Ivan.

At some point, Micah had unbuttoned the top of his white shirt. He didn't know it, but when he'd been roughhousing, his shirttail had worked out of his trousers. A light breeze ruffled his hair, disarraying its absurd, deep side-part. A tender, protective feeling welled up in Megan. He was much better looking than she'd ever given him credit for. She could understand why Joy Ann and Lori were smitten.

He must have sensed her watching him, or else he'd known that the women were talking about him. He brushed her with a soft gaze and quirked the corner of his mouth. And Megan couldn't deny being his biggest supporter.

After Micah left the picnic, Ivan took the men to the barn to look at some new farm equipment. Katy and Elizabeth put the babies in strollers, and the women took a leisurely walk past cornfields and ditches covered in spires of purple loosestrife. Although Megan's nose tickled and a dull headache settled in behind her eyes, she kept it to herself. She didn't want to spoil one of the rare moments when the friends could all be together.

CHAPTER 22

Megan's headache had increased by the time she returned home. Deep in her thoughts, she entered the house through the kitchen and walked toward the refrigerator.

"Just look at the floor! And I mopped it yesterday."

Megan whirled, following her mom's gaze. "Was that me? I'm sorry."

"Not just you. Everybody!" Mom exclaimed. "And I suppose you're hungry now?"

Megan took out a pitcher of iced tea. "No, I was just getting something to wash down a painkiller. I told you I was going over to Lil's, didn't I?" For the life of her, Megan couldn't figure out why her mom was acting snippy.

"Yes. You told me. Guess nobody else is hungry, either." Mom placed her hand at her temple. "I didn't mean to snap. I'm sorry you have a headache."

"I'll be fine, but are you feeling all right?"

Mom's face reddened. "'Course I am. I was thinking about making some homemade ice cream tonight, but we're out of rock salt."

"You always work hard. Why don't we go to Dairy Queen later? I'll treat."

"That would be nice, honey. I got a new *Country Living* magazine. Think I'll just go sit on the swing and relax a bit. Your grandparents are coming over later."

"I'm going to wash my hair. We went for a walk today, and Lil's road is so dusty. There must be some pollen in it, too."

"That's the same thing Micah said. He sure does get hives a lot."

Megan nodded and went upstairs, glad to get away from her mom's bad mood. As she washed her hair, she wondered if having Micah around all the time was starting to wear on Mom. She'd always enjoyed having friends over, the relatives, too. Often she hosted the holidays. Megan blotted her hair on a towel. Everybody was allowed a few grumpy days. She just hoped there wasn't anything wrong that Mom wasn't telling her.

By the time she'd finished, the bathroom was steamy. The summer heat always rose and made the upstairs hotter than the rest of the house. Megan opted to dry her hair on the porch and give her mom a chance to redeem herself.

"Can I sit with you?"

"Sure, honey." Mom scooted over, gave her a wary glance, then turned the page to her magazine. "See this quilt advertisement? It's machine stitched. Now why would somebody want to buy this when they can make one themselves—a much better one, too?"

Megan drew the hairbrush down through her long, straight locks. "Don't know, Mom."

"You ladies trying to solve the world's problems?" Micah asked, stepping up onto the porch and obviously not realizing the tension surrounding the women.

Feeling his gaze on her hair, Megan self-consciously tossed it behind her back and dropped the hairbrush onto her lap.

"No, I was just asking Megan why somebody would want to buy a machine-made quilt when they can make a better one."

"Probably for convenience."

"I suppose. But shortcuts don't make things better."

"Unless it's Dairy Queen," Megan teased.

"You don't like my ice-cream recipe? Honestly, Megan. You're a piece of work right now." Mom rose. "I'm going to ask Bill which he'd rather have. There's still time to make a batch before your grandparents get here."

Thought we didn't have any rock salt.

~ ⌒

Micah watched Anita go into the house. On the porch, Megan sighed.

"Sorry. Guess I have bad timing."

She stared at the screen door. "It's not like Mom to be rude. Something's bothering her. We used to be able to talk about things. But lately. . ." Her voice trailed off.

"She's withdrawing?"

Megan shrugged. "Maybe it's me."

"I talked to her this afternoon. She seemed stressed. I hope it's not me. Or the cat."

"Phooey. Mom loves to entertain and play the hostess. She always enjoys having my grandparents over, too. Whatever it is, I'm sure it'll pass." She glanced at him and patted the swing. "Sit?"

"I'm good here." He lowered himself to the top step.

Megan shrugged. "I'm glad you could spend time with my friends."

"You all grew up together except for Fletch?"

"Yes. Katy and Jake loved each other since first grade."

"Jake told me how he helped fix up the doddy house. It reminded me of my cottage, here."

"Believe me, the doddy house needed more than a day's work. It was a major project."

"So you girls lived together?"

Megan fiddled with her hairbrush. "Katy and Lil moved in together while I was still at Rosedale. I couldn't afford my share of the rent until I graduated and got a job. I lived at the doddy house with Lil for a while, but then she got married and took it over."

"You sound disappointed."

"Not really. It was Lil's dream. And she loved the place. After she met Fletch, her dreams changed." As Megan got invested in her memories, she involuntarily drew her half-dried hair to the front of her shoulder and ran her hairbrush through it.

Watching her made Micah's mouth go dry, and he struggled to push away his own dreams, the ones of Megan with the silky long hair. It was good the root cellar had been dark; it had helped him maintain his self-control.

She tilted her head, realized what she was doing, and shook it back over her shoulder. "You all right?"

"I'm fine," he managed.

"Good. I saw your sneezing fit at the picnic."

"I saw yours, too."

"I know. It's weird how we're allergic to the same things. Except I don't have any food allergies."

He clamped his arms around his bent knees. "You don't get hives every Sunday morning, either."

Megan leaned forward and waved her hairbrush. "Why do you think that is?"

He gave a harsh laugh. "If I knew, I'd put a stop to it."

"You think it's something at the church? It's only on Sundays," she reasoned aloud. "Could it be stress or nerves or something you wear?"

Micah shook his head. "I've been stressed and nervous before. Never had hives. But something I wear? Hmm." His eyes widened. "I did get my suit coat dry cleaned just before I came to Plain City."

Megan eyes sparked with excitement, "That's got to be it." Then her shoulders sagged. Beautiful shoulders that were making it hard to concentrate on their conversation. "No. That can't be it. You wear it more often than Sundays."

He stood, rubbing his clammy hands on his trousers. "No, I have more than one. I think you just solved the mystery." As difficult as it was, he needed to put some physical space between them. "Enjoy your ice cream."

"Don't you want to stay for Dairy Queen? At least let us bring you back something."

"Thanks for the offer, but Anita's already stressed. And your grandparents just pulled in the drive. I'll give you some family time."

Megan stood. Her pale hair fell forward and caught a shimmer from the sun that was dropping low in the west. "All right. 'Night, Micah."

" 'Night." He curled his fists and strode to his cottage. His cat leaped from the window seat to greet him, rubbing against his trousers. "She's an angel, Purrty, and I feel like the devil."

~~~

Megan went to Volo Italiano for lunch. "All week long, Mom's been snippy and withdrawn. She goes to bed early, and Dad's been spending more time in the shop. Micah must have sensed something's wrong, because he'd grown scarce, barely taking any meals with us. I don't know what he thinks of us," she bemoaned.

Lil touched her friend's arm. "I know what you're going through." She referred to her own mother's long, painful bout of depression two years earlier. "I never dreamed it would happen to Anita. You better talk to her. Try to get at the bottom of it, before she slips into a downward spiral."

Lil wasn't helping matters. Megan hadn't felt this scared since her frantic drive with a funnel cloud barreling after her. Her heart clenched as though destruction was peeking its head in her rearview mirror and gaining momentum, even as they spoke. "I'll talk to her."

"Good. Or I could send my mom over."

"No, not yet." Megan pushed the idea away, almost sorry she'd brought up the matter. "Did you have your romantic picnic this week?"

"Tomorrow. Fletch doesn't have to work. At least, as far as we know."

"Has it been hard getting back into the grind?"

"Not bad. Giovanni's patient."

"A good thing," Megan teased. Lil had tried the patience of every boss she'd ever had before Giovanni. Of course, that was back when Lil's mom was going through depression. The thought of her own mom having that condition troubled Megan.

"I only saw Chance once this week. He hasn't left yet?"

"No. two more weeks. His stay got extended." Megan debated asking Lil's opinion about the movie that Chance had pestered her about all week. But when she saw Lil glancing toward the kitchen, she knew their time had ended. She pushed up from the stone bench. "I'm glad you're back. Thanks for the penne."

"I'll pray for Anita." Lil pushed up and straightened her black slacks. The two friends hugged, and Megan left the restaurant with a heavy heart.

That evening, Megan fidgeted through an uncomfortable supper.

"I can't believe I burned the potatoes," Mom apologized.

Micah examined the food on his fork. "Parsley potatoes are supposed to be crispy, aren't they? And if they aren't, then you're on to something good with these."

"A little charcoal's good for the liver," Dad teased.

Mom tossed her napkin on the table. "Don't patronize me."

Soon after that, Micah slinked away to his cottage. But there was no place for Megan to go. This was her home. It used to be happy. "I need to know what's going on with you two. Nobody will look me in the eyes anymore. Mom?"

Mom grabbed some plates and went to the sink.

Dad sighed. "Come back here. Sit down and tell her."

An army of dread marched up Megan's neck. Dad hardly ever spoke sternly.

With slumped shoulders, Mom set the plates on the counter and returned to the table. "It isn't a pleasant story." She clenched her lips.

"Dad?" He shook his head, and Megan looked back at Mom.

"You know that I'm adopted."

Megan nodded, nearly numb with fright. Surely they weren't going to tell her she was adopted, too.

"What you don't know is that I know some things about my blood relatives on my birth mom's side. They come from Reading, Pennsylvania. They have kept in contact a little bit."

Relief swept over Megan, and she strived to understand. "Do I have grandparents that I don't know about?"

"No, they aren't living. But you have a great-aunt."

"Did something happen to her?"

"No." Mom's jaw tightened. "She's coming for a visit."

A boulder of burden rolled off Megan's shoulders. "But that's wonderful!" So Mom's irritability was worry about meeting her relative? She wasn't depressed, and her parents were still getting along? Only relatives visiting. It was a good thing. But Mom didn't act like it was good at all.

"Not so wonderful. Let me tell you the rest."

The weight returned and pressed heavily. Megan kneaded the base of her neck.

"I didn't tell you about your relatives before now because I thought it was something we could brush under the rug. But it refuses to stay where it belongs. Now I wish I'd told you about them before."

Dad's eyes shone with sympathy. Folding her hands on the tabletop, Megan whispered, "So tell me now."

Fidgeting with the cloth napkin, Mom nodded. "Your great-aunt is English. I come from a family that is not Mennonite, never was. My blood mother was not even a Christian."

An ocean of shock washed over Megan, disabling her movement and speech.

Mom dabbed her eyes with her napkin. "I'm an imposter."

Dad reached across the table and stilled Mom's hand. "That's ridiculous. You're a wonderful woman. You may have been born into the world, but you were raised Mennonite. Megan and I don't have any regrets."

Megan struggled filled with confusion and frustration. "Not Mennonite?"

"Of course she is," Dad maintained. "She was baptized in the church just like you were."

Truth strangled Megan's neck. "Then I'm not Mennonite, either. I have the outsider's blood." Tears pressed behind her eyes. She stumbled to her feet and clutched the table. "This is a shock. But I have to know. Who are we?"

Mom blew her nose on her napkin. "If I hadn't been adopted, my name would be Lintz. My mother's family was Witherspoon."

The word *adopted* reminded Megan that none of this was her mom's fault. Mom couldn't help that her parents had been killed in a car crash, either. Megan softened her voice. "How do you know they weren't Christians? Did you meet them?" She refused to believe that her mom would secretly stay in contact with her family and keep it from her.

Once Mom opened up, the story spilled out. "My parents weren't even married. My grandparents attended some church, but my mom didn't want to have anything to do with their faith. She went wild and lived with my dad without the blessing of her parents. I don't know much about the Lintz family. When the accident happened, my grandparents rejected me."

"Maybe they were too old to raise a child?"

"Not that old. They knew about the Mennonites through a friend's housekeeper. They made some inquiries and found a home for me." Her voice glittered with resentment. "One that was far away, in a different state. So they could hide their shame. But now they're gone. My aunt Louise wants to bring me some of my grandmother's things."

"Did she tell you all this?"

"No, Mom told me."

Megan knew her mom referred to Grandma Bachman, the woman who had raised her. With Dad's parents gone, she was the only grandmother Megan had ever known. "When?"

Mom gripped Dad's hand. "When I was about your age, Mom told me about my background. It was hard for me to accept their rejection. Now this Louise is sticking her nose in where it doesn't belong. I told her not to come. She wouldn't take no for an answer. She's bound and determined to drag up my past. What good can come of it now?"

Feeling as though she were crawling out of a dark shroud and viewing the light for the first time, Megan blinked. "Who all knows about this?"

Mom shrugged. "I suppose most of the older folks in church."

Resentment that she'd been kept in the dark, Megan cried, "I can't believe nobody ever told me."

"It's one of those things that died down."

"You know that everyone loves your mom." Dad patted Mom's hand. "And they adore you. I know it's a shock to discover some genes you didn't know about, but these people gave you and your mother some good genes. A cheery disposition, for one."

Megan pushed in her chair and gripped its back, disgusted by how he could refer to an entire clan of living people—her people—as a gene pool.

He explained, "You can't discount the good just because a young girl made some poor choices."

"When is our aunt coming?"

"Next month."

Megan forced a smile. "Don't worry about it, Mom. Somehow, we'll make do."

Mom's expression filled with gratitude. She shot to her feet and pulled Megan into an awkward embrace. Megan woodenly patted Mom's back. But inside, she felt broken, as if everything she'd always believed in had been snatched away from her. She pulled back. "Thanks for telling me. I'm tired. I think I'll go to my room now." She shifted her gaze to the kitchen sink.

"Go on to your room. You don't need to help with the dishes."

Megan didn't have the strength to argue and sprang up the stairs and down the hall. In her room, she slammed the door and crumbled.

CHAPTER 23

The skeletons in Megan's outsider closet rattled their bones, making sleep elusive. She squinted at the digital clock. It was barely after midnight. Anger and resentment added to the clatter in her brain, and after hours of struggle, she threw back the covers. She tossed her legs over the side of her bed.

Her room was hot and oppressive. She snatched up her robe and stole downstairs. Mom claimed lemon tea helped her occasional insomnia. In the kitchen the demons of the conversation she'd had with her parents haunted the air. Through the window, the cottage light glimmered. Her lips formed a grim line to think that she'd once considered Micah repulsive. In truth, she was the faulty piece. With her outsider genes, she was no longer a prize for any decent Conservative man.

The whistle of the kettle drew her from the window. She quickly removed the teapot from the burner, lest she awaken her parents. She didn't want to face them or their sympathy. With resentment she fixed her tea and bought the steaming cup to her lips. Micah's light twinkled into the surrounding darkness. What had he told her in the root cellar? *"When it's dark enough, you can see the stars."* She bent and looked up toward the sky, but it was blocked by shrubbery.

She padded barefoot onto the front porch, flinching when she heard the creaking chains of the porch swing. "Micah?"

"It's me."

She hesitated. "What are you doing here so late?"

His soft voice was laced with amusement. "Probably the same thing as you. I couldn't sleep." His brown gaze swept over her night robe.

"Sorry for disturbing you. I better take my tea back inside."

"Is Anita upset with me?"

"No. It's nothing to do with you."

"Are you sure?"

His pleading tone beckoned. With brief hesitation she rationalized that even though she wore a robe, her body was fully covered. They had survived the root cellar without causing a scandal, and he was the preacher. Her bitterness scoffed that her good name was already smirched, anyway, so she sank down beside him. "I found out what's troubling Mom."

"I don't mean to pry, but it's obviously upset you."

With her forefinger, she twisted her hair. "Mom's adopted. I always knew that, but tonight I found out that she kept some things from me about her real family. We have an aunt who's coming to visit us. Mom's been worried about the visit and also about me finding out the truth about her family."

"That explains her behavior."

Her bare feet fell into sway with Micah's tennis shoes, and the story flowed forth in hypnotically bitter waves. "We're not sure why my great-aunt wants to meet us. But I found out that my mom's family is not Mennonite. They aren't even Christians. Funny, Dad just told me a couple weeks ago that Dirk Willems is in our blood line." She laughed bitterly. "I was so proud of it. And I didn't even know who I really was."

Micah gave a short whistle. "Dirk Willems *is* a hero. I heard the story in college. It stirred me, too. It's easy to believe that a man like him would be in your bloodline."

She pulled a sarcastic face. "Hardly."

"Regardless of your mom's people, he's still one of your ancestors."

Megan lowered her gaze, and her hair fell into a silky curtain that veiled her shame. "No. I'm lucky if I got any of those genes. Don't you see?

I've been living a lie. I'm so angry at Mom for not telling me sooner. I feel so deceived. Confused."

Micah removed her cup from her hands and set it on the ground. Then he folded her hand in his, intertwining their fingers. "Despite what you're feeling, this doesn't change who you are. God holds each of us accountable for ourselves, according to our talents and our own faith. That hasn't changed."

She tightened her grip. "Hasn't it? For nearly two months, I've fought off an attraction for Chance." Her throat constricted painfully. "Just because he's not a Mennonite. But he's a Christian. If he knew about this, he would despise me for my hypocrisy."

Micah caressed her hand with his thumb. "How could he, when you just found out? But you're still a Mennonite. You haven't changed just because you found out some things about your relatives."

She pulled away from his touch and thrust her hand up in anger. "I can't just slough this off. If something like this came out about your family, do you think you'd still feel confident about your job at the church?"

"First of all, I'm not confident about it. Secondly, maybe your aunt is coming to help you work through it."

Megan shook her head. "Mom says she's coming to stir up the past."

"Anita's a typical parent, trying to protect you. She's probably afraid that if you visit these people, you'll see something you like and be tempted to leave the church."

"What if she's right?"

—◌—

Micah saw that Megan's faith was being sorely tested. Doubts and emotions were blurring the truth that had been the foundation of her faith. The timing of this news couldn't be worse. Anita couldn't have known about Megan's infatuation with Chance. It was up to him to place Megan's hand back on her anchor.

"Being Mennonite is a way of life that reflects certain beliefs. It's not something genetic. Now more than ever, you need to pull strength from your beliefs. Let them ground you."

"I've been thinking about this all night. It's like a ripple that widens into eternity. I can't comprehend how it's going to affect my life. But I know one thing. It was wrong for Mom to keep this information from me. People at church knew about this and didn't tell me, either. Don't you understand how betrayed I feel?"

"I'm sure nobody wanted to intentionally hurt you. They probably saw your mom's adoption as a blessing. The church family was an extension of her adoptive family. Then when she married a man of the church, her grafting in was even stronger. All that was set in place before you were even born. Your family is a strong unit, providing leadership in the church."

"Whenever I asked Mom about her real family, she always made some comment that made me believe she didn't know anything about them. How could she cut off ties with her real family and assume that I wouldn't want to meet them?"

A night owl hooted. Another owl gave answering calls. Micah's heart melded with the mournful music and Megan's pain, seeking to ease the latter. "She'd already weighed everything and made those choices before you were born."

"My grandparents are dead. She made the choice of shunning them. And because of that, I never knew them."

His own grief identified with Megan's pain. "That's hard. I loved my grandma." He still missed her cheery hugs and gentle guidance. She'd been good-natured like Anita. He hoped this disclosure hadn't caused a breach in Megan's relationship with her mom. He asked tenderly, "Did you have an argument with your mom tonight?"

"No. She was upset. I wanted to think through everything before I said something to upset her even more."

"That was a smart thing to do."

Megan tossed her hair over her shoulder. The simple gesture aroused a physical reaction that he tried to tamp down. Everything about her affected him, but lately it was becoming a natural habit to gravitate toward her need as much as her desirability.

"Chance thinks I can find a job in Ecuador."

Her bitter remark splashed cold water on his foolish hopes and drove a knife into his reckless heart, but he understood what drove her. The sifting and weighing of her faith had shattered her self-control and caused her to lash out at the restrictions of her upbringing. His frantic heart leaped, willing her to realize that her life didn't have to drastically change.

She hardened her gaze, ineffectively warding off his unspoken intervention.

Her world had tilted, giving Chance a small window of opportunity to step into this new realm of Megan's life and prey on her vulnerability. When Micah saw his words were powerless against her instability, he slipped his arm around her, anything to anchor her to the Conservative world, his world. "Don't run from your family, from the people who love you."

Megan wiggled out of his embrace and pushed to her bare feet. She narrowed her eyes into thin glacial slits. "We shouldn't be out here."

He gave a sad sigh. "I suppose. It's just that I want to protect you."

"Thanks. But I need to figure this out myself. And I need to tell Chance the truth."

"Do you think that's wise?" She swept her chilly gaze over him as if he was from an enemy camp. "All I meant was you shouldn't do anything rash. Give yourself more time to think things through."

"Chance invited me to his place to watch a movie about the Aucas. It will help me work through my new identity. Spending time with him and learning more about Ecuador will help me make some decisions so that I *don't* do anything rash."

"I understand that. But proceed slowly while you're still emotional."

"We don't have much time until he leaves the States again."

"Surely you can take a few days?"

"Fine. I won't talk to him about it until the weekend, when we watch the movie."

Balling fists of frustrated energy, he pressed, "You shouldn't go to his apartment while you're feeling confused."

"Micah, how is it any different than being alone with you, like we are now? Don't you trust me?"

"It's different because you're not attracted to me." Rays of moonlight revealed her embarrassment.

"What if the timing of Mom's news was meant to make me more open-minded toward Chance's offer?"

"And what is his offer? Has he offered you marriage?"

Megan eyes glittered. "My blood grandmother wasn't married when she had my mother."

Her unanticipated slash drew blood, but it only made him more obstinate to play the hero and shield her from her own foolishness. He parried, "Or maybe God sent me to Plain City to keep you from ruining your life."

She placed one hand on her hip, looking regal in her white night robe. "Now you're just being manipulative."

"I'm being your friend. If our friendship means anything, then at least consider my advice."

Tears glistened, softening her eyes. She sucked her bottom lip between her teeth.

"Meg," he breathed. He drew her close. She melded into his embrace, clutching the back of his shirt. She sobbed against his chest. If he had manipulated her, it was for her own good. But his conscience licked wildly at his ears. And he wrestled with his scruples, as he comforted the object of his desires. A broken barefoot woman wearing a robe with her hair immodestly streaming down her back. He struggled with the impulse to whisper that she didn't need to go any farther than her own porch to find a man who would love her and help her find her identity. Instead he whispered, "Your identity is in Christ. Be sure to pray about it." And then he released her.

Megan nodded. "Of course. Thanks for listening. For everything." She bent and picked up her tea then gave him a wobbly smile. "Don't lose any more sleep over it, Micah."

He smiled and watched her disappear into the house. Sleep was the last thing Micah had on his mind.

⸻✺⸻

"You look terrible." Paige tilted her face, studying Megan. "Like you cried all night."

"Personal problems," Megan muttered.

"Wanna talk about it?" Paige lowered her voice and leaned over Megan's desk. "Is it about Chance?"

Megan shook her head. "No. And I don't want to talk about it. But if

I fall asleep at my desk, bring coffee."

"Sure thing, honey. Hope you work things out."

Megan had gotten to work a few minutes late, and the door to Chance's office had already been closed. Until she talked to him about the movie, she wouldn't be able to calm the restless river that flowed through her veins, making it difficult to concentrate on her work.

As soon as Paige left, Megan scooped up a stack of paperwork and knocked on his door.

"Come in." She pushed the door open and allowed it to close behind her. Chance looked up with pleasant surprise. "Hi."

"Can we talk?"

He nodded toward a side chair. "Sit down."

Megan slipped into the welcome support of a masculine leather side chair. "I'm sorry I was late this morning."

"No problem. Usually you're early. Everything all right?"

Now Micah's warnings were sharks circling her mind and confusing her, but she couldn't break free from the promise she'd made him. She clutched the files and drifted into unchartered waters.

"Something wrong?" he repeated.

She wet her lips with her tongue. "Some personal stuff that I don't want to talk about right now. But I wondered if the offer still stands about viewing your movie *The End of the Spear*?"

Chance's face lit with undisguised pleasure. "Of course, Meg. Do you want to do dinner first?"

She drew a line in the sand. "Oh. Just the movie, if you don't mind. And could we do it during the day?"

Chance acknowledged her wishes. "Sure, no pressure. We can just watch the movie." Then he tried to gain control again. "You want me to pick you up on Saturday? Two? Three o'clock?"

"If you give me the address, I'll drop by around two."

He quickly scribbled the address on a yellow sticky note, and she exchanged the address for her files. "Thanks. These need signatures."

Accepting the paperwork, he replied, "Let me know if I can help. With the other."

"I think you already have. I'll explain it on Saturday." Relieved to have maneuvered the situation to her satisfaction, Megan stepped out of his office. But her brief buoyancy fled when she saw Paige waiting near her desk. The other woman's gaze narrowed as if she saw right through Megan's intentions. "I don't advise crying on his shoulder."

"That's not what I was doing." Megan resented the way everybody interfered, treating her as if she wasn't an adult capable of making her own choices. If her mom hadn't been protecting her for all these years, she wouldn't be feeling so rotten now. "Why does everybody want to run my life? Do I need to wear a No Trespassing sign on my back?"

"I guess you never heard the story about Little Red Riding Hood?"

Slipping into her chair, Megan rolled her gaze toward the ceiling. "Yes. A lot of wolf stories are circulating, but thinking about them doesn't get my work done."

Paige gave a sulky toss of her head and departed.

CHAPTER 24

Megan stood at her bedroom window and looked down over the peaceful country landscape, but it did little to ease her internal restlessness. She'd spent the remainder of the workweek consumed in private thoughts, feeding the idea that she needed to explore the part of the world that she knew so little about. Fifty percent of her genetic background came from the outsiders' world. She couldn't just ignore it like her mom had done.

She had to find out if those genes were responsible for the unexplainable stirrings she sometimes felt. She needed to identify the source of her restlessness so that she could determine if they were God-given or sinful urges. She had no intention of shucking her Christian faith, but she needed answers. Now that her eyes had been opened, she was rethinking her personal destiny. Was she still to follow the Conservative road or did another road beckon? The mission field? More specifically, was God calling her to join Chance in Ecuador?

Just as she released the gauzy curtain to move away from the window, she heard the sound that could be none other than Lil's old rattle clap. A quick look verified it. Only Lil never dropped by these days, not since her marriage. They always met at Volo Italiano or the doddy house. She hurried downstairs and moved with haste to answer the door.

"Hi. You busy?"

Easily sensing that something had occurred to upset Lil, Megan drew her friend inside. With a warning finger to her lips, they snuck past the hall, almost losing Lil to the aroma of freshly baking cinnamon rolls.

Upstairs in Megan's room, Lil sank on the bed with a sigh.

"What on earth's wrong?"

"Fletch cancelled our picnic. He has to work again. I thought my dad had the market on pigheadedness, but I was wrong. My husband thinks he's always right about everything. I always have to give in."

"Fletch had an emergency?"

"Vic had an emergency, and Fletch feels like he has to cover for him at the clinic."

"Why don't you just take the picnic to him?"

"I didn't think of that." Lil shook her head. "The picnic's off now. He's mad because I second-guessed his decision. And according to him, I'm *never* supposed to question his decisions. I'm not in the mood for a picnic."

Although Megan hated to see Lil angry and upset, she had a strong inkling that it wasn't a coincidence that Lil had stopped by. "I don't know about *never*. But this time, I think he made the right choice."

"What?"

"I think I'm the reason Fletch has to work today."

Lil looked at Megan as if she'd lost her marbles or wasn't following the conversation at all.

"Because I need you to go with me this afternoon. I thought about asking you anyway. First I thought about asking Micah, but that wouldn't have worked." Micah would have gone with her to watch the movie. But after telling Chance that Conservative men were nonresistant, putting those two men together would have been setting a foolish trap for Micah. After nixing that idea, Megan had thought of Lil. And here she was, delivered right to her doorstep.

"Slow down. Go with you where?"

"I'm going to Chance's apartment to watch a movie with him."

Lil jumped off the bed and grabbed Megan by the shoulders. "What? You aren't even allowed to watch movies. And going to his apartment is asking for trouble. Have you lost your mind?"

"Not my mind. Just my identity. Sit down. It's a long story."

Lil drew her brows together in concern. She eased onto the edge of the bed. "Okay, spill it."

The story unfolded more easily the second time around, and Megan only strayed from it long enough to answer a few of Lil's well-placed questions. "And this is your aunt?"

"My great-aunt Louise. My instincts tell me that her visit is going to reveal some things that could change my life. There has to be a reason why she's coming to visit us now, after all these years. Although Mom's skeptical, I want to hear everything my aunt has to say."

"But what does this have to do with going to Chance's house?"

"I want to weigh all my options with an open mind."

"Your mind may be open, but your emotions are all over the board."

"You sound just like Micah."

Lil arched a brow but didn't press. "Don't worry. I'll keep you accountable."

"Then you'll go?"

"Of course I will."

"I'm probably not the friend to advise you about husbands and marriage. Katy would have more experience in that department. Sometimes I even feel sorry for myself, that you are both married. I'm sorry I've been so engrossed in my own life that I haven't noticed your struggles."

"You drop in at the restaurant all the time. If I needed a shoulder to cry on, I would have told you. I came today, didn't I? And I don't want you thinking we have marriage problems. I'll admit we both have self-control issues. But if God led me here today, then I owe Fletch an apology. I haven't been a very understanding wife." Lil leaned close. "Fletch really is pigheaded. But then, so am I."

Megan smiled.

Lil grinned back. "Movies aren't forbidden at the church Fletch and I attend. It'll be fun." Lil suddenly giggled. "I can't wait to see Chance's face when I walk into his apartment with you."

Megan laughed. "Poor Chance. It will be a surprise."

⸻ ❧

Chance shook his head and burst out laughing. "Of course you brought a friend." In a sense, he was relieved. He didn't want to do anything to chase Megan away, and she'd come up with the perfect solution. One that made her feel safe to set foot into his bachelor apartment. He didn't know why he hadn't suggested it himself. "Come in, both of you."

As Lil passed by him, she whispered. "Just remember I'm watching you."

His smile deepened, and he whispered back, "I think I can take you." Then he flinched, for he'd almost referred to his air force experience. Revealing that information before he'd won Megan's complete trust would have shot their relationship out of the sky, sending them in a downward spiral with no recovery.

Lil flounced by, and Megan shrugged. "Lil showed up at my house today, and I thought she'd enjoy the movie, too."

"Believe me, I understand. I'm glad she came."

Megan gave a slight nod and entered his apartment, which he'd spent the morning cleaning. He knew that she kept a tidy desk, and by the way her hair was always perfectly swept into that bun and net thing, he was pretty sure she even bordered on the neat-freak side.

His gaze swept over her, as hers took in the results of his cleanup campaign. Megan usually carried herself with confidence, but today her shoulders were soldier straight. Normally her serene expression and pale skin gave her a feminine appeal, but as she perused his apartment, her face tilted upward, revealing a strong square chin and a don't-mess-with-me attitude.

To Chance, it was a challenge. He watched her move about the room. She wore a dark print dress, black stockings, and black shoes. Her clothing was always too baggy for his preference. He figured she did that on purpose to hide her figure.

"In Ecuador, is your apartment this sparse?"

"Small and sparse. Except for my tapestry collection. My favorites are a gray elephant print and a blue tree of life."

"What's an elephant print?"

"The design has rows of elephants." He thought how to best describe it. "Along the lines of an Egyptian motif."

Megan nodded.

"I'm sure they're nothing like the quilts we're used to," Lil interjected.

"Do you hang them on the walls or use them as rugs?" Megan asked.

"Both. I hope I can show them to you someday."

She glanced at the floor of his apartment—a short-piled, neutral carpet—and back up at him. He saw a glint in her eye that made his heart race, but he tried to keep his voice casual. "Sit down, ladies. Can I get you something to drink? I have soda and water bottles."

Megan and Lil shared the couch, and he brought them water. As they made small talk about Lil's recent trip, he watched the petite brunette with the stylish haircut swing a jean-clad leg. Not for the first time, he wondered about the women's friendship. They both had the same Pennsylvania Dutch huskiness to their voices. Were they relatives? After listening for a polite period of time, he asked, "How did you two become friends?"

Megan replied, "We grew up in the same church. After Lil got married, she started going to a different one, with fewer restrictions."

A spark of righteous anger flared up in him, he turned to face Lil. "Then why are you so dead set against me? You do realize I'm a Christian?"

Lil replied, "I was never satisfied in the Conservative church. But Megan is."

He caught a flicker of disagreement in Megan's gaze. His pulse raced to think that she no longer felt that way. "But it's her choice. I know she's interested in missions, like you. That's why I invited her to see the story of the Aucas."

"Um, I'm sitting right here," Megan interjected.

Lil ignored her. "My husband is the one interested in missions. But I support him in it."

Still feeling that Lil's attitude was a bit duplicitous, he took the DVD out of its case. "I'll start the movie."

The picture began, and vivid jungle scenery flashed onto the screen. As the plot escalated, it contrasted the beauty and dangers of the jungle, focusing on its hostile tribes. It delved into the missionaries' faithfulness to their callings, no matter the hardships. Chance couldn't help but get caught up in the wonder of the story again, feeling a strong desire to return and continue the work he loved. A glance told him that the women were swept into the plot, oblivious to their surroundings, and he wasn't surprised to see them cry when the missionaries were killed.

After the movie concluded, the women sat in brooding silence until Chance sought to lighten the mood. "It had a good ending, don't you think? In real life, the grandson is now a Christian and works with the missionaries."

Megan's voice was huskier than usual. "Grandson?"

—⟡—

"Yes, although the grandfather was heathen, the grandson has helped to reach many souls," Chance explained.

"That's good to know." As dismissive as Megan's statement was, the idea was momentous, taking root in her mind: the grandfather was barbaric, but the grandson became a Christian. It was as if God whispered in her heart, *You don't have to follow in your grandmother's steps.* It wasn't the direction she'd expected from God. And after viewing the hardships the missionaries incurred, she wasn't so sure about the jungle lifestyle, either. Swiping her eyes, she gave Chance a tremulous smile. "This movie touched me. But I need time to think about it."

His expression told her he understood she was talking about more than the plot.

When Megan stood, Chance tried to detain her. "You ladies don't have to rush off. Let me take you to dinner."

Megan needed more time to process her thoughts. Before she came to his apartment, she'd had every intention of telling Chance the truth about her background and even revealing her feelings for him. She was growing to despise secretive behavior of any kind, lest it fester and spread its malignancy to the unsuspecting. But the movie had planted some reservations in her about rushing forward with her earlier plans. "Dinner? No thank you. Perhaps another time. Lil needs to get home to Fletch."

"Yes. I also have a cat, a basset hound, and a rabbit to feed. Fletch is a vet, and he came to me with an entire entourage of animals."

"I won't keep you then." But when they reached the door, Megan felt his touch on her arm and turned into his low growl. "What if I want to spend some time with you?"

"Lil?"

Megan's accountability partner arched a warning brow. "I'll meet you at the car."

As soon as Lil was gone, Chance joked, "She packs a big wallop for her size."

"I don't know about that, but she's a good friend."

"At work you mentioned a personal problem. The preacher's not bothering you, is he?"

Thinking that Micah's advice was more detrimental to their relationship than anything, she shook her head. "No, nothing like that." Micah meant well. Why, he'd opened his arms to comfort her even though he lived beneath the congregation's microscope. If her dad had walked onto the porch and misunderstood, Micah might have lost his position at Big Darby. No, Micah wasn't bothering her, but his harsh advice sometimes presented a nuisance. Both men found pleasure in cutting the other down.

"Then what?"

"It's a long story, and Lil's waiting in the car." But she owed him an explanation. "I'll keep it brief. You see, I've always known my mom was adopted. But this week, I found out that none of her relatives are Mennonite. Or even professing Christians. I always thought I had a strong Mennonite heritage. I was wrong. I came today looking to find some answers."

His eyes rounded with understanding. "Because this sheds new light on our friendship. I've known all along that you were attracted to me. And now you're wondering if there's a way that we can be together?"

His quick assessment set her pulse racing. "Pretty much. But I'm not ready."

He placed his forefinger beneath her chin, tilted her face upward so that she could look into his yearning gaze. "We're running out of time. Soon I must return to Ecuador. You must come with me. Find your answers in Ecuador. Like I did."

"What do you propose? Exactly?"

"Whatever you need. A trip to Ecuador. Friendship. Love. I want it all, but I'll take whatever you can give me."

She watched his earnest expression, waiting for the word marriage, but it wasn't uttered. Realistically, it was too soon for him to consider it. They hardly knew each other. But Megan had to make sure the word was in his vocabulary.

In her hesitation, he urged, "I hope it's love." His gaze darkened, and he lowered his head and brushed his lips against hers. His arms encircled her and drew her close. The kiss was surreal. With it, many things went through her mind. He kissed her again and tried to deepen it, but she drew back with a slight gasp. "But are you the marrying type?"

He smiled. "I dream of sharing my life with you. I'm not opposed to marriage, but I see it farther down the road for us. Somewhere after dating. I believe the more appropriate question would be, are you willing to take the next step?"

She placed a hand on his cheek. "I know you have to go back to Ecuador soon. But I'm not ready to give you an answer. If our feelings are real, they'll last. My aunt's coming to visit. She wants to tell us about the relatives we never knew. I'd like to hear what she has to say before I make a decision."

Placing his hand over hers, he assured, "I'll wait. I'll give you whatever time you need."

The doorbell rang, and Megan withdrew her hand. "Lil." His smile held disappointment. "I'll see you Monday."

Inside the car, Lil apologized, "I'm sorry about the doorbell. I just wanted to give you a way out."

"Don't worry about it. It was perfect timing."

Lil started the car and glanced sideways. "So what happened?"

Megan sighed. "I told him about my mom's real family. He asked me to go to Ecuador with him. I asked if that included marriage. He said yes, that he dreamed of spending his life with me. Oh. And he kissed me."

"All that!" Lil shook her head. "He's fast. I'm glad I didn't leave you alone with him any longer."

Megan smiled. "I kind of cornered him when I asked him if he was the marrying type."

Lil burst out laughing. "Good for you. But let me tell you that the marrying type needs plenty of patience."

Megan burst into laughter, feeling lighter than she had in weeks.

As the city turned into countryside, the Ecuador decision tiptoed back into Megan's mind. Gazing at the fields and mailboxes that held names of lifelong friends, she asked herself if she could really leave the familiarity of Plain City. The movie imprinted her with a fresh perspective of a missionary's life and hardships. It wouldn't be like her college mission trip. The sacrifices she'd make for Ecuador would be permanent. Life-altering. If not Ecuador, then some place similar; for she was certain Chance wouldn't be comfortable living in the States. He thrived on adventure and blue skies.

Pulling into the drive, Lil pointed. "What's Micah doing by his car?"

Megan craned her neck. "I'm not sure."

"Do you think he's the marrying kind?"

Megan sank back in her seat and rolled her gaze toward the car's peeling ceiling. "How would I know?"

"Just asking. I imagine that's what your entire congregation is wondering."

"I suppose. But there's no sense putting the cart in front of the horse." Yet their midnight rendezvous flashed across her mind. "Micah's a nice man. He deserves a good woman. I'll miss him when he moves out of the blue cottage. It's been nice to have a friend so close at hand."

"When I wasn't there for you."

"I didn't mean that."

"All I'm saying, Chance isn't the only fish in the ocean. And there're probably even more where Micah came from, too. Remember how the Lord brought Fletch right to my door?"

With a sad sigh, Megan replied, "I wish you liked Chance."

"I'm sorry. I'll try harder. My family didn't like Fletch. Yet you helped us get together. You were the one who convinced me to give him a second chance. You deserve the same support from me."

"Thanks. It means a lot to me. And thanks for going with me today." Megan reached for her door handle. "Coming in?"

"No, I'm going home to make myself presentable for Fletch. We have some making up to do. Anyway, I think your preacher friend is lingering over there, hoping to talk to you."

Megan threw Lil a kiss and backed away from the car, waving. Then she saw Lil was right. Micah was watching her.

CHAPTER 25

Micah curiously observed the women, not that it was any of his business where they'd been. When Lil finally drove away, Megan started toward him.

"What are you doing?" she asked. "Hopefully not packing up your car?"

"You probably wish I was. But no, I'm cleaning it. It was filthy." He straightened and tossed his drying rag over his shoulder like a tote, noticing that she'd shed her heavy spirit. "You look happier."

"I am. I learned something today."

Micah crossed his arms. "I'm all ears."

"Lil and I went to Chance's apartment to watch that movie I told you about."

Relief washed over him that she'd not gone alone, like he'd imagined. "I'm glad you took someone along. That was the smart thing to do."

"I figured you would think so. Anyway, as I told you before, the story was about the Aucas natives who murdered some missionaries. It turns out that a native who threw one of the spears had a grandson who became a Christian. Now he tells people about the Lord. I felt God showing me that it doesn't matter what my grandmother was like. I can be whoever I want to be. It doesn't answer all my questions, but. . ." She shrugged.

Micah's arms relaxed to his sides, and he quietly thanked the Lord for answering his prayers. "That's what I've been trying to tell you. But we probably shouldn't judge your grandmother, either. Usually the rumors or hearsay about someone is worse than the actual truth."

Megan nodded thoughtfully.

"So what did you think about Ecuador?" Micah chose to ask that instead of what he really wanted to know: After seeing Ecuador, was Megan still interested in the missionary pilot? Was she planning to run off with him?

"The film wasn't actually in Ecuador, but in a place with similar climate and terrain. It's jungle. Very primitive. I enjoyed my college mission trip, but I'm not sure if I want to live permanently in such a wild and dangerous place. If I'm interested in Chance, it's my only option. He's committed there. That's the kind of life he's offering me."

Micah clenched his fist and snapped his towel off his shoulder, running it through his other hand. "So you talked about marriage?"

"Sure."

His jaw hardened with jealousy.

"He wants me to go to Ecuador and spend time with him, take it slow. He's not opposed to marriage."

He blurted, "Not opposed?" His throat released a harsh objection. "That sounds like less than you deserve, Megan. You do realize that?"

"How do you know what I deserve?"

He tore his gaze from her hurt expression, focusing on the towel. Reminding himself that he possessed no rights to Megan beyond those of a friend. "I think you deserve a clean car. Want me to wash it for you?"

Her resistance slowly melted away, and she looked at him with gratitude. "Yes. But only if I help."

He twisted his rag and lightly snapped her skirt with it. "That depends on your skills, missy."

"Ouch! Hey! Do not call me after your cat." Tossing her purse aside, she tried to snatch the rag away from him, caught the end of it, and held on. "I think I'd better be the drier."

Enjoying their tug-of-war contest, he started to reel her in. His breath catching, he wondered what she would do if he reeled her in close enough to kiss. But when their faces got within inches of each other, she released it so fast that he stumbled back.

"You don't play fair," she pouted.

"And you need to play more."

"Is that so?" With a mischievous glint in her blue eyes, she grabbed the half bucket of sudsy water and started toward him.

Micah's hands went up to shield his face, allowing the towel to slip from his hands to the ground. He made a pass for it, but missed. Megan eyed the towel, too, and he could tell she was undecided whether to make a move for it or to drench him with her pail of water. His gaze shifted from the towel to Megan, trying to anticipate her moves.

She darted forward, letting the pail go. It rocked and sloshed but remained upright. She snatched the towel off the ground and dashed after him with it.

He dodged her and went back after the bucket. Megan understood his intentions too late. He started toward her, holding the bucket while its contents slopped sudsy water onto his shoes.

"Oh, no. No you don't," she said, backing away. Micah stopped advancing just as she backed into something solid. With a shriek, she turned. "Dad!"

"Is it recess?" he asked.

Feeling foolish, Micah explained, "We're just in the middle of car washing." He glanced toward the shop, referring to Bill's Nova. "Want us to wash yours?"

Megan brought the towel close to her face to cover her grin.

"No, thank you. Carry on." With that, Bill strode toward the house.

As soon as he was inside, Megan keeled over in laughter. When she could finally speak again, she said, "He'd never let us touch that car. Did you see the expression of stark terror on his face when you asked him?"

Micah set down the bucket and thrust his finger at her. "Young lady, you were born to get me in trouble." Then he motioned, "Come on. Let's see how good you are with that rag."

He pushed his damp shirtsleeves above his elbows and reached into the bottom of the soapy bucket, retrieving a sponge. He washed, and Megan dried. As they worked, he tried to concentrate on the task and not the woman beside him.

They were partway through Megan's Nova when she said, "You must have your sermon ready."

"I do. And I took my suit to a new dry cleaner. Hopefully tomorrow will go better."

"You deserve a good day."

He cast her a flirtatious glance. "And how do you know what I deserve?"

"Oh, it's easy to see into your heart, Micah. Because it's so big."

Her remark couldn't have been further from the truth. Because if she really could see into it, she would see her own reflection.

⁓

Late Sunday afternoon, Megan quietly read in the living room, keeping alert for a familiar creaking that would signal Micah's presence. She wanted to return his straw hat to him. She eyed it on the floor by the door. About halfway through Chapter 5, she heard the chains groan, so she laid aside the novel. She swept up the hat and stepped onto the porch. But Micah's slumped posture faltered her steps. "Excuse me." His head snapped up. "Oh, hi."

"You left this on the swing the other day."

"Thanks."

Megan seated herself on the top step. "Why so sad?"

"Have you been to Joy Ann's house for Sunday dinner?"

Trying not to laugh at his expense, she admitted, "Not lately. She made you do the dishes, huh?"

"I'd have gladly done the dishes. Instead, it was a checkers competition, but more like a ploy to spend an hour alone with her while everyone else found excuses to leave us alone. The looks she kept giving me. . ." He shook his head and ran his hands through his hair.

As she watched him, Megan wondered when she had quit noticing how his hair was parted way too far on the side. Suddenly it seemed important to her to fix it, and it was all she could do to keep her hands out of the brown, haphazard mane. She looked away, stared at the crooked floorboard planks. She kept her gaze diverted until she'd counted three missing nails. When she looked back up at him, the anguish she saw made her sorry she had joked about the situation. "Poor Micah." His hands dropped, and she had his full attention. "Could you like Joy Ann, if you weren't focused on your job? You know, later after you get settled in?"

He shook his head. "No. But I don't want to hurt her."

"Well, if you're not worried about burning any bridges with her, I think honesty is the best policy." She remembered telling him that before when they discussed the librarian, but he hadn't had the stomach for it.

"Back at Rosedale, you told me the truth, but I wouldn't listen."

Megan sighed, remembering their encounters at Rosedale. "Everybody responds to rejection differently. You just get more obstinate."

"I'm not obstinate."

"Yes, Micah, you are. You also have the gift of perseverance."

"Well, this isn't about me. You don't think I'd hurt her?"

"I think it's more likely you'll make her mad. But you can't keep leading her on."

"She's leading herself on. But you're right. I have to do something. The way things went today, I'm going to have to say something to her this week."

Megan nodded, having already experienced what he was going through. It hadn't been easy to give him that set down. And now that she knew him, she felt even worse about it. Scrambling for something to brighten his mood, she said, "At least you didn't get the hives during your sermon."

His gaze darkened. "But did you hear what I said?"

She'd forgotten all about that. Now she covered her mouth to keep from laughing at the gaffe he'd made at the end of his sermon. He'd told the congregation to "go home and breed the Gospels." When she thought she could keep a straight face, she said, "Well, at least it's not on tape. At Lil's church, they record the sermons."

"Right." He rolled his gaze toward the porch ceiling. "I didn't even realize what I'd said until I heard people snickering; then when I sensed something was wrong, I backtracked in my thoughts. I could still hear the phrase floating in my brain. So I tried to cover it by saying, 'go and have a good day,' which really brought down the house. More than one man asked me how to"—he cleared his throat and cut off his remark, as if remembering he was speaking to a woman.

"Don't be so hard on yourself. You're doing fine."

"Oh yeah? Did you know that your dad told me after church that the search committee is going to call monthly meetings?"

"No."

"Yep. They want to discuss how it's going. Give me their perception of how the congregation's responding to me. Bill tried to make it sound like the meeting was for my sake. But I don't believe that for a minute. It's for their protection."

"Whose?"

"The point is, it wasn't part of the original agreement. I already meet with the elders regularly. I expect the search committee wants to give me some specific dos and don'ts. Or a hand slap."

"Honestly! Sometimes I wonder if my mom doesn't give Dad any advice at all." Megan released an angry sigh. "I'm sure the committee doesn't mean to be disrespectful."

Micah propped his elbows on his knees and leaned forward. "It's not that I blame them. But I have to believe that it's a sign that I'm failing."

"You don't know that for sure. Let's think about something else. Remember how my friend Paige came up with those man repellents?"

He eyed her warily, leaned slightly away from her. "The ones that didn't work for you? Yeah?"

She moved closer. "I have one that might."

He gave her a reluctant grin. "I'm listening."

"If you parted your hair about a quarter-inch deeper on the side than you already do, like this—" She reached out and ran her fingers through his hair, making a deep and even sillier part than he normally wore. Then using both her hands, she brushed the rest out of his eyes.

He froze at her touch, but she ignored it. She leaned back and bit her bottom lip, studying him. A few wisps stuck straight up. She carefully brushed them into place. Releasing her lip, she smiled. "Then our worries would be over."

But Micah didn't return her smile. His eyes narrowed and darkened. "And what about you, Megan. Would that chase you away?"

Feeling confused and slightly embarrassed, she snapped, "No. If your hairstyle mattered, I'd already be gone. Honestly, you can use my help."

His gaze took on a glint. "If I repel one woman, I might repel them all.

What if I don't want to repel you?"

"Don't be ridiculous. I'm trying to help. It's just that you part your hair way too deep. And if you didn't, you'd be rather handsome. But either way, it doesn't affect me."

He snatched her wrist and scowled. "Are you sure?"

She jerked her hand away, wretched that he'd felt her racing pulse and saw the truth that curled deep in the pit of her stomach. She wanted to see him at his best because she actually enjoyed staring into his face. Disconcerted, she wheeled and started to the door, tossing over her shoulder, "Or wear it the same. And everybody will just make do. 'Night."

Behind her, he got in the last word. "I'll think about it. Don't want to make any rash decisions. We must guard our steps, Megan. One wrong move, and life can become a jungle."

Her face now burning, she stepped into the darkening room, snatched up her Christian novel, and headed upstairs. Maybe she needed to take Micah's advice and draw a line in the sand. For him! Because she didn't want to hurt him again. But mostly, she didn't want to get her own heart broken. Yet she might. If Micah didn't get the position at the church, she was going to miss him. Unless, of course, she was living in the jungle.

—ဢ—

That night Megan prayed about her future but remained torn. Every time she envisioned Chance's hopeful smile, the way it had been when she'd left him on Saturday, Micah's sad expression chased it away. She knew she'd hurt him badly. Wished she could turn back the time. Wondered why it bothered her almost as much as her indecision. What was it about Micah that disturbed her?

Was it the way he'd pinned her with his black scowl, after she insisted that she wasn't affected by his looks? He'd almost sneered when he'd asked, *"Are you sure?"*

She flicked on her lamp and went to the foot of her bed. She knelt in front of her hope chest and opened the lid, taking in the scent of cedar and the pull of nostalgic dreams. A pang of regret saddened her, to think of the many ways that Ecuador would change her life. How would her parents react if she married Chance and moved out of the country? The news would be shocking. She was their only child. Folding back her grandma's quilt, she searched for the journal she'd kept in college, the year she'd known Micah.

It was beige with green vines. She took it back to her bed and slipped under the covers, thumbing through its pages, looking for the entries pertaining to Micah. As she read, she felt ashamed. The entries were no longer humorous. She must have hurt him deeply. Why had he been so obstinate? That's what she'd called him today. It was true.

Otherwise, he'd never have returned to Plain City. She let the journal drop onto the covers and lay back on her pillow, staring into the past. Once he'd told her that she had awakened something inside him. She felt something similar. She wished her dad and the search committee weren't making things difficult for him. She hated to see him despondent. Even if she moved away, she wanted to think of him happily ministering at Big Darby. She sat up and reached for her other journal. Lately prayer had replaced her journaling, but she'd missed it. Still, she found herself unable to do anything more than jot down her prayer requests:

1. *Direction regarding Chance.*
2. *Forgive Mom.*
3. *Accept whatever Aunt Louise brings us.*
4. *Micah getting the desires of his heart*
5. *Randy being able to save his marriage*
6. *Lil getting along better with Fletch*
7. *Be with Katy and Jake*

CHAPTER 26

Megan drove into Char Air's employee parking lot and parked in a partially shaded area about sixty yards from the front of a row of sleek buildings. When she opened her door and stepped out of her car, the sight of Chance striding toward her sent a surge of alarm. Dread curled in the pit of her stomach because he would press her to go to Ecuador. A longing pushed her toward the thrill of his kiss and the remembrance of his sweet promises.

"Does this old girl have air-conditioning?" His admiring glance swept over the Nova then rested on her.

"No. Sorry to say." She reached back for her purse. "So why does something old and classic have to be a she?"

With a shrug, he admitted, "If it's something appealing to a guy, it's usually female. No air-conditioning and yet you always look so pretty and fresh." He leaned close and brushed a kiss on her ear.

Megan shivered. "Better not do that here."

"But we only have ten more workdays until I leave. And if you go with me, then who cares?"

Megan studied him regretfully. "Ten days isn't long. But you did remember that my aunt is coming to visit?" Did he really think she'd pack up her life in two short weeks?

"Yes. You want to talk to her before you decide about Ecuador. But what does that have to do with us?"

Megan drew her purse strap over her shoulder as they started toward the office building. "It's just a mystery that I have to explore."

"So she's coming this week?"

Her steps faltered. "No. Late next week, and we don't know how long she'll be staying."

Chance grabbed her arm and wheeled her around to face him. "But I'll be leaving."

Reading the alarm in his expression, she softened her voice. "If you really care, you'll make do." She remembered saying something similar in his apartment, feeling as though they'd already had this conversation once.

"I know. I'm just disappointed."

"Chance! Hey. Wait up, buddy!"

Megan flinched at the unexpected intrusion. A quick glance revealed Randy and his wife Tina walking toward them.

Almost protectively, Chance whispered, "Go on ahead."

His words yanked her out of the clouds and dropped her back to her lowly station, where she was merely a Char Air employee. Thinking she'd do well to remember it, she nodded. She gave the approaching couple a little wave and went on toward the entrance of the office building. With a soft grunt, she tugged the long door handle and entered the building. Why were Randy and Tina here? The question troubled her, because it was the first time she'd seen Randy since his leave of absence.

"Hi, Summer." She passed the receptionist. The hallway opened into a space with several modern cubbies. Her space carried an uncomfortable feel now that she'd been to Chance's apartment. There was nothing safe about it. He had invaded every inch of it with his smile and his adventuresome style. She felt like she had lost her grip and was now only along for the ride.

If she bailed, he would still fly off to his jungle, letting her crash. And when she hit the ground and crawled back to her space, she'd find it vacant and meaningless. She sank into her chair. She could always buy a plant to place on the corner of her desk where he liked to perch. She could go on a vacation. No, Randy would need her.

"Hello, Megan."

Megan snapped her head up and quickly pasted on a smile. "Tina." It felt awkward to be addressing Randy's wife, given the private knowledge that their marriage was falling apart. "Good morning. Can I get you some coffee?"

"Oh no. I already had some." The tall, thin woman gave a little wave with a tanned, manicured hand. "We stopped for breakfast on the way over. Randy just needs to pick up his passport for our cruise." Silence pervaded for a few moments. Tina said, "It's my first one. Randy's always been too busy for getaways. But you know how everybody raves about cruises?"

Megan dropped her gaze, for the people she knew didn't go on cruises. Mostly they worked for people who went on cruises. When she looked up again, she noticed that Tina's eyes bore more sadness than anticipation and wondered if the cruise could restore the happiness the couple had lost.

"How's work going?"

"We're keeping Randy's customers, but I can't deny that he'll have a few pieces to pick up when he returns."

Tina tucked blond hair behind her ear. "Yes, he's been doing a lot of that lately."

Thankfully Megan didn't need to respond to the bitter comment because Randy and Chance entered the office and strode up to her desk. Randy paused long enough to give Tina a peck on the cheek before heading into his office. Outside the door, Chance hesitated. He gave Megan a tender expression that assured her everything was fine.

Her blue eyes suddenly glittering, Tina stared at Megan. "I can't believe what I just saw."

"What?"

"You two." Tina narrowed her eyes. "There's something going on between you guys."

Megan knew exactly what the other woman meant. She had just lumped Megan in the same category as Randy's previous assistant, whom Tina detested. Her expression shot sparks of blame as if Megan was responsible for her marriage problems.

"It isn't what you think," Megan defended, but it sounded like the cover-up it was, and she knew that eventually the truth would surface. It always did. For all she knew, at that very moment, Chance could be spilling out everything about their relationship to Randy.

"I don't know you that well," Tina continued, her eyes spewing accusation, "but when Randy hired you, he assured me that you were chaste because of your religion."

Chaste! Anger bubbled up Megan's throat like bile; one kiss didn't make her promiscuous. And her personal life wasn't any of Tina's business. She fought for control of her tongue. *I can't fly into the boss's wife. She's hurting and pathetic.*

"Anyways, I thought Mennonites were some sort of pacifists."

"What?" Megan's head spun from Tina's baffling and unjust allegations.

"I'm just shocked that you'd lower your morals and fall for an air force fighter pilot. That's all."

Stricken by the words *fighter pilot*, Megan clutched the underside of her desk. Her thoughts swirled to make sense of Tina's rebuke. *Fighter pilot?* She panted slightly then felt her heart clench. When she could speak, she repeated, "Chance is a fighter pilot? He told me he was a missionary pilot."

"Now he is. But he served in the air force. Even received a medal."

Megan read the truth in Tina's eyes. "I didn't know that."

Tina lifted her chin in justification. "I see. Let me tell you something for your own good. Women are fools around men. But not me. Not anymore. Don't be a fool, Megan."

Looking up through burning eyes, she nodded. "Thanks for the tip. If you're sure you don't want coffee, I'd better get back to work."

Tina tapped her flamingo-pink fingernails on Megan's desk. "I'm serious. If he lies to you once, he'll do it again. Anyway, he's not the settling-down type. Never has been."

The door to her husband's office opened. Randy and Chance stepped into the room, oblivious to the undercurrents. Megan watched Tina's gaze turn icy, before she averted her own. The bitter woman had pushed her out of the plane, and she was plummeting, but Megan determined not to crash until she was alone. With wooden movements, she changed her calendar and pulled out her to-do list.

"See you soon, Megan. I've heard some glowing reports about you," Randy said.

Megan felt Tina's smirk and gave her old boss a weak smile. "Just doing my job, sir." She lowered her gaze back to her desk.

When the space around her cubicle grew silent, Megan lifted her eyes. Randy and Tina were gone, and Chance had disappeared into his office. She stared at his door, feeling belittled and deceived. When Tina shoved her out of the plane, her decision about him and his jungle had been made—the painful way.

Her phone rang, bringing her thoughts to the present. She answered it and then worked frantically for the next hour, refusing to dwell on the painful disclosure, because if she did, she'd crash. Megan didn't want to do that at work. Didn't want to see the sympathy in Paige's eyes. Didn't want to hear, *I told you so.*

Megan went through an entire stack of paperwork before she stalled. When she did, she was unable to proceed. As much as she fought it, her mind sank its teeth into the information that Tina had divulged. Chance was a fighter pilot, turned missionary pilot. How little she knew about him. Tina's loathsome words held merit in Megan's case: *"Women are fools around men."*

Shame burned her cheeks to think how she'd succumbed to his advances. He'd taken advantage of her inexperience. He'd wrapped her around his little finger, while she blindly turned her eyes from the truth. No matter how much outsider's blood she possessed, she was a Mennonite at heart, and she could never fit in or feel at ease with him. He must never have intended for their relationship to be permanent. It had all been a game with him. For if he loved her, he wouldn't have taken her into the sky without a parachute.

She recalled the conversation where she'd confided in him about her nonresistant beliefs. He'd scoffed, putting down Mennonite men. Now she understood that he'd only probed into her beliefs so that he could skirt around them. He intentionally kept his military past a secret.

She clasped her head, shaking with anger so that she couldn't focus on anything but the man who'd played her like a fool. Pushing back her chair, she strode to his door. She squared her shoulders and knocked.

"Come in."

Megan stepped into the room and gave the door a shove. It banged behind her. As she stood trembling, Chance's eyes went from surprised to wary.

"Megan?"

She strode to his desk and speared him with her furious gaze. "When were you going to tell me that you were a fighter pilot?"

His eyes closed and fluttered opened, filled with regret. "That was a long time ago. I didn't think it mattered."

"I don't believe that. You knew it mattered. You purposely deceived me."

Chance rose and came around his desk. Megan jerked away from his touch. His hand moving upward in appeal, he explained, "When we first met, I thought we were like night and day. But the more we worked together, the more we connected. And lately, it seemed that we might be able to meet somewhere in the middle and actually have a wonderful future together. I was only taking it one day at a time. Just like you were."

An image of rows of red x's flashed into Megan's mind. With it came the idea that he'd been bored, using her to while away his time. She pushed him aside and ripped off the top page of his calendar. She crumpled it with her dreams and flung it at him. "That's what I think of your one day at a time!"

The wad hit his chest and bounced onto the floor. Chance stared at it then looked back at her. "Whoa. You're way too angry to think clearly. You need to cool down."

"I won't be deceived."

His hands went up in appeal. "Look. I meant it when I said I dream of us together making a happy life in Ecuador."

Happy when she let go of her beliefs and blended in with him and his lifestyle. "You knew I didn't want to date you. But you pursued me anyway. You took advantage of me because I work here. I'd no place to go to get away from you, and you were relentless. You wouldn't take no for an answer. What kind of boss is that?"

"When you say it that way, it sounds bad." He shrugged and gave her a contrite smile. "I couldn't help it. You're irresistible."

"That's sick. Just admit it. It was only a game for you."

"All right. Maybe at first I was curious. But I fell for you." He touched her again, and she was too exhausted to pull away from his pathetic appeal. "You make it sound as though we're finished. We can work through this, just as we have every other difference. This is no game, Megan. It doesn't matter if I made mistakes getting to this place. Now we're talking about our future life together."

"Futures are built upon honesty and respect. You played a dangerous game. Couldn't you see that there would be no winners?"

"There aren't any rules with love."

"Tell me, Chance. Have you changed since you were in the air force? Are you now nonresistant?"

"I won't lie to you, I'm not. But yes, I've changed. That's why I resigned from the military and use my career to save lives instead of to kill. We're both Christians, and we can disagree on a few things. People do that, you know."

He had killed. Even if she could forget that, given their personalities, she'd be the one who'd always have to adapt. The fight went out of her. She took a calming breath. "Look. I respect what you're doing with your life now. But today's broken the spell and opened my eyes. I see you differently. I know that going to Ecuador with you won't make me happy." She shrugged. "I've been starry eyed for a long time. It wasn't your fault."

"Meg, honey. You're just emotional. Don't say anything more until you've had time to really think about this. It's not about who we were then, but who we are now. Together. We make a great team."

"That's what I'm telling you. We aren't a team. We're finished."

"Two weeks. Don't decide yet." The irresistible charmer now came across as a spoiled, begging child.

She thought about how she'd threatened Micah she'd call in the church elders if he didn't quit pursuing her. It seemed childish, too, but it was proof that she could have resisted Chance. She had chosen to encourage his advances. If anything, she had courted a dream. "I'm sorry I led you on." She pulled away from his touch and stepped away. "I was wrong to give you hope."

He shook his head and advanced. "I'm not letting you go."

"Then I'll go to my desk and write Randy my resignation." She started to go.

"Wait."

She hesitated, her shoulders sagging.

He released a loud sigh. "You're really serious?"

"Yes."

"Don't resign. You stay, and I'll go."

"What about Char Air? And what about Randy?"

"I won't stay here and pretend to ignore you and your pious little net cap. Now get out before I change my mind."

Stung, Megan lifted her chin and marched out of his office. She sank into her chair, sick to her stomach, waiting for his door to fly open again. She expected him to storm past and make a dramatic departure. What would Randy say when he found out that she'd chased his replacement away? Would the cruise get canceled? Would she lose her job, anyway, because she'd caused such a fiasco?

But when the door finally opened, Chance emerged looking repentant, without his briefcase. He perched on the corner of her desk, squashing her imaginary plant and looking at her as if it was business as usual.

Megan tensed, hoping he wasn't going to beg.

Lines tugged the corners of his mouth down, and even his voice sank. "You go home. Take a couple sick days. Come back on Thursday, and I'll be gone."

Her mind leaped at the opportunity to escape, but his kindness flung a shackle of guilt around her ankles. "I really do feel sick."

He rose into a stance that made her wonder how she could have missed his military background. "The war changed me. You changed me, too."

"We've both changed." She lowered her gaze and heard him walk away.

With a burst of adrenalin, she moved toward flight. In a few strokes, she tidied her desk and grabbed her purse. On the way out, she told the receptionist that she felt ill and was going home. "Chance said he'd take care of things for me."

"Take care of yourself, honey."

"Yes. That's what I'm doing."

Micah had just stepped outside his cottage to exercise the cat when he noticed Megan's Nova pull into the drive. His brow furrowed, thinking it wasn't like her to come home in the middle of the day. When she got out of the car with a lowered gaze and sagging shoulders, it confirmed his suspicions that something terrible had happened. He darted across the yard toward her.

"Megan?"

She stopped, looked up in confusion, staring at him with vacant, red-rimmed eyes.

"What's wrong?"

She shrugged, and pain replaced the emptiness in her eyes. "I just came to my senses." He could only hope she was referring to the pilot. Her gaze flitted briefly over to the kitchen window. Sensing she didn't want her mom watching them, he nudged her elbow. "Come with me." He guided her around the front of the house past the porch to the buckeye tree that would shield them from public view. "Megan?"

"I broke it off with Chance. I found out that he had an entire past that he'd kept secret from me."

Images of a wife and family back in Ecuador came to Micah's mind. He had an un-Christian urge to place his hands around the man's arrogant neck, but instead he tried to remain calm.

"He had a military career. He was a fighter pilot."

"Hmph." That was the last thing he'd expected to hear. But it didn't surprise him. Although they were nonresistant, Micah didn't think Chance's military career was that shocking. She'd known all along that he was a man with feet firmly planted in the outside world. Micah wondered why, in her mind, his military career overshadowed his current mission work? And then it hit him, it was the timing of the deception, so soon after her mom's disclosure.

"He kept it from me. And I had dreams of marrying him. But when I heard that, I realized he'd manipulated me. I let him draw me away from my faith. I set my heart in the wrong place. What was I thinking, Micah?"

"We've been praying for God to reveal His will to you."

"I know. But it doesn't make this any less painful. I wanted him."

Her confession cut through the freshly laid scars of his never-healing heart, but he gently kneaded her shoulders and whispered, "I'm sorry." And when she eased into his arms, he comforted her, placing his chin on the top of her golden-spun hair. He closed his eyes to their merging pain. They both ached because they loved somebody they couldn't have.

"He told me to take some sick days. When I go back to work, he'll be gone." She clutched his shirt and mumbled, "I'm sorry I keep crying all over you."

He drank in her citrus scent. "I understand."

She released him. "Thanks."

He wiped her tears with his finger. "I admire your strength and determination to do the right thing."

She squeezed his hand and stepped away. "Thanks. I gotta go." Then she brushed past him and went into the house. Feeling exasperated, he stared at the door. The cat mewed. He looked down and scooped up the feline. *Why do I want her when she only wants him? I'm such a fool.*

—◠—

Later that evening, Megan poised her pen thoughtfully.

Thank You, Lord, for revealing that Chance is not the man for me and Ecuador is not the place You want me to go. It hurts, but I accept it.

She scanned her other prayer requests and added:

1. *Heal my pain.*
2. *Direction for my job at Char Air.*
3. *Healing for Chance.*

She set her journal aside to read from her Bible, pausing at Job 17. Verses 11 and 12 jumped out at her. "My days are past, my purposes are broken off, even the thoughts of my heart. They change the night into day: the light is short because of darkness." It was so similar to Micah's quote: *"When it is dark enough, you can see the stars."*

CHAPTER 27

Micah pulled his blue Honda Civic into Big Darby's parking lot. Sometime during the night, he'd realized that Megan's crying all over him had been a good thing this time. It'd been the last and final straw, opening his eyes to reality. Sure he was glad that she'd finally made the right choice. But the depth of Megan's feelings for the pilot had created an impenetrable wall. It was time he realized she was still inside the walled fortress of her own making, desperately needing to heal. Micah had been prowling and pacing around its perimeters, ever since the Fourth of July parade, waiting for a breach. It was sickening. Disgusting. It needed to stop. And it would.

He stepped out of his car and strode purposefully to the church building. He resolved to give his job the priority it deserved. He opened the door and moved down the hall. If he didn't confront Joy Ann, then he was treating her no better than Chance had treated Megan. He'd face the situation head-on and wouldn't be soft. She'd survive rejection. He was living proof it wasn't a fatal disease.

Inside the secretary was already busy at her desk. He was positive that Joy Ann had started arriving early merely to create a private time with him before Ruthie's arrival. Today that worked in his favor. He paused at her desk. "Morning, Joy Ann."

"Hi, Brother Micah. I guess you don't want to see yesterday's bank deposit slip?"

"You're right about that. My job doesn't require knowledge of church finances."

"I can see that, but—"

"But you don't like change?"

"I thought I did. But I guess I fell into the same mind trap as everybody else."

He saw that as his opening. "You're just trying to do a good job."

She involuntarily dusted her phone buttons with her fingertips. "Thanks."

"Sometimes you even go beyond what's expected. Take, for instance, how you always come to the office early."

Her face glowing, she explained, "I like to get things set up before Ruthie arrives."

"I understand, but I need to ask you not to do that anymore."

"What? But why?"

"This is a little awkward for me. It's because it doesn't look good for us to be here alone together."

Misinterpreting his caution light for a green one, she fingered the edge of her caped bodice. "I suppose it wouldn't do for people to start talking about us, especially before you hire on for good."

"Exactly. People might get the idea that you and I have something going, even though we don't." Joy's face reddened, whether with embarrassment or anger, he couldn't be sure yet. "I have a one-track mind right now. Focused on my work, you understand."

"Oh." He saw that she didn't understand. And she wasn't going to let it drop until she pushed him for more clarity. "So for now, we should. . ." She looked up at him with frustration.

"Joy Ann. There's no we."

She blinked furiously.

"I want to keep things strictly business at work, and outside of work, I'm not looking for more than friendship with you."

Her lower lip drooped for a second before her eyes darkened into stormy slits. She pushed back from her desk and stood. She planted her hands on her hips. "Just because I'm nice to you, doesn't mean I have my cap set for you. Preacher or not, I think you're a little big for your britches."

"Maybe I was out of line. But when we were playing checkers, I got the distinct feeling that—"

Her hand flew up. "Just stop. Just—" Her voice broke.

Micah touched her arm. "You're a great secretary."

Joy Ann lunged at him, burying her face against his shirt and slipping her hands tight around his waist. Micah froze. Not again. Did every woman think he was their weeping pole? He must be the only preacher who got himself in these scrapes. Joy Ann shuddered. He glanced toward the hall, wishing he'd closed the door, yet that would've been even more inappropriate. And what he saw in the doorway made him cringe and quickly pry Joy Ann's arms from his waist. Susanna Schlagel was staring at them with astonishment and pursed lips.

⁓

The next morning, Megan strolled through her mom's flower garden, pausing to enjoy the rugosa roses that were blooming after the third or fourth flush of the season. After crying on Micah's shoulder the previous evening then telling Mom the entire story, she'd spent hours alone in her room engaged in prayer and contemplation. Now she was positive that she'd done the right thing by ending it with Chance.

She also felt strangely tranquil in the certainty that God would guide her in the days ahead. She set down her weed pail and placed her gloved hands on her hips. Despite her lingering grief, she was unable to ignore the way the honeysuckle danced against its white trellis. She caught the scent of lavender and vowed that when she had her own home, she would plant a garden like this one. The scents and colors were healing to the soul. She envisioned imaginary conversations with her mom, comparing techniques and varieties. She followed the flight of a butterfly, amazed that she'd been so willing to exchange all that she was familiar with for an outsider's jungle.

Her mom had urged her to spend the morning in the flower beds, acting like they needed urgent care, but she'd known it was a ploy to cheer her. Megan's gaze lifted farther out to the big garden with its routine upkeep, which was now focused on tomato worms, squash borers, and flea beetles in the eggplant. As precarious as their relationship had become this summer, Mom remained kind and giving.

Pushing back her long hair, still wet from her shower, Megan knelt and began picking faded flowers and seed pods and ungainly stems, tossing them with soft thuds into a metal pail. As she worked, she began to hum the chorus of "Great Is Thy Faithfulness." She snapped off some ungainly stems and moved farther down the row, when unexpectedly an exuberant male tenor provided words to her tune: "'All I have needed Thy hand hath provided, great is Thy faithfulness, Lord, unto me.' I need that assurance right now, too."

Smiling, she paused from her work to look over her shoulder. "You have a nice voice."

"And you have a pleasant hum."

Megan softly laughed. "Hardly. But what are you doing back from church so soon?"

He knelt down. "It was too awkward at the office after my talk with Joy Ann."

"Oh. How did she take it?"

"At first it was hard for her to accept."

"She got angry?"

"Yes. She cried. But worse than that, she latched onto me just as Susanna Schlagel showed up at the office."

Latched onto me? Had he felt the same way when she'd clung to him after breaking up with Chance? When she'd cried about her outsider genes. When she was wrought with fear in the root cellar? She flung a sprig of hardy ground ivy into her pail. Brushing off her gloves, she asked, "So Susanna saw the two of you?"

"Mm-hmm. After that things went downhill. Let's just say I'd rather be pulling weeds than back at church cleaning up the mess I made."

"Actually, this is therapeutic. Even if it does kick up my allergies."

"We can't let the sniffles keep us from living." His gaze traversed the length of her hair, followed it all the way down to her waist. Then his jaw hardened, and he looked away.

Feeling his disapproval, Megan wished she'd braided it instead of enjoying the nakedness of sun and breeze. She didn't even have on her covering. The whole conversation had reminded her that he was more than a friend. He was a man. And he was a preacher; one who didn't appreciate women latching on to him. She'd do well to remember that. "So there's the pail. Help yourself to some therapy, while I go in and fix us a soda."

Yanking out some quack grass, he called after her, "You better come back. I hope this isn't a trick to get me to do your work."

She composed herself and returned with her hair primly bound beneath her prayer covering. Although she was sure he'd heard her approach, he kept working until she offered him a tall glass of the iced beverage.

Thoughtfully, she sipped her own cool refreshment. "I'd like to have a garden like this someday."

"I can picture that." He stood and brushed the soil off his pants. "A man could be happy with a property like this."

She wished happiness for him. "Dad is, but his cars have something to do with it. If you stay, the parsonage has a big property. Enough to enjoy the outdoors, but not enough to keep the preacher from doing what he's supposed to be doing."

Micah seemed thoughtful, almost distant. "Sister Barbara seems pretty attached to her place."

"I know. I wonder how the elders will handle that? Have they mentioned housing to you at all?"

"No." He pointed toward the apple trees and changed the subject. "Does your dad spray those?"

"Yes, he does."

"I can do that for him."

"You like gardening?"

"I've been keeping up my grandma's place for a long while. My place," he softly corrected.

Megan felt a tug of sympathy. She looked into Micah's eyes, and before he schooled his gaze, the depth of compassion and sadness she saw almost made her feel like a trespasser. But he quickly schooled it, and next he flung a tiny clod at her. It hit her skirt and fell to the ground. "Yes. I like gardening."

The boyish gesture beckoned her. Her lip curled, all intentions of revering her preacher fled. She was just about to pay him back good when she noticed the change in his appearance. Her mouth gaped in astonishment. She squealed with delight. "You did it! You parted your hair in the right place." She made a slow and complete circle around him. He rolled his gaze skyward in minimal toleration. She smiled. "If you're not careful, next you'll be almost average looking."

"Megan!" Mom appeared from nowhere, shaking her head. "Remember, you are talking to our preacher."

Waving her hand through the air, Megan dismissed manners. "Oh, Mom, you know we're old friends. Brother Micah," she mocked, "our lunch must be ready." She turned her back to him and strode toward her mom. "He wants to spray the apple trees next."

Mom called, "You coming, Micah?"

"I have some leftovers in my cottage. Thanks anyway. But when you're finished, you can show me where you keep the spray."

"Oh, sure."

At the screen door, Mom paused. "You sure you and Micah are only friends?"

"I'm sure. Micah just makes me feel better."

Mom nodded. "I just thought. . .never mind."

CHAPTER 28

The next day Megan awoke rubbing her eyes, a hangover from her gardening spree. Grabbing a tissue from her nightstand, she wondered how she could fill the hours of another day with no work. Then she remembered the promise she'd made to herself at Brother Troyer's funeral, to spend time with Barbara. Somehow since then, she'd gotten caught up in her own affairs and neglected that promise. Megan's romantic disappointment had to be minor compared to the older woman's loss of a lifelong companion.

At breakfast while she and Mom lingered over coffee, Megan brought up the matter. "I'd like to go see Barbara this morning unless you have other plans for me."

"That's a great idea. If you're up to it. You don't look so good."

"It's just allergies. I took a pill, and I'll be fine."

"Would you mind stopping at the store for me on the way home?"

They made plans, and an hour later, Megan found herself ringing the parsonage doorbell, while juggling a small watermelon Mom had sent along.

Barbara's eyes lit with delight. "Nobody can grow those like your mom. Come on in."

They set the fruit on the countertop and settled in at the kitchen table, where Barbara's Bible lay open.

"How are you doing?" Two months earlier, Megan wouldn't have had the nerve to ask the older woman anything so personal. But given all her own soul-searching, the question came out so naturally, it almost asked itself.

"I have moments when I feel sorry for myself. But even though I'm lonely, there are new blessings every day. To think that a young thing like you takes an interest in an old widow like me. Well, that's a blessing."

"I'm not so young." With all she'd experienced since she started working at Char Air, life had caught up with her.

"Something's happened." Barbara pushed up from the table. "I've been cooped up all morning. Let's take a turn around the garden. I want to show you my hydrangea bush. Then you can tell me what's going on."

Not bringing up her allergies, Megan followed Barbara's spry steps, thinking that her back was more stooped than usual. When they reached the eight-foot-high bush, equally large in diameter, Barbara plucked a stem with a pink cluster. "Just look at this. Did you ever see anything happier than this bush?"

Biting back a smile, Megan took the happy bloom in her hand, gave its stem a twirl, and brought it to her nose. It was fresh and sweet smelling. "Mom had me weeding her flower garden yesterday. The lavender smelled so good we took some inside. We added some roses to the bouquet."

"It sounds lovely. But shouldn't you be at work?"

"I'm taking a break from my boss."

"And he pays you for this?"

Megan laughed. "He told me to take a few sick days." She briefly filled Barbara in on what had happened with Chance. The widow listened without batting an eye. Megan was in the middle of explaining about her great-aunt Louise's portending visit when she was silenced by a series of sneezes.

Barbara snatched the stem from her hand. "Oh honey, I forgot about your allergies."

"It's probably because I was in Mom's garden yesterday. I should've known better."

"Well, let's go inside." A bluebird swooped into a blueberry bush. "I

wanted Eli to build me a bluebird house, but he never got around to it."
Inside, Barbara placed the stem in a tall, narrow vase of water and bent to
rearrange her refrigerator to make room for the watermelon. "I guess you
see how this melon is white on the bottom? A sure sign it's ripe and sweet.
Sometimes, life is like that. I think you're still on the vine, honey, but very
soon now, things are going to change for you."

Later at the store, Megan got the few items on Mom's list, while going
over the strange conversation with Barbara. The widow enjoyed hinting at
things, as if she was privy to some prophetic insights. While she was there,
Megan should have asked her if she thought that Micah would get voted
in as permanent pastor.

Micah heard the low din of male conversation drowned out by his own
footsteps clattering across the linoleum hallway. When he got close to the
doorway, he heard a cough followed by dead silence. Stepping into the
meeting room, the hair on the back of his neck bristled at Vernon Yoder's
guilty expression. Micah took the remaining chair and folded his hands on
the sterile gray, rectangular table.

He nodded at the five men who had assembled to discuss the state of
his interim pastorship. Bill sat on his immediate left. Vernon and a grim-
faced Leon Beachy sat across the table. The painter had some white speckles
on his wrist that he must have missed when he'd showered. *Normal people
just like me,* Micah tried to reassure himself.

Next to Leon was Ray Eversole. They were on good terms since Micah
had learned not to put him on the spot, asking for songs that weren't on the
agenda. To his right sat Noah Maust, the professor who had recommended
him for the position.

Bill cleared his throat, which wasn't necessary since the room was
already quiet. "Vernon, you wanna pray?" There were a few mumbled
*Amen*s when the prayer was completed, and then Bill turned his gaze
toward Micah. "Do you have anything to share with the group? Want to
tell us how it's going?"

Being the specimen on display, Micah sought for something that
would put himself in a good light. "I still believe God led me here, no

matter the outcome. It's been humbling to break out in hives two Sundays in a row, and then make that embarrassing blunder last week. . . ." He had to pause when they broke into laugher. "But I've also been blessed with affirmations. Brothers and sisters telling me how the sermon touched them or spoke to their needs. I see God in it."

Bill nodded. "That's true. People come to me with good things to say about you."

There were some affirmations along that line, and then Bill continued, "I've probably gotten to know you the best, and I respect and admire you as a godly man. I'm quick to always put in a good word for you."

"We think he just wants to keep you around to spray his apple trees," the professor teased. Micah had learned back at Rosedale that the professor had a good sense of humor when he felt like applying it.

The song leader smirked. "It isn't all roses over there, from what I hear. Not with a cat in the shop."

The men chuckled at Bill's weakness for nice cars without cat scratches.

Bill winked at Micah. "Let them have their jokes."

Micah figured it was best to remain silent and keep them in good humor.

Bill yanked at his button-down shirt. "All in all, the committee feels positive about your preaching and your character. But some rumors have reached us. We'd be at fault not to bring them to your attention."

Assuming he knew where the conversation was headed, Micah nodded. "I understand."

"So Leon, why don't you tell Micah what your wife heard this week at the quilting."

"Sure." He turned his gaze onto Micah. "My Inez, she doesn't gossip. Just so you know. But she overheard the widows talking at their corner of the quilt, pretending to keep their voices low, but Inez said she thinks everybody heard them when Susanna Schlagel told Ann Byler that she went to the office on Tuesday and saw you and Joy Ann Beitzel in a heated embrace."

"Where was Ruthie?" the professor asked.

"She hadn't arrived yet," Micah interrupted. In spite of the committee members' startled gazes, he continued, "Let me explain. I thought Miss

Beitzel had a crush on me. I believed that's why she always managed to come in early before Miss Ropp. I saw the infatuation from the start but wasn't sure how to handle it, not wanting to hurt her or offend anybody. I've tried to show her that I wasn't interested, but after Sunday's dinner invitation at her home, I realized I was going to have to be more direct with her. On Tuesday she was there early again. So I explained as kindly as I could that I wasn't interested in a relationship with her. She didn't accept it. I tried to explain that I appreciated her as a person and a secretary. That made her even more upset."

Several eyebrows lifted, and Micah was certain that if the men knew Joy Ann at all, they were imagining her reaction. "At first, she argued. Then she cried. Before I knew what had happened, she clapped her arms around my waist. I didn't know what to do and looked up, frightened that somebody might see us, and sure enough, there stood Susanna Schlagel in the doorway."

Leon shook his head. "That explains it. Bad timing, that's for sure."

Micah felt beads of sweat on his forehead. "I disengaged Joy Ann and went to the door to speak with Susanna, but she stormed off and wouldn't listen to my explanation. After that Joy Ann returned to her desk. She was embarrassed, but we were able to speak more calmly about the incident. I affirmed her work again, and then I went into my office until Miss Ropp arrived. After that, I left the church because the atmosphere was strained."

"Too bad," Leon repeated. "But there's more."

With surprise, Micah jerked his gaze to the painter. "More?"

"The widows claim that you stare at them while you preach. They want to know why you stare at them."

"I don't stare at them!" Micah objected, feeling a flash of resentment toward the widows, Susanna in particular.

"They claim it makes them uncomfortable and self-conscious, wondering if you are trying to lay some conviction on them. It makes them feel like the congregation is watching them."

Micah wanted to say, *if the shoe fits*, but instead he shook his head. "I'd never single out a person and preach at them. If I had something to say, I'd tell them privately to their face."

"Good." The professor quickly came to his defense. "The incident with

Joy Ann verifies that."

The other men nodded thoughtfully.

"Like I said, my Inez doesn't gossip. Trust me on that. But if I were you, I'd make sure you don't look at the widows' section anymore when you preach. Leastwise, until this settles down some."

Vernon cleared his throat and spoke for the first time. "The real issue's not your character, Micah. I hope you don't feel like you're on trial. We can only hope that the congregation's ready for a single preacher. It's a tricky situation. A big change. But the younger folks are behind you. Katy and Jake have nothing but good things to say about you."

"There's still time for the congregation to settle in and accept the idea," the professor replied.

Bill interrupted. "I'm not sure this will die down on its own. I'd like to take this information to the elders committee. They may have some helpful advice. The last thing we want to do is embarrass any of the women if we can help it."

After that, Micah wondered if he was capable of doing his job in a way that would exhibit the constant decorum and discreetness that it required. All that came to mind was the many times he and Megan had spent time alone together, how they'd embraced. And how he secretly loved her. If someone confronted him about that, there would be no way to deny it. In a sense, Susanna wasn't that wrong about his character, only she'd attributed his weakness to the wrong woman.

<hr />

When Megan returned to Char Air, Paige wasted no time to single her out in the coffee room. "Feeling better?"

"Much better."

As they prepared their hot drinks, Paige waited until they were alone and then probed. "I guess Chance must of caught whatever it was you had."

"Did he?"

"That's what I'm asking you."

Megan sighed. "If I tell you, can you keep it to yourself?"

"I always told you that I'm here for you."

"We were getting close, and he asked me to go to Ecuador with him."

Paige's face stretched in disbelief, partly horrified yet greedy to learn more. "All that right under my nose! I'm getting lax."

With a wry grin, Megan replied, "Maybe you should trade in those contacts for some reading glasses." Paige swiped the air with her hand. "Anyway, he was relentless, and I was even considering it."

"I guess my man repellants didn't work? Nor my big bad wolf speech, either?"

"No."

"So what happened, honey?"

"The other morning when Randy and Tina came to the office, she told me that Chance was a fighter pilot."

"Well, yeah. I thought you knew that."

"No. Actually, we'd talked about my beliefs, and he purposely held back that information. It helped me understand that he wasn't being honest and open with me. It wasn't all his fault, but it helped me understand that we needed to end it."

"So you did have the same thing."

Megan nodded grimly. "It's my own fault. But it's going to be dull around here without him."

"I don't like dull, either, but I can tell you from experience. Sometimes dull is restful. I know you have a sweet tooth. Maybe you should put a dollop of whipping cream in your coffee today and an extra spoonful of sugar. That'll help."

"Do you see whipping cream?" Megan joked. "No thanks, but I am going to Lil's restaurant for lunch today. Want to come along?"

They started walking out of the coffee room. "Maybe next time. I need to get my work in order for the real boss when he returns after next week." Before Paige returned to her own desk, she shook a manicured finger at Megan. "Now I know why you snapped at me the other day. You need to trust me more."

"I'm sorry about that. I did confide in someone who I thought would give me good advice."

"Who?"

"The preacher who lives in our little guest cottage."

"And did he?"

"Yeah."

"Well, I'm no preacher or even a saint. That's for sure." With a huge chuckle, Paige left for her own cubicle.

On Megan's desk were stacks of work that Chance had organized for her before he left. Brief sticky notes topped each one. She peeled off the first one and brought it up to her face. *Dead ends.* Rather fitting. Was he on a plane now headed for Ecuador? How long would he think of her? With a sigh, she grabbed the stack of files and headed to the file cabinet.

The morning went surprisingly fast, and she soon found herself at Volo Italiano, confiding in Lil. This time, Lil had taken her back into the employee's snack and lunchroom, and they ate together.

Lil waved her sandwich. "You're a strong woman. I'm proud of you for sticking to your beliefs. I like the part about how God opened your eyes and you just knew."

"That was amazing. I'd been struggling for so long and didn't seem to be getting any direction at all, but at the office that day, I just knew." Megan frowned. "Is that a peanut butter sandwich?"

"Yeah. I like them." She leaned closer. "Get tired of pasta every day."

"Last night Dad said that Joy Ann resigned from her secretary duties. Ruthie did, too. And guess who's going to be the new secretary?"

"Not you?"

"No. Barbara."

Lil smiled. "That's perfect."

"I know. At least it'll keep her from weeding Brother Troyer's grave plot."

"She still does that?"

"Mm-hmm. And I think they'll make a great team."

"I hope it works out for him. Maybe Barbara will put in a good word for you."

Megan sighed. "Let's not go there." Everybody wanted to match her up with Micah. No one understood how numb she felt. Even if she grew interested in the preacher, there was no way that he would forget how she'd cried over Chance.

CHAPTER 29

The next week sped by because both Megan and Paige had more than their normal amount of work to do with both Chance and Randy out of the office. Megan was glad because it helped her not worry about Great-aunt Louise's scheduled visit that weekend.

After lunch on Saturday, Mom replaced the tablecloth on the dining-room table three times, finally settling on the antique white with the scalloped edges. The center of the table bore a beautiful bouquet of lavender and roses that Megan had refreshed. "It's beautiful," she tried to reassure her mom. "But she probably won't even remember anything about our house. She's coming to look at us."

Her hand going up to her hair, Mom gasped. "I see a car in the drive now. It must be her."

"Don't worry. It'll be all right."

Only moments later, their aunt had swept in and taken control of the get-together. "Louise means *warrior*, you know. But don't let that bother you. I'm a warrior for the real King." She pointed toward the sky.

"I'm happy to hear that," Mom replied, but Megan could tell that she wasn't happy at all. Mom was pure nerves. Megan herself wasn't much better off.

Seated together on the sofa, they faced their warrior aunt, who leaned forward from the edge of the chair that was a garage-sale purchase. Louise had short, bottle-blond hair and bright blue eyes, which openly studied them. "I suppose you're wondering why I waited all these years to contact you?"

Mom's hand fidgeted with the sofa pillow. "You mentioned something about my grandmother passing."

"Yes. My sister, Mary, rest her soul. A good woman."

Things were not going at all as Megan had envisioned. Warrior for God? Good woman? Where were the wild ancestors? Surely she hadn't conjured up that vision? No, Aunt Louise hadn't mentioned Mom's birth mother yet.

Mom placed both feet firmly on the floor and leaned forward. "You don't know what it feels like to be given away. It doesn't seem like something a good woman would do. In my church, we take care of our own."

Her finger dancing through the air, Louise said, "Mary knew that the Mennonites were good people, and that's why she allowed them to adopt you. About the time you were born, there was so much strain between Mary and her daughter. Janice broke Mary's heart when she left the church and rebelled against all she had been taught. Mary was going through a bit of depression herself at that time. Then when Janice and your father were killed, Mary grieved because she wished they hadn't broken ties."

"Yet she was willing to break ties with me."

Louise flicked her tongue in and out as if it stoked her thoughts. "She regretted it once the depression lifted. It was a sad time. Mary and I were close as two sisters could be."

"We wouldn't know," Mom quipped.

Louise tilted her head and glanced at Megan with confusion.

"Mom was an only child. I am, too. But I have two close friends so I understand the type of relationship you are describing."

Louise looked back at Mom, who finally shrugged.

"I'm here for Mary. I want to bring a piece of her to you. So I've collected some things that I thought you might want to keep."

"So Mary didn't really set these aside herself?"

"Now, Anita, your grandmother didn't want to bring you pain by stirring things up and thought it best she not contact you. But I found your address among her belongings. I'm sure she put these things together for you."

"She sounds like you, Mom," Megan noted. "Not wanting to stir things up."

"But not me." Louise thrust her fist into the air. "I forge ahead, and I felt God tugging at me to do this, so here I am." She settled her gaze on Megan. "You resemble our family."

"I can tell."

"You both do, but Megan even more so. You look like Janice."

That would be the rebellious girl. And maybe she did carry some rebellious genes that had been handed down to her, but she'd already made her choice to resist them. "What about you? What's your life like?"

"I am at that stage in life where I'm defying my age. I do that by traveling. I have a widow friend. We go to wonderful places. I even put my house up for sale. May I send you tokens from my future travels?"

"No! Yes!"

"Well, you'll just have to share yours with your mother then, dear."

Mom looked contrite. "You've come a long way. My manners have been poor. May I get you something to drink? I have cookies."

"Oh, no. I'm fine on those accounts." Louise stood. "Now, if you'll follow me to the car, I'll show you what I've brought."

They followed Louise to her rental car, and she pulled a hinged velvet box out from the passenger's seat, handing it to Mom. Then she riffled through her purse for paper and pen and jotted something on paper. "Megan, here's my address. Let's stay in touch."

"I'd like that." Megan didn't dare glance at Mom.

"Good. Anita, I know that my sister would want you to have those things. Mary must be smiling from heaven even now."

"She was a Christian?" Mom asked.

"Oh, yes. A Methodist!" Louise spread her arms to include their property. "This is a pretty place. God must have planned all this for you. Nothing gets by Him, you know."

Megan admired the twinkle that brightened her great-aunt's eyes when she spoke. She admired her zest for life and God.

"But I speak for the entire family when I say that without you, something was missing. We all missed you. And you'll never know how much it blesses me to see you. If, after you look through those things, you have a change of heart, I'd love to stay in touch."

Megan held her breath, hoping that her mom didn't refuse to accept the box. More than anything, she longed to see what was inside.

"We have your address," Mom replied. "Thank you for your good intentions."

Louise smiled. "You're welcome. Now, may I hug you both before I go?"

Reluctantly Mom allowed the gesture, but Megan meant hers. "Thank you for coming." She wanted to say more, to say that having Louise contact them had changed her life. But it might be better to write her a letter instead. Tokens of affection seemed to matter a lot to this sweet little warrior woman.

They watched the car until it drove out of sight. "Did that really happen?" Megan ventured.

With a deep sigh, Mom said, "Let's go inside and see what's in the box. What she thought was so important that she had to cause all this trouble."

Megan's heart leaped joyfully. She hoped it would contain something that would ease Mom's pain.

They took the box to the dining-room table. Mom ran a shaky finger across the stitched ribbon edging. Slowly she opened its hinges. The lid was lined in red velvet on the inside, too. The first thing she removed was a small Bible.

"It's worn, like she used it," Megan said hopefully.

"A Methodist!" Mom imitated Louise's comment, and when they both laughed, some of the tension left the room.

"Open it."

Mom opened the cover and gasped. On one of the cover pages, Grandma Mary had made a hand-drawn family tree, and Mom's name was there: *Anita Mary Lintz.*

"They gave me my dad's name."

"Mary never knew you, but she loved you," Megan reminded her.

But Mom's eyes darkened. "It's just a name, says nothing about love.

Love is what your Grandma Bachman did for me. For us."

"I know that. But Grandma Witherspoon carried the loss in her heart. Surely, she did." Megan examined some photographs of her mom's parents. "They were so young."

"Young and foolish, I suppose."

They took turns studying the photographs, trying to decipher any resemblances.

"We should have asked about your dad's family," Megan said with disappointment.

"Please, don't ask about that. I'm not ready for that yet."

Nodding, Megan decided in her heart that someday she would ask Louise. She had a right to know, even if her mom didn't want to deal with any more information.

Next Mom drew out a lacy handkerchief. The antique was tiny and delicate. She unfolded it and smoothed out its creases. It looked yellow against the white tablecloth. The handkerchief was trimmed in blue and had hand-embroidered blue initials on it. Suddenly, Mom's hand fluttered at the side of her face. "Do you see it?"

"What?"

"It has your initials."

M.W. "It does."

"You must have this. If you want it?"

"Oh, yes." Mom handed it over, and Megan drew it to her face and took a deep breath, inhaling the musty sweet smell. "What does it smell like?"

Mom found a sachet and brought it to her nose. "Roses."

"I'll bet that's hand sewn, too. I'm glad Aunt Louise brought these, aren't you?"

Mom whispered, "Yes."

"Do you think you'll ever go to Pennsylvania?"

A sarcastic laugh quickly replaced the tender moment. "No. My family is here. This is all I need." Then her hand went out to touch Megan. "But you may stay in touch with Louise. That would be nice."

"Thanks, I'd really like to do that. But what is that bundle of papers?"

"I don't know if I'm ready to find out."

"May I?"

Mom hesitated then nodded.

Megan removed the ribbon that bound a two-inch stack of stationery. She unfolded the top paper. "It's a letter." Silently she read then laid it down and took up the second. "Mom, they're love letters between Mary and your grandfather. His name was John. They must have had some sort of long-distance relationship."

"But we shouldn't have those."

"Why not?"

"Let me see it. I believe you're right. Listen to this. 'Dearest Mary, I can't wait to see you in two weeks. I'll take you for a ride in my convertible. I love to see the wind blow through your blond hair. You look like an angel.' " Mom stopped reading. "It doesn't seem right to read this."

"I'd really like to look through them."

"Fine. You can have them. I need to go start supper."

— ᧒ —

The next week Randy returned to Char Air. When Megan got to work the first day of his return, there was a note on her desk:

Come into my office.
        Randy

Not knowing what to expect, she wasted no time, but grabbed a note pad and knocked on his door.

"Come in."

Megan stepped inside. "Welcome back. We missed you."

"Oh. Did you?" He didn't meet her gaze. Rather, he kept it averted to the legal pad on his desk—on top of the blank calendar that wasn't on the right month because she'd wadded it up and destroyed it. "Chance left me some notes. Sit down and we'll go over them."

Sliding into the leather side chair, she felt her face heat at his rebuff. He went through the list so quickly, that she could hardly keep up, scribbling notes as they went. He never made eye contact until they were finished. Then he studied her. "Now that my playboy brother is gone, are you ready

869

to get back to work?"

She met his gaze, feeling resentful because she hadn't loafed, but carried a heavy load in Randy's absence. Yet he made a valid point about her foolish behavior. "Yes."

All week long, Megan was bombarded with an almost impossible workload, and she had to wonder if Randy was trying to break her, push her to quit. Or maybe it was Tina who wanted her gone. But she was determined not to give her boss another good reason to fire her. If she left the company, it'd be her choice.

In spite of his gruff behavior toward her, it was obvious Randy had missed, possibly even mourned, his job. His enthusiasm drove him to be everywhere at once, righting things and even pushing Paige harder to drum up new business. His thirst was unquenchable. Yet there were isolated moments when Megan caught glimpses of turmoil on his brow, sad determination in his eyes. Generally speaking, he'd aged. She had no idea if he was still with Tina.

Their most personal conversation had been minimal, when Megan had asked, "Did you enjoy your cruise?"

Randy had set his jaw and replied grimly, if not sarcastically, "Had the time of my life." And the look he'd given her indicated the conversation was finished forever—unless she was masochistic, and she wasn't.

There were no lunches with Lil. Megan dragged herself home every night, too tired to field any questions her parents or Micah wielded at supper. After helping with the supper dishes, she excused herself and went straight to her room. She wrote in her journal and read her great-grandparents' love letters. She discovered that her great-grandfather loved to quote poets and well-known love sayings. Among her favorites was a quote from Elizabeth Bowen: *"When you love someone, all your saved-up wishes start coming out."* Her great-grandparents' letters were the bright spot of Megan's existence.

CHAPTER 30

Thursday evening on his way home from work, Fletch stopped at the Weavers on Lil's behalf. He invited Megan to join them for a picnic and softball game at the doddy house. On Friday Megan held her breath, hoping that Randy wouldn't ask her to work on Saturday. He didn't.

Lil set up the picnic much like she had the one earlier in the summer. After the meal while the toddlers napped, Fletch numbered off the guests to form softball teams. Gleeful that it wouldn't be like in grade school, when Megan was one of the last to be chosen, she joined Fletch's even-numbered team. Ivan and Elizabeth were on her team. Each team had two couples and a single person. Micah joined the Yoders and the David Millers.

Lil was first up to bat. "Get it over the plate, chump," she taunted her cousin.

"And what good will that do you," Jake shouted back, "if you don't know how to hold the bat?"

But Lil did know, and she met the ball with a loud crack. Her bat sailed through the air as she hastened to first base, nearly knocking Fletch's feet out from under him. When she saw she was safe, she did the garbanzo dance to the amusement of everyone, even their opponents.

"You shouldn't throw your bat like that, honey," Fletch admonished, stepping up to take his turn.

"Sorry, sugar," she replied with a sheepish grin.

He brought Lil in, and the score was 1–0.

Next, it was Megan's turn. She warmed up her swing then waited for the perfect pitch. To her surprise, she connected and even sent it over Micah's head at second base. When she saw Fletch go for home, she made a bad choice to try for second base. She heard her teammates' groans, but there was no turning back.

"Run, Megan!"

She sped up, even though she saw she couldn't possibly make it. Micah planted himself over the base, and she barreled into him.

"Oopfh!"

The man was a brick wall and had barely budged. His free arm had even snagged her and kept her from falling at his feet. When he saw she was steady, he lifted his glove and cried, "Out!"

Breathing hard from the sprint, she looked up. His eyes were hidden behind dark sunglasses, but his lips quirked just before he repeated more softly, "Out."

She jerked her arm away, wanting to wipe off his silly grin.

"Watch out how you act around the preacher," Lil warned.

Megan sloughed it off and joined her on the grass. "Whose side are you on?"

"Yours. I missed you this week."

"It was rough. Randy came back with a chip on his shoulder. I get the feeling he regrets hiring me. I'm not sure if Tina wants me out of there or what's going on."

Jake's arm improved, and Ivan and Elizabeth both struck out. The girls pushed to their feet, and Megan walked toward the outfield. Beside her, Lil adjusted her glove. "I'd miss our lunches if you ever left your job, but sometimes change can be a good thing."

Megan wasn't so sure. She hated job hunting. "I'm all right. Since my great-aunt Louise came to visit, Mom's back to her old self. I think her contentment is rubbing off on me."

"Oh yeah? You looked pretty intense out there with Micah a minute ago."

"He was laughing at me."

"I know. We all were."

"It's just that he's always so capable." And she was always the needy one, hanging on his shirttail or using it to wipe away her tears. "Sometimes his perfection is just plain aggravating."

"I know exactly how you feel. It gets even worse after you marry them. But loving Fletch is better than hanging on to my pride." Megan was glad Lil was happy, until her friend put in a parting jab. "I see you and Micah drove separate cars. A waste of fuel, if you ask me."

Megan rolled her gaze skyward, but she had to admit that she would've enjoyed riding over with him because they hadn't talked all week. Unless you counted a few snippets over supper with her parents in the room. She hoped he didn't think she was avoiding him. But if she recalled correctly, he'd missed a couple of meals, too. Her gaze traveled over the Millers' yard until it located him, standing in the home team area, trying out various bats.

He wore jeans, which in itself was an unusual sight. More often, she saw him in his dress clothes. He also had on a solid gray, pocketed T-shirt and a pair of sunglasses that prohibited her from knowing where his gaze was focused. As he made some test swings, his shirt lifted a bit, revealing a small waist. She felt a strange sad yearning, but it was as fleeting as it was strange. As his legs found their stance, his strength drew her interest. He had fascinated her from the moment he'd stepped onto the Weavers' property. Now his arms bunched under his shirt as he took several fake swings. Finally he took his place at home plate. Tapped the plate with the tip of his bat.

Ivan's first pitch was outside, and Micah let it go by. Fletch was catcher. He lopped it back to Ivan. The next pitch was good, and Micah drew back. He hit the ball high into centerfield. Megan's gaze followed it, until she saw that it was going to fall behind her. Both she and Lil ran for it, but it hit the ground beyond them. Lil scooped it up first, probably because she could run faster in her jeans.

Panting, Megan bent slightly to catch her breath and watched Lil toss it into the infield. It was an overthrow that sailed over Ivan's head. Micah rounded third, his long, churning legs never slowing. Megan watched the play unfold, found herself rooting for Micah even if he was aggravating and playing for the opposing team. He hit the ground and slid, uprooting some grassy clods, his feet hitting home just before Ivan finally recovered the ball and threw it to Fletch.

Micah stood and clapped Fletch on the arm, both men grinning. Then Micah brushed off his jeans and looked up, and although she couldn't be certain because of his sunglasses, she thought he caught her staring. Quickly, she dropped her gaze and returned to her position.

"We're tied," Lil called over with disappointment.

But in Megan's estimation, Micah's home run outshone anything their team had done. Her admiration diminished, however, when the odd-numbered team's runs began to stack up against them, inning after inning. And when the babies woke up and the game ended, Megan was glad to be finished with it.

Lil and Fletch served homemade ice cream topped with strawberries, and Megan was content when Micah stretched out on the grass beside her quilt. "You're good. Did you play in school?"

"No. Just lucky," he replied.

She didn't think so. "Normally we have a church picnic and ball game on Labor Day weekend."

"Really?" Micah got excited. "No one's mentioned it."

"Only the men play ball," she clarified. "It's always been the last hurrah before school starts, kind of an early harvest celebration."

"Why should this year be any different? I think we should do it. Who plans it?"

"Brother Troyer and his wife always did."

"I'll talk to Barbara about it. A church ball game might ease some tension."

Megan nodded, wondering what tension. She took a spoonful of ice cream, felt his gaze on her.

"Do you think I stare at the widows?"

Almost bursting into laughter, she asked, "What?"

"When I preach?"

She saw he was dead serious and tried to envision his last sermon, when suddenly her eyes lit with understanding amusement. "I believe you do. But I always thought you were watching the clock."

"Of course." He shook his head, and a clump of bangs fell playfully over his sunglasses. He gave it a quick brush of his hand. "That's it."

"Guess you'd better put a watch on the pulpit."

"Now I can give the search committee an explanation." He rubbed his chin thoughtfully, and she noticed that he had ice cream under his lower lip.

It was all she could do not to reach out and remove it. She quickly glanced away, watching Katy scoop up little Jacob. Why was she always wanting to fix him? Help him when he was already practically perfect? The idea troubled her. "Glad I could help. I need to go talk to Katy." She stood and brushed her skirt. "I'll be on the swing later if you want to drop by and gloat about getting me out on second."

His voice sounded grave when he replied, "It's tempting."

As she strode toward Katy, she felt her face heat and wondered how she could be so bold, but she missed him and their quiet talks. From the start of Micah's return to Plain City, God had drawn them together. She found rest in his quiet strength.

She was certain he would never offer anything other than friendship, like everyone seemed to hope. He might wish to, but he wouldn't. She had ruined her real chances with him when she had acted the fool over Chance. No, Micah was too honorable, too perfect to make that kind of mistake. When had she started thinking of him as perfect? That night in the root cellar? Certainly not back in college.

"Megan, have you heard what Jacob did last night?"

She tore her attention away from the preacher and saw the joy in Katy's eyes. Marriage and motherhood agreed with her. Megan fondled the baby's soft squirmy arm and shared in Katy's delight. "No. What did he do?"

Micah pushed his notes aside. How could he study his sermon when Megan might be waiting for him on the porch swing? Had he really caught her staring at him throughout the ball game? Or did she merely need another sounding board, a tear blotter. If so, he'd be smart to think ahead and stick a hanky in his pocket and keep her off his shoulder and out of his arms.

Megan had been distant all week, which had suited his desire to quit chasing her. But he'd been disappointed that she hadn't been there for him when he'd needed to vent after his search committee meeting. Today, however, she'd redeemed herself, by solving the mystery about why the widows thought he stared at them when he preached. Not only that, she'd told him about the annual church picnic and softball game.

With a touch or a word, she made things right, providing the exact type of encouragement he needed. He sighed and laid down his pencil, hating to admit that she'd helped him as much, if not more, than he'd ever helped her. And surely her motives were purer than his own.

With things intensifying at church, he didn't need the extra stress of Megan messing with his emotions. She didn't realize how she affected him. Her naïveté was deadly.

What he needed was his grandmother's sweet advice. She'd been more than motherly, she'd been a saint. The past week, working with Barbara, those memories had returned. He could hardly face the idea of failing at Big Darby and having to return to live in the quiet old house alone. It would stir up the sad memories of her last weeks. He knew that he would need to go back and deal with the house sometime, no matter what happened.

His traitorous thoughts returned to Megan. Why had she asked him to meet her on the porch? With a disgusted sigh at his male weakness and one-track thinking, he pushed back his chair. Scooping up the cat, he went toward the door. Once he was outside, he'd be able to tell if Megan was there. Usually his body came to alert anytime she was on the property. He'd know, all right. He'd take the cat out, but he wouldn't sit on the porch and wait for her, for pity's sake.

Miss Purrty meandered toward the back of the property, and something akin to static electricity danced across his arms. But his heart throbbed with a dull pain, like arthritic joints before a rain. Megan was his rain. She was nothing if she wasn't bittersweet. He paused, listened. Smiled at the swing's groan. Stuffing his hands in his pockets, he gravitated toward the rain.

When he reached the porch, he saw her hair was backlit by the moon, giving her face an ethereal appearance. "Hey."

She looked up. "Fireflies will soon be gone."

"Like me."

"You're in a bad mood for being on the winning team."

He didn't ask for permission, just slipped onto the seat next to her. Oddly, she didn't slide over, like he'd expected, which left their shoulders lightly pressed against each other. He already regretted their touch, and he would suffer from it. But if she wasn't going to move first, he certainly wasn't going to go wimpy. He'd already done that earlier in the afternoon, when he'd gotten a sneezing attack the second time he was up to bat. He'd made it to first, and as he'd waited for the next batter to hit him around the bases, he'd heard Megan sneezing in the outfield. Though his allergies always made him feel less than manly, it gave him a perverse sense of satisfaction that she shared his symptoms.

"I saw your light. Working on your sermon?"

"Mm-hmm. It's about patience."

"You're good at that one, aren't you?"

"Not so good."

"I'm anxious to hear your sermon. But lately, I have this feeling. . ."

"What?"

"That everything will turn out right in the end. Is that patience, you think?"

"Sounds more like faith. Was it something your aunt said? Did she leave you with an inheritance or something?"

She ignored his sarcasm. "I think it had more to do with finally agreeing with God, instead of resisting Him. The past two weeks seem like years. Another lifetime, actually. I don't think I loved Chance." She turned, searched his face. "Do you think that's fickle?"

He wanted to kiss the fickleness right out of her lips, help her find her way. But she trusted him with her shoulder snuggled against him. "Nope." When her eyes widened, he realized he'd said that out loud. "No. Not fickle. I know what it's like to lose someone. Feel disappointed and confused. To receive God's peace in the midst of it. I understand."

"Your grandma?"

He missed her dearly, but he was thinking about his struggle to get over Megan. It was exhausting, so he directed their conversation to a safer place. "I don't want to lose this position." Had he really agreed with God, as Megan finally had? Or was he still resisting Him?

"What can I do to help?"

Kiss me. Keep your distance, and for crying out loud, don't be inviting me to meet you on the porch swing. He glanced at her moonlit face, wondering if he could tell her that. Would she understand if he explained how hard she was making it for him to concentrate on his job? Or would it frighten her and make her loathe him for pretending friendship when he really loved her. She looked at him, waiting expectantly. "Just be a good sport and hold my hand, I guess."

She took him literally and slipped her hand in his. "I'm glad we're friends."

He eased away. "We are, Megan. But difficult as it will be, we need to quit meeting like this. Like you said before, we need to agree with God, not resist Him, and I don't think our actions honor Him."

She rubbed her rejected hand down her skirt. "I guess. But it feels right. I don't understand why I feel so comfortable with you? Do you?"

He wished he could say the same. But comfortable didn't quite fit the bill for him. He clamped his knee so he didn't give in and put his arm around her. He heard Purrty's mew, and knew that their moment was ending. That he had to take his stand against the pull of the flesh. "I'd better get back to my sermon." She turned, looking hurt. Somehow, he found the strength to say, "I'm glad that we could get over the awkwardness of college. I appreciate all you've done to help me. Your friendship, your kindness. But we're not children, and we can't play with fire, Meg. We need to keep our distance, for both our reputations."

"Is this what you told Joy Ann?"

Surprised to hear the edge in her voice, he studied her eyes. Even softened by moonlight, they held flashes of anger. "Of course not. But if you really want to help me—"

"Stop," she interrupted, as she stood. "I get it."

"I don't think you do. You don't realize how you affect men."

"Are you insinuating that I enticed Chance?"

"No. I'm just saying I can't go around protecting you." He sighed, ran his hands through his hair. "I need to practice what I preach. In all honesty, we both know we need to grow up."

Her head dipped. He hoped she wasn't going to cry again. Because he refused to comfort her the way he had in the past. He waited. Slowly she raised her head. There was a trace of moisture in her eyes, but thankfully, she kept her composure.

"You're right. I've been selfish. It's impossible to continue this way. But I hope you won't think badly of me if I see you staring at the clock tomorrow and make a face. It won't do, you know, to keep staring at the widows."

Grateful for her brave attempt at humor, he whispered. "I'd be honored for your help."

"It's late. 'Night."

He scooped up the cat and headed for his cottage without even attempting a reply. He wanted to get as far away from his temptation as possible. He knew there'd be some kneeling time before he could get back to his sermon. But he felt good about taking a stand. It was up to God now to give him the strength to abide.

$$\sim \hspace{-0.5em} \circ$$

Added to everything else that had happened, Micah's rejection devastated Megan. She'd never expected him to give her the brush-off. She deserved the humiliating set down for using him the way she had. She'd been selfish and horrified when he told her to grow up. But worse was the loss of a valuable friendship. Kind, gentle, perfect Micah, always trying to do the right thing. He was not a weakling. He was the strongest man she knew. And she'd driven him away.

Rolling onto her back, she stared into the darkness and pulled the covers up under her chin. She was positive that he still cared about her, but he'd been man enough to resist her. He wouldn't settle for less than what he deserved. Someone who adored him, some pure-hearted woman who could share his life and bring honor to his position as head of the church. Who would he choose? Lori Longacre? He admired her and found her attractive. It was painful to imagine the two of them together. Why had it taken her so long to realize Micah's worth? She'd been such a fool. Twice over.

She would take his advice to heart, as if it was from God Himself.

Micah was her preacher, after all. She would pick herself up and be a better person for it, even if he did marry the librarian. She would do everything in her power to help and not hinder him. He deserved that much from her.

She thought she understood the quotation in the latest love letter by her great-grandfather that she'd read: "There is no remedy for love than to love more"—Henry David Thoreau.

CHAPTER 31

The next morning at church, Megan watched Micah preach his best-ever sermon, his gaze never veering toward the clock or the widows' section. Afterward, he announced his plans for the church picnic and what he now called the Brothers' Baseball Outing. At the announcement, a general buzz fell over the congregation. On one hand, she was happy that his idea was being accepted, but on the other, she was a bit disappointed that Micah presented the idea with enthusiasm and didn't appear to have lost any sleep on her account.

"Clever name, Brothers' Baseball Outing," Inez whispered to Leon.

When the general din waned, Micah surprised the congregation further by delegating those men seated on his left to be on the white-shirt team, and those on his right side to be on the blue-shirt team. He encouraged them to choose their own captains. As she listened to Micah's plans, she was surprised to hear that Joy Ann and Ruthie were organizing some games for the children. And Barbara was working with the hostess committee to plan the food.

After the meeting, feeling generally left out and disagreeable, Megan started across the parking lot to find Katy, hoping little Jacob would lift her spirits. She'd only taken a few steps when she heard David Miller planning to recruit Chad Penner, who was home sick with a cold. She wondered if Micah's new method would foster unhealthy rivalry and contention amongst the men. But with Micah's rejection still heavy on her heart, she didn't have it in her to warn him about it. *Men. Let them work it out.*

"Hi, Katy. Can I hold him?"

"Of course. He loves you."

Megan bounced Jacob until he giggled.

"I have news. Elizabeth Miller is thinking about taking a job, and I offered to babysit for her if she does." Katy's dark eyes flashed with joy. "Won't that be fun?"

Megan kissed Jacob's cheek. "I thought you hated that nanny job."

Tucking a strand of black hair beneath her covering, Katy quickly explained, "That was different. Those children were raised differently and I didn't know how to handle them. I've also developed a little patience since then."

Megan's mind went to Micah's sermon on patience, but she quickly reined it in. "From living with Jake?"

Katy laughed. "That, too. But enough about me. I heard Randy's been rough on you. I've been praying for you."

"Thanks. I'm not sure what I'll do if things don't change soon."

"Have you talked to Micah about it?"

"No. He doesn't want to have much to do with me, either." Megan didn't wish to turn Katy against their preacher candidate, so she quickly added, "It's not his fault. Our friendship isn't really appropriate, right now."

"Are you still unwilling to admit it might be more than friendship?"

Trying to speak while Jacob poked her cheeks, seemingly fascinated with adult speaking mechanisms, Megan replied, "I was foolish to tell him about Chance. Now I wish I hadn't. He knows everything, and I don't think he can get past that. He needs somebody with a good reputation, somebody like Lori."

"Oh." Katy's dark brow suddenly quirked in warning, just before Susanna swooped in and landed beside them.

"Young ladies, the quilters are helping the hostess committee with the picnic. Isn't it exciting? Anyway, I wanted to ask you, Megan, if you'd bring that three bean salad that Barbara raves about."

"Of course. But it's really Lil's recipe."

Her arm swept a graceful but fierce wing through the air. "Well, work it out between you. Hopefully Lil will come and bring something a little more. . ."

"Scrumptious?" Katy supplied, and Megan's feelings weren't in the least bit hurt.

"Exactly. We certainly don't want to tie her hands, now do we?" Susanna's laugh croaked. But when she walked away, Megan asked, "Did she hear us talking about Micah?"

"I don't think so, but then her hearing is extraordinarily sharp."

─❧

Micah watched the tender scene transpiring across the parking lot, how Megan gave Katy a friendly hug and then lifted baby Jacob into her arms. It caused a bittersweet pang, knowing that Megan would make a wonderful mother.

"Brother Micah?"

He quickly tore his gaze away from Megan and rested it on the pretty brunette woman facing him. "Yes, Lori?"

"I believe that resurrecting the picnic and ballgame was the perfect thing for the congregation. How do you do it? Always anticipate the needs?"

"I sense a *but* coming next."

She smiled. "See what I mean?"

He waited, curiously. Lori had been helping him with research for his sermons. He no longer worried about her stepping out of line. She was easygoing, and in working with her, he'd learned that her advice was usually timely and valuable. It was too bad her perfume always tickled his nose.

"There's a cold bug going around and a few families traveling to family reunions. I overheard some men scheming to snap up the better players upon their return. There's some competition brewing. And I was just wondering if you were going to let them get away with that?"

"I can tell that you have a different idea."

"I do." She urged him closer with her finger. "I think I can help."

He leaned close, strangely intrigued.

—⟋⟍—

The following Sunday, Megan slid into the pew next to her mom and watched Micah deliver a sermon on peace, another fruit of the Spirit. She jotted down a few notes but often found her mind detouring, fixed on the way his jaw hardened when he stressed a point. It was his tendency in the next breath to soften his jaw by allowing his lower lip to droop into a bit of a smile. She knew him well enough to recognize it as one of his pleading smiles. Often he admitted his own shortcomings to the congregation. But his humility only made him more loveable.

She crossed her arms and wished his smile wasn't the last thing she thought about before she fell asleep at night. She'd tried to tell herself that she was only attracted to him because he was a preacher, just like she had been attracted to Chance because he was a missionary pilot. After all, weren't God's men the most appealing?

But it wasn't his occupation at all. He'd wiggled his way into her heart, little by little, revealing his true nature. And now when she looked at him, that's what she saw, not the gawky outer shell she remembered from Rosedale. His physique had become pleasing as well. Now her competition was plentiful.

She uncrossed her arms, took a tissue from her purse, and blotted her forehead. Maybe this fascination with him was the result of reading her grandparents' love letters every night before she drifted off to sleep: "To love another person is to see the face of God"—Victor Hugo. What better way to describe what she felt for Micah?

He sneezed twice, drawing her from her private thoughts. "Anyone wishing to play softball who wasn't here last week when we designated teams can draw his team placement from a jar in the library. Lori Longacre will monitor the drawings after the service and each week until the event."

Megan frowned at the affectionate look he shot Lori.

"In fact, I'm headed there to draw a team for myself after the Doxology. This way the teams will be formed in a fair manner, even if they end up lopsided, for I'm sure the team who gets me will be at a disadvantage."

There were a few chuckles. *Hardly a disadvantage*, Megan thought, remembering how he'd hit a home run the day they'd played at the doddy house. Micah went on to stress that this was first and foremost a friendly competition.

Suddenly Megan felt the forewarning tickle of a sneeze. She brought her tissue up to press under her nose, hoping to ward off her irritating connection to Micah. When she felt it was safe, she lowered her hand, and her gaze involuntarily followed those of the majority of the congregation's to Lori Longacre's pew. It shocked Megan to see the woman's undisguised admiration directed straight ahead toward the pulpit.

Clearly, Lori and Micah had conspired to come up with that plan. It tugged painfully at Megan's heart to imagine him going elsewhere for advice. She'd recognized the admiration they shared for each other from the beginning. She certainly wouldn't go anywhere near the library after the service. Let them have their fling!

___⌒___

After that day, Megan intentionally kept out of Micah's way. As if in unspoken agreement, he followed suit, accepting more food offerings, keeping to his cottage most evenings. If her parents noticed a change, they didn't comment to her about it.

Megan's workload lightened. One noon she dashed over to Volo Italiano. Two men standing beside a silver SUV eyed her Nova as it rumbled into the parking lot, and she felt their gaze follow her all the way into the restaurant. Inside it seemed busier than usual.

Lil darted around a corner. "Just a minute!"

"Sure." Megan turned to the hostess. "Seems busy today."

"A conference. Bunch of engineers."

"Think Lil's too busy for me?"

"I doubt it. They made reservations, and we increased our staff today."

Lil strode up, tucking some straying hairs back into their pins. "Sorry about that."

"Just when I get a break, you're busier than normal."

Lil brushed a hand through the air. "The worst is over; it's mostly some stragglers left. I was glad when you called. So Randy's off your case now?"

"He's eased up. But work's different. It's just a job now. You know what I mean?"

"Sure. The honeymoon's over." Megan glanced at Lil to see if her comment was a jab at Fletch, but it didn't appear to be. Especially when she added, "That's not always a bad thing."

"'There is no remedy for love than to love more.'"

"Huh?"

"Henry David Thoreau. From my great-grandpa's love letters."

"I like that. I guess you could say there's no remedy for work than to work more."

Megan laughed. "You're right about that, too. Tina dropped by the office this week. She acted like we were old friends. It's weird. But at least now I know they're still together. That's a good thing." Megan shrugged. "Did your family tell you Big Darby's having their annual picnic and softball game?"

"Yeah, Mom mentioned it."

"You and Fletch should come. See the old crowd. It'll be fun. Susanna hopes you'll bring something scrumptious."

"Susanna misses me?" Lil glanced over her shoulder. "Before I go, I've been thinking about something. Remember when Fletch and I were dating? We broke up for a few months because he needed time to work things out so he knew what he had to offer me."

"I remember. It was a hard time for you."

"Maybe that's what's going on with Micah. He needs to concentrate on his job now. Some things are worth the waiting. You know, like my veal spinach ravioli."

CHAPTER 32

It rained the night before the Big Darby picnic. By noon the sky remained ominous, but the grassy field at Inez and Leon Beachy's home had dried somewhat. The congregation held the annual softball game and many other church outings at the Beachys' farm.

Years earlier, before the couple's children had left the vicinity, Leon made a ball diamond with softball dimensions. It became a community gathering place. Leon finally gave up trying to fill in the bare spots. Though weedy, it could easily be resurrected for a game just by mowing the sparse grass lower than normal.

Inez, a starkly conservative but take-charge woman, knew how to set up for an event. When Megan arrived, several of the women's black tied shoes had already stomped down the grassy area in and among the folding tables. Megan quickly jumped in to help them with the tablecloths.

Inez twisted her mouth, placed her hands at her hips, and studied the picnic site. A breeze swirled the hem of her skirt and her covering strings. "This will never do." She pointed. "See those small rocks at the base of that tree?" Megan shifted her gaze. Tree roots twisted through an undergrowth of wild ground ivy, but she saw some stones protruding from the tangle. "Those can secure the tablecloths."

Susanna lifted her hawkish nose, which presided over her oval face, and sniffed the humid air. "I'm going to make some quilts to use at these events. They'll be heavy enough that we don't have to use dirty old stones."

"Nonsense! Where do you think our food comes from? The ground." Inez huffed. "Anyway, they'd get ruined."

"It wouldn't be any different than using white tablecloths." Susanna lifted the hem of the closest cloth. "You know these have seen their better days. We'd only need four or five at the most."

Inez swiped her hand through the air. "I suppose it might work."

Megan left the bickering women and washed the stones at a nearby water faucet, making sure to put one at the ends of each table.

A huge cloud rolled in over the farm, cooling and darkening the air. Susanna shook her auburn head. "This is going to be a disaster."

"Maybe so, but the food's arriving. You head up the dessert table," Inez instructed the widow. "I'll arrange the main table, and Rose can handle the drinks."

Megan eyed the dessert table regrettably, but followed Rose to the drink table, knowing that when Lil arrived, she'd pitch in and help there. Wooden sawhorses with planks supported crocks of lemonade and iced tea. Coolers were stuffed beneath the tables and emptied of their contents. Side dishes and cold salad arrived in heirloom dishes to fill Inez's tables. Crowd-sized roasters contained sliced or shredded meats. Susanna hovered over the desserts of fluted, flaky pie crusts baked to perfection.

Lil arrived carrying homemade bread, and Susanna intercepted Fletch.

"What do you have there, young man?"

"Lil's veal spinach ravioli."

The widow lifted the foil and eyed it greedily. Then she pointed. "Take it to Inez. Over there."

When Fletch returned, he said, "Hon, I think it cut the mustard. I'm going after our lawn chairs."

Megan looked away from the tender exchange and watched guests vying for places to set up their folding chairs. Her gaze took in the bright old quilts strewn across the ground and the sports equipment propped up against rough-barked tree trunks. But the person she'd been longing for was still missing. She scanned the cars that lined the dirt driveway, some all the way out to the weed-fringed, faded barn. The rickety structure still held some old farm antiques, but was mostly used for Leon's paint business. And then she saw it. Micah's Honda.

Quickly scanning the yard again, Megan spotted him with a small cluster of men from the search committee. They were all glancing skyward. Megan looked up, too. Though there had been moments of sunlight, the sky was mostly hidden in fast-moving clouds.

Lil nudged her. "What's so interesting?"

"Nothing."

Lil quirked the corner of her mouth. "Right. Hey, there's Katy. Let's go over."

Megan followed Lil, and they dropped to the quilt where Katy had laid Jacob. "Where's Jake?"

"Tossing a ball with Ray Eversole. They're taking this game way too seriously to suit me."

"Really?"

Katy's sulky lips thinned. "The men were not happy to be mixed up."

Although Micah had gone to everybody but Megan for advice, even after the picnic was her idea, she still came to his defense. "He didn't know about the tradition. That they already had teams."

"I know. But they don't like change."

"Nobody does. But it doesn't matter who the next preacher is, there's going to be change. We all knew that."

A loud whistle rent the air. Megan looked to her right, and her heart gave a sad twinge. Oblivious to the undercurrent of complaints, Micah's face was wreathed in enthusiasm. He stood on a stump and waved his hand as the din around them quieted. A few childish squeals broke the silence. Then as parents drew the youngsters, hyped from their first week back at school, to themselves, a reverent hush fell over the group.

Micah prayed, thanking the Lord for Brother Troyer's years of service, dedicating the day to his remembrance, and asking for strength for his widow Barbara. There arose a soft murmur of affirmation. Afterward, he told the group to enjoy their meal and fellowship and, Lord and weather willing, they'd assemble for the game around 1:30 p.m. Megan knew he was rushing it a bit, hoping to beat the storm.

"We'd better get to play," Ray Eversole shouted out, "I hope I haven't conditioned the last couple of weeks for nothing."

Hoots of laughter came from the men. "What kind of conditioning?" Mark Kraybill asked.

"I'm not giving away my secrets," the song leader replied.

"Better just go and fill your plate. You'll need your strength," Mark urged.

Megan got in line next to Joy Ann. "So what do you have planned for the children?"

"We're having some relay races. I bought some pencils and prizes they can use at school."

"That was thoughtful."

"It was Brother Zimmerman's idea to get the prizes. I was happy to do it." She pushed her glasses higher on the bridge of her nose. "Ruthie's helping. And some of the young moms."

Somehow Micah had made his peace with Joy Ann, who now took a plate and turned her attention over to her choices. Megan made sure she got some of Lil's veal spinach ravioli before Susanna cleaned the platter. When they'd lived together in the doddy house, she'd seen firsthand how painstaking the recipe was, with Lil making everything from scratch. She noticed with a bit of glee that her own bean salad was also getting devoured—word must have gotten out that it was Lil's recipe.

Megan took her food to join her friends. Their men assembled nearby, and Elizabeth's little one toddled back and forth between his parents. He took bites and shyly watched the older children who would rather play than eat.

"Jake got rained out early yesterday, and I ended up doing an extra load of laundry last night to get rid of all the wet clothing. That man can make a mess. But after the baby went down, he surprised me with a new Christian novel. We stayed up late reading it, when we really should have been studying for our Sunday school lesson."

"I love hearing Ivan's perspective on the lesson. You can always study tonight," Elizabeth said. "Isn't that what Saturday evenings are for?"

"If nobody has a sick animal emergency," Lil piped up. Then coloring a bit, she quickly added, "I'm not complaining, just saying."

Megan couldn't help but feel left out, getting such vivid imagery of her friends' married home lives. The three young couples seemed settled in like old shoes, yet she could see by the sparkle in their eyes that there was still plenty of romance in their relationships. The honeymoon wasn't over, as Lil had insinuated. Micah ate with the Kraybills, while jostling one of their little ones on his knee. He was good with kids. Megan remembered that he had worked with teenagers back in Pennsylvania. She had no doubt about his reading and Bible study abilities.

Passively listening to the conversation, Megan's plate emptied first. "I'm going for Mandy Penner's blackberry pie before it's all gone." The young woman worked at the well-known Berry Farm on the Mitchell-Dewitt Road.

"Could you bring me a piece of blueberry?" Jake called over.

"Sure." Megan grinned, amused how the men honed in on their conversation when it involved food. She brushed off her skirt and went to the dessert table. Her gaze went over the rows of glass pie pans, searching for the mouth-watering blackberry. A familiar scent tickled her nose. She froze at the sound of a recognizable male voice. She had been unaware that Lori Longacre and Micah were inching together along the opposite side of the table. How had he moved so quickly from the Kraybills?

"Those lemon bars have to be yours," he purred.

Megan lifted her gaze. Not seeming to notice her, Micah placed a lemon bar on his plate, his head bent.

Feeling the heat creep up her neck and scorching her temples, she would have slunk away if she hadn't promised Jake his pie. She quickly got two clean dessert plates and filled hers with the blackberry and then moved to the blueberry tin.

"That's right. I baked some for you when you first arrived. I'm surprised you don't waddle by now."

He had plenty of room on his sharp bones, Megan thought. Even called him Stick Man at Rosedale. Keeping her gaze down, she hurried to get done with the pie and away from the sickening conversation.

"I don't waddle. I do worse things. I. . ."

Megan's pie slipped off the spatula. It plunked onto Inez's starched white tablecloth. "Aye, yi, yi!" She stared at the mess she'd made.

A masculine hand touched her arm. "Let me help. You hold the plate, and I'll serve the pie."

"What a waste." Lori dipped her finger in the glob of blueberry and licked it off with pleasure. "I'll go get something to clean it up before it stains."

"I'll do it," Megan argued. *Tablecloth's seen its better days anyway, according to Susanna.*

"I don't mind."

In resignation, Megan held the plate, trying to keep her hand from shaking. Micah slid a perfect piece onto Jake's plate. "Thanks." She couldn't help but glance up and was even more distressed to see the crinkling around his eyes. Returning his look with one of low toleration, she hurried back to the refuge of her friendly circle.

But Micah followed her and lowered himself next to Jake, balancing his plate of Lori's lemon delights on his knees. "Who's ready to work off their meal?" he asked the men.

Megan turned away, so that her back was to the other quilt. She stared at her pie. Her appetite had vanished. Obviously she wasn't as ready as she had thought to give Micah over to Lori. And even though her eyes couldn't watch the intruder, her heart felt his presence, and she felt naked and vulnerable as if everyone could interpret what was churning inside her.

But Lil was giving Katy tips on pasta sauce. And Elizabeth was chasing the baby, who'd gotten bold enough to finally venture after the older children.

Megan took a forkful of pie, willing herself to taste it. Took a second bite and soon found herself scraping another empty plate. Lori was right. A waste of good food. The image of Lori's slender finger dipping into the blueberries made her set her plate on the grass beside her. She shouldn't resent Lori's quick reaction, coming to her rescue. But everything about the librarian irked her lately.

Behind her, she heard rustling and the general din of men, clad and divided by white and blue shirts, doing their manly maneuvers to prepare for the game.

"Let's move the blankets closer to the game," Lil suggested.

With Megan's dad and Fletch on the same team with Micah, she was able to cheer for the white team without embarrassment. By the second inning, her dad had struck out twice, but Fletch was usually able to get on base. In the fifth, Micah lost a ball in the outfield and scored a home run. The game lagged in time out as several men combed the field of grass and wildflower to recover the ball. The fuss Micah received was more than Megan could bear. She jumped up. "Want some lemonade, Mom?"

"Sure. Thanks, honey."

Megan strode purposefully toward the house to fetch it. The man was good at everything. Sure, there'd be complaints and lots of change, but he'd overcome. She, on the other hand, might not. She placed her cup beneath the crock's spigot.

"Too much excitement for you?"

Megan flinched and pivoted. "Just parched. And you?"

"Actually, I'm good." Lori smiled at Megan.

"How nice."

"But I might as well get some iced tea while I'm here." Lori filled her cup, swirled it, then gazed at her with sympathy. "I don't need a man to make me happy."

Megan narrowed her eyes and set her cup on the table. "What's that supposed to mean?"

"Don't be blind, Megan. Micah's all yours. But respect God's timing. Micah has more important things on his mind these days."

Even though Lori was her senior, the unbidden advice hit Megan as condescending. "Oh, yeah? You two seem chummy."

"Really?" Lori's mouth twisted in disgusted sarcasm. "That's just the sort of rumor that could ruin Micah."

"No kidding."

Lori's anger vanished as quickly as it had been stirred. "It's true we share a friendship, but there's nothing romantic going on between us. If it appears that way, then I'll be more careful."

Megan blinked back unwanted tears. "I'm sorry. It's none of my business. You've done nothing wrong. I don't want to hurt Micah."

The librarian's touch gentled Megan further. "Really, my life is complete without a husband. I'm not desperate for a man." Lori lifted her chin. "I've had offers."

"I didn't mean it that way."

Lori's hand fell away wistfully. "If I married, I'd have to give up the things I enjoy. My freedom. My books. I'm one of those people the apostle Paul talked about. Sometimes the single life is best."

Megan bit her bottom lip, taking in the other woman's sincerity. "Thanks for sharing that. Maybe I should consider a single life."

Lori smiled. "Or maybe you should be more patient toward the right man. Micah's been preaching on patience, hasn't he? I hope he gets the position. We need young thinking. I'm using all my resources to help him."

Lori had always been progressive in her thinking. Some of her family had moved to churches like the one Lil attended. Her candid honesty warranted Megan's respect. She was ashamed over her jealousy. *"There is no remedy for love than to love more."* "You've given me a lot to think about."

"Looks like the game's starting again."

Lori's perfume lingered after she'd left. With a sigh, Megan filled her cups and trudged back to the sidelines.

"I thought you'd gotten lost," Mom chided.

Shifting the attention away from herself, Megan pointed. "Look, Dad's up next."

When her mom turned her interest back to the game, Megan quietly pondered the unusual conversation with Lori, wondering if in time Micah could forgive her for chasing after Chance. Could he let go and allow himself to fall in love with her? But then Lori didn't know about all that. Or did she?

"Look!" Mom pointed upward.

Almost instantly, the sky cast a dark shadow over them. Even the ball players fidgeted as the stormy wind caught several loose lawn chairs. Inez jumped, grabbed her skirt, and ran toward the tables.

Micah raised his hand. "We better quit now. The women could use our help."

"But it's mid-inning. It's not fair!"

Some of the men ran in from the field and huddled around Micah. Megan saw some gesturing and a glove slammed down to the ground. Although she couldn't hear the hot debate, she saw Micah plant his feet and shake his head in that obstinate way of his. Soon after that, the players formed a line and shook hands.

Fletch walked over to Lil. "They're calling it a tie."

"But the white team's a run ahead," Lil argued.

"Yeah, but it's mid-inning. It's only fair."

Megan hoped that was the general consent, but she didn't wait to find out. She went to help with the food. The wind whipped the tablecloths at every unsecured edge. Megan spit hair from the corner of her mouth and tried to tuck it behind her ear and secure her covering, but the effort seemed useless. Inez rushed bundled tablecloths to the house, and Megan went to help Katy and Jake get the baby and all their belongings to the car.

She was amazed at how quickly everything cleaned up and everybody dispersed. Hastening her gait to a near jog, she started toward her own car, giving a few final waves. She'd parked on the far side of the lane, and before she'd made it the barn, the real downpour began. It drenched her and made it hard to see more than a few feet ahead.

"Megan!"

CHAPTER 33

Micah lunged for Megan's hand and drew her into the shelter beneath the barn's overhang. "It's dry here."

"Whew! I guess I was too slow."

"I saw you helping back there." He leaned his back against the rough barn wall. "Let's just wait it out a little. Maybe it'll let up in a minute."

With a shiver, she backed up against the damp wall next to him. Overhead, water dumped on the barn roof and ran off the eaves. Her hand fluttered around her face, tucked a wet strand behind her ear. "I'm already soaked."

"I know. But you might get run over out there." Thunder rumbled above the roar of water. "Or hit by lightning."

"I can't even see the driveway."

All he could see was the woman next to him. Dripping as if she'd just taken a swim, Megan was totally fetching. She silently watched the rain, her damp bodice still heaving from the run. Sudden blasts of pinpricks occasionally peppered them, but mostly they were sheltered. In fact, too secluded for his raging testosterone. Water cascaded off the roof, creating a wall between them and the elements, a paradise for the two of them—Tarzan and Jane and their own private waterfall. He tried to focus on something other than Megan and his junior-high novel reading list, turning to the obvious. "Looks like Leon needs to fix his rain spouting."

She grinned. "You offering?"

"I should. He's on the search committee."

Her smile widened, revealing fine even teeth. "Is there anything you can't do? Or won't do?"

"Yes. There is."

She lowered her gaze as if reading his mind. Lori had warned him that Megan was jealous earlier. After that, he'd hardly been able to concentrate on the game. He supposed it was foolish to hope that Megan could grow to care for him as more than friends. Ever since he'd pushed her away, for his own sake, he'd missed her. As their silence prevailed, rivulets of water transformed the ground around their feet.

"You're a home-run hitter," she said softly. "Next thing to a hero."

"Hardly. Most of the men don't like the way I handled things. And I even dented Professor Maust's car. I'm thankful it wasn't your dad's."

"You did? I must have missed that when I went to get lemonade. Wasn't he the one who gave the search committee your name?"

"Yeah. So I wonder what he needs fixing around his house?"

Megan laughed softly, tucked her hair behind her ear again. "I don't think it's going to let up, Micah. Maybe we should make a run for it."

"Not yet." He reached for her hand. "I've missed you."

She gave a soft gasp. "Remember what you said? About playing with fire?"

His own words boomeranged, hitting him as sharply as they must have struck her, earlier. He regretted them, but they reminded him of his good intentions. He dropped her hand, and his voice came out harsher than he intended. "You're right. Give me your keys. I'll bring your car around for you."

"You don't have to do that. I'm already soaked."

He reached out and touched her shoulder. "Please, Meg. I want to."

She nodded and silently riffled through her purse. Keeping her lips grim, she thrust them at him. "Here."

"I'll be right back."

"Brother Zimmerman? Would you get my car, too, while you're at it?"

Micah froze. Watched in horror as Susanna inched her body carefully around the corner of the barn then blinked her eyelashes at him. Her unwelcome appearance brought him back to that day in the church with Joy Ann Beitzel. And it was obvious by the cunning look in the widow's gaze that she'd heard every word that had just transpired between him and Megan.

⁓

Megan watched Micah turn pale and angry, but he left them without uttering a word. The moment he was gone, Susanna looked down her dripping beak. "Cozy under here, isn't it?"

Feeling like a rodent stalked by a capable hunter, Megan squirmed under Susanna's brown gaze that held the same fiery highlights as her hair. "It's not what it sounds like."

"Sounds like a lot of first names flying around." The thin lips pressed together in accusation.

"We knew each other at Rosedale College. It's hard to break old habits. We're just friends." Megan inwardly cringed at the partial lie. "As you probably heard us talking, Brother Zimmerman pointed out to me a few weeks ago that even though we're friends, we need to be careful around the house not to tarnish his. . .our reputations." Megan bit her lip, regretfully setting up some imagery for the widow's sharp mind.

"Or his chance for the position he's after? I didn't just fall out of the nest, young lady. I was married. I know exactly what playing with fire involves."

The rapturous widow circled, fearsome with her extended claws. Megan squeezed her eyes closed, trying to think of something that would keep her from shredding Micah to pieces. "But you didn't hear our earlier conversation. Brother Zimmerman merely pointed out to me that because I was naive, I was too trusting of men. That even though I could trust *him*, I shouldn't. That I needed to show more discretion."

"Such as not kissing under the barn eaves?"

Megan gasped. "Kissing? Susanna. We never!"

"Then why is your hair all messed up?"

"Because it rained. And yours is messed up, too!" Only the widow's ruffled appearance made her all the more frightful. Megan heard the approach of her Nova's rumble.

"At least he had the sense to bring your car around first."

Megan bit her tongue. She'd already fueled the woman's cruel imagination and ruffled her feathers. She would've been better off to just keep quiet like Micah. "I'm sorry if I was rude, just now. I don't want to cause any trouble for Brother Zimmerman."

"That's obvious, dear. You had to remind *him* not to play with fire?" She patted Megan's arm. "I commend you for that. He needs to be stopped before he ruins someone else. First poor Joy Ann Beitzel. And now you. Who will be next?"

Micah suddenly appeared, and Megan clamped her mouth closed. Looking distraught in his wet clothes and with water streaming off his hair and down his face, he urged, "Hurry."

"Thanks." Megan gave him an apologetic look then made a dash to her car. She slammed the door, all thoughts of the weather gone. Her windshield wipers were already swishing, so she put the car into DRIVE and prayed for Micah and what he had yet to endure.

⸺⸙⸺

His career at risk from Susanna's barbed threats, Micah changed into dry clothing and grabbed his umbrella. The downpour continued as he sprinted across the Weavers' yard to the main house. When he stepped into the kitchen's warmth, Anita turned in surprise.

"Micah! Come in. I just put on a pot of coffee."

Closing the umbrella and propping it against the door, he went to join Bill at the table.

"Too bad about the rain. We woulda beat them," Bill said. "But I suppose the tie warded off bad feelings. Probably the best thing, in the end."

Although the men's competitive fervor was an earlier concern, now Micah's worries had shifted. "Yeah, you're right about that. Is Megan here?"

Bill's voice filled with suspicion. "Yeah. She's upstairs changing. Why?"

"I need to talk to you."

Anita brought both men steaming mugs of coffee. "That's the same thing Megan just said."

"Does this involve her?" Bill probed, his expression starting to resemble the thunderclouds.

"Yes."

"Well, what happened?"

"It's probably best to wait for her to join us."

Bill glanced at his wife. "Why don't you go check on her."

Mrs. Weaver wiped her hands on a striped linen dish towel and scurried from the room.

Meanwhile, Micah didn't feel like making idle conversation so he took some fortifying sips of the dark, strong brew. After weeks of sitting as a guest at their table, one of the refrigerator magnets that Anita collected from her garage sales had driven home its message taken from Walt Whitman: "Either define the moment, or the moment will define you." Regardless, when Anita quickly returned with Megan, he hardly knew where to begin. "There's been an incident."

Bill shot a gaze at Megan, whose wet hair had been slickly brushed back into semblance.

"Back at the picnic during the confusion of the storm, I found shelter under the barn's overhang. I'd only been there a few moments when I saw Megan running for her car. I called out for her to wait it out with me."

"I could hardly see the road in front of me," Megan interjected, fiddling with the sleeve of a soft gray sweater. "It was lightning, too."

Anita plopped another cup of coffee on the table and pushed it toward her daughter.

Micah continued. "We were only under there for a few minutes. We didn't know it at the time, but Susanna Schlagel was also taking refuge there, just around the corner of the barn. We found out later that she overheard our entire conversation."

Bill's hand moved away from his cup and swiped through his wet hair. "What exactly did she overhear?"

Micah met Megan's gaze. "I think we need to tell them everything."

Her voice held resignation. "I was going to anyway."

Bill's jaw clenched. If there was a refrigerator magnet to describe the emotions on Bill's face, it would have read. "Nobody messes with my daughter."

"What's going on?"

Anita's hand went out to stay her husband. "Now, Bill. Micah's trying to explain. I'm sure it's not what you're thinking."

He shrugged away from her touch. "How do you know what I'm thinking?"

She tilted one eyebrow reproachfully. "After all these years? Believe me, I know what you're thinking."

"Please," Megan interrupted. "It's not."

"What is it then?" Bill's eyes snapped angrily.

"When I first came to Plain City, Megan was one of the few people I knew. We quickly became friends. Remember how she saved my life with her EpiPen? Sometimes I need someone to talk to, and we hang out."

"Hang out?" Bill's voice was harshly judgmental.

"We talk on the porch swing."

"Micah is always full of good advice," Megan explained. "I talk to him about work."

Bill's nostrils flared. "Sneaking around right under our noses, taking advantage of our hospitality."

"We did give Micah the run of the house," Anita reminded.

Bill shot his wife a withering look.

"But a few weeks ago, I was convicted about it. I warned Megan not to be so trusting around men." Micah sighed and plunged into what might be his defining moment. "I told her our behavior was ultimately playing with fire. So we quit meeting like that."

"That's why you don't come in to supper anymore?" Anita shifted her gaze from Micah to Megan. "And why you've been moping?"

"Mother! You know I've just been extra busy at work."

"So what exactly did Susanna hear?" Bill's voice was somewhat calmer but filled with dread.

Micah exchanged a glance with Megan, and she gave an encouraging shrug. "Like I said, we were just there at the barn a few minutes. Megan wanted to make a run for it, but I asked her to wait. Told her I'd missed her. She reminded me of my own words, how we shouldn't be playing with fire. I knew she was right. So I offered to go get her car for her."

Megan jumped into the story. "Then Susanna came around the corner of the barn and asked Micah to get her car, too. We knew she'd heard everything. When Micah went after my car, Susanna accused us of kissing." Her face reddened. "Which we didn't, of course. I probably said all the wrong things to her, but she's coercive. The last thing she said was that she didn't blame me. That it was Micah's fault, and she hoped he didn't ruin any other girls. I'm sorry, Micah."

Bill slammed his fist on the table. "I trusted you, young man. And now you've embroiled my daughter in one of your escapades."

Even Anita looked at him with disappointment.

"Susanna's trying to stir up trouble," Megan said. "Can't you see that?"

"Of course I do. But if Micah's foolish enough to play with fire. With my daughter. Under my own roof. Then maybe he deserves to get burned!"

"Dad."

"No, he's right," Micah replied, then shifted his gaze from Megan to Bill. "There'll be trouble. I wanted you to hear it from me first."

Bill folded his hands on the table. "What are your feelings for my daughter?"

Micah met Bill's unflinching gaze. "I admire her. And I respect her. I'm not blind. Megan's an attractive woman, and I've felt fortunate to become friends with her."

"If you respected her, you wouldn't have gotten her involved in this."

"But he was doing the right thing by me," Megan argued. "He was protecting me. Giving me good advice about Chance, too."

"At the barn when you were ready to go, he asked you to wait. Was that the right thing? Tell me. Do you love him?"

"Dad. Don't do this."

"Are you willing to let Susanna smirch your reputation? If you two are falling in love, then the logical step would be an engagement."

<hr />

Megan had never seen her easygoing dad so obstinate. "People don't believe everything Susanna says. And if you ask me, the elders need to talk to her about her gossiping."

Brushing that aside, Dad said, "First, I need to know Micah's intentions."

Humiliated that Dad was backing Micah into a corner, Megan jumped up and gripped the edge of the table. "But I'm not ready to get married."

"Engaged," Dad corrected.

"And it's the farthest thing from Micah's mind, too."

"So you've talked about it?"

"Sir," Micah interrupted. "I'm not sure that friendship and attraction are the basis for a good marriage. As you know, my heart's set on preaching and ministry. I need to marry the right woman for all the right reasons." He turned his gaze to Megan. "As much as I like you, I'd rather get voted out than do something we'd both regret."

"Yes, you can leave Plain City. But Megan has to stay and weather this through. This may ruin her chances to marry a good man."

Megan lifted her chin. "Maybe I don't even want to get married. A woman doesn't have to get married to be happy. Today at the picnic, Lori Longacre and I were talking about that very thing."

"Nonsense!"

Megan restrained herself from arguing further.

"You were right about one thing, Micah. You were both playing with fire. I'll call the other elders tonight. See what we can do."

Megan mumbled, "Thanks." She gave Micah an embarrassed glance then went to her room. Fighting back anger toward Susanna, she moved to the window and drew back the curtains. The rain enveloped her in a wall of sound. How long ago it seemed since that Christmas season when she stood at this window with Katy and Lil. They'd watched the snow with high hopes of moving into the doddy house. So much water under the bridge since then. Now both her friends were married. And she was floundering, making a mess of her life.

Micah couldn't have made it any plainer. He'd reinforced what she'd already known. He was attracted to her, but he would marry the right woman for all the right reasons. He would stick to his convictions. And she'd become an old maid like Lori, that is if Micah didn't marry Lori. Megan had been nothing but a jinx on Micah, creating problems for him. She placed her forehead against the window pane, remembering the John Dryden quotation in her great-grandparents' latest love letter: "Love is not in our choice, but in our fate." She was fated to misery.

CHAPTER 34

The next morning, Megan would have preferred to skip church. But on the other hand, she didn't want to mope at home while Susanna spread gossip. Mom encouraged her to face the situation and get it behind her as quickly as possible, so Megan made the choice to go. But poor Micah had no choice. He had to face the congregation.

Megan slid into a pew as inconspicuously as possible. Mom followed her, leaving a space at the end of the pew for Dad to join them later. Megan opened her church bulletin and noticed the topic was faith then scanned through the announcements until the opening hymn.

After the singing, Micah stepped to the front of the congregation. He took a sip of water and cleared his throat. "I apologize for my voice. I've caught a bit of a cold." Megan conjured up the image of him bringing around not only her car, but also Susanna's, and then running after his own. "Today's topic is faith." Micah raised the Bible in his left hand and recited from memory. "Hebrews ten, verse thirty-eight says, 'Now the just shall live by faith: but if any man draw back, my soul shall have no pleasure in him.'"

He coughed and took another sip of water. "Fruit is an agricultural term. The Christian life is not based on the fruit we bear but on the Lord who gives the vine its fruit. When we walk in His Spirit, He produces fruit in us. He gives us the measure of faith we need for our circumstances, as we need it. Some may only need a cherry, and somebody else might need a watermelon."

The congregation chuckled, and Megan figured she definitely needed a watermelon.

"This varies from day to day. I lean on faith, same as you. I trust God for my future. You trust God for the future of this congregation. The day is coming when you must decide if I will be your permanent pastor. If we follow God, we can trust Him for our best. Remember faith is unseen, but not unfelt." He paused and looked over the congregation. His gaze rested briefly on Susanna, included Megan, then moved away.

He ended his sermon with an admonition. "In Acts, the church gathered together to talk about God. The early church gave us an example of what we should be doing. When we leave the auditorium, we should be sharing how God answers prayers, reminding each other of the glories of God, building each other up in the faith, and not tearing each other down."

"A good reminder," Megan whispered to her mom.

"Yes." Mom stood. "Your dad's got a five-minute meeting with the elders. I'm going to go invite Barbara for lunch."

Megan watched Mom leave and made her own way to the center aisle, catching up to Katy. Everyone was talking about how the storm had brought their church outing to a screeching halt. When they stepped outside, Katy whispered, "I have something for you."

They stepped aside so others could pass, and Katy dug in her diaper bag and then handed Megan an envelope. "Micah asked me to give this to you. What's it about?"

"I don't know." She drew Katy off to the side and briefed her about Susanna.

"Oh no. I'll pray for you. But I wonder if it has anything to do with the envelope? Are you going to open it?"

"Not here."

"I understand." Jake waved, and Katy frowned sympathetically. "Stop by the house or call if you need to talk."

"Thanks. I'll keep in touch."

Inside her car, Megan tore open the seal with shaky fingers, removing a note card of the masculine persuasion:

Megan,
"When it is dark enough, you can see the stars"
—Ralph Waldo Emerson.

Micah

Her lips formed a sad smile.

—⸎—

After the Weavers' Sunday noon meal was finished, Dad offered to help Mom with the dishes, so Megan took Barbara outside to the porch swing.

"I always wanted one of these. Guess it's one of those things we never got around to. I've driven by a few times and seen Micah here studying. Usually, he's so caught up in what he's doing, he doesn't return my wave. It's been nice working with him at the church. Reminds me of when Eli and I first started out. There wasn't any church secretary, and I helped him a lot."

Megan's legs fell into rhythm with the older woman's. "I'm glad that's working out for you."

"Your mom's a good cook. Micah has it good here. After he leaves, you think your parents would consider taking on a permanent resident?"

"Why, I'm not sure. It all happened pretty spur of the moment. They seem open about it."

Barbara's shoes scuffed the floorboards as her blue gaze traversed the Weavers' yard. "I love my home, but someday it's going to be too much for me to take care of."

"I've heard Dad talk. The men don't mind helping out at the parsonage."

"Oh, I know. But it seems impractical, don't you think? I'm sure they don't want to boot me out, but I sure don't want them to think they have to wait around for me to die."

Shocked, Megan shook her head. "Nobody's thinking about that. Everyone loves you. You've served the congregation in many ways. For a long time, too."

"Exactly, I'm no spring chicken."

The swing creaked, filling in a gap of silence, and gradually Megan understood. "You want to move into our cottage?"

"I'd do my part. I'm no slacker."

"That's the least of anyone's worries. Do you want me to talk to Mom and Dad?"

"Not yet. After the church votes in Brother Zimmerman, then I'll talk to your dad."

"So you're asking me to keep a secret?"

"You might as well get used to it if you're going to be a preacher's wife." Before Megan could object, the older woman asked, "You think Anita's bringing our dessert out here, or do we need to go back inside?"

Megan jumped up. "You stay here. I'll go see."

But the moment Megan was inside, she paused to compose herself. Preacher's wife? Was Barbara actually prophetic? She'd seemed so sure that Micah would be voted in. By the abrupt manner in which Barbara changed the subject, the topic was closed. Perhaps the old woman was more brilliant than senile.

⁘

Relieved that he wasn't the first to arrive at Susanna's two-story, gray-sided residence nestled beneath large evergreens, Micah harbored mixed feelings about the meeting. The elders were bringing the barn incident out into the open, and they wanted both Micah and Susanna present.

He needed to be there to stand up for himself. But his honesty was apt to provide more fodder for Susanna's voracious appetite. At the least, it would aid her justification. He'd already reckoned with the fact that he deserved whatever might come, but he also knew that God was merciful and forgiving, even if Bill Weaver wasn't. There was no turning back. The incident needed to get resolved. Especially if by some miracle of God's grace he ended up being Susanna and Bill's preacher. Megan's.

The air smelled of damp soil, stringent from the recent storm. He couldn't help but notice that Susanna's yard needed lots of work. The storm had broken some tree limbs, and the flower beds were weedy and rampant with decaying litter. The porch, however, was freshly swept.

Susanna answered the door and curtly invited him in. He wasn't late, but he was the last to arrive. He took his place at the end of one sofa beside the professor, who gave him a brief pat on the arm. On the other side of him was a round end table, shined to perfection so that he could almost see his own trepidation. A glass lamp and a Bible were the only items on top. A mean thought struck him—that Susanna would profit from reading the holy book.

She came to hover over him. "Would you like some tea? Or are you a coffee sort?"

A quick glance told him that the others had already taken her up on refreshments. "Coffee, if it's no trouble."

She speared him with a look that assured him, he was extremely troublesome. But she went into the kitchen and returned shortly with his beverage. She placed a tray of snickerdoodles on the coffee table. "Please help yourselves. I miss cooking for Charles, you know."

"How long have you been a widow?" Micah asked curiously. She was young for a widow, couldn't be any more than in her early forties and still carried a trim figure. In spite of the earlier incidents with her, he hadn't heard her story.

She went to the fireplace mantel and returned with a framed photo, which she handed Micah. "Two years now."

"He was a handsome man. I'm sorry for your loss."

She nodded, took the photo, and placed it back on the mantel. Then she turned and placed her hands on her dark skirt. "I have a hunch what this is all about."

"I'd feel more comfortable if you sat," Micah said, not liking the way she presided over the room.

She snapped her gaze in his direction. "I'm not really concerned about your comfort, young man."

Bill leaned forward. "That's hardly the way to speak to one of God's anointed. Actually, we're all your church leaders. And we'd all feel better if ya relaxed and took a seat, Susanna."

She transposed from gracious host to a red-tailed hawk ready to strike at its nearest victim. Eyes glittering, she perched on an antique side chair near the hearth, keeping herself separated from the men. "Perhaps you should have brought your wives along. I feel like a cornered rabbit."

It was all Micah could do not to roll his eyes at her dramatization. It was more like she was the bird of prey and they were all the rabbits.

Bill replied, "We could have done that, but we felt this was a personal matter that didn't need to go any further than the people in this room."

"Hmmph. There's one woman already missing who was involved. And are you telling me that your Anita doesn't know about Micah's behavior?"

"Let's pray before this discussion goes any further," Bill said.

Thankful, Micah bowed his head.

Afterward, Bill returned to the previous conversation. "It's true that Micah and Megan came to me after the picnic and told me and Anita what had happened. Perhaps we should start with your perception of what you saw and heard that was so troubling."

Susanna repeated the conversation she'd heard and gave her perception of how loose Micah was around the single women, bringing into it the earlier incident with Joy Ann Beitzel.

"What you claim to have heard validates Micah and Megan's story. As an elder board, we urge you to consider the fact that Megan and Micah knew each other from Rosedale. Because he's staying in our guest cottage, they've spent time together in our home. After the incident, I asked them if they've any intentions of marriage. Neither of them has thoughts along those lines. All they've done is have some private conversations. Even then, either Anita or I was at home. They haven't done anything wrong."

"Micah specifically said they were playing with fire."

"Which is pretty smart for a man his age," the professor interjected.

Micah flinched and quickly whipped a handkerchief from his pocket and sneezed into it.

The professor restated, "We all think Micah's mature beyond his age."

"Well, you're allowed your opinions," she said.

"And it is the consensus of the elders that you need to look inward and examine the source and motives of your opinions."

"Well, I never! Brother Troyer would never have acted like this. This church is going to pot."

"With your husband now gone, we're here to encourage you in your walk."

"I'm sorry for the misunderstanding." Micah was almost embarrassed over the staunch support the elders gave him. He supposed his set down was coming later.

Susanna gave Micah a cold look. "Noah is right. You're young. Maybe this has taught you a lesson."

"You're right," Micah said, pretty sure it hadn't taught her anything edifying.

"The snickerdoodles are tasty," Bill said, bringing the meeting to a close. "One of my favorites."

"Yes, we all have our favorites." Susanna rested a calculating gaze on Micah.

Outside Susanna's house, Bill followed Micah to his car. "Guess we didn't have to drive separate."

Micah wasn't positive Bill was ready to make jokes about the situation, but he couldn't resist. "Wouldn't want you to show any favoritism."

Bill smiled. "Look. I'm sorry I jumped down your throat last night. You caught me off guard. And Megan's our only daughter."

"I expected and deserved everything you said."

"Anita and I were talking about it afterward. Sometimes women have better insight into these kinds of things. We see what's going on between you and Megan. The undercurrents. We think it would be a healthy thing, if you'd take meals with us again."

"Undercurrents?"

"Don't get the wrong idea. We're not trying to matchmake. We're not pushing Megan off on you. I'm talking about your friendship. We all miss you." Bill shrugged. "Anita suggested it. She's usually right."

"Tell Anita I'll be in for supper tonight."

"Good."

Micah got in his car. While he was sitting in Susanna's living room, the Lord had whispered in his heart what he needed to do regarding the widow. He wasn't looking forward to it, but he was going to be obedient.

After that, when Bill had walked him to the car, he'd been expecting another set down. Bill's change of attitude was a mystery. Was it godly forgiveness or was it because of those undercurrents he'd mentioned? He said he wasn't matchmaking, but it seemed like that to Micah.

He remembered Megan admitting that she'd talked to Lori. It had almost sounded like the two had conspired against him, with their anti-marriage sentiments. But maybe that had all been a bluff. Because Megan was warming.

He started his engine, never having imagined an hour earlier that he would leave the widow Schlagel's house with a grin on his face and a dinner invitation. Indeed, God was merciful.

⁂

As Megan set the table, her mom said, "Be sure to set a place for Micah."

"I doubt he'll come in tonight."

"Your dad invited him, and he accepted."

Megan swung around as her mom took a berry cobbler out of the oven. "Why would he?" Then she shrugged, answering her own question. "I suppose we all need to make amends."

Mom kept her gaze lowered. "Something like that."

Moving to the cupboard above her mom's slow-cooker chicken and dumplings, Megan got the extra plate. She'd just placed it on the table when her dad came in from the shop with Micah. Amazingly, the two men bantered as if Saturday had never happened.

Micah took a chair then sneezed into his handkerchief.

"Sorry about your cold," Mom empathized. "You taking anything for it?"

He shook his head, stuffing it back into his pocket. "I think it's allergies. And just when things had settled down for me."

"Oh, probably the start of fall allergies," Mom said. "Your resistance is probably low. Maybe from the storm?"

Micah looked at Megan. "You don't have any symptoms?"

"Not yet."

Micah frowned at her as if she was letting him down. Her lack of the sniffles had probably been his basis for assuming it was a virus.

"Medicine makes me drowsy."

"Work makes me drowsy," Megan quipped back, but when she saw everyone's gaze rest on her questioningly, she quickly added, "But it's getting better, now that Randy's back." The incident had left its mark, making her feel as though she were walking on eggshells, afraid to say the wrong things. But when Micah didn't react negatively, she relaxed. Maybe everyone had gotten past Saturday's argument after all.

Mom speared Dad with her gaze. "Can't the newspaper wait till after supper?"

"Oh sure." He folded it up and handed it to Megan with a sheepish grin. "I'm tired, too."

Megan took the newspaper to his favorite chair in the living room, and when she returned, everyone was waiting.

After Dad's prayer, they passed the food. "Good sermon," he said.

"I didn't get it," Megan differed. "Is faith something we have to do? Or something God gives us?"

"Both," Micah said. "You inhale to breathe, but air is a gift from God."

"How do allergies fit into your analogy?"

"Or exercising?" Mom arched an eyebrow.

Micah grinned. "They're darts from the enemy."

"Amen!" Megan said, grinning back.

Across the table, Mom smiled, too.

Dad shrugged. "What? When dinner's so good, who's got time to breathe?"

CHAPTER 35

Micah drove into Plain City, down Madison Street, to a small house in the heart of the village and parked on the street. He made his way up the rippled sidewalk and climbed three stairs to the exterior stoop. Then he rang the doorbell. He waited, staring at the floor and noticing it was in bad need of paint. When he didn't hear any stirring, he rang again. This time, the door opened.

"Micah. What a surprise. Come in."

"I've been meaning to stop in, sir."

"Glad you did."

Micah followed his professor into the adjoining room that looked more like a library than a living room. One corner of the room held bookcases. Beneath a window was a massive desk. But Noah Maust took Micah to a set of masculine armchairs.

"A wonderful room," Micah observed.

"Yes. For years I studied back in one of the bedrooms. Then one day, I decided to make myself comfortable. Most of my visitors feel more comfortable in this atmosphere, anyway."

"Yes, sir. I could certainly make myself comfortable here."

"It's time to dispense with the titles. If anything, I should defer to you now."

"That doesn't seem right. How about first names?"

"Done. So what brings you here, Micah? Making your rounds?"

"No. I came to find out how much I owe you to fix your car."

Noah brushed his hand through the air. "No need. I'm more concerned about function. Your ball didn't destroy that."

"You don't intend to take it in for body work then?"

"For one little dent? Don't be ridiculous. I'm just glad to have the ballgame behind us. Never relished playing."

"But you did fine. You got on base several times."

"It's not something I enjoy, but I do my part."

"It's tougher than I imagined trying to fill Brother Troyer's shoes."

"Nonsense. Lori Longacre says we need young blood. And all that bluster with the widow will soon blow over."

Micah studied the professor thoughtfully. "You and Lori talk?"

Noah laughed. "Women love talking better than anything."

"I'm discovering that. Talking and crying."

The professor laughed. "Lori's the studious type, and we have a lot in common. We're actually kind of in cahoots, trying to put in a good word for you whenever we can."

"You two are friends," Micah repeated. "So you think men and women can just be friends? I'm finding bachelorhood is getting me in trouble."

"Even though I never married, I enjoy several female friendships."

"If you had to do it over, would you stay single?"

"Good question. It's lonely. But my job at Rosedale places me around people all day long. So home is my retreat. I like it. I'm used to it. I know what Bill said at the meeting, but is it really over between you and Megan?"

Micah felt Noah's probing gaze. "I can't believe I'm so transparent."

"Something tells me you didn't come here to talk about my car. I'm sure it's lonely for you in your position. I make a pretty good sounding board."

Micah met the professor's gaze and decided he was good as his word. "I could use a mentor. I talk to Bill, but not about Megan. I can't get her out of my mind."

"How does she feel?"

"Even though she despised me in college, we've become close. When

I first came, she was in love with her boss. She came to me for advice. She gave him up because he wasn't a Mennonite. She cried on my shoulder. Actually, she does that a lot." Micah decided to omit the information about the night in the root cellar.

"So you don't know if she's over him?"

"She's over him. But I don't know if she could ever think of me as more than a friend."

"That's complicated. I understand your thinking. You're a perfectionist. And now your idea of the perfect woman conflicts with reality, especially because you weren't Megan's one and only."

"I hadn't admitted that to myself. Of course, I live by grace and extend grace to others. But maybe you're right. Maybe it bothers me more than I thought."

"On the other hand, you love her. Marriage would make your job easier, and from what I hear, there's not a perfect relationship out there."

Micah gave the professor a half grin, wondering what a bachelor like Noah really knew about love or marriage. "Is that why you never married?"

Noah's gaze drifted up to his left toward the window. "I proposed once. A long time ago. Obviously she refused. But I didn't regret it because it freed me to get over her. And if you're going to live in Plain City, you either have to marry her or get over her like I did and move on."

"You're right. But I don't want to rush her."

"Again, the perfectionism. Waiting for the perfect time. But from what I hear, you can't rush a woman, anyway." The professor gestured toward the adjoining hall. "Can I get you something to drink? I'm a pretty good cook, too."

Micah rose. "Next time. Thanks for listening. Now, what would be a good day for me to show up with my paintbrush?"

"Excuse me?"

"I'm painting your porch floor."

Amusement crinkled the corners of Noah's eyes. He studied Micah almost long enough to make him squirm. Then he finally replied, "Any weekday, now that college is back in swing. Just be sure it's dry before I get home. And make sure it matches the siding. Oh, and whatever you do, don't show up with any of Leon's leftover blue paint."

Micah laughed. "It's a deal."

"You don't owe me for anything, except taking so long to get over here."

"I wish I'd come sooner."

Micah saw himself out, whistling all the way to the car. The professor was right; he should have visited him when he'd first arrived in Plain City. It was his own loss that he hadn't, for an hour with his old mentor had revealed many things.

_____

Megan arrived at work, glanced at the clock, and saw that she was fifteen minutes early. As she waited for her computer to boot and did a few rote tasks, she wondered what it would be like to move into Barbara's parsonage with Micah. Was the woman really prophetic? Or had she made her observations while working alongside Micah? The idea of supporting Micah in his ministry put goose bumps on her arms. She rubbed them, thinking Barbara wasn't the only person pushing her toward the idea.

Lori and Lil saw her and Micah together, but insisted the timing was wrong. If that was true, Megan needed patience. She bit back a smile, thinking that the other night at the table, she should have asked Micah about patience rather than faith. She imagined him catching her hidden meaning and taking great pains with his explanation, even throwing in a love quote or two. No, she'd been reading too many of Great-grandpa's letters. That wasn't real life, not her life anyway.

She didn't even know when she'd fallen in love with Micah, but she had. She loved his sense of humor, his compassion, and his perseverance. She sighed and picked up a small stack of complaints. The one on top was about a bumpy ride. How could bad weather be the fault of Char Air? She'd have to make the phone call and apologize, regardless.

Tapping a pencil against her chin, her thoughts returned to Micah. Did he know that her lifelong dream had been to marry a missionary or preacher? Would that information help him understand why she'd fallen for Chance? It reminded her of Abraham taking Sarah's servant woman when he didn't think Sarah would be able to produce the son he was promised. Settling for second best from what God intended all along.

"Megan?" Near her desk, Paige stood with a hand on her tight-skirted hip.

Megan dropped her pencil and snatched up her white ceramic cup. "Yes. I want coffee."

On the way to the snack room, Paige told her what she'd done over the weekend and then asked if Megan had done anything exciting.

"If you call instigating a church incident exciting, then yes."

Inside the coffee room, Paige shut the door. "Come on, girl. Don't leave me hanging."

As Megan told the story, Paige's expressions varied, but mostly she bore a look of frustration. "What?" Megan finally asked.

"I just think sometimes your people make a mountain out of a molehill."

With a sinking disappointment in her inability to explain things fully so that her outsider friend could understand *her people*, Megan turned away to fill her coffee cup.

"But then, I never knew a preacher personally. I guess Micah's even holier than you?"

Megan cringed and faced Paige. "Nobody deserves grace, but I suppose it appears that way." Had she fallen into the trap of believing that lie? That she wasn't good enough for Micah?

"You're a riddle. That's what I love about you." Paige fixed her coffee. "So did you see what's on the bulletin board?"

Megan walked over to a mishmash of photos and business cards, expecting to see something from the recent newsletter or a customer's thank-you note. She followed Paige's red fingernail to a sheet of lined yellow paper. Curious, she stepped closer. The signature at the bottom made her heart do a little trip. *Chance Marshall*? Her gaze scurried to the top of the page:

> *Hi, Char Air friends,*
> *I'm back in Shell, trying to get things in order. I suppose it's been the same with Randy picking up the pieces since I left there. Don't let him downsize the charity flights! I'll hold you accountable if I ever come back to the States.*

I hit the rainy season here, if there's such a thing. Having some downtime now, waiting for the weather to break so I can fly in and pick up a snakebite victim. A child. The missionary family from the compound assures me that God gives life and takes it away. Not to take our losses personally. I try to trust God's timing, but sometimes I just have to go with my instincts. . . .

Megan paused with understanding. How difficult that must be when it was a matter of life and death—someone else's.

Thanks for all your hard work. Remember, you keep Char Air successful, no matter what my brother claims.
    I've no regrets for spending time with you all, but I'm tickled as blue skies to be back in the thick of things here where I belong.

Happy flying,
Chance

"Whatcha think?"

Megan tore her gaze from the letter. "He sounds happy."

"Yeah, but he was thinking about us on his downtime."

"With no regrets."

"What about you, honey? Because if you have them, you can still change your mind. Let your preacher and church members work out their problems while you are knee deep in jungle and love. Why, Randy would probably fly you over there, himself."

Megan grinned. "You noticed it, too? He wants to get rid of me, doesn't he?"

"Nonsense. That's not what I meant."

"I've got my heart set on Micah."

Paige nodded. "Just wanted you to admit it."

Megan was glad for the note's closure. "Don't worry. I'm over Chance. But things are complicated with Micah."

Paige brushed her hand through the air. "He's a man, isn't he?" Then she got her cup and opened the door.

Back at her desk, Megan reflected briefly on Chance's message. It validated her feelings. She was over him but wanted the best for him and his ministry there in Ecuador. And he would be fine.

As she went back to work, peace stole over her, the kind that came with agreeing with God. With it came a whisper of knowledge that shocked her. God had given her the job at Char Air for a reason. She might never understand the reason, but once her purpose was finished, He would open a different door. If she hadn't been so positive that the message came from God, she might not have had the courage to speak so boldly to Randy when he called her into his office.

"You look discouraged," she said.

His gaze flashed up at her with bitterness. "You may be my assistant, but you're not a confidante."

She rested her hand on the corner of his desk. "And I'm a great assistant. Without me, you'd have a bigger mess on your hands right now." She hoped he'd remember that he'd created his own mess and quit disrespecting her.

"So you've been here a year. Now you run the place?"

"You've worked hard to make your company successful. But I do know some things that you don't."

His jaw nearly unhinged. "Like what?"

"Spiritual truths."

He laughed out loud. "Now you sound like Chance. That why you two had a thing?"

"I guess. But we were smart enough to do the right thing."

He leaned back in his chair. "Wish I could say the same. I don't seem to know when to quit."

The pain in his eyes prompted her to say what she'd been thinking for months. "The only thing that will save your marriage is turning to God for help."

"Why would God help me? Because of a few charity flights? I do that for publicity."

That was information she regretted hearing. But Randy was hurt, and she knew people said crazy things under duress. "Because He created you. Did you know God sees right into the hearts of men? He can see into Tina's heart, too. That's why He can help you win her back."

"I don't think she has a heart. Don't try to convert us." He laughed. "I can't see Tina in a bonnet contraption."

Megan felt her face heat. "There are other churches where you can find God."

"Then why didn't you leave yours and go with Chance?"

"Because I like my church." Megan pinched the inner corner of her eye to keep the tears at bay. "Just think about it."

"Oh, don't cry."

She squared her shoulders, trying to oblige him. He softened his voice. "I'm sorry I've been hard on you. You signed on here at a bad time. And Tina's jealousy puts pressure on me."

A thought flew into Megan's mind so swift and hard that it almost knocked her off her feet. She blinked, wanting to resist it, but she was sure it came from God. The missing piece of what he was already showing her. She wet her lips. "Maybe you should offer Tina my job."

Randy's eyes snapped open with interest. She watched his inward struggle. It was almost amusing to see the wheels of his mind turning over the idea.

"Just a thought."

He looked at her with gratitude. "Thanks. I'll think about it."

"Think about God, too," she said, before pivoting and leaving his office.

Two hours later, Randy emerged from his office and bent over her desk. "Would you train her?"

Biting her bottom lip with disappointment, Megan nodded. "Of course."

"Maybe we could find you another position? Assistant to Paige?"

She gave him a weak smile. It was a demotion. How would she ever get anything done sitting next to Paige? "Follow your heart. And I'll make do."

He nodded with a whisper, "Let's keep this between us. I need to think about it. I'll talk to Tina. It just might be the trick that finally wins her trust."

She cringed at the word *trick*. Randy needed a lot of help. "Don't forget about church."

Randy strode back to his office with a grin.

Megan sank back in her chair. "Aye, yi, yi."

CHAPTER 36

Micah opened his cottage door and stepped into Bill's workshop, espying a pair of tennis shoes and about six inches of blue jeans sticking out from beneath a dark blue Nova, Bill's current restoration for a lawyer from Columbus.

Not good timing. But the professor had chided him about his propensity toward perfection. Micah stood in indecision. On the other hand, this was important and needed the perfect lead in. He didn't want to pour his heart out to a pair of shoes. He put his hand back on his door handle.

"You need something?" Bill called out from beneath the vehicle.

The question sent adrenalin spurting through his veins. "Yes, if it's not a bad time for you."

The mechanic's gurney squeaked and moved until Bill's face was visible. With a grunt, he said, "I need to talk to you, too. Give me just a minute." He slid back beneath, made a few quick adjustments, and then slid back out, sitting up.

Micah reached down to give him a hand, but he brushed the offer away. "Too dirty."

Waiting patiently, Micah's gaze slid over the shop's tools without really taking them in. He watched Bill move to a sink and wash his hands with a harsh soap. "Wanna go in and see if Anita's got any lemonade for us?"

"No." Micah blurted out much too quickly. "I mean what I want to talk about is personal." He glanced at the door to his cottage. "How about my place?"

"Too dirty. Pull up a seat." Bill closed a huge toolbox and perched on it.

Seeing an empty bucket, Micah plopped it upside down and sat across from Bill, who eyed him with curiosity and what he hoped was respect. "I've been working through some things. What I once told you about Megan wasn't completely truthful." At Bill's growing frown, Micah quickly continued. "About my feelings for her. The truth is I love your daughter, sir. Have since the day I saw her on the steps at Rosedale." He sighed. "It's a long story."

"I've all the time in the world."

"She didn't return the attraction, so I learned to hide it."

"That why you came to Plain City?" Bill's harsh voice interrupted.

"No. At that time, I didn't harbor any hope that Megan would change her mind. It was more of a nuisance for both of us."

Bill nodded.

"But then we became friends and helped each other through some stuff. I gave her advice. She gave me advice."

Bill got a slight smile on his face, and Micah thought Bill was reading too much between the lines. "Anyway, I knew I'd fallen for her again, only I wasn't sure about her feelings. When you brought up marriage, I didn't want her to find out about my feelings that way. Didn't think the timing was right."

"I can understand it happened prematurely, but as far as the church is concerned, the timing could be the key to your future."

"That's just it. I started out not wanting Megan to interfere with my chance at the job, but now I don't want my job to interfere with my chance for Megan. I don't care if it means losing this position. I'm more worried about losing her."

"Have you talked to Megan about this?"

"No. We haven't been alone since the incident. I don't know if I'm reading her wrong, but I have to find out. And I wanted your permission first."

Bill rubbed his chin thoughtfully. "Permission for?"

"To pursue her." He ran his hand through his hair. "To figure everything out."

Bill's smile showed his teeth. "You have it. As long as you don't go breaking her heart. I'd be proud if things progressed and you became my son-in-law. I'm assuming that's your goal?"

"Well eventually. Long term, yes, sir."

"Your guess is as good as mine to what this congregation wants in a preacher. From what Inez told Leon today, Susanna didn't take the elders' advice. She's trying to turn the older people against you. Just being a little more subtle than normal. Pushing the idea that you'll bring too many changes."

Micah hated to hear it. He thought about what he'd done after he'd left the professor's home. How he'd gone over to Susanna's and started cleaning up her yard. She'd come out of the house, spewing, *Don't think that's going to change my vote.*

His thoughts went over the conversation they had that day.

"No, ma'am. I'm not here to change your vote. Just to show you I'm not the bad guy you think I am."

"Same thing."

"What's wrong Susanna? What've I done to offend you?"

"For one, you stare at me when you preach."

"I'm looking at the clock. I'm sorry you thought that."

"You can just go. My son takes care of my yard every time he comes to town."

"I'm going to finish what I started."

"So am I," she'd said, marching to the house and slamming the door.

Bill interrupted his thoughts. "She's right about that. There'll be changes."

With only a week and a half until the big vote, Micah had done some planning. "I was thinking of having a communion service, then taking the vote afterward. Do you think that would be appropriate?"

"Sounds perfect. I hope the congregation doesn't make a big mistake. Because you're the right man for the job. God will have to deal with Susanna."

"He's given me a word on that, but it's not mine to tell yet."

Bill arched an inquisitive brow.

"I thought I'd ask Megan if she wanted to go with me to a fall festival out in Galena-Sunbury way." He'd wanted to take her someplace romantic, away from every reminder of church and daily grind. Some place where she might catch the passion.

"God bless you, son."

Micah reached out his hand, and this time Bill took it, shaking it firmly. Then Micah left him and strode toward the house. Now that he'd been given the go ahead, nothing could keep him from going after the woman he loved. He knew that she was home from work, and he wanted a moment alone with her before supper to instigate his plan.

Inside the kitchen Anita was humming. She turned at the sound of the door closing.

"Hi. You hungry?"

The aroma of freshly baked homemade bread wafted over him. "Getting there. Is Megan home?"

"Yeah, she's up in her room."

He moved up beside her. "I'll stir the pot for you, if you don't mind getting her for me."

Anita handed him the spoon. " 'Bout time."

It was getting hard to ignore Anita's little matchmaking attempts. He stirred the taco soup that he'd grown to love, thinking it would be nice to be a real part of this tight-knit family. He'd liked the way Bill called him *son*, earlier.

"You wanna see me?"

Anita stepped up and snatched the spoon. Probably would have pushed him, too, if he wasn't already physically drawn toward her daughter. Swallowing, he nodded. "We need to talk." Without waiting for Megan's reply, he started toward the living room. When he heard her footsteps behind him, his heart began to race.

⸻ ❦ ⸻

Megan glanced back at her mom. She gave her a frantic nod to follow Micah, who was acting strange. On the porch, she touched his arm,

"What's this all about?" One glance into his anxious face and trepidation crawled up her spine.

"Sit with me?"

Shrugging, Megan settled onto the white porch swing. When his movement swayed the swing, she grabbed the chain with one hand. Their shoulders touched, the same as they had that last time they'd shared the swing. She glanced at him. "You're not going to give another lecture about playing with fire and growing up, are you?"

He grinned. "Hardly."

Her thoughts went to the rumors she'd overheard Dad tell Mom about, rumors that he wasn't going to get an affirmative vote, and wondered if this was some sort of farewell. She didn't want to lose him now. "What's wrong, Micah?"

"Your eyes are gorgeous. When you look at me that way, it's hard to breathe, much less talk."

She shifted her gaze to the floor. "Is this better?"

"No."

She looked back up with confusion. The adoration in his gaze was unmistakable. Her heart leaped with hope. "I'm listening."

"I'd like to take you someplace romantic. I heard about a farm a county over that gives hayrides. Wanna go out Saturday night?"

The hope inside her exploded into fireworks that warmed and spread. But it seemed too good to be true. She had to hear more, to be sure of what he was offering. "Go on a romantic date?"

"Uh-huh." He fastened his soft brown gaze on her in a way that started the fireworks all over again. A corner of his mouth lifted playfully. "Want to?"

How could she convey that the prospect of a hayride with him made Ecuador with Chance inconsequential? His eyes were so boyishly hopeful, and she wanted to remove every qualm. To erase any lingering memories of her past mistakes and poor decisions. Moments passed as she groped for the perfect response. In the lapse, his gaze grew dismayed. She needed to say something before he started wheezing.

"Only if you let me kiss you in the corn maze."

His gaze opened in understanding. He beamed. Shook his head with wonder as if he'd been given a gift. "Now that's a promise."

CHAPTER 37

Megan skipped through the remainder of the week, feasting on her great-grandpa's love quotes and Micah's lovesick glances from across the dinner table. Neither of them sought out private conversation with each other, not wanting to burst their bubble of infatuation, but directing all their romantic energy toward their date on Saturday.

When the day finally arrived, Megan dressed in a warm skirt, blouse, and light wool coat. Micah wore jeans. When she slid into the passenger seat of his Honda Civic, she grinned. "This is my first ride in your car."

"First date," he reminded her with a look that held plenty of promise, a look that wasn't going to let her back down. "Hopefully, a lot of firsts tonight."

This openly flirtatious side of him was new. It was as though he'd rent the veil, and his adoration poured over her in a massive warm wave. She should have known he'd be flirtatious and fun. He'd probably be eloquently expressive in a relationship, too. After all, he was a preacher. But it was hard to believe that he was finally throwing decorum to the wind. She cast a skeptical side-glance at him. "How long do you think it will be until everybody hears about this?"

"It doesn't matter. We have your dad's approval."

"I know." She felt strangely nervous.

He sensed her hesitation. "Anyway, the Lord says not to worry about tomorrow."

"If we date, will you always quote scripture to me?"

"Not in the corn maze." He grinned. "I was thinking we'd better do that first, before it gets dark. I don't want to miss it."

Megan laughed and turned her gaze to the window. Everything familiar whizzed by, but she felt as though she was starting a wild adventure.

When they reached the farm, Micah paid their admission and raised his gaze to the jean-clad teenager who took their money. "Point me to the corn maze."

Aye, yi, yi. What was she getting herself into with such a determined, one-track man? She couldn't wait to find out.

"You can buy that ticket here, if you want."

"I want," he replied, looking deep into Megan's eyes. Blushing with delight, she clasped his hand, now stamped to get them inside the maze. They strolled along a wide path flanked with pumpkins and corn shocks. "I've waited a long time for this."

"Yes, autumn is my favorite season. Especially after a long hot summer."

"Hot and dry. Absolute drought-ridden."

They passed some food booths. It almost frightened her to imagine how such a parched man would quench his thirst, and with thoughts of her own inexperience, she slowed her pace. The pleasant aroma of kettle corn wafted over them, and he misunderstood. "Hungry?"

She paused to watch the man who ran the booth. He smiled at her. She didn't really want popcorn in her teeth for their first kiss. "There's more to life than food," she paraphrased, shooting scripture back at him.

He caressed her hand with his thumb. "I can't wait to get you alone."

A breeze swirled some fallen leaves. Megan shivered.

Micah turned to face her. He gently took her by the shoulders. "I'm only teasing you. I'm a patient man."

The tenderness in his gaze drew her. "Yes, well, I should probably tell you, about now, that sometimes I'm more words than action."

He dropped his hands, then tucked her hand in his arm and started walking. "Don't worry. I don't even know what to do in a corn maze.

I'm a city boy."

She doubted that. Micah was good at everything he attempted. They passed a stand that sold apple butter and Ohio maple syrup. "Will it be hard for you to adjust to small town? To Plain City?"

"I loved it when I was in college. In Allentown, we lived in the suburbs."

"Tell me about your grandma's house. Your house."

"It's small but quaint. In an old shady neighborhood."

"Sounds nice."

He squeezed her hand. "*Very* nice."

"You're *very* one-tracked."

He pointed at his chest. "Me?"

They reached the maze entrance. He showed another teenager the stamp on his hand. The kid motioned them in. Megan stared at the large red sign that read Enter. With a chuckle, Micah grabbed her hand and tugged her through its opening onto a path. Walls of corn instantly towered above her head. Children's voices carried to them over the beige tousled heads, and Megan relaxed. She felt almost childish again. In truth, it had been a long while since she'd actually been inside a corn maze.

Micah slipped his arm around her waist and drew her possessively to his side. "Wonder where the closest dead-end is?"

She lowered her voice and thickened her Dutchy accent. "I'll bet you do."

They followed the well-trodden path. On either side of them, sticky green and beige arms with stringy fingertips waved them along. They walked until the titters of children grew quiet around them. Rows and rows of tall brittle stalks, silent strangers except for the rustle of breeze or the thrashing of birds.

Suddenly Micah stopped. His arm still around her, he drew her close. "Thanks for coming with me tonight."

"I was thrilled you asked. I thought I had run you off for good."

"It's been complicated."

"Painfully so." She saw his eyes sadden and wanted to explain that she wasn't talking about Chance. "I've so many regrets that I didn't get to know you back in school. Things could have been different."

He leaned down and rested his forehead against hers. Whispered, "I'm not complaining. I like the way things are. You here, in my arms." He tilted his head and sought her lips.

She melted into his kiss, her hand going up to the back of his neck. She allowed him to quench his thirst, but he gave her more than he took before he drew away. He stroked her cheek then dropped his hand and gazed at her with adoration.

With his tenderness, he had completely stolen her heart. She felt like doing Lil's garbanzo dance. Or Paige's cha-cha step. She tucked her bottom lip in her teeth. "I guess that was a good idea, huh?"

He burst into laughter. His eyes lit with mischief. "Just so you know. That was your kiss. The one you requested. The next one will be mine."

Her eyes widened in speculation, his promise whetting her appetite.

"Come on." He tugged her hand, and they started back through the maze.

Megan dropped her gaze to the black soil strewn with dry matter. Like their steps, her mind covered many paths. When she looked up, she said, "It's hard to shake the feeling that we always have to watch over our shoulder."

"We aren't going to do that anymore."

She nodded, wondering about Micah's intentions for their budding relationship.

On the hayride that wound through a colorful display of woods, he brought up the subject. "By now, you must know how much I adore you. But we need to take things slow." She nodded, although she didn't fully understand, and recognized the look when his eyes took on a steely glint. "Will you trust me in this?"

Megan couldn't begin to grasp what his question entailed, but she was sure it had a lot to do with the congregation's vote. She also sensed his urgency.

"Yes, I will."

His eyes slid closed in relief. When they opened again, he said, "That means everything to me. I'll do my best not to disappoint you."

She thought he wanted to kiss her again, but he didn't. And she realized he wouldn't do that in a public setting. His steel extended beyond his gaze. Mettle ran through his veins. And from the memory of their kiss, there was hot lava in there, too. She wanted to ask him if he'd still stay in Plain City if the vote was negative, but she'd just assured him of her trust, so she squelched the question.

⁓

Megan didn't see much of Micah the next week. Her dad mentioned Micah was spending time in his cottage, fasting and praying about the vote. But on Wednesday morning, she'd just started her Nova's heater when she noticed a small paper sack on the bench seat. It wasn't any ordinary bag with its large blue ribbon. Her heart panting with thoughts of Micah, she drew it to her lap. She shot a look toward the cottage, but the drapes were drawn tight. Relishing the gift, she slowly pulled the ribbons. Peered inside. To the delight of her soul, she pulled out a clear plastic bag of candy corn. She opened the candy and placed one on her tongue. Closed her eyes, remembering their kiss. Wondering when she was going to get the next one.

Another glance toward the cottage told her that it wouldn't be until after the vote. But in the meantime, she'd savor his gift, one kernel at a time. She stuffed the bag in her purse, thinking that with Tina coming into the office to begin her training, she was going to need all the sweetness she could get.

⁓

Megan stood in the church foyer, looking for Micah. She'd hoped to give him a word of encouragement before the big church meeting. With disappointment, she gave in to the fact that he must be cloistered off some place with the elders or search committee.

"Not me. I don't like having the vote right after communion." Susanna shook her auburn head.

Megan retreated into the sweet-smelling library and shrank against the nearest bookcase filled with inspirational nonfictions. She hadn't set out to eavesdrop, but she didn't want to step into the middle of that conversation. She feigned interest in a book of sermons. From her hidden vantage point, she could hear Barbara's gentle protest.

"The date for the vote was set a long time ago."

Megan could imagine Susanna's eyes snapping as she argued, "Yes, but Brother Zimmerman set fall communion for the same night."

"We don't know that. It could've been the elders' idea."

"You're saying you don't know where the idea came from?"

"No. But I think it's a good one. It'll remind us to search our hearts for sin. And once our hearts are right, God's will can be done."

"That's puttin' God in a box. He can do His will with or without communion. Crackers and grape juice won't make that young man a better preacher all of a sudden."

"Susanna!"

The discussion ended, and Megan eased a peek around the corner. With relief, she saw Susanna moving toward the fellowship hall.

"She's bitter." Lori stated softly.

Megan turned, thinning her lips in disapproval. "She's not even hiding it anymore."

Lori removed the book from her hands with a grin and shoved it back into place. "Wanna sit together?"

It was an invitation to do the foot washing ceremony with her. Usually, Megan and Katy were partners, but she knew Katy would understand. "Sure."

Communion happened two or more times a year. The procedure had changed somewhat after the congregation sanctioned its integrated seating. Entering the auditorium, a quick glance assured Megan that families were going to sit together for the first part of the service, where they took the cup and bread.

Lori went to the singles' pew about halfway up the center aisle, and Megan slid in beside her. Shortly after that, Micah strode past and took his place in front of the congregation. He quietly stood, allowing his gaze to drift across the assembly. It paused on Megan and warmed. He smiled.

Megan beamed back at him, surprised and thrilled that he'd openly sought her out.

His gaze dropped from Megan to the Bible that lay open on the podium in front of him.

Lori hissed, "What was that about?"

With heat rising up her neck, Megan lowered her voice so Joy and

Ruthie wouldn't hear. "We're dating."

"I see." Lori's reproach reverberated her warning, not to rush ahead of God's timing. "Micah did the asking. He talked to my dad."

Lori's tight-lipped nod ended the conversation. The librarian fastened a stern gaze on Micah.

He reminded the assembly that communion symbolized the Lord's sacrifice at the cross, taking their sins upon Himself, so that they might have forgiveness and eternal life. He urged everyone to search their hearts for sin before taking communion. For the folks at Big Darby, it was a solemn, contemplative moment.

For an ugly instant, Susanna's remark about crackers and grape juice tormented Megan's mind. She quickly dispelled it. Felt a nudge at her arm and saw the communion tray. After she partook, she passed it to Lori without making eye contact.

Afterward, Micah instructed the women to move to the left of the auditorium and men to the right. Ray led the congregation in hymn singing as, row by row, women and men slipped into their respective side rooms.

Inside the women's anteroom, the women removed their shoes and stockings and waited barefooted, quietly whispering with each other, until one of the six chairs became available. The actual ritual was done with somberness. The foot-washing practice reflected the Lord's actions, when He washed His disciples' feet.

Lori took a chair, and Megan carefully dipped each of the librarian's bare feet into a round porcelain basin filled with soapy water then dried them with a fluffy white towel. Afterward she helped Lori stand. They kissed each other on each cheek, saying the blessing: "God's peace be with you."

The ceremony held significance for Megan in many ways. She felt acceptance and healing in her friendship with Lori and a solidarity in their desire for the good of the church and for Micah's victory.

When everyone had gathered back in the sanctuary, Micah stepped to the front. "You may take a ten-minute recess, and when you return, the elders will lead you in the voting process." He gave no parting pep talk but quietly left the podium.

An air of reverence still filled the sanctuary, and the congregation slowly came to life, milling quietly. Megan and Lori stood with the other singles. From the corner of her eye, Megan saw Barbara huddled with the widows. Above their bent, whispering heads, the clock's minute hand had only moved two marks since Micah had closed the service.

Lori nudged her. "He's coming."

She shifted her gaze, and her heart tumbled to see Micah moving toward her, but taking care to greet others along the way. He glanced up at her repeatedly, and she knew he would not be deterred.

When he reached them, he touched her arm. "Hi, Meg." Her emotions soared giddily to see his unveiled admiration and to hear the shortened endearment of her name. His brown eyes also held concern. "All I can think about is your mom's refrigerator magnet."

"Oh?" A mishmash image of her mom's garage-sale magnets ranging from ceramic flower buttons to die-cut vintage sayings gave her another delightful glimpse into Micah's complex nature. "Which one?"

" 'Either define the moment, or the moment will define you.' "

"Walt Whitman," Lori murmured.

"You have my vote," Joy Ann said softly, while toeing the hardwood flooring.

He smiled. "Thanks. That's good to know."

Lori touched Joy Ann's arm. "I believe my lip balm fell out of my purse in the anteroom. Would you help me go look for it?"

Joy Ann furrowed her brow. "Now?"

"Yes. I need it now."

Megan tucked her lower lip in her teeth until the two other women moved out of sight. "I know you and Lori make a good team, but the two of us aren't bad together, either."

"I noticed. But I hope you don't want to follow her footsteps. Whatever you do, don't switch to her brand of perfume. I love the citrusy scent you wear."

She smoothed the side of her upswept hair. His eyes softened as he followed the movement. "Thanks for the bag of candy corn you put in my car."

He sucked his bottom lip then grinned. "It was symbolic."

"Yes, I got that." She smiled.

His jaw slightly tightened. "I'm sorry I did a disappearing act this week."

"I understand."

He glanced at the clock. "I better go."

She touched his arm to detain him. "Can I come with Dad when he brings you the news?"

"Yes." He hesitated, his expression contrite. "But I may need time."

"I know."

CHAPTER 38

After the communion service, Dad continued the meeting with a short introduction and reminder that only members could vote. The process was simple. He asked those who affirmed Micah as preacher to stand.

Megan hurried to her feet. Beside her, Lori also stood. The entire singles' pew affirmed Micah. Two elders counted heads from the front of the room, allowing Megan just enough time to quickly scan the auditorium. She tried to get a general feel for the vote without honing in on individuals, lest she develop hard feelings toward those who remained seated. Susanna's row was behind her, out of her view, but she thought that Micah had the majority of votes.

"Be seated. Those opposed, please stand."

As skirts rustled, Megan wished she'd asked Micah what percentage he required to accept the calling. Some preachers required 100 percent, not wanting to take a position where there might be a rift. She kneaded her hands, remembering the church was requiring 80 percent in favor to extend the invitation. Would that be enough for Micah? She was sure the vote would not be unanimous.

"Thank you. Be seated." Dad turned to confer with the other elders, then returned to the podium.

Her dad's words had never held more significance for Megan. And then she saw the smile in his eyes and sank with relief. "He got it," Megan whispered.

"What?" Lori's hand clutched Megan's arm.

"The vote is positive," Megan's dad announced. "Big Darby Conservative Mennonite will be offering Micah Zimmerman a permanent ministerial position. We'll ask him to give us his answer next Sunday from the pulpit. You're dismissed. Go in peace."

Megan stood and squeezed Lori's hand. They knew better than to make a display of their emotions for the sake of the people who had not voted for Micah.

"Now it's up to Micah," Lori said. "Please do what you can to convince him to stay."

"He asked me to trust him."

"Just do your best."

Megan moved in a daze for the door, anxious to see the matter through, to get home to Micah. An arm snatched her in the foyer. She turned, and Barbara leaned close to her ear. "You take good care of my hydrangea bush. You hear?"

"Don't put the cart in front of the horse."

"And don't topple the cart."

Shaking her head with amusement, Megan stepped out into the brisk September evening.

"Megan."

She turned. "Mom. Where's Dad?"

"Still talking to the elders. Let your dad be the one to tell him."

"I will, but try to hurry him along. Don't let him be the last one to leave again."

"I'll do my best. Put on the coffeepot when you get home." She leaned closer. "This calls for a celebration."

They exchanged a victorious look; then Megan started toward her car. She'd only gone a few steps when Katy intercepted her. They spoke briefly and parted. She was halfway across the parking lot when she saw Susanna sitting inside her car. Mixed emotions rushed over Megan, resentment and triumph followed by guilt.

The woman looked rigid as a stone statue, and Megan wondered if something was wrong besides the outcome of the vote. Megan struggled with her conscience then veered to the left where her feet did not want to go. Even as she approached the widow's car, Susanna didn't notice her. She didn't move. Megan rapped lightly on her car window.

The widow jerked, raked a glance over Megan, then rolled the window. "What do you want?"

"Are you all right?"

"No. I'm not." Susanna gripped the steering wheel and lowered her forehead to the top of the steering wheel.

"Can I help? Drive you home?"

Susanna shook her head then lifted her gaze to Megan. "Just go home to your preacher. Someday you'll understand."

Megan sighed. "Susanna."

But the widow was done talking. She put her car in REVERSE.

Megan stepped away. For the first time, she felt pity for the widow.

Micah had been waiting in his cottage for over an hour. And after the previous week's seclusion, he was good and sick of it. He knew there was fellowship and driving time involved, but he'd hoped Bill would make an effort to bring him the results in a prompt manner. Megan's car had arrived at least twenty minutes earlier. She was doing the right thing by letting her father bring the news, but the waiting was almost more than he could bear.

He stationed himself next to the window. Even Miss Purrty paced and switched her tail. Finally the Weavers pulled into the driveway. And then they went inside the house! Micah sighed. Stood and paced, stepping on the cat. She yowled and leaped into her crate. He started after her, but then he heard the fervent rap at his door.

Diving for it, he swung the door open. He gave Bill a sheepish smile and gestured the Weavers into his apartment. From another world, Micah felt the cat's motor as it wove in and out of his legs.

The older man's eyes brightened, and he offered a congratulatory handshake. "Big Darby wants you."

Micah blew out a deep sigh and relaxed his shoulders. "That's good news."

Megan rushed to hug him. "Congratulations, Micah."

He rested his chin on top of her head, closed his eyes, and drank in the promise of love and a glorious future. There was a joyous flash of Sunday sermons, baptisms, communions, and softball picnics until he felt Megan's gentle pat on his back. Reluctantly, he released her.

Anita hugged him next. "Come in for coffee. We have to celebrate."

He nodded and choked, "I'll be right in."

As soon as they left, he sank to his knees where he'd already worn a fuzzy spot in the rug and leaned his head against the tiny bed. When he had control of his emotions, he rose with thanksgiving still on his lips. He stroked the cat. "Stay."

Inside the Weavers' home, his first clue that something wasn't entirely right was when Bill said, "I told them you'd give your answer next Sunday over the pulpit."

Disappointment settled over him like a familiar companion, but he bit his tongue until Anita finished serving the coffee and joined them at the table. "What was the vote? The percentage?"

Bill fiddled with his cup. "It was eighty-three. But given the timing, you can have every hope that a few years down the road, you'll have one hundred percent support. Change takes time. We talked about that."

Micah nodded. "I know. But I had a number in mind. It was a lot higher than yours."

Megan's face paled. Her eyes searched him over the rim of her cup. She gave a trembling smile.

He looked at Anita. Tears had sprung to her eyes, and he knew why. She didn't want her only child to move away from Plain City.

Bill gave him a forced smile. "You have all week to decide. The elders and search committee are unanimous. They want you. You have to keep in mind that it's a small congregation. That's why the margin is so big."

"I know."

Anita cleared her throat. "There's a pumpkin in the garden that's bound to be a prize winner. Have you seen it?"

Micah swiveled his gaze in confusion then caught the glint in her eyes. "No. But may I take your daughter and check it out?"

Anita nodded. "It's getting dark, but there's a flashlight in the junk drawer."

Megan pushed back her chair and went to the drawer.

Micah stood and faced Bill. "Thanks for the news. As soon as I have an answer, this family will be the first to know."

The atmosphere was hardly celebrative. Megan followed him out the door. Without speaking, his left hand sought hers, and his right flicked on the flashlight. Its beam zigzagged across the yard but did little to lift the descending gloom.

Megan broke the awkward silence. "So what happens next?"

"I thought God and I had a number in mind. But the last couple of weeks, my thinking's changed." He knew what needed to be done. He just didn't know if Megan would support his decision.

Megan walked beside Micah. Her heart leapt with joy at his words: *"I thought God and I had a number in mind. But the last couple of weeks, my thinking's changed."* Surely he was referring to their growing relationship. He was going to change his plans for her.

"It's not so much the number, anymore. I'm not staying unless I can win Susanna's vote."

"What?" She stopped walking and shrugged away. "But that will never happen!"

He flicked off the light and stuffed it in his back pocket, then took both her hands. "I have to try."

"But you only have a week. You'd need a miracle."

He caressed her hands. "I know. You still trust me with our future?"

Her mind exploded in possible scenarios of what such a trust might entail. They'd only had one date. She couldn't run off with him. "Are you staying here if you don't take the job?"

"Let's take this one step at a time."

That sounded too much like Chance's philosophy. It had ended up in a dead end. And her heart had been broken. But Micah was different.

"I have to have a job, Meg. And you know what kind of job I want."

"What about us?"

"I've waited for you a long time. I want to take it slow. I want to grow into our future."

"That's what I mean." She couldn't chase after him. "I have a job here."

"People do survive long-distance relationships."

Long distance meant periods of separation. That could stretch on for years. Was that what he'd been trying to warn her about all along? Her heart resisted, but her mind raced ahead to weigh her options now. She gripped his hands, not wanting to lose him.

She'd already fallen in love with the man. She thought he felt the same way, though he'd never told her he loved her. But now she needed to decide if she could live with and support his ministry and everything it would bring into their lives. It could be a rough row to hoe, living from one miracle to the next. She'd already faced the reality that the missionary life wasn't as she'd dreamed. Would being a preacher's wife be as disappointing?

Micah was here in the flesh now. She could either reach for her dreams or shrink back in fear. She was too invested to do that.

"I spoke with Susanna after the vote. She seemed depressed. Do you have a plan?"

"Yes." He touched her cheek. "You're so beautiful in the moonlight. Even when you're brooding. I love the way your forehead gets those little wrinkles."

His fingers traced them and sent shivers down her neck. His hand found her cheek again, and she cradled her face into his touch and breathed into his palm. "Yeah, I'll trust you."

He scooped her close, whispered against her ear, "Thank you." Then he lifted her chin and brought his lips to hers. He kissed her gently, urgently, then peppered her with kisses of promise. "Everything will be fine," he murmured.

"I know." His lovemaking made her so dizzy it was impossible to object. He might want to take it one day at a time, but she'd think of it as one kiss at a time. That would get her through. Her thoughts took her to the corn maze, comparing the kisses. "So that was the kiss you warned me about?"

He sighed. "I'm afraid so. Was it wimpy?"

"I'll make do." She stepped away and crossed her arms. She lifted her chin in determination for whatever lay ahead. Her gaze drifted to the garden, and sudden amusement bubbled up in her throat. "Bless Mom, that's the puniest pumpkin patch she's ever had."

Micah looked at the scrawny pumpkins and laughed.

CHAPTER 39

On Monday Micah trimmed Susanna's trees. When he first got started, she'd pulled her drapes closed, but just before he'd left, she stuck her head out the door and yelled, "You're doing nothing but making a big mess!"

On Tuesday Susanna's car was gone all day. He borrowed Leon's flatbed trailer and hauled off the trimmings and trash. Leon stocked him up with painting equipment to do the professor's porch.

On Wednesday morning Micah stayed home, drew the curtain and fasted and prayed. It wasn't any ordinary prayer but a struggle of sprit and flesh, for his flesh wanted to forget about Susanna, to give in and make a home for Megan here in Plain City. Late afternoon, he'd made his peace again and rose from his meditations.

On Thursday he went to the church, heartened by Barbara's kind face.

"Morning, Micah. Coffee's ready. And the professor already stopped in on his way to work. He said to tell you that Saturday does suit, after all, for painting his porch."

"Good. I want to do that before I go."

"Nonsense. I already told you you're not going anyplace. And don't be moping around and slacking off keeping up that cottage. I don't want a mess on my hands when I move in."

"Barbara, I thought I knew what God wanted me to do, but now I think I heard Him wrong."

"See, that's what I'm talking about. Moping. I heard you say it right over your own pulpit: 'Faith is unseen, but not unfelt.'"

He hadn't told anyone but Megan what he was doing at Susanna's. Or even that his decision hinged on her change of heart. He wasn't seeing any evidence of a changed heart, and now his feelings were becoming wishy-washy, too. But Barbara's faith remained intact; the woman wouldn't be deterred.

On Friday Micah unpacked his gardening tools and let himself through a creaky gate into Susanna's backyard. A flagstone walkway went from the house to a weedy, vacated garden patch. He'd noticed the grass was trodden down where Susanna veered from the flagstone to the clothesline. He'd start by clearing the walkway for her.

He sat on his haunches and moved along the flagstone, pulling weeds from the cracks and opening up the footpath. After twenty minutes, he removed his jacket and got his hoe. He headed for the worst neglected area, the garden patch.

"Just what do you think you're doing?"

Micah flinched. Bracing himself, he turned with a smile. "I'm back to finish what I started."

Susanna straightened her back and marched up to him. She was a beautiful woman, all ruffled and fierce. "You got the vote. Why are you still here?"

"I wasn't after a winning vote. I was after the congregation's love and support. But for some reason, you have hated me from the start. So I failed."

Susanna clenched her jaw, shifting her brown gaze away.

"I can still turn down the church's offer, you know."

Surprise lit her eyes. "Will you?"

"That depends on you. Don't get me wrong, I'm not worried about the damage you could do to my character or even my failure. But God never fails. So I have to obey Him. And He's telling me that I need to put my choice in your hands."

"What?" She eyed him skeptically. "Then I guess you'd better pack your bags."

"God cares more about you, Susanna, than He does about me getting the job. He sees your pain. He sent me here to give you a message. He loves you."

She lifted her chin, but her words came out shaky. "Don't make this about me."

Micah wet his lips, searched for the right words. It was another defining moment, even more important than the last, because this one defined a woman's soul.

"He wants you to love Him back."

Susanna flinched. Confusion clouded her eyes. She lowered her gaze, and it was the first time Micah had observed real weakness in the woman. Hesitant, yet feeling God's urging, Micah touched her arm. "God loves you."

Susanna looked at him. "Why?"

"Why wouldn't He?" Miraculously, her defenses shattered, and she gulped back sobs. Tentatively, Micah patted her back. There in front of the forsaken garden, God's love infused the autumn sunshine and warmed them, as Micah ministered to the woman's broken spirit.

When she could speak, she flattened her palms against Micah's chest and pushed him away. "I gave up on God a long time ago."

"But you still came to church?"

"It's all I know. It's where my friends are."

"I'm sorry we didn't realize you were hurting. Do you want to tell me what happened?"

"You know how to wear a woman down." She strode to a wooden bench near the garden. "Aren't you coming?"

Biting back a grin, Micah joined her. They sat in silence, both their gazes fixed on the tangled mass of past gardens. Then she began to talk. "When I married Charles, I had hopes of love. But he never loved me. My entire marriage, I felt like I was trapped inside a cage. But there was nothing I could do. The only people who ever loved me were my boys. But they moved away." She sniffed. "My bitterness drove them away."

It became clear that Susanna had been starved for affection and used her gossip to win a following. With a heart hardened toward God, it had been an effective tool. But it hadn't brought her love or acceptance. She was a lonely woman.

"Did God really send you here? You didn't just come because you're some perfectionist and you have to win my favor?"

"Only God's love enabled me to come here today."

"And it's up to me if you take the job?"

"Yes. I'll go away if that's what you want."

"No. I want you to stay. You're the only man who's ever been kind to me."

"Thanks, Susanna. You really need me. Your yard's a mess."

"Like me."

"Can I pray for you?"

She nodded, and holding her hand, Micah prayed for God's forgiveness and grace in her life. When they were finished, she stood and straightened her skirt. "You've got to quit going around hugging women and holding their hands. You do know that, don't you?"

Getting a glimpse of her inner loveliness and a long-suppressed sense of humor, Micah replied, "I'm making you an exception, along with my Megan."

Her eyes widened, and she opened her mouth to say something, but clamped it shut again. She shook her head. "It's going to be hard to break my old habits."

"You have the rest of your life for that. God doesn't expect perfection." He'd do well to remember that, himself.

"Well then," she said, swiping her hand across her face. "I'll go inside and get you some apple cider. Would you like that, Brother Zimmerman?"

"Why don't you call me Micah?"

"Brother Micah," she said, turning and hurrying toward the house.

Micah stooped and retrieved his hoe then looked toward heaven with a broad grin. "Thank You, Lord." He looked at the tangled mess of Susanna's garden and rolled up his sleeves. He couldn't wait to give Megan the news. And he knew just how he'd do it.

CHAPTER 40

Megan peered into the back of Micah's Honda Civic. "How did you cram all this stuff in here?"

He put his arm around her waist and shifted her to the side. "I have all kinds of talents you haven't discovered yet."

She eyed him skeptically. Ever since Friday night supper, he'd been acting like the cat that swallowed the bird. She could only hope that was a good thing, but she knew better than to press him. The stubborn man had the patience of Job, and he would do things in his timing. When he'd invited her to help him paint Noah Maust's porch, his chest had puffed out as though it was the best second date anybody had ever proposed to their girl. She didn't mind, really. He was probably just trying to give her a taste of what life with him would entail. He might even be testing her. She'd prove her mettle. Wouldn't let doubt color the decision that still loomed over them. The one he had to make before Sunday morning service tomorrow.

"Hold this?" He handed her a bag bulging with rollers, trays, and tape.

"Want me to take it up on the porch?"

He looked her in the eyes. "No, I don't." He glanced at the porch and back. "You can set it at the bottom of the steps, though."

She shrugged a brow and went to do his bidding. When she turned, he was standing directly behind her. He dropped a five-gallon can of paint at her feet like a caveman peace offering.

"What's up with you?"

The mischievous glint that shot in his eyes made her gasp and back up a step. She hit the railing.

He advanced a step and closed the distance between them. "I just wanted to make it special." His gaze never leaving hers, she felt his hands grip her waist and pull her close.

"Micah!" Without warning, he swept her off her feet and into his arms. She squirmed. "What are you doing? In plain sight of the entire neighborhood." Had he finally reached his limit and gone from discreet to throwing all caution to the wind? Of course she had no idea what he was capable of, so early into their relationship. *Oh!* He was carrying her up the steps and nuzzling her neck, and she found it hard to remember why she had tried to prevent him.

"I'm carrying you up over the threshold, sweet. Consider it a promise of things to come. No matter what happens, all right?"

His charming gesture and use of a pet name quieted her resistance. At the top of the porch, she decided to show him her mettle and swung her arms around his neck, pulling his face down. But he kept the kiss brief and set her suddenly, unexpectedly on her feet. She looked up at him with surprise.

He grinned. "Wondered how long it would take before I swept you off your feet. I thought it might happen that day the tornado came through. I'd hoped. But you got away from me. I guess it's taken about three-and-a-half years. I just want you to know that I never quit trying."

She clutched the front of his shirt. "Well, you missed a good chance that night in the corn maze. For a while, I thought you might get away."

Looking down at her, he said, "That night, I told you I wanted to take it slow. That I wanted to enjoy dating you."

She relaxed her grip. "I remember."

"But I'm giving you permission to try and change my mind. You might even find it easy to do since we won't be having a long-distance relationship."

Megan squealed. "You're staying? Oh, glory be."

"I'm staying, but I need you to promise me something."

"What?"

"Give me enough time to shower you with my love. I want to do it in a million different ways before I pop the question."

"Write me a love letter, Micah. My aunt Louise gave me my great-grandparents' love letters. My great-grandpa told my great-grandma that the poet Charles Morgan understood love. He said: 'There is no surprise more magical than the surprise of being loved. It is God's finger on man's shoulder.'"

~⌒~

Winter came. The bean patch and Brother Troyer's grave lay buried in snow. The folks at Big Darby Conservative Mennonite were adjusting to change. Bishop Heinlein came to fill in while Micah went back to Pennsylvania to wrap up some loose ends. Megan missed him but kept busy with her wedding plans.

She swept through the living room to check the mail for the Butterick patterns she'd ordered and came to a halt. Back stepping, she retraced her steps to her mom's small, round side table. A smile tugged her lips as she lifted the frame that hadn't been there earlier. It was the photograph of Mom's birth parents, and beside it was the small worn Bible. *A Christmas miracle!*

Snow swirled magically through the picture window, and Megan drew her coat up tight against her before she stepped outside. Everything was pure and beautiful, reminding her of that Christmas Eve when Lil and Katy had come over to exchange gifts for their hope chests. At the time, none of them even had a boyfriend. So much had changed since then. She'd been a bridesmaid twice over. And soon Katy and Lil would do the honor for her.

Her boots tapped down the steps and trudged through the yard to the road. She brushed the snow off the mailbox with her sleeve and pulled the latch. She bent to peer inside. No patterns. But a small parcel rested on top of some envelopes. *From Aunt Louise!* Excited, she gathered the rest of the mail and started back to the porch.

The cottage light caught her eye. Barbara waved from its window. She waved back and hurried up the porch steps to the swing. She quickly brushed off the seat with her gloves and sank into its comfort. Placing the bulk of the mail at her side, she tore open the wrappings.

She swept away the tissue paper. It was a Christmas ornament. A smile of delight spread over her face. A bride with wings. A wedding angel. She'd never seen anything like it. She remembered how excited Louise was that Megan planned to carry her great-grandmother's handkerchief the day of her wedding. Her something blue.

Sometimes she thought the day would never come. How she missed Micah. He'd only been gone for two weeks, but it seemed like an eternity. He'd already moved into the parsonage. February would be here before she knew it, and there was plenty to do. She swooped up the mail to go back inside and show her mom the bride-angel, when she saw it. A letter from Micah.

To her heart's joyous leap, she sank back into the swing. She drew out a sheet of gray stationery and read:

Dearest Meg,

I was able to spend a few days at my brother's and invite him personally to our wedding. He says they wouldn't miss it for the world, and they're anxious to meet you. I visited your aunt Louise. She says the twenty-five miles between Allentown and Reading is not a problem. She's excited about renting out my house whenever she's not traveling. Says to look for a package from her.

I miss you. It's barren and cold without you. I've thought a lot about the love letter you requested that day we painted the professor's porch. I've written at least a dozen since then but was never satisfied with any of them. They're inadequate to express my feelings. I can't compete with your great-grandfather. But if you want them, when I return, I'll give you the entire stack. Maybe they'll tide you over till our wedding night.

Megan felt her face heat, but read on:

In the meantime, some scripture from Song of Songs 4:9–11 is the best this preacher can do to keep you warm until my return: "Thou has ravished my heart, my sister, my spouse; thou hast ravished my heart with one of thine eyes, with one chain of thy neck. How fair is thy love, my sister, my spouse! how much better is thy love than wine! and the smell of thine ointments than all spices. Thy lips, O my spouse, drop as the honeycomb; honey and milk are under thy tongue."

Megan clutched the letter and fanned her face, while all around her snow swirled. *Aye, yi, yi!*

MEGAN'S JOURNAL

January

Tina and Randy are snug as two bugs in a Cessna, but working from the cubicle next to Paige is driving me bananas. She hums annoyingly, curses every time she breaks a fingernail, and gives me all the cold calls. She wants to spend every spare moment revising my wedding plans. But I guess I'll make do since the demotion came with a significant pay raise.

February

Aunt Louise sent us to San Diego, California, for our honeymoon. I'm madly in love, and Micah's obsessed with carrying me over anything that vaguely resembles a threshold. I found out that he's a hopeless romantic. Not that I'm complaining. One night we took a quilt to the beach to prove Ralph Waldo Emerson's theory: "When it is dark enough, you can see the stars." It's true.

March

Joy Ann Beitzel went with Ruthie Ropp to her cousin's wedding in Lancaster County. They had some car trouble and stayed longer than they originally intended. But when they returned, Joy Ann informed me that she's now in a long-distance relationship with the man of her dreams.

Maybe now she'll finally get over the crush she's had on my husband.

April

Micah and I are miserable with spring allergies. As much as we love the parsonage gardens, we had to suck up our pride because Barbara initiated a workday for us. It was the day that I found out Lil's pregnant. She did the garbanzo dance. Calls the baby her little bean.

May

Went to a garage sale with Mom and found a wonderful bookcase for Micah's never-ending collection of books. Jake removed a wall between two bedrooms and set up Micah's office to resemble the professor's. Even put an outside door to it. Lil thinks I should demand a kitchen update to even the score, but I'm content. Every Monday night, Lori stops by to see what he'll need for his sermon. We've become best of friends.

June

Gardens everywhere are in full bloom. Mom and I are having the discussions of my daydreams. Susanna's even got a garden this year. Micah's organized a group that helps out the widows. But he goes to Susanna's himself as long as his allergies allow it. The four of us—Mom, Barbara, Susanna, and I—are getting together to put up Lil's three bean salad.

July

One of Dad's Nova clients begged him to drive his Nova in the Plain City Fourth of July Parade. At first Dad refused, but Micah talked him into it. We watched the parade from the professor's porch.

August

It was the annual Big Darby picnic and softball game. Have I mentioned how stubborn Micah can be? He kept his white shirt/blue shirt teams. His team forgave him when he hit another home run. Now he'll have to come up with something to appease the rest of the men.

Joy Ann's boyfriend helped with the children's relays. Susanna was proud of her new quilted table coverings, and Inez admitted they were way better than rocks. There wasn't any rain this year, but Micah stole with me into Leon's barn for a few moments of reminiscing. Only this time, there were no regrets.

September

Fall allergies. Monday night Lori teased us about our his-and-hers inhalers. Micah's a hands-on preacher and keeps a "To-Do for Others" list. He employs my help whenever possible. This week we cleaned out the root cellar for Mom. He suggested we sneak back in after dark that night, light some candles, and spend the night for old time's sake, but I was having nothing to do with it. Normally, he's full of good ideas, but that wasn't one of them.

October

We went to the corn maze, and on the drive over, Micah teased me about chasing him and demanding a kiss on our first date. I told him if he didn't get the story right, he wouldn't be giving me any candy corn later. That shut him up even though he was right. I did ask for that first kiss. After that, my obstinate husband seemed to know what to do on his own.

November

Micah painted the spare bedroom blue. Stubborn man! I told him that it was too early to know what color it needed to be. I thought little Hope Marie would favor a light pink room. But in a way, I hope Micah's right. Wouldn't it be fun to raise a miniature Ichabod Crane?

December

David Miller gave us an early Christmas present. He set it up for Micah and me to go on a winter's sleigh ride. So I added horse handling to my husband's amazing talents. Afterward the entire church met at the Stucky's farm for a bonfire and ice-skating party on the Big Darby Creek.

January

Lil's little bean arrived. She's cute as a button. She still sleeps too much to tell if she's as strong willed as her parents. Something new is happening at their house. First, they traded Jezebel in on a new car. They're looking for a bigger home. It's kinda sad because the doddy house holds a lot of memories for us.

Today Aunt Louise sent us something blue for baby Isaac Michael's growing nursery. We were unanimous on the name Isaac. Micah says it means *laughter*. And we are certainly riding the giddy wings of joy these days. For me it's a precious pet name, shortened from Ichabod Crane. I never told Micah about the nickname, but somehow it lives inside me to symbolize my all-inclusive love for my husband. I envision this little life within me growing into a gangly tree climber, all arms and legs. I hope Isaac's just like his dad in every way. Well, it'd be nice if he didn't have our allergies, but that would take a miracle.

February

For our anniversary, we dressed up and went to Volo Italiano for dinner. Giovanni's anxious for Lil to return to work, though she's undecided about it. Micah held my hand and quoted Song of Songs to me across the lasagna. Honestly, I don't know how I ever made do without him.

Dear readers,

For more of Megan's journal entries, please visit my website at: www.diannechristner.net.

DISCUSSION QUESTIONS

1. Which of the following adjectives best describes Megan: principled, adventuresome, naïve, or late-bloomer?

2. Megan's family didn't have television or the internet. Imagine all you would have to delete from you mind if you'd never experienced such technologies. How did it shape her worldview?

3. Would you say Megan and her mom's relationship was close, normal, or dysfunctional?

4. Who was your favorite minor character?

5. After one of Micah's sermons, Megan tried to set her heart. Did it work?

6. Do you think Micah acted honorably around Megan? Why or why not?

7. Did you learn anything new or unusual about the Mennonite faith?

8. In line with the title *Something Blue,* what blue things were mentioned in the story? How were they symbolic?

About the Author

Dianne Christner enjoys the beauty of her desert surroundings in Phoenix, Arizona, where life sizzles when temperatures soar above 100 degrees. She and husband, Jim, have two married children and five grandchildren. Before writing, Dianne worked in office management, in admissions, and as a teacher's assistant in a Christian school, and owned an exercise salon in Scottsdale, Arizona.

Her first book was published in 1994, and she now writes full-time. She has published several historical fiction titles and writes contemporary fiction based on her experience in the Mennonite church. Her husband was raised on a farm in Plain City, Ohio, in a Conservative Mennonite church. Dianne was raised in an urban Mennonite setting. They both have Amish ancestors and friends and family in various sects of the Mennonite church. Now Dianne and Jim attend a nondenominational church.

You may find information about her other books at www.diannechristner.net, where she keeps a blog about the Mennonite lifestyle.